DARE

DARE

KEN RAND

FAIRWOOD PRESS
Bonney Lake, WA

DARE

A Fairwood Press Book
August 2021
Copyright © 2021 the estate of Ken Rand

First Edition

Fairwood Press
21528 104th Street Court East
Bonney Lake, WA 98391
www.fairwoodpress.com

Cover and book design by Patrick Swenson

ISBN: 978-1-933846-15-6
First Fairwood Press Edition: August 2021
Printed in the United States of America

DARE

CHAPTER ONE

*T*he skinny little announcer smiled at Ian, bright-eyed and mouth full of crooked teeth, as he stuck his microphone in his face, waiting for Ian to answer the question: "Why do you do it?" He waited breathlessly, as his listening audience waited, the "thousands of K-95 listeners and fans out there in central Iowa." Pimply-faced, earnest, the kid looked maybe sixteen.

"Why do we do it?" Ian smiled his showtime smile back at the fussy little teenager, changing the question from "you" to "we." He tapped his hearing aid and shook his head as if he hadn't heard right. The hearing aid always acted up in the heat and dirt and humidity.

"Yes, yes." The announcer danced from foot to foot, excited. A blob of sweat flew from the tip of his mini-hatchet nose. "Why?" He either had to pee or the station was coming up on network news.

"Why do we do it? Well—" Ian paused, smiling, scuffing his toe in a practiced aw-shucks manner against the packed dirt on the floor of the flag box on the grandstand side of the clay track where they stood. He squinted out, brow furrowed, as if for inspiration, over the crowded grandstand, maybe three thousand people jammed cheek to elbow, lit in the glow of the high overhead stadium lights, the light banks fuzzy with drifting smoke and fluttering late summer moths. "You know, we call what we do a thrill show—"

"Uh-huh." The kid's hair bobbed, a comic imitation of Elvis Presley's pompadour, his toothy smile gaped, and he squirmed like he was sitting on a load of dynamite. Ian wondered if this was his first real job.

"—because," Ian said slowly, enunciating the well-practiced semi-slogan, "it's as much of a thrill for us to do as it is for folks—like the good folks listening to K-95 right now—"

"Uh-huh." No, Ian decided. The kid was the station owner's son or nephew.

"—for those good folks to see."

Ian glanced across the track, where his own announcer and clown and his son Joel were deep into the funny-car routine, keeping the crowd's attention focused on them rather than the mundane preparations for the show finale. The ramp crew had finished setting up the catch cars and ramps for the T-bone on the track and had the hood up on the jump car in the infield. Shaun was bent over a fender, his big head in the engine, doing something, gesturing animatedly with Tink, who sat in the car behind the wheel. The car revved and gray smoke mushroomed from the exhaust. Sounded throaty, balanced, tight, all pistons firing.

It was almost time. Showtime.

The thick, smoky air above the grandstand smelled of gasoline, burnt wood, popcorn, and hot dogs.

Ian's daughter Hanna had been watching the timing too. She gave a secret little tug low on Ian's sleeve, a signal: "Showtime, Dad."

Ian gave her a quick nod: "I got it. It's me."

She smiled back at him, dimples, white teeth, and dazzling blue eyes. Her mother's smile and eyes, but her father's solid chin. Tall, like both Ian and Grace. Not for the first time, Ian found himself awed at his own daughter's stunning beauty. So like her mother.

The announcer was asking him some fool question about the stunt but Ian hadn't heard. It was showtime.

"Sorry, uh—" He'd forgotten the boy's name. "—but the show calls. I got to go."

He opened the little wire mesh gate that separated the cramped flag stand area, like a tiny concrete bunker, where the flagger stood during stock car races, from the track proper, and stepped through, Hanna at his elbow. "Just watch," he said to the announcer. "You'll see."

A pace inside the track, he turned back to the announcer and found the microphone still six inches from his nose. He thought maybe the announcer had asked one last question as he'd turned away, but if so, he hadn't heard it. His hearing aid battery was fading again.

"You tell your listeners to stay tuned for the biggest thrill of their lives. They'll never forget Sunday, August 20, 1978. Tell them next time to come out to the track themselves and see it in person. There's nothing like the Ian McGinnis Auto Daredevil Thrill Show, nothing on Earth like it. Just watch." Then he turned, with Hanna beside him, and started across the track toward the infield, where the jump car waited.

Ian had timed it just right, as he'd intended. His announcer and clown and Joel had finished the funny-car routine and Tink and the other hands were lining up, facing the grandstand from the infield, a tidy row of competent, healthy, smiling, clean, well-trained, well-mannered, all-American, entertainers dressed in red, white, and blue, you're getting your money's worth, folks, from the national anthem opening to the thrilling grand finale, yes sir, you are.

Grace gave him the thumbs up from over by the trailer in the infield where she'd laid out a cardboard box of souvenir T-shirts, photographs and programs on a folding table to sell after the show. Shaun had dropped the hood of the jump car, wired it down, and waved Ian's helmet in the air, smiling as he walked out to join the crew line-up. All was ready for the show finale, the T-bone crash.

Hanna said something to him as they walked slowly across the track, Ian moving as gracefully as a gunfighter stepping onto the street for a showdown, the very picture of competence and confidence, not too fast, not too slow, but he didn't hear.

"What?" He cupped his ear.

"Why *do* you do it?"

Ian laughed aloud, a deep-throated guffaw, his smile crinkling up the skin around his eyes. "How many years you been with the show, darling? Eighteen, isn't it?"

"Dad, you're dodging the question."

"I can't hear worth diddly, honey. Ask me later, okay?"

As Ian walked across the track, his lovely young daughter on his arm, his announcer declared: "Ladies and gentlemen! Here's the producer and manager of our show! From Rock Springs, Wyoming! Ian! McGinnis!"

Perfect timing.

Ian waved, smiling, as the crowd roared, applauded, whistled, and the broad wooden grandstands thundered under their stomping feet. Hanna joined Grace by the trailer where she grabbed her change apron, ready to put it on, right after the jump, ready for the post-show peddling routine. Ian took the microphone from the announcer, who stepped back, joining the crew lined up on the infield. Ian stepped a few paces toward the grandstand and put the microphone to his lips.

"Thank you!"

The crowd applauded again.

"Are you enjoying the finale of the 1978 Iowa State Fair?"

Roars, applause, whistles, thunderous stomping.

"How about a special round of applause for the announcer of our show, Mr. Keith Whitmore from Port Chicago, California!"

Whitmore took a step forward, smiled and waved, got his due smattering of applause, then stepped back in line.

"And our crew—Mr. Mike Stern from Price, Utah, our high-flying motorcycle stuntman and wheelie expert—" Step forward, wave, smile. Applause. Step back.

"—Mr. Terry Flynn from Seattle, Washington, our dynamite expert— he's okay now—" Flynn shook his head as he waved, still dusty and a bit groggy after walking away from the Russian Dynamite Death Chair less than an hour earlier. Applause.

"—Mr. Galen Washington from Denver, Colorado, America's only full-blooded Indian stuntman, and the best crashman in the world—" Tink stepped up, took his applause, and stepped back.

"—Miss Connie Coulson from Casper, Wyoming, our lady driver—" Connie barely managed a smile and wave.

"—my second-in-command, my right-hand man, my nephew, the best stuntman I've ever met, from Green River, Wyoming, Shaun McGinnis!" Shaun trotted forward, waved, gave Ian his helmet, and then stepped back in line.

Ian introduced Joel, Hanna, and the clown, and Grace; each got their own moment to bask in applause. Then he gave the mike back to Whitmore and turned to walk toward the jump car.

Ian was pleased with the jump car, a 1964 Nash Rambler wagon, six cylinder, automatic, of course—couldn't have a gearshift sticking out where it could hurt somebody. They'd found the Nash in a junkyard before their last show at Storm Lake and bought it—a steal at fifty dollars because it hadn't been running, but Ian knew he and Tink could get it going—and hauled it to Des Moines, here, for the season finale. Long experience told Ian that the '64 Nash Rambler wagon with a six made the best jump car. Lighter front-end with the six, longer than a sedan, sturdy frame, more steel above the rear, nice balance bumper to bumper. Good aerodynamics. Ian never depended on his bookers or sponsors to find a really good jump car because they didn't understand what to look for. He praised his lucky stars when they had one waiting for him before a show, but he never counted on it. When he found the right car between shows, he snatched it up and towed it along.

Iowa State Fair Board member Devon Rowe of Rowe Brothers Ford had meant well when he provided a sharp-looking 1972 four-door flat-top Caddy for use as the jump car, and Ian had been polite, even enthusiastic in receiving it, as well as the other two junkers Rowe had provided, all runners, but the flattop Caddy had a tendency to spiral in the air—it was too heavy in front—and the skinny posts always collapsed like cardboard. Dangerous. He'd opted for the Nash as his T-bone jump car, the Caddy relegated to first catch car. The Caddy would tear apart spectacularly under the Nash.

All the crash cars were painted with the Rowe Bros. Ford logo in splashy, bright spray paint, Tink's pre-show artistry.

Shaun walked at Ian's side as he approached the Nash's driver's side. Whitmore's description of the upcoming stunt to the audience had turned to mush in his ear as his hearing aid faded further. This was Whitmore's second season, and he knew the routine. He could take as much or as little time to talk about the stunt as Ian needed or wanted. He was one of the best announcers Ian had ever had, with a natural sense of show timing. Ian didn't need to monitor him.

He pulled the hearing aids out of his ears and tucked them in his shirt pocket. That familiar underwater feeling enshrouded him again.

After he'd lost his hearing in an early experiment with what eventually became the stunt known as the Russian Dynamite Death Chair, Ian lost a pair of hearing aids in a T-bone crash. The crash jarred the plastic lumps loose and they got ruined. He learned to take them out before doing a jump or a crash. Or the dynamite chair. Put them in your shirt pocket—wear shirts with button-down pockets where you can find them twice in a row— then stick them back in your ear when you get done with the stunt.

At Ian's side, Shaun started to say something, but Ian couldn't hear.

"What?" Ian cupped his ear.

He fell.

He grunted in pain as his right foot twisted sideways and he slammed hard to the ground, like he'd stepped on a patch of ice. He sat up and saw the culprit, a greasy black knob of machinery near his foot. Ian groaned through gritted teeth and grabbed the offender, an AC pump.

It was the pump Shaun had been starting to talk about a second ago. He'd taken it out of the Nash at the last minute, probably thinking, Ian guessed, that losing the extra couple pounds in the front end would help the stunt. Not guessing, Ian thought, that leaving it lying around after he took it out was a bad idea.

Swearing through gritted teeth, Ian tossed the greasy lump away without watching where it went or who it might hit.

Details, Ian thought as he tried to stand, Shaun and Tink helping under each arm. Keep the infield neat. Account for everything. Double check. Take care of the other fellow. Have a plan in case shit happens. Details.

"Are you okay?" Tink asked. Ian lip-read more than heard the strained question.

Whitmore kept up his muffled spiel. He probably hadn't seen Ian fall, he'd gone down so fast, and Whitmore was facing the audience, his back to Ian. Ian tried to put weight on his ankle, but the ankle screamed in sharp reply, and Ian tasted blood in his mouth where he had bit his tongue, crying out in pain.

"Of course I'm okay," he grunted.

He'd twisted his right ankle, and he wondered if he could manage the accelerator and brake with his left foot. He'd done it before, driven a car with a broken ankle, and he had plenty of track, so there was no hurry.

But when he'd done it before, it hadn't been a few seconds after breaking the ankle. And this hurt like hell.

He tried to stand on it again, leaning on Tink and Shaun, and he did his best to stifle a scream. It hurt like all hell.

"Ian, maybe I should," Shaun said, "you know—"

"What?" It sounded to Ian as if Shaun was talking under water, but Ian knew what he was saying. "*You* do the jump? Is that what you're going to say?"

Shaun nodded. "Yeah. That ankle looks—"

"Like hell." Ian pushed Shaun and Tink away awkwardly but forcefully and stood, sweating, teeth clenched, wobbling like a newborn calf. "I'm ready. I can do the goddam jump. I can do the—" He took a step toward the car, and pain lanced up his right leg like fire. He fell. It hurt like hell.

CHAPTER TWO

*T*he previous November, Ian had driven his road show car to the Iowa State and County Fair Convention in Des Moines. His road car was a 1976 Ford Maverick, two-door, three-speed, six-cylinder. He'd repainted it days before in red, white and blue stars and stripes after a design Grace, with help from Tink and Joel, had come up with. After he arrived, Ian washed off the bugs and road grit at a drive-through car wash. He spent an hour hand polishing it. Then he drove the last mile to the motel and parked the flashy show car as close to the motel front door as he could so people could see and marvel.

He'd already been booking through Nebraska and Kansas in the previous two weeks, missing Halloween at home with the kids. He planned to drive straight to Oklahoma tomorrow morning for the Oklahoma fair convention the following weekend, stopping at a few stock car racetracks on the way to see if he could fill in a date or two in the process. After Oklahoma, he'd swing through Colorado and then home a week before Thanksgiving. Then he'd take a long break: return whatever calls he had waiting, wait for his phone to ring, see to his cattle, winterize Gran's house, tend to McGinnis's Big D Tires in Green River, take in odd paint and repair jobs in his garage, and work on his show equipment through the bulk of the winter. He'd get back into serious booking mode in February, on the road and on the phone. He'd book through March, then finish getting ready for the season.

He'd set out in mid-April, if he had a good season.

He hoped he wouldn't have to wait until May to start. A late start cut into the wallet, but there weren't enough fairs early in the summer, and he'd have to book racetracks to fill empty days. That way always took more time to set up and was more risky financially. For the filler gigs, or "fill dates" as he called them, where he rented a track for a show and promoted it himself rather than coming in sponsored and at a fixed fee, Ian would have to do his own advertising and promotion, buy his own junkers, rainout insurance, and so on. Sometimes he made out like a robber baron, but sometimes he lost his shirt when the stands didn't fill or there was a rainout and he'd gambled by not buying insurance for the date, or something else happened. There was always risk.

The end of the season was also important. It was easy to find he'd booked two good dates in Texas in mid to late August before he discovered that there were six better ones in the Dakotas or the Corn Belt, dates that he had to pass up because he'd already compromised them in Texas. It was delicate work, booking.

Iowa, he knew, as he set up show posters in the Ramada Inn lobby, could be pivotal and difficult to work out. It was theoretically possible to book as many as a dozen dates in Iowa, but not realistic. There were plenty of county fairs in the state, but many were clustered on the same three weekends in August. If he accepted a contract, say, in Council Bluffs for August 12, what should he do if he got an offer from Dacorah for an afternoon show August 13?

Back-to-back shows were hard enough on equipment and crew, especially late in the season when everybody got tired, lost their edge. But a back-to-back with the second date an afternoon show, and after a long overnight haul?

If Ian needed the money, it might be worth the risk. But he couldn't know that—or the condition of crew and equipment at season's end—before the season started. It would be a tough call, and he hoped it never happened.

Then again, he might get a repeat booking in Oskaloosa and Washington—those gigs had worked out well last year—followed by alternate-day swings through, say, Cedar Rapids, Waverly, Madison City, and then maybe wrap up in Sioux City. That would put the show headed west, headed home, on the last weekend of August, a grand finish. A good dream, but it could happen. No five hundred mile hauls between dates, no afternoon gigs, no back-to-backs in August.

Such were Ian's thoughts as he checked the list of fair dates on the letter he'd gotten from the fair board in September, announcing the convention date and location, and as he studied the Rand McNally road map spread out on his bed in his room at the Ramada.

Snow fluttered and gusted in the parking lot, and the hotel lobby windows sweated with the over-heated air inside as Ian set up a poster in the lobby announcing "The Ian McGinnis Auto Daredevil Thrill Show! Thrills! All-new for 1978! Chills! In its 15th Consecutive Season! Spills! Meet Ian IN PERSON! *in rm. 205.* Fun for the whole Family! Affordable Arrangements!"

Ian had put the poster out early, even before he unpacked, so he'd get a good spot next to the elevator. He noticed a few other shows had arrived even earlier then he had—The Jordanaires, Carlos "The Great Escape" Lombardi, Patterson's Carnivals, The Oswald Family Band—and they'd clustered their posters closer to the stairs and the entrance to the restaurant, thinking most people would use the stairs in the three-floor hotel since the stairs were closer to the lobby and so they'd see their posters, but Ian knew better.

Years ago, back when he'd been working with Sid Hirsch, after his first season—that long ago—he'd been booking with Sid in Fargo, North Dakota. It was early December and Ian's first time booking in the off-season. He'd noticed the room next door to them was getting serious traffic and Sid Hirsch's Tournament of Thrills wasn't getting much. Curious, Ian left Sid and his bottle of gin to study.

The next door neighbors, an Italian acrobatic act, "The Flying Lazzarinis," had a lot to teach Ian as he sneaked a peek into their room. He took mental notes of the bowls of candy, the booze placed so that it could be brought out or hidden depending on whether the fair delegation visiting had liquor already on their breath or if they had kids in tow. There was a buxom teen-aged girl in the room, one of the performers maybe, and Ian took note of her scanty costume and how she placed herself in the room with men bookers. And how she donned a demure coat when those men had wives with them. And the secret winks in any case.

Music, posters, lots of color, brochures, ribbons, a running film. The smell of hot buttered popcorn wafting through the air, aided by a small fan strategically located for the purpose. Food. Drinks. Details.

Ian's mind reeled when he realized that Sid didn't have a clue how to promote a show. He decided to make a list of things, of details, to write it all down so he never forgot.

He went down to the lobby, passing Sid's room where the door was, stupidly, half-closed. Inside, he could hear Sid's slurry twang extorting the virtue of his own show over that of his competitor, Crash Dick. Sid sounded whiney, defensive. He was doing a good job of selling Crash Dick and the Death Dodgers. Ian shook his head in amazement and walked down to the lobby, still studying. There, he noted the professional job some acts had done with their posters compared to the amateur job evident in Sid's. Sid's poster was too small. And in the wrong place.

People going upstairs, Ian discovered, watched their feet so they wouldn't trip. They didn't watch posters extolling the virtues of "Augie French's Amazing Trained Dogs" or "Wailin' Joe Wilcox" or "Buckskin Jack's Wild West Show."

People who used the stairs were in a hurry, too big of a hurry to wait for the elevator, let alone read posters. When they went to the hotel restaurant, their minds were on food, and even if they saw an intriguing poster before they got seated, they would forget about it by dessert.

On the other hand, people going up the elevators sometimes had to wait for the next car, and their eyes drifted as they waited. They had time to read the poster Right There, extolling "The Flying Lazarinis," who waited in a room Right There, just after you got off the elevator.

The next year, Ian's first on his own, he got the details right, and he booked a good first season.

Now, fourteen years later, in Des Moines, Ian was surprised to see three members of the Iowa State Fair Board Entertainment Selection Committee shuffled into his room, straw cowboy hats in hand, just before lunch.

"Heard about your show," one twanged, looking around the room, ill at ease. "What do you got?"

Ian had heard that Jimmy Hapgood's Auto Thrill Cavalcade had the state fair sewn up, so he hadn't expected to even have a chance to pitch the state fair. He stifled his excitement. The state fair was a plum date. He could book it for three times the going county fair rate and make out like a bandit selling programs and T-shirts and souvenirs to a larger crowd after.

Part of Ian's pitch was a sixteen-millimeter film showing brief glimpses of the different show stunts, something he'd paid a small fortune to have put together professionally at KSL TV in Salt Lake City in the off season two years before.

The three men in the committee were all bulky, clean-shaven, middle-aged with deep tans from the middle of their foreheads down, farmer tans. They dressed in pearl-snap plaid shirts, new jeans, big leather belts with dinner plate buckles, and cowboy boots. They smelled of Mennen.

They watched the film without expression, munching Ian's popcorn and pretzels, sipping his Coke. No boozers among them.

They watched the film and Ian watched them watch. They sat in a row on folding chairs, staring, munching, sipping, expressionless.

The T-bone crash was only a twenty-second segment toward the end of the five-minute film, but Ian saw one of the men lean forward and squint at the screen at that point. Ian altered his pitch and focused on that stunt and the interested fair board member.

It turned out the man was Devon Rowe of Rowe Brothers Ford, a big Des Moines car dealer who did his own TV commercials and had small-time political ambitions. Another fair board member, who didn't make the booking trip because he was busy working overtime in the wake of a recent ice storm south of the city, was Perry Wallberg of Wallberg Towing and Wrecking. Both were new to the fair board.

Ian found out that the two had lobbied their colleagues hard and fast for a car show as a finale for the fair. It made sense to them because the two could use the show to promote their businesses. They'd sold the notion to their colleagues who'd been burned in back-to-back seasons by over-priced famous-name country and western singers who didn't draw decent crowds and lost the fair serious money.

They'd tried to book Jimmy Hapgood weeks ago, but Hapgood apparently told them he had a conflicting date, so they'd turned their attention to Ian, Hapgood's only competition, besides Terrible Tom Tolliver, who wasn't available let alone affordable. Hapgood was famous, but they'd heard about Ian, heard that he was good too. Ian said the appropriate magic words but couldn't get an on-the-spot commitment.

The three left. "We'll talk it up and get back to you." An hour later, after lunch, they came back.

In his pitch, Ian had casually promised he'd do a T-bone for the show finale, but he really didn't want to. "You sure you don't want the car carrier jump?" he asked again, pen in hand, smiling. His boilerplate contract stipulated that Ian had the right to change the show, but everybody knew details could be inked in. Ian didn't want to get sidetracked this late in the game pitching the car carrier jump over the T-bone, or arguing contractual details, but—

"No, sir," Devon said, shaking his head, lips pursed. "We got our hearts set on seeing that T-bone."

Ian later discovered that Devon Junior, who'd just gotten his first drivers license and a brand new Mustang for his sixteenth birthday, had seen an amateur try a T-bone during intermission at a stock car race the previous summer in Fairbury, Nebraska. Some local racing celebrity had nearly gotten killed trying to do the stunt, but Devon Junior wanted to see it again.

"Can do," Ian said smiling, and he signed, inking in the T-bone as the show finale for the 1978 Iowa State Fair.

He signed Storm Lake and Sioux City too, later that day.

Sitting in the dirt beside the jump car, Ian reached out and massaged his twisted ankle. Grace had seen that something was wrong from the other side of the trailer, and she'd come running.

"Ankle?" she asked, kneeling. She'd gotten the small Johnson & Johnson first-aid kit from the van before she ran across the infield to Ian.

Ian nodded, grunted. Grace started to unlace Ian's boot, but he pushed her away. He signaled for help and Tink and Shaun helped him stand. Shaun had Ian's helmet in his hand.

"Put it on," Ian said.

"What?" Shaun looked baffled. Then: "Oh." Brightly. "The helmet. You want me to do the—"

"Do the goddam stunt, yeah. I'm afraid I'll faint trying to hold onto that last corner."

"Okay, boss, I got you."

Shaun was already climbing through the driver's side window, snagging his pants on the twists of bailing wire they used to seal the door—they never trusted door latches on junkers. Tink deftly unsnagged the pants and rewired the door as Ian grabbed Shaun's shoulder before he could snap the heavy-duty seatbelt on his lap.

"Listen up a sec," Ian shouted.

"Yeah, I'm listening," Shaun said, or Ian thought he said, but he busied himself securing his helmet and seatbelt. Fidgeting. Nervous. Blinking the sweat from his eyes. He'd never done a T-bone before. He had done well enough in rolls and the head-on, but Ian wasn't quite ready to let him do the T-bone.

"Remember to keep her at fifty-five," Ian shouted a foot from Shaun's left ear. He didn't need to shout, but his hearing aid was an inert lump of soggy, dirty plastic in his pocket and he couldn't hear himself. Whitmore would tell the audience that the car was going to travel at seventy miles per hour, show hype, because fifty-five wasn't as exciting or daredevilish as seventy, and few people could really tell the difference anyway. And fifty-five was plenty fast.

Shaun nodded and said something Ian didn't get. He was adjusting the helmet strap.

"Watch your speedo. This one works." Some speedometers didn't. In those, a driver had to go by feel, a matter of experience. "You got plenty of straightaway on the front stretch and you'll tend to get lead-footed as you come out of corner one." Adrenaline flows down the leg like piss, Ian knew, right to the accelerator, and it took a professional touch to ease up when that happened, something that came from experience, which Shaun didn't have, at least with the T-bone. "So relax when you come out of that last turn and watch the speedo, okay?"

Shaun nodded, started the engine, gunned it, and said something Ian didn't catch.

"Hold on," Ian said. "Let me see your reach." The crew had already adjusted the seatbelt for Ian, not Shaun, who was four inches shorter than Ian.

Shaun turned off the engine, then stretched across the front seat, grabbing the seat by the passenger door, fingers digging into the seat foam. He held the grip for a moment. Ian called it "stuffing yourself in the glove compartment," where the driver needed to be when his crash car hit, down low and under the posts so when the car flipped and the top came in, the driver didn't get his ribs crushed or his neck broken, which might happen if he was still sitting up behind the steering wheel at the time.

It meant the seatbelt had to have enough give in it—not too tight so Shaun couldn't make the reach quickly as he hit the ramps. But not too loose either, because that could rattle bones in a jarring impact, jerk a back bone loose.

The lap belt was a heavy, webbed airplane seatbelt, chained at each end under the car's frame through two holes Tink had poked in the floorboards earlier that day with a tire iron and a hammer when the crew were preparing the car, removing the glass, visors, mirrors, back seat, spare tire, and other dangerous and unnecessary items, and cleaning it out.

Two years ago, Tink had found a calculator they'd missed while stripping a car. It dislodged from under the seat in a head-on. It had raised a goose-egg knot on Tink's forehead as it dislodged on impact and got under his Bell Star and bashed him. Grace still used it.

The seatbelt that came with the Rambler had been rotten. Ian had long ago learned never to depend on factory equipment in a jump car.

"I think it's a tad too loose," Ian shouted. "Shaun, you got to take it up a notch, hear? Maybe three, four inches."

But it appeared to Ian as if Shaun hadn't heard, as if he was saying something to Tink, or listening to Tink, who was under the car, under the driver's side, maybe adjusting the seatbelt chain under there, pulling it tighter by a link. But he couldn't hear well enough, and as he started to repeat himself, Shaun restarted the engine, revving it. Tink got out from under the car, said something to Shaun, who turned to say something to Ian, but Ian didn't hear.

Shaun started out, with a fist *thump-thump-thump*ing with eagerness on the dashboard, all fire and vinegar, as excited as Joel on his first bicycle. He started the car forward toward the front stretch, in front of the grandstand, where Whitmore would give him a rousing send off, coax up a blast of applause—and maybe come to recognize and deal with the fact that it wasn't Ian in the car but Shaun.

Details. Ian went over the details in his mind as Shaun sped down the track in a smoky, dusty roar and into corner number three, counter-clockwise around the track. Seatbelt—did he get it tight enough? Speed—what if the cable broke in the front stretch on the final approach? Helmet—did Shaun get the chin strap adjusted?

Approach and take-off.

Shaun had to line up on the ramps straight, but the take-off ramps and the parallel catch cars on the other side of those ramps had been set up angled a bit toward the infield inside the fourth corner, so the crash car would tumble away from the audience at the left end of the grandstand—left from the audiences' point of view—a safety measure, in case car pieces flew or the crash car got out of control. Shaun would have to adjust his aim and speed right after coming out of corner one as he went wrong-way around the track.

Shaun drove clockwise, instead of counter-clockwise as the track was usually used for races. Crashing clockwise made for a better view for the audience on most tracks, like this one, and it made takedown and clean up after the show easier, faster.

For the moment forgetting his ankle, Ian tried to take a step so he could get a better view of the backstretch—the trailer and his sound van were in the way—to see how Shaun was doing.

His ankle screamed and he found himself sitting abruptly on the ground with Grace yelling something at him, her anger as evident as his pain. She jerked his laces out and slapped Ian's hand away, brooking no nonsense, as Ian tried feebly to protest. Instead, he let her take off his boot, and he tried to watch Shaun in the backstretch under and between the wheels of the van and the trailer.

"Too fast," he said to nobody in particular. "He's going too fast." Shaun slid low into corner two and nearly lost control of the car. But his speed dropped as he recovered and accelerated into corner one and into the front stretch, high and outside this time, close to the grandstand, where he'd get the longest and straightest approach to the jump ramps, have plenty of time to adjust his speed and aim straight for the ramps.

Ian twisted around where he sat and saw Tink inside corner number one, waving his arms above his head at Shaun, gesturing frantically.

Grace yelled something like "warm-up lap," as she jerked off the boot. Ian winced in pain and tasted blood in his mouth under his bit lip.

"He should take two laps," Ian said. He didn't really care if anybody heard him. He could barely hear himself. He was talking away the pain. Sometimes it worked. "Maybe stop on the infield after the first lap, to milk—"

Even as he said it, Ian heard the Rambler engine gear down and the dust rise as Shaun slid into the infield almost directly in the front and center of the grandstand. A concerned Tink and Flynn and Stern dashed over, talking to Shaun in animated hand gestures, lots of broad body language so everybody in the audience could see "Something Is Wrong."

Whitmore, Ian could tell by the tone of his voice on the PA, was milking the interruption, grimly intense, with something like "Ladies and gentlemen, we may have a problem—The crew is working over that engine—it's critical that the engine work at peak efficiency—young daredevil Shaun McGinnis knows his very life depends on—professional engineers working frantically—" And so on.

Details. Ian had forgotten to check the time as he'd dispatched Shaun into the finale.

The show was contracted for two hours. Too short a show and people complained that they didn't get their money's worth. Go too long and people got bored. You wanted to leave them excited, breathless, ready to come down on the infield after the show and look at the crunched cars and the shiny new stunt cars all lined up in a neat row and buy lots of programs and photos and T-shirts and get the smiling, carefree and charming daredevils to autograph them and go home happy enough to tell the fair board that they should book the show again next season.

Ian had forgotten to check how much time he needed to kill with the stunt. Usually he did that after he got into the jump car, checking out the belts, helmet, engine, and so on. But this time he hadn't gotten that far. He'd gotten flustered with the sudden injury and had forgotten to check the time.

Now, he glanced at his watch, wiping dirt and sweat from it, and saw that the stall had been a good idea. The show had been running fast because the roll cars had collapsed too quickly earlier in the show.

Or had Shaun in fact found something wrong in the engine? Shaun understood show well enough—he was a good actor—but maybe this wasn't show. Ian tried to listen to the crash car engine as Grace babbled to him, swearing at him as she wrapped an Ace bandage around his pale ankle, swearing in her genteel but earnest way as only she could when Ian got unbearably and stupidly stubborn.

Shaun revved the Rambler six dramatically and the crew poked and prodded under the opened hood, shaking their heads, lots of body language projected to the good folks in the back row. He couldn't hear anything wrong in the engine's deep roar—they'd removed the air cleaner, of course, and holed the exhaust to get a gutty roar out of the otherwise tame engine—but that didn't mean Shaun hadn't felt the engine miss or sputter alarmingly under the accelerator in the back stretch, and the whole world sounded to Ian like he was underwater anyway.

At last, Grace finished bandaging the foot, the crew finished wiring the jump car hood back down, Shaun gave an impatient wave, thumping the dashboard, and revved the engine into a greasy roar. Whitmore whipped up more applause from the audience, Grace helped Ian stand, and the show got back underway.

"One more test lap," Ian said to himself. Grace had wrapped her arm around his waist, holding tight, standing with him as they rotated around slowly, minding the sore ankle, facing and following the Rambler as it turned into the backstretch from corner three. Ian leaned on her shoulder, appreciating the soapy smell of her long black hair. He wanted the support now, and needed it, though he'd never admit to either.

"That first lap," he said, "he had trouble rounding into the front stretch, lost his angle and speed. Dirt's a bit greasy there. He'll need to check one more time."

Grace shouted: "He'll be okay." Or words to that effect.

"Especially if he found a problem in that last lap with the car." They'd tested the Rambler earlier that day, after they'd stripped it, to see how it performed. Shaun and Tink had driven laps around the track, then Ian had taken it. It felt good, sounded right. All systems looked good.

But junkers were junkers. This was a '64 Rambler they'd bought from a junkyard, and it hadn't been started in years, not until Tink and his crew got to it. Things could go wrong.

In any high-speed stunt—fifty-five miles an hour was considered a high-speed stunt for show purposes, like the head-on or a carrier jump—there was what Ian called "a point of no return." That point was an instant when the crash car is committed to finish the stunt, where there's no chance of aborting. At that point, if a wheel came off, or the engine stopped or the steering wheel snapped or snagged, or something else happened—and a lot could go wrong in a junker—all the driver could do was dive for the glove compartment, grit his teeth, hold on for dear life, and pray.

Ian had long ago stopped counting the times he'd missed or wiped out jump ramps because his crash car had gone out of control or quit running at the last second. He had the broken ribs to prove it. One summer, he'd gotten loose and he'd hit a sponsor's brand new Caddy, with the sponsor sitting in it.

That's why details were important, why Ian still mentally tightened his muscles, from broad shoulders to bowels, as if it were him in the car, not Shaun, driving—"too fast, goddam it, too goddam fast—"

"He's just doing show, Ian," Grace yelled into his ear. "Backstretch show. He's okay."

—and that's why Ian wasn't really blowing smoke when he told interviewers, like the pimply-faced teenager Radio Boy Wonder he'd spoken to a few minutes ago, that the show "is as much a thrill for us to do as it is for folks to see."

"Too fast," Ian mentally coached Shaun from a hundred yards away. "Ease up, ease up, ease up." Shaun was doing maybe seventy as he entered corner two. Way too fast.

At the last possible instant, Shaun hit his brakes and slid into the second corner, the back end of the Rambler slithered snakelike, and slowed just as much as he needed to keep from spinning out, a show no-no. He came on into the first corner in full control, rounding into the front straightaway, facing the ramps. He hit the accelerator again at the top of the turn and blue smoke and flying dirt followed him toward the jump ramps.

Suddenly, Ian felt his heart sink into his wounded ankle. "Oh, shit," he muttered, throat dry. "Oh, shit, shit, shit." He started running—hobbling—toward the crash set-up where Shaun would land. Grace did her best to follow-carry-support his awkward but determined hobble.

Too fast. Too goddam fast.

The T-bone is set up like this: parallel, even ramps are set in front of two cars that are set parallel to each other but perpendicular to the ramps. The ramp top ends are about a foot and a half off the ground, the right elevation. The crash car gets up to the right speed—fifty to fifty-five miles an hour on takeoff—as it hits the ramps. It flies off the ends of the elevated ramps, and hits the first catch car in the side.

If you get the right catch car, one with lots of thin metal in the side, like a big rusted out '67 Buick Skylark wagon or a '69 Chrysler Imperial flattop, the one with no center post between the front and back doors, and your jump car has the right speed and you get the right angle off the ramp and the ramp height is right and the distance between the end of the ramp and the first catch car is right, then the jump car rips completely through the first catch car, ripping it clean down to the floor boards, and tips its nose against the inner side of the second catch car, parked a few feet beyond and parallel to the first car. The crash car's momentum is then sufficiently spent that it rises in the air, nose down, truck up, to form, for an instant, a perfect inverted "T," which is the point of the stunt and where it gets its name.

Then the crash car, if everything has gone right to this point, drops spectacularly into the dirt or asphalt, but preferably dirt, on the far side of the second catch car. Forward momentum almost fully spent in the first and second impacts, the car comes to rest. It stops rather than crashes.

The driver, belted into his steel-framed cocoon, helmet secured, latched with an iron grip across the front seat and into the glove compartment, then emerges from the car, dirty, waving his helmet in triumph, but not until after a sufficient time for the announcer to dramatically wonder if he's survived the stunt, and for the ramp crew, or "safety crew," as everybody gets called at this stage, to gather around animatedly checking to see if the driver is okay, waving fire extinguishers, waving desperately to the standing-by ambulance crew for a false start, milking it, milking it, milking it, all for show.

It's a grand and spectacular stunt, if everything goes all right. But by 1978, Ian was the only daredevil show still doing a T-bone, and that only rarely, like when he got cornered into signing for it while booking shows the previous winter, as he'd done with this show. Ian didn't like to do the stunt because it didn't come off spectacularly—didn't come off *right enough*—often enough to afford the broken bones, bruises, and damage to crew and equipment. It was a bone-breaker stunt, and people were just as happy to see a motorcycle jump or a junker car jump over his car carrier lengthwise. Easier stuff, but crowd-pleasers.

Mike Stern had done the show finale most all season, jumping ten cars with his motorcycle, routinely, sometimes more, and giving Ian a rest, though Ian did a few car carrier jumps when he felt like it and had a good car to do it with. But Ian had booked a T-bone for this show, inked the contract in November, and he had to do it.

Shaun had to do it.

And now, he was doing it wrong. Ian's gut roiled as he muttered between steps toward the coming crash, "Too fast, too fast, too fast—" Grace puffing at his side, the crew converging, Whitmore shouting in cadence with the pending crash, his voice machine-gun fast.

Too fast.

Ian knew what too fast meant with the T-bone. He'd been there, still had the scars.

Seconds, now, and nothing Ian could do about it.

Shaun sped toward the takeoff ramps, still accelerating, Ian could tell, out of the corner. Too much straightaway, he thought. Needed a pro's touch, Ian's touch.

Too late, too late, too late—

There was a pause as Shaun hit the ramps. Time froze.

Whitmore's breathless, shotgun narration over the PA had risen to a fever pitch. Then, as the crash car hummed to within twenty feet of the ramps, Whitmore went abruptly silent and let the hushed, breath-holding, eyes-agog crowd gape in wonder and listen—really listen—to the *silence* before the horrific impact of metal on metal, a sound like a train wreck, a menacing, awesome sound that needed no hype to register.

But that instant wasn't exactly silent. Whitmore knew this, and Ian knew it. The crowd had hushed, Whitmore had hushed—and the abrupt shift from whiplash carnie barker narration to sudden silence emphasized that silence. But there *was* sound, even if at the moment Ian couldn't hear it over the sound of his panting muttering, "—too fast, too fast, too fast, too fast—" and Grace saying something in his ear as he hobbled helplessly toward the coming disaster. He couldn't hear the faint girlish scream coming from somebody in the Ferris wheel in the carnival behind the grandstands, or the *pop-pop-pop* of a carnie shooting gallery or the tacky hurdy-gurdy music from the carnie midway, but those sounds were always there.

He couldn't hear the woody thump as the Rambler's front wheels hit the jump ramp approach boards. He couldn't hear the distinctive high-pitched whine of tires spinning in the air as the car left the end of the ramps and hung in midair for a split second, poised to hit the first catch car—poised as if frozen in molasses—"too fast, too fast"—or the bone-jarring metallic *whack* as the crash car slammed into the first catch car.

Ian fell again, either catching his wounded ankle on a hole or bump in the uneven ground, or because his heart had fallen into his injured foot and he couldn't stand the thought of staying upright at that instant.

From fifty yards, an instant before Shaun hit the first catch car, an instant Ian wanted to freeze in his mind, to rewind and try again, only with him in the driver's seat—doing it *right*, goddam it, him, not Shaun, doing it *right*—Ian *saw* Shaun.

Saw him.

That was bad. Real bad.

If he could see Shaun in that snapshot instant before the Rambler hit, than Shaun wasn't in the glove compartment. For whatever reason—things went wrong, that's why you paid attention to details, why it's called a thrill show—Shaun was sitting up.

The crash car hit, and the first catch car imploded in stunning bright steel, ripped like tissue, and dust and shrapnel flew. The first car split with a heavy metal shriek clear through to the floorboards, but Ian knew what would happen next, knew it as Shaun had turned into the front straightaway "too fast, too fast, too fast," knew the second car would split too, rather than catching Shaun's car and spending its momentum.

Shaun would either land on his wheels and go careening farther on down the track, completely out of control—down there, a wrecker parked, Wallberg Towing and Wrecking, with Perry Wallberg himself at the driver's seat, and his kids, two little girls, "free tickets, and you get to watch from the infield, ain't that a thrill?" A few spectators always managed to get onto the track at the wrong place and at the wrong time no matter how much energy you spent on security. There they were, two teen-aged boys inside the fence, watching, beer cans in hand.

Out of control.

Either that, or Shaun's car would slam down into the dirt on the other side of the second catch car so hard they'd end up scooping him out with spoons and sponges.

Ian felt rather than heard the crashes, felt them in his bones. The first, in the first catch car, high-pitched, like a woman screaming, and the second, another woman's abrupt scream but more brassy, as Shaun clipped the second car, sheered it almost in half.

Then the third crash.

From his vantage, Ian couldn't see Shaun's crash. A billow of dust rose from beyond the battered, gutted, raw-edged catch cars, and a piece of loose chrome, like a silvery baton, rose and spiraled into the air, flashing, straight up and straight down into the dust and acrid smoke, and there was a scream.

A man's scream.

Ian had heard it distinctly, despite no hearing aid, as clear as if it had been his own voice, or Grace who'd screamed, running, limping beside him, her face contorted in anguish.

She'd heard it too.

CHAPTER THREE

Nick Cassidy revved the '75 Kawasaki Big Horn 350, feeling the power under his leather-gloved hands through the throttle, a palpable kinetic energy cranked to the max and barely leashed. The two-cylinder engine rapped to a piercing high pitch and a tight vibration coursed through his arms and thighs and butt. He closed his eyes, taking a private moment to savor the sensation, a familiar tingle, a high. The dirt bike smelled of burning gas and hot rubber. Sweat drenched his thin cheeks and plastered his long, stringy blond hair to the back of his neck. The bike felt like it wanted to explode from under him, launch to the moon, and he felt ready to let it.

But was the crowd ready for the jump?

Nick eased back on the throttle, gut-roar to gentle buzz, flipped up his helmet visor, wiped the sweat off his pale forehead with a thumb, and scoped the scene around him. He stood straddling the bike at one end of the raised rim of Ingersoll's Quarry, a semi-oval, stadium-sized, crater-like dirt bowl. Half a thousand members of the Confederacy of Angels and their cohorts and hangers-on ringed the bowl rim, all watching him, jumping up and down, waving their arms, yelling. In the blast furnace hot, clear late August afternoon, sticky-humid, half the crowd—mostly men but a few women—were shirtless. Most were drunk or stoned or both.

Nick couldn't hear them yahooing over his breathing inside his helmet and the engine rapping. Didn't want to, or need to.

They were almost ready, anticipation cranked to near fever pitch. Almost.

Where was Danny?

Dozens of granite boulders from the size of dead dogs to some as big as trucks haphazardly pocked the floor of the bowl Nick faced. In the non-stop party that had raged the past few days, thousands of motorcycle treads had packed the bare, grassless ground among the obstacles into asphalt-hard dirt, perfect for bike racing and assorted invented-for-the-moment two-wheeled games and tomfoolery.

The playground was an abandoned rock quarry on the remote edge of a ratty farm three miles east of the gravel road between Red Lick and Till-man, Mississippi, twenty-five miles east of the river. A dense pine forest in low rolling hills surrounded it. The weedy, twin-rut dirt path from the main road to the run-down farm and quarry wasn't marked by so much as a "private property no trespassing" sign, but the Angels and their friends knew where it was.

Nick spotted Danny's lanky frame amid a cluster of rowdies and their bikes at the far end of the bowl, battered lime-green helmet held high, waving it. As Nick watched, two big bikers stuffed what looked like handfuls of dollar bills into the helmet, and Nick got the impression that the money bucket was near full. Danny was at the landing site so he'd made a full circuit of the crowd. Almost ready.

The Confederacy of Angels was an outlaw motorcycle club, mostly white, mostly out of Jackson, but their colors flew from Mobile to Natchez and many of the tiny bergs in between. The Angels' raucous parties weren't welcome in most places in southern Mississippi, their turf, and definitely not in New Orleans, a rival gang's territory.

This was a private party, members only, and on private property, member-owned. But under the club's loose notions, anybody who knew it was going down, knew how to get there and wanted in, was welcome. Cops excepted, of course.

Bring beer, women, and dope.

Nick had heard about the party a week before at a legal, sanctioned and sponsored motocross in Oxford, an all-American, clean-cut, chamber-of-commerce kind of event. He'd played by the rules there and had lost, but he made back most of his loss in a bet with a bunch of fellow losers in an unofficial, un-chamber of commerce-like post-event beer bash that night. He'd bet he could jump his bike over a dozen of their bikes lined up side to side. They'd seen him wreck his Kawasaki that morning and spend the day frantically trying to get it running again, with noticeably poor success, so they felt confident that he couldn't do it.

The take had been good, but not good enough. After the jump, Nick heard about Ingersoll's Quarry.

Buddy Ingersoll was an Angel. He'd inherited a farm, Nick had learned, but had to give it up for taxes or something. Didn't matter. Ingersoll had it for a month before the tax collectors moved in so he decided to throw a party.

Nick arrived after the party was in full swing, brought and gave away a dozen bottles of whiskey for good will, and set about showing off what a daredevil he thought he was, playing the smartass. Did some impressive, showy wheelies but he fell off once in a spectacular fashion. He was loud, cocky, and clumsy. Tried a mediocre jump and crashed. Spread gobs of Ben-Gay on supposedly bruised joints and wrapped himself in yards of Ace bandage. Spent that night fixing his bike, loudly proclaiming that he was going to try the jump again the next morning.

Nobody noticed he didn't drink or get high.

A gangly, pimply-faced kid had come up to him while he was fixing his bike, offering to help.

"Name's Danny." Toothsome grin. Firm, confident handshake, if a bit bony. "You sure know how to put on a show." Thick Big Muddy accent.

Was the kid saying that he wasn't fooled?

"How old are you?" Nick had asked. He feigned a muscle twinge, and Danny grinned, shaking his head. Unfooled.

"Eighteen. I'd like to learn how to take a fall like that. How do you do it?"

Nick snorted. "You're fourteen." Nick had just turned twenty-one.

"Seventeen." Danny huffed, Adam's apple bobbing, indignant. "And ain't nothing wrong with your bike. I don't get that either. What's up, man?"

They finally settled on "fifteen and a half," and Nick recruited him, cutting him in for a percentage of the take, briefing him that night on his part in the show.

Nick tried the jump again just after sun-up and failed again. Danny helped him wrap more bandage and "fix" the bike, again, and spent the rest of the day shilling for the evening's planned main event. For right now.

Almost. Another minute, or two.

The sun started to dip into stringy pink clouds laced low over the river when Nick made his move.

He revved the bike again, a mechanical question hollered to Danny a hundred and twenty yards away: "Ready?"

As if he'd heard and understood, Danny turned to face him and waved the money-stuffed helmet over his head, a signal: "Bring it on." Then he stalked down the rim slope, knees and elbows bobbing like an animated scarecrow, toward the far side of the big boulder where Nick would land in a few seconds. He disappeared behind the boulder and Nick revved again.

Showtime.

Nick took off his helmet and waved it high, ready to go. The crowd cheered, yahooed, whistled and stomped. Nick put his helmet back on and focused on the path ahead, and the next few seconds. If aliens had kidnapped the entire crowd, Nick would not have known or cared.

Focused.

The jump Nick faced was the longest anybody had tried during the week-long party, but Nick had paced it out and he knew what he could do. To a casual observer, it looked dangerous, maybe even impossible, but he had jumped longer, twice, and he felt sure he could handle this one.

That was part of the trick: make it look hard but make sure you can do it.

He faced a thirty-five foot long, twenty-five degree downslope of even, hard-packed clay, onto the bowl floor, then a straight, level stretch of ninety-five feet before he hit the upramp. The upramp, close to thirty degrees but not quite, was two four-by-eight pieces of plywood nailed together end to end and propped up against a boulder about the size of a station wagon and seven feet high. The center of the upramp had been braced with rocks and two-by-fours. Nick had hammered the boards into place himself.

The station wagon boulder over which Nick would jump was eight feet wide. Beyond it was a stretch of relatively open ground and then, a hundred and ten feet away, another boulder. Nick called the second big rock the Oldsmobile because it looked like one. It had almost the same dimensions as his take-off boulder. At the far side of the Oldsmobile, a sloped plywood ramp, twin of the take-off ramp, waited for Nick to land on. Beyond the landing ramp, Nick had a clear-enough shot, eighty-five feet, to the far rim of the arena, near twin of where he now sat.

If Nick missed, and went wide of the landing ramp, to his right, an irregular mass of refrigerator-sized boulders waited to shatter his bones. Flanking the landing ramp on the left, a low pile of square hay bales piled up around somebody's make-do campsite.

After he landed, he'd ride up the far arena rim, using the thirty feet of upslope there to help dampen his momentum. Then he'd take off his helmet, shake out his blond hair, and wave his helmet to make sure everybody saw him, saw that he'd done it. He'd turn off the bike so he could hear their cheers, close his eyes and soak in the sound for a moment. Applause: his other aphrodisiac.

Then he'd put Danny on the back of his bike—Danny had said he'd hitchhiked in—with the money bucket and they'd ride out of Ingersoll's Quarry, put distance between them and the large, rowdy, and unpredictable crowd. They'd get out quick; delay might tempt some of the more intemperate to think about robbery. They'd count the loot after they got to the gas station in Tillman where Nick would give Danny his cut, plus a generous tip, if there was enough. Then they'd part company; Danny had said something about needing to get back to his uncle's farm north of a town called Jack in Alabama.

"Jack?" Nick laughed. "Is that really the name of a town?"

Danny had blushed and stammered, unusual for him. "I don't come from there," he'd said. "I'm a city guy, mostly. Montgomery. Mobile. Bright lights and city ways."

Nick had laughed and Danny had changed the subject.

If all went well, Nick would have enough to cover fall semester.

Showtime.

Nick took a deep breath, eyes on the path ahead, mind already in the air, his entire body wired on adrenaline. He revved the engine to a screaming peak, brake hand aching with the strain. He let the bike go. It tried to jerk out of his hands, but it was part of him now, an extension of his body and will. In seconds, he was airborne.

The roar of an engine between his legs, all that power. That got Nick high. The sound of applause after he'd done something amazing, spectacular, even impossible. That too was a high Nick craved. But neither compared to the thrill that coursed through his veins like heroin when he got airborne, when he was flying.

He hit the takeoff ramp solid and straight at the right speed—he felt it. He launched into the air, leaning forward into the launch. He soared like an eagle, flying free. He tried to freeze the instant at the top of his arc, before gravity pulled him back down to earth.

Freeze it, savor it.

At the top of the jump arc, in that frozen, weightless moment, Nick saw the dog on the landing ramp.

CHAPTER FOUR

Shaun was Ian's nephew, the youngest of Ian's older brother Brian's three sons. Shaun's older brothers, Erroll and Fred, had had seasons with the show. Erroll had gone out two consecutive seasons, as a sophomore and as a junior at Rock Springs High School, before a drunk driver on I-80 outside Fort Bridger killed him at 3 a.m. January 1, 1971.

Fred did two seasons, '73 and '74, then graduated from high school and joined the Army. He served in Nam, got wounded, discharged, and came home a local hero. Now, he lived in Salt Lake City with his wife and two daughters. He drove a milk truck. He took the family to see Ian's show when it was in the area, anywhere within two or three hundred miles, which happened every couple of years.

Traveling with the Ian McGinnis Auto Daredevil Thrill Show for a season or two was a sort of a coming-of-age ritual for Erroll and Fred, during a summer in their high school years. Ian took other local boys with him on the road from time to time, sometimes after quiet discussions with concerned parents, and on two occasions, after talking it over with school counselors. Twice, he'd taken on a boy as a ramp hand after a talk with Sweetwater County Sheriff Ed Clarke. One boy was the sheriff's own son, headed for trouble. Ian, as expected, turned his charges around. That was the point.

Ian never pressed Erroll or Fred to join the show, or to stay with it once they'd been out for a season. He understood that life on the road wasn't what most people wanted, at least as a long-term investment of time and energy. So he was always prepared, at least mentally, to spend a large part of each winter replacing talent, or planning to do so. It was a bonus when Brian called or dropped by the house with one of his boys packed.

It seemed inevitable that Shaun, being the youngest McGinnis nephew, would be the last to work a season on the road, but in fact he'd joined up the summer after Erroll's death and helped show Fred the ropes when Fred signed on later, Shaun's precociousness mitigated by native charm.

Ian tried to do a show in the Rock Springs area at least once every other year. He did it sometimes to help warm up a new crew, sometimes as a fill date at the end of the season if the weather still held up and his equipment wasn't too shot, or he wasn't hurt too much. But he always did it because he felt it was a good policy for his friends and neighbors and family to see what he did for a living when he was away all summer. Let them know that it wasn't all crazy stuff, and that he wasn't an irresponsible whacko. They'd heard stories about Terrible Tom Tolliver, and Ian wanted to make sure they didn't think he was like that.

It was about credibility; it was about family. It was about payback, and it helped business at the Big D in Green River and at his own garage behind the house during the winter. His banker liked to see the show too.

Family always got in free, of course. But Ian never hesitated to put family—his own and Grace's sisters and their husbands and kids, and Fred and his wife and their kids, but only if they wanted to, and they usually did—to work on the show, painting, toting ramps, selling tickets, helping strip cars before a show, or clean up afterward. There was always a family dinner at Gran's after a local show, dozens of relatives and shirttail relatives showing up for Gran's big pot of beef stew and homemade apple pies and homemade ice cream, made from her own beef and her own apples and berries and from Beauty's milk.

By the time he was ten, Shaun had seen the show four times and had pestered his dad relentlessly to go on the road. "Wait'll you get to high school," Brian would say.

But Shaun took Erroll's death hard and became a discipline problem at home and at school in the winter and spring of '71. "He's getting a bit ragged around the edges," Brian had told Ian, "if you know what I mean."

"I hear you," Ian said. He knew. Send me a boy in March and I'll bring back a man in August. Brian had seen it.

So Shaun had become a working daredevil at the age of ten.

He dived into the work as if he were born to it. He was interested, genuinely interested, in how things worked. Others were fascinated by the adventure, the adrenaline rush of the show, all the circusy glitter and the hint of danger.

Ian could see that others loved seeing the show, but not doing it. There was a difference, he knew, between the way the show got appreciated by the people who did it as opposed to those who merely watched. "The show is as much a thrill for us to do as it is for you to see." The line was more than a slogan.

Even at the age of ten, Shaun seemed to understand.

Shaun was big and strong for his age, and after Erroll had died, he'd become a bully, getting into fights after school, hurting people. Breaking things at home. Running away.

Now, on the road, Shaun became eager to please his Uncle Ian and Aunt Grace, eager to learn all he could about the show and the stunts. He wanted to know everything and do everything. He pestered Ian with constant questions, getting in the way as much as helping. Ian encouraged the questions, did his best to stay patient with the energetic boy, and keep him from getting hurt.

Shaun served as a ramp hand that first year, carrying and setting up ramps and blocks between stunts, participating in the clown stunts, and functioning as part of the safety crew in the jumps and crashes, carrying a huge fire extinguisher with hawk-like vigilance—nothing would burn with him on guard.

He behaved as if he were sixteen, not ten, that first season, and as big as he was, he almost looked it. He insisted he'd carry more blocks than anybody, lift his end of the hundred and twenty-pound, sixteen foot-long wooden ramps, and get to the scene of a crash sooner than anybody else. He became a holy terror in stripping a car, competing with the other older and more experienced members of Ian's crew in contests to see who could get a crash car prepped faster, do it cleaner, spray paint it fancier. He was a super car washer, ramp painter, and sign putter-upper, and Ian was not surprised that he could move a junker around on the infield like a miniature grownup, same as he did his dad's field tractor back home, carrot-topped scatter-haired head peeping above the steering wheel, with professional competence.

Keeping Shaun from doing stunts that first year was impossible, he was so eager to do everything.

"I can do stunts, Uncle Ian. Just watch."

You got a driver's license?"

"No, but I can drive good. You just watch me."

"You're too short."

"I can put stuff under the seat, and tie a block to the accelerator, and—"

"But I won't let you."

"But you let me move the junkers around when we're setting up for a show."

"But I won't let you drive in the show."

"Why not, Uncle Ian? I'm good enough."

"Setting up and showing are different—"

And so it went, day after day, that first season. The crew started calling him "Muhammad Ali," but they shortened it to "Moo" in jest. He got mad at that and he'd yell and jump them, little fists flying when they did, and he bloodied a lip or two, so they stopped.

Ian would get exasperated, so he'd invent some task for Shaun. "Go get me a left-handed crescent wrench." Off the boy would run, only to come back a few minutes later—"There ain't no such thing, Uncle Ian. You were fooling with me and the guys are laughing and—"

"Laughing at you, huh?"

"Yeah, Tink and even Joel and—"

"Well, what did you do about it?"

"I kicked Tink right in the knee and he chased me and—"

"All right, all right—"

"Uncle Ian, can I help you with that? What are you doing? Do you need any help?"

And Ian would send Shaun off to reorganize the toolbox or adjust the van mirrors or help Grace do the laundry or go to the printer or put up posters or get the mail or something to get him away for a few minutes.

One afternoon in late August that first year, while setting up for a show, their second to last that season, Ian had been busy tinkering with the engine of his jump car, a '66 Ford Fairlane two-door. It had a gutsy engine so it would fly well, but the top was weak, so Ian opted for a carrier jump as the show finale rather than a T-bone. The junker had run well earlier in the day, but the carb throttle arm had jammed open, so he was under the hood tinkering. Tink was helping him.

He didn't see Shaun, all by himself, set up a ramp on the infield fifty yards away. Tink had been moving the ramp where it was supposed to go for the show when Ian had called him, exasperated with the jammed carb, and Tink had dropped the ramp and come running. Shaun saw his opportunity.

Just one ramp, not two. The ramps were heavy, but Shaun was strong and he'd learned how to move them without straining, and this one was practically set up already, at least enough for what he wanted to do. All he had to do was shift it a few inches and lay in an approach board at one end. Shaun was determined to show his Uncle Ian that he was ready to do a real stunt. Opportunity knocked. Shaun answered.

He set up the single ramp, the high end atop two wooden blocks, which made the high end not quite two feet off the ground, not quite enough, but it would do and he was in a hurry, wanting to get the task done before anybody stopped him—Ian and Tink had their noses in an engine. The rest of the crew was busy washing equipment on the other side of the back-stretch. Aunt Grace and eight-year-old Hanna, and Joel, the newborn, were off laundering uniforms and getting burgers for lunch.

So he got his jump ramp set up, got into a junker that he'd helped strip earlier that morning, and started it up. This one, a '49 bathtub Ford, earmarked for the rollovers, sounded quiet enough, which is exactly what Shaun wanted. He started up the Ford and was halfway around the track before anybody noticed.

"Omigod, Ian," Tink said, looking up from the jump car engine, "Shaun's got a car."

"What the hell?" Ian bumped his head on the underside of the hood as he rose to look.

Two of the hands with him that season, Eric and Leslie, as well as his announcer and clown, had started running across the track to intercept Shaun as he rounded toward the ramps, rooster tail of dust following, but they were too late and too far away. Ian stopped Tink as Tink was about to go over and kick the ramp down. "No," he said. "Watch."

Tink gave him a glance as if to say, "Are you crazy?" Then he got it and smiled. Tink was only thirteen at the time, but he'd been with the show for six years and Ian knew Tink understood.

Ian and Tink and the other hands watched as Shaun hit the ramp. He was going too slowly, and he hit the ramp crooked, knocking the ramp down rather than rising the car's driver side up it so he could cock the wheel and do a roll. Instead, the car flopped back to the ground with the grace of a dump truck and Shaun steered it as best he could—he had borrowed Tink's Bell Star and the helmet had turned around backwards on his head and he couldn't see—a few feet farther. The car collided with a soft, dusty *frump* into a pile of old white-painted truck tires, a crash barrier at the foot of a light pole. Shaun grunted as he jolted in his too-loose seatbelt.

Ian wasn't certain, and he never asked, because it could have been his hearing aid acting up, but he thought he heard Shaun utter, as he hit the tires, a very grownup "Oh, shit."

"You all right?" Ian said as he leaned into the driver's side window. Ian tried to turn Shaun's helmet around, but the boy slapped Ian's hand away.

"I'm okay," Shaun said, and he pulled off the helmet, his red hair scattering upward like straw in an electric storm. He gave Ian a look that could have been parts of triumph, chagrin, anger, frustration, and maybe a little terror. Ian had never raised a hand to spank him, but Ian could see the dread of that possibility in the boy's eyes. His dad had paddled him once or twice. Three times.

Instead, Ian laughed. Which, of course, made Shaun mad. And the other four members of the crew, standing by, relieved now to discover that the precocious boy was unhurt, laughed too.

"Hey, what are you laughing at, huh?" Shaun's face turned an angry red, his freckles standing out, and he undid his seatbelt and was halfway over the steering wheel, climbing out the windshield to attack Tink when he tripped and fell off the hood into Ian's arms.

"You did it wrong," Ian said to the struggling Shaun.

Shaun stopped struggling—Tink would live another day—and looked at Ian, puzzled. "What? What did I do wrong?"

Ian chuckled, amazed that Shaun seemed to understand not only that he did the stunt wrong, but that if he listened to Ian, he might find out how to do it right.

"Well, let's see." Ian sat Shaun on the hood of the car with a grunt—Shaun was very heavy, all chunky, compacted muscle, not fat. "Tell me what *you* think you did wrong."

Shaun blinked, sneezed a blast of grit from his pug nose, and nodded. "The blocks," he said. "I could only get two full blocks under the high end because I wanted to get going before anybody stopped me—"

"And what's wrong with that?" Ian shooed Tink and the others back to their jobs.

"Should have a half block under the high end too. Two and a half blocks for a roll. It was too low."

"So if the ramp high end is too low—"

"Well, then, either I got to go faster, or cock the wheel harder or—"

Ian shook his head.

"What, then?"

Ian explained. Rolling a car is a matter of precision, not speed. You set the ramp up high enough so that the roll car gets to a point where its equilibrium is in jeopardy for a critical instant. In that instant, the driver must cock the steering wheel *into* the roll, which undermines the equilibrium beyond the point of no return. If it's done right, the car will cascade onto its passenger side, then its top, then the other side, and back onto its wheels. If it's done right, when it stops rolling and lands upright, the engine will still be running, the wheels still attached and aligned, the steering okay, and enough metal remaining above the driver and the steering wheel to do the stunt again. If done right, with a good roll car—and some were better for the stunt than others, and a '49 bathtub Ford, with its rounded contours, like an inverted bathtub, hence the name, was better than most—a driver could roll the same car over and over again.

"But folks instinctively try to cock the wheel the other way, and that rights the car, so it doesn't roll. But what about the speed thing?"

"If you go too slow, you don't got enough—um—"

"Momentum. Same as if you go too fast. It's got to be the right speed, and that's about twenty-five miles an hour. Most folks think the car will roll if you go faster at the ramp," Ian said. "It ain't so."

"Why twenty-five miles an hour?"

"I'll tell you if you promise me you'll get an A next year in science."

"What's that got to do with—"

"Promise?"

Shaun promised and Ian tried to explain. Shaun frowned at the words "gyroscopic action" and "laws of thermodynamics," and Ian told him to look it up when he got home and "just keep her at twenty-five. Too fast or too slow and you don't roll. Then, you have to hit the ramp straight, dead straight, all the way up. Then, when you reach the top, you've got to cut the steering wheel—cut her real hard, mind—to the left, toward the grandstand, toward the ramp. Then, when you feel the top tilting away and you're looking at sky out the driver's side window, you dive for the glove compartment."

"The glove compartment. I've heard Tink talk about that."

"Show me your reach," Ian said.

"What?"

Ian told Shaun to get back into the car as he explained. Shaun demonstrated that he was too short to grab the far side of the front seat.

"See," Ian said, "that's why I don't let you do rolls in the show. Because you're too short."

"But, Uncle Ian, that's a good thing, being short."

"No, if you can't get under the posts when the car hits—"

"But I'm too short to *need* to. See?"

That stopped Ian cold and Shaun showed Ian that he had only three or four inches of head exposed above the posts, "so even if the roof comes all the way down to the bottom of the window frames, I won't get hurt, cause I could bend over easy."

Ian, impressed, changed the subject. He berated Shaun for not bracing the jump ramp with a block in the middle, without which his roll car might have broken the ramp. He berated Shaun for not cinching up Tink's helmet tight enough, and for not using a block on the accelerator so he could reach it more easily.

"But, Uncle Ian, you said that would be dangerous, having a block on the accelerator. Besides, I was in a hurry."

And so it went, for almost an hour, Ian giving Shaun an impromptu but thorough lesson in how to roll a car for show, all the details Shaun would need to know to do it right.

Looking back, Ian didn't really know when he decided to let Shaun do it for real, but it was some time about when he stopped Tink from knocking down the roll ramp that Shaun had set up, or Shaun saying "Oh, shit," or Shaun's insistence that being small was a good thing if you were rolling a car.

Ian coached Shaun for another half hour before he let the boy start the car again. Ian and Tink set the ramp back up—aimed away from the light pole this time—and Shaun had another go at it. This time, he went too fast and flopped off the end of the ramp and rolled to an inglorious halt a hundred feet away.

He tried four more times. He got it on the fourth, rolling the car onto its top, not a good roll, but he'd done it.

A week later, Ian rented the Sweetwater County Speedway for a Saturday night show. He put out word, deliberately mysterious, that there would be a special feature. Still, only a few hundred people came. It was cold and Ian had done a show the year before.

Ian insisted Brian attend.

That night, a brisk and windy night, rain threatening under hammerhead clouds, under the glaring track lights, the announcer announced preparations for the rollover contest midway into the show. Leslie Horst and Eric Mattson had done the rolls throughout the season, both quite adept at the task. "But tonight, folks, Eric Mattson has unfortunately suffered a debilitating but minor injury, so he'll be unable to participate. Instead, it gives me great pleasure to introduce to you, for the first time ever, the World's Youngest Daredevil Performer! Ladies and Gentlemen! Please welcome! The One and Only! Shaun! McGinnis!"

Shaun emerged from his hidey behind the van, spiffed in the show's fancy glittery, all-American tri-colored uniform. He waved a Bell Star helmet, one Ian had gotten for him a week ago when he decided to give Shaun this show.

Shaun ran out to his place by the roll car. The announcer hyped the stunt and the crowd "oh"ed and cheered. Shaun got into the car. Ian failed to stifle his laughter as Brian, watching from the grandstand, dropped a box of popcorn and spilled his Bud as he stood, sputtering and pointing. People nearby laughed at Brian's expense, pulling him back into his seat, slapping him on the back and teasing him as he watched, goggle-eyed and helpless as his youngest son got into the junker, started it up, and pulled it around onto the track in front of the grandstand, where everybody could see, spray-painted on the passenger side, "Hi, Mom & Dad! Love, Shaun."

Brian, Shaun's brother Fred, and the rest of the family McGinnis, those who weren't in the know about the surprise—Ian had told Brian's wife—sat stunned, shaking their heads in amazement as Shaun wheeled around the track, turned and came around for the stunt.

Ian later determined that Brian, of course, beet red at all the attention, was privately proud. Ian had done it again. Send out the boy, bring back the man. The surprise stunt was just icing on the cake. Ian had known that Brian would be angry, but the anger would be as much for show as anything else.

No, Ian had figured, Brian would be proud of Shaun. But he'd still chew Ian a new asshole for pulling off the surprise without Brian's permission. Ian had considered all this when he decided to do the Rock Springs show. He lost money on it, and he knew Brian might pop him in the eye, but he did it anyway.

He did it for Shaun.

Shaun did a show-perfect roll the first time. The car, a '63 Chevy Corvair Monza coupe, ended up on its wheels in a magnificently showy dust cloud, hardly a scratch on it. The hood was slightly wrinkled on the passenger side, but still wired down, and the engine had stopped.

"You okay?" Ian asked Shaun through the slightly crumpled driver's side window after the stunt.

"Hell yeah," Shaun said.

"Watch your language," Ian said. "The car looks good. Do you want to go again?"

"Hell yeah." Shaun started the engine and headed out.

The crowd roared, Brian beamed, and Ian and the safety crew got into position.

Yet another perfect roll.

"You okay?"

"Hell, yeah. I want to go again."

But the engine had conked out and the right front wheel had ripped loose from the rim. Ian checked his watch and declared the stunt over. Shaun climbed out of the car to the sustained whoop and roar from fans, including his father, mother, older brother, and cousins.

After the show, Brian's pop to Ian's nose lacked enough oomph to even draw blood, and it was followed quickly by a brotherly hug, beer from Brian's half empty paper cup spilling down Ian's back.

Brian asked the boy if he wanted to go with the show again.

"Yes, sir," Shaun said. He gave Ian a comic-serious look as if to say, "See, I heard you. Not 'Hell yeah,' but 'Yes sir.' I listen."

There had been a time when Ian had considered Tink as his obvious successor, someday, when he retired. If Ian ever retired, of course. Tink was intelligent and focused. But Tink had bad bones that broke easily. He was okay for rolls and even the head-on, but Ian wouldn't trust Tink's weak bones in a carrier jump, let alone the unpredictable T-bone.

Besides, Tink had made it clear that he wanted to go on to college and get a degree. In what, he wasn't sure, but in something. Tink had been adopted, didn't know who his parents were, except that they were Indian, Shoshone or Arapaho, from the Wind River Reservation. He wanted more. A couple of years before Shaun had come onto the scene, when Tink was himself being groomed for doing stunts as either "The World's Youngest Daredevil!" or "America's Only Full-Blooded Indian Stuntman!" and before Tink's weak bones became evident, Tink had made it clear that, after high school, he was off to college, the best he could find. Ian didn't begrudge the boy's ambition. "Go for it," he'd said. He helped Tink save money.

Joel was not quite a year old at the time.

So Ian had started grooming Shaun to assume a greater role in the show, maybe take it over someday. Shaun had the right stuff, even then, even as a ten-year-old kid.

Now, nine years later, here he lay inside a ton of crunched metal in the middle of the track at the Iowa State Fairgrounds, busted like a watermelon dropped off the back of a pickup.

They had to pry sheet metal apart with a crow bar and use a hydraulic jack to extricate Shaun. The crowd had gone dead-white silent after the stunning crash, sitting still and goggling at the upside-down car, its wheels spinning in the gasoline-fragrant night air. Shaun groaned loudly in the wreckage now and then, punctuating the near silence. A few people in the audience openly wept.

Whitmore was stuck, alone and improvising, out in the open, in the middle of the track, linked to his audience by a microphone at the end of a fifty-foot cord to the sound van, not able to really see what was going on in the wreckage.

What could he say?

The show's tone turned from excitement to quiet, stunned horror. Like a war turns from "There goes our heroes," to "Here comes the first boxcar full of dead boys." Whitmore did his best with the microphone, given the situation, one that he'd never witnessed before, but Ian couldn't hear. He was busy trying to get his nephew out of the wreckage and into the ambulance.

In the crash, the seat had ripped loose from its floor mounts and crushed Shaun against the steering wheel, which had bent like a pretzel. Shaun suffered broken ribs, a broken collarbone, both arms broken, a mild concussion, multiple bruises, and some internal injuries.

The worst injury, a doctor told Ian, was "an acetabular fracture."

Ian had heard doctor talk before; often it was just Latin-sounding tempest in a teapot, but this sounded familiar. "What's acetab—" And dire.

"Common in collisions," the doctor said, "where you strike an immovable object head on. The force drives the head of the flexed femur—that's the ball—" the doctor pointed at a colored anatomy chart on his office wall,

"—through the relatively thin bone of the acetabulum—"

"The hip socket," Ian finished. He remembered now. Common in collisions. He'd seen a few. "So what does—"

"He'll have some numbness and tingling, not to mention protracted convalescence."

"We'll take care of him," Ian said, mouth dry. "We got family."

"It's very painful. He may suffer a permanent limp."

Ian nodded, mute. Shaun wouldn't take well to being gimpy, let alone having to use a cane.

The crew stayed over an extra day before Ian sent them home. Grace drove the Freightliner hauling the car carrier alone; her younger days trucking her dad's cattle up to the range near Pinedale coming in handy once again. Ian stayed with Shaun at Iowa Lutheran Hospital. Shaun's fiancé Amanda flew out the next afternoon and Ian picked her up at the airport, one of the few times he was not at Shaun's bedside or in the hallway outside his room.

That evening, the doctors declared Shaun in stable condition and Ian finally got a chance to talk to him.

"You okay?" Ian asked, leaning over the bed. Ian had smelled hospital antiseptic, freshly starched sheets and bandages too often.

"Feel like shit," Shaun muttered through a drug-induced haze and an oxygen mask. His eyelids fluttered and his jaw drooped.

"Watch your language."

"Go to hell. Want to go again."

Ian went home the next day, assured Shaun was on the way to recovering. Amanda would stay until he was ready to go home.

Two weeks later, Ian drove back to pick up Shaun and Amanda and drive them back to Rock Springs. He drove the van instead of the road car, fixed it up so Shaun could lie down in the back.

Days later, Ian got a bill from the hospital. He'd expected to see the astronomical figure run up in Shaun's recovery because his injuries had been extensive and severe, and he'd expected that his insurance wouldn't reach far enough and that he'd have to dip into reserves. He called his insurance agent and got more bad news. He was right. Not enough.

Long ago, back when he was with Sid Hirsch, Ian had learned the practical and shrewd ins and outs of managing show insurance. Rainout insurance was iffy, damned if you did but sometimes damned if you didn't, like hail insurance in the Corn Belt. Liability was necessary for fair dates; they wouldn't book shows without it. You could take chances on some fill dates, but not all. Ian never bothered to insure his vehicles, except for liability. He was the best mechanic he knew, Tink almost as good, so there was no edge there.

But health and accident for his crew?

Insuring the health of people who deliberately crash cars and drive motorcycles through flaming walls, let themselves get run over by trucks, blow themselves up with dynamite for a living, let alone log twenty-five thousand miles driving big rigs on the road, mostly at night, in four months—it wasn't easy.

Ian had shopped for a good insurance agent, the right one; he found her in Wendy Wilding of Farmers Insurance in Salt Lake City. He made a point of inviting her to see local shows, made it a point for her to come early so she could see his set-up and safety prep, know the behind-the-scenes details. She learned that all the death and danger hype she heard during a show on the microphone was just for show, that Ian did everything in his power to ensure nobody got hurt, not only because hospital bills were costly, but because there was a show to do tomorrow and the day after; people with broken arms didn't drive as well. She learned that, when it came right down to it, Ian was a businessman doing business. Show business.

Wendy did her best to help Ian get coverage without busting him. Still, health and accident insurance cost Ian an arm and a leg. Always a risk involved.

As September turned to October in 1978, Ian sat at the kitchen table at home, a doublewide trailer that he'd bought used, had refurbished, and had added two bedrooms. A gloomy gray snowfall swirled listlessly outside the frosty window. Grace sat across the table, Tink's crash calculator in hand. Bills spread out in piles between them on the table as they went over the figures again, but the figures wouldn't budge.

"Looks like we're bust," Ian said.

CHAPTER FIVE

Ian had already inked a half dozen dates for the next season, and he'd booked rooms later that winter for the fair conventions in North Dakota, South Dakota, Kansas, and Nebraska.

"We could sell more stock," Grace said. She flipped open a file folder marked "Cattle."

Ian snorted. "Prices are pretty shitty." They kept a small herd on leased land over in Uinta County. Hobby farming.

"Still. The household budget won't stretch to Christmas. And you need money to book with."

"Not the cattle." Ian shook his head. "Not yet. I'll sell one of the show cars, and make some calls, see if I can hustle up some work in the garage. Maybe I can make Darrell Schumacher a deal to paint his fleet. Maybe I could put in some clock time at the Big D. Pay myself a decent wage."

Grace laughed at that. There was an oil boom, and the tire business was brisk. The store employed nine people in peak season, and winter wasn't peak, despite the boom. They didn't need Ian.

"Maybe we could get Hanna on a newspaper route," Ian said. Another joke.

"Hold off on the cattle, then," Grace said, laying the folder aside. Ian knew Grace understood the cattle market better than he did, growing up on her dad's ranch. She was just jogging him, getting his mind focused, was all. It worked.

"I'll take in sewing," she said.

Ian said nothing. Grace's winter sewing and doll making had never come close to meeting her household budget needs.

A long silence followed, and the kitchen clock ticked, the refrigerator hummed. From the living room, the flickering glow and subdued chatter of the TV came. Hanna was watching *Charlie's Angels*. Joel was in his bedroom, reading.

"What if you don't go out next summer?" Grace seemed hesitant to ask such a question, given Ian's dark mood. Doing bills always made Ian uneasy so she usually did them. But this was different. Shaun's spectacular mishap was catastrophic.

"I have to go out," Ian said, distractedly. He was looking out the window, thinking hard.

Ian had not tried to get a room at the Iowa convention. He'd taken a lot of flack from the fair board after Shaun's botched stunt. Apparently, the fair board had gotten complaints. Ian's show, remembered only for the bloody finale, had caused considerable emotional distress among a number of people in the grandstand, and the fair board had a few letters, some from people's attorneys. The board was doing what it could to squeeze calm and quiet out of the various provisions of the contract it had with Ian, but while it appeared that no lawsuits would materialize against the board or Ian, it was clear that Ian was better off staying out of Iowa for a while.

The Iowa county fair people had gotten word and they'd been spooked, Ian had discovered after making a few cursory phone calls. Maybe he could book a fill date or two in Iowa, later, but nothing more than that.

"We paid back the bank," Grace said.

"Oh, happy day." Ian often joked that Fred Weeks, at Rock Springs National Bank, was his best friend twice a year—in the spring when he borrowed heavily to buy new equipment and to have operating capital in his pocket before going on the road, and in the fall when he came home flush with cash and paid off the loan.

"But we're still short with Iowa Lutheran," Ian said, tapping the hospital bill. "And we still got all these others." He tapped a file marked MISC. DUE. "We can stretch, of course, but if something else goes wrong—"

"What else could go wrong besides Shaun?"

"—if it does, we ain't got leverage."

They both sighed, then burst out laughing as they realized they'd done so in perfect comic chorus, like something you'd see on the *Mary Tyler Moore Show*.

"Tighten the belt another notch," Grace said. "You book shows, work the garage and the store, and I'll pinch pennies." She stood, rubbing bloodshot eyes, and yawning. "We'll keep belly button and backbone apart, somehow."

Grace left to shoo Hanna off to bed. Hanna had just started her freshman year at Western Wyoming College up on the hill only a few days ago and she was still excited about the new adventure, first-day-of-school excited, like she'd been each year through high school, and before. She'd been studying hard for a quiz in her journalism class, seriously aware that the scholarship she'd won was all she had in her pocket.

Money. Always a problem, like a nagging toothache.

Ian sat amid the bills and tried to conjure up in his mind, not for the first time in the last ten years or so, what he'd do with himself if he wasn't doing a show.

He was a farmer, yes, and a crackerjack mechanic and painter. But he was a daredevil, and more that than anything else. It had been his life, what he did.

From the living room, he heard Hanna complaining, arguing in her falsetto whine with her Mom about having to go to bed. Grace gave in to Hanna's insistence that she was not a little girl anymore, "and besides, this test is a killer and I need to relax." Ian wondered if there was a boy in that class, a boy he didn't know about. Yet.

Which reminded Ian that he was not just a daredevil. He was a dad.

He went in to check on Joel, asleep with *Wizard of Oz* lying open on his chest. He left the bills strewn on the table, didn't want to touch them. Organizing those files and folders, that was Grace's job. She had a system.

In the next two weeks, Ian signed two more contracts, fill dates in Rawlins and Riverton, and he did the math and decided that he had his minimum—if he got no more dates at all, he could go out and at least break even. He got two paint jobs for the garage. If nothing went too catastrophically wrong, he'd be able to keep the wolf at bay, maybe through next fall. He booked three more shows before the month ended.

Just before Halloween, he got a call from his announcer. He'd hoped Whitmore would come back for another season, his third, but that's why Whitmore had called.

"I got an offer from Salt Lake, Ian," Whitmore said over the phone, gushing his excitement, "from KWMS, the news station. They want me. I start next week."

Ian took a deep breath, and congratulated his now-ex-announcer. After he hung up, he began flipping through his little black notebook where he kept names, phone numbers, and addresses. He took out a pen and under the section marked "poss. anncrs" he began ticking off contacts. He had seven prospects. He made seven phone calls.

Ian hadn't expected to connect right away. One contact said he "might think about it," but Ian had reached only two names on the list in that first try, so his hopes hadn't bottomed out.

He decided to see what the rest of last year's crew was doing, who he could count on, although he knew it was always iffy until the last week no matter what they told him this early in the winter. The call from Whitmore had made him antsy.

Buster Bledsoe, his clown, admitted he was thinking of staying on with his brother in his brother's meat packing business in Sioux City. "I don't really know, for sure, Ian, but I guess I could give you a 'for sure' maybe by February, maybe. If that don't strap you none, I mean. But I got to have me a job, you know."

Ian smiled over the phone and promised Buster that he'd keep the job open. After he hung up, he started calling names listed in his black book under the heading "clowns poss." He had nine prospects listed. Two sounded "poss," worth following up. One said, "I'll get back to you." None committed.

Terry Flynn said he'd be back, but Stern begged off. There was a girl, you see, and well . . . Ian understood.

So. Flynn, his dynamite man. Tink, who did crashes well enough, given his fragile bones. Hanna or Grace, or both, could be brought on to the track for some of the stunts, the simpler ones, like the rolls and the crew jump and hell driving.

He considered working with Joel on his mini-bike, to see if the boy was ready to do a flaming boardwall. If Joel wanted to do it for the show, it could help some. Some.

But not enough. Flynn, Tink, Ian, Grace, Hanna, and Joel. He needed an announcer and a clown and at least one more hand, preferably a motorcycle man, if he could find one.

There was a kid he'd heard about, Nick Cassidy. Ian had heard the kid handled a bike well on the motocross circuit back East, did good wheelies, had some good show qualities, but Ian had no contact number. Maybe he'd call around. Somebody might know how to reach him.

Unless the kid had already signed with Hapgood.

Ian picked up the phone again and called Shaun. Amanda picked up on the second ring and passed the phone to Shaun.

Shaun was recuperating at Amanda's mother's house. Mrs. Davis, Amanda's mother, was wheelchair bound, a result of the accident that killed Amanda's father five years ago. She liked Shaun and liked having him in the house. Having him bandaged up like a mummy, though, where she could keep an eye on him, and keep him out of mischief with her daughter, seemed like a good idea. Both of the kids were two years out of high school, and were pumping adolescent hormones like premium unleaded. They couldn't get married too soon, if you asked them. Shaun's accident had prompted them to postpone the wedding.

Shaun had sold his car, a '65 Mustang, and Amanda had taken on a job driving a parts truck for a drilling outfit south of town. She cashiered at the Big D on weekends. Belt-tightening. They were trying to save money for that wedding. Next month.

"Are you okay?" Ian asked Shaun.

"Hell, yeah," Shaun yelled, as usual, into Ian's earpiece. It wasn't just Ian, because of Ian's hearing aid. Shaun was always loud, boisterous, high-strung.

"Watch your language." Ian's hearing aid whistled and he adjusted it.

"Okay, boss. I'm doing great. How about you?"

Ian tried not to sigh, but he failed. "I just got a call from Whitmore. He's out. Know any good announcers?"

"Screw Whitmore." Shaun snorted. "He was a wimp. I might know a few people. Who else wimped out?"

Ian recounted his losses, and Shaun promised to see if he could make some contacts. "I think I know a couple of kids who would make good ramp hands. Let me check, boss."

"So, how are you doing?"

Shaun hesitated before answering, and in that silent second, Ian heard the truth. "I'm doing great, like I said. I'm ready to hit the road tomorrow. Well, maybe the day after, but what the hell. I'll be ready, count on it."

"Great. Let me talk to Amanda."

Pause. Then Amanda came on: "He's cranky, foul-mouthed, and he can hardly go to the bathroom by himself." In the background, Ian heard Shaun snort. "That's the truth."

"He says he'll be ready," Ian said. He cupped his ear. He wanted to hear her response clearly.

Again, the hesitation. "Well, you know he's got the constitution of a horse." She sounded tentative. "And he wants to go."

In the background, Ian heard Shaun say, "I'm damn sure going, and you damn well know it."

Ian bantered with Amanda a minute more and hung up.

Shaun would go with the show whether Ian or Amanda liked it or not, even if he was still wearing a cast six months from now, which wasn't likely, unless he hurt himself more in the meantime, which *was* likely. They'd be married by then and Amanda would no doubt be pregnant by spring and campaigning to keep Shaun home. But Shaun would go anyway.

But could he perform?

Shaun did have the constitution of a horse—with the disposition of a mule—so there would be no arguing about him going on the road, but Ian could out-stubborn his nephew, or anybody else for that matter, when it came to the show. If Shaun wasn't ready to do stunts, if his game leg was too much of an impediment, Ian wouldn't let him. They could come to blows, had done so more than once, but if Ian said no, then there was nothing to discuss but "What part of 'no' don't you understand?"

And the way Shaun hesitated on the phone, and Amanda too—Ian had a hunch that Shaun wasn't recovering as expected. He had no idea what might be wrong, but he sensed it in his bones. He decided to make a surprise visit to the Davis residence. "I was just in the neighborhood, so I thought I'd drop by and—"

He'd bring Mrs. Davis one of Gran's homemade pies.

It was mid-afternoon, a couple hours before supper, when Ian left the garage behind the house where he'd telephoned Shaun and walked across the field to Gran's side gate. Grace was shopping with Joel, and Hanna wasn't due home from classes for an hour.

Seven years ago, Ian's mother Emma had moved to Salt Lake City to live with her second husband, Ernest Hawthorne. She'd been widowed ten years before when Ian's father Angus died in a mining accident. Emma's decision to marry a stranger and move to Utah, which seemed a thousand miles away, stung Ian.

But his grandmother was always there, in her house right next to his, across the field, like an old cottonwood, roots deep in the soil. Ian saw his mother now and then, called her often, and had reconciled with his mother and Hawthorne, but he saw Gran every day. She was his rock.

Gran's name was Nora but everybody called her Gran, including Ian and his crew. She lived in a smaller, older house on twenty acres south of Ian's converted, rebuilt and expanded double-wide and his modest allotment of land. Angus McGinnis, Ian's father, had inherited the house, and the land, including Ian and Brian's acreage, from his father, Ian McGinnis, who's father, also named Ian, had come over from Scotland on the boat at the turn of the century. That first Ian had worked his butt off for a piece of the American pie. His wife Nora and his one surviving son—three others had died, two in World War Two—had inherited the fruits of those labors. Two hundred and forty acres of good bottom land north of town on the banks of a branch of the Green River, where a guy could grow a little alfalfa, maybe some hay or corn, cattle and pigs, and plant a good apple orchard and do right by his family if he worked hard enough.

After Grandpa Ian died in 1960, Ian's widowed mother gave his son Brian sixty acres, and Ian took forty, even though he was just a teenager at the time. Brian managed Ian's allotment until Ian was eighteen. Gran kept twenty acres, all she said she needed or wanted, and they leased and later sold the rest. Ian later sold twenty acres of his property to Brian when he was in a pinch the third year he'd started his show, in 1966.

Brian raised dairy cows, grew alfalfa, and grazed a hundred head of Hereford on his own land and leased land over in Uinta County.

Gran had Beauty, her milk cow, a yard full of chickens and a rooster named Tarzan, half a dozen beef cows, a massive garden, the remains of the McGinnis apple orchard on five acres, and she had a countywide reputation for making the best apple pies anybody ever tasted. She had a wall full of county fair blue ribbons to prove it.

The gate squeaked as Ian unlatched it and pressed it open—Ian had decided not to oil it because it functioned as a sort of door bell for visitors coming from Ian's house—and Gran looked up through the kitchen curtains over her sink, where she was running water. She smiled when she saw Ian and waved, the loose skin under her flabby arm jiggling.

"Coffee's on," she said as he came through the kitchen door. She turned off the water in the sink, where a dozen apples lay, and he gave her a hug, crushing her ample bulk tightly. Her cramped kitchen smelled of baked apple and brown sugar and her graying hair smelled soapy. She grunted under his hug.

Ian grabbed his mug in the cupboard by the side counter. "You baking pies?" he asked as he poured coffee, adding a dollop of Beauty's cream and a lump of brown sugar.

"Applesauce," Gran said, wiping her hands on her apron. She sat stiffly and shifted her broad butt on the chair and winced—the arthritis—but said nothing. She had her own mug steaming in front of her. "I gave Joel two pies yesterday."

"I know. I wanted something to take to Mrs. Davis. Shaun."

"How's my great-grandson? He hasn't called since yesterday morning."

"Amanda says he's as cranky and foul-mouthed as ever."

"Gets that from you."

"Gran—"

"Spill, Ian. What gets said here stays here."

And Ian spilled. About Whitmore's call, and his calls to the other boys, and to Shaun. About his suspicions that Shaun was more stoved up than he admitted, and that Amanda knew it and that Ian wondered if—" Well, if Shaun is ready. I mean, *ready*. You know what I mean?"

"Do *I* know what you mean? Me, a stockholder in Johnson & Johnson? Me, who's bandaged more scrapes, wiped more tears of pain and frustration—"

"Yeah. Ready. Not just the injury, and not just for next season, but—ready."

"Let me ask you this." Gran took a sip of her coffee, holding it tightly in both hands for a moment, her plump fingers caressing the mug for warmth. She set the mug down with a thump on the old scuffed table, and pushed it aside. Making room between her and Ian. "When did *you* know you were ready?"

"To start the show? Well, I—"

"No, I know about that. Your ma. Your dad, dying—"

"Gran—"

"No, I don't mean that. I mean, to end it. To quit."

"To—what?"

"You heard your grandmother, Ian McGinnis. You've been thinking about cutting back—hell, you've been pondering retiring altogether—for at least the past four years, far as I can tell. That's what you mean by 'ready.' You're trying to figure if Shaun is ready to take over so you can cut back. Or retire."

"Three."

"Say what?"

"I've been seriously thinking about it for the past three years, Gran."

"Four. I know. I'm your Gran."

Ian laughed and shook his head, amazed.

Gran was an essential part of his life and therefore of the show in ways that he could never convince the IRS or anybody else. In the spring, in the final weeks before Ian got ready to hit the road, he and Tink and members of the crew, whoever he had with him that year, worked in Ian's garage, painting and repairing and getting ready. Every day at noon, the phone in the cavernous, noisy, oily, smelly garage would ring and Gran would tell whoever answered that "Dinner's ready and it's getting cold," then hang up and set the table. The crew, sometimes as many as a dozen including Grace, Hanna if she didn't have a class, Joel, and whoever happened to be on hand at the time, would drop whatever they were doing and traipse across the field fifty yards to Gran's house. Dinner—some of the crew called it lunch—never had a chance to get cold.

Main course was chicken or beef stew, always from Gran's own stock, never store-bought. Vegetables were from her garden, milk and butter were from Beauty, and there was always apple pie for dessert, covered with Beauty's whipped cream. Nobody ever complained that the menu seldom varied much. Nobody ever left the table hungry, although some often took an extra slice of pie for later.

The conversation was always congenial, and the most vulgar-mouthed of Ian's crew somehow understood without being told that they were At Table and managed to mind their manners, leaving their vulgar tongues back in the garage. Everybody knew you were at Gran's and she got treated with respect. Ian never had to fire anybody for violating the sanctity of Gran's kitchen or dinner table.

And privately, Ian looked to his grandmother for counsel when he couldn't figure his own way past a problem, or when Grace couldn't figure either.

"I didn't stop you when you wanted to do your stunts," she said. "I won't stop you when you want to stop doing them."

Ian nodded again. "I guess you're right—"

"I *know* I am."

"But this next season is going to be rough. New people to train, if I can find them, the money's tight, I can't really count on booking Iowa, and who knows if fair boards in other states have gotten word and are going to piss backwards."

"And there's Terrible Tom. And Hapgood."

"Goddam them both." Ian told her what he'd heard about the two famous daredevils, his only real competition. Tolliver was still soaking up enormous limelight wattage with his spectacular, well-publicized but infrequent jumps. And Hapgood Junior was still living off his dad's reputation, although his show had deteriorated into a forty-five minute fest of fancy cars racing around the track, what they called "hell driving," with no crashes, no motorcycles.

"Both of those frauds," Gran said, rising slowly with a groan to fetch the coffee pot, "will be extinct in three years, mark my word. You can outlast them." She poured for Ian and herself. "You damned well know it."

"But is Shaun ready?" Ian asked again. Cream and sugar.

"I get it now." She sat. "You want an excuse to go over and check him out for yourself. That's why you asked for a pie. I get it. Will applesauce do?"

"Mrs. Davis likes your applesauce."

"So does Amanda. So does Shaun." Gran pushed her chair back again and rose, and Ian stood. She pointed to the quart Mason jars of applesauce on the counter by the sink and Ian scooped up two jars.

"Take one for yourself," she ordered and Ian complied. He headed for the door, where he hesitated, arms full, and turned as if to say something.

"Don't say diddly," Gran said. She had already returned to the sink and turned on the water, to resume peeling more apples. "You'll do right. You always do."

Ian smiled, kissed Gran on the top of her head, said nothing, and left.

At the gate, before he opened it, Gran tapped on the kitchen window to get his attention. He turned and looked and she lifted the window a notch. "You tell that lazy great-grandson of mine that if he don't call me this evening—no, before supper—that I'll come over there and spank his butt."

An hour later, at the Davis', Ian got a phone call from Grace. Gran had suffered a stroke.

CHAPTER SIX

I nearly killed that goddam dog," Nick said; then he swore to himself. *If Hapgood freaks out at swearing, I'm off on the wrong foot.* "The poor critter." He tried a sorrowful headshake at the memory, and a smile, but it felt wooden, forced. Nerves.

"Uh huh." Expressionless, Jimmy Hapgood Junior, who said he preferred to be called "James," took another sip of his A&W root beer, slapped the half-empty glass mug down on the picnic table, and licked the froth off his mustached upper lip. "But you didn't, right? It got away okay?" He bit into his paper-wrapped cheeseburger.

Jimmy Hapgood's Auto Thrill Cavalcade had many sponsors—Buick, Goodyear Tires, and A&W Root beer among them, hence the huge glass mugs. Free burgers and fries everywhere they went, and root beer in glass mugs, not paper cups.

"I guess," Nick said. He set his smile aside and bit his own burger. Thick and juicy, and warm. "The pooch was gone."

Nick and Hapgood sat on a freshly painted white picnic table in a grassy patch of ground behind the backstretch of the Lincoln Park Speedway in Putnamville, Indiana, Hapgood's hometown, under the shade of a row of giant yellow poplars. The show crew, three men and a woman, all about Nick's age, were on the front stretch, doing close-quarter maneuvers in four red, yellow, and orange flaming eagle motif '79 Buick Skyhawk hatchbacks, revving their engines, bouncing over low ramps, zigzagging around the corners and skidding into showy slides. White-haired and grizzled Hapgood Senior, the legendary daredevil himself, coached from the flag stand with a bullhorn, his gravelly voice rising and falling indistinctly in the distance.

No one else besides Hapgood's show people were in the stands or on the grounds. It was a Tuesday afternoon, and the racing season didn't start until Saturday. For Hapgood, this was home turf. He'd raced his first car here, back before Korea; he was a local hero. He had a long-standing agreement with the owner to show and train here.

Less than an hour ago, Junior had picked up Nick at the Greyhound depot in Indianapolis in a new white Skyhawk hatchback along with a package that looked to Nick like posters, but Nick didn't ask. They'd stopped at an A&W Root beer drive-in stand in the western suburbs to pick up lunch for the crew. The stop was short and Nick didn't get out of the car; apparently, the A&W people had expected Hapgood.

Hapgood Junior had tooted the car horn when they pulled under the trees: "Lunch is here." Senior seemed oblivious as he continued coaching his crew. The '79 season was only a few weeks away and Nick guessed that at least two members of the crew were rookies; they needed the training.

Junior popped the hatchback, left it up, took out a cardboard box filled with paper sacks, and laid it on the picnic table. Nick carried out another box, filled with drinks and mugs. He and Nick sat and started in, not waiting for the crew.

"The pooch was gone, huh?" James grunted, expressionless. No eye contact. Nick sipped his mug, watching. He couldn't read the man. Frustrating; this was a job interview, even if they were in the small talk stage right now, and it mattered. No expression to read meant he'd get no edge to exploit.

Nick had set up the interview by phone just the day before after frustrating weeks of trying to get in touch with Hapgood, either Senior or Junior. They were seldom at their phone. When he finally talked with Junior, he was told that he'd have to come out to Indiana to talk, and be there the next day. "Call me James," Junior had said. "We're pretty busy right now, but it's the only time we have to talk. Can you make it?"

Without thinking, Nick said, "Sure, no problem. James." He hung up and sat in his apartment in Decatur, Georgia, traffic on College Avenue whooshing by in one ear, the phone dial tone in the other, six hundred miles away from Putnamville, Indiana. He had no car, couldn't borrow one, and there was no way he could ride his new dirt bike, a Yamaha 400, there by noon the next day.

He could hop a Greyhound that would get him there on time, if he moved quick. He called back, told the Hapgood answering machine when he'd arrive, and hoped somebody would be at the bus depot to pick him up. He tucked his last fifty in his pants pocket just in case he had to take a taxi from the bus depot to the track; who know how much *that* might cost?

Nick felt uneasy about using Hapgood's bike to show his stuff at the track, but it would have to do. No choice. This was his audition, and he had to make it go.

He'd pick up his own bike later, after they hired him, or send for it. Details: he'd work them out later.

He was nervous about the meeting, and he hadn't eaten since he'd left his apartment, so the smell of hot cheeseburger wafting from the bags in the back distracted him as they drove to the track. James didn't say much so he babbled.

Small talk. He said something in passing about Ingersoll's Quarry.

"You were there?" James said as they swung out of the A&W and back onto highway 40, heading west to the track.

"You heard about it?" Of course. It was in all the papers and on TV. "Yeah, but I left before *that* happened." Police arrived in droves the night of Nick's jump, looking for an underage runaway. Things got out of hand. A shooting. One killed, two injured. Riot. Dozens arrested. "I read about it too, later. I was gone before all that."

"You left before, huh?"

And Nick started to tell James about the jump as they drove to the track. Nerves.

Gunmetal-gray clouds hung low and threatened rain, but it was an unusually warm day for late March, windless and muggy. Nick was hungry and thirsty.

Nick sweated. James didn't.

"And you didn't get hurt?" No eye contact.

It was as if James didn't believe the story, as if he was interrogating a suspect in a mugging. Where were you when the lights went out in Mississippi? Any witnesses to your alibi? Along with James' expressionless demeanor, the questions felt creepy, and it made Nick even more nervous. He wondered how many times he'd sworn without realizing it, a bad habit. Maybe that's what rankled Hapgood.

"Nope. Didn't get hurt."

Nick sat at the picnic table facing the track, facing James. He saw no motorcycles among the equipment scattered about the infield—a 50-foot container trailer with the Hapgood fiery eagle-winged car logo painted on its side, and loading ramps down at both the rear and side. A Freightliner cab-over, a small house trailer, the four show cars on the track, and a Dodge van. Maybe the bikes were in the big trailer. It might hold the four cars, if it had racks inside, with room to spare. Yeah, that's where the bikes were.

"Not a scratch." Nick had sprained ankles, wrists, shoulders and other body parts in the jump, had bloodied his nose and lip, and suffered more bruises than he could count, but no broken bones. Cracked ribs, maybe, but nothing worse. "Tore my leathers all to hell and—" *Damn.* Nick suddenly remembered he'd heard that Nick Senior—*or was it their grandpa?*—had been some kind of minister.

James gave Nick a quick look, but Nick couldn't interpret it because it came over a mouthful of burger, James' cheeks bulging and jaw working.

Baby-faced handsome, probably in his mid-twenties, James Hapgood Junior had beefy, rounded shoulders and arms, more fat than muscle. He had slicked-back black hair and a pencil-thin mustache that made him look like a dude from a melodrama about to foreclose on Li'l Nell. A dab of mustard coated his left mustache tip. He smelled like Mennen aftershave.

"Tell me again," James said as he bit the burger, "about the falling part."

Nick noted the skeptical tone in the question, but he told it again anyway. Nerves.

The dog sitting in the middle of Nick's landing ramp in Ingersoll's Quarry had been a black lab with a red bandana collar. It had sat facing away. It didn't see that it was about to get smashed by a flying quarter-ton motorcycle dropping on it at sixty or seventy miles an hour.

Nick would kill the dog and the dog would kill him. Simple.

It seemed odd to Nick, when he thought about it later, that he should remember that the lab wore a red bandana—or even that he should remember that the dog was a lab—but nothing about that instant seemed ordinary on reflection. How had he managed to notice such a trivial thing as the color of the damn dog's collar?

Time froze at the top of his jump arc when Nick saw the dog. Without conscious thought, he leaned his upper body to his left, raised his right leg high and out of the way, tucked his left foot up and against the gas tank and pushed against the bike sideways with his left foot as hard as he could, as if trying to throw the bike away. He kicked it to his right, away from him.

He fell to his left and stuck his arms out above his head like a diver. He tried to lie down in mid-air, keep his legs and arms straight, so that when he hit, he wouldn't tangle up and tumble helter-skelter, bones snapping like dry spaghetti.

He'd slid before in races, dropping off a bike that was headed for a crash. He'd done it three times, had walked away; but he'd never done it so far off the ground.

Same principle. Get off the bike, get low, relax, and slide.

He tried to relax.

He rolled over in mid-air, a full 360. Timed it right. He arched his back and held his arms and legs out straight—just so, a nice dive, only horizontal rather than vertical—and came out of it almost flat on his stomach as he hit the sloped ramp. He slid, relaxed.

The same instant he hit the plywood ramp, the bike also hit, six or eight feet to his right. As he rolled, he caught a glimpse of the bike, and tongue-lolling, white-eyed, stupid bewilderment from the lucky dog. Red bandana.

How did I notice such a detail?

The bike hammered the plywood with a heavy woody crunch, the dog yipped, and Nick grunted with the impact.

The impact was blunted by his improvised mid-air dive-slide, by his helmet and leathers, by the smooth, sloped wooden ramp and by the hay bales along the left of the landing area, where he rolled to a gentler stop than he would have had if he'd hit the misplaced dog.

The bike flipped, crashed and exploded; shattered as if hit by artillery amid the congregation of refrigerator-sized boulders flanking the right side of the landing site. Wood splinters and broken bike parts scattered to the breeze.

Nick lived.

Dazed, it took him a while to stand up. His legs wobbled.

He hurt all over; blood gushed from his lips and nose, but nothing had broken. A few cracked ribs, maybe, but nothing broken. Probably.

"Yeah, I got through it okay," Nick said. His voice quaked.

From across the track, Senior bellowed on his bullhorn. "Hey, Jimmy Two, bring lunch over here. We're starving."

Jimmy Two? James Hapgood Junior had told Nick he preferred to be called "James."

Nick and "Jimmy Two" reloaded the white hatchback with A&W

cheeseburgers, fries and root beer, and with the trunk lid up, drove across the infield to Senior and the waiting crew in the front stretch.

"Heck of a story," Jimmy Two said as they drove. Nick caught the disbelieving tone again, clearly this time. Nick had suspected he might not like Jimmy Two, or "James," back at the bus depot, had been unsure at first, or maybe just nervous, anxious to please, but now his trepidation was confirmed.

"No story," Nick said. He felt angry at himself for being nervous in front of the pale errand boy; that's all Jimmy Two was. An errand boy.

"It happened, Jimmy Two." Nick tried to smile as he said it, but it didn't take.

And Nick didn't want to talk about what had happened next.

After he stopped rolling, Nick stood, fell down, rose again, and fell into the arms of a gang of cheering drunks. They poured beer on him, offered him cans, bottles, pills, joints, slaps on the back, and the occasional crotch rub with some tattooed cutie, yelling and cheering all the while. He didn't hear a thing.

Several men tried to hoist him on their shoulders, a triumphant hero, but they fell in a pile of drunken, smelly flesh, yahooing and laughing, and Nick spent another few minutes getting untangled.

Hurt all over, but no medical expenses to speak of.

Danny was gone. He'd split with all the money.

Nick sold his shattered bike for parts to a drunk for forty dollars and hitchhiked home to Decatur.

When he got home, he discovered that Tammy had split. He'd expected that. She knew he loved his bike more than her. She'd threatened to leave if he went to the Oxford race, and she did. She hadn't stolen anything; just a few LPs. She'd even left a note and locked the door.

He read about the riot in the papers. It had been a big deal, and he'd been there, just hours before it happened.

His cousin Virgil gave him his old job back at McIntyre's Performance Shop, or just plain Mac's to the regulars; Nick knew how to fix a bike better than most.

Had Danny planned to sting him from the first? Nick worried about that for weeks after. He had no sense for business, and the lack nagged at him. He'd been taken in by a goofy-grinning, gap-toothed, fifteen-year-old con man, if Danny was really that young. Incidents before and since reinforced the point; Nick knew bikes but he didn't have a clue about business.

As he worked through the winter of '78-'79 at Mac's on other people's bikes, saving money to buy his own, he came to realize that, if he wanted to be a daredevil showman, his dream, he'd have to hook up with somebody who knew the ropes.

Somebody like Jimmy Hapgood.

"What kind of bikes do you use?" Nick asked. He thought he saw a front wheel and fender peeking out from behind the side door of the open container trailer as they drove past.

"Kawasaki," Jimmy Two said.

Sure, Jimmy Two wasn't the one Nick should be trying to impress anyway. That's why he'd said so little; he was just an errand boy, in charge of nothing and he probably knew it, resented it. The real interview would be with Senior, and Senior, even though he didn't travel with the show anymore, would tell Jimmy Two what to do.

Terse introductions. Two members of the crew didn't bother to offer handshakes; they just grunted a semblance of a hello and dived into lunch, ravenous, sitting on the track next to the cars. Nick tried to remember names, but his attention was focused on Senior and he forgot instantly.

After Jimmy Two handed Nick off to dad, nobody but Senior paid him much attention. Jimmy Two resumed eating, sitting alone a short distance from the four daredevils, with his back slightly toward them. None of the crew seemed particularly friendly toward Jimmy Two, but that didn't matter.

What mattered was the impression Nick made on Senior.

Nick offered and got back a firm handshake. Senior gave up a toothsome, squinty smile; sun-freckled skin corrugated around his bright eyes. White hair, Marine recruit haircut. Senior had earned his reputation as a pioneer in the auto daredevil business after Korea, doing things with cars that nobody had ever dared to do. If anybody was The Man, it was Jimmy Hapgood Senior.

But he'd gotten banged up in early '76 and hadn't healed well. A limp. Junior had finished the '76 season and had been the show's on-the-road supervisor since.

Senior didn't eat. He and Nick sauntered slowly across the track, a private conversation, small get-acquainted talk, away from the crew, and Jimmy Two.

This is the interview.

Finally: "So you want to be a daredevil, huh?" Senior said. He squinted, eyes disappearing, as he looked over the track. No eye contact, and Nick saw where Jimmy Two got it from.

"I do, yeah." *I already am. I just need a show is all.*

"Pretty good with a bike, are you?"

Nick nodded. "Wheelies, jumps. I can do boardwalls if you like, but they're hard on equipment sometimes."

"And jumps aren't?" They climbed into the grandstand and sat in the first row, Senior grunting as he sat.

"Not if you're good."

"And you're good."

Nick nodded, smiled. *I'm the best.*

"Better than Tolliver?"

"He doesn't know it. Yet."

Short pause. "I heard about Ingersoll's Quarry," Senior said. Before Nick could answer, Senior stood up, grunted, and yelled, "Carl, bring your Kawasaki over."

One of the crew, a big man with a rolling gait, long black hair and a sour expression, got up from his picnic and walked slowly across the infield toward the container trailer.

"Now," Senior said, "let's see what you got under the hood." He started back across the front stretch toward the infield and Nick followed.

Senior began barking orders to his crew to set up a jump and landing ramp. The three daredevils had finished their lunch and stood in a huddle that didn't include Jimmy Two, who busied himself looking under the hood of one of the show cars, nor Carl, who'd gone into the trailer to get his bike. The three moved onto the track and began to set ramps.

Nick took over supervising the set-up, arranging the heavy plywood ramps, each sixteen feet long and two feet wide and braced with three four-by-four lengthwise stringers, atop adjustable wooden support blocks and metal A-frames. He set the landing ramp seventy-five feet from the take off ramp.

"Not very far, is it?" Senior asked, squinting.

"On a strange bike, I want to see how it flies." Nick eyed the track, fore and aft of the takeoff and landing ramps. He had plenty of track to do more than a hundred feet, if he wanted to. "Then we'll see."

Senior squinted, said nothing.

The crew spoke to Nick only in grunts and terse questions as they set up the ramps. Nick helped lift and tote, demonstrating to Senior that he wasn't afraid to get his hands dirty, do the hard lifting too—*I'm a good hand, see?* The labor also served to channel Nick's nervous energy.

Jimmy Two didn't pitch in; he just stood aside, watching, expressionless. Like Senior.

Nick quickly became aware that none of the three crew helping had set up motorcycle jump ramps before. He had to explain minor details. Were *all three* rookies?

As they finished, Carl rolled his Kawasaki up and set it on its kickstand. Carl got off, handed his helmet to Nick, stood nearby, folded his arms, expression sour, and said nothing.

Nick inspected the bike. Carl had maintained it well enough, though Nick could see it could use a more professional tune-up and a couple new spokes. He checked the fluids, kick-started it and revved it, listening to the engine.

Yeah, a tune up; just a hair off, but it would do for now. He put on Carl's helmet and adjusted it. It fit well enough. Smelled oily.

"No leathers?" Senior asked.

"I'll be fine," Nick said. He wore work boots, jeans and a denim jacket; he didn't intend to crash. He rolled the Kawasaki out onto the track.

He did a couple high-speed passes to get used to the bike and the track. When he felt comfortable, he did some fast wheelies, slowing one pass in front of the grandstand down to where he was almost motionless, feeling like the Long Ranger, standing high in Silver's saddle.

Finally, he sped down the track into the third corner.

There, he turned and made a fast dash down the track. He narrowly missed the takeoff ramp and sped past the landing ramp high on the grandstand side. He did it again. Practice runs.

Then he sped back toward the third corner, doing a wheelie as he passed in front of the grandstand and took his place high in the corner where he turned and faced the jump. He hesitated, revved, then leaned, gunned it, and sped forward.

He hit the ramp fast, as if he intended to jump right then, but powered back down suddenly at the same time that he jerked the bike up into a wheelie on the narrow slanted ramp, and rode up on his back wheel. At the top of the ramp, when it looked as if he might fall off the end, he rolled slightly back and dropped the front wheel, inches from the ramp end, and stood straddling the bike.

Nick had practiced the tricky stunt a lot and had noticed that it produced gasps from on-lookers, who were sure, at first that he was going to jump *right now*, and then that he was about to dump the bike off the ramp end in an inglorious and clumsy crash. Nick's masterful control of a motorcycle, at high and low speeds, impressed people who knew their machines.

Carl, jaw dropped and eyes wide, was impressed. Ditto the crew. But it seemed as if the Hapgoods, Senior or Junior, were not. Poker-faced, expressionless.

Nick eased the bike back down the ramp, went back into corner three, turned, revved, and did the jump.

At the apogee of his jump, he stood in the saddle, took his hands off the handlebars and raised both arms high, two fingers spread in a Nixon victory salute. Then he retook control of the bike, landed it, returned to the center of the front stretch, and slid into place.

Simple, flawless, accurate, well timed, showy. Fun. *God, what a rush.*

Nick turned off the bike, set the kickstand, got off, and walked up to Hapgood Senior. "You want to see what I can do at a hundred feet?" He took off his helmet. "Or a hundred and twenty-five?"

Senior hesitated, then chuckled, eyes disappearing in cheek skin folds. "Not today, son. But thanks anyway." Then he stepped forward and patted Nick on the shoulder. "Let's talk more." He started walking away, back toward the grandstand.

"Reset those ramp for show," Senior hollered over his shoulder. "We got two weeks."

The crew got back to work and Nick followed Senior, who said nothing until they sat down in the fourth row, facing the track and crew.

"Carl was our bike man last year," Senior said. "He's not going with us this year. But he doesn't know it yet. I haven't told him. You understand what I'm saying?"

"Yeah."

"Good." Long pause. "You handle a bike good, Cassidy."

"Uh huh."

They chatted for a while longer, nothing consequential, except wages. Senior named a figure and Nick said okay without hesitating; this was no time to be difficult. Besides, it was better than he'd been making at the bike shop.

More small talk, then Senior stood suddenly, a mercuric change in demeanor that Nick had started to suspect was characteristic of the man.

Nick hoped he'd hear "You're hired," but he didn't.

"Go home," Senior said instead, as he started back onto the track. Nick followed. "Rest. Get ready, you and your bike. Always be prepared, words to live by, especially in this business. We'll call."

Nick had a round-trip ticket.

Jimmy Two gave him a ride back to the depot; he said little during the trip. Nick felt elated about the interview, his mind on getting ready to go on the road, so he didn't try to talk him up. He went home.

He told Virgil about the gig. They had a strong relationship, which had grown since Virgil's parents died three years before. Virgil's folks had adopted Nick when he was four and Virgil six; he and Virgil had always been close. Nick was the best mechanic at Mac's, but Virgil understood as probably no one else did how important being a daredevil was to Nick. As long as Virgil owned Mac's, Nick would always have a job to come back to.

His girlfriend didn't understand. She left.

Jimmy Two called three days later and left a message on Nick's answering machine, saying Senior wanted to check and see if he made it home okay. Nick called back and left a message on the Hapgood answering machine saying yes.

Nick tuned his new bike, notified the phone company, the garbage company, the utility company, his landlord and others, and he packed. Then he waited.

Four days before the first show of the season, he came home to find a message from Jimmy Two on his answering machine.

"Listen, we've decided to not use a bike in the show this year. At all. Uh, good luck."

CHAPTER SEVEN

A friend dropped Hanna off in the lane in front of Gran's after classes at the junior college in town. Hanna rode to and from her classes with a friend who lived a mile farther down the lane, and it had become a habit for her to visit Gran first thing. She'd chat and eat a piece of pie and gulp a glass of milk before walking across the field to home, where she'd do chores and finish her studies.

Hanna had found Gran on the kitchen floor, halfway between the kitchen sink and the telephone, which hung on the wall by the back door. Gran was barely conscious.

"Are you okay?" Ian asked his daughter hours later at Sweetwater County Memorial Hospital, when he finally got a chance to talk to her, where they waited for word about Gran's condition. Grace hugged Joel, who unabashedly cried and clutched his mother. The waiting room was crowded with family and friends, all with pale, grim faces. Word had gotten out.

Hanna nodded, stifled her tears—she'd cried her fill after the ambulance had arrived and taken Gran away—and then she'd crushed her dad in a hug and cried more, nodding and muttering, "I'm okay. I'm okay."

Hanna had knelt by Gran on the floor of the kitchen, relieved to discover that she still breathed. She'd fought back a moment of panic before she grabbed up the phone and called 911. Then she'd called Grace, who was home and came running over. Hanna had tucked her coat under Gran's head and pushed stiff, gray hair off her feverish brow, muttering tear-soaked, unintelligible endearments as she stroked Gran's papery, pale skin. Gran's eyes fluttered alarmingly and she groaned weakly, like a newborn calf, her jaw slack.

Grace moved the kitchen table aside and propped open the front door so the ambulance crew could get Gran out quickly. Then she'd called Ian.

Shaun would not be dissuaded from coming to the hospital, and it was a struggle for Amanda and Ian to get him out of bed, into a car, then out of the car and into the hospital. If they hadn't helped him, they knew Shaun would have tried to walk to the hospital, which stood in town on a hill, by the college, overlooking the freeway.

Later that evening, family doctor Tom Swenson met with Ian and Brian. Minutes later, the McGinnis brothers briefed their families who sat and stood about anxiously waiting in a nearby conference room.

"She'll recover," Ian said, "but she ain't going to be able to move around like she used to."

"The stroke partially paralyzed her left side," Brian added. "Doc Tom says she may be able to get by with a cane." He shrugged. "Or maybe not."

"She's alert," Ian said, "but Doc Tom—"

"Can we see her?" Shaun asked.

"Doc Tom said she's asleep," Brian said, "pretty drugged up and all."

"Truth is," Ian said, "we don't know how she'll do."

"There may be some memory loss," Brian said, "or speech problems." He sighed and his big shoulders rounded, slumped. "Hell, we just don't know, truth to tell."

"Truth to tell," Ian added, "we need to be prepared for—well, for whatever."

A week later, during which the fair board from Mitchell, South Dakota, called and Ian booked the show, hardly bothering to check his calendar to see if he had the date free, the McGinnis family learned more about their matriarch. Gran's memory and speech were not impaired, but she would never walk again. Her left hand quaked and she'd need help feeding herself. She'd never work in her garden again.

But Gran's spirits were high. Amanda's mother had a spare wheelchair and the two talked about doing wheelies on the dirt road in front of Gran's house. Grace and Hanna would tend to Gran's personal needs—hiring a nurse was out of the question—and they'd tend Gran's garden under her supervision. Amanda would help as much as her two-job schedule would allow. Brian and his wife made a schedule to drop by daily. Ian's mother Emma would drive out from Salt Lake at least once a month. The family rallied.

Joel volunteered to milk Beauty.

"You sure you want to get up at 4:30 every morning?" Ian asked. Joel was nine, but he was a McGinnis.

"Yes, sir," Joel said solemnly, and that was that.

Shaun boiled in frustration, trying desperately to find ways to help. "You just get your own self better," Gran scolded him. "That would help."

Friends stepped forward. Cards, flowers, and money overflowed tables at Gran's hospital room. Food filled her cupboards at her house. Casseroles and the like. No pies.

Ian built a wheelchair ramp to Gran's porch from the front gate, and a ramp to his own back door for those occasions when she might want to come over. He fixed Gran's back door so she could come and go out the back way when she pleased. He paved the walkway between the two houses and oiled the side gate. Neighbors dropped by to help. He had more lumber donated than he could use.

Shaun and Amanda thought about postponing their wedding, but Gran wouldn't have it. It was a big wedding, held at Brian's. Family and friends pitched in to plan and decorate. Grace's sisters and Amanda's sisters made the wedding a memorable occasion. Some two hundred guests attended and nobody got in fights and there were no accidents.

It snowed Christmas morning. Shaun went out sledding with Tink and Joel in the road in front of Gran's where the family had gathered, his limp so slight it went unnoticed, mostly. He refused to use a cane.

He twisted his right ankle and had to be helped, cursing a blue streak, back into the house. Ian counted forty people in the small stuffy house, filling themselves with mountains of food on the kitchen table and lining the counters, coming and going between the cold outside and the warmth inside, laughing and singing and talking—family—before he stopped counting. It was a good day.

Ian decided to wait until two days after New Year's Day, 1979, to talk about the show with Grace.

"We're bust," he told her.

They sat at the kitchen table, the kids in bed, bills stacked high, crash calculator at hand. "I can't do it. I have to cancel. The show. I can't see any other way."

"I'm sorry." Grace reached across the table, to squeeze Ian's hand. He pulled away, reflexively, annoyed. He didn't need comfort now, he needed answers. "I know how much the show means to you—"

"I'm going to call everybody tomorrow morning and cancel. I'll sell the Freightliner, the car carrier, all the Mavericks, the van, the trailer—"

"We can use the trailer—"

"—and the wrecker—"

"Not the wrecker. Ian—"

"And if we sell off our cows—"

"Ian, we need—"

"Goddam it all to hell," Ian slammed a fist down on the table, startling Grace. She blanched and blinked. "Work with me on this. I don't want to quit, you know that. But we got to. We can't afford—" He picked up the bill from Sweetwater County Memorial and waved it.

"I talked to Wendy today," he said, quieter. He took a ragged breath, to get control of himself. He told her what the insurance agent had said. Not good. Insurance went only so far.

First Shaun, and now Gran. "The only thing we got to decide," Ian said, his voice strained, "is how to squeeze as much money as we can out of what we got. And I can't go on the road with Gran the way she is."

"Everybody is helping—"

"Goddam it, Grace—"

"No, damn *you*, Ian—I *am* trying to work with you on this."

Ian blinked, startled, and Grace continued. "Okay, we can sell the trailer, but not the wrecker. Use your head. We can use the wrecker for business. You want to stay at home and work in the garage, fine, then you'll need the wrecker. And we sell only half the cattle. Keep the rest. The market may swing. And if we quit the lease over by Mountain View and bring the cattle, what we don't sell, back over here—"

"Slow down, slow down." Ian held out a hand in a warding gesture. "We need to make some notes. You got a pen? Write this down—"

And so it went, until past midnight. Details. They argued, drank more coffee, and argued more. The crash calculator got a good workout, and they figured out what they could sell, how they could make extra money—details.

Grace could get a fulltime job in town. She still had her license, could get a trucking job. The oil companies always seemed to need a driver. They argued about that.

"You got to be here for Gran," Ian argued.

"Not if you're working in the garage," Grace countered.

"Yeah, but what about when I'm out with the wrecker?"

"Shaun could come over."

"What if he's with me, on the wrecker?"

And so it went. Long after midnight. Details.

The Ian McGinnis Auto Daredevil Thrill Show wouldn't see a fifteenth season. It wouldn't end with a bang, or a crash, or thunderous applause from a thrilled, excited audience. It would end with a few quiet phone calls, a few deals made with neighbors, with Fred Weeks at the bank quietly offering a loan extension, with Whittington Ford buying his cars. What to do with the uniforms?

The show was over.

Ian did not sleep that night.

CHAPTER EIGHT

*I*n the morning, after the school bus picked up Joel, and Hanna's ride picked her up, Grace asked Ian, "How will Shaun take it?"

Ian snorted a weary laugh. That question had kept him awake until Tarzan had crowed. "Maybe we oughtn't to tell him until he shows up here all packed when the snow melts."

Ian sat at the kitchen table, wearily sipping coffee. Grace sat across from him, pulling on mud boots to go to Gran's, help her get breakfast, and do morning chores.

Joel had milked Beauty and seen to the full milk pail, and Hanna had already helped Gran with her morningly personal business, all before Tarzan crowed and Ian gave up on sleeping.

"Best call him." Grace stood, gave Ian a peck on the top of his head. "Or see him. Get it over with." She left.

Ian sighed after the door closed. "I know, I know."

Still, it was early, and while Shaun was probably up and helping Amada get off to work, and Mrs. Davis might still be asleep, it wouldn't do to agitate Shaun, who'd probably yell his damn fool head off, get dogs barking a mile away.

Shaun had started working part-time at the Big D, enough to siphon off some of his energy. He'd probably be on his way to work now, Ian thought, or soon.

He'd deal with Shaun later, after he dealt with all the other details. After it was a done deal, it might be easier to deal with Shaun.

Ian sat sipping tepid, bitter coffee, mentally planning the day. He had a few chores to do and a car to paint. He'd get some painting done early, kill a couple hours that way, and then hit the phones at about eight o'clock. About eight o'clock here, it would be an hour later in the Corn Belt.

First things first, Ian decided—cancel the dates. Then call Whittington, see what he could get for his cars and the van. And the Freightliner. Maybe go in to see Weeks at the bank this afternoon, right after dinner, or later, after he'd painted more on the car in the garage.

He'd talk with Gran over dinner first, though.

Ian did his morning chores quickly and got started painting the car. Milton Cramer's '59 T-bird hardtop coupe was in good running condition, but the original robin's egg blue had faded, and Milt wanted it refreshed and a small dent and scratch repaired. Ian thought the car was too ugly for words, but Milt, who owned a thriving vet business with offices in Green River and over in Mountain View as well as Rock Springs, paid cash in advance, and if he'd wanted the car painted in fresh babyshit, Ian would have done it, smiling. He cleaned the car and started masking the windows and chrome. He checked his watch. Nine o'clock. Time to start phoning.

He started for the house, to make the calls from there, where he'd have his date book and address book and calendar handy, when the garage extension rang.

"McGinnis's." Ian's hearing aid whistled in his ear and he adjusted it so he didn't hear what the voice on the line said. "Say again, please," he said.

"I said," came a tinny voice, like a child's voice, "is this Ian McGinnis? Of Ian McGinnis's Auto Daredevil Thrill Show?"

"Well, yeah, this is Ian." He put a smile into his tone, as he tried to do when on the phone with prospective dates, bookers, and reporters, forgetting for the moment that he intended to end all that in a few minutes.

For a second, it sounded like a rodeo clown he'd met the previous season at a show in Norfolk, Nebraska, a dwarf named Boo who'd impressed him enough to add to his list of "clowns poss." in his black book. Boo had said, "I'll get back to you" when he'd called a few weeks ago, after he'd learned that he couldn't count on Buster Bledsoe. Boo hadn't gotten back to Ian.

"My name is Parry Reynolds. I'm in charge of special projects for Landini Tires." There was a long pause. "Mr. McGinnis? Did you—"

"Yeah, I heard. Landini Tires, huh?" Ian felt mildly annoyed. It was about tires. The guy on the phone—Reynolds—he should be calling the store. It must be a problem, Ian decided, and his stomach clenched. More problems. Just what he needed.

"What can I do for you, Mr. Reynolds?" He couldn't keep the annoyance out of his voice.

Ian used Big D tires in the show, of course. He'd worked a deal with the company, through the store, to advertise the tires on the road. In exchange for a season's supply of rubber for his vehicles, he put up big banners at shows, used the Big D logo in his newspaper ads and posters, and made sure the announcer mentioned the tires at least twice in each show—it was in the contract—once during the high skis, and at least one other time. Ian and his probably-now-ex-clown Buster had worked up a clown routine around a talking truck tire.

"Yes, sir. Landini Tires. Mr. McGinnis, I'd like to talk with you about—"

"Call the store. I'm only part owner, you know."

"Yes, Mr. McGinnis, I know, but this involves the show, not the store. Landini Tires has a proposal for you that—"

"Look, I get all my rubber provided. You think Big D would get a kick out of me using Landini Tires?"

"I'm sure they wouldn't, Mr. McGinnis, but—"

"You call the straw boss at Big D, Mr. Reynolds, and you work a deal with them. If you can do that, then you call me back and we'll talk rubber. Until then, I'm sticking with Big D."

"Yes, sir, Mr. McGinnis, I can understand your loyalty. It's a good thing in this day and age—"

"So I'm sticking with Big D. And so, where does that leave this conversation, huh?"

"Uh, well—"

"Look, we don't got a lot to talk about here, now, do we?"

"Well—"

Ian hung up. He stalked to the house in a foul mood, Hobo nudging him, the mutt's tail wagging.

The annoying phone call reminded him of yet another detail he'd have to deal with in canceling the show—sponsorship. He had a contract with Big D, had one for the past four years, but he hadn't read it since he signed it, didn't remember what was involved in canceling the show. He wondered if in canceling the show he might end up owing somebody something or getting into legal trouble—breach of contract or whatever.

That thought led him to another—would he get into any legal trouble from fair boards and bookers that he'd already inked deals with when he cancelled? He'd thought of that, one of the many nagging thoughts that had kept him awake, but he'd forgotten since he got up and the annoying little man on the phone—Ian felt certain the man was a little creep with horned-rimmed glasses and a pocket protector and a plastic clip-on tie—reminded him, and he felt angry. And tired.

He decided to brew a fresh pot of coffee and delay phoning people until tomorrow. Instead, he'd spend an hour before going back out to the garage studying contracts. He *thought* his show contract would be okay, but he wasn't sure about the Big D PR contract, and maybe there *was* going to be a problem with breaking the dates. His stomach growled as he sat at the kitchen table and began reading the arcane language in the contracts.

It was almost ten when he'd finished reading the contracts—there were clauses he could use to cancel shows—and was drawing up a list of calls to make when the phone rang, startling him. He almost spilled coffee on his lap.

"What?" he barked, then immediately remembered his show smile and said, "I'm sorry—may I help you?"

"Mr. McGinnis?" It was the tire guy, Landini Tires. Ian surprised himself by remembering his name.

"Ah, Mr. Reynolds. Parry, right?"

"Yes, sir, Mr. McGinnis. I—"

"Sorry about dropping the phone back there." Ian forced a laugh. Habit. "We get lousy service out here. Didn't mean to cut you off."

"It's okay, Mr. McGinnis. Look, I wanted to talk to you about your show. I do have a proposal for you—that is, Landini Tires does—and I hope you'll just hear me out. Just a minute of your time. That's all. Please."

"One minute?" Ian knew he was going to tell the wispy-voiced little man to buzz off, but he decided that he'd take his time before doing that and practice. This was the first person in the business he'd say "no" to, so he'd practice doing it gracefully. What the hell.

"Promise. One minute."

Ian shrugged. What the hell. "Shoot."

"I saw your show in Davenport last July. You did an excellent show. You're to be complimented."

"Thank you, Mr. Reynolds, but—"

"Please call me Parry."

"Yeah, right. Parry. Listen, I'm pretty busy right now." That wasn't true—Ian could take a couple days to finish painting Milt's T-Bird and he wasn't anxious to start phoning people yet. "So if you could get to the point, I'd appreciate it."

"Why I've called, yes. We at Landini Tires have been, as I said, very impressed with your show and we'd like to sponsor you next year."

"You want me to dump Big D?"

"In a word, yes. But please hear me out. I think it's in your best interests. Now, there are details that need to be worked out—"

Details. Ian had just read his contract with Big D. It was fluid enough to break easily, but he wasn't eager to let the Landini Tire rep—Parry— know that.

"Did I say something about 'loyalty' last time we talked?"

"You did, Mr. McGinnis—"

"Call me Ian."

"Yes. Ian. Loyalty. But doesn't your family come first?"

Ian found himself suddenly speechless. Of course, the little twit on the phone was right, but his pushiness still irritated.

"You know," Ian said, "I got relatives that work at my store. I employ upwards of—"

"Yes, Ian, I know. Shaun and Amanda, and others. You're good, working with the sheriff and counselors, and that's the kind of people that Landini Tires wants to represent—"

"Shaun?" A trickle of dread crept along Ian's arms like a line of sweat, the kind of feeling he got an instant before something went seriously wrong during a show, or on the road. Like the moment before Shaun's T-bone. Had the guy been to Des Moines? Did he know what happened there?

And the guy knew about working with the sheriff, taking on trouble kids in the show. *That* was supposed to be on the QT. Ian never talked about that to anybody. The sheriff had agreed to keep quiet about it. "What do you know about—how do you know about Shaun?"

"Believe me, Ian, I'm sorry about his injuries. I hope his recovery is going well. And your grandmother."

"How do you know about—"

"I can imagine the pressure you're under. The doctor bills, the insurance. It must be horrific."

"Listen, you little—" Ian took a breath, and held it. Then, with a smile: "I gave you one minute. I'm really busy right now."

"Oh, sorry. Yes, Landini Tires would like to buy out the Big D sponsorship. We'll make it worth your while, I promise. But I'll need to talk to you to work out the details."

"Details."

"Yes. An hour, at your convenience. I'll show you the numbers, our proposal. You won't be committed to anything, I promise. One hour, that's all I ask."

"Where are you, Mr. Rey—Parry?"

"I'm at Little America, in Salt Lake. I just flew in from our corporate headquarters in Saint Louis. I can be in Rock Springs this afternoon."

Ian snorted. "Have you checked the weather over the Sisters?" If Parry Reynolds was a flatlander, driving I-80 through Echo Canyon and up and down the Three Sisters east of Evanston would scare the daylights out of him, especially if the weather was iffy.

"No, I haven't—"

"You check it out. And if you think you can make it—what kind of car do you have?"

"I've rented a—uh—it's a Buick. I think."

"Riviera?"

"Well, I don't know—what does that have to do with—"

"Whatever." Ian snorted. A guy in the tire business who didn't know cars. Ian realized that Parry Reynolds wasn't really knowledgeable about cars, or tires. He was a PR man, nothing more. And that impressed Ian not at all.

"Look, Parry, if you want to drive over to talk, then I'll talk with you. If you survive the trip. I mean, winter? I-80? In a Buick? Your call, but I'd be mighty careful, if I was you. A guy could get hurt."

"I'll keep that in mind, Mr. McGinnis." Parry took a deep shuddery breath, and Ian almost regretted playing with his mind. It was unkind, like verbal roughhousing. The weather was good enough, there probably wasn't a lot of traffic, the guy had a tank Buick, new, with good tires. But Ian couldn't help himself. Ian pictured him showing up trembling, oozing sweat. It made up for the frustrating interruption.

"And we keep it under wraps, you hear?" Ian wondered how the guy knew about Shaun, and Gran, and the sheriff. He wanted to quiz the guy. And with that thought, his irritation returned, itchy as ever. "I have business in town, with the tire store and other folks. I can't have rumors about making deals."

"I understand the need for confidentiality—"

"So we'll talk. If you show up. If I ain't busy."

"That would be fine, Ian. I'm looking forward to it."

"Good." Ian hung up. He chuckled to himself as he walked back to the garage. He'd deliberately not said goodbye, deliberately not told the guy his address or how to get to the house, which was a problem if you didn't know your way around, since he lived out in the country north of town. But the guy knew Shaun and Gran.

If the phone rang again, Ian decided as he turned on the radio—Johnny Cash singing "Ring of Fire" on K-95—and got ready to spray the T-Bird, he'd let the answering machine take it. He'd paint until noon—the phone would ring promptly then, Gran calling as usual, and he'd answer that one—then go for dinner at Gran's. Then maybe he'd go downtown, check in at the Big D, see how Shaun was doing, maybe stop at the bank.

Amanda was at Gran's for dinner. She'd arranged her schedule at the IGA so she could be with Gran during the afternoon, when Hanna had classes and Grace was also likely to be busy. Ian decided not to talk about the PR man who'd called. It wasn't that he distrusted Amanda to keep a secret, but Ian couldn't be sure that Amanda understood as he did the need to keep these kinds of business deals close to the vest. She could innocently say something that might cause problems with the tire store, where, of course, she worked tending the till on weekends.

They talked about Shaun, who was on the mend, or so it sounded, and he was driving parts for the tire store, and trying to get on part-time with UPS, "until the season starts," Amanda said between bites of chicken pot pie, "but Cunningham—he's the overseer at the local UPS office—he says UPS don't need no daredevil drivers in those big trucks, and Shaun, he says—"

Ian decided to finish the T-Bird before Joel and Hanna and Tink came in, if he could. Grace had been in the house, left a note on the garage door— "picking up some doll stuff at Horizon's"—but she didn't say when she'd be home.

There were no messages on the answering machine after dinner.

Ian worked until three, when Tink came in to help, and Joel came in to ask to go play at a neighbor's house, and Hanna stopped by to borrow some money for a school dance that evening. Grace was going to chaperone, but there'd be pizza with Hanna's friends after, and a girl needed pocket cash— but nothing from Grace all day.

It came to be suppertime, just after five, and Ian was famished. Milt's T-Bird was all but finished. Tink went over to check on Gran, help her get supper ready, and Joel came home without being asked. Hanna, antsy about her school dance—there would be boys there—started puttering, getting supper ready. It got to be five-thirty, Grace was late and Ian began to get worried. If she had been delayed in town, she would have called.

It was almost six and Hanna had gone ahead and started heating a tuna casserole when a car drove up in the driveway beside the house. But it wasn't the Maverick. It was a Buick, a Riviera. Grace was in the passenger seat, and Ian couldn't see who was driving, but he knew.

"Son of a bitch," he said.

"Dad," Hanna said, "watch your language."

CHAPTER NINE

Ian glared at Grace, but he kept his smile fixed as he shook hands with Parry Reynolds, the Special Projects Manager for Landini Tires. Reynolds was bigger than Ian had expected, tall, muscular but slender, Ian's age, mid-thirties, maybe a bit younger. He had a ready smile, a firm, dry handshake, a casual, confident air. His skin was light brown and his eyes were black, his eyebrows and mustache thick and black. Latin, maybe Italian. Ian didn't ask. He wore new jeans and tennies, and a down-filled jacket; casual duds, but on him the duds looked rich.

"So, where you from, Mr. Reynolds?"

"Tacoma. But I live in Saint Louis now."

"And you made it out I-80 okay?"

Parry Reynolds nodded and sat at the kitchen table with the McGinnis family, with Ian, Grace, Tink, Hanna, and Joel. Pizza for dinner, pepperoni and mushroom that Grace had gotten from the Pizza Hut in town. The casserole Hanna had started would be on tomorrow's supper menu.

"So, how did you meet Parry?" Ian asked Grace.

"At the tire store," she said. They'd been in a hurry—the dance started at seven in the college student union building. "I stopped by to get the Maverick aligned. It's been pulling to the left, you remember. Parry was there."

"I stopped to ask directions," Parry said, talking around a bite of pizza. He wiped his mouth with a napkin and smiled. "I did okay until I got to town. Found the store okay." Ian was impressed. Parry was relaxed, eating like he was with his own family, not with people he was trying to hustle for a PR scheme.

"I heard him ask for directions," Grace said, "and I offered him a ride."

"You left the Maverick?"

"They were backed up," Grace said. "That's the good news, the store being busy and all—and I was ready to bring the car back tomorrow, because I couldn't wait there because we need to get to the dance and all, but Parry offered to drive me home in his car, so he can talk with you—he said it was important—so here we are." Grace raised her hands and eyebrows and smiled a small triumph. "I think I might have a part-time job at Horizon's, working the till Saturdays."

"So you'll drive the wrecker to the dance?"

"The van. If that's okay."

It was okay with Ian. "A job at Horizon's, huh?"

"Maybe. I'll fill you in later."

Grace and Hanna went straight to the dance in the van, Tink went back to Gran's to visit for a while, and Joel disappeared into his room.

Ian made coffee.

Weariness, the result of a day's hard work in the garage, and the weight of his gloomy thoughts and gloomier plans on his shoulders, settled into Ian's bones as he sat.

He sighed. "Look, Parry, I'm sorry I let you come all the way out here. I should have told you on the phone."

"Told me what?"

"I'm not only not interested in changing sponsorship for the show. I'm flattered at your interest, but like I said—"

"Loyalty and all that. I understand."

"Yeah, that." Ian sighed. "But." He realized that he'd been avoiding saying it. He tried to recall if he'd used the words with Grace, or with anyone. He couldn't remember. But now, he decided, he needed to do it, get used to saying it. Get it done and move on.

"But what?" Parry said.

"I quit," Ian said. The words sounded alien, as if somebody else had said them, or as if he'd read them off a Cheerios box.

"Quit? I don't understand."

"I'm quitting the show. I'm not going out this season."

Parry looked puzzled, his thin brows furrowed, his jaw slightly slack. "But you've booked shows."

"I was going to call today and cancel. I got busy; I have a car in the garage I'm painting. But I'll do it tomorrow, I think. Cancel the season."

"You can't be serious." Parry sounded alarmed, as if this somehow involved him, personally.

"I can. Look, Parry, it's none of your business, but I got problems at home. Shaun's little—well, he got hurt on the road this year, I guess you knew."

Parry nodded, said nothing, sipped coffee.

"And Gran had a stroke. She's—well, damn it, it's none of your business. And how the hell did you know about Shaun and Gran? And you said something about the sheriff. I take troubled kids on the road with me from time to time, I guess you know, but that ain't something I brag about. What's your story?"

Parry sat his coffee mug aside, spread his fingers on the table, and looked Ian in the eye. "Landini Tires is looking to make a major corporate surge into the domestic marketplace in the next year. We want our name to be on everybody's lips by next fall. It's ambitious, but we have new blood in the head office, and they want to conquer the world."

Parry leaned over the table, stared at Ian with intense dark eyes, and said, "Starting with you."

"With me?"

"With your show. We considered Jimmy Hapgood because his reputation is taller than yours, you'll admit."

"Yeah, his dad was a hero of mine, but the kid is souring the market. Their show's gotten pretty weak. More and more folks are finding out. You found out. And I guess you looked at Terrible Tom too?"

"He's flashy, intense, colorful, dramatic, all that, and draws media like Elvis, but he's—he's—"

"He's an asshole. He's a womanizer, a thief, a drug addict, a mean-tempered barroom brawler, a drinker—and he's an asshole. You checked it out."

"We want a family show. We want people to see Landini Tires as something that they'll use on their family station wagon, their fleet vans and delivery trucks and school busses and cop cars. We want to see people ask for them because they've heard they save lives and are reliable and have been tested under professional conditions—tested by professional daredevils who are also family folk, just like they are—and who're working hand-in-hand with Landini Tires to make America's roads safer for American drivers. We want to show pictures of girls like Hanna and little boys like Joel smiling and riding safely on Landini Tires. We want American tire buyers to see Ian McGinnis thoughtfully putting Landini Tires to the roughest tests he can provide, and laying his life and limb on the line in his dedication to serving American motorists. We want to see—"

"Jesus Christ," Ian said. Parry's voice had risen and Ian knew that the man had had some professional speaking background, even if his voice was a bit squeaky, maybe in radio, maybe in TV. His intensity was—there was that word again—impressive.

Parry sighed, gave a weak smile and a shrug. He sat back in his chair. "I'm in charge of the project, so I'm excited about it. I hope you catch fire too."

Ian stood to refill their mugs from the coffee pot on the counter by the kitchen sink and spoke over his shoulder, gathering his thoughts. "So you looked around for a vehicle to carry the corporate logo and fortunes."

"That's how I know about Shaun and Gran—I want to meet her, by the way. And your work with what you call 'the trouble kids.' We checked. We want to make a major investment, so we checked."

Ian poured, returned the pot, and sat. "What about Big D? I have a deal with them and I own part interest in the store. And there's Gran. Parry, I can't see how I can afford to go on the road and take care of her at the same time."

Parry smiled, his eyes disappearing behind wrinkles in his cheeks, and sipped.

"Don't tell me," Ian said, "that you've cleared those obstacles already."

"I came a long way to tell you exactly that."

Parry stayed more than a hour. He was there when Tink came home, when Grace and Hanna came home, and he was there when Joel went to bed. Grace joined Ian and Parry at the kitchen table, more coffee got served, Parry got his first taste of Gran's apple pie, and time passed as Grace weighed in on the discussion.

"Good," Grace said, stifling a yawn. "Shaun will be pleased." She stood.

Ian stood too. It was almost midnight. "We could put you up on the couch—"

"I already have a room at the Motel Six." Parry grabbed his coat from the peg by the back door, and he turned and looked at Grace and Ian. "You two need to talk."

He shook hands with Ian. "I'd like to be able to give my handlers a tentative report tomorrow morning. We can take our time getting a contract written, iron out details, a couple of days, but if I could phone home tomorrow with good news, I'd appreciate it."

Grace and Ian exchanged a look. They nodded in unison, and stifled a laugh at the unintended near-comic gesture. "Sure," they both said. "We can hammer out details, but you can go ahead and say yes."

CHAPTER TEN

Among the details that needed hammering out was the show finale. "We want something spectacular," Parry had said, "something that we can advertise in advance, like a 'coming attraction,' for the season finale, a show everybody will look forward to, nobody will be able to miss, and that they'll talk about for years after. Maybe we could build this enormous Landini Tire and you fly a car through it. Something like that."

Ian and Grace had laughed about Parry's enthusiasm, his naiveté, but they did it later, when he wasn't there, and wearily, as they were both tired. They talked in the dark, laying in bed until after three a.m. about it.

"I'm sure as hell not going to let some corporate suit design a stunt for the show," he said. "He'll get somebody hurt with his big ideas."

"His talk about booking shows, though, and doing PR for us, maybe getting other corporate sponsors. That sounds good."

"Maybe we'll get Motel Six and Denny's," Ian said.

"And Texaco."

"Nah. Exxon."

"Do you believe he can do what he said about bookings?"

The sheets shifted crisply as Grace shrugged. "Maybe he can get dates you can't. Maybe he can get dates in Iowa."

Ian snorted a laugh. "Hapgood owns Iowa next season."

"What'll folks think about the store?"

"Well, that's a toughie." Ian sighed. "McGinnis's Big D becomes McGinnis's Landini Tires. Don't know how people will take that, folks being brand loyal and all."

"We can make sure the contract doesn't hurt anybody. At the store, I mean. No job changes—"

"No revenue drains. Yeah."

Long pause.

Finally they slept.

Ian didn't voice his greatest fear—that letting some outside corporation get involved with the show would erode his vision of what the show, *his* show, was supposed to be. Loss of control, that was it. In fact, Ian didn't identify that fear in his own mind until days later, when Parry, who'd stayed in town to meet Shaun and Gran and had joined them for dinner the previous day, sat down with Ian and Grace to discuss specific contract terms.

Ian stopped Parry often in the conversation. "Good God, this stuff is worse than insurance contracts."

Parry would laugh and explain.

"Oh," Ian would say. "Now, *that* I understand. Why didn't you say so in the first place?"

The contract had a sunset clause—a provision for either party to cancel under certain conditions. It was something Ian always looked for, lest he find himself in indentured servitude to a corporate sponsor forever. He also read carefully the renewal clause for the next season, but it was loose and Ian had expected it that way. Renewal clauses on endorsement contracts were always loose. Corporations wanted to be able to cancel in case something happened to "the party of the second part," like indictment, bankruptcy, or death. Ian expected no more than a token supply of tires and posters for the year following Landini Tire's big campaign for the summer of '79.

Clause after clause, in nine pages of tiny single-spaced type, the three went through it, Parry's patience a balance to Ian's antsiness. Grace helped as she could, but she broke off the talks after two hours, sent Parry away, and promised they'd resume later—they'd meet for supper at the Sizzler downtown.

"What's up?" Grace asked Ian after Parry left.

Ian paced the kitchen between the fridge and the far side of the kitchen table, about four steps in his stocking feet, big strides. "PR's getting pushy," he said. "I don't know, I just don't know, is all."

They'd nicknamed Parry "PR," both his initials and his job.

"You're afraid of what? Of losing control?"

Ian stopped pacing and looked at his wife, sitting at the kitchen table, arms crossed. Once again, and so much like Gran often did, Grace had hit the nail on the head. He *knew* there was something wrong, but he'd refused to name it. Grace did. And now that the problem had a name, Ian faced it head on.

"Yeah. That's what. First, he's going to start telling us where to go—"

"Booking shows we can't get."

"—then he's going to tell us what to do in the show."

Grace shook her head. "I think PR knows he doesn't know show stuff, at least not like you do. And you're smart enough to deflect interference if the company tries anything. In fact, we can make a stipulation in the contract that says—"

"Yeah, that says I'm in charge of the show and my decisions are final. Something like that. Like this spectacular finale they want. I don't know about that."

"We might have to bend somewhere."

"I don't know—"

"We're getting our bills paid, we're getting equipment, bookings, advertising—we're getting bailed out, Ian. You're going to have to bend somewhere."

Ian sat, weary, still unconvinced. He shook his head.

Grace sighed, took his hand across the table. "We'll watch that contract like it was Beauty calving in a snowstorm. We won't let them screw us."

Ian's trepidation didn't end even after they signed the contract late the next afternoon, after two more long, grueling conferences, and even after PR left town. But Ian's ill ease was at least silenced—or pushed back in his mind—when Parry wrote him a check to cover the latest bill from Iowa Lutheran and from Sweetwater County Memorial before he left town.

On the last day of January, 1979, McGinnis's Big D became McGinnis's Landini Tires. Word had spread around town that Ian had a new sponsor, and that they were ladling out the bucks. Ian's concern that people would grumble about changes at the store were unfounded. His friends were farmers, like he was, and miners and ranchers and small business owners, like him. Most were hard-working people with families. The economy was teetering for most of them, even if the oil business was booming, and while they all instinctively held anything that smacked of "corporate tyranny" in near-open contempt, they understood that a man did what a man had to do for his family.

For the next few weeks, Ian kept busy, and he was happy keeping busy.

Flynn showed up early and he got on part-time at the tire store so he could help Ian in the garage. PR had arranged for Ian to buy a new trailer and van, and the company had footed the bill to repair and repaint the entire fleet, from Freightliner to the Mavs, including the wrecker.

And the phone kept ringing. Booking agents, promoters, sponsors, fair boards, track owners. He'd be working in the garage, under the new engine hoist he'd bought with Landini Tire money, when the garage phone would ring and he'd grab it, greasy-fingered, say, "McGinnis's," say, "Yeah, this is Ian McGinnis," say, "Let me get to another phone, please," say, "Tink, will you hang up when I get to the house?" and go to the house, grab the phone off the kitchen wall, say, "Okay, Mr.—um, what did you say your name was?" And then he'd juggle dates, distances between shows, and other details. One day he booked three shows in a single day, one right after breakfast, and two before supper.

Hiring help became a problem. By late March, less than a month before the show's first scheduled date, a fill date at the fairgrounds in Rawlins, Ian had no announcer and no clown. PR tried to help, sending a couple of prospects to Ian for interviews, but none worked out. Ian had final say about show personnel, something that he insisted on in the contract. He was getting desperate because the announcer and clown held such critical roles in the show. And it wasn't just a matter of finding somebody who'd go out on the road for three or four months. Announcer and clown demanded special talents, and Ian knew those talents were rare. PR didn't.

Ian also wanted a motorcycle man but PR was no help in that department. Landini Tires had little interest in the specialty tire market.

"I think I finally got your clown," PR told Ian on the phone one afternoon. "Unless you've hired somebody since yesterday morning."

"Tell me about him," Ian said. He smiled over the phone, his show smile, suppressed a sigh, and adjusted his hearing aid. Ian often let Grace handle PR's calls because PR called so often and Ian was often busy working when he called, as it should be. But Grace was at Gran's so Ian took the call.

"Her," PR said, and got Ian's attention.

Bonnie Brunner was twenty-two years old, blonde, buxom, and brassy. Nickname was "BB." She had a broad face, broad shoulders, and a broad, bold laugh. Unpretentious. Not extraordinarily pretty, but charming and friendly. Good show qualities. When she showed up for her interview, just before dinner, Ian could see that everybody took to her, including Grace and Gran.

But Ian could see that she wasn't clown material. Her movements were awkward, stiff, her timing a bit off.

On a hunch, right after supper the next day, Ian hooked the ski car up behind the wrecker and took BB and Flynn out to the county fairgrounds track north of town. There, he and Flynn set up a high-skis ramp and they unloaded the ski car.

"What we're going to do," Ian said, "is take this car, and I'm going to drive it around the track on the two side wheels, as far as I can go before I fall over. We call it 'the high skis.'"

"Uh-huh," BB said. She chewed a mouthful of Dentyne, her big, heavily mascaraed eyes wide, taking in everything. It was like she'd never been out of Shelby, Montana, her hometown, where she worked on her family's horse ranch.

"I hit the ramp, driver's side up, and drive the car on the two passenger side wheels like it was a bicycle, you see—"

"Uh-huh."

"—and you'll be my passenger, okay?"

"Uh—" she looked at him. "Huh?"

Ian got in the car. "Hop in," he said as he strapped in.

She did.

Ian watched her more than he did the ramp and he almost missed his approach. But he got up all right, hitting the ramp with a gentle wooden *thrump* and gently settling the Mav into the delicate balance he felt through the steering wheel. He could hear Bonnie Brunner at his side chomping on her Dentyne like she was in a cud-chewing contest.

A couple seconds on the side wheels and Ian had found a good groove, had control at least for a few more seconds, at least until he got into the first corner, fifty yards away. He looked down at BB and knew. She was in. He could see it in her eyes that she was hooked.

"So," he said, sounding like he did this sort of thing every day, real casual, "what do you think?"

In answer, she let out a raucous whoop, and her gum popped from her mouth and bounced off the inside of the windshield, and she shouted something Ian didn't catch but that sounded like "This if more fun than beating the shit out of cowboys."

After Ian dropped the car back onto all fours, she turned to him and said, "Let's do it again."

Ian appeared to think about it as they drove back around the track where Flynn waited, putting on a show, and finally, reluctantly, shook his head. "I don't know—"

"Aw, come on, Mr. McGinnis—"

"Ian. Call me—"

"What can you tell in one pass, huh? I mean why are you really doing this? Testing the tires, or the engine or the suspension or me or what? Let's go again, really, I think we should do it again, don't you? At least one more time, pretty please, just one—"

Relentless. Ian went twice more with the whooping cowgirl daredevil-clown at his side, but put his foot down after the third pass and he nearly put the car on its top when he hit a jarring rut at the foot of the back stretch before coming down hard on all fours and said "no more."

BB sighed, but her enthusiasm didn't diminish. "So if I get to be your clown, do I get to ride in the ski car like that?"

Ian thought about it. He saw in his mind's eye a possible clown routine involving the ski car, a vague notion now, but it might work, something he hadn't considered before, but he'd have to talk that up, but later, and it would depend on what kind of a clown he eventually got.

This one, this broad-shouldered, bouncy, chesty, vivacious rodeo clown was daredevil material, but not clown.

Ian assigned BB to help Flynn with some busy work in the garage after they got back home while he went to visit Gran.

"She's not clown material, Gran, but I can use her."

"I like her too. You'd best make sure Grace says okay."

"I plan on it."

"And Hanna. If Hanna gives you even a clue that she don't approve of your stunt gal, drop her like a soggy taco."

"Hanna? What's she got to do with it?"

Gran chuckled, and shifted in her wheelchair. "Never mind. Just tell Grace what I said, and ask Hanna. You ask, and make sure Grace asks too, hear?"

Ian shrugged and did as his Gran said.

Grace approved. Her enthusiasm surprised Ian. "Your daughter," she said, "in case you hadn't noticed, is grown up. It'll be good for her to have a mature woman on the road to talk to, somebody other than her mom. Girl talk."

Ian frowned his skepticism, as much as his lack of understanding, and Grace dismissed him with a hand wave. "Never mind. Just hire the girl. Use her in the show as you see fit. I'll see to Hanna."

Hanna liked the idea too. "I like BB. She's funny."

So, at dinner, over dessert of Gran-made apple cobbler with store-bought vanilla ice cream, Ian told her.

"BB, I can't use you as our clown—"

Her face fell, and Ian could see her fighting back tears, so he moved on quickly.

"—but I can use you as a stuntman."

For a long second, BB sat immobile, wide face frozen, mouth open. Then she smiled, her back straightened, and she looked at the others at the table, one at a time. Ian, Tink, Joel, Flynn, Grace, and then Hanna.

"Stunt*woman*," she said. And she was in.

Three days later, Boo called, the dwarf rodeo clown Ian had seen in Norfolk last season, the one who'd said "I'll get back to you" before Thanksgiving. Two days later, Ian picked him up at the Greyhound bus station, suitcase as big as he was and sleeping bag in hand.

"Know where I can get me an announcer?" Ian asked Boo as they drove back to the farm. It had rained and the lane off the highway that led to Brian's and Ian's and Gran's and other farms down that way was muddy and slippery. Ian fought the wheel constantly, but he knew the ruts and was never in any danger of sliding off the road into the irrigation ditch on the left or the wire fence on the right. Still, Boo gripped the passenger side armrest hard, white-knuckled, his head tilted back so he could see above the window and his wide eyes fixed on the road ahead.

"Nu-nah," he said. "I seen me this one g-guy, but he got this radio job, I think. He did a f-few shows I did, a good rodeo announcer. He was good, but, but he got this other j-job."

Ian had heard Boo's stutter on the phone before, but he knew it wasn't nerves because he'd seen Boo kick a bull ten times his size in the ass with his little foot. A good clown, lots of animation with his stubby little arms and legs, and good broad stage presence. He played the audience well, but Ian's driving scared him. Go figure. Ian slowed a bit and Boo relaxed.

"Well, maybe I could talk to him anyway," Ian said. "Do you have a number?" Ian was thinking that maybe he could get PR to front a higher salary for the announcer than Ian might otherwise have been able to afford. Maybe that would shake loose a few good prospects from Ian's little black book. And maybe BB would know a guy or two.

Grace and Flynn knew Boo from watching him work at Norfolk and meeting him after the rodeo. Ian had gotten his number for his book. Ian introduced him to Tink, Joel, Hanna, Flynn, and BB. Ian thought it was his carrot hair at first, the same shade as Shaun's, but now Boo revealed the reason for his nickname when he shook BB's hand, blushing as bright red as a stop light. BB and Boo were the same age.

Gran loved him instantly.

Boo didn't know the announcer's number, but the guy, Hal Dunn, had gone to work for a station in Saint Louis. That was all Ian needed.

He called PR.

"I got a lead on an announcer," he said. "I got a name and where he works, but that's all. Can you look him up for me?"

"Can do. What's the name, and where is he?"

Ian told him.

"I know the guy," PR said. "He's with KWMU, here in town."

"Is that good? I mean for us."

PR snorted over the phone. "It's a public radio station, NPR and all that. He's not making money, believe me. I'll talk to him."

"No, just give me his number and let me—"

"It's not a problem. I'll talk to him."

It galled Ian to suspect that PR still hadn't gotten it into his head that he, Ian, would be responsible for hiring. It was difficult to get under the promoter's enthusiasm and get him back on track, but it was necessary. "Look, PR, when it comes to hiring crew—"

"I understand, Ian. You know performers and I respect that. But I know announcers and promotions. That's my business—"

Ian wanted to interrupt and snarl something along the lines of "Then why haven't you found me an announcer yet, smart ass?" But he didn't.

"—and I know this guy. Just relax and let me talk to him."

"PR, you're not getting the message—"

"I'll talk to him *first*, then you check him out. Your decision, final, I understand. No problems. Just let me talk to him—*first*. Okay?"

"PR, I'm telling you—"

"Just relax. You got final say. Okay?"

Ian remembered to smile. "Yeah. Okay."

Three days later, PR drove up to Ian's in a rented Buick and introduced Hal Dunn, "Your new announcer."

CHAPTER ELEVEN

Nick replayed the answering machine message again, but it didn't change. "Listen," Jimmy Two said, "we've decided to not use a bike in the show this year. At all. Uh, good luck."

Nick paced, his pulse racing, breath ragged. Then he phoned the Hapgood number.

He got their answering machine.

"Shit."

He tossed the phone receiver across the kitchen; the cord brought it up short, and the receiver and phone clattered to the tile floor. He stalked to the back door, jerked it open, stopped—"Shitshitshit"—went back for his denim jacket, put it on, picked the phone up off the scuffed floor and dialed the Hapgood number again.

Answering machine.

"Shit." He gripped the receiver in his fist like a club, like he wanted to break it, teeth gritted. He hesitated, took a deep breath, and felt dizzy. He'd had a beer or two at Baker's Bike & Grill. After he'd clocked out of Mac's for the last time until fall, he'd borrowed Nancy's Dodge van to dump thirteen cardboard boxes of his stuff in Virgil's garage, to keep over the summer. Then he returned the van and went straight to Baker's to relax.

He'd been among biker friends at Baker's, people who wished him well; most of them seemed to understand what he was about. He'd gotten a buzz on, had felt good. He'd walked home alone, just ten blocks, enjoying the nippy, damp night air, taking his time, hands in his pockets, whistling as he strolled. He'd left Baker's at ten so he could get plenty of sleep before the long trip tomorrow.

He steadied himself against the battered Formica kitchen table, took another deep breath, tasted stale beer in the back of his throat, like bile, unknotted his muscles, hung up, and set the phone down on the table, gently this time.

Except for the kitchen table, sofa, and the phone, all of which came with the place, Nick's apartment was empty now. The night before, Nancy had helped him vacuum the ratty carpet and clean the toilet, sinks, windows, and fridge so he could get his cleaning deposit back. Mrs. Griswold would come by in the morning, check the place, give Nick his deposit, and buy his answering machine and a toaster oven she'd wanted. Then Nick would take off.

Nick had sweet-talked Nancy into agreeing to drive him and his bike in her van all the way to Muncie, where he'd join up for the Hapgood's first show of the season in three days, on Monday afternoon. Before he'd talked her into making the trip, Nick had contemplated the dire prospects of riding his Yamaha 400 dirt bike cross country, a butt-numbing, back-breaking notion; the bike wasn't meant for the road. When he first met her at Baker's the night after he got back from Putnamville, he noticed she fancied herself bold and brassy, an adventurer. Pretty enough, with big doe-eyes, full lips and long legs. A dancer. She had a Ferrari body but a dump truck mouth. She had a van and had just broken up with a boyfriend. Nick made his move, and she moved in.

She wouldn't be around when he got off the road. But by then, Nick wouldn't need a van.

He had his show leathers packed in his custom-made canvas satchel, and his Army surplus road duffel bag with his travel gear in it, propped in the corner by the back door. Now this.

What now?

Nick had long ago learned that he thought best while riding, cool wind in his face, a bike humming to him and massaging his legs and butt as open road rolled under him and mundane, anonymous, who-gives-a-shit country receded to either side. White lines flicked by on black pavement seduced him and soothed him. Sometimes he'd just go, even in the middle of the night, didn't matter where. Just go.

Nick buttoned his denim jacket as he crossed the apartment's unkempt backyard—crusty weed patches, trash, a row of dented garbage cans, and his neighbor's rusted '67 Ford F-150 up on cinder blocks—went to the little storage shed by the alley, got the key from atop the door frame, opened the shed and rolled his Yamaha out.

He rode east, not keeping track of where he was or where he was going, trying to loosen up, let his mind drift in the wind, figure *what now*. He found himself on Stone Mountain Road north of Belmont, absolutely alone for the moment, no lights in either direction. He turned off the bike and took off his helmet, listened, inhaling the fragrance of thick pine forest around him, his own sweat, and the hot, oily scent of his bike. Crickets chorused, a horn honked far away, a dog barked somewhere in the brush, his bike ticked as it cooled down.

He straddled his bike in the middle of the lonely, dark road, marveling at the answer that had come to him, as clear as a lightning flash. What he had to do.

Crash the Tolliver Omaha jump.

Of course. It was obvious.

The moment felt just as if he was in a big jump where all his senses hummed razor sharp and he didn't miss a thing—not a goddam *thing*—wired into the center of the universe, his mind and his spirit and his body and the bike and the jump—the very *air* he flew through—all one. Such clarity as he realized in a jump, that heady feeling of certainty, or total control, total *involvement*—that's what it felt like.

You can't describe it. You only feel *it.*

And if there was a damn dog in the way when he came down on the landing ramp, metaphoric or real, maybe this time he'd just have to kill the fucker. In any case, if he tuned up his bike proper, got a good run at it, gunned it hard, kept his eye on the takeoff ramp, kept relaxed and his wits sharp, and made the jump clean, he'd land okay.

And that's what he had to do. *Had to.*

"Why the hell not?"

Terrible Tom Tolliver was scheduled for a big televised jump at the Omaha Speedway Sunday night, day after tomorrow. Nick would be there.

He'd show Tolliver that he needed Nick as part of his show, and he'd do it in grand style. Tolliver would have no choice but to take him on, maybe doing pre-jump exhibitions, wheelies, and the like, a warm-up act. Something like that.

Maybe Tolliver would chicken out and Nick would replace him and jump for the cameras.

His mind clear, Nick focused forward, on the jump in Omaha at Tolliver's show. Focused. In a way, he started the jump from that lonely road north of Belmont, Georgia.

Past midnight now. Nancy would be home from her job.

He rode straight to the apartment, put the bike away, and found Nancy asleep under the sleeping bag on the air mattress on the living room floor. He woke her and they made love, though Nick didn't call it that. He rode her roughly, not caring if her cries were from pain or ecstasy, his mind miles away.

"What the fuck's gotten into your pants, asshole?" Nancy asked after, pushing him off of her with sharp elbows. "I'm not a goddam motorcycle." Her voice went whiney, as she did when she got irritated. She sat up, stiff back to him, brushing her long black hair with her fingers, and Nick knew there was nothing he could say that wouldn't end in an argument. If that happened, she'd walk out, take the van with her.

So he wasn't surprised when, less than an hour later, she was gone. He didn't fight it. He had a backup plan, a plan he'd found in the road north of Belmont a couple hours before.

He slept peacefully.

The doorbell razzed and he woke up, the light of day hurting his eyes, puffy and gunked shut, muscles stiff.

He pulled his pants on, finger-combed his stringy, long blond hair, and, shirtless, let Mrs. Griswold in. It was just past seven, Saturday morning. She asked, "Where's your *nice* little girlfriend, whatshername," inspected the apartment briefly, her grandma smile parting rosy cheeks, "My, my, I'm so *proud* of you, how you *did* make this old place shine," gave Nick a check for his deposit, "Don't spend it all in one place, now," and ten dollars for the toaster oven and answering machine, "So *nice* of you to let me have them." Nick would have to wait until after nine to cash the check.

But even that might work out.

He lashed his gear to his bike and rode to the Pantherville Truckstop for breakfast. He sat in the cafe near the payphones lining the wall near the hallway to the "Trucker's Only" area, where long-haulers found showers and other amenities. He listened to truckers on the phones as he ate eggs and sausages, toast and coffee. Before he'd finished his third cup of coffee, he heard one trucker ten feet away raising his voice on the phone, angry and frustrated. Something about a missing wallet, no money to make it out to Omaha, going to miss his delivery and so on. An unlucky trucker, stranded with no money, pleading with somebody, his boss or wife or whoever for help, heading west.

Help is on the way.

Nick rose from his table, turned to the trucker, ahemed to get his attention, took out his wallet from his back pocket, held it up and shook it. It took a few minutes to convince the trucker—Ivan Perkins, from Atlanta, father of three, a Nam vet, but more significantly, as Nick found out later, an ex-biker—that he wasn't pulling a scam on "Ivy," that he, Nick Cassidy, would pay for the trip west if Ivy would take him and his bike and gear to Omaha.

It took only a few more minutes before Nick left a still somewhat skeptical but curious Ivy standing beside his load of steel pipes, went to the bank and, at ten past nine, got Mrs. Griswold's check cashed. He returned to the truck stop where he intended to hand Ivy a couple twenties to seal the deal.

Nick's heart sank as he entered the truck stop parking lot; Ivy's truck was nowhere in sight. He went into the cafe, the restrooms, the showers, and the back room where there was a pool table, pinball and poker machines, and other games for the truckers. No Ivy.

"Shitshitshit."

"There you are." Ivy, who'd just entered the cafe.

"Yeah. I'm here. Where were you?"

"Getting in line." Ivy pointed over his shoulder with this thumb at the sprawling truck-filled parking lot and the rigs waiting in line in front of the pumps to fuel. "Need to gas up now. You ready?"

They stashed Nick's bike and gear into a compartment behind the truck cab and below the sleeper; they fueled, and they were on the road before eleven.

Nick chatted with Ivy much of that afternoon, napping only in short fits. Ivy encouraged him. The older man had raced once or twice, had broken a bone or two in crashes, before Nam. He understood about riding high into the wind, about flying. Nick bought dinner in Paducah, and they drove on west. Nick dozed and woke up in a truck stop parking lot outside Saint Louis. It was two a.m. Sunday morning.

"How long are we going to be here?" Nick asked.

Ivy curled up in the sleeper behind the driver's seat. "I drop this load here in the morning," he said. "Then I pick up another across town, and then on to Omaha."

Ivy stuffed cotton balls in his ears and grinned. "Helps me sleep."

Nick ran numbers through his head. Miles to go divided by average speed of an eighteen-wheeler. Subtract time for off-loading one cargo and loading another, and time for Ivy to sleep. He needed to be in Omaha no later than, say, three or four the next afternoon.

"How long will it take?"

"Couple hours." Ivy frowned in thought. "Geez, Nick. You might not make it. Sorry, man."

Terrible Tom Tolliver's "Missouri River Challenge," as it was being hyped by ABC Sports, who would broadcast the jump live, was scheduled for nine Sunday night. The jump would take place at the Omaha Speedway and had nothing to do with the river, miles away, but somehow word was out that Tolliver was jumping over the river itself. Nick knew better. He anticipated that Tolliver would later say that, "Hell, no, man, I never intended to jump the goddam river—today. This was just a rehearsal, kind of." Something like that.

Hype. Tolliver was a showman, the best. He knew how to hype show. Nick could learn a lot from Terrible Tom.

Nick had figured he'd need time to finesse his way into the situation, and when he left Ivy at Saint Louis to get his sleep, he knew it would be a close thing. Still, he remained focused, eye on the jump ramp, steady.

The Yamaha was street legal, but Nick knew it didn't look like it belonged on the freeway; it looked like a dirt-track racing bike with the skinny tires, high fenders and long forks, even if it was loaded down with travel gear. It didn't look like a low, fat road bike and it didn't sound like one. Nick had papers, but who knew which Missouri laws trumped Georgia laws? He couldn't afford the time to be stopped and hassled by curious and maybe hostile cops. So he took the back roads to Omaha. North from Saint Louis on 67, west on 36, and north again on 75. He found long, empty stretches where he could crank up and make good time.

An accident twenty or so miles south of Omaha stopped him cold in backed-up traffic, the road clogged for miles ahead. The clock ticked toward showtime; Nick, desperate, found a side road, and ended up going west to Marysville, then north through Lincoln before turning back east to Omaha.

He arrived at the Speedway in time to discover that the show had been cancelled.

Tolliver had been busted just minutes before Nick arrived. As he pressed forward through and around people leaving the packed Speedway parking lot less than an hour before the show, Nick caught enough from the drifting, grumbling and often angry chatter in the rowdy crowd to know Tolliver had been busted, but not enough to know why, exactly. Rumors.

He'd beat up his own promoter over money. He'd busted a chair over a fan's head when the fan taunted him. He'd punched out Howard Cosell. He'd gotten into a fistfight with an under-aged teenybopper chick's dad, or brother, or boyfriend. The teenybopper was only fourteen, twelve, ten. He got caught with his pants down smoking a lid of weed in a port-a-potty; he had a key of smack hidden in his bike.

Tolliver was on his way to jail, to the emergency ward with a busted skull, on his way to Mexico with a helmet full of money, run away with the teenybopper on the back of his motorcycle.

Rumors.

But clearly, the game was over. Nick had made his desperate, bone-numbing, sore-ass, cross-country ride for nothing. For nothing.

"Shitshitshit."

The lot Nick had entered felt more like a turned-over anthill than an after-the-big-football-game parking lot exodus. Cars were jammed at the exits and people milled around between cars, shouting and jostling. Groups of young, drunken rowdies drifted aimlessly looking for trouble. Nick heard a bottle break on the pavement somewhere off to his left. He heard a ragged impromptu drunken chant, indistinct but probably vulgar. A woman's scream. A siren. He smelled beer, pot, and popcorn. In Ingersoll's Quarry, he'd experienced something like what was happening here, a nasty edge to the crowd that could erupt into a violent mob any second. He wondered if Danny were here.

Game over.

Dirty, sweaty, muscles aching and vibrating like banjo strings from the almost non-stop bike ride from Saint Louis, chasing the clock, Nick almost screamed in frustration. But he wasn't finished.

"Not by a goddam long shot, I'm not. Not by a god*dam*—"

Gritting his teeth, a growl in his throat, he revved his bike, stood on a wheelie, awkward with his gear lashed to the back fender, and gunned the bike forward through the crowd. He heard a woman's high-pitched scream, and a bottle bounced off his front fender, but people got out of his way. He dropped the bike down off the wheelie and angled toward the far side of the grandstands, revving now and then when he had to scatter a cluster of pedestrians slowing him down.

There was a service road that Nick suspected would take him around back of the track and that's where he headed. Fewer people got in his way as he progressed; they were all going the other way. In a few minutes, he found a gate to the track backstretch. He entered and stopped.

The grandstands were nearly empty; only a few people milled about cleaning up trash. Men dismantled a scaffolding of lights at each end of the front stretch and Nick saw two vans with the ABC symbol on the sides parked on the front stretch, their side and rear doors open, people loading equipment into them.

Nick sat on his bike high in the long, flat asphalt backstretch and eyed Tolliver's jump set-up in the grassy infield. The jump was to arc over a row of bright new 1979 Ford Mustangs—courtesy of Atchley Ford, the ubiquitous banners read—from left to right, as the fans in the grandstands would see it. *Would have* seen it. The take-off ramp, sturdy four-by-four beams interlaced to support flat plywood plates, was eight feet wide and maybe fifty feet long from its foot to the high end, maybe twenty feet up.

No landing ramp.

The landing ramp, a twin of the take-off ramp and maybe a hundred and fifty feet or more from the take-off ramp, had been dismantled. Worker bees were loading the pieces onto the back of a flatbed truck parked next to where the ramp had been inside the track first and second corners.

A group of men wearing matching mustard yellow blazers and baseball caps, probably Atchley Ford people, were driving their Mustangs away, lining them up to load them on two car carriers parked high in the third corner.

No landing ramp.

"Shitshitshitshit."

Bile rose in Nick's throat and he realized how long it had been since he'd eaten. He'd stopped to piss twice, maybe three times, and to refuel, in the trip from Saint Louis, but had he eaten? He didn't remember. He stifled the urge to retch, turned the urge over to a blind, muscle-clenching scream that burned his throat like broken glass and blurred his vision.

"Hey, you!"

Nick turned. Two cops stalked his way from behind him, intent, hands on their batons. Behind them, a black and white was parked just outside the backstretch where Nick had entered a minute before.

When the cops were twenty feet away, Nick revved the bike, the cops broke into a run at him, and he gunned the bike north, into the third corner. He didn't hear if the cops were chasing him, didn't care. He broke into a wheelie as he arched into the third corner, nearly bowling down a couple of pedestrians standing by one of the car carriers, but he didn't slow.

He dropped the bike on the high side of the track and eyed the take off ramp for only a second. People started running at him, yelling indistinctly, waving their hands in the air. Trying to warn him.

Nick ignored the pain in his jaw from his clenched teeth as he gunned the bike and aimed straight for the takeoff ramp. He leaned far over the front fender, opened up the throttle and poured it on, not letting up until he was in the air.

He launched.

There, fifty feet above the ground where a long row of Athley Mustangs once faced the grandstands, Nick stood high above his Yamaha and raised both hands in his victory salute to the cleaning crew, the car salesmen, a few bewildered cops, camera people packing up, and Brent Musberger.

He gripped the bars again as the bike started falling, faced forward, stood, leaned back, arms and legs loose and ready, back as far as he could over the gear-laden rear wheel, front wheel raised high, and braced for the impact that he expected to shatter the Yamaha and send him tumbling down the pavement.

The bike hit solid pavement on the back wheel with a rubbery *skeetch*, the rear forks collapsing all the way until the wheel scraped the inside of the rear fender. Nick's arms and legs accordioned too as he hit. His head snapped forward like a bobble-head doll, but his solid death-grip kept him from toppling over the front wheel, and his balance had been perfect. The front wheel came down, almost gently, also helping absorb the shock of impact.

Nick focused on not hitting anything in front of him as he quickly throttled down, leaning back again as he did so. Whoa, Nellie.

He lived.

All done in a split second, and Nick was on his way out of the track, fast, aiming across the infield, dodging between parked trucks and vans, and people still waving and shouting who-the-hell-knew-what and who-gave-a-shit?

He made the backstretch, the side access road, and the lane outside the speedway before he drew breath and slowed down.

The bike wobbled and bobbed as he slowed and the engine had a raspy edge to it, wounded. He'd probably bent every spoke in both wheels, and the shocks were now so much mangled steel, but she still moved. He rode her to the first gas station he could find, drove around back, got off, and inspected the damage.

Not as bad as it sounded. Still, he needed to tend to it if he wanted to ride anywhere further, at least tonight. And it would be good for him to sit still and focus on something routine for a while, something not moving. He had spare parts in his kit, and could jury-rig a solution for the problems he couldn't fix until he could get to a good shop.

He sat on the curb in the parking lot behind the gas station and fixed his bike, focused on the intricate details, the mechanical minutia that his fingers knew so well he didn't have to think as he worked.

In time, satisfied that he'd done all he could do, he stood, wiping his hands on a rag, and walked into the station. He bought a hotdog and a Coke and ate, ravenous, standing by the front door, watching traffic whoosh by in the glaring neon night.

What now?

Nick's muscles throbbed sore and stiff and he felt dizzy, drained. He thought about finding, a rest area, someplace to pull off the road, to sleep. Or a motel. He still had some money, but how far would it go?

Leaning against the gas station front wall, a crushed Coke cup in one hand, the remnants of a hotdog wrapper in the other, shoulders sagging, Nick heard somebody out by the pumps say something about a motorcycle.

"—and Tolliver's a pussy." A guy, pumping gas into a battered Dodge pickup, Nebraska plates.

"No way, man. He'd primo." Another guy, leaning on the side of the pickup by the first guy, arms folded.

"Nah, McGinnis is better. I saw him in Des Moines last year and he—"

"Bullshit, man." Both were kids, maybe Danny's age, wearing ball caps, denim jackets, jeans and cowboy boots. "McGinnis' got people to do his stuff for him. He's too fucking old, man. Tolliver ain't a chicken shit like McGinnis."

McGinnis? Ian McGinnis?

"Yeah? Just wait and see, dude."

"Fuck it, man, and fuck you. I ain't going to no Wyoming. No goddam way, man."

The Ian McGinnis Daredevil Show?

"You chickening out on me? Huh?"

Nick tossed his trash in a barrel and listened to the argument unfold, one that had maybe been going on for a while and was maybe escalating toward a fistfight between the two men. Boys, not men, maybe Danny's age, maybe a little older.

The McGinnis show, Nick discovered as he listened, was opening in a few days somewhere out in Wyoming.

One of the boys had a pickup and was going West. And his partner was chickening out of the trip.

Nick smiled, crossed the lot to the pair, ahemed to get their attention, took out his wallet, and shook it.

CHAPTER TWELVE

*T*he first chance Ian got after suddenly and unexpectedly meeting his new announcer, he took Grace aside on the pretext of "getting something out of the freezer," which was against the side of the garage, away from the house, and said through gritted teeth, "Why didn't you tell me?"

He knew Grace knew. PR called at least once a day from his office in St. Louis, sometimes twice or three times a day, but Ian had stopped answering the garage extension and PR most often talked to Grace. If Ian needed to know what the call was about, Grace would tell him. She'd come out to the garage if Ian was working there, which he usually was, to tell him about the phone call, if it was important for Ian to know about it immediately, or she'd tell him over dinner or supper, or later that night when they sat at the kitchen table going over their books, which had become a daily ritual in the weeks since they'd signed with Landini Tires and the closer they got to heading out on the road.

"I *told* you," Grace hissed back at him. She had her arms crossed over her chest, which Ian knew meant that she was being stubborn and would argue if he pressed the issue. "I *told* you," she repeated, which meant she had probably told him and Ian hadn't heard, or had forgotten.

"When did you tell me? When I was in the shower?"

"I told you, is all, right after he called. You said, 'I know' and 'we got it covered,' or words to that effect. Anyway, I figured you knew, so I didn't say anything else."

"We really needed to discuss this."

Grace shrugged. "I thought you already did."

"I don't mean me and PR. I mean me and you. And Gran. We need to see how he fits in with the crew."

Grace shrugged, all she could do. "Well, PR looks happy as a flea in a doghouse. What can you do?"

"Cut loose," Ian said. He discovered that his fists were bunched, and his neck muscles were knotted. He was pressing close to a damn good headache, and he stopped himself before he made any decisions. He took two deep breaths, then said, "I'll see if I can chat with PR private and see what kind of promises he made to Hal Dunn, ace daredevil announcer. Then I'll talk with Dunn. Maybe he ain't daredevil material. PR will understand that. I'll make him understand."

Grace tugged on his shirtsleeve. "But what if he is good? What if everybody likes him?"

Ian sighed. "Even me?"

Ian took PR aside later that afternoon. Ian talked about doing a rehearsal show, something to help the new performers, BB, Boo and Dunn get used to the stunts. The announcer and clown would have to work on their routines and BB would need to learn some basic stunts—hell driving, the fire slide, and maybe the rolls, if she was up to it.

"We always try to do a show for the hometown crowd," Ian told PR as they drove out in the road Mav to the fairgrounds track. "Either before or after the season."

The stock car racing club had their own track nearby, The Sweetwater County Speedway, but Ian preferred the county fairgrounds. The Speedway was good hard clay and the fairgrounds track was mushy sand, hard to compact. The stock car track people were always easier to deal with than the county, but the stock car track didn't seat as many people and the track was much tighter, with not enough front stretch and it was too steeply banked in the turns.

"Good," PR said. "It'll give us a chance to work out some of the on-site banner ad details."

During the trackside inspection, Ian found out what he wanted to know about Hal Dunn and his deal with Landini Tires. Dunn was being paid by Landini Tires, not a penny of his salary coming out of Ian's pocket. But Ian was still the boss.

"So he's on for just this summer, then," Ian said.

"We have him under contract for the duration of the Landini Tire daredevil show campaign, right."

The Landini Tire daredevil show? Ian didn't like the sound of that, but he said nothing.

PR continued. "His contract ends when the show season ends. He's free to go after that, and you're free to re-hire him for the next season, if you want to, or he wants to, or hire somebody different."

Ian liked the sound of that. "But he works for me. Announces my show, answers to me."

"Absolutely. But we pay him, so he promotes Landini Tires during the show—we're good on that, right?"

"Right."

"And we'll have him doing radio interviews, taking some of the load off you in that regard, and some other off-track stuff for us, PR at local stores, that sort of thing."

"But I'm the boss come showtime."

"Absolutely."

"Good." Ian intended to keep looking for an announcer, but on the Q-T, and this time, he was looking for the rarity—somebody he could hire on a moment's notice, to replace Dunn the minute Dunn gave him or the show any grief. Whatever assurances PR gave Ian, however the promoter made it sound like he wasn't usurping Ian's position as The Man—*the Landini Tire Daredevil Show, my ass*—Ian seethed inside, and he resolved to get rid of Dunn at the soonest pretext, as soon as he had a replacement lined up.

If the guy screwed up in a show, or anywhere near one, Ian would send him packing in a heartbeat. PR had crossed the line in interfering with Ian's hiring prerogative, and Ian would not stand for it. It was his show. *His*.

The next morning, Ian took Dunn aside, this time in the van. They headed downtown to Anderson Lumber to pick up some tools and nails and a supply of wood to make motorcycle fire-crash boardwalls with. "So, what do you think of the crew so far?" Ian asked him as they drove.

Dunn said something Ian didn't hear.

"You got to speak up," Ian yelled. "I got this hearing aid. From the dynamite chair."

Dunn shifted in the van seat, leaned toward Ian. His voice sounded good, even in the noisy, hollow van. The announcer from last season, Keith Whitmore, had a high-pitched voice, and he talked too fast. But he was a hard-worker, quick-learner, knew his pacing, and he got along with everybody. All were important ingredients on the road, along with good health and a rugged constitution.

"I said," Dunn yelled, "I like your crew. I used to travel a lot, did I tell you?"

Ian shook his head. If Dunn had, Ian either hadn't heard or he'd forgotten or he wasn't paying attention. Or maybe PR had told him. Dunn had been a rodeo announcer.

"One of the things I guess Parry—PR, that is—one of the things I guess made him decide to take me on. But I understand I work for you, right, answer to you in the show, right? I mean, you were the one who told PR to call me, right? I don't understand the relationship between you and Landini Tires, but I guess if everybody is good with it, so am I."

"Answer to me," Ian said, nodding vigorously. "I know the show, know what works and what doesn't. I'll teach you what needs doing."

"You got it," Dunn said, and Ian sensed his willingness to take orders. Problem one didn't seem to be a problem.

Ian quizzed him about how he felt about his co-workers. In particular, he looked for red flags, trouble waiting to happen. If Dunn felt even the slightest bit contemptuous of Flynn's slowness or Boo's dwarfism or Tink's Indian heritage, or he made any boorish remarks about BB, or if he sounded arrogant or disparaged the show or anybody in it in any way, red flags would pop up and Ian would cut him out, contract with Landini Tires be damned. *His* show.

But Dunn seemed to genuinely like everybody and Ian discovered everybody seemed to genuinely like him.

He was older, almost thirty, a bit pudgy and pale, but he pitched in with the hard work, the lifting and painting of ramps, washing cars, and so on, all grubby work, unfamiliar to him, as if he may have been as born to hard work as Flynn or Shaun were but had missed the privilege for the past five years. He wore a neat beard and little round glasses, and had a bald spot in longish graying brown hair. Tink dubbed him "Radar" like the character on *M*A*S*H*, because of the little round glasses and round, innocent face.

Radar and Boo got along well. In the days following Radar's abrupt hiring, the two worked in the yard between the garage and the house, rehearsing their routines two or three times a day. Tink or Flynn or Ian would occasionally watch and offer suggestions to sharpen the routines.

Sometimes, in the evenings, Radar would go off by himself and announce the show to Joel's rabbits and to Hobo, the daredevil dog, in the dark.

Gran liked him.

The second day of April, 1979, a Monday, came in with cold battle-ship gray skies and ended with wind, frozen rain showers, and mud. The crew had been working hard putting finishing touches on the show equipment before hitting the road Thursday morning. There would be a rehearsal show at the fairgrounds in Rock Springs Wednesday afternoon, then the first real paying gig in Rawlins Friday. Ian had repainted all his vehicles, and bought a new Mav ski car—Landini Tires had bought it, rather—and he'd had the ramps out in the yard, painting new blocks, approach boards, and ramps a pristine, bright white, double-coated, with a four-inch wide red stripe down the middle of the approach boards and the ramps. Everybody had been busy, trying to beat the coming rainstorm, so they'd been working hard.

The whole place reeked of paint and thinner.

When the storm hit that afternoon, and everybody was exhausted from moving some of the still-wet boards inside the garage and covering up the rest with tarps, Ian gave everybody two days off—"Don't nobody do a lick of work until Wednesday morning, hear?"—and gave up the Mav and the van to his crew. "Go to town. Have fun, meet some girls. Drink if you want, but don't drive."

The crew left to see a movie, shop, lollygag, eat out, and visit bars and chase girls.

PR stayed behind. Days earlier, he'd flown in again and had returned the rental and announced that he was going on the road with the show. "I can do my job as well from on-site than I can from my office in Saint Louis," he said. "Besides, you could use an extra hand in the show, am I right?"

Grace, Ian discovered, had already sewn a uniform for PR.

"Right," Ian said, smiling. Seething behind the smile. Yet another instant where somebody made a show decision without consulting him—*consulting* him. Ian gave Grace a "We'll talk later" glare. "We'll start you with the dynamite chair and move you up to the T-bone. How's that sound?"

They all laughed, PR a bit apprehensively. PR had seen the Davenport show the previous summer, had seen the stunts on film and had seen Ian, Tink, and Flynn working with BB out at the fairgrounds track, showing her how some of the stunts got done, and she had learned quickly. Half-jokingly, Ian had offered to let PR do a fire slide, but PR balked, his nervousness evident, like Boo's. Now, stewing in his anger juices at again being passed over on a decision on his own show, Ian mentally resolved to get PR inside a stunt sometime during the season, something to rattle his bones. Revenge, or something like it.

But Ian did need another hand, and PR had proved himself a willing worker, if a bit weak, and Grace always needed help doing bookwork and advertising and all that.

"So," Ian said. They sat at the kitchen table, sipping coffee, the regular evening book updating and strategy session, with PR sitting in on the last few, "we got me, Grace, Hanna, Joel, Tink, Flynn, Radar, Boo, and you. And Shaun."

"Ian," Grace said as she stood, "help me get something out of the freezer. Fish for supper tomorrow. It's stuck to the bottom. S'cuse us, PR."

When they got outside, Ian said, "What now?" He opened the freezer.

"It's about Shaun. About him coming on the road."

Ian took a big screwdriver that hung on a hook by the freezer, there for ice-chipping purposes, and jabbed at an ice-encrusted lump in the freezer, an old Westinghouse. "Come on, Grace, goddam it, don't be lollygagging on me. Tell me what's up." Jab, jab, jab.

"I don't think he should go."

Ian stood, screwdriver in one hand, dead trout in the other. "What?" He shook his head. His hearing aid whistled. "What did you say?"

CHAPTER THIRTEEN

*I*an fumbled, putting the screwdriver back on the hook and it fell into the weeds on the muddy ground. "Shaun?" he said stupidly as he retrieved the screwdriver. "He shouldn't go?"

"I've been talking with Amanda." Grace whispered, hissing, and her voice sailed off into the cold wind. The crew had gone to town, Joel and Hanna were watching TV, PR was thirty yards away in the kitchen, and nobody but the rabbits and Hobo were close enough to hear. Grace whispered anyway, and the wind blew her words off into the field behind the house.

"And?" Ian prompted when she didn't reply instantly. She didn't meet his eyes.

Grace sighed and faced Ian. "He's not as healthy as he says. He ain't ready."

"What are you saying? He's driving, out of his cast, no limp as far as I can see, working part-time at the store—"

"I've been talking with Amanda, and he ain't ready."

"—He's been helping in the garage—"

Grace snatched the frozen fish out of Ian's hand. "I *said*, goddam it, that he ain't ready. Now, you listen." She aimed the fish at Ian, shaking it like a rolling pin.

Ian listened.

Doctors at Iowa Lutheran, and later at Sweetwater County, had told Ian that Shaun's horse-like constitution helped him make a speedy recovery. Shaun wanted to recover so he'd willed himself past pain that would have crushed a lesser man. But his injuries were more serious than Shaun wanted to believe or admit, and he had to be restrained from getting up out of bed too soon, taking off his bandages before his fractures had healed enough, and taking off his casts too soon. He was, in general, a pain in the ass to doctors and nurses, if a charming pain-in-the-ass.

He did recover faster than normal, except for one thing. He hadn't coped with the pain as well as he claimed, and he'd been on pain medication, specifically Darvon, a lot longer than normal. He was hiding it.

The truth dawned on Ian slowly as Grace spoke to him, intensely, as they leaned against the humming freezer, huddled close, whispering. Wind stirred weeds at their feet, and they ignored the cold nip in the air, more rain due later that night.

"Shaun is—" Ian swallowed in a dry throat. "He's addicted? He's a drug addict?"

"Amanda is trying to do something about it, get him therapy or something, but you know Shaun. He won't admit he's hooked."

"I know Shaun, yes, but—" He fluttered his big hands as if to snatch the words out of the wind. "But *this*. It don't make sense. Shaun—he—"

"I know, I know." Grace set the trout on top of the freezer with a damp thunk and embraced Ian. He shuddered and returned the embrace. It was a cold afternoon.

Finally, he pulled away. "I'll have to think about this. You could be wrong, you know."

"Ian—"

"You and Amanda. Both of you. You could be. What do either of you know about drugs anyway? I'll have to think about this." He grabbed the fish and stalked back to the house.

Ian called Shaun the next morning.

"I'm chomping at the bit, boss," Shaun roared into the phone. "Packed and ready."

"Great. You might as well bring your bags over right now. We got a special project, you and me."

They understood at McGinnis's Landini Tires about Ian's crew leaving suddenly. There were always people who needed work, even if it was only part-time, even if it paid poorly. The economy was booming because of the oil patch, and McGinnis's Landini Tires made its own positive impact, however small. Everybody understood what the show meant to Shaun and he had no problems leaving the store.

Shaun arrived at Ian's in an hour, driving his mother-in-law's puke green '76 AMC Pacer. He was alone. Ian didn't bother to ask how he intended to get the car back home if he wasn't driving it. Instead, he barely gave Shaun time to refill his Thermos with coffee and unload his duffel bag and sleeping bag on the living room floor before he revved up the road Mav and waved for Shaun to "Quit lollygagging and get in."

Shaun did and Ian took off from the yard, spitting gravel, swerving onto the long, narrow dirt road that ran past his farm as if devils dogged him. He looked grim.

"So, what's up, boss?" Shaun lost his smile, maybe puzzled by Ian's abrupt, in a hurry, no-nonsense dash down the road, mud spitting up from the back wheels.

"We got to get down to Vernal in a hurry," Ian shouted. He checked his watch, almost without taking his eyes off the road. "There's been a screw-up in a delivery. From the good folks at Landini Tire. Sent a box up to Vernal instead of Rock Springs. And we got to hustle."

Shaun gave a cracked, nervous-sounding laugh. "How long is this going to take?"

"Couple hours." He turned to look at Shaun. "Why? You got a hot date?" Shaun wiped sweat off his upper lip. Wispy traces of clouds trailed last night's storm eastward and it would warm up later in the day, but it was still cold, the car's heater struggling to catch up, but Shaun still sweated.

"Nah," Shaun said. Ian barely heard him.

It was a ploy, of course. While Ian had Shaun out on a wild goose chase, Grace would search Shaun's duffel and sleeping bag for drugs. The plan was for her to find them and take them. Later, with the pills in hand, Ian would confront Shaun and talk to him. Or beat the hell out of him, whichever Shaun allowed. Truth to tell, Ian's plan didn't go past the finding out stage and then the confrontation stage. Truth to tell, Ian had no idea how Shaun would react.

The wild goose chase would also let Ian isolate his nephew from his drugs for a few hours—all day, if necessary—to see how Shaun took it.

Halfway to Vernal, at the Flaming Gorge Dam, Shaun asked to stop to take a piss. Ian pretended not to hear, feigning hearing aid problems, and didn't get it until after they got another few miles down the road. Then Ian heard and pulled over by a copse of cottonwoods. There, Ian went with Shaun into the brush to water the sage. It was clear to Ian that Shaun wanted to be alone, and that Ian being with him bothered him. It bothered him a lot.

Okay, so he has stuff in his pockets.

"How about you drive?" Ian said, zipping up. "My back is getting crampy." He tossed Shaun the keys.

"Sure," Shaun said, sounding anything but sure.

It was almost eleven before they rolled down the steep, winding grade out of the Ashley National Forest and into Vernal, and pulled into the Greyhound bus station. Ian managed to inquire about the missing package without letting Shaun get out of the car—he talked to an agent from the window—and discovered that there was no package for him there. Ian made an excuse to get Shaun to use a payphone to call home and find out where the package really was while Ian did a charade with the agent, stalling, keeping one eye on Shaun, keeping Shaun busy for a few more minutes.

Just as Shaun hung up and was trotting toward the restroom, Ian broke off his charade and grabbed Shaun, arms waving. "They sent the damn package off to Salt Lake," Ian yelled, dragging Shaun to the car. "It was here but they didn't take it off. We can intercept it in Roosevelt."

A Highway Patrol cruiser just ahead and heading west on Highway 40 slowed them, and Shaun began to twitch.

They missed the bus by five minutes.

They were almost to Duschesne when Shaun, clearly, had figured out what was going on.

"Pull over, dammit, Ian."

"Why? We got to get that—"

"Bullshit. Bull*fucking*shit."

Ian slowed, clicked the turn signal to enter the rest area.

In silence, they stopped, and Ian turned off the engine. Shaun got out of the car, shoving the door open like he wanted to break it, face flushed with anger. Standing with his back to the car, he jammed his beefy hand into the bottom of a pocket in his down-filled vest. Shaun then raised his hand to his face—Ian heard a plastic rattle—tilted his head back, then put his hand back into his pocket.

Shaun stood motionless for a long time, highway traffic whooshing by, the cooling engine ticking.

Then he got back in the car. He sighed.

Ian waited.

"Ian, they're Darvon. It's prescription—"

"You know how I feel—"

"*Goddam* it, Ian." Shaun thumped the dashboard with a fist. "Goddamdamdamdam—" He hit the padded dash repeatedly, denting it, splitting the vinyl. He stopped, suddenly. He raised his fist to do it again. The muscles in his neck and upper arms bunched and quivered. He hesitated, unballed his fist, lay his head back on the headrest and seemed to sag into himself, deflated. He uttered something that sounded like a sigh or a sob. Both.

"Amanda acted funny this morning," he said, dry-throated. Ian sat quietly, listening, unmoving. "I never got a chance. She wouldn't let me out of her sight. Now this. I'm slow, Ian, but I got it now. Goddam it. Goddam."

"Yeah. We talked, me and Amanda." Pause. "Your turn."

Shaun was slow to get up to speed, but he did. He knew that Ian wouldn't let him go without getting it all out. It was something Shaun understood from being on the road, something Ian tried to make everybody understand.

"If you smash a thumb with a tire iron," he'd say, "cuss it out. Swear like a drunk sailor, beat the shit out of a junker fender, jump up and down, do whatever it takes. Get it out of your system, put on a Band-Aid, then get back to work. We got no time to let wounds fester."

And if two of his crew didn't get along, Ian encouraged them to talk it out or fight it out, whichever, but get it out of their systems. The crew lived too closely, in each other's pockets day and night, for four months. Festering wounds, jealousies, anger, other pains, if left untreated, could become dangerous. Ian had seen it, and he wouldn't tolerate it.

They talked.

It took a lot of talking to work it out, but they did. Shaun would join the show when he was ready, really ready. Gran would decide when that was.

To save face, Shaun would do the Rock Springs show tomorrow, but opt out of going on the road of his own accord. "I'm staying home to help Gran," Shaun would say, and nobody would fault him.

But it left Ian with a hole.

"I need me another man," he told Grace later, recapping the harrowing day. Part of the adventure had been distracting PR so the company man didn't get wind of Shaun's problem. That was one of the reasons Ian and Shaun started out so early. And Grace invented a problem—something to do with a new logo design—and got PR's attention. All he knew that day was that Ian and Shaun were on show business and they'd be back that evening.

Ian dropped Shaun off at Mrs. Davis' after Shaun coughed up his bottle of Darvon. Ian knew Shaun had another bottle stashed somewhere, or could get more, and Shaun probably knew that Ian knew, but they let the pretense go for the moment. Shaun had a battle to fight; Ian knew now wasn't the time to make a stand.

Ian said nothing about his adventures to PR when he got home, just before supper.

"Yeah," Grace said. They lay in bed, lights off. Quiet. The house clicked and ticked, and the fridge hummed and Grace sighed. "Yeah, I know, I know."

"If only I had me a motorcycle man," Ian said.

Ian had three options for a show finale—a motorcycle jump, a car jump, or a T-bone. Which option he used depended on track conditions, what kind of junkers he had, his own health and the health of his crew, and other factors. He tried to vary the menu so nobody got overly stressed, so nobody got overly cocky, thinking they were the stars.

With no motorcycle man, that finale wasn't an option. Ian was good with a bike, but he wasn't as good as many other riders.

Shaun was ready for the T-bone, Ian had decided in the past few months, despite the fiasco at the Iowa State Fair. Ian had hoped to alternate the '79 season with him doing a car jump here, then Shaun doing a T-bone there, conditions permitting, of course. But now, that wasn't an option.

Short-handed.

Ian would have to do a car jump at every show.

The motorcycle jump was an easy stunt. It was easy for the crew to set up for and take down. It was easy for the announcer to pump up, given Terrible Tom Tolliver's high-profile stunts. It was easy on the motorcycle man, given that Ian had found a way to make a ten-car jump look exciting and spectacular and dangerous, yet keep his riders from breaking bones, and do it so that it could be repeated show after show.

It was easy on Ian because he didn't have to do it.

The car jump was hard work to set up. Three junkers, used in the rolls and the head-on earlier in the show, had to be manipulated into a line in front of the car carrier to serve as catch cars. If they weren't aligned right, Ian could land in the dirt, not on the softer top of a station wagon. The carrier that Ian jumped was sixty feet long and twelve feet high. A heavy, intricate, elaborate takeoff ramp affair had to be arranged at the foot of the carrier, anchored securely, and aligned just so.

It took a lot of time and energy to set it all up, and sometimes Ian got hurt. Some landings were harder than others, and over the years, the hard ones had taken a cumulative toll. Ian dreaded doing the carrier jump, deep in his creaking, cracked, and too-often mended bones, but he never let on. His show smile covered a lot.

The T-bone was easy to set up for but harder on performers. While the carrier jump most often went off without injury, the T-bone had proven to be a bone crusher. The landing couldn't be mitigated or softened. The driver always hit hard, always took the brunt of slamming into the seatbelts, and almost always came away with bruises. The motorcycle jump almost never hurt, if done right. If done right, the car carrier jump seldom hurt much. The T-bone almost always did. It was that simple.

Shaun wanted to do a T-bone for the hometown crowd, and Ian was obliged to let him. Under Uncle Ian's probation, Shaun hit the mark at speed, did the stunt without mishap, and walked away.

Radar and Boo did well, not missing a cue. Flynn lost a few inches of skin when gravel got under the dynamite chair and ripped his shin, but he didn't bleed much.

Supper at Gran's after, a show tradition, went well. It was there that Shaun announced he was staying home to see to Gran.

Joel had given Beauty-milking duties to a friend who lived a short bicycle ride down the lane in exchange for doing his friend's water turns all next winter, no matter what time of day or night Joel had to get up to open the gate on his friend's fields, plus tend to Beauty. Ian was impressed with the deal Joel had made. He talked to Grace about giving Joel a raise for the season, maybe buying him a new mini-bike.

Hanna's grades had been almost perfect the last semester, so she'd earned her summer on the road. She enjoyed school, an oddity in the McGinnis family, but one Ian and Grace were proud of. Hanna packed a couple of textbooks to bring with her on the road to get a jump on fall semester.

The next day dawned warm and cloudless.

Ian fired up the Freightliner, gave a toot, and pulled out, the carrier with the three show cars and the ski car and the motorcycles and the ramps riding high and rocking in the open carrier framework as Ian squeezed the big rig out of the gate into the lane. Grace and Joel rode with Ian. Behind him, Flynn drove the wrecker with the clown car chained down on the fifth wheel trailer and the rabbit in its cage and all the other clown gear in the clown car. Tink rode with Flynn. Next came the sound van, Radar at the wheel, with Hobo, Boo, and PR as passengers, pulling Ian's new thirty-foot house trailer. Bringing up the rear, in the road Mav, came BB and Hanna.

Gran and Shaun waved from in front of her house.

They set off on the road for the 1979 season, the fifteenth consecutive for the Ian McGinnis Auto Daredevil Thrill Show.

CHAPTER FOURTEEN

Nick broke his second to last twenty on a room at the First Choice Inn minutes after he arrived in Rawlins and left the Jorgensen boys, Tom and Andy, who decided they weren't going to stick around for the McGinnis show after all. In Cheyenne, they'd heard about a rock concert in Oregon and they'd argued since about whether to stay for the daredevil show or travel to the coast. They didn't have time to do both. The concert won—Jefferson Starship and the Kinks headlined—and off they went in their battered pickup, yammering incessantly, westward down I-15, leaving Nick in front of the motel.

Nick was a bit more than a day ahead of the McGinnis show and in desperate need of a shave; he hadn't shaved since he left Decatur. He also needed a shower, a serious night's sleep, and a little peace and quiet.

The two boys he'd talked up in Omaha had decided to stick it out together for their cross-country adventure; Nick learned that their constant bickering meant nothing. It was a game between the cousins, both just out of Fairbury High School and drifting for the summer, "Or until we get our heads together, like." Maybe, eventually, they'd go home and work their dad and uncle's farm, "Cause they like need us, man." Or join the Army, "See the world and all that shit." Or go to San Francisco and be hippies, "Get us some of that free-love pussy." Or hitchhike across America, "See us some goddam sights, fuckin' A, man."

They bickered and babbled on matters mostly trivial, their chatter more for entertainment than anything else, a self-made high, and cheaper than fixing their busted radio. Nick sat on the hard, tattered bench seat between them in the pickup and got little sleep for most of the trip. Four speed with floor-mounted gearshift. His knees were always in the way. He'd tried to sleep back in the bed, but his bike and gear and the kids' gear took up too much space, and the damn machine was practically springless. No way could he get comfortable on the metal floor, and it seemed like they drove through downpours every half hour across Nebraska, and the boys found reasons to stop every hour or so—bathroom, beer, gas, food, change drivers, whatever. So Nick had to sit up front.

They'd stopped for a day and a half in Chadron to visit a friend, "who's got some righteous weed, man, grows it in his fucking ditches," but Nick begged off. He took out his bike, checked it over, tuned it, gave it a good workout up and down a dirt road between cornrows, then slept in the pickup while the boys got stoned.

They woke him before dawn and discovered the pickup wouldn't start. The boys weren't mechanics. Nick had visions of driving across Wyoming on the bike, his back ached in anticipatory sympathy, and he dove under the pickup hood desperately determined. Frayed wiring. The boys scrounged from their dealer cousin, Nick fixed the problem, and they got a late start that day. Nick had to dive under the hood later in Cheyenne. Busted oil pan. That took all day because the boys had to buy a replacement from a junkyard and they didn't have the tools to fix it. Nick used his.

A gaudy circus-like poster advertising the McGinnis show hung below the registration desk at the motel. In stark reds and blues, the poster featured a cartoon-like Maverick flying through a flaming hoop. Smaller pictures along one side depicted "The Famed Russian Dynamite Death Chair!" and "Lugnuts, the Daredevil Clown!" and "Death-defying Head-On Crash!" A row of posters hung in the lobby window, obscuring the view of the dusty and cracked, nearly empty parking lot and Main Street beyond where few cars and trucks drifted by.

Nick registered, broke the precious twenty, locked his bike to a lamppost in front of his room, unloaded his gear, went in, took off his boots, lay back on the soft bed, just to rest for a minute, that's all, just rest his eyes, and fell asleep. He'd arrived shortly before two. When he awoke, it was dusk.

No—it was *dawn*. He'd slept—*what? Fifteen, sixteen hours straight? Jesus H . . .*

It was show day. But Nick was ahead of the curve this time by a good fourteen hours.

He took a long, blissfully hot and soapy shower, shaved, changed clothes, went to breakfast at a JB's across the parking lot, and thought about his next move over coffee.

It might be a good idea, he decided, to do his laundry now, while he had time; there was a laundry at the motel. Checkout wasn't until noon, and he'd left his gear in his room. It would also be a good idea to tune his bike, check it out, give it a test run. He didn't want any last minute glitches when he showed his stuff for McGinnis. Just get on the bike and fly. Competence, that was the ticket. There had to be a shop in town if he needed parts.

He looked in his wallet. Breakfast and laundry would break into his last twenty. He sipped coffee, slowly, added sugar, and snuck three packages of crackers from the table dispenser into his jacket pocket.

He'd also have to scope out the track, maybe see if he could get a leg up on the show, on McGinnis, his crew, what they expected, what he needed to do to get on with them. If he could find an edge—

Nick snorted and sprayed coffee. He wiped it off the table with a napkin as a waitress, a dumpy middle-aged Mexican woman—MARIA, her name badge read—smiled at him with rosy cheeks and tobacco-stained teeth. She refilled the napkin dispenser and added more crackers. Nick didn't smile back. Distracted.

He'd been in this place before, with Hapgood, and "edge" hadn't figured into that fiasco. In a way, he'd been in the same place with Tolliver. With Hapgood, his plan—Nick stifled another snort—was more like a fantasy. He'd just show up and get hired. Because—well, *because*, that's why. Nick was good at what he did, so he deserved the chance, and Hapgood would be a damn fool not to hire him. It was obvious, so it didn't require much thought, so Nick didn't think about it much. No plan.

Tolliver had been totally thoughtless, totally planless. Result for both: disaster.

He sighed, poured more coffee. Nick knew he had no head for business, had had sufficient occasion to remind himself, but the really bad part was that he always forgot. He'd screwed up with Danny in Mississippi and hadn't planned well enough—*again*—with Hapgood—*I didn't read either of them well*. Tolliver had been a mindless, long-distance, spaced-out wet dream with nothing rational involved in any aspect of it except the sheer animal desperate need to *do something*, even if it was stupid on reflection, which is why he didn't *think*, dammit, just didn't damn well *think*.

And here he was, nearly broke, out in the middle of the goddam desert, hoping that Ian McGinnis would take him on with the show. Like Hapgood. *Do you* ever *learn?*

"He might," Nick said aloud.

"Que?" The waitress.

"Nada." Nick knew Spanish as well as he knew business. Nada. Mama Maria smiled beatific, replaced his coffee pot with a fresh one, wiped the table and left, smiling.

What if he doesn't?

So Nick sat, lingering over coffee until his nerves fairly rattled and he found his leg twitching like a sewing machine.

He thought, painfully aware that thinking or planning wasn't his strong point, but he did his best to think. He made some notes on a stack of napkins with a pencil stub that Maria had thoughtfully provided.

Laundry. Tune up. Stow gear? Where? Scope track. When to approach McGinnis? Approach *him* first, or find his announcer, or some other?

What if he already had a bike man? Plead poverty. "Let me do one jump, just to earn some pocket change to go home with. Please." Nick knew he wouldn't—couldn't—beg. Didn't know how. But he also knew he was a spit and a holler from being flat out desperate broke.

"All right, then; scope the track—" *Maybe somebody at the bike shop would know about the show. I can scout even before I go to the track. Yeah.* That's *smart thinking.*

Feeling better about himself, Nick folded his napkin notebook and stuffed it into his breast pocket. He left Maria a dollar tip, stole another handful of crackers, and left.

He returned to his room and learned that the motel washing machines were broken. The clerk at the desk sent him to Rawlins Family Cleaners across town on Jade Street. He asked about a bike shop. Big Al's motorcycle shop was across the street from the laundry.

Great. Nick loaded his gear, left his room, rode to the laundry, parked his bike at the curb next to Big Al's Cyclery, New & Used Motorcycles and Off-Road Supply, toted his dirty clothes duffel across the street, and started a load. He was the only person in the laundry, a tacky plastic room, long and narrow, with chipped tile and old rattletrap machines in long rows. Hot, dusty, humid and noisy. It smelled like old dishwater. He sneezed.

It was still early, just after nine. He got his load started, ate his crackers, and walked back across the street to Big Al's. More posters. He'd seen

McGinnis show posters in the laundry window too. It seemed to Nick as if every flat surface in town had a show poster on it.

Have to remember that. Posters. Wonder who put them up? What do you pay people to do that sort of thing? Do they have their own Danny?

Nick entered Big Al's where he found a linebacker with a black pirate beard spread bib-like across his barrel chest defending the goal line from behind a neat, clean, glass-top counter. Behind Big Al lay rows of shelves with parts in well-organized wire mesh boxes. In the smaller front room, a half dozen new-looking bikes lined up facing the window. Yamahas, Kawasakis and Hondas, two each. A lone Harley. All used but bright and clean looking. A display of helmets, leathers, gloves and other gear lined the walls floor to ceiling.

"Help you?" Big Al asked. With the soprano voice and used car salesman smile, the pirate image vanished. More like Mrs. Griswold if she had skulls tattooed on beefy biceps.

"Yeah." Nick pointed over his shoulder with his thumb. "That daredevil show. You know anything about it?"

"Some."

"I don't see any motorcycles on the poster."

"They don't do bike worth shit, man," Big Al said, wagging his beard. "Used to. I knew Ian back when he was tops, you know. But this Tolliver guy—ever seen his show? He was supposed to do a jump a couple days ago back in Omaha—"

"No bike man in the McGinnis show?"

"Well, they do *some* stuff, you know. They got this stunt where they crash through these burning walls, and they got two of them, one right after the other. The walls, I mean. On fire. I seen McGinnis last year in Nebraska, in Scottsbluff. Anyway, Ian doesn't do the big jumps like he used to, you know. Man, I remember in 1970—or was it 1971? No, it was '70. McGinnis had this old Indian. I know what that bike could do cause I did some work on it—"

"Jumps?"

"Huh?"

"Does he have anybody in his show that does jumps? You know, like Tolliver?"

"Nah, nothing like that." Big Al looked sad, as if they'd torn down the Rawlins Family Drive-In Movie Theater where he first got laid. He sighed, remembering. "Just crashes and stuff. I mean, he's pretty good with the crashes, don't get me wrong, pretty cool stuff, you know, and they do have some motorcycle stuff, but—" He wiped his chest with his beard bib and frowned. *Ah, the good ol' days.*

Nick discovered that one of McGinnis's men had been in the day before—*they were here!*—to pick up some parts. The guy, who's name Big Al didn't get, seemed a good enough guy, gave him two free passes, knew something about motorcycles, but not like he was a real *bike* man, you know—shake of beard, frown, sigh.

"What do they do for their show finale, then?"

Big Al's eyes bugged under raised caterpillar eyebrows, he spread his beefy arms wide and his tattoo skulls yawned. "*Big* car crashes. Ever heard of a T-bone? Ever *seen* one? Man. But mostly, you know, he just jumps a junker car over his truck and lands on a bunch of junk cars. It's pretty spectacular, don't get me wrong, but—" Shake of beard, frown, sigh.

Big Al loved to chatter and it was early so he had no other audience, or customers, so Nick let him chatter. Big Al had been a flat-track bike racer but he never got into motocross, not much. Another Nam vet, like Ivy, didn't want to talk about that stuff, much, you know. Ex-Hell's Angel, from L.A., had a lot to say about those days. He'd heard about Ingersoll's Quarry, but Nick quickly changed that subject.

So the show *was* in town, arrived yesterday, probably a couple hours before the Jacobsens dropped Nick off at the First Choice. They were at the fairgrounds, at the east side of town, can't miss it, you know, big sign down Main, turn left a half mile past the Country Kitchen, you can see it from the road.

A clock behind Big Al told Nick that his wash cycle was probably done. He muttered something to Big Al about maybe needing some parts after he checked out his bike, which he intended to do while the dryer ran, run it up and down the street a bit, but later, and he turned to go. He got as far as the door, and he stopped, hand on the doorknob. Stopped cold.

She stood there.

She. The most beautiful girl Nick had ever seen in his whole life.

Through the front door glass of Big Al's Cyclery, New & Used Motorcycles and Off-Road Supply, partly obscured by another McGinnis show poster and the shop's open/closed sign, Nick saw her. She stood across the street, in front of the Rawlins Family Cleaners, a plastic laundry basket on her hip, opening the back of a Ford Econoline van at the curb.

Nick gasped and held his breath.

A loose helmet of wavy red hair framed a pale, oval face dominated by blue eyes. She was saying something to somebody Nick couldn't see and her head bobbed and her hair shook and her mouth moved, flashing bright teeth, full lips, laughing as she talked. Long, slender model neck. Tight blue jeans accented long slender legs. Battered cowboy boots. Tucked into her tight jeans, a pink and white checked flannel cowboy shirt, the kind with the pearl snaps, twin pockets stretched over her small breasts, pointed like twin ack-ack guns straight at him fifty feet away, aimed right at his pounding heart.

"Oh, shit."

The van the girl was loading was painted with the show colors and insignia of the Ian McGinnis Auto Daredevil Thrill Show.

"She's quite a babe, you know?" Big Al had come from around his counter and stood gawking through the window, grinning and giggling like a schoolboy at a peephole in the girl's locker room, over Nick's shoulder. Nick hadn't heard him approach. He'd startled Nick. "Yes, sir, quite the babe."

Suddenly, Nick felt angry with Big Al. *Fucking crude bastard.* Didn't know why, but Nick instantly resolved to not do business with the giggling giant. He smelled like old grease and Mennen aftershave. Fat guy. A flat-tracker.

"Yes, sir," Big Al whispered, stripping the girl with his eyes, licking his lips. "Quite the babe."

Nick gritted his teeth, stifled a comment, balled his fists, and stalked back to the counter, the first leg of anger-venting pacing. But it was only four paces and he turned, still charged, to say something stupid to Big Al.

The van was pulling away from the curb.

Nick pushed Big Al— "Hey, man, what the fuck—" aside and went outside. He watched the van as it drove east down Jade, kept watching it until it disappeared from view at Main Street.

CHAPTER FIFTEEN

Ian started worrying about the show finale at about three o'clock, four and a half hours before showtime. A veil of high, wispy clouds mitigated the bright sun and a slight breeze cooled the sweat on his forehead, and on the crew, some working shirtless, who had been hard at it, washing cars and setting up, since late morning.

"Are you Ian McGinnis?"

Ian was deep inside the engine of his jump car when he heard a voice, and at the moment, he was upset by the way the engine sounded so he wasn't interested in being interrupted. He was concerned about the engine failing him coming out of the third corner come showtime as he made his final approach for the car carrier jump, failing at the wrong time and making him land on top of the carrier upper rack rather than clearing it. That would be rough. But worse than that, he was concerned that the car would give out in the backstretch even before he could reach the front stretch and he'd have no finale at all—not good for the show's reputation. The jump car had to reach fifty miles an hour to clear the deck.

Of course, Radar would jack that up to seventy in his spiel.

You can't do a jump with a deadstick. You can push a car with the wrecker for the rollovers after the roll car engine quits, and Ian had done it for the head-on a time or two, although it made for a lousy-looking stunt, but there was no way you could get up enough speed for a jump with a deadstick. The jump car had to run, and had to run well.

"Ian McGinnis?"

It had to be the carb. "Shit," Ian muttered. He jiggled the choke butterfly plate. Sticky, filled with gunk. "What do you want?" He didn't look up.

Joel, Tink, BB, Radar, and Boo were washing show cars beyond the fairgrounds backstretch in the spotty shade of a cottonwood grove next to a livestock barn. Flynn was by the trailer making the dynamite chair. Grace and Hanna were in the trailer. PR was off on some errand or other in town.

"My name is Nick Cassidy," the voice behind Ian said.

"Good for you."

The jump car was a '63 Buick Skylark, a two-door hardtop. The other three junkers set aside for the show were four-door sedans with sturdy center posts, good tops, so they'd roll well. The Skylark had the best engine, or so Ian had thought after the cars had been stripped a few hours ago when he determined this was his jumper. He'd taken it around the track, concerned at first that the corners were too tight and the ground a bit slippery coming out of the third corner. But that concern changed when, in the backstretch, the Skylark had coughed like an asthmatic old man and nearly died.

"Maybe you've heard of me," the voice said. "I ride motorcycles."

"Good for—" Then Ian remembered. "Cassidy?" he said without looking up from the engine. But he'd stopped tinkering. "Nick Cassidy?"

Last season, Ian had heard of a kid named Nick Cassidy who did good wheelies and jumped cars at motocross intermissions. He never got a chance to scout the kid, but rumor was that he had real show flair, could be the next Terrible Tom Tolliver. Ian had quizzed Mike Stern, his motorcycle man last season, about Cassidy, but got nowhere, except for a vague reference to some biker rally fuss in Mississippi. Either Stern didn't know about his competition, which would be a surprise because Ian knew that motocross fanatics like Stern knew who was on the circuit and what they were doing, or he was jealous and didn't want to own up to it.

Stern was a competent motorcycle performer, but Ian knew from the start that Stern's heart wasn't really into being on the road, and he'd started scouting for options before they'd finished their first couple of shows.

If Stern was impressed enough with Cassidy to tell Ian that "I never heard of the cat, man, except for that thing down South," then that piqued Ian's interest. Also intriguing was the fact that Cassidy chose to do wheelies and jumps during motocross intermissions rather than to race. Cassidy preferred the limelight; he was a showman.

But he never got to meet Cassidy last season and he'd figured, shrugging mentally, that he'd either gone back to junior college in Atlanta, or had signed with Hapgood or was on the racing circuit.

"Nick Cassidy," Ian said. "You did an intermission for the motocross at Bismarck last summer, early June, county fair." He still hadn't looked up from the engine. "Jumped twelve cars. Nearly spilled on the landing ramp."

"Thirteen. And I didn't nearly fall. That was for show. So you were there?"

Ian rose from the engine and squinted at Cassidy, who stood between him and the sun. He wiped his greasy hand on his jeans and offered it to Cassidy, who shook it. Firm, dry. Confident.

"I was busy working that day," Ian said, eyeing Cassidy closely, "but I heard about it."

Cassidy stood two or three inches shorter than Ian, maybe five-ten. He was slender and wiry, like Tink, only more mature. Broad shoulders, thin waist, no fat. He had a cat-like grace to his movements, barely-contained energy under his deeply bronzed skin, ready to explode. He had bright blue eyes and thick brows, a strong chin and a ready smile, but it was his blond hair that Ian noticed. Long, flowing to his shoulders, and golden, almost white. Like a lion's mane.

He'll draw the dollies, Ian thought. He forced a smile. Cassidy smelled like cologne. Ian smelled like oil.

"What can I do for you, Mr. Cassidy?" Ian already knew why Nick Cassidy was in Rawlins, Wyoming, in the middle of the afternoon, Friday, April 6, 1979.

"Nick." He wore a clean blue and white plaid pearl-button Western shirt, jeans, leather belt with a dinner plate buckle, and polished cowboy boots. Not a trace of dust or dirt on him.

"I'm Ian. What can I—"

"I ride motorcycles. And I'm here."

"Yeah?" Ian leaned his butt on the Skylark's fender and crossed his arms.

"Yeah. If you heard of me, then you know I'm the best there is. I'm here to join your show. Where do I put my gear?"

"So you just thought you'd drop by and take a look?"

Cassidy's smile didn't waver as he added a chuckle, and a shake of his golden mane. He waved a dismissive hand. "Take a look? I'm here to work. In the show. With my bike. Jumps. I'm the best, and I'm here."

"Uh-huh."

"Thirteen cars is routine, all in a day's work. I figure, this track, maybe fifteen."

"Fifteen, huh?" Ian snorted a laugh. "You see how tight these corners are? What kind of bike did you ride in on?"

"Yamaha 250." Nick flipped his thumb over his shoulder and there, parked at the high end of corner three was a lime green motorcycle. Sitting behind the bike was a stack of luggage—two duffel bags.

"Where did you come from?" Ian asked.

"Atlanta. I live—"

"You rode all the way from Georgia on *that*?"

Nick snorted a laugh that was a near-perfect imitation of Ian's snort. "Nah, I flew to Cheyenne. Rented a car from there. I had the bike shipped before. Dropped off my rental and picked it up. I drove it here, the bike, about two miles."

"You flew—you shipped—" Ian was flabbergasted. "How did you know where we were?"

Nick shrugged and shook his mane, a gesture Ian sensed might have been practiced in mirrors often. "You advertise, don't you?"

"Yeah, but not in Georgia."

"Whatever." Nick shrugged. "So where do I put my gear?"

"Not so fast, hotshot. I do the hiring around here. And I'm not sure I want you in my show."

"Oh?" Nick smiled, and Ian saw stubbornness in flashing eyes. Test me, that stare said. Go ahead and test me. Ian knew that look. "Think I'm not good enough?"

"Are you?"

"Set me up a ramp."

"How far apart?"

"S'cuse me?"

"How far do you want your landing ramp out?"

Cassidy shook his head. "No landing ramp."

Cassidy turned away and started walking toward his bike. "Set me up a ramp," he said. "One ramp." He didn't look back.

Flynn and Tink and Joel had come over to eavesdrop and had heard what Nick had said.

Cassidy sat on his bike, revving it, waiting, as they set up a ramp in the front stretch. By now, everybody in the crew was watching. BB didn't watch, Ian noticed; she ogled. Hanna and Grace stood outside the trailer, arms crossed, watching.

Cassidy sat on his bike as he had come dressed, no helmet, no gloves, no leathers. When Ian finally gave him a wave and the crew backed away, Cassidy shook his head and said something nobody heard. Ian cupped an ear as if to say "What?" and Cassidy shook his head as if to say "Never mind," and shot forward.

The bike's knobby-tired front wheel lifted off the hard-packed dirt of the track and Cassidy leaned forward to balance it quickly, and he aimed for the ramp. He had only thirty or so yards to hit it, and he took no practice run. He just gunned the engine, leaned into it, hit the ramp, probably doing thirty or forty or so, and he flew. In the air, he raised himself up, standing on the pegs, faced the grandstands, let go of the handlebars and raised his hands in a Nixon-like gesture of triumph, held the victory pose for a long time, then sat down and quietly brought his cycle to the ground, back wheel first, then front wheel.

He turned back in the first corner, popped a wheelie that he sustained until he dropped the bike in front of Ian and the crew, where he slid expertly into place. Smiling, shaking his golden mane. A quick glance at Hanna and Grace.

"Wheelies look okay," Ian said, quietly. He was impressed, but he wasn't going to let it show.

"I did with what you gave me. Ten cars is what I did. If you raise that ramp high end maybe two foot—I guess that's two of your little wooden blocks, right?—I can get down to about thirteen cars, easy."

"Ten cars?" Tink said, frowning.

"You measure. You'll see. Where I dropped was the equivalent of a ten-car jump."

Flynn went over and walked off the distance from the end of the ramp while Tink, Joel, and Ian raised the ramp high end two blocks.

"Nine cars," Flynn reported. "A guess. Three of my steps make the width of a Maverick. He jumped nine cars."

Cassidy had been listening. "You mark the spot again, and we'll see."

He revved his bike and took off into the corner. This time, he went high into the banked clay between the third and fourth corners. There he revved the bike, popped the clutch, stood into a wheelie, and shot out of the corner, head down, faster this time than he had done before. He hit the ramp straight on and flew.

A bird. Graceful.

In the air, at the top of his arc, Cassidy raised both hands in his Nixon salute, standing on the pegs, and he shouted. "Nick Cassidy!" Then he landed. Smooth as grease. Turned in the first corner, wheelied back, and slid into place. As if the grandstands were full, he then turned off the bike and saluted the invisible crowd.

Tink took the bike from him like a valet car-parker and Cassidy turned to Ian. "Now, measure *that*." Smiling. He'd hardly broken a sweat.

Flynn already had. "Almost fourteen, looks like."

"No landing ramp?" Tink said. He was looking at the bike in awe.

"That's the beauty of it. What you just saw was no more than a good motocross jump. The audience doesn't know that. Hell, a landing ramp just gets in the way, something else to go wrong. I learned that in Omaha from—well, I learned it is all. And landing ramps take a long time to set up. This stunt is easier on your crew."

Ian nodded, said nothing.

"Now, it'll look better if you park cars in front of the ramp, but you don't need too. And if you don't have enough cars, you just space them out to give the visual equivalent of ten or twelve cars or whatever. I've given this a lot of thought. You got a good announcer? He hypes up the distance, the speed, and all that. You hype the hell out of the fact that I don't use a landing ramp and that's more dangerous than using one—even better than Tolliver, if you want to say that—because I'm landing on the hard, hard ground, right? Of course, I take a few practice runs, check the engine, all that sort of stuff. And then you get your man, what's your name—"

"Flynn. Terry Flynn."

"—get him or this other guy to hold a stick down where my back wheel hits and you hype the hell out of the fact that it's the equivalent of fifteen cars or sixteen or whatever, and they can come down and see for themselves. The crowd, I mean. And the crowd goes wild."

"What if you got a short track?" Ian said.

Cassidy snorted. "This is as short as they get."

Ian shook his head. "You've been working stock car tracks and speedways and motocross tracks. We work the occasional rodeo grounds. Believe me, they get shorter."

"Then you either don't use any cars at all or you tilt the front ends of the farthest cars back so that if I come up short, at least I don't do it on the hood of one of the cars. I hit dirt, as planned, short or long. And the crowd loves it."

Ian scratched his chin, looking thoughtful.

"Hell," Cassidy said, "the audience won't see that the end cars have been pulled back. We hype the speed, the danger, all that. We pull back the end cars so I don't get hurt if I come up short and it still looks good."

"It would be easier to set up for," Flynn said.

"And take down after," Tink added.

"You guys get back to work," Ian told them. "We got to talk, me and Mr. Cassidy here."

And they talked.

Ian let Cassidy assume that he was going to take him on, but in the back of his mind, Ian was planning exactly when and how to break the news, that Nick Cassidy's presence wasn't required, thank you very much, but here's a free ticket to the show, hope you enjoy yourself. He planned to do it when PR got back to the track from his downtown errand, whatever it was, Ian couldn't remember. He wanted PR to see it happen, so Ian could see the look on PR's face when he did it.

Ian knew that PR was behind Cassidy showing up like he had, packed and ready to go. He'd probably assumed that Ian would have no other choice but to hire him. PR had pulled the same stunt in hiring Radar and then himself. Oh, there was no doubt that Cassidy was a good bike man, good with the wheelies, and his jump was stylish. He had real show flair. In the absence of Shaun as an option, having Cassidy along would take a load off the crew, and Ian. With Cassidy, Ian didn't have to do a car jump show after show.

No doubt PR had probably figured so, too. Maybe he'd even planned to celebrate the coup as a pleasant surprise, flashing his promoter pearly whites. But Ian would turn the tables, pop PR's balloon. He'd been looking forward to the opportunity.

There was another element that Cassidy's presence represented. Not only would he help by taking a load off Ian's shoulders with a motorcycle jump finale, but also he would allow for more shows, including some back-to-back gigs that otherwise Ian might have turned down. Cassidy's presence in the show would help everybody make more money. And that, Ian concluded, was probably the main reason PR had dispatched Cassidy to Rawlins.

Back-to-back shows were a sore spot with Ian. PR had already pissed off Ian by booking a back-to-back that Ian hadn't wanted. Joplin to Sikeston, in late July.

"You trying to kill me?" Ian had shouted at PR.

"I'm trying to make us money, Ian. This second gig is worth three times what you usually get. It's a guarantee against percentage, too."

"Two car jumps in two nights? A two hundred and fifty mile haul? What happens if I get banged up the first night?"

The kitchen table conversation cooled when Grace intervened and got PR to prearrange show set-up for the second gig. PR got on the phone and bought four top quality junkers, and he hired people to strip the cars. He also got the Sikeston Boy Scouts to do a car wash, including Ian's equipment, as a fund-raiser. With that, he confirmed his PR wings by getting TV coverage out of St. Louis. The crew would find half their work done when they arrived. He also moved the show back to an eight o'clock start.

Cassidy solved some problems, yes, but Ian wasn't listening to any voice of reason whispering in his ear. Instead, quietly fuming behind his smile at PR for setting him up again as they chatted, Ian continued to string Cassidy along until it was time to sadly shake his head and say no. It would be worth every bruise and bump he might get doing a car jump to see PR's face when he did it.

Something else bothered Ian. Hanna and Grace had come out of the trailer to watch Cassidy show off his stuff. They'd gone back in when he'd finished. Cassidy had glanced more than once at the women before his jumps and had seemed disappointed when they'd disappeared, looking all over for them. Cassidy did seem to have an eye for the dollies, always a problem on the road.

They talked and Ian checked his watch. Where was PR? Ian didn't recall where he'd gone or why or if anybody had even told him when PR had left shortly after dinner.

Cassidy, Ian learned, had been riding motocross since he was twelve. He was twenty-two now and ready to take on the world.

Curious, Ian asked why Cassidy didn't join Hapgood. "He works out your way, back East and down South."

Cassidy—*Nick*—shook his head. "Hapgood's show—there's something wrong there since Senior retired. I've seen it. Maybe you've heard. Too focused on Jimmy Junior and too tame for my blood. I don't know.

This could be their last season. Something wrong there."

Nick told Ian that he'd done a few solo shows last summer, freelancing, "just tinkering around back home."

"How'd you come up with the idea of no landing ramp?"

"I was at this one place where the promoter was a bit crooked, if you know what I mean—"

"I think I do."

"—and as I'm getting ready for my jump, he tells me he doesn't have enough money to pay me. I asked him how much ramps cost and he told me, and I said 'Don't put up one of the ramps and pay me the difference,' and he says 'Which one?'" He laughed. "The crowd went wild." Nick had the bug. "But I'm more of a stuntman than a promoter, you know? Can't do this on my own. I'll be candid with you, Mr. McGinnis—"

"Ian."

"—Ian. I need a show like yours—and there ain't any quite like yours; but you know that—"

"Get your steady thrill fix, make the big bucks, and impress the dollies?"

"Are we into salary negotiations?"

The kid was quick, and Ian couldn't help admiring that. And he had cast-iron balls. Ian couldn't suppress a chuckle.

And Ian understood. He even sympathized, seeing in Nick's story a bit of his own. Ian had started out with no clue as to what to do next, or how to do it, with nothing more than an itch that could only be scratched with speed and thrill, the roar of a crowd and the smell of burning oil and hot rubber. He understood.

When PR pulled up in the road Mav at about five-thirty, Ian took particular note of the looks on Nick's face, and on PR's, when he introduced them. Ian had expected to see it in their faces that they knew each other, but that didn't happen. What Ian saw surprised him.

They *didn't* know each other, and with that knowledge, evident as the two shook hands warily, like two bare-knuckle boxers meeting before a bout, Ian changed his mind. Hiring this upstart would piss PR off. So that's what Ian did.

"Nick's going to do the finale," Ian said offhandedly.

"What?" PR had said, genuinely surprised. "I thought you were going to—"

"Nah," Ian said. "This track is too short, the corner is too tight. And the Skylark runs like a chili fart."

PR sputtered and took a few seconds to rearrange his face from surprise to something more casual and in control. "So we got ourselves a motorcycle man after all, huh?"

"Yep," Ian said. Ian desperately wanted to bust out laughing out loud but he didn't. "A daredevil show without a motorcycle is like a pig without dirt."

"What's this about a motorcycle jump finale?" The question came in a gravelly voice from a man who got out of the passenger seat of the Mav. Ian had given the man a cursory glance since he'd been focusing instead on spoiling PR and Nick's day.

Seeing the man now, Ian suddenly remembered what Grace had said PR had said when he took the road car an hour ago. PR was going to pick up a big shot at the airport, somebody higher up in Landini Tires, a suit from the St. Louis head office, who'd come out to see the show for himself.

At the time, Ian had just gotten the Skylark towed back to the infield to see why it had quit him in the backstretch. He was irritated and hadn't paid much attention. Now he remembered. Suit from St. Louis, come to see a show.

"Ian," PR said, recovering his cheery demeanor, or remembering he had one, "this is John Runzoni, Landini Tires Vice President for Promotions. John, this is Ian McGinnis."

Ian shook hands with PR's boss, a short, red-faced, round-faced, round-bellied, middle-aged man, who looked like he needed a new toupee and a stiff drink.

"I heard a lot about you, Mr. McGinnis," Runzoni said. Damp handshake, a bit nervous. Maybe a drinker. Runzoni wore a sweat-soggy white shirt with a loosened tie. Neat slacks and wing-tipped shoes, the shine already giving way to the pervasive dust. Out of place, Ian thought. And: *What's he really want?*

"Call me Ian." Big smile.

"I'm John." Big smile, right back at you.

"So, John," Ian said, "you come all the way out here to see a show, huh?"

Grace was nearby, like she belonged there, listening, as was Radar and Nick, but Ian noticed that everybody else had found something to do as far away as they could get. Suits. Some folks instinctively distrusted suits. Ian understood.

Nick looked around, frowning, and again, Ian got the impression he was looking for Hanna, who was apparently still in the trailer. Nick kept glancing toward the trailer.

Guess I'll have to have a little chat.

"More than that," John the promoter from Landini Tires headquarters in St. Louis said, "I'm here to work out details about the show finale. We've got to get an ad campaign going. What's this talk about a motorcycle? I thought we were going to do something with a car. Landini Tires doesn't have much of an interest in specialty tires."

From the very beginning, PR had been pressuring Ian to describe the big stunt they were going to do at the end of the season so Landini Tires could launch an ad campaign leading up to the big day. Ian had been vague, which frustrated PR no end. In truth, Ian had no idea what sort of stunt would fit the bill, and PR's pestering him about it didn't help.

"You mean at the end of the season?" Ian opted to play dumb. He tapped his hearing aid. "*That* show finale?"

"Yes, sir. How we're going to end this season. How we're going to put Ian McGinnis's Auto Daredevil Thrill Show on the map, and Landini Tires. I mean the big finale, the season showcase, the big stunt. I understand you and Parry have been calling it—" John held up both hands and crooked two fingers on each hand like quotation marks, "—The Big Stunt, with capital B and capital S, am I right?"

He laughed, an abrasive, machine-gun bray. "Bahahahah! B and S. B-S. Am I right? Bahahahah!"

Then his rubbery jowls hardened as though there had never been a smile there in the first place, let alone a laugh. The wrestler that he may have been in his younger years showed through. He put his hands on his hips, a belligerent gesture, and gave Ian a challenging look. "So what's all this shit I hear about a motorcycle finale?"

CHAPTER SIXTEEN

Ian introduced Nick, who explained to Runzoni all about the show finale, and that he was the best motorcycle man in the world, and why Ian and Landini Tires were so lucky to have him along.

"It means more shows," PR said, getting into the spirit of things. "More exposure."

"But we're understood," Runzoni said, "that the season finale, the Big Stunt, won't be a motorcycle skit, right?"

They understood.

It was an hour before showtime and PR took his boss on a walking tour of the show set-up. He showed him the flashy new show cars all equipped with Landini Tires and the ski car. He explained what the junkers were for and how they were prepared, about the dynamite chair, the ramps and so on, and introduced him to the crew one by one.

Grace called Nick into the trailer where she quickly fitted him with a spare uniform.

"Uh, that girl who was here?" Nick said, waving his hand vaguely, standing in front of the trailer's tiny wardrobe mirror.

"Um?" The pants cuffs were too long. Grace hemmed them with safety pins.

"Uh, I wasn't introduced to her. I mean, uh—"

"Hanna," Grace said. "My daughter." She stood.

"Oh." Nick smiled, looked away from Grace, and fiddled with the shirt-sleeves.

"Just roll those up for now," Grace said.

"And Joel is your son, right?" Nick fiddled with his collar—too tight.

"And Tink. He's adopted. Are you okay, Nick?"

"Hm? Oh, it's this shirt. Kind of tight under the armpits. I might rip it."

"It's just for today. I'll fix it later. Or Hanna will."

"Ah."

When she finished, and Nick had left to prep his bike and stow his gear in the van, Grace leaned out the door, caught Ian's eye, and waved him over. He went into the trailer and they sat at the little fold-down table.

"What are you doing?" Grace whispered.

Ian shrugged. "Nick will save my weary butt a lot of wear and tear."

"I don't like it, Ian."

"You'd rather I get busted up?"

"I don't mean that and you damn well know it. I mean him coming out here like he owns the place. Taking us for granted."

"He is cocky, sure, but he's good. He'll save us a lot of time and damage and make us some money."

"That's not why you hired him, not really, is it? It's PR, isn't it? You've been trying to knock him down a peg since he hired Radar, haven't you?"

"We've had this talk before. Whose show is it?"

Grace nodded sharply, as if Ian had just proved her point. She folded her arms over her chest, crossed her legs, and tapped a toe in the air, frowning. Ian had seen the look before.

"What?" he said.

"So you hired this guy to prove this ain't the Landini Tire Daredevil Show, but maybe now it's the Nick Cassidy Daredevil Show? Is *that* what you've done?"

That took Ian back a notch.

"There's more," Grace said.

"Goodie, goodie."

"Did you see the way BB and Hanna looked at him? Your golden boy, Mister Prince Charming?"

"Uh." It was all Ian could think of to say, and he dare not even shrug.

"You'd better have a talk with Nick Cassidy."

Ian nodded, ahemed, and left the trailer, speechless. He stalked over to the Skylark, to move it back into place, ready for the show. *What the hell just happened?*

Nick *would* benefit the show.

But Grace was right too. The kid was cocky, acted like he owned whatever he touched or looked at, and he was a pretty-boy.

"What the hell just happened?"

Irritated now for outsmarting himself, Ian got down to the routine of last-minute show prep. He got on his uniform and walked the infield, inspected the set-up, and he talked with Radar about the new routine, and with Boo. Later, maybe Boo could find a way to add to the finale, but right now, he was just to keep out of the way.

Radar began playing pre-show music on the loudspeakers, echoey upbeat rock and roll, Alan Parsons, rattling in the wooden grandstands. People started arriving, bringing with them the smell of hot-buttered popcorn from the concession booth under the grandstands and the fluttery feel of butterflies to Ian's stomach. Showtime butterflies. He tinkered and puttered, getting ready, checking and double-checking here and there, tinkering and puttering. Details.

"So, what do you think of Cassidy?" Ian asked Tink as Tink spray-painted the last of the junkers.

Tink kept spraying, didn't look up. "Ah, leave him behind and hire Baha."

"Baha?"

Tink looked up and laughed, shaking a spray can. Rattle, rattle, rattle. "I'm kidding, of course."

"Baha?"

Everybody in the show got a nickname eventually. Tink usually came up with the names, as if it were his responsibility to do so. He'd named the clowns over the past five years, after Gazebo moved on. Lugnuts. Dipstick. Crankshaft. Boo was a good enough nickname for the new clown.

The names were often just CB handles. Ian was "Number One" on the CB and Grace was "Her Nibs." Hanna was "Tiger Lady," something to do with a pet cat. Joel had balked at being called "Number Two," so he was the only one who didn't get a nickname. And Flynn.

Of course there were BB and Radar and Boo and PR.

Nick would be named "Trigger," Tink told Ian. Tink's own joke, it was, something about Nick's hair, something to do with Roy Rogers' golden palomino. Tink and Nick had already talked, instantly bonded, and Tink came up with the name on the spot. "He liked it right off," Tink said.

"Baha?"

Tink's eyes hid under a broad, squinty smile. "Yeah," he said. He held up two fingers on each hand, squiggled them like quotation marks and said, "Bahahaha." Ian laughed, then looked around to see where Baha was.

In the stands, front row center, beer and popcorn in hand, watching and taking notes in a little bitty notebook.

The show went off with few problems, including the finale. Radar narrated the dramatic show finish well, although he'd never done it before, coming up with a few impromptu lines that Ian promised himself to try to remember since they were good enough to keep. Nick did some spectacular wheelies, proving that his exhibition hours ago was just warm-up, thrilling the crowd into a fever pitch, even before he started looking at the jump ramp like it was some kind of towering Matterhorn. He also inspected his probable landing site with grave intensity. Radar quickly caught on to what Nick was doing with his body language, and he articulated it for the slower on-lookers.

"Nick Cassidy is now looking at his proposed landing site," Radar said in a grave, intense whisper as if he were narrating a golf tournament or a funeral, "and you can see the concern on his face. Will this be where he meets his doom? Can he survive the tight corner, the short approach, to land here, safely—or—" Significant pause, then change of pace. "We have an ambulance standing by—" And so on. Milking it, milking it.

Then, when Nick nailed the landing, and came back in front of the grandstand and took off his helmet, shaking out his damp, golden hair, the applause meter broke. Big hero.

They made a small fortune in souvenir sales after the show.

The only snag had been the motorcycle flaming boardwalls, which Tink did. Tink got whacked on the back of the neck with a board, and got a cinder down his neck. It burned a nice dime-sized blister on his neck, but as usual, he didn't let anybody know he needed a little salve on it until they were packed up after the show and ready for supper.

Grace put on a salve, scolded Tink uselessly, and that was that. Tink and Grace had been here before. Tink had forgotten to wear a scarf. It was a warm night.

Nick had wanted to do the boardwalls, made it clear right away that he wanted to do everything, learn the daredevil business from the inside out, including car stunts and the dynamite chair, but Ian said no. He said no because he wanted to establish right off who was boss. Nick could ask, but Ian could say no and Ian's way was the only way. Nick—*Trigger*—needed to understand this up front.

And we need to have that talk.

Besides, Ian didn't know if Trigger had ever done a boardwall before. It was different from a jump. You had to do it right, hit the ramp in front of the wall aimed straight and with enough velocity to break the boards solidly, and you had to get your head down at the last second, and you had to do it now, no lollygagging, or the fire would die down and the stunt would look silly. Ian had seen riders approach so slowly, so tentatively, that they'd almost been knocked over by the flimsy walls, and he'd seen rider's approach the walls crookedly and nearly crash. He used two walls, one right after the other, *bam, bam*, the second about fifty feet from the first, and both followed off low ramps so the crash took place in mid-air, made it more spectacular that way, and if a rider approached the first ramp crookedly, he might hit the upright two-by-four supporting the wall or even miss the second one. Ian had seen it.

He resolved to set up a boardwall in Riverton, their next stop, before the show, and see what Trigger could do. If he could do a decent boardwall, he might give Tink a breather there. And if Trigger persisted, he might let him do a roll or two.

"Why do you do it?" Baha asked Ian after the show.

"Well, Mr. Runzoni—John. The show is as much of a thrill for us to do as it is for—"

"Yeah, I heard that. We got tape, going to use some of it in a radio commercial, but what I want to know is—" Baha's smile dropped from his face in another of his sudden and startling apparent emotional shifts. "Why. Do. You. Do. It?"

The pot-bellied man's intensity startled Ian, but he recovered and matched sober for sober. "You want to know—why? For business or is this personal curiosity?"

"Maybe a little of both." Baha shrugged round shoulders. "Which would you prefer to answer?"

Before Ian could respond, a small gang of fans and reporters interrupted them. Ian immediately forgot the question. And deliberately forgot it.

An hour later, Baha brought up the subject of the Big Stunt, or "B-S" as everybody was now calling it, over supper. It was almost midnight, and the daredevils and their paunchy guest from St. Louis, now dressed in a cowboy hat and jeans and tennis shoes, were sitting around a big table in the back room of Denny's in downtown Rawlins.

Ian had made sure that everybody understood that the Rock Springs show had been just for practice, not a real show. That way, if anybody screwed up, it wouldn't weigh on their minds like it might otherwise if they thought it really counted. But Rawlins was a real show, a real audience, and it had gone well, and everybody felt it, and they were all a little giddy after the show. They had drawn a huge crowd, largely due to PR's campaign, and some of the daredevils had their first real chance to meet fans, sign autographs, and be stars, which didn't happen in Rock Springs after that show.

Baha, who had seen his first real-live auto daredevil show, felt some of that giddiness, which prompted his "Why do you do it" question earlier. Now, Ian was relieved to see he seemed to have forgotten, caught up in the babble of conversation around the table.

It was in this giddy, post-show, excited atmosphere, sitting around a big table at Denny's, tired but happy, that Baha brought up the Big Stunt.

"Tell me about the Big Stunt," he said. The tone was as close to an order as Ian had ever heard, and Ian knew that he would not sidetrack Baha as he'd done with the other question. Baha reminded him of a bulldog.

Ian had delayed this conversation long enough with PR. It weighed on his mind and he had to come up with something, now.

"Okay," Ian said, wiping mashed potatoes off his lower lip, "I'll tell you." He hadn't a clue.

"A while ago," he said, "Parry here talked about setting up this big ol' Landini Tire for me to jump through. Can you do that? Make a big enough tire?"

Baha made a note in his little bitty notebook. "World's biggest tire," he said. "Bahahaha. I like that. What else?"

"Well," Ian looked pensive, frowning, "we use fire in the show a lot, you saw tonight. I don't know what you'd think about setting your world's biggest tire on fire—"

"How about if we have the car on fire?" PR said.

"With me in it?" Ian said.

"Yeah, we fire the trunk," Tink said. He and Ian had from time to time talked about doing more spectacular stunts and varying the show routine. Some of their brainstorming ideas had had merit, others had not. "We light up a hay bale in the trunk of the jump car."

"Wouldn't that be d-dangerous," Boo asked, "being so close to the g-gas tank?"

Ian started to answer, but Joel took the floor, sleepy but exhilarated by the first show.

"There ain't enough gas to matter," Joel said. "But we could set off Roman candles along the launch ramp. Maybe dynamite." Joel understood brainstorming, and he wanted to play too, tired or not.

With a pang of nostalgia, Ian now recalled brainstorming sessions he'd had with Shaun, how much they'd both enjoyed those sessions, and he wondered how Shaun was doing. Shaun hadn't made the trip up to see the Rawlins show, and Ian decided to call him tonight, right after he dealt with the B-S.

"As long as it doesn't hurt the big tire, right?" Baha said.

"Yeah," Flynn said, "but where's the tire? I mean is it part of the landing or the takeoff? And if it's at the takeoff end, what does Ian land on? Tires?"

"He lands *in* tires," Hanna said. "There's like this big pile of tires for him to land in."

When Ian heard Joel and Hanna join in the conversation and the energy level ratchet up another notch, he relaxed. He'd let his family and crew design the season finale, the B-S, and he'd sit back and supervise, modifying as needed. This way, everybody got to feel part of the show—everybody except Trigger got worked up in the animated table talk; Trigger seemed pensive and distracted—which was good for morale.

Ian noticed with relief that Baha was busy taking notes and getting involved, so involved that Baha failed to notice that Ian hadn't come right out and said, "This is exactly what were going to do," that Ian was winging it, designing the stunt on the fly.

Of course, Ian thought, as he listened to Boo offer a way for the clown to be involved, if you didn't listen too closely, it might sound like Ian's family and crew were re-designing Ian's original idea. That led Ian to believe that whatever cockeyed idea they came up with now, Ian could modify on the fly later.

Meanwhile, Baha was getting a notebook full of ideas to take back to Landini Tires headquarters.

"But it's got to be a jump, right?" BB said. "That's what everybody wants, isn't it?"

"Yeah," Flynn said, "the longer the better."

"So, maybe we do the world's longest jump through the world's biggest tire," Radar said. "But what do we jump? Cars? Trucks? Tires?"

"Jumps are old," Tink said. "Everybody jumps stuff, even we do. We need a twist."

"A jump with a twist," PR said. "That's it. The takeoff ramp is corkscrewed, not straight."

"Corkscrewed?" Hanna.

"So the jump car spirals in the air," PR said. He twisted his hand to demonstrate, the Red Baron describing an aerial dogfight to his colleagues on the ground. "Like this."

Ian counted three side conversations. People were setting up jump ramps with plates and using forks for jump cars. They were scribbling on napkins. Baha hijacked PR for an animated side conversation about the giant tire Ian would fly through. "Can we make two of them?" he was asking.

"I don't know about a twist," Ian said. "That would be a bear to build. It'd have to take a lot of stress and—"

"But a j-jump," Boo said. "I mean, it's so common."

"Yeah," Tink said. "Everybody does jumps. We need a twist. Maybe not literally—"

"How about a loop?" Flynn said.

"Like at the carnivals?" BB asked. "With the motorcycles in the globe thing?"

"I saw one show," Trigger said, "where they called it 'The Circle of Death.'"

"A loop?" Grace said.

"Now, *that* would be tough to engineer," Ian said.

"Yeah," Trigger said. "For a car, but if you used a bike, it wouldn't be such a problem. Less weight, less stress—"

"But we're doing a car in the B-S, right?" BB asked.

"It's the length," Flynn said. "That's what people get excited over. The longer the jump, the more it looks like the driver is going to die—Sorry, Ian."

"No, I understand. It's how far, that's what excites people these days."

"So, how about this," Tink said, getting everybody's attention. "We have Ian launch off this huge loop ramp—"

"That starts in the parking lot," BB said, "and goes up and over the grandstands and back under—"

"Yeah," Tink continued, "and then the ramp twists, like the corkscrew you said," he nudged PR, "and then Ian flies through this giant tire—"

"And there's fire everywhere," Joel said.

"—and Ian lands in this huge pyramid of Landini Tires. What do you think?"

Flynn took over, and Ian was glad to see that the discussion was turning silly but that Baha didn't seem to notice that nobody was being serious. "Yeah, the twist and the loop and the fire and the tires, right, but remember it's the length that counts—" He held his hands apart, a fisherman describing the big one that got away, only he managed to make it vulgar. Lots of laughter. "So here's what we do."

Flynn used a napkin holder for the jump car as he talked. "World's longest jump, right? Okay, Ian jumps the car out of one airplane and it lands into another airplane, one of those big cargo planes with the big door in the back—you tire guys can rent one of those, right?—and this second plane flies across country where Ian drives it out of the plane with a parachute, and he lands it and then—*then*, he drives it up a loop from the parking lot, over the crowd and under them, *then* through a spiral ramp, *then* you get your fire and dynamite and your big tires and all that. Voila, the world's longest car jump, *with* a twist *and* a spiral. Now, *that*'s a stunt people will talk about."

Flynn made his animated presentation with such finesse that everybody at the table roared with laughter.

Baha was the first to sober. "So, tell me, Ian, which is the hardest to build? The twist ramp or the loop?"

CHAPTER SEVENTEEN

*H*anna McGinnis. The boss's daughter.

"What was I thinking?"

Nick shook his head and sighed. *Not* thinking. Again.

He stood over the urinal in the Denny's men's room, relieving himself and rubbing the back of his neck. Still riding the high of the successful bike jump finale, the dinner conversation about the "B-S" had at first intrigued Nick. Was there a role in it for him? But the talk shifted quickly until it became just a noisy word game, something the Jorgensen boys might do for road trip entertainment but with almost a dozen players. He lost interest quickly and he felt out of the loop, so to speak, so he just sat back. By and by, simple disinterest congealed to cold boredom, which became restlessness in a heartbeat. Nick wanted to move on to something else, or just leave, just go.

They had a show up in Riverton—*was it tomorrow or the day after*?—it was now past midnight, the caravan was loaded, gassed and ready. Shouldn't they be putting some road under their wheels?

Nick excused himself from the table with a mumble; nobody said anything to him. Napkins, spoons and knives and forks and plates and glasses and cups and salt and pepper shakers and sugar dispensers and catsup bottles flew, spiraled and crashed across the table, everybody yakking and laughing at once. The carnage kept two harried teen-aged waitresses busy running back and forth between table and kitchen, struggling to keep smiles on their faces. Nick knew from dating a few waitresses that big tables often meant lousy tips.

As he stood, he noticed a crink in his neck, and he massaged it as he walked to the men's. For a second, he thought it might have been from the jump, but he'd landed without complications just as he had in Omaha, neat and smooth as a French kiss. Matter of fact, he'd had the bike's shocks and tires adjusted to take the landing impact better than in Omaha, so that wasn't it.

The crowd *had* gone wild, thunderously, and the accidental discovery he'd made in Omaha—no landing ramp—had been a big hit. A wonder nobody had thought of it before. Maybe somebody had, but nobody was routinely using it in a show. He'd patent it. Maybe they'd call it "the Cassidy Way," or something like that. He'd have to think about it, see if he could get something worked into Radar's script.

Nick hadn't heard much of Radar's spiel before the stunt over his engine growl and his own breathing in his helmet and the track's bad acoustics and the tinny sound system. They'd communicated mostly by hand signals, announcer and performer, signals worked out in advance. But Nick clearly saw the crowd cheer in response to the warm-up laps and wheelies he did before the jump and knew it resulted in large part from Radar's hype. Radar was a good announcer, seemed to love manipulating a crowd, getting them frenzied up. Nick would talk to him.

The Cassidy Crash? Cassidy's Cruise?

Trigger's Triumph?

Nick snorted and zipped up. He didn't like the nickname. He hadn't said anything at the time Tink brought it up, but he'd resolved to change it as soon as he could. Today wasn't the day, though, to begin hassling anybody.

The cheers after the stunt weren't Radar's doing. That was all Nick Cassidy.

Nick had been good. Damn good.

The crew had been impressed too, even Flynn. Nick had wondered if the show's until-now prime bike man would be jealous of him, but Flynn didn't seem so. Flynn was easy-going, relaxed, admirably at ease with himself. A giant Buddha, Nick decided soon after meeting him.

But as they loaded up after the show, Nick realized that he'd tried so hard to do the best show he'd ever done in his life not for the cheers of the crowd, which was an amazing high, true enough, like nothing he'd ever experienced, but he'd really done it for *her*. She'd watched, he knew. He'd looked and had to force himself to concentrate on the stunt after he spotted her standing by the sound van, watching.

She'd seen, yes, but after the show, everybody had gotten busy and

Nick didn't get a chance to ask her what she'd thought.

Now, combing his long blond hair in the mirror, he realized where the crink came from. From trying to see *her*, to look at *her* at the supper table.

Hanna McGinnis. The boss's daughter.

What had he been thinking?

"I know what I was thinking," he said aloud. *But what body part was I doing the thinking with*?

They'd taken a long table in the back room at Denny's and Nick had tried to maneuver himself so he could sit next to Hanna, but it hadn't worked out that way as the crowd shuffled in. He'd ended up sitting on the same side of the table three seats down from Hanna. Couldn't see her, except if he sat forward at an absurd angle and damn well *gawked*. His glimpses were few and somewhere toward the last fork of mashed potatoes, he realized how he'd behaved: *downright fucking adolescent*. Trying to sit next to the little red-haired girl in class, passing her notes, holding the door open for her, "May I carry your books, pretty please?"

"A crink in my goddam—"

A guy walked in and Nick gritted his teeth.

Talking to myself. Jesus H.

Nick barely got a hello when Grace first introduced him to Hanna in the family's small trailer that afternoon after Ian agreed to hire him. Grace stood back a step, standing in the narrow doorway, after she'd introduced him, smiling, arms folded. Nick didn't know whether to shake Hanna's hand or not. She sat behind the little fold-up table in back of the trailer as she opened and sorted boxes of souvenir T-shirts. She had both hands full at the time so Nick opted for a quick nod.

"Uh, 'lo." He put his hands in his pockets.

"Hi." She looked up from counting T-shirts and smiled and caught his eye. Perfect teeth. Perfect eyes.

Grace took him out of the trailer and showed him where to stow his duffel bag in the van. She then introduced him to Radar and Boo who were way off in the backstretch, practicing a clown routine with the tricky car, an old Fiat painted in red and blue polka dots on a white field. Looked like the toy cars you see in circuses where eighteen clowns climb out of it, or a squashed Wonderbread truck.

As he walked across the infield to meet the two, he heard the trailer door bang shut and he turned to see if Hanna had come out. He stumbled on a rock. Grace barely glanced at him and kept on chatting about the show. How Ian got into the business. "Been at it before you fell off your first tricycle." How the crew works together on the road, before shows, during a show, and packs up after. "Everybody has a job, but we help each other." Teamwork and all that. And how they behave in front of the media. "Smile a lot and watch your language." Ian's insistence that, no matter how tired they get, "Nap when you can because sometimes you don't know when you can't," or how little time they have, or how scant the facilities, everybody washes equipment and themselves before each show. "Comb your teeth and brush your hair." And so on. "Tuck in your shirt."

It wasn't Hanna.

"Have you ever had to sponge bathe in a horse water trough?" Grace asked.

Had Mrs. McGinnis—Grace—seen me looking back at her daughter?

"Not on purpose," Nick said.

While Nick shook hands with Radar and Boo, and chatted a bit, Grace stood aside, arms folded under her lemon-sized breasts, like Hanna's—*Jesus, I'm gawking at the boss's wife!*—smiling, waiting. Then they'd moved on. Grace turned him over to Flynn, who showed him where to stow his bike and leathers and helmet bag.

Then he'd tinkered with his bike, tuning and prepping it for the jump, getting a feel for the track, talked with Radar again about the bike jump, with Grace about pay—he got an advance—helped Tink and Joel and BB and PR finish cleaning out the junkers that would be used in the roll-overs and head-on crash, and generally got himself ready for his first real daredevil show. All the while, trying to see where Hanna had got to, and when she was in sight, trying to keep her there, and scheming ways to get closer to her.

He stumbled on another rock.

Come the show, Tink and Flynn and Boo and Ian, each in their turns, kept Nick on schedule and in the right place for his part in each stunt and the take-down and set-up between acts. He'd been too busy to keep track of Hanna. He found himself during one stunt holding the opposite end of a twelve-foot long inflatable plastic hotdog, part of a clown gag, with Hanna on the other end, and barely glancing at her, before Boo "ate" the hotdog and they moved on to the next act. They exchanged not a word during the whole show.

After, fans came down to the track and milled about the front stretch and infield, inspecting the wrecked cars, and the new stunt cars and the bikes and trucks and the scene of the dynamite chair explosion, and talking to the daredevils, taking pictures, and buying souvenir programs, hats, T-shirts, and posters from Hanna and Grace. At one point Nick was surrounded—*engulfed*—by fans, pressing in on him three deep on all sides.

Everybody in the show signed autographs, even Radar and Joel and PR, but Nick was aware that he was the most popular performer by far. He got more fans around him than even Ian did, clearly, and for an awkward moment, Nick wondered if Ian noticed, or cared—or worse, if he was jealous. But Ian didn't seem to notice. And if he did, he apparently didn't care.

Nick had signed autographs before, but this was like nothing else he'd ever experienced. Dozens of fans, and quite a few attractive young women among them, and the look in their eyes, the way they stood, lingered, spoke—touched him. Nick could have had his pick of any of a dozen pretty women that night simply by asking.

Two particularly determined tarts, not too young, maybe, and reasonably attractive, had hung around long after almost everybody else had cleared away and the rest of the crew were deep into the loading-up routine. Nick indulged the babes for a while, not sure how to get them off his arm— they literally clung to him. He felt tempted to indulge himself, and them, but the timing was wrong. Nick needed to pay attention to his new job right now, learn the ropes, but he didn't want to be rude to fans. Grace had said something about the show's image. Smile and don't swear. Besides, they had a show tomorrow. Or was it the next day? Was it up in Riverton? Where was that? Grace had given him a schedule and he'd put it—somewhere.

Ian solved the problem when he walked up to the threesome. "You ladies are going to have to let my man go now. Sorry. We got work to do. No rest for the wicked."

Ian smiled as he said it, his eyes disappearing in cheek skin folds. He let the disappointed gals linger a bit, pouty, and drift off with significant glances over their shoulders until they stood in the grandstands watching like wives at the dock seeing their sailors off to sea.

Ian chuckled and pointed to a ramp on the ground. "Take that end," he said, "and I'll show you how we load these little puppies."

Nick knew the long wooden jump ramps were heavy, had helped shift one setting up for the roll-overs, but he was impressed with how easily Ian and everybody on the crew, including pencil-necked Radar and even tiny Boo, handled the task of organizing and loading the big ramps and the piles of large wooden blocks, used to prop up the ramps.

"Everything has a place," Ian said as he and Nick stowed the ramp in its slot on the car carrier. "Ramps, blocks, cars, bikes. Dollies. All have their place."

"Dollies?"

"Those gals." Ian laughed. He laughed a lot after a show. And before. But not during. Nick noticed that Ian, during a show, seemed to be everywhere, seemed to see everything without looking, even when he was behind the wheel doing a stunt.

Ian told Nick about "shipboard romances."

"I started out doing bike stunts for Sid Hirsch's Tournament of Thrills. About Tink's age. Back then, jumping over four cars was a big deal, and I was one of the best. Anyways, I didn't know much, but I learned. Show stuff, how to do the stunts—all the stunts. Business. Advertising, promoting, stuff like that. And getting along with folks on the road. That was the most important lesson."

They stood leaning against the end of the car carrier, where a plastic five gallon water jug sat with a cup tied to the handle, taking a breather while the others worked on stowing gear, loading and cleaning up, like gandy dancers, a rhythm to their efforts. Everybody dirty and sweaty, working hard, but seemingly content, even happy, in their shared effort. Nobody seemed to mind that he and Nick had stopped for a chat.

"Yeah, I confess," Nick said, looking around for Hanna—over by the van, helping Radar stow sound gear—"I don't know much about business— I mean, about people."

"We had a girl driver in the show, a real looker." Ian gestured with his hands in front of his chest in the universal sign that meant she had huge hooters. "The girl driver, Doris was her name, and another stuntman, guy named Henry, hit it off strong before the show hit the road. Doris and Henry were an item and everybody knew it. They slept together in the sound van when they didn't have motels and took a room separate from the rest of the crew when they had the chance to motel up.

"After the first month, the clown, don't remember his name, fell off the carrier deck and broke his leg and had to leave the show. We hired us a new clown quick enough, fellow named Peter, but we'd've been better off to forget about clown routines for the rest of the year, as it turned out.

"See, Doris and Peter hit it off. They became an item, and the friction between Henry and Peter simmered. I got concerned—crew morale and all that. Talked with Sid about it, tried to catch him when he was sober, but the old fart brushed it off."

Ian paused and his eyes fogged over and his shoulders went slack. Nick filled the water cup and drank cool coppery-tasting water, waiting, while Ian remembered. It looked to Nick as if Ian didn't want to remember.

Ian continued, voice changed, infused with something like awe, or dread. "Last show of that season, during the routine ol' Sid called The Freeway of Death, what I call Hell Driving, it happened."

Took him a minute, but Nick finally recognized the tone, the body language. He'd heard it before, most recently from Big Al, the Rawlins bike store guy, and before that, from Ivy, the trucker. Nam. When people remembered, something odd happened to their eyes, their bodies. Like Nick saw in Ian now.

"You watched the Hell Driving?" Ian asked.

"Yeah. You told me to."

In Hell Driving, the first stunt in Ian's show after the national anthem and the crew is introduced, two parallel ramps are set up in the front stretch, one set near the fourth corner, the other near the first corner. Ian had four hell-driving cars, used almost exclusively for this one stunt. Four drivers, usually Ian, Tink, Flynn, and BB or sometimes Grace or Hanna, raced right-way around the track, in a tight group, two-by-two, inches between the front bumper of the trailing car and the leader's rear bumper, but the inside pair was four feet or so away from the outside pair.

The four cars hit the fourth corner ramp set, inside and outside, hard and fast. The infield side pair hit their ramps with the passenger side wheels. The grandstand couple hit the ramps on the driver's side. The ramps are raised at the high end so that the cars tilt into the air until it looks like they'll fall over. Of course they don't. They crash back to the track and repeat the over-the-ramp maneuver quickly on the first corner ramp pair. Zoom, zoom.

They then come back wrong-way-round in a crisscross maneuver between the ramp groups and slide into position before the grandstand, pop out of their cars, wave and smile to the crowd, and move on to the next show event.

The cars are loud, flashy and colorful, they drive close together, and the speed looks magnified in the limited space of the front stretch between the ramps in the two corners, but if not for the announcer hype—and some announcers were better at it than others—or the fact that a clown sat on the second set of ramps, looking to the audience like he was about to get his silly, geeky Howdy Doody butt run over, the thrill of the stunt would be diminished. Hirsch, clever showman when sober, added the clown to the stunt years before Ian joined the show, and since then, it took on an aspect that was both dangerous and crowd-pleasing.

The clown sat on the high end of the infield side ramp of the first corner ramp arrangement, facing the audience and the grandstand side ramp, casually reading a newspaper. People would scream in anticipatory fear as the cars bared down on the poor fool at top speed. But the cars always missed.

The clown, startled out of his leisurely lollygagging when the cars passed inches from him, tossed his newspaper into the air where it disintegrated into a thousand glittery confetti fragments, thanks to the magic-shop device the clown gripped hidden in one hand for that moment, his pants fell down and he ran off the track, stumbling over his suspenders, clutching his clown hat, and screaming about needing to change his underwear.

And the crowd goes wild.

The clown never got hurt. "Well, not *never*," Ian said.

"What happened?" Nick had an idea where Ian was going.

"You know how we see to it that Boo doesn't get hurt?"

"The infield side driver—that's you—you hit the ramp where Boo sits, and you've got to make sure you miss the clown, because the clown is sitting on your passenger side—"

"And I can't see diddly, so how do I know I'll miss Boo?"

"You miss the high end entirely. You drop off the ramp halfway up, and the crowd can't see that because it's masked by the grandstand side car—"

"That does go all the way off the high end, so it rises higher and you can't see."

"This Henry guy," Nick said, "he didn't—"

"He did. I was on the grandstand side, which is easier and less of a responsibility because the infield side driver has a life in his hands, you know, which is why I do that side now. My show and all that. But I was new then, a rookie. The infield side driver, Henry, he deliberately drifted over on the ramp and stayed there, deliberately hit Peter. Tried to kill him. He nearly succeeded."

"Jesus H."

"Peter recovered. You hardly notice the limp." Ian shrugged, seemed to come out of his war story funk. "Shipboard romances," he said. "I don't tolerate them. You see why, now?"

Nick nodded. He drew water from the jug, something to do with his hands. "Listen, those dollies—"

"I ain't worried about them. Dip your wick as you please, when it don't cut into your work, but if I get a pissed off poppa come to the next show with a shotgun, I'll turn you over for a dime reward. They got plenty of rubbers at the truck stops, I guess you know. And if a gal says she's eighteen and a half, you frisk her and check her ID. Some states under 21 is jail-bait, so double check at the border."

"Okay, I got you." Nick folded his arms and feet and leaned back against the side of the carrier. He's listened because he was new, still learning, and Ian was his boss and it seemed politic to listen, but Ian's tone seemed— what? Disrespectful? Or something like that. *Does he think I'm stupid?*

"As for the crew," Ian said, "we're elbow to cheek every day for four, five months, gals and guys. And we got work to do, hard work."

"All right, I'll try to—"

"You'll do more than try. When it comes to show, you keep your dick in your pants, hear? I told you that story because I want you to believe me that I won't tolerate shipboard romances, and I damn well mean every word. If I catch you—well, I won't kill you. Much. I'll just fire you. On the spot. I've done it before. Ask any of the crew, if you don't believe me. Except BB. She don't know shit. Yet."

"Have you had this talk with her?"

"Grace did."

"All right, I got it."

But it wasn't until he left the bathroom to return to the B-S at the supper table, rubbing his neck, that Nick really got it.

As he strolled down the hallway, BB and Hanna walked toward him. For an uncomfortable second, Nick thought they were heading for him, maybe to talk to him about something, but the second passed as he realized the women's room was next to the men's room he'd just left and that's probably where they were heading. He was jumpy in the presence of the two women; realizing that he was jumpy irritated him.

As they passed him, he stuffed his hands in his pockets, and tried on a smile. It wasn't quite a real smile, not really.

Two things happened as he passed the girls in the not-quite-wide enough hallway. BB looked at him with a longing, a familiar gaze, and Nick realized that it was BB that Ian had been worried about; BB had taken a shine to Nick. Instantly, Nick recalled her looking at him when they were introduced—*how had I missed it?* Nick would have to fight her off with a stick. If she'd looked at him like that before the show, during it, or after, Nick hadn't noticed. He'd been busy. He'd been busy doing show, working, and gawking at Hanna when he could. But now it was clear: BB wanted his bod, and Ian knew, or so it seemed, and Nick would have to deal with this, sooner or later.

The second thing Nick realized as the two girls passed was that he rather liked his nickname.

"Hi, Trigger," Hanna said.

"Hi, yourself." Damn good nickname, Trigger.

Nick stopped at the end of the hallway where it joined the main dining room and looked back. Both girls were watching him over their shoulders. Hanna was watching him. Nick recognized the look, had seen it a thousand times.

Turning, he tripped over the edge of the dining room area carpet.

CHAPTER EIGHTEEN

So it came to pass, without anybody really knowing how it had happened, that the Ian McGinnis Auto Daredevil Thrill Show, whose principal sponsor was Landini Tires, would perform at the end of the 1979 season, probably in late August although a date hadn't been fixed yet, or the place, a daring, never-before-attempted stunt that would involve a car flying through a loop-the-loop ramp, through the world's largest tire, over twenty or so Landini Tires delivery trucks, which would set a new world's record, and landing in a pyramid of Landini Tires, which would later be auctioned off to an as-yet unnamed but worthy charity, an event that would itself attract still more media attention.

Details to be worked out, of course.

Later that night, when Ian and Grace were alone in their room at the Rawlins Motel Six, they talked.

"You're not serious, are you?" Grace asked.

Ian snorted. "Baha is happy and he's gone away. PR is happy, for now. And everybody had a good time."

"So you *weren't* serious."

"A loop-the-loop ramp? I haven't a clue how to build one, or if it can even be done."

"But PR doesn't know that. He thinks—"

"And he's happy thinking what he thinks. I'll do some drawings, drum up some figures, give him a dose of reality. I'll show him it's out of the question, and we'll come up with some modification. Something that *will* work."

"You'd better get on it, and quick before you find yourself committed to jumping out of an airplane in a flaming car into a vat of sharks."

The Landini Tire PR folk under Baha's guidance went to work on the ad campaign even before Ian did the Riverton show two days later. By the time they reached Sheridan on April 10, word was out. Ian faced a small army of microphones in Sheridan before the show, unusual for such a small town, because word was out about the Big Stunt, and word was vague enough that people wanted details, were begging for details, which is exactly the reaction that Landini Tires wanted at this stage of the game. Ian smiled his aw-shucks showman smile, and did his best to sound like he had a clue, but he said little enough, and committed to nothing. He started drawing on napkins, talking with Tink and Trigger about engineering a loop-the-loop ramp. Nobody had a clue how to build it.

Flynn got some flash burns on his leg from the dynamite chair but otherwise the Sheridan show was a success. It was so successful, in fact, that Grace ran out of souvenir stock, and PR had to make phone calls.

Trigger did the double flaming motorcycle boardwall jumps that night, and he did them well, even though the first time he'd ever done anything like it was earlier that afternoon when Ian and Tink set up a wall—one wall, and no fire on this one—to see how he did. The boardwalls are scheduled early in the show and Ian understood right away, given the audience reaction, a lot more lively than when Flynn or Tink did the stunt, that it was a good idea to give the audience a taste of Trigger's wavy, golden hair and winning smile early, and use the moment to hone their desire to see the motorcycle jump later. Trigger would do the boardwalls for the rest of the season.

"Are you good with that?" Ian asked Flynn.

"Hell, yes," Flynn said.

"Watch your language."

"He makes us all look good. Besides, it's a bike stunt and he's the bike man, so he should do it. I'm backup. I got no problem with that."

That night, PR got a call. "You are now co-sponsored," PR told Ian, "or maybe the word is 'sub-sponsored,' by Denny's and Motel Six."

The crew was jubilant. On the road, they most often slept in and on the rigs and trailers. Flynn bunked in the wrecker back seat, Tink on the deck beside the wrecker boom. Boo slept in the ski car, Radar slept on top of the ramp rack in the back of the car carrier, BB slept in the van, Trigger slept in the Freightliner sleeper, and Ian, Grace, Joel, and Hanna slept in their tiny trailer. It kept costs down. They could pull in at a roadside rest area, a truck stop, outside a fairgrounds, or track or wherever they found themselves at three a.m., drop anchor, and sack out without fuss.

But when they had time and one was available, and they were in desperate need of a hot shower, they tried to find a motel. Until now, it had been a crapshoot both in terms of finding one at all and in terms of cost and quality. Now, both were reasonably assured. Still, they would end up sleeping outside and in and on the equipment most of the time. Motel Six was a pleasant luxury.

Now, they'd eat free when there was a Denny's, and there was always a Denny's.

They scheduled to film a Motel Six TV commercial in Spokane in mid-May.

Billings on April 13 was also a fill date, heavily promoted by Landini Tires, and a financial success. The crowd was bigger than Sheridan, but Ian expected it to be because Billings was a bigger town.

The Miles City show, two days later, even though the night was cold and dreary, drew an even bigger crowd than Billings, and Ian had to admit it was PR's doings. That afternoon, Flynn wrenched his back while stripping junkers, so Ian did the rolls that night in one car, Tink in the other, and Ian did the dynamite chair. PR arranged for a doctor to look at Flynn the next day in Glendive, and Flynn was well enough to do the rolls and the chair the next night. Tink opted to let Trigger do the rollover.

Trigger had seen a couple rolls done and Ian and Tink had briefed him, but Ian expected the first few tries to go wrong. But Trigger performed his first roll flawlessly.

"Are you left-handed?" Ian asked Trigger after that first rollover.

"Yeah, why?" Trigger asked.

"Just that it takes lefties longer to learn how to do this stunt." Trigger had gotten it right the first time. "You want to do it more? You can if you want."

Trigger wanted, and Ian now had at his disposal three daredevils—four, counting himself—that he could call on for rolls. He enjoyed the luxury.

Ian also had begun to enjoy the luxury of letting Trigger do the show finale. But in Glendive, Ian decided to do a car carrier jump instead—or rather, PR decided for him to do it. There were TV cameras at the show, a crew from KTVQ out of Billings, stirred to action after a producer had scouted the show in Billings and in Miles City and stirred up by talk of the Big Stunt—and PR's effort to get them stirred up. PR wanted footage of a car jump, just a taste of the B-S.

He also wanted footage for a commercial, for which he paid the film crew extra. Ian did a few takes in the parking lot that afternoon, getting into and out of the ski car, saying things like, "Buckle up," and "Seatbelts save lives," and "Drive without Landini Tires? I wouldn't dare."

Ian had a good car for the jump, a '74 Olds Cutlass coupe. PR had bought it for five hundred dollars, tapping his seemingly bottomless Landini Tire budget. Ian would have never paid such a price for a junker, but this car was no junker and he didn't have to pay for it. Whether Ian liked it or not, PR and Landini Tires were coming through, as promised.

For the price, PR demanded results. Ian could only smile, and comply.

But not without a fuss. "I don't know about this track, PR," Ian said. "The corners are pretty tight."

"So we can put the carrier farther down the front stretch, couldn't we?"

"Yeah, but it would be harder for folks in part of the grandstands to see if we did that."

"We could announce what we were doing early so people could move over."

"What if the stands are so crowded nobody can move over to a better seat?"

"We move the carrier further infield. That gives you a longer straight-away and the audience a better view."

"Well, I don't know—"

And so it went. Ian wasn't seriously trying to get out of the stunt. He would rather have had the motorcycle jump in the first place, of course, but he wasn't backing out. He just wanted to assert his authority, keep PR aware of who was in charge. It was *his* show, and PR had once again taken over. It galled Ian and he did his best to regain control, even while realizing that he had to do the jump anyway.

Trigger, as Ian predicted, chaffed in the wake of the decision to make the Glendive finale a car crash featuring Ian McGinnis rather than a motorcycle jump featuring Nick "Trigger" Cassidy. He pouted before the show. In part, his pouting helped convince Ian that he really wanted to do the car jump.

Trigger did his best to hide his pouting, but Ian saw through the forced smiles and bravado. The pouting got to be annoying, so Ian tried to get Trigger to focus his disappointment on PR instead of Ian, but Trigger didn't rise to the bait. To keep him content, or at least reasonably quiet as well as busy, Ian gave Trigger his first head-on.

"How about that?" Ian said. "You end up with more stunts during the show than anybody."

"I don't know—"

"You do the crew jump, the boardwalls, rolls, head-on. Do some wheelies."

"Hell of a deal."

"Watch your language."

Trigger had to accept the deal and like it. Ian knew Trigger in fact wanted to learn as much as he could about dardeviling, and learning how to do a good head-on crash was a major step forward. Just as Ian made as much of a show as he could complaining about the carrier jump, Trigger made a show of being aware that he'd been slighted, but was putting up with it, gallant man that he was.

During the show, nobody would have known he was being an ass about being passed over, or that in fact he even knew how to jump a motorcycle. He flashed his smile and shook his golden mane, and strutted his stuff when it was his turn in the limelight and he did it, as he always did, as if he owned the limelight.

So Trigger did his first head-on. He did a poor job of it, but Ian had expected him to do a poor job of it. The head-on was a difficult stunt to pull off well. Ian knew Trigger wasn't ready to do it, and he was right. Tink had coached Trigger on the stunt, but Trigger still botched it. Ian got a perverse pleasure in seeing the cocky golden boy fail.

But Trigger rose to the occasion. He blamed the car, saying the steering went loose as he approached the track and that the speedo cable was off, saving face. Or maybe it was true. Junkers were junkers. Anyway, Trigger got Tink aside to coach him on it more, and resolved to do it again.

Ian just nodded. "We'll see," he said. He smiled.

Tink and Flynn did the rolls.

Ian's car carrier jump went well enough, at least as seen from the grandstands and the TV cameras. After the show, Grace applied half a jar of Ben-Gay on Ian's zebra-stripe bruises where the seatbelt had ripped his skin raw. Nothing broken.

When Boo dropped an approach board on his toe, Ian decided they needed another ramp hand. BB mentioned a friend who might be available on no-time notice, and Ian put PR on it. PR made calls and did his magic and Larry Thornock, from Havre, joined the show the next day.

Thornock and BB were close, good friends, old high school chums, and Ian thought maybe there had been a romance there once, maybe still was, although they acted more like brother and sister. He was of two minds: cringing at a possible shipboard romance between BB and Thornock, but relieved if it meant that BB might stop salivating over Trigger.

Grace was no help. "Give Larry your 'shipboard romance' talk," she said, "and we'll try to keep track. Maybe we'll print programs."

Ian had known that he was taking a risk heading north so early in the season, catching the tail end of winter in Montana, but he also knew that he'd done well in previous years there. Track owners and audiences knew him and had welcomed him back. But the weather in April in Montana could turn vicious. Ian lost two shows in a row to a gully washer that seemed endless.

It started as they set up for the Havre show. BB and Larry had grown up in Havre. Local media, including the now ubiquitous TV, this time out of Great Falls, focused on her, and to a lesser extent, new ramp hand Larry, who was still too new to have a nickname. BB took to the attention like a pro, having observed Ian and Trigger and PR doing their things and after they'd all coached her. Queen of the daredevils, local girl makes good, and oh, yeah, the Thornock boy, too. Grace and Hanna made sure that BB's makeup and hair looked good; makeup wasn't BB's thing.

But the show rained out and hundreds drove home disappointed that night. Ian took a chance, largely for BB's sake, and stayed over another day, hoping the clouds would move on—there was a fifty-fifty chance—but it was still raining the next evening so the daredevil show moved on to the next stop, scheduled for the next day, Saturday, April 21, in Polson, a show sponsored by the Flathead Indian Tribal Council.

It rained, still, in Polson. The drenched and weary showmen left early for their next date, in Spokane, where they had time—three days—to dry out, rest, and maybe see blue skies again.

The weather cleared a bit as they set out, but it didn't last. As they drove south to Missoula to catch 90 to head west, they hit a particularly bad pocket, rain so intense it threatened to wash them off the highway. Ian made a few calls—he had lots of friends in Montana—and arranged to hole up for the night at a county garage in Missoula, wait out the storm.

The next morning, they arrived in Spokane under clear blue skies, where the B-S TV ad campaign started in earnest. Ian missed the first showing of the ad because he was filming an ad for Motel Six. The crew told him about it that evening, some of them as giddy about being on TV as school kids, but he didn't get a chance to see it until the morning of the show at the speedway.

And there he was, in his red, white, and blue uniform, holding his helmet under one arm, smiling, wind from a wind machine blowing his hair back, and behind him, rapid-fire flashes of show stunt clips, mostly the crashes and a gut-wrenching heavy drum and screaming-guitar soundtrack under it all.

Ian: "Drive on anything but Landini Tires? I wouldn't dare."

Announcer: "Where will *you* be when Ian McGinnis attempts the world's most daring stunt—on Landini Tires?" Behind Ian, engineers talk earnestly over a huge drawing, like a blueprint, and a scale model of the loop-the-loop ramp, like a scene from one of those "The Making of" movies.

Ian vaguely recalled PR saying something about Landini Tires hiring engineers to work on the jump ramp. He hadn't paid attention. Maybe, he thought, as he watched the intense activity around the model and the drawing in the commercial, with a model of a daredevil car in one engineer's hand, a Ford Maverick, looked like, his other slicing the air like a fighter pilot describing an aerial maneuver to two other intense engineer types, maybe he should have.

"Buckle up," Ian advised viewers as he snapped his shoulder belt into place with an amplified audible click. The camera pulled back to show the array of cars, trucks, vans and motorcycles, and Landini Tires banners surrounding Ian. Words formed on the screen: "See the Ian McGinnis Auto Daredevil Thrill Show tonight, 7 p.m., Rocky Mountain Raceways." Exciting, bassy music up and out.

Later, Ian would have time to discuss the ad with PR.

"You give the impression that the 'greatest stunt in the world,' or whatever that ad says is going to happen right there, instead of at the end of the season. That's deceptive advertising, PR, far as I can see."

PR promised to look into it. There were other versions of the ad in the days and weeks that followed, and some made it clearer than others that the Big Stunt was still in the planning stage, but the original was still among the ad rotation. If anybody complained, Ian never heard about it.

The crowds kept getting bigger show after show as Ian moved into Washington—Spokane, Wenatchee, Yakima, Spanaway. The Montana rain-out losses got washed away in a flood of money.

Ian did his best to avoid car jumps, which pleased Trigger but made PR antsy. "We need the variety," Ian would say, "and besides, some of these tracks won't do." Besides, it kept Trigger busy. Trigger was a dollie magnet, and that concerned Ian. Trigger was a grownup, but still—all those babes, all that sexual tension, needed proper channeling.

"The B-S is a car jump, Ian," PR would say, "not a motorcycle stunt."

"And I have to be in reasonably good health to do it."

"Yeah, but—"

"The sugar days of a day off between shows are coming to an end. You keep booking shows back-to-back like you're doing toward the end of the season, and a guy runs the risk of getting hurt. The motorcycle jump, that's where it comes in."

"But you have to do some car jumps."

"Well, yeah, when conditions are right."

"And I'm booking good tracks, you have to admit."

The same discussion, with minor variations, happened several times. It almost became a ritual between Ian and PR, a struggle for ascendancy. Whose show *is* it?

PR occasionally asked about a T-bone. Ian did his best to discourage such talk, or sidetrack it, or even to pretend he hadn't heard. Ian had no intention of doing a T-bone this season. Being partially deaf was often useful.

Most of PR's bookings were in the Corn Belt late in the season and most were fill dates—Ian was convinced now that with Landini Tire backing, a fill date was a better way to go than the guaranteed gates he usually tried to get—but PR managed to hijack three fair dates in the first two weeks on the road, an impressive coup. He'd done this by keeping the word out that if any fair board lost a booking for any reason this late in the game, that the Ian McGinnis Auto Daredevil Thrill Show, with a little help from Landini Tires, would bend over backward to help out. Hapgood unintentionally helped Ian in one instance where, so the story went, he'd cancelled because he'd found himself double-booked.

Ian called home three or four times a week. He talked with Gran; "How's the farm? How's Shaun? How are you?"

"Shaun is a pain in the butt cheeks," Gran said when Ian called after the

Spanaway show. "He wants to go on the road so bad he can taste asphalt."

"Is he ready?"

Long hesitation. "He will be." Gran understood.

He called Shaun. "How are you feeling?"

"I'm great. How about you?"

"You know what I mean."

Long hesitation.

Ian could see through people well enough that few could successfully lie to him, but it was good that the people Ian loved and trusted most loved and trusted him enough not to try.

"Give me a couple weeks, Ian," Shaun said. He sighed. "It's—it's tough, you know?"

"Yeah." Ian didn't know, hadn't a clue. "We got a segment on *Wild World of Sports*. I don't know when, but you watch for it, hear?"

Ian made that call from a pay phone outside a gas station near Fort Lewis, where the crew was gassing all the vehicles before the haul down to Portland, where they had a two-day, three-show stand, including a matinee, all at a racetrack that doubled as a drive-in theater. He hung up and headed for the trailer, where he intended to get a jacket because it had started to rain, a typical chilly, drizzly Washington mist. He stopped at the corner of the trailer when he heard Trigger's voice coming from ten feet away, around the other side. At the side of the trailer, he saw two shadows.

"—T-bone crash," Trigger was saying, his voice hushed. "I *know* I can do it, but your father is so damn stubborn—"

Two shadows. Close to each other. One shadow was Hanna's.

CHAPTER NINETEEN

*I*an looked around for Grace and saw her inside the gas station, standing with Joel at the checkout counter. PR was on a payphone outside by the ice machine and newspaper rack. The rest of the crew were—elsewhere. In the wrecker, checking the tie-downs on the car carrier, in the Freightliner. Elsewhere.

"Yeah, but you don't know how to do a T-bone." Hanna's voice sounded odd to Ian. Soft, frilly. Odd.

Trigger laughed, and Ian felt something clench in his stomach, some dread, some feeling that he didn't at first recognize.

"I'm the *man*," Trigger said, voice syrupy, oddly gentle, but giving the last word a husky emphasis. "I can do a T-bone. *You* know I can."

"I know what you can do," Hanna said and Ian had heard enough. He rounded the corner at a brisk walk and confirmed what he'd heard in Trigger's and Hanna's startlement. They both gasped as if they'd been caught literally with their pants down, and they stepped away from each other. Ian repressed his anger. He barely looked at the two as he went into the trailer, grabbed the coat, and came back outside.

"You left the trailer unlocked," Ian said to Hanna. He stood close to her with his hands on his hips, a challenging, belligerent stance, intimidating. Deliberately so.

"Sorry, Dad. I just came out. I was just—"

"Well, never mind." Ian waved a dismissive hand. He handed his coat to Hanna. "Take this to Her Nibs. So she don't get herself wet."

Hanna left without another word and Ian fixed his attention on Trigger.

Trigger stood leaning casually against the trailer with one outstretched hand, his other on his hip, one foot crossed over the other. He looked like a gunfighter in a spaghetti Western. He looked away as if studying the big flickering Conoco sign at the edge of the road, glowing red and white in the drizzly night.

"Hey, Nick," Ian said, "I've been wondering." He feigned a casual lilt, wasn't sure if it took.

Trigger looked at Ian, raised an eyebrow and a light smile. He didn't shift his relaxed stance. He's better at this than I am, Ian thought. "Oh? About what?"

"You want to learn about the show, how the stunts get done, right? The rolls, the head-on—you're doing a pretty good job there, by the way."

"Yeah." He shrugged, stood, and faced Ian, armed crossed. "No secret about that."

"Even though you're a motorcycle man."

"Even so."

Ian stood silent, waiting for Trigger to take Ian where Ian wanted Trigger to go. The kid bit.

"Look, Ian, I'm the best, you have to admit, but I'm new and I can get better. I know motorcycles better than anybody on two wheels alive today, but I don't know show—I'll admit that—as well as you, and all your experience. And if I want to know how to do really good show, I'll study with the best. Hell, you combine my talent with what you've learned about running a show—I mean, as soon as I learn what you know—"

"I get the picture."

"But I've got to *experience* the stunts, you know?" Trigger bunched his fists in front of him for emphasis. "Not just watch, but experience the stunts from the inside. You know?"

Ian nodded. "Would you be willing to do the dynamite chair? We got three shows in two days in Portland. Me, you, and Flynn. What do you say to that?"

Trigger's face shifted between surprise, giddy joy, suspicion, shrewd calculation, and back again so fast Ian could hardly keep track. "I say let's do it."

"Do you want the matinee or one of the night shows?"

The gears in Trigger's head whirred loud enough for Ian to hear, hearing aid or no. Matinees drew smaller crowds. Trigger knew this. "I'd prefer an evening show," he said, thoughtfully.

Ian nodded, satisfied. He started to walk away toward the Freightliner.

Then stopped and turned. "Oh, hey, what about the T-bone? Have you given any thought to the T-bone?"

"Yeah, some." Casual shrug. Eyes hooded, cautious.

Ian shook his head, looking down. "I don't know—"

"I know you don't want to do it, but *I* do."

Ian looked up, smile in place. "Maybe we can work something out." He turned and walked away.

Ian told Shaun about it the next night and spent the last few minutes of their conversation trying to calm Shaun down.

"I'll come out there and beat the holy living shit out of that son-of-a-bitch—"

And, in talking with Gran, Ian discovered that Shaun could come out. "He's ready," she said. "Do you want to tell him, or shall I?"

Ian thought a moment. "Let's wait. Until after we clear California. Couple weeks more. The wait'll do him good anyway."

Portland was cold and overcast, but it didn't rain. The crew found twelve junkers waiting for them underneath the big, berry-vine enshrouded outdoor screen at the speedway-cum-drive-in movie, already half-stripped by day laborers PR had hired in advance. The crew took a day off, all except for Ian, Grace, Radar, and PR, who hit the interview circuit. They did two local TV sessions, a radio call-in talk show, and visited three Landini Tires stores in the day and a half they had before the first show. Phone lines to the talk show were busy, most of the questions circulating about the loop-the-loop. When, Ian got asked, and where? Fans and reporters demanded details.

PR sprung a new element on Ian during the talk show concerning the B-S.

"Ian McGinnis engineers are," he said, "even as we speak, building a full scale test ramp at an as-yet undisclosed location somewhere in the Southwest, and Ian's going to test the ramp within a month."

"Exactly where?" Ian was asked, and, "Exactly when?" Give us details. Ian aw-shucked his way through the show. He kept his show smile on, but cornered PR after the mike was off.

"You keep surprising me like that," he said, smiling, smiling, smiling, "and I'm going to bust your chops."

"Sorry, Ian," PR said, dripping sincere contrition, "but I just got word this morning and we didn't have time to talk."

Ian admired how slippery PR was. But he logged in his mind yet another strike against him, and resolved once again to give PR his comeuppance, whatever form it took, and whenever. Maybe he'd tie PR and Trigger together, put them in the same dynamite box and touch it off.

Conoco signed. Free gas and oil for the rest of the season.

It didn't rain and the crowds were more than Ian had ever seen anywhere. The first show was a matinee. Ian did the dynamite chair and a car carrier jump. A good gate, and no problems beyond Radar's finger, cut on his own pocketknife when he set up the sound system. That evening, Flynn did the dynamite chair, and Trigger did a bike jump finale. The next night, Trigger did his first dynamite chair, did a professional job, no hitches. Ian wrapped up the last Portland show with a car carrier jump, and took a lump on his left elbow that hurt like hell for the next week.

Ian found himself looking at a day off followed by an unprecedented three shows in three days, something PR had arranged. The three were close together—Eugene, Bend, then Medford—no long hauls involved, and the weather cooperated, but Ian made PR feel his displeasure about the tight schedule.

"Is it as bad as three shows in two days?" PR said.

"We didn't have to drive between those shows," Ian said. "All that driving takes a lot out of a guy."

"So let Trigger do a motorcycle jump each night. I'll bet he's up to it."

"I'll bet." There would be TV at all three shows, local news. It had become routine, the TV cameras, even in the smallest venues.

Trigger, of course, enjoyed the limelight as much as Ian enjoyed the respite. His elbow quit bothering him by the time they entered California, where PR had set up a schedule that would occupy the rest of May and probably garner them the largest per-show crowds of the season until they hit the B-S; that would outshine by itself any whole season Ian had ever had, including this one.

To feed the media feeding frenzy PR had helped create, he leaked that the big stunt would be held somewhere in Arizona.

Ian could tell Trigger was eager to talk about the T-bone back in Eugene, but Ian ignored his hints, feigning either hearing aid problems, or being too busy to talk about it right now. Indeed, they were busy, and Ian made a point of keeping Trigger as busy as possible, and keeping an eye on Hanna at the same time. He gave her a few tasks with BB and talked with Grace about helping.

"So you just discovered your daughter has grown up," she said. Ian had decided he'd better tell Grace what he saw—or heard, or thought he saw or heard—at the gas station at Fort Lewis, and do so right away. He knew he had been out of his element.

"Hell, Grace, this isn't a laughing matter."

Joel had fallen asleep in the sleeper as they talked in the Freightliner, headed south, the windshield wipers shush-shushing a backbeat to the diesel's monotonous gut-rattling groan.

"I ain't laughing. I been keeping my eye out, believe you me. And I've talked to Hanna. Have you?"

"Well, no. I wouldn't know what to say."

"And I got BB on the job too. Ain't that one of the reasons you took her on?"

Larry, who still hadn't found a nickname, and BB seemed to get along well, Ian had observed. Even though it didn't look quite like a romance between the two—they acted almost like brother and sister—the relationship did clearly serve to keep BB from drooling over Trigger, at least most of the time.

"One of the reasons you insisted I take her on," Ian said. Grace's assurances served to smooth Ian's ruffled feathers some, but not enough. Grace hadn't been there, hadn't seen Trigger's arrogant attitude—hell, his goddam calculating *intent* in his cold, blue eyes. Ian had seen. And he resolved to keep Trigger too busy to scratch his balls.

So if he wanted to do three jumps in three nights, let him. And two dynamite chairs, too, and a head-on. Trigger, no surprise, ate it up, and asked for more.

He asked, specifically, for a T-bone.

Which Ian finally got around to discussing at dinner the night the crew arrived in Eureka. They arrived two days in advance of their Friday, May 10, show and everybody took time off, except, again, Ian and Grace and Radar and PR, doing PR.

At supper that first night at Denny's, Ian quite casually brought up the T-bone.

"So, PR, you ever seen a T-bone crash?" A forkful of apple pie, good but not as good as Gran's, disappeared into Ian's mouth, got chewed vigorously.

"Seen a—yeah, on film. Your film, that is. And we got—we at Landini

Tires, I mean—we got a copy of a few stunts on film that other shows have done. Crash Dick way back in the '60s, and Sid Hirsch. But not live." PR's face shifted under sudden realization, and he added, "What are you saying?"

"I'm thinking about a T-bone crash," Ian said. He tried to make it sound like he was thinking about ordering another helping of pie. He chewed thoughtfully and pushed a bit of crust around on his plate with a fork. No eye contact. Let's see where this thing goes.

"You mean," PR said, his voice nearing a squeak, "in the show? Doing one in a show? Our show? You—"

"The Ian McGinnis Auto Daredevil—"

"—you want to do a T-bone? *You*?"

Shrug. "Just asking for your input. What do *you* think?"

PR sputtered incoherently for a few seconds and Ian enjoyed both his and Trigger's expressions, restrained excitement and dread, mixed and fleetingly exposed in their eyes. He read in Grace's eyes "Quit teasing," but he persisted.

PR recovered and tossed back his own bombshell. "Before or after you fly to Phoenix to test the loop-the-loop ramp?"

Ian tapped his hearing aid unconsciously. "Say what?"

"We'll have a structure ready for you to look at by the time we reach San Bernardino. We have three days off there, and we have lots of big media, including network, but I've been in touch and that looks like the best window to fly you to the site and look at the ramp, maybe test it. Now, *that* will hit prime time, more than a T-bone in Modesto. We'll film you talking about it with the engineers, looking it over, maybe even giving it a test run, we'll see. But it's in the works, what we got planned."

"Ian." Trigger couldn't resist the opportunity. "Let me do a T-bone. That way, PR gets to see one, and you don't get—you know—" He left unsaid: "All busted up so you can't show," but everybody at the table heard it clearly.

"Nobody does T-bones anymore," Ian said, an edge to his voice. "There's a damn good reason for that."

"Ian," Grace began, a warning tone. Ian knew she knew he was getting frustrated and wasn't handling it well. He wanted her to interrupt, needed her to, but that part of his mind had been chained to a wall.

"Because people get hurt doing it, that's why. These new cars we get—" He waved a dismissive hand. "—they got no steel on top, crush like beer cans when they hit. And the older cars are rusted and can't run for shit."

"Ian—" Grace tugged at his sleeve.

"I can't afford to have my crew all bunged up—" Ian stopped and realized that he was thinking of Shaun, thinking as if he'd been asked to let Shaun do a T-bone, something he'd been on the verge of letting Shaun do last season. But he *had* let Shaun do a T-bone. And the result—

Ian laughed and shook his head. Frustrated once again by PR's taking over the show, telling him what to do, where to go, and when, and by PR's surprises, Ian had forgotten his fiendish little plot to set up Trigger for a T-bone then get Shaun down to do it. He took a couple of breaths, felt Grace's restraining hand retreat, and he got back on track.

"PR, a T-bone *is* a dangerous stunt," Ian said, quiet, intense, "make no mistake. I expect we ought to do one this season, or two, but you got to calculate the odds of success. You need the right track, the right car—hell, there are a *truckload* of variables."

He looked straight at Trigger as he continued. "Including the driver." He shrugged. "And the fact that we need to be healthy for the next show." Another shrug. "And this year, well, we got this extra agenda we need to work into the show, don't we, this B-S. So maybe we ought to think about it."

PR shook his head, dismayed. Trigger fidgeted like a kid who had to pee.

"The right track," Ian ticked off the points on his fingers, "the right car, both the jump car and the catch cars, the right crowd. Weather conditions too. The right driver." He looked at Trigger yet again. "We can do it. Maybe we should. I know we get folks asking about it all the time. But it has to be right, no doubt about that."

PR nodded. "Of course."

"And one final thing. I have final say. When and if. And who."

PR nodded again, as if satisfied, and Trigger failed to keep his disappointment off his lips, thinned to a knife-edge.

"Can we at least wait until after the ramp test?" PR said.

Ian shrugged. It was fine with him if it got delayed until the Second Coming.

"That way," PR continued, "we don't dilute our PR campaign. We're starting right away to tease the market about the ramp test. That's in three weeks, toward the end of the month. After that, then maybe—if you approve, Ian—we start talking about a T-bone. In July, late. Just teaser talk is all. This way we stay focused. First on the test ramp. Second, and after, on the T-bone. Maybe. When, where, and who to be discussed. How's that sound?"

Ian shrugged and ate pie. And if PR and Trigger took his shrug and smile as agreement that the show would do a T-bone in July, so be it. He had no such intention. Trigger would eat up considerable energy campaigning for the T-bone. And in so doing, he'd stay away from Hanna and maybe give PR a ration of crap.

That's how Ian saw it.

Ian called home after dinner. Shaun answered.

"What are you doing up so late?" Ian asked.

"Watching Johnny Carson with Gran. But my bags are packed and I'm ready to go. How about I meet you in Las Vegas?"

"Hold your bladder," Ian said. "But that might be exactly what's needed."

Ian told Shaun about the test jump in Phoenix, and how it seemed to have put Trigger's campaign to do a T-bone on hold. "So I don't want you to show up too soon, you see?"

"Damn it, Ian, let me come down and I'll keep that little piss ant in line."

"You just cool your jets a few more days. Now, let me talk to Gran."

Gran got on the phone. "How's showbiz?" she asked. "I keep seeing things on TV and in the papers."

"Too much fuss for my blood, Gran, but hey, it's a payday. How's Shaun?"

Ian listened for the pause before the answer, and the change in Gran's voice that would tell him more than her words could. But she answered without hesitating. "He's ready to show, Ian. I wish you'd get him out of here."

"Soon enough, Gran. And you can tell him that from me."

CHAPTER TWENTY

Nick kissed Hanna on Sunday night, April 22, a freezing cold, rain-slick night in Missoula, Montana, and the kiss knocked him on his butt, literally.

No, *she*'d kissed *him*. At first. But it still knocked him on his butt.

He'd been busy, had never been busier in his life, during the early days that season as the show traveled up from Wyoming and through Montana. Even when they got rained out, which seemed to happen so often that Nick wondered if the show was going to go broke before the end of the month, Nick kept busy, as did everybody in the show. Ian seemed to have a knack for knowing when his crew needed to relax, take a day off, and let off steam, or when he needed to give them busy work to keep their minds and hands occupied.

The constant hard work exhilarated Nick, who'd never been afraid to sweat, but it frustrated him. He seldom got to exchange more than a few words on any given day with Hanna, and he was never alone with her.

His anxiety about BB had abated though, and that was a relief. BB and Larry went way back, it turned out. High school chums, maybe sweethearts, it was hard to tell the way they joked and jostled each other. Still, with Larry in tow, helping tote ramps like the good ranch hand he was, BB seemed to drool over Nick a lot less.

A sudden thunderstorm so severe that it made driving hazardous stopped the caravan in Missoula in the late morning hours the day after the Polson show. Ian made some calls—he had a lot of friends in Montana—and finagled access to the Missoula County garage at the fairgrounds until the storm abated. The fairgrounds sat on the west edge of town north of the freeway amid gently rolling hills and a thick forest of tall pines.

Intermittent hail and freezing rain hammered the metal roof of the cavernous garage in sweeping gusts. It felt and sounded like they were inside a giant tin drum.

Ian had the crew unload all the equipment, spread it out, and had everything examined, cleaned, dried out, repaired, polished and painted, as needed.

Using his cheerleader voice, Ian talked about taking advantage of "this nice weather we've been blessed with" to catch up on a few chores and "busy hands keep folks out of trouble" and "besides, this town shuts down on Sundays and ain't nothing worth seeing anyways so might as well open up a few hoods and clean the squirrel cages," and "maybe we ought to paint up a bit, put a shine on." Ian took apart the Freightliner engine during the long, miserable cold gray day. The garage wasn't heated.

They'd been on the road for only two weeks but Nick was surprised at how ragged some of the equipment had already gotten. So they worked all day until after dark, breaking at mid-day for burgers and fries and shakes and at supper for pizza and Coke that Grace and Hanna had picked up on parts errands into town.

That day, typical of the preceding days, Nick barely exchanged five words with Hanna. Six. "Hey." "How you doing?" "Hi, yourself." He'd counted.

It rankled. Occasionally, Nick's frustration had peaked and he'd beat hell out of a junker fender with a tire iron for a minute or two or hop on his bike and ride it out of his system. Nobody bothered him when he was on his Yamaha, and nobody questioned him when he cranked it up and said he needed to check it out, tune it, or just warm it up. He was the bike man.

The rain stopped abruptly, like somebody had turned off a faucet, late in the afternoon and just before pizza supper, and silence ensued, a stunning change in the environment. Suddenly, everybody felt giddy and loose. It had been a long, hard work day, and Nick needed to relax. Everybody did.

"Let's pack up now," Ian said as they ate pizza, ravenous, around two big picnic tables in the garage. "Pack up everything and get ready for an early start tomorrow morning. We got business in Spokane."

They packed up quickly and BB and Larry and Joel started a squirt-gun fight with makeshift pistols Joel had made with foot-long plastic plumbing pipes he found in the garage and balloons he stole from Boo's clown car. The rest of the crew cheered them on, clapping and hollering.

Nick walked to the big garage doors, which had been opened wide all day for ventilation despite the cold. He looked out, hands on hips, scanning the gray clouds shredding like cotton candy in the west, the sky quickly changing from copper-toned to crimson and on to darker hues as the sun set among the pines. A streetlight came on by the garage door and others followed down the gravel lane to the county road beyond the fairgrounds and here and there in the spacious parking lot behind the grandstands.

The air smelled fresh, clean and crisp. Nick decided to take a little ride. He fired up the Yamaha and dodged out into the dusk. Didn't put on a jacket or wear his helmet. He'd gotten used to the cold, and he wanted the freedom.

The sweat on Nick's face and under his thin T-shirt chilled as he ran the bike up and down the gravel lane in front of the garage, but the gravel was loosely packed and sucked at his wheels, made it feel like he was dragging a plow.

He tried a few wheelies across the adjacent fairgrounds parking lot, which was broad, concrete, relatively free of obstacles and had better footing than the gravel lane closer to the garage. He splashed through the occasional puddle, spitting water to either side like a speedboat and drenching himself in the process. Some puddles, deeper and bigger than others, caused the Yamaha to hydroplane, threatening his balance. It felt good, that instant when he teetered on the edge of going *this* way instead of *that* while riding the back wheel, so he aimed for the puddles, riding the edge of stability. In a small way, it felt like the top of the arc on a long jump.

Felt real good. *Fun.*

He rode to the garage door and revved the bike. "Who wants to go for a *ride*?"

The water fight had turned into a general melee in the few minutes Nick had been gone. A garden hose and water balloons had been added to the mix. Boo, Flynn, Tink and Hanna had joined with Larry and BB and Joel in the fight while Ian, PR and Grace stood by, laughing and shouting and dodging, their giddy voices bouncing echoey off the garage corrugated steel walls.

So nobody objected when Nick revved his bike and hollered, "Who wants to go for a *ride*?" Joel went first, dropping his squirt gun and hopping on the back of Nick's bike.

In a few minutes, during which night descended fully and the sky cleared, mostly, they came back soaked and whooping like wild Indians. Joel dismounted, dodged a tossed water balloon, and quickly rejoined the water fight, although it seemed to be winding down, only BB and Larry and Hanna participating.

"Who's next?" Nick hollered. He tossed his stringy, wet hair off his forehead.

Hanna, giggling, bounced across the floor and straddled the bike behind Nick before he could take a second breath. She grabbed around his waist and clung tight, fingers digging into Nick's chest. She wore bulky coveralls but Nick could feel the warm, firm pressure of her breasts against his shoulder blades as she squeezed him and said something into his ear that he didn't catch. She panted from playing hard, her breath warm on Nick's chilled left cheek and she smelled like pepperoni.

"What?" Nick said.

"I said, what are you waiting—" Something went *splat* on Nick's shoulder, a water balloon or the like. Hanna squealed like a little girl. "Go, go, go!" She slapped his shoulder, and Nick roared off.

He dashed the length of the parking lot once, reveling in Hanna's warm body pressed against him, surrounding him. She shouted into his left ear as they rode, but he couldn't hear over the engine whine and the splash of the tires as they plowed through puddles. Maybe she was only squealing in delight. Didn't matter. This was a moment, an unexpected moment, and Nick found himself—

Distracted.

—when the bike's back wheel suddenly, unexpectedly, slipped sideways in a puddle and Nick had to counter, turn the front wheel into the loose skid, gear down, break, counter-lean against the momentum—a lot harder with a hundred and some-odd pounds of squealing woman over his back fender, resisting his efforts.

Pain lanced his shoulders and upper arms as he managed to stop the bike, still upright, without losing it, or his passenger. It felt like he'd tried to bench-press the Yamaha. And succeeded.

"What happened?" Hanna said. Nick realized that he'd grunted, maybe call it a scream, in exertion, to keep from crashing. "You okay, Trigger?"

He revved the bike as he sat straddling it, Hanna clutched to his back like she was pasted there, warm.

"Yeah. You?" He was okay. The bike was okay. Hanna was—

"Let's do it again." Giddy, her lips two inches from Nick's cheek. She didn't realize that she was shouting in his ear. He didn't mind.

"No, I don't think—"

"Do a wheelie." Pepperoni.

"I don't—what?"

"Yeah, with me on the back, you know?"

"Hanna—"

"Come *on*." She squeezed him, fingers digging into his chest, pressed against him. Warm.

Nick hesitated, but for only a moment. He knew from long experience that to hesitate was to be lost. He hesitated only long enough to realize that if he balked further, he'd not do it, he'd surrender to the inertia of standing still, straddling the bike in the cold night, a warm, giddy woman pressed against him, and he'd never know that feeling ever again.

He seized the moment.

He revved the bike, balanced it between throttle cranked as full on as he could get, and braked, held until his aching muscles corded and threatened to tear apart under the pressure. Then he let loose.

The bike stood up. Hanna's grip tightened claw-like as he jerked forward. She squealed in his ear, and Nick had never heard a sound so sweet.

He balanced the bike in the wheelie, compensating for the added weight perfectly, and rode down a stretch of concrete under perfect control, angling between the larger puddles he could see. He kept the Yamaha on its hind wheel for what felt like an eternity. It felt like the end of an era when he had to bring the front wheel down as he neared the far end of the parking lot, near the fairgrounds front gate and the road beyond.

When he slammed the front wheel down and stopped the bike, spreading his legs to balance, Hanna stepped off the back of the bike, stepped around the side, gripped his jaw with both hands, and kissed him full on the mouth. Her tongue probed, hungry, and he responded, head reeling.

"Have you ever done *that* before?" Hanna said in a husky whisper as she let him up for a breath. She released her grip on his face and stood a step back, brushing her damp hair with her fingers, smiling, rosy-cheeked, bright-eyed.

"Wheelies with a pass—"

She kissed him again, and this time, Nick reached for her to engulf her in his arms, crush her against him, return the kiss with all his attention.

The bike fell.

Nick lost his balance and tried to grab the bike, but it fell and he fell on his keester. He pulled his right leg out from under the bike in the nick of time, let go, fell to the side on the asphalt, and pulled Hanna down on top of him. Or she pulled herself there. She lie straddling him, laughing, unhurt.

They kissed again. And again.

"Do you remember Missoula?" Hanna whispered in Nick's ear.

They lay, their slim, sweaty bodies entwined and partially covered in an itchy, old woolen blanket in the back of a '62 Mercury woody station wagon that had been stripped for the last show at the Portland drive-in-cum-stock car track the next night. The car was too big and flat for rollover duty, and too bulky and sluggish for the car carrier jump, which Ian would do, so Tink had pegged it for the head-on that he'd do.

Nick had helped strip the car. He knew that the meeting he and Hanna had planned—promised themselves—since Missoula would take place in this car. He wanted to make sure the car—at least the back—was extra clean.

As he cleaned it the afternoon the crew arrived in Portland, he caught Hanna's eye across the track and nodded at the car, raised his eyebrow a half inch. Hanna smiled, gave a half-inch nod, and the date was set.

Now, here they were, snuggled in the warm afterglow of their first lovemaking.

Godzilla roared and stomped Tokyo on the big screen behind and above them. A few hundred popcorn-munching drive-in patrons gazed wide-eyed up at the screen or necked in the back seats of their cars oblivious to the action taking place behind the screen.

The junkers for the Portland show had been lined up and stripped behind the big screen in a narrow, grassy corner flanked by the back of the towering wooden screen and the back fence of the huge lot, all covered with tangled blackberry vines. The area was hidden, concealed from view. Debris and parts from the stripped cars got loaded into a dump truck to be hauled off later.

The show vehicles and equipment got hangered in a garage under the grandstands at the far side of the lot. The grandstands were opened for stock car racing patrons but cordoned off while the drive-in movie was on. Because they had three shows in two days, Ian had opted to keep crew with the vehicles on-site rather than get a motel in town.

"Yeah. I remember."

Nick had wanted to prolong that moment in Missoula, that first kiss, but Hanna pushed him away and made him go back and take BB for a ride. Reluctant, rubber-legged and foggy-headed, Nick had done as urged. He didn't do a wheelie with the heavier BB on the back, but she had been delighted with the bike ride anyway. BB had yahooed like a cowboy in Nick's ear as he sped across the parking lot a couple of laps and Nick wondered if he'd ever hear anything but ringing in his ears again.

"Did she kiss you?" BB hollered at Nick as they rode back to the garage.

"What?" Nick said.

"Never *mind*," BB had said, slipping off the bike at the garage door. She said something about "dumbass men" and laughed as she walked away to help Boo load the clown car.

"How can I forget Missoula?" Nick fondled Hanna's breast, cupping the marble-hard nipple in his fingers. "It's only been a couple weeks." He stroked her back and butt with the other hand. "First time for me."

Hanna giggled as she rubbed Nick's scrotum between her thumb and forefinger, a gentle rhythmic stroke. "Didn't feel like it to me."

"I *meant*," Nick said, rolling on top of her, straddling her, "it was the first time I'd ever done a wheelie with a passenger."

Nick kissed her, softly at first. Their tongues entwined, and their passion resurged. Arms and legs groped, tangled.

Nick rolled his thick cock side to side against Hanna's belly and she moaned, grabbed him, and guided him into her.

At the last second, she pushed him aside.

"What?" he said.

"You forgot your helmet." Hanna handed Nick the rubber.

Nick sighed, rolled onto his back, opened the pack of Trojans, tossed the wrapper aside, and rolled out the rubber. Hanna helped him put it on. Then she straddled him.

She lowered herself half way, then withdrew almost all the way, then impaled herself. She began to ride, slowly at first, savoring each stroke, then she began to rock, probing with frantic urgency. In a moment, almost ready to come, she eased herself off Nick, lay down on her back, and pulled him onto her.

Nick remounted and thrust. Hanna cocked her legs back high and pushed against the roof of the station wagon for leverage. She thrust back, meeting Nick, matching him stroke for stroke. She clawed Nick's butt cheeks, forcing each frantic thrust deeper and deeper into her.

Minutes later—or it may have been hours later; who was counting—they muffled their conjoined orgasmic moan into each other's shoulders. Drive-in patrons yards away on the other side of the screen ate popcorn, necked, or gawked as Godzilla roared and stomped Tokyo into balsawood kindling. The daredevil show crew slept on farther away in their usual places amid the daredevil vehicles; Ian, Grace and Joel in their beds in the little trailer. BB slept in the road Maverick back seat, PR slept in the Freightliner, Radar and Boo in the van, Flynn in a sleeping bag on the carrier deck between the ramps and Larry slept cocooned in a sleeping bag on the ground under the carrier.

"Yeah, I remember Missoula," Nick said, panting. "And Snoqualmie Pass, and—"

Hanna giggled.

Nick and Hanna had managed to sneak away for a few frantic, passionate minutes at the top of Snoqualmie Pass en route to Spanaway during a rest stop there, and again before the show in Spanaway, and at a gas stop near Fort Lewis and once, later, just before the first Portland show. They'd talked. Kissed. Groped. Promised themselves tonight.

"We'd best get going," Hanna said. She sat up and started tugging on her pants. She hadn't worn panties, or a bra.

"Just like that?" Nick sat up. He couldn't keep the disappointment out of his voice. He reached for his own pants.

"The show's about over and I got to get back." Hanna had told Ian and Grace hours ago that she was going to stay up and watch the movie from the grandstands with BB. BB would cover for her, she'd told Nick. Nick didn't know why BB had, seemingly all of a sudden, slackened off her interest in Nick, but he wasn't about to ask. Maybe BB was romantically involved with Larry after all, despite their apparent brother-sisterly relationship. Didn't matter. BB seemed to be an ally, a friend.

"The show ain't over," Nick said, dressing. He didn't mean Godzilla.

Hanna got dressed quicker. "Yeah, not over." Something in her voice—regret? Disappointment?

She got out of the station wagon and stood, waiting for Nick.

"When can we—" Nick started, but stopped. Who knew when?

"I don't know." Frustration. That's what he'd heard in her voice. Incomplete, guarded conversations. Quick, frantic groping while watching over their shoulders. Who knew when?

"Nick, we—"

He kissed her. Held her. As long as he could.

Who knew when?

CHAPTER TWENTY-ONE

The swing through California was rigorous, as PR had planned it, and enormously profitable. Ian found himself once again grudgingly admiring PR's efforts. Overall, PR had arranged a route throughout the whole season that was as intensive as it could be, giving the show more opportunity to make money than Ian had ever seen in a season, not just in the number of dates booked, and the bigger gates, but in the economy in which the dates were arranged.

The swing north in Montana, west through Washington and south through Oregon, then California, would bring the show aimed east at the end of May. From that point on, PR had filled dates in a near-perfect spiral route through America's heartland. The show traveled east through June to Arkansas, with most of the dates in Texas, then north through Iowa to Wisconsin in late June and the first half of July, then west to Bismarck, North Dakota, in mid July, then south zigzagging through the Corn Belt, ending in late August in Tulsa, Oklahoma. Tulsa would be the season-ender, except for the B-S on Sunday, September 2.

To be sure, there were plenty of back-to-back shows, and two dates where they showed at the same site back-to-back, and the inevitable matinee, a half dozen of those. But the routes were so close together, so tightly arranged, that in one case, they could do three shows in a row without refueling, and in another case, they could do two different dates and stay in the same Motel Six between those dates. In any case, PR had arranged for good junkers and in most cases, they were already prepared when the crew arrived.

Trigger's motorcycle jump finale was catching on and Ian did fewer car carrier jumps. Trigger's intensive antsiness was reflected in his eagerness to do stunts, anything Ian could throw at him. It seemed to Ian that Nick was constantly attached to some kind of electric switch, always in the on position. He seemed downright—twitchy, alive with tension. Ian didn't really understand it, but he tried his best to channel that hyper energy into show.

PR's awareness of the toll his rigorous schedule would take on crew and equipment helped mitigate Ian's desire to get Shaun on board. Without Trigger's motorcycle jump finales and PR's efforts to ease the workload and pressure on the crew, Ian would have been tempted to put Shaun on the payroll back in Portland.

Maybe. Gran had assured Ian that Shaun was ready to show, but Ian wasn't convinced, not entirely. He would never tell Gran that he doubted her, and it wasn't that—if she said he'd kicked the monkey on his back, then so be it. But Ian wasn't sure if Shaun was ready to *show*. That was something that couldn't be measured, that he couldn't rely on Gran to determine, or Grace, or anybody else. He had to see, to judge for himself, whether Shaun was ready to show.

Las Vegas. He couldn't put Shaun off longer than Las Vegas.

Ian looked at the schedule and the map and shook his head in grudging admiration. He couldn't have booked a better season by himself. With Tink's junker calculator in hand, Grace informed him that, if they kept up their current pace, and didn't get rained out too much and nobody got seriously hurt, they might be able to pay off their bills before mid-July. It usually took them to mid or late August before that happened, and they'd had seasons that ended in the red.

Yreka was their first stop in California, a small track with a smallish crowd. PR had booked it rather than opting for a day off before the next date, Red Bluff, not because the show needed the revenue but because PR was promoting Ian as a humble servant of his fans. Ian was a rural farmer himself like most of those in the Yreka crowd who didn't wear ties, who took to country ways, who were humble—all traits PR wanted associated with Landini Tires. Plain folks. Aw-shucks folks.

Ian understood.

"This show," PR explained to him and Grace as they set up in Yreka, "and to a lesser extent Eureka and Red Bluff, will prepare us for a lot of media fuss when we do Sacramento and Fremont and points south. Those dates will be big-lights, big-star events. We're looking to get celebrities on hand, limos and red-carpet stuff, like at the Oscars. That sort of thing. The humble shows in northern California will help offset some of that glitz."

"I'll go you one better," Ian said.

"How's that?"

"I'll step back when we hit deep traffic down south and let the crew take the limelight." Ian understood. "Only natural."

Ian hoped PR would take the hint and give him a break with all the interviews and PR appointments, but it was a thin hope. PR was a media pimp.

The shows went well enough, the crowds were there, packing the stands. TV and reporters were there as usual, and nobody got hurt too much. Tink gashed his leg in a head-on in Eureka, bled a lot, causing a lot of stir. Paramedics staunched the shallow cut. Tink limped gallantly away from the scene, blood-soaked bandage around his leg, waving to the crowd, and got his moment in the sun.

In Red Bluff, Boo bashed his thumb with a tire iron as he helped strip a junker. Boo was not given to swearing, but he'd come to understand a show maxim Ian repeated often. "If you injure yourself," he'd said, "you yell a lot, beat the hell out of a fender, or whoever is standing too close, and then you go back to work. You don't bottle up pain or anger. Let it out, then go back to work."

Boo, a Baptist, had been listening to the crew's colorful language for weeks, and he expressed himself eloquently for four or five minutes, before he realized what he was doing. He stopped in embarrassment when he noticed a TV camera filming his tirade. The film was never used, but the crew got a kick out of teasing Boo after that.

"Watch your language," they'd say, more to watch Boo blush than to admonish him for an offense they themselves committed regularly and with vigor.

Loading up after Red Bluff, Larry dropped an approach board on his foot and badly mashed a big toe. Before he quit limping, he'd earned his nickname—Hopalong. Tink decided the name and "Trigger" fit together. In due time, it got shortened to Hoppy.

Tink and Hoppy got along well.

They rained out in Sacramento, but stayed over and took rain checks the next night. As it turned out, the extra day helped fill the stands because the night of the rainout, somebody tried to steal Hobo, the daredevil dog. The culprit, a zealous animal rights advocate, gave the press an earful of radical invective when she got caught, and it gave the show more publicity than PR could have hustled on his own.

Ian was an animal-lover. That was the gist of the message. The fact that he didn't press charges against the dognapper helped his image as a humble, peaceful, forgiving man of the people. The contrast between him and Terrible Tom Tolliver was left as fill-in-the-blanks.

In Fremont, Coke signed an endorsement contract. PR managed to let it leak to the press that Ian had turned down an endorsement proposal from Anheiser-Busch. It fit the show's family image, PR told Ian and Grace, turning down a beer endorsement, and the image Landini Tires was trying to create for itself. Ian never found out if there really was an endorsement offer, but if there had been, PR had guessed right—Ian would have rejected it.

"Sales are up," PR told Ian and Grace after the Merced show, after he got off the phone with Saint Louis. "We're thinking of doing the ramp test live, CBS or maybe ABC. They're in a bidding war, imagine that." He danced like he had to pee and rubbed his hands together in comic glee.

"You got a date set for that?" Ian asked. He gritted his teeth as he asked, his neck still stiff from the hard slam he'd taken in the car jump an hour before. He'd jumped in a '64 Chevy Biscayne two-door sedan with a good engine, but the steering decided to go squirrelly on him at the last second and he hit the take-off ramps slightly askew. He bounced off his catch cars and toppled onto the track, hard, on his top. Whiplash.

He intended to exhaust their supply of Ben Gay, let Trigger do a bike jump at Laguna Seca and Bakersfield, and get back in the saddle for San Luis Obispo. That was on Sunday, May 26. They had time from then until the next show, San Bernardino, Orange Speedway, on Tuesday, the 29th. Ian could use the time off in case he got banged up in San Luis, so doing a car jump there made sense. And he felt the need to get Shaun on board.

"Yeah. We'll fly you from San Luis Obispo right after the show to Phoenix, get some good film by that afternoon, and fly you back to San Bernardino by supper that night. Plenty of time to rest for the show the next night. Sound good to you?"

Ian nodded. He tried on a smile, but it didn't take. He was tired.

"Then we start looking at a T-bone," Trigger said, trying to appear very casual about it. "Right? Two or three weeks after San Berdo. Where does that put us?"

"Somewhere in Texas," Grace said. "Did you lose your schedule?"

Grace gave everybody schedules at the start of the season, all nicely typed out on her IBM electric typewriter, with show dates, times, and locations, except for Trigger and Hoppy, who'd joined the show late. She'd scribbled a schedule for them in haste. Until Portland in early May, PR often told the crew over supper that they needed to add such and such a date to their schedules. After that, the only booking that came in was the big Phoenix show. After that, PR changed his focus from booking shows to promoting the B-S. The loop-the-loop ramp test was an interim stage in that process.

"Yeah," Trigger said. "But which one? I mean, we got a dozen shows in Texas, so which one do we do the T-bone at?"

"Relax on that," PR said. Ian felt relieved that PR had taken up the gauntlet and Ian didn't have to feign deafness. "Let's get through California, get this ramp checked out, then we can focus on other stuff."

Which satisfied Ian. PR didn't want a T-bone and Trigger did. They'd irritate each other and give Ian a mental break for at least three weeks.

On the flip side, he'd have to tell Shaun to wait it out for two more weeks and be ready to join them in Texas. "Surprise, Trigger. Shaun is here and *he*'s going to do the T-bone, not you."

Monterey went well, though it was unusually cold. Blonde bombshell actress Kim Novak, who lived in Carmel, came out to see the show and met Ian after it was over in front of a gaggle of TV and newspaper cameras.

Bakersfield went well too, with the exception of Hanna, who sprained an ankle during one of the clown acts she was involved in. No sooner had Hoppy recovered from his toe-jamming affair then Grace was back in the first-aid kit for more Ace bandages. Hanna had been hinting that she was ready to do the rollovers—"Why not, Dad, huh?"—but Ian saw the sprained ankle as a good excuse to postpone it.

It wasn't that Ian didn't want Hanna to do the stunt. She was a good performer, conscientious, and hard working. She did the hell driving sequence, handling the Mav like a pro, did the clown routines, and was out there for the crew jump and helping with the boardwalls and after show. Did what was asked of her. Her main role was to help with selling souvenirs, but she was a driver too.

Hanna was no braggart, no puffy-chested alpha male show-off. She could do the rollovers, do them well, and move on, like a pro. Ian had no problem with Hanna doing the rollovers. In fact, he'd contemplated getting her to do more stunts earlier in the season. But now—

Now, Ian had Tink, Flynn, Trigger, BB, and Hoppy to do rolls. He didn't need to get Hanna under a helmet. And, now, he didn't want her to do a crash stunt.

Ian feared that Hanna's increasing insistence on getting into a junker might have been the result of Trigger's influence. He talked to Grace about it on the way to San Luis Obispo while Joel napped behind them in the Freightliner sleeper.

"I told you I'm keeping her busy," Grace said. "And BB. I got her on the job."

"Well, good for you."

"But I don't think you not letting her do rolls is going to help much."

"She's got that bad ankle."

"I don't mean that. You don't think she got her stubborn streak from my side of the family?"

Ian thought about that for a couple miles. There had been a fire off the side of the road, a sooty smudge amid the rolling, golden-grassy hills.

"So," he said, "you think that by not letting her do the rolls, that maybe she—"

"Ha," Grace said. "Sometimes you're quicker than others."

Ian thought about it for a few more miles. The sooty air hurt his eyes. "I'll think about it." But he wasn't convinced.

Hanna's ankle was taped up well enough that she could run on it, more or less. Ian watched her to see if she was in any pain, hiding it under a slightly twisted smile, something he might have done, but she wasn't.

He told Hanna to grab a helmet at the last minute. He did it so late that Radar had already introduced Flynn and Tink as the two performers competing in the rollover contest. Boo dashed over to Radar as he was telling the audience how the rolls were done, and breathlessly broke the news. Radar shifted gears and got on board.

"Ladies! And Gentlemen! For the first time anywhere! The world's youngest woman daredevil performer! Ian McGinnis's only daughter is about to perform her first crash stunt! Let's give a big round of welcoming applause—" And so on. PR watched and Ian could see his PR gears moving. BB had already gotten her share of PR, and now Hanna would too. Maybe a few interviews, a little TV. She did have nice hair, a nice smile.

He only hoped Grace was right.

Hanna botched her first try, going too slowly, flopping down off the end of the jump ramp and landing in an inglorious plop, the engine dead. They couldn't get the car started, so Ian got into the wrecker and pushed Hanna in her next attempt. This time, she didn't crank the wheel hard enough. Same result.

Ian got out of the wrecker and talked to Hanna. "Do you know what you're doing wrong?"

Hanna was almost in tears when she answered. "I cocked the wheel too soon, before I got off the ramp—"

The ramp had fallen apart and the crew had to reset it.

"Do you think you know when to do it now?"

Hanna nodded.

"Wipe your eyes so you can see good and let's go again."

Hanna nodded and went again.

And flopped again.

Ian talked to her again. "Do you want to do this or not?"

"I do, Dad, I really—"

"I don't know. You cranked it too soon again. You're busting up my ramps. I think maybe you're afraid of—"

"I am not, Dad." Hanna thumped her little bunched fist against the steering wheel. "I am *not* afraid, damn it."

Ian smiled. "Watch your language."

Hanna took a big breath. "Tell me again."

Ian did. "Relax. You're tense, scared. We all get that way. It ain't fear, so much as it is excitement. This may sound like a contradiction, but you got to wait until *after* you do it to have fun. *When* you're doing it, well, it's work. It's the job. You do it, then you can whoopee after."

"I don't—"

"Think of it like—like kissing—"

She looked shocked for a second.

"Until you let yourself go, it ain't going to happen. Know what I mean now?"

A slow smile lit up Hanna's face, illuminating the inside of the Bell Star helmet she'd borrowed from Tink. "I *think* I got it. Let's try."

The inspiration to compare doing crash stunts with kissing had come to Ian on the spot, and while he was pleased that apparently Hanna understood—"it's as much of a thrill for us to do as it is for you to see"—he now wondered if that was a good thing or not.

Damned if you do, damned if you don't. He was tired of out-maneu-vering himself.

He got back in the wrecker, got in position behind Hanna's car, and wait-ed for her signal. She stuck her hand out the window, waved and Ian pushed.

It worked.

CHAPTER TWENTY-TWO

*J*ust before midnight, after the show, Ian and PR flew out of a small municipal airport just outside San Luis Obispo in a corporate Lear jet Landini Tires had hired.

"We're looking at leasing our own jet," PR told him after they took off. They ate steak on board, hot and juicy. "Or maybe buying one outright."

Ian had a good appetite despite a nagging shoulder pain aggravated in the car carrier jump a couple hours earlier. Grace had applied Ian's ration of Ben Gay and drove them to the airport as the rest of the crew packed up and went off to a local Denny's. Here I sit, Ian thought, eating thick steak while the crew eats at Denny's. But the thought didn't spoil his appetite.

"Tell me about this ramp," Ian said around a mouthful of steak. "Who you got working on it? Who are these engineers I got working for me?"

PR barked a laugh, spitting mashed potatoes on his lap. "Believe it or not, we got a genuine NASA engineer on the job. Name of Orland Cartwright. Heard of him?"

Ian shook his head, chewed, drank glacier cold water from a wine glass. The plane hummed in quiet grace as they passed over the scattered flickery yellow lights of some mid-sized town in western California, or Nevada, or maybe they were already in Arizona. The night was clear, starry. He felt sleepy, intended to nap some right after dinner. And maybe dessert.

"He designs space stations, I hear. Studied at Cornell, a big Ivy League university. Anyway, he's retired, teaching at the University of Arizona. We made some calls, lucked out when we found him." He shrugged. "But mostly, it's his students doing the work. For credit."

"For *credit*? Class credit? You're not paying them?"

"Hey, they're making out like bandits, plus getting good lines on their resumes and a lot of PR. There's a reporter from *Parade* there and I expect somebody from *Car & Driver* too, plus the usual newspapers and TV. They're not paupers."

"So tell me about the ramp."

In a few minutes, Ian determined that PR didn't really know much about the loop-the-loop ramp, at least not the kind of information Ian wanted. So Ian dropped the conversation with a "Let's wait to see it, okay?" and decided against dessert—strawberry ice cream—and took a nap.

He didn't nap long.

They landed at the Glendale Municipal Airport and stayed at the Hampton Inn at the big airport closer to town, where Ian slept well.

The next morning, Ian called Gran. She was well. "And so is Shaun," she said. "And he's antsy to get on the road."

Ian toyed with the notion of telling Gran to tell Shaun to meet them in Las Vegas. He told her so.

"No, Ian, you should tell him. He and Amanda will be here for dinner. Why don't you call him right after you do your loopy ramp thing? I'll keep my mouth shut."

Ian agreed.

Ian and PR ate a quick breakfast, where Baha and another Landini Tires suit met them. Ian phoned Grace—all was well with family and crew—then they motored out to the site.

So far this season, the weather had been reasonably kind, Ian thought, except for the Montana rain-outs and Sacramento, but that show had been saved for the next day by the dognapper's antics—rain check shows usually drew less than regularly scheduled dates. It had been cold and damp in western Washington, but that was expected. It didn't seem to cut into the crowds, and it presented no problems for the show. The real heat of the season hadn't arrived yet, except for a sticky, hot stretch in Fremont and Merced. In the last few days, it had been quite cool.

Here, the heat assailed Ian like a wet blanket. It was supposed to be hot in Arizona in the summer, he knew, but it was supposed to be a dry heat, not this syrupy thick air, a steam bath heat you expected further east in the Corn Belt. The Hertz rental car's air conditioning tried to keep up.

"How you going to get a crowd in this heat?" Ian asked.

Baha sat in the back with PR. Another company man, a southwest regional manager or whatever he was titled, Sam Something, drove. "Bahahaha," Baha said. "Wait'll you see. We'll sell a lot of Coke and ice cream. We're lining up sprinklers for the kids to play in. We'll sell umbrellas. We got it covered."

"It'll be hot, all right," PR said. "But we'll take care of it, don't worry. You just worry about the jump."

PR briefed Ian on the site as it came into view. It was on a leased section of scrubby-looking land a few minutes southwest of the city. Ian could see downtown Phoenix's skyline behind him, shimmering in the heat, like a boilerplate even this early in the day. That close to town.

Like many big cities in the West, Phoenix went from intense downtown urban high rise, to pastel ticky-tacky sprawl, mall, and suburban spread, to fringe rural with barbed-wire fences, cows and haystacks, and then abruptly to barren, dry desert, sagebrush and wind, the transitions coming in a heartbeat.

They drove a short stretch of the freeway—Interstate 10, the Maricopa Freeway, they called it—before they dodged south on a side street, 19th Avenue, and turned off on the lesser Dobbins Street, which took then through a crossroads called Laveen, then to the jump site a mile south, just off 51st Avenue.

They turned off the rural two-lane onto a sagebrush-flanked, rutted dirt road interrupted fifty yards in by a barbed-wire fence and a wire gate. There, they stopped and PR got out to open the gate.

Ian could see activity farther down the road, a half-mile or more. People working on some kind of scaffolding among spotty sage and stiff clumps of dry yellow grass. A crane lifting something there. Cars and trucks parked helter-skelter and stacks of supplies of some kind.

"Let's walk from here," Ian said, getting out. "I want to see the lay of the land, feel the ground."

At Baha's look of impatience, Ian added, "From here on, I'm in no hurry."

He got out and Baha did too, muttering something Ian didn't catch about the heat. PR opened the wire gate and Sam Something drove through.

"Go on," Baha told Sam Something. "We'll met you." Sam drove in, raising a fine veil of dust in his wake.

Ian stood inside the gate for a moment, looking around, PR and Baha standing nearby, quietly waiting.

Landini Tires had leased the large square of so-called farmland, or ranchland, from a probably desperate and dirt-poor farmer or rancher. Ian felt a pang of sympathy for the poor bastard and resolved to meet him and see that he and his family got to at least see the show. Sometimes that small courtesy got overlooked.

Maybe the farmer had once raised grain here, or alfalfa, or hay, or maybe he grazed stock. But the owner of this land had fallen on hard times. Ian could see it in the clumped dirt clods lining the recently graded dirt access road and the sage and the clumps of stiff, dry grasses. Hard times meant hard dirt, and hard dirt meant desperation. "Lease the land for a daredevil show?" Ian could hear the man say. "How much and where do I sign?"

The sky was clear, cobalt blue, and cloudless from horizon to horizon, interrupted only by a blazing sun.

"That's the Gila River Indian Reservation," PR told Ian as they looked south. "We're thinking about Tink doing something or other." Ian said nothing. He wasn't sure how Tink would take to that, nor how the local tribe would take to it. He made a mental note to talk to Tink about it later. If Tink opted out of the limelight, Ian would back him.

"And over there," PR pointed east to a range of jagged purple ridges shimmering in the heat, "the South Mountains. There's a park, and we had to do a song and dance to make sure the environment folks are well fed. So to speak. As we did with the tribe, too. But you don't want to hear about all the paperwork it took—it's still taking—to get this site, do you?"

Nobody had secured the gate, so Ian did it. "Never leave a gate open," he said. "Stock'll wander off."

"No stock here," PR said. He was sweating. They all were.

They walked in, raising powdery dust with each step, and Ian looked around, thinking of details.

"Is this the only access road?" he asked.

"There's a road to the east," PR said, "that we'll have to secure. Hire some people, put up banners, new fence, that sort of thing. Paying customers will come in through this road."

"Parking?"

"See those flags?" Baha said. He pointed to a thin forest of knee-high little red flags scattered around to the left and right of the road, which seemed to bisect the field neatly. "Parking. We'll hire a local club—Sammy's on it—to help with parking. Maybe sheriff's posse, maybe Boy Scouts, whatever."

"What about security at the jump?"

"Fences," PR said. "Plus security people."

"Fences can get climbed over," Ian said. The oppressive heat, the hike, longer than he'd anticipated, was sapping his energy, and his left knee was aching. "And security people are usually the ones who get in the way."

"We'll hire security people to watch the security people," Baha said. "Bahahaha."

"Don't worry about the details," PR said. "You just worry about the jump."

They walked on in silence, except for their steam engine huffing and puffing, until they came up on the jump site proper, the loop-the-loop ramp itself.

It looked like a huge tire sitting upright in the desert, with a gang of Lilliputians frantically crawling all over it and roping it down.

The top rim of the loop was maybe a little over a hundred feet up. The floor was made of bare plywood, the underside reinforced with lengths of four-by-four beams crisscrossed with two-by-four bracing. The ramp was maybe twelve feet wide, which would leave about two feet on either side of the jump car. A thigh-high chain link barrier edged the ramp, something to keep a jump car on the ramp if the driver lost control. The wire guardrail looked spidery, frail.

A complex of spindly-looking metal beams braced the whole thing in place. More thin metal beams bolted sideways and at angles between the upright and sideways braces reinforced the dozens of thin upright beams. It reminded Ian of high voltage power poles.

Or an Erector set.

Ian thought the beams looked too spindly to hold the loop up when it was just standing there, let alone take the stress of driving through it at a high rate of speed in a big car. He thought the loop looked a bit tight too.

On either side of the ramp, fifty yards out, piles of temporary stadium seating lay scattered about, most still in huge wooden crates. Two sets of bleachers, Ian could see, would flank the jump, facing each other south and north—the stunt would go west to east. He was used to seeing grandstands only on one side of the show. This would be something different, though, something new, even for him. He wondered how many people they intended to get into those seats.

Ian met his chief engineer, Orland Cartwright, who struck him as an earnest, honest, energetic man. Built squat, stout but not flabby. Balding, sandy fringe of hair askew, Ian saw when Orland took off his yellow plastic hardhat to wipe his brow. Broad, wrinkle-laced face, deep-set eyes. Warm handshake and smile. A working man, Ian saw, jeans and sweat-soaked T-shirt, nothing like the Landini Tires suits. His worker-bees looked like a gaggle of college students, some with hippie-like long hair and beards, stripped to the waist to accommodate the intense heat, except for one girl student who seemed to be in charge of a clipboard and a tape measure who wore a halter-top and no bra. Everybody wore hardhats.

Somebody handed Ian a hardhat. A TV camera crew, also wearing hardhats, descended on Ian immediately and began filming and taping everything. Landini Tires would use what film they got here, Ian understood, to promote the B-S over the next three months, so he put on his show smile and watched his language. He wiped his forehead and said something about the heat, smiled, and got to work.

PR and Baha left Ian to talk PR business with Sam Something while Cartwright showed Ian the jump ramp, TV crew hovering on the sunward side.

They walked around it slowly as Cartwright spoke. "Part of the trick," he said in a Southern drawl that Ian thought might be Texan or maybe not, "is trying to figure out how long the loop needs to be. That is, how fast do you need to go to clear it? See, the tighter the loop, the slower you need to go to get through, but you got this jump on the other side, so you don't want to go too slow.

"On the other hand, if you got the loop too big, there's a chance that you'll lose momentum trying to get through it and come down with not enough speed for the jump."

"I need to be going seventy miles an hour when I clear that loop," Ian said.

"Well, you'll have plenty of time to get up to speed," Cartwright said. "You can start way off back there." He pointed over his shoulder, to the west, vaguely.

"What kind of car do you have in mind?" Ian asked.

"Well, you're the car expert," Cartwright said. Ian noticed that Cartwright deferred to the cameras, the way he stood, placed himself in relationship to Ian and the jump ramp, making for good camera angles, as well as any practiced showman Ian knew, and he wondered if that came from his work with NASA. "Why don't we take a look at what we got for today's test and you tell me?"

The Landini Tires people had gotten Ian a '65 Mustang fastback, painted it in show colors and with the Landini logo, and stripped it down expertly. They'd even gotten the seatbelts right, Ian noticed as he inspected the car.

He unwired the hood, lifted it, and inspected the engine, which was unusually clean.

"Big engine, looks like," he said. "Modified?"

The engine had been stroked and bored, modified to crank more power than the 271 horses advertised. A stud on the road.

Ian said nothing as the cameras rolled. He was the expert daredevil, checking out his trusty steed, hands on his hips, hardhat cocked back as he inspected the engine, smiling, smiling, smiling.

Seething inside. The engine was too big.

He pulled out the dipstick and confirmed that it had oil in it, clean. Then he got in, crawling in through the driver's side window—the door had been properly wired shut—and started it. The Mustang roared to life, like a lion. Ian punched the accelerator a couple of times and the hood lifted slightly, powerfully, big engine—*too big*—ready to race.

Ian smiled for the cameras, then turned off the engine and got out. "Where's my helmet?" he said.

Ian had expected a camera moment, a dramatic piece of film, when somebody would race up and hand him a helmet, then he'd put it on, say something memorable, take the car down the way, drive back and forth to get a look at the approach, then maybe get the camera to go along inside as he raced toward the approach, practicing.

But it didn't happen.

There were no crash helmets at the site.

Ian was hard-pressed to keep his smile and finally gave up. "Jesus Christ," he said, "you mean you guys forgot a *helmet*?"

"We got hardhats—" somebody said, but Ian shook his head.

"Okay if you ain't moving sixty miles an hour," he said, "but a guy needs a real helmet for stunt work, you understand?"

Ian told the camera crew to take a lunch break, to find PR and see if they could rustle up a helmet. "Until you get one, boys," he said, "show's over." He was as much angered as amused at the oversight. "Hell, it ain't even starting, until."

What else did they overlook?

The car, for one, Ian thought. But that could be changed come B-S showtime, three months away. For now, it would be a good idea to get Cartwright and PR and whoever else needed to know on the same game page, and do it out of camera range.

"Listen, you guys," Ian said. They'd retreated into the air-conditioned interior of a tiny plywood-walled construction trailer shack, where they slugged down bottles of cold Coke and sat around on metal folding chairs. He put as much sincerity into his voice as he could command. It helped that a little anger showed through. "It ain't just the helmet, but you got a lot of problems. That car for instance. It'll never do."

"Well," Cartwright said, "that's why you're here. What's wrong with it?"

"The engine's too big. If I get it up to speed—and there ain't no doubt it'll get me up to speed—but it'll come down nose first, the engine is so heavy. Hell, maybe it'll even go over on its top. You guys ever seen a T-bone? You don't want that here. What you want is a flat landing, land on the bottom of the car. You got to distribute your weight so the jump car floats. There's more to it than just speed. You got to land right."

"What do you suggest?" Cartwright asked.

Ian told them, and they took notes.

"And besides," he finished a few minutes later, "I think it might be a good idea, for this stunt, at least, to put in a rollbar. I don't use them in the regular show, because we don't got time to weld them in and it's not as thrilling for the crowd to come down afterwards and see a rollbar. We brag up that the jump cars are ordinary street cars, like the kind folks drove to the show in, just without glass and with better seatbelts. And with helmets. But for this show, for the B-S, I think maybe we have time. And since we're aiming for some kind of distance record, I figure we ought to put in a rollbar just in case."

They resolved to let Ian select the appropriate jump car. Experience had long ago told Ian that the '64 Rambler station wagon, six-cylinder, auto, was his best bet for a jump like this one. He promised to find the right car, and do it before the end of July so they'd have time to prepare it. PR jumped on the idea of using the dilemma for PR purposes—Ian taking his time shopping for the right car, finally finding it, then shipping it to Phoenix—all steps that PR could capitalize on in his story.

Somebody had gone into town to buy a helmet, but did so in such a hurry that they forgot to ask what size or type was wanted. The errand boy returned with four helmets, one of which fit Ian well enough to proceed.

Cameras back on, dinner over, the sun a blazing spot high overhead, no wind to speak of, Ian did a few practice dashes at the loop ramp. He stopped after the first one to talk with Cartwright and one of his students about the approach road. It needed to be graded and surfaced, he said. There were a couple of mushy spots that needed to be filled and one rocky lump that would lift him off the ground, compromise his traction at the wrong time. Ian joked about paving it, but wasn't surprised when Cartwright and the student didn't laugh.

He took the cameraman for a ride in quick dashes at the ramp, turning aside at the last moment. First, the cameraman sat in the back seat, filming over Ian's shoulder, then he filmed from the passenger seat. Ian narrated for the mike as he dashed down the approach lane.

Then it became time to do it.

Before the jump, Ian demanded that everybody take a half hour break, rest up, shade up, drink some liquids, cool off, relax. "You all get wound up in knots," Ian told them, "you don't perform worth beans." Cameras caught it, yes, but Ian meant what he said. "It's the same in daredeviling, the same in engineering. Life's like that, you hear?"

Ian took his own advice, shading up in the construction shack, slumping in a metal chair, rotating his shoulders, trying to loosen his stiff muscles. He needed Grace there to give him a good back rub.

"Are you sure, Ian?" PR whispered, almost reverently. Good, Ian thought, that reverence. About time they started taking this stuff seriously.

"About what?"

"I mean, what you said about this car, the Mustang. And it doesn't have a rollbar. Sorry about that. We could cancel—"

"The take-off is flat, not raised, so I won't go airborne, so I don't expect to get squirrelly. Unless the ramp collapses when I'm up at the top. But that won't happen," he turned to Cartwright, who leaned against the little refrigerator, rolling a Coke can across his sweaty forehead, "will it?"

"Well, I don't think so, Ian," Cartwright said. "We got the stress patterns down, I believe. See, it's like a bridge—"

"I got you," Ian said. He trusted Cartwright. "So let's go do it."

They set up, cameras and spectators taking their places, and Ian checked out the Mustang again, as thoroughly as if he'd never seen it before, walking around the loop ramp and part way up it, thinking about details, last minute details. Then he got into the car, started it, and drove down the track.

He turned to face the ramp, took his hearing aids out of his ears, and tucked them into his shirt pocket. Seen head-on, the ramp looked like a circus diving tower, or an airport traffic control tower set against the low mountains to the east. It looked rickety, spindly, like it might topple in a good sneeze.

He revved the big engine, stood on the brake as he cranked up the RPMs, feeling the gut rumble through his bones, and then shot forward, engine screaming, spitting smoke and dirt in a frothy rooster tail, aimed at the ramp.

His speedo read sixty-five as he hit the ramp straight on with a solid wooden *thump*.

When he hit the ramp, Ian experienced once again as he had so many times over the years that feeling of time stopping. Molasses time. Everything took place in slow motion.

Instinct honed in hundreds of jumps and crashes told him that he should be diving into the glove compartment, yet he was still on the take-off ramp—*too soon, too soon*—so he gripped the wheel and concentrated, jaw clamped, muscles tight, on keeping the car straight. It was a long, *long* take-off ramp, and time crawled as he rumbled up it.

Up it. *That* felt different. In molasses time, Ian reflected on the difference between a loop-the-loop jump and a straight car jump. Nobody had ever done a loop-the-loop jump, as far as he knew. This was a first. He was making history.

The wooden floor under him rumbled, strained under the car's weight, that weight magnified by pressure caused by the tight inward curve.

The g-forces surprised Ian—he hadn't expected such force. Usually, he felt a lifting sensation as the car floated over whatever he was jumping. But he wasn't jumping yet. He was still on the takeoff ramp, an unusually long takeoff ramp that curved back on itself and pushed him into the driver's seat.

Unprepared for the sudden surprisingly strong pressure, his grip loosened on the steering wheel, and his head dropped down and forward. For a critical instant, he couldn't see, and he was concerned that he'd turned the wheel when his grip loosened and that he'd shoot off the ramp side into the air—upside down. He tried to concentrate on keeping the wheel steady. If he hit the wire-mesh guardrail, he might not hear it but he'd feel it.

Molasses time crept onward as the car shot into the first arc of the wooden takeoff ramp and hit the top at maximum momentum. He was upside down, centrifugal force keeping him in place.

There, Ian realized as it happened, helpless to do anything about it, the ramp was under the greatest stress. The top was the farthest from the ground, and Ian realized, the beams holding it up would be their weakest at this point.

And, in molasses time even as he felt rather than heard the floor change pitch and *groan* rather than rumble, giving way under the stress as he was upside down and in that fraction of a second before the car started on the downward arc, he thought that Cartwright did a good job of bracing the structure up.

But he didn't do so hot about keeping it down.

The g-force pressure forcing him into the seat stopped with head-on crash suddenness and the floor became mushy and Ian thought—he *knew*, and he swore that he *felt*—that the beams holding the loop structure up were being pulled from the ground, pulled at least enough to weaken the whole thing.

Momentum drove the car through its final arc. But the entire loop structure had been compromised by the pressure at the top that had pulled its support beams out, and when the car came down, it *slammed* down, hard, bouncing off the rear wheels, spitting split shock absorbers, suspension, and miscellaneous body parts out the rear like a leaky garbage truck.

Then the wounded Mustang shot out the end ramp, rose into the air, torqued to the right, and began to roll. Side to side to side.

Ian didn't have time to dive for the glove compartment before molasses time ended and the roof and sides of the car came in at him, again and again and again.

CHAPTER TWENTY-THREE

*T*he next time Nick and Hanna got together turned out to be in San Luis Obispo, the night Ian flew to Phoenix with PR to test the loop jump ramps.

The crew had settled in for the night in their rooms in the San Luis Obispo Motel Six. At three a.m., Flynn's buzz saw snore shifted pitch, or some errant sound intruded from outside the room. Whatever. Nick awoke. He quickly dressed and quietly left the room he, Flynn, and Tink shared. BB and Hanna shared a room. Hoppy, Boo, and Radar shared a room and Grace and Joel had another room.

Nick crossed the parking lot to the vehicles. The night was warm, humid, and he wore only a thin short-sleeved shirt, unbuttoned, and jeans. No underwear. He went barefoot. He didn't expect be gone long. The room had been stuffy, airless. He toyed with the idea of unloading the bike. Or maybe not; all he wanted to do was stretch his legs.

They'd parked the rigs at the fringe of the broad paved truck lot around back of the motel, away from traffic. The lot was isolated but secure; well lit and fenced from a busy nearby street and accessible only to vehicles that passed in front of the motel office where a bored night clerk sat reading a paperback and sipping coffee from a Thermos. A row of giant, old eucalyptus trees lined the lot between the rigs and the street, shedding bark and leaf litter between the daredevil rigs and a chain link fence, branches rustling stiffly in a breeze.

Halfway across the parking lot, Nick saw Hanna climbing down from the side of the carrier. She saw him and she froze, halfway down. Nick looked over his shoulder back at the motel. It was night. Nobody else up and about. *Just we two.*

Neither had planned this rendezvous; they'd both just been restless is all, and at the same time.

Or maybe they had unconsciously sought each other out. Moments together had been rare, moments alone ever rarer; Nick had resigned himself to that reality. But was there some kind of power, Nick wondered, behind their mutual attraction that made moments like these possible at all? *Maybe even inevitable.*

Nick saw in Hanna's sudden mischievous smile, as she turned to him standing atop the carrier holding onto the side of one of the Mavericks tied down up there that she understood that they weren't about to let the scarce opportunity pass. Nick climbed up the carrier where Hanna had already ducked into a Maverick, one of the three two-door Mavs on the upper deck. She left the door ajar and Nick joined her. In the back seat. They chose the middle Mav with little thought; it was mostly hidden by shadow from the eucalyptus. They couldn't be seen from the motel or from the road.

In the shadowed and cramped backseat, they closed the distance between their bodies in a hurry. Who knew how long the moment might last?

They kissed frantically and groped, as they'd done eight times since Portland. Eight times. Nick had kept count. In all those scattered, frantic, and eventually interrupted minutes, since Portland, he'd not gotten so far as to even undo Hanna's bra.

Now, as he fumbled for the bra clasp between her shoulder blades, Hanna pushed him away from her lips to whisper huskily, "Did you bring your helmet?"

Nick froze, dizzy. "What?"

"*You* know. A rubber." Hanna stiffened, grew a degree colder in Nick's arms. "What did you think I meant?"

"No, I—"

"Damn it, Nick, what the hell do you think this is?" Hanna pulled further away from Nick—he'd learned that she was a lot stronger than she looked—and they ended up sitting side by side, facing more forward than toward each other. Traffic hummed on the nearby street.

Nick's mouth went dry and he felt numb. "Watch your language," he muttered.

"If you've been listening to my dad, you know safety—"

"Shipboard romance, I got that." Nick rolled down a window. "Hanna, I don't have a goddam—"

"You can't go through life without a landing ramp, Nick." Her voice went as rigid as her body and Nick lost all hope of getting laid, or even touching her again, at least tonight.

"Well, *you* don't have one either, do you?"

"No, I *don't* have any rubbers, Nick."

"Well, there you go." No hurry now anyway; his erection had wilted.

"Huh? 'There I go?' What the hell—"

Nick shut Hanna out with a sigh as she babbled on, ragging on him for not having a rubber that she didn't have either. *Like it's my fault?*

He'd experienced this sort of thing before. The last time? Was it Nancy? Anyway, he knew when women stopped making love to talk, it was all over.

His shirt was on the floor and his fly was unzipped.

Frustration had mounted for both of them. They'd checked schedules, plotted, schemed, but every chance they'd had to get together had been foiled.

"Now this." Why hadn't they planned to get together tonight? Nick grabbed up his shirt and tugged it on. He was sweaty in the muggy heat and the shirt stuck to his skin.

"Now *what*?"

"Nothing." The thin shirt tore at the shoulder as he jerked his arm into the sleeve. "Shit."

Well, they'd been busy with show business, doing the show, loading and unloading. A lot of media types around. It just slipped by is all. Frustrating, but nothing you could do about it now.

"Look, Nick, you're frustrated, I'm frustrated—"

"Then why the hell—"

"You damn well know—"

"No I don't. I don't know anything. Ask your father. He'll tell you. I don't know shit."

"Is that what's got your drawers in a bunch? My father?"

"Your father—"

"My father—"

What could have been a romantic rendezvous turned into a loud argument. A revealing one.

Nick had no idea how long their talk lasted; he didn't bring his watch. It shifted, as these conversations inevitably did from knee-jerk gut-instinct loud and angry verbal punching to something more rational and calm if no less infused with anger. Knowing this, Nick had often walked out before it got to this stage. Most often, he'd force his bed partner of the week, or day, to stalk out on him.

But this time Nick stuck it out, refused to be the first to walk away. He wasn't sure why he stuck it out, even knowing instinctively where the talk was going, but he did.

They quieted, and through gritted teeth, sullen intense glares, and stiff tones, Hanna moved a step down the agenda. She dropped interest in Nick's apparent lack of prudent foresight in not stocking a supply of rubbers in his shorts in case of emergency, and pressed on to Nick's relation with Ian.

"I know how you feel about my dad," she said, sounding like a goddam school counselor, sympathetic and self-satisfied at the same time.

"What the hell—"

"You can quit showing off and join the show—"

"What the goddam hell—"

Nick learned that he was jealous of Ian, and that his interest in Hanna was because it was the only way he could get back at Ian. The revelation shocked Nick for a moment before he found his tongue.

"Psychological bullshit." Dumb move; it only incited Hanna to further anger and more psychological bullshit.

She shifted gears again. "That's why you're jealous of me getting more involved in the show."

"Huh?" Nick began to regret indulging Hanna, not walking out when he'd had the chance. She was making him crazy.

"Jealous. You want to be the star of everything, can't let anybody else have the spotlight. You think that somehow diminished you—"

"Oh, that's a bunch of—"

"Which is why you want to do the T-bone crash."

"That's—that's—" For a long second, Nick felt speechless. What she'd said was bullshit, of course, but there was something in what she said—*or the way she said it?*—that prompted him to hesitate, to stifle his knee-jerk response.

"Hanna, I want to do the T-bone because—"

"You want to show up my dad, show up me, show up the world. Be a big star. Now's your chance with Landini Tires and all this media fuss. You want it all, Nick, but you damn well don't want to earn it."

"Earn it? *Earn* it? I drove half-way across the country—"

"Oh, don't tell me your Horatio Alger story again." Hanna's voice turned sing-songy, mocking. "Jumped off my bike in Mississippi to save a doggie, out-jumped Tolliver in Omaha, drove across country—"

"You don't believe—"

"I don't know *what* to believe, Nick. Tell me." She held his gaze, her eyes glistening in the reflection of the lights of traffic passing by. "How much is for show and how much is—" She took a breath. "How much is real?"

Silence hung in the air like smog. Nick finally sighed and climbed out of the Mav.

"Nick—"

"Forget it."

"Nick—"

"I said *forget* it."

He slammed the Mav door, jumped down from the carrier and went back to the motel. There, he discovered he'd not brought his room key with him and was locked out. He looked back to the rigs, saw Hanna stalking across the parking lot toward her room, shoulders hunched, head down, arms folded across her chest.

Instead of pounding on the door to wake Flynn or Tink to let him in, he walked back to the rigs and unloaded his bike.

CHAPTER TWENTY-FOUR

*I*an suffered assorted bumps, bruises, minor cuts, strained muscles, and a broken left ulna, but it could have been worse. When the Mustang stopped rolling, he discovered that somehow, he'd dived across the front seat, had gripped the far edge of the passenger seat frame—they'd taken out the passenger bucket seat, of course, but the floor mount, a two-inch wide bar, was still there, and Ian found it. Instinct saved his life. The top had been smashed in all the way to the bottom of the window frame. They had to use a hydraulic jack to get him out.

While they'd been dumb enough to forget to have a proper crash helmet on hand, they had been smart enough to have an ambulance standing by for the test jump. They hadn't expected to use it. It was there so PR could get some footage. Paramedics treated Ian on the scene, reporters hovering over their shoulders. They took him to Phoenix Baptist, checked him over, and released him. The episode made the evening news nationwide.

It was after six o'clock when Ian checked out of the hospital. PR was there and offered to take him to supper.

"We're late getting back to California," Ian said. "We'll eat on the plane." He'd split his lower lip and it hurt to talk. "Or after we get to California." He wasn't hungry.

"Yeah," PR said. "Okay. I called Grace and told her that you were running a bit late."

"Did you tell her what happened?" Ian hadn't objected when a nurse insisted he ride in a wheelchair out of the hospital, although he felt well enough to walk on his own. He'd been in a few wheelchairs, and he respected nurses, made it a point to try not to give them a hard time. He itched under his cast.

"Well, yeah, I had to tell her." PR sounded apologetic. "I couldn't hardly not tell her, could I?"

"I'd better call her." He did, from a pay phone at the hospital entrance. All was well with family, crew, and equipment.

Ian called Gran and told her what happened. "How's Shaun?" he asked.

"We got a water turn. He's out at the gate now." All the farms along the lane that ran past Brian's, Ian's, and Gran's houses tapped the ditch to irrigate their fields, orchards, and gardens. Everybody got a turn to divert the water at a gate across the lane by their property, a rigid schedule. Sometimes it took place in the middle of the night. If you missed it, you didn't get any more water until your turn came up next. It was like milking Beauty—no excuses.

"Tell him I'll call tomorrow. I got some business I need to take care of here."

PR drove to the airport and they ate turkey sandwiches after takeoff. Ian discovered his appetite was enormous and he wolfed down his food. Adrenalin, he was sure, fueled his appetite. That and anger.

"Here's what's going to happen," he said to PR after he'd finished eating. The plane was a few minutes from landing. "You're going to fire Cartwright—"

"But Ian, he—"

"You want to work with me on this, Parry?" Ian's voice rose and he bunched his right fist, his glower menacing.

PR nodded, lips a tight line, eyes wide.

"Get somebody who knows what they're doing. Hell, I know nobody builds loop-the-loop ramps, so there *are* no experts, but this guy—" Ian waved a dismissive hand. "The problem was that he'd been thinking of keeping that ramp *up* when the problem was keeping it *down*."

Ian used a water glass as a car to show PR what happened, and what needed to be done about it.

"And that ground is too soft. The beams pulled right out, didn't they?"

PR nodded. "Cartwright said two side beams, the main—"

"I figured. You got to think holding down, not holding up. Think guy wires, like they use on radio towers and stuff like that. Hell, all over the Midwest, they get tornadoes and those guys know how to keep their radio towers from blowing away. Get somebody who knows how to wire things down in a tornado." When PR nodded, he added, "You better write this stuff down."

PR took out a notebook and started writing as Ian ticked things off on his right-hand fingers.

"Keep Cartwright. I changed my mind. He got it wrong, but he's no fool. He'll not make the same mistake again, especially after you tell him how pissed off I am. Then tell him to get somebody who knows how to keep the ramp down."

Ian said he believed that the loop was too tight, which caused more pressure on the structure and, worse, too much pressure on him, compromising his ability to control the car.

"A wider loop means we'll need a bigger car, a mid-sized sedan. Can you get me a Torino or a Grenada with a six? Second best thing to a Rambler, but I think we need to go bigger. And I don't need a ton of bricks under the hood either. I'll need to test it again, maybe do a low jump. And the ramp. I guess we'll have to come up with another test."

It suddenly occurred to Ian that maybe there wouldn't be a B-S after all, that this failure would discourage Landini Tires. He asked PR about it.

PR shook his head. "No, we still got time. And maybe we can play up the drama." He shrugged. "I don't know. Believe me, I'm in new territory here."

And so was Ian. As he realized that Landini Tires was already looking for ways to continue with the project, so was he. He could have said "no" after the crash, but instead, he'd come up with a dozen specific ways to improve the stunt, to make it work. It had never occurred to him to quit. He didn't have an "I quit" gene.

Ian also suggested they look into using metal plate for the ramp floor, the kind the military used for runways and bridges, instead of plywood. Maybe it would be lighter and stronger, he suggested. "The lighter the jump ramp is, the easier it'll be to hold it down. Maybe aluminum. I don't know."

The plane landed at San Bernardino International where Grace met them and drove them to the Motel Six.

An hour later, PR tapped on Ian's door.

"I've been on the phone with Saint Louis," PR said. He sat on a wooden chair by the window, sat on the edge, nervous and tired. "I gave them your notes. They were all for firing Cartwright at first, but I told them what you said. They say he's mighty apologetic."

Ian snorted. "Good."

"And we're going to go car shopping in Dallas, a Ford dealership there, for your car. We'll film it." He shrugged. "Might as well get some PR mileage out of this, right?"

Ian didn't smile. Grace got busy in the tiny kitchen.

"Right," PR said, sobering. "Anyway, we're working on it. We'll let you do the jump car, strip it and prep it, and a back up if you think it's necessary—"

"Good idea."

"And maybe we can do a test jump with it, maybe in Saint Louis, or so, see if it flies well enough for you. Meanwhile, we're rebuilding the ramp—building a new one, I mean. We're going to have to do another test as soon as it's up."

"When?"

PR shrugged his narrow shoulders. "I say we ought to have a month or so in case anything goes—that is, in case we need to make any, uh, last minute adjustments. So no later than mid-July or so. How's that sound to you?"

"It'll have to do, won't it?"

PR left.

Ian called Shaun. "Are you ready to show?"

"Well, boss—" Ian was surprised to hear the hesitation in his voice. "Can you wait a day or two?"

"Sure. What's up?"

"Amanda's sick. I think she's pregnant. I just found out. I think I need to deal with that before—well, before I leave town. You know?"

"I'll call from Las Vegas," Ian said.

He talked with Grace. "Maybe Amanda will be pissed if I take him away," he said.

Grace laughed. "She'll want him around when it's time to drive her to the hospital and for three a.m. feedings, but right now, she'll probably jump at the idea of getting him out."

"I don't get it."

Grace laughed and said, "Never mind."

The San Bernardino show came off well enough, big crowd, good gate, and only one mishap. PR had used news about the test in Phoenix, failure or not, to help generate a lot of media buzz to pump up the crowd, and nobody was surprised to see Ian in an arm cast. He took the microphone early in the show to announce that they'd see a motorcycle jump finale instead of a car crash. This garnered a groan from the crowd, but it didn't last.

The single mishap turned out to be planned, not an accident, and it helped rather than hurt the show. Trigger hit something on the asphalt track while doing wheelies before the intermission and right after Ian announced there would be a motorcycle jump finale, and he fell. The crowd oohed as he rolled, arms flopping, across the track. He stood up, with help from Tink and Hoppy, wobbly but all right, waved to relieved applause, and picked up a shock absorber strut. Trigger shook his head in dramatic dismay and tossed the offending debris to the infield. The crowd roared in approval.

But Ian was suspicious about the incident. Trigger didn't look all that shaken up, and he was usually cautious about checking his track for such problems. And Orange Speedway was asphalt. How had he missed it?

"How did that strut get there?" Ian asked Trigger a few minutes later.

"I put it there," he said, smiling.

And Trigger knew how to fall, knew how to make it look like a bone-breaking major disaster, tricks he'd learned on the motocross circuit. Showmanship. He wore knee and elbow pads.

The motorcycle jump finale, over eighteen cars this time—a bit of a stretch, but they had a long straightaway—included a pointed search of the ground by the landing site, where they determined that no obstacles had accidentally come to rest.

After the show, they went to a Denny's for supper.

"Now," Trigger said over apple pie alamode dessert, "can we talk about a T-bone?"

Under the conditions, everybody sitting around the same table, Ian could not easily claim hearing problems, and he was caught off guard so that he had no diversion at hand.

"You said," Trigger said, "that we could talk about it after the loop test jump. Well, that's now."

He turned to Tink, who sat next to him, poking him with a fork. "Don't you think so?"

So Ian found himself promising to do a T-bone in about two weeks. Trigger had done his homework and he knew that would put them in Dallas, on Friday, June 15. "If that's where you're going to buy your B-S jump car, maybe we could snag a T-bone car at the same time. What do you say?"

Something irritated about the way Trigger approached the discussion, which he'd initiated; it set Ian's teeth on edge. Trigger was pushy and annoying in his own right, but usually that was his ego on display. Now, he seemed to be selling something, like a door-to-door Fuller Brush man, like a sophomore version of PR in his glory.

Oddly, too, there was a hint of desperation in his voice.

It was the T-bone, the damn T-bone again.

And Ian remembered their earlier talks about this subject, and the way their attitudes aligned.

Ian didn't want to do a T-bone for a lot of reasons, all of which he'd already explained to Trigger and whoever was in earshot at the time, more than once. But somehow, it had been determined that the show would do at least one T-bone before the season was over and the B-S occurred. Now, under Trigger's relentless, sugary sales pitch, he couldn't remember how he'd been talked into it.

Then he remembered. He was going to stall as long as he could, set up a T-bone, then let Trigger believe it was his to do, then snatch it out from under him at the last minute. Maybe let Shaun do it. Ian remembered the plan. He remembered he'd been unusually pissed off at Trigger at the time, catching him flirting with Hanna, and had hatched the scheme in revenge.

Now, it looked as if Trigger had taken the momentum and was behind the wheel, steering to the takeoff ramp too fast.

He looked at Hanna pointedly but silently. She didn't catch his eye, apparently fascinated with the cake crumbs on her plate.

And what was up with Tink? He and Trigger and Hoppy hung out when they had time off, but so what?

Ian felt uneasy, like he was missing something going on around him, but he didn't know what it might be. He resolved to talk to Grace about it after.

He gave up thinking about it and sighed. He was stiff, sore, and tired, bone-tired.

He remembered an incident back when he worked with Sid Hirsch. He was driving a car carrier between shows one night, heading south on 283 south of WaKeeney, Kansas, and he was tired, when he spotted something in the road ahead. He stopped the rig in the middle of the deserted two-lane and got out. In the headlights, Ian watched a wagon train crossing the road, headed west. It was a long wagon train, and the oxen-pulled covered wagons moved slowly, so Ian took a leak and checked the tie-downs. When the last man crossed the road, a tall, rail-thin farmer in overalls and carrying a long rifle, who waved at him, Ian got back in the rig and drove on.

He woke up in Dodge City, lying in the cab in the fairgrounds parking lot. He felt rested, refreshed, as if he'd driven asleep. He was convinced it wasn't a dream, that it really happened.

Ian understood tired.

"A T-bone," Ian said. "In Dallas. But I do it. Then, if we do another, maybe somebody else can do it. Maybe."

Later, he asked Grace what had happened.

"You were tired," she said. "One T-bone. I think you have to do it. PR wants it, we're getting a lot of media questions about it. Trigger wants it. Do it to shut them all up."

"Trigger wants to do it."

"Now. Wait'll after he helps you off to the hospital. Then ask him if he wants to do it."

"Shaun wants to do it," he said.

"I'm surrounded by fools," Grace said. "You guys sort it out, and I'll push your wheelchairs after."

Ian laughed. It hurt to laugh, his busted lip and sore ribs, but it helped.

He called Shaun—Amanda wasn't pregnant after all, not yet anyway—and brought him up to date on the plan. Shaun wanted Ian to set a date for the second T-bone, the one Trigger would be fooled into believing he was going to do, and the one that Shaun would show up to do instead. After hearing Ian's stories about the cocky, pretty-boy motorcycle daredevil, Shaun was clearly relishing being a part of Ian's comeuppance plot.

"Let's wait and let Trigger set the date," Ian said. "He'll think he's in charge, getting one up on me."

Shaun laughed with devilish glee, and once again agreed to wait before hitting the road. "Besides," he said, "I need to butter up Amanda before I leave. Who understands women? Like it's my fault she's not pregnant. She's really getting bitchy, you know?

"Watch your language."

They drove to Las Vegas, where they had three days before the show. The crew got a lot of time off, but as Ian had come to expect, he and Grace and PR kept busy doing PR. Film from the disastrous test jump in Phoenix had come out and media interest intensified. Ian dealt with it as best he could, show smile in place, but in the back of his mind was the T-bone stunt and Trigger's pressure about it, and Shaun's pressure to get out on the road again.

On top of it all, for some reason, Hanna had turned moody. Ian noticed but said nothing until Grace mentioned it. "I asked her what was wrong," she said, "but she isn't talking."

"You don't suppose she's—"

"No, she's not pregnant, Ian. Jesus H. We've talked about *that*."

"Oh. Good."

"She talks with BB but BB won't confide in me. I won't ask, you know? Maybe she's bored with the road already, thinking about school. She really enjoyed school, you know? She's talked about transferring to Laramie. I don't know."

The Las Vegas show attracted a small herd of celebs. Wayne Newton got a ride in the ski car in the parking lot at Caesar's Palace.

John Travolta, Kate Jackson, William Shatner, and a half dozen other famous people, some of whom Ian didn't recognize, came by to schmooze and flash their pearly whites and soak up camera light. As PR had promised, it was bright and glitzy, and Ian was hard-pressed to whip out his country, aw-shucks, just-folks image on demand. It was tiring.

Trigger, on the other hand, took to the limelight like a budding starlet.

Gran was well, Amanda was not pregnant, and Shaun was antsy to hit the road.

CHAPTER TWENTY-FIVE

Ian let Grace drive the big rig east while he nursed his broken arm. Hopping eastward across the southwest, dripping with sweat in hundred-degree heat more often than not, the show pressed on. Flagstaff, Albuquerque, Roswell, Lubbock, Odessa, San Antonio, Houston, then Dallas. The Dallas show got pushed back a day to Saturday, June 16, because PR found himself with more interviews and PR events than he could handle in the original time schedule. Ian wanted the crew to get time to rest, and he needed to fix a busted suspension in the ski car. And the equipment was getting ragged again, ramps scarred and busted. PR hired painters, and the crew went off to tour Dallas while Ian, Grace, Hanna, Radar, and PR went off to promote the show.

Trigger tried to insinuate himself into the PR campaign without success. Both Ian and PR wanted to maintain focus. Trigger tried not to show his pout, but Ian saw.

In Dallas, Ian found the car he wanted, both for the B-S and for the upcoming T-bone. The B-S jump car was a '75 Mercury Capri coupe, plenty of energy and good steel all around. For his T-bone car, Ian chose a '66 Chevy Biscayne, a six-cylinder sedan, an old blue and white police car with a faded shield on the door that said "Chicago Police" and "8352"—a solid crash car.

At the speedway, Landini Tires had set up a pyramid of tires as a landing site for Ian to test the B-S jump car. They expected the car wouldn't get hurt too much if it landed in a bunch of tires.

The car jump into the tire mound would take place just before the T-bone, and since they expected an enormous crowd, possibly the biggest to date, they scheduled a motorcycle jump in the show as well. Trigger performed what for him was a modest fourteen-car jump just before the loop-the-loop jump car and landing test, basking in as much limelight as he could muster under the circumstances.

Despite the butterflies gathering in his gut, ready to flock into his gullet for the T-bone, Ian felt good all day.

Even before the Tire Jump, as Radar had been calling it, PR had gotten it into his head that having Ian do a stunt involving a pile of Landini Tires was a good idea, and he sound-boarded the notion many times since Odessa the week before. Hours before the Dallas show, he told Ian what he'd come up with.

If it worked for this show, they'd do it again "up the river," as PR put it, when there was a good chance it would help boost Landini Tire sales locally. "There's a couple markets we're dying to penetrate more," he said, as if Ian cared, "like Little Rock, Kansas City, and Minneapolis. Big shows, all of them, so we ought to go all out, don't you think?"

"Right." Ian was cleaning corroded battery cables on the head-on car, a '60 Chevy Corvair sedan.

"We don't have to use the actual jump car," PR said, talking fast as if he'd gulped a gallon of coffee, "but one that looks like it, if we can get one. I'll check around. And we don't have to do it every show, just those big ones, where we need to penetrate market share. And it doesn't have to be much of a jump, just a low ramp and into a pile of tires. Then—and here's the big thing, y'see—after the show, after each show, *we give away the tires*."

He paused for Ian to appreciate the wonder of it all. "Isn't that great?"

"Yeah, great."

"Yeah, we invite the audience down to take a tire or two from the stack, take them home with them. That way, maybe the tire ends up as a swing in somebody's front yard, maybe it ends up as a planter for some granny's mums, or maybe they decide to buy two or three more for the family station wagon. Anyway, it'll get tongues wagging and maybe sales hopping. So, that's the hope at least. Good idea, huh? Great idea, I say."

Ian, feeling good, didn't have to fake his smile. "Great, PR. But we don't know how the crowd will take it, do we?"

"Well, not yet, but we will. And they'll love it, believe me. I've been working with Radar on it. He's got a crackerjack routine, trust me. And Joel suggested we wire some Roman candles on the jump ramp, the back of the car. Boomers and sparks is what he called them. What do you think of that?"

"We got some fireworks."

"Great." PR jumped up and down like he needed to pee. "Great." He ran to get Flynn and Tink to rig the fireworks.

The dozen worker-bees PR had hired to unload tires and stack them took longer than PR had estimated. The group was day laborers hired through a local temp service. Most looked shabby, down-and-outers scrabbling for minimum wage and feeling damn lucky to get even that. Ian made sure they all got dinner on the house and a handful of free tickets.

But they really didn't know what to do or how to do it. Tires rolled away across the track, people tripped and fell. A Keystone Cops routine played out until Ian went over to supervise.

He organized a stacking brigade, like sandbaggers at a flood, and built a shallow mound of tires, not the pyramid PR had envisioned, wider than it was tall. The tires were roughly interlocked, and the mound seemed stable enough. Ian had never landed a car in the middle of a pile of tires before, so he really had no idea of what to expect; his supervision of the stacking of the tires was more or less a matter of pretending he knew what he was doing. The work crew trusted him and the mound got formed. They finished an hour before showtime.

The mound lay in the infield between the first and second corner. The plan was for Ian to go wrong-way around the track, cut hard out of corner four, just inside corner three, into the infield and then to the jump ramp. It was a tight turn, it would sap momentum, and the ground wasn't right. But they'd moved obstacles to ease the approach as much as possible, graded down a hump in the way, and filled a soft spot on the approach, then they'd marked the approach lane with little yellow flags so Ian wouldn't get disoriented when he came around and so other people wouldn't get in his way.

"And we'll get security to make sure the road is clear, too," PR said.

"Be sure the security people don't get in the way," Ian said. He told PR about the curious rent-a-cop who got too close and got run over by a motorcycle in Mankato four years ago. The bike stuntman who was with Ian at the time didn't get hurt, the cop emerged unhurt, and the show emerged unsued, but Ian made it a habit to repeat the story as needed, and to whoever needed to hear it.

The show went well. BB and Hanna did the rollovers, as they had since Las Vegas. Both were doing good rolls, and the crowds loved it, so they got pegged for the routine more often than not. Boo stumbled while running across the track after the crew jump and bloodied his nose, but nobody except Grace, who administered first aid in the trailer, and Radar who had to make do between stunts for a while without a clown to play off of, knew it had happened.

Ian had taken off his arm cast the day before, maybe sooner than he should have, but nobody argued with him, not even Grace. His grip seemed a bit weak, but he could hold a steering wheel and he could drive. He would be okay, he insisted.

His problems in performing the high skis stunt weren't related to the weak grip. He kept dropping the car back onto the four wheels at a soft spot just past the first corner. He had the crew shift the takeoff ramp a few feet so he hit a different part of that corner, lower down, and he got through, and just as he was entering the backstretch, he found a rut in the hard clay and put the ski car over on its top.

He was unhurt. He had the car righted without getting out, then he did another two-wheeled circuit of the track, this time making it all the way around, dropping right side up in front of Radar, and the grandstand, which exploded in applause as he got out of the car, triumphantly waving.

After that, all the stunts went well. Trigger's motorcycle jump lifted the crowd spirits to new heights, the Tire Jump got good applause when Ian hit and tires by the dozen squirted from the mound, rolling helter-skelter across the infield and track. As they set up for the T-bone, crew and security gathered tires and rolled them out of the way.

The T-bone went off without a hitch. The jump car flipped, as it should, smacking down on the trunk and back window on the other side of the second catch car, and gently settling on its top. Ian felt nothing more than a series of hard jolts.

"Are you okay?" Trigger was the first of the safety crew at the side window.

"Yeah," Ian said. He recalled his conversation with Grace about the stunt, how maybe if he'd gotten hurt maybe Trigger would have been discouraged from campaigning to do it. "I'm okay." But he'd decided that even that wouldn't have discouraged Trigger, so there was no point in faking anything.

"Let's milk it," he told Trigger as Flynn and BB and Boo and Tink and Hoppy came up to the inverted car windows to peek in. Boo had the ubiquitous fire extinguisher in hand, the red canister almost as big as he was. "Boo, you make a start for the ambulance, and Tink, you go stop him, then come back and climb in. Then, Boo, you go tell Radar I'm trapped inside, then grab the fire extinguisher and blow it off. Everybody got that?"

They did.

Boo jumped up, hollered something incoherent, and started dashing, his little legs pumping, short arms swinging, toward the ambulance, which was parked on the infield, engine running. But just as the ambulance started forward, lights flashing, Tink dashed out after Boo, grabbed him, and waved the ambulance off. The ambulance stopped, red lights still strobing, just on the verge of the infield, next to Radar, whose breathy, excited narrative had become filled with pauses and dramatic hums and haws, as if he too was totally surprised by events and had no idea what was going on.

The crowd sat in shocked, attentive silence as Tink grabbed the fire extinguisher from Boo's hands and began spraying the interior of the car. Then Ian jumped out in a cloud of rising dust and smoke, coughing, waving his helmet, and the crowd cheered their heads off.

Ian took the microphone and explained, "I'm all right. The stunt worked as planned, but my seatbelt got jammed and I couldn't get out. The crew did the right thing when they thought I was hurt." Then, with a planned tension-reliving laugh, he added, "But we got to talk about getting an itchy trigger finger with that fire extinguisher."

With the tension expertly broken, post-show souvenir sales reached an all-time high, and the daredevils spent an hour signing autographs, posing for photographs, and chatting with fans and media. Every tire in the Landini Tire Jump Pyramid got removed, but a fight broke out; cops broke it up, but PR resolved to forego the tire-giveaway in future shows. "We'll donate the tires, sure," he said, "but no more free-for-alls."

Somebody tried to steal Hobo again and got arrested. Fans tried to strip souvenirs off the jump car, but security intervened. Ian's toolbox got stolen.

And the show moved on.

"Kansas City," Ian told Shaun that night. "Saturday, July first. Be there. Aloha."

Shreveport, Vicksburg, Little Rock, Springfield, Poplar Bluff, and Saint Louis.

Saint Louis was a PR fest, with Baha and other Landini Tires suits getting into the act. PR had let out the rumor that there would be another B-S test in Phoenix after Kansas City, and the media responded like a stirred beehive.

Ian's weariness had reached a breaking point and he snipped at some minor Landini Tires exec on the morning of Wednesday, June 28, the day before the show. PR finally noticed and let Ian off the hook, let him relax, disappear, and be a tourist.

Ian took Hanna to the zoo that afternoon.

"What do you think?" Ian asked her.

"About what?"

Ian laughed. They stood chucking peanuts at chimpanzees. "The show. The T-bone. The B-S. Everything." Pause. "Trigger."

"I don't care about Trigger."

Ian heard a petulant tone in her voice and remembered the romantic clinch he'd interrupted weeks before. "Oh? That so?"

"If Trigger gets to do the T-bone, Dad, can I do a head-on?"

"I'm going to put you in a goddam convent." So she'd had a crush on a good-looking guy. But it seemed that it had played out of its own accord, naturally.

"Dad, watch your language."

Probably a good idea I didn't get in the way. "You think these monkeys care?" Or maybe Grace had said something, or BB.

"I'm kidding about the head-on," Hanna said, chucking peanuts. "I'm busy enough as it is. We all are."

"Yeah." *My little girl.*

"Nice to have a real day off." She smiled, radiant. "Let's not talk show, okay?"

They saw *Star Wars* that evening, had supper at a JB's, and got back to their motel after six.

Clouds threatened rainout come showtime, and it was unusually windy. PR blamed the weather on the smaller-than-expected turnout. The wind was bad enough that Trigger agreed to forego a motorcycle jump, though his disappointment was evident. Ian's car carrier jump satisfied and no other problems reared.

Ian called home after the show. Shaun was ready to go, suitcase already in the car, alarm set for five a.m., to get an early start. He'd be in Kansas City the next night, day before the show. Ready to do a T-bone crash.

The next morning, along I-70 a few miles east of Columbus, Ian got a message on the CB from a Missouri State Trooper asking him to pull over.

Ian pulled off the freeway at a wide spot called Kingdom City. Behind his car carrier, the wrecker towing the clown car on the fifth wheel pulled in. Behind that, the van and trailer parked, and the road Mav pulled up the rear. Everybody got out, stretching, eyeing the trooper who stood next to his cruiser up ahead by the side of the road.

He walked up to Ian as Ian got out of the Freightliner.

"What's up, officer?" Ian asked. He had all his permits, all his road equipment was up to snuff—no broken lights or turn signals. PR and Grace had made sure their books were clean before they left the track the night before. None of the crew, as far as Ian knew, was wanted by the law.

The officer took off his Smokey bear hat and Ian's heart sank. He knew. Gran. Heart attack.

CHAPTER TWENTY-SIX

Kingdom City was just a wide spot in the road, a cluster of shabby old buildings around a gas station and general store and a huge barn-like garage. A half dozen houses lined the road, two trailers sat back on a low hill amid tall pines, and a cluster of old cars lay helter-skelter in a fenced yard behind the garage. There was a pay phone.

Nobody answered when Ian called Gran's, hoping. Nobody was home at Brian's. Mrs. Davis answered on the first ring.

"Shaun is at the hospital with Gran," she said, voice wavery. "I don't know who-all's with her." She'd been crying. "They took her to University Hospital in Salt Lake in an ambulance. Your mom's there. Nobody's called since they left. We've been trying to get a hold of you."

Ian got the hospital number from Mrs. Davis and called. After a maddening delay, being switched several times, Shaun finally came on the line. He sounded tired, worried.

"The doctors aren't too optimistic, Ian," Shaun said. "And she looks bad, really bad. She isn't conscious, and they—they think she isn't going to—"

Shaun broke off and Ian heard noises on his end of the phone. Indistinct voices, and somebody calling on an intercom. And a kind of muffled snort. Shaun blew his nose.

"Sorry, boss," he said, sounding nasal. "I got a cold."

"Is there a doctor I can talk to?"

"Everybody's busy. You know how doctors are. Like cops. They show up when you don't want them, can't find one for love nor money when you do."

Ian talked to his mother, who couldn't speak, could only sob. He talked to Brian, who seemed less tense and more articulate and informed than Shaun or his mother.

Gran had suffered a heart attack in the middle of the night, but had somehow managed to pick up the bedside phone and call 911. A deputy happened to be just down the lane at the time and responded within minutes. He acted quickly. Gran was lucky to be alive, but Brian made it clear that her luck might not last.

"I'll be there this afternoon," Ian said. He hung up. Grace had been listening. Hanna and Joel had retreated to the trailer, and the other members of the crew, including PR, had respectfully kept their distance.

Ian found PR. "I'm taking the road car back to Saint Lo. I'm going straight to the airport. Grace'll book me on the first flight out to Salt Lake. I don't know when I'll be back. Grace is in charge. You guys go on to KC. I'll call later."

"You're not going to drive back to Saint Lo," PR said, his jaw clenched.

"It's closer than—"

"And you're not going to take a commercial flight either." PR pushed past Ian, heading for the pay phone. "I'm going to charter a jet. The Columbia Regional Airport is fifteen minutes from here," he said over his shoulder.

Twenty minutes later, Ian drove the road car south on a back road to the airport, Grace with him. Ian hadn't even grabbed his suitcase. They didn't talk much on the way. They waited another twenty minutes, then a jet landed.

"Call," Grace said as she kissed him. The jet waited, doors open. "When you can."

Ian nodded, not trusting his voice. He got on the plane and left, heading west.

Amanda was waiting for Ian at the airport in Salt Lake and drove him to the hospital. It was mid-afternoon and Ian was ravenous, but he didn't want to stop or even ask about dinner. He wanted to know about Gran.

"Sleeping," Amanda said, voice gravelly with weariness. Bags under her eyes, hair stringy. "You'd better talk to the doctor. And your mom's not taking it well."

The doctor, an earnest-looking young man with an engaging but apologetic smile and an alarmingly bald head, whose name Ian immediately forgot, described Gran's condition as "critical" and warned that she might not wake up. Ever.

Which was why Shaun was in Salt Lake City and not on the road headed for Kansas City, and why Ian was not going to be there for the show the next night, Saturday, July first.

PR had phoned the hospital while Ian was in the plane and left a number for Ian to call, a Motel Six in Kansas City. Grace answered on the first ring and he briefed her.

"I'm staying here," he said. "At least for a couple of days, until Gran comes around. Tell PR we ain't doing a T-bone. Trigger can do a motorcycle jump finale, and Tink can do the Tire Jump. Or you can skip the tire jump, if you want. It's up to you, Grace. You're in charge."

"Okay. You'd better talk to PR."

Ian did. He briefed him on Gran's condition and his plans. The plans didn't extend past the next day.

"I'm really sorry about Gran, Ian," PR said. Ian was certain that PR meant it. They had gotten along well while he was in Rock Springs, a regular at dinner at Gran's place in the days before the show hit the road. Ian couldn't think of anybody who ever met Gran who didn't like her.

"I may miss Lincoln," Ian said. "Better plan on it, just in case. But I'll plan to be back for Norfolk, if you can fly me out."

"I'll work out the details. And we have a day after Norfolk so we can delay—"

"Nah, that'll be plenty of time. I just need to see that she's okay, see to Mom, see to the farm, that sort of thing. Brian and Shaun are on it, but, well, I got to help, you know?"

"Yeah, I know."

"If I know Gran, after she wakes up, she'll be chewing my butt for not being with the show."

"Yeah, I know."

Ian talked with Grace. All was well with the crew and the show, but she'd had to cancel a few interviews and she had questions about buying a new toolbox.

"Let Tink do it," Ian told her. "He knows what we need in the box. Tell him to make a list. You go with him. Bring the card. It'll cost." He told her how much he estimated it would cost to replace the stolen toolbox and she whistled.

"Uh, Grace, I want to thank PR. You know? Will you—"

"Yeah, Ian. I'll do it for you. But I think he knows."

Gran's condition didn't change much through the next day, but Ian did get some rest.

Grace called Ian that afternoon before the Kansas City show. "Trigger wants to do the T-bone," she said.

"Tell him I said no."

"I did, but it's like he doesn't hear. He's been talking it up with Radar and Tink and PR. It's like he's taking over, you know what I mean?"

"I know. You just got to put your foot down, Grace. Don't take no shit from anybody."

"Ian, if you could just talk to him—"

"That wouldn't work worth beans. I've been there, and believe me I know. I know this guy. You just got to be firm with him is all."

"I don't know, Ian. I'm trying, but I don't think the guys respect me."

"Dammit, Grace, you got to act like you know what you're doing. You let them know that *I* respect you. And that you trust yourself. It's a leadership thing. You get me?"

Grace sighed into the phone.

"Dammit, Grace, listen here. You got to think like you do when I get stubborn and you have to slap me upside the head to get my attention. Kick ass. You just wait'll one of them gives you the opportunity to kick some righteous butt and have at it. They'll get the message and start asking instead of telling."

Pause. Then Grace said, "Like that time I had to hit you with the frozen fish?"

"Exactly. Call me after the show."

Ian checked on Gran again, but there had been no significant change. The message was clear: there's nothing you need to do here. Ian resolved to tell PR to go ahead and arrange for his flight out the next day.

He talked with Shaun. Holding a paper cup of hospital vending machine coffee, Ian's nephew looked depleted, saggy, washed-out. They sat on plastic chairs in a waiting alcove by the gift shop.

"I can't, Ian." Shaun stared at the floor, leaning forward, elbows on his knees. "I got to stay. You understand."

"Yeah. I understand."

"I mean, Brian, he's doing all he can, and Amanda's helping and your mom and other folks are helping, but—" He looked up, eyes narrowed, that stubborn look Ian knew so well. "But I got to be here, for Gran. For as long as it takes."

Ian nodded. He understood how much Shaun wanted to get on the road.

As he tried to find something to say—his throat was clogged with something, maybe a cold coming on—he also understood how much he had been looking forward to having Shaun with him on the road.

But Gran came before show. It had always been that way.

"I'm going to head back tomorrow, fly out to Lincoln, if PR can arrange a flight. He does magic with that sort of thing, arranging things, I mean, PR does. Sometimes he goes too far, but give him that."

Shaun nodded. "I'll be with Gran, don't worry. And if things change—"

"We can talk about that later."

Maybe Gran would stabilize and recover, but who knew when. Worse—who knew *if*.

Ian's mother Emma had offered up a spare bedroom, but the Hawthornes lived too far from the hospital, way down south by Point of the Mountain, and the family wanted to be closer. They rented a room at a motel closer to the hospital, where they slept and showered and stayed with Gran in shifts, Shaun and Brian and Ian. Amanda and Brian's wife had gone back home. Ian was there, napping, when the phone rang just before midnight.

Grace. "We got a problem, Ian," she said. "It's bad."

CHAPTER TWENTY-SEVEN

*T*he morning of the Kansas City show, cloudless, windless, and dripping, sticky hot, Nick paced out the track front stretch step by step for the bike jump. He'd done the same thing the afternoon before when the crew had arrived and again later the evening before. But the math wouldn't work no matter how he tried. A bike jump at this track—bad idea; not enough room.

"It's practically a goddam rodeo arena," he muttered to nobody in particular. Sweat dripped into his eyes.

PR had been standing nearby when Nick first looked at the track the afternoon before and had heard.

"Well, Nick, maybe we could take down that fence—"

"Not your best work, PR. Kansas City." Nick snorted, hands on his hips. "Supposed to be a big gig. Big city, big crowd."

"Yeah, well—"

PR had had to cope with a last minute change forced by some kind of sudden and unexpected structural problems with the grandstands over at the fairgrounds—county officials had abruptly closed it down—where they'd been originally scheduled. "That's what I was told," PR explained to Nick. "This arena was the best we could get on quick notice. Maybe we could get them to knock out that fence—"

"Yeah, right." The fence PR so hopefully and pathetically pointed to was a stout wood rail structure used to pen livestock. Behind it, twenty feet behind, another fence stood, as stout as the first.

Since that first look, PR had kept his distance from Nick, busy doing his PR thing. Nick was certain PR sensed his foul mood. Nick didn't care.

The show had appeared at rodeo grounds before, always a hassle. Horse people complained about the fumes and the noise and tiniest bits of metal left on the ground that would hurt their horsies delicate footsies so you had to be extra careful with clean up after shows; you had to spend a lot of time holding hands with hay-burner fans. Rodeo arenas were too cramped and the ground too loose and unstable. Made for horses, not cars.

Always too short.

If rodeo grounds had any virtue, Nick had learned, it was that rodeo fans had a more healthy respect for wild on-the-loose livestock then race fans did for runaway, out-of-control cars. Which meant fences on rodeo grounds, often in the wrong places.

This wasn't a rodeo track, not exactly, but it looked like it had recently been converted from one into a tight quarter-mile dirt oval racetrack. No, Nick amended as he kicked up a new ten-penny nail in the dirt at the foot of the grandstand; it was still being converted. That corral in the way, just off the fourth corner. And the grandstand smelled of fresh paint and the wire mesh around the flag stand was new and shiny. Nick saw ragged clumps of fossilized horseshit here and there.

A Cat was parked smack dab in the infield, broad yellow blade facing the third corner, and a grader stood just past the backstretch. The infield had been recently bladed flat, bare dirt neatly scraped naked the length of the field, with small brown hillocks at the corners, like fuzzy eyebrows.

The track had been graded and packed, but the soil was sandy. Nick poked at the loose soil with his boot toe. *Gonna be like riding on a beach.*

Too short. No traction.

"A T-bone finale, then," Nick muttered. *Has to be. Carrier jump is out, we got no tires for that silly tire jump gag, and I'll just look silly with a bike jump in this toilet bowl.*

"Pardon?" Hoppy stood nearby; Nick hadn't noticed.

"Well, just look," Nick said. He recounted his reasoning and Hoppy nodded and grunted, hands on his hips, squinting in the hot sun.

It was a cloudless morning, probably above a hundred degrees already, breezeless. It would get hotter come showtime.

Flynn, Boo, BB, Joel and Radar were stripping junkers behind the backstretch. PR was off somewhere doing PR while Grace and Tink were shopping for a new toolbox. Who knew where Hanna was?

"Yeah," Nick muttered, "and who cares?"

"Pardon?"

"A T-bone, Hoppy," Nick said. He'd forgotten Hoppy was there, again. He waved his hand. "You can see that, right?"

Hoppy shook his head. "I don't know. Grace said—"

"Well, we'll just have to talk to her, won't we?" Nick felt irritated at Hoppy for being so bone-headed. *Can't you see?* "I mean, just *look* at this."

"Yeah, sure. But—I don't know."

"Shit." Nick walked away. He decided to see how the others felt about it.

As he stalked over to the group stripping the junkers, Nick realized there was yet another problem needed fixing. Only two of the four junkers were runners, twin '58 Olds hardtops, one red and one blue. Bastards to clean with all that chrome; which is why they called them "Chromemobiles."

"And with no posts," Nick said tossing a length of twisted chrome into a pile of debris growing in two wheelbarrows. "We got us one roll each before the tops come in and they become catch cars."

"But not both," Radar said. He wiped his little round glasses on his stained coveralls, squinting into the stark daylight. "We got to save one for the head-on."

"Gee," BB said, dripping sarcasm, "which one? The red piece of shit or the blue turdmobile?" She'd just smashed a thumb with a tire iron and was in no mood.

The two deadsticks had good metal, and would make good jumpers if they could be made to run.

Big if.

One was a rare '56 Hudson sedan. Its once stylish tri-tone paint job was rust-spotted, the upholstery rotted out, but the top was solid. The other was a spiffy '62 Chevy Corvair Monza station wagon that somebody had apparently once tried to salvage—lots of Bondo under the right front fender—and had given up halfway through.

Nick dived in, helping strip the junkers with characteristic gusto. Hoppy joined in and everybody worked hard. They finished early, well before noon. Nick and Flynn tested the two runners with brief dashes around the track as they all waited for Hanna and Tink to return with dinner.

Where the hell is—

Nick battered the red Olds trunk with a tire iron to work out the frustration. He didn't want to think about Hanna, had resolved since California not to; he'd moved on, or was trying to. But she damned well wouldn't let him go.

"Shit." Whack. "Shit." Whack. "Shit." Whack. The iron flew from Nick's sweaty hand and almost hit Boo.

"Hey!"

"Sorry."

"Pull your trigger over here," Flynn said from under the Monza hood he'd just opened. "Let's see if we can get this fucker running."

They puttered under the hood of the Monza but quickly gave up. Some of the parts, including the wiring, looked new, but the damned thing refused to turn over.

"Let's ask Tink," Flynn said, tossing a rag aside. "Maybe he can work some of his magic."

Tink and Grace returned from shopping shortly after noon. Hanna had been with them. Nick ignored her and she ignored him right back.

The crew had worked themselves into a ravenous thirst and hunger in the oppressive heat, and they took to the provided burgers, fries, and Coke dinner without prompting. They sat in the dirt in the thin sliver of shade by the carrier and ate.

"Gran is doing a little better," Grace said as she doled out burger bags. "Ian sounded good, said Gran looked—okay."

Grace's smile looked odd, and she sounded overly cheerful. It took a moment before Nick thought maybe she was lying, that maybe Gran wasn't doing well, but Grace didn't want to say. Or couldn't bring herself to say.

"When will Dad be back?" Joel asked.

"He'll be here when he gets here," Grace said. Irritation, concern. Something like that, Nick concluded.

Hanna's expression was unreadable, but then Nick had given up trying to read her.

As for the crew—everybody concentrated on eating and it was hard to read their mood. Joel was the most obvious, and his distress over Gran was evident; Joel fairly twitched, on the verge of tears.

Tink didn't eat. He claimed he'd eaten in the car coming back to the track. He lugged the heavy, new toolbox to the side of the Monza to resume his tinkering with the beast. Since the afternoon before, Tink had spent considerable time and energy under that hood.

"I'll make this thing work," he'd declared loudly, "or I'll eat the front seat." He'd skipped breakfast to get an extra hour at the task. Now, brow furrowed, stripped to the waist, sweat-streaked dirt caking his thin bronze face and bony chest, he leaned over the engine with a wrench in one hand, a length of wire in the other, and wire-cutters clenched between his teeth like it was a Bowie knife and he was after scalp.

He'd tinkered some that first night before supper and a little after, until he lost daylight. He seemed obsessive, driven, Nick thought, but he wrote that off to anxiety over Gran. Tink took his worry out on the engine; he couldn't fix Gran, so he'd fix that goddam engine or bust.

Nick dismissed the idea of offering to help. No, this was Tink's way. Even Flynn, always right there under the hood at Tink's elbow, kept his distance.

PR returned a few minutes after the crew started eating. He looked brighter than he had before he'd left, but not by much.

"I called off that TV interview," he told Grace, who sat with the crew, eating. "And the other ones. I stopped the ads." He looked around the track, squinting. "Might help. Some."

"Some," Grace said, munching.

"The way this track is built, maybe we can keep cameras away, say—" he pointed "—over there, or—"

As PR muttered, mostly to himself now, Nick realized that PR's task that morning had been to do all he could to get this show ignored, if not by those who might attend—if those people got the word about the venue change, which might not happen for many because of the cancelled ads— then at least by the media, especially TV.

For a second, Nick felt a pang of sympathy for PR. He was good at attracting crowds. *Tough job for him trying to make crowds go away.*

An engine suddenly roared nearby, a rusty growl. The Monza had fired to life.

"I knew that sucker could run," Tink hollered from the driver's seat as he revved the engine, smoke gushing from the tailpipe. Tink gave a rebel yell, slapped the dashboard, *thumpthumpthump,* and the crew applauded and whistled his triumph.

Tink drove the Monza around the track, a greasy smoke streak trailing his victory lap. When he got back to the infield, everybody was standing, cheering. After the anxiety over Gran, uncertainty about this track, Nick felt relief, and saw his relief reflected in the demeanor of the rest of the crew. It had been needed, this small triumph.

"Do you think it'll fly?" Nick asked.

"It better," Tink said, face flushed. You'd have thought he'd won at Indy. "If it don't, I'll eat the brake lining." He coyote-howled again and grinned, dancing from foot to foot.

"Think it'll fly?" Tink asked Hanna, poking her roughly in the ribs.

"Yeah, sure," Hanna said. She laughed. "If you say so." She'd caught Tink and the crew's infectious cheery mood.

"What do *you* say?" Tink asked Grace. Nick was certain that if Grace said anything positive that Tink would drive off in another victory lap, howling. Or wet his pants.

"I'm sure it'll fly, Tink—"

Howl—

"—but it'll make a good head-on, too."

"Well, yeah," Tink said, deflated, "but what about the finale? I mean, we can use a deadstick for the head-on."

"Nick's got the finale," Grace said.

"Well, that's the thing," Nick said. He rubbed the back of his sweaty neck and frowned.

"What?" Grace asked.

While the crew went about their business preparing for the evening show, Tink's giddiness toned down by Grace's apparent antipathy to a crash finale with "his Monza," Nick took Grace aside, walked out to the front stretch, and made his case. She listened, silent, looking at the ground mostly, arms locked across her chest. She grunted and nodded, said little. Listened. Tink glanced over at the pair occasionally, as if trying to read their lips. Nick thought he didn't look happy.

"Besides," he concluded, "with Ian not here, we got no high skis and we're short for hell driving—"

"I'll fill in."

"—and we'll have to milk everything we've got."

"Ever thought of doing it wrong way around?"

"Huh?"

"Your jump. Go clockwise, not counter, like you usually do. You got take-off room that way."

Nick felt flabbergasted that he hadn't thought of that alternative. But—

"But the landing. I got no room with that fence—"

"Maybe we could take down the fence?" Grace gestured in unconscious imitation of the way PR might have made the same case. "And put down some hay bales; you could slide in. You've done that before, haven't you? Think you could do it here?"

Nick remembered Mississippi and that damn dog and for a moment felt speechless. Yeah, he could do it, but— "Not on purpose." He shook his head. "This dirt; it's pretty sandy. I don't know. If it don't kill me—"

"A short jump then. Best way to go."

"—I'll just look silly."

"We got no other options."

"We can do a T-bone. That Monza—"

"Ian said no."

"But *look* at this track. I mean, just *look*."

And so they continued, Grace doing her best to sell the bike jump to Nick, who ordinarily wanted the limelight, and Nick doing his best to sell Grace on the notion that a bike jump finale was a bad idea.

It took a while before Nick noticed that Grace had gone stubborn. Her lips had gone knife-thin, her stance belligerent, challenging. She was a rock and wouldn't be moved. Reminded Nick of Ian when he got pissed.

Reminded Nick that she was Hanna's mother, and he couldn't figure out Hanna either.

As he realized Grace wouldn't budge, was getting pissed off at Nick, he felt himself getting pissed off right back.

At that realization, he hesitated, sighed, pasted on a smile, hoping Grace hadn't sensed his anger, and gave in. Or professed to.

"Okay," he said. "I'll do what needs doing. But let's just put out a couple cars, nothing special. Maybe the junkers. Yeah, just the junk. Easier to pack up after if we use junkers instead of our rigs."

Frustration boiled under Nick's smile.

"Good," Grace said, and she turned and walked away.

The show was a disaster before it started. It was to have started at seven, but Ian had long ago learned to wait for fifteen minutes, sometimes twenty, to accommodate stragglers. The wooden grandstands could hold no more than a thousand or so, fewer than half what they'd counted on at the fairgrounds, but at 7:25, the stands were less than a quarter full, maybe fewer than two hundred people. Radar stood in the middle of the front stretch with microphone in hand, ready to go, and the crew milled about, restless.

Grace sent PR to check with the track owner, who was under the grandstands, in his little office next to the ticket booth.

PR came back in a few minutes to report there had been a crash that blocked the long two-lane access road to the track, and traffic had been slowed to a single lane squeaking through.

"They say it's backed up a mile or so," he said, panting. "Nasty accident, they say. I don't know, maybe we should—" He shrugged. "Cancel?"

"What? You got us this contract, PR." She gave him a loaded look, and PR looked as if he'd rather be anywhere else.

"They're selling beer in the concession stands," he said.

"Cancel?" Grace frowned.

Nick translated in his mind: *If we cancel, this crowd could get ugly.*

Grace chewed on the thought for a while, jaw muscle twitching, and nobody spoke.

People trickled into the stands in groups of three and four, Steppenwolf's "Born to Be Wild" blaring from Radar's sound system counterpunched by the occasional indistinct yell of male voices and tinny radios. Many in the stands carried plastic beer mugs and big coolers; they seemed to be a tad more rowdy than normal for so early.

"What would Ian—" Grace muttered to herself; Nick barely heard her. Then she suddenly brightened, and said, "Let's go."

She addressed the crew, gathered in a loose huddle at the infield edge of the front stretch. "Get out there and do the best you can. Make Ian proud. But don't lollygag. We do the minimum—one hour; it's in the contract— and move on. Use the short gags, Boo. Radar, keep it snappy. BB, Hanna, one roll each, good ones the first time. One lap on the head-on, Tink, and hit it hard. Flynn, blow the chair on the first count and get up; no heroics. Nick, we'll see what we have for time after the intermission—and we'll do a short intermission; just ten minutes, Radar. Maybe we'll skip the wheelies, or just do one pass. We're lining up the junk for the finale, Nick's idea, so we'll load quicker. Everybody, get ready to pack fast."

Grace looked at each of them one by one. "Make it good, but make it quick. I don't like the look of this crowd, but we're here to do show and that's what we're going to do."

They left the huddle with a communal shout of grit and determination like they were going into the kickoff of the Rose Bowl.

Radar started the show with all the enthusiasm he could muster and the show got underway. Three minutes later, Hanna's car lugged in the hell driving sequence and Grace, inches behind her, smashed out the front lights of her Mav against Hanna's rear. Quite a few members of the audience applauded and howled with laughter as shards of glass splattered across the track with the impact.

The hay-burners would be pissed, the crew would have a hell of a time picking up the glass, but what bothered Nick more was that the accident embarrassed Hanna. Nick wanted to go up into the grandstands and beat the hell out of one particularly loud, drunk group of four men.

Fucking rednecks.

Instead, he bunched his fists and moved on. The entire crew looked grim. Nick felt certain that, like him, they wanted to go up into the stands and kick ass.

Joel slipped and fell off the side of the carrier during intermission, hitting his head so hard he lost consciousness. The EMTs loaded Joel on a stretcher and the crowd, which had by now grown so big it overflowed the grandstands—people sat on the fence behind the backstretch, and atop the grader and Cat which had been moved back before the show—howled and yipped in barbaric, drunken delight as the ambulance crew bent over Joel.

Before she climbed in the back of the ambulance, Grace pulled Nick, Hanna, Tink and Radar aside. "Hanna, you're in charge. Do your best."

Grace stood close to them in a huddle, shouting above the noise of the intermission rock and roll music—Rolling Stones, "19th Nervous Breakdown"—amplified from Radar's sound system, and a stereo tinnily competing from the grandstands, Steve Miller, "Living in the USA" and a lot of shouting and booing.

She gripped Nick's arm. "Finish this as best you can." Her grip was iron, her jaw set, her face pale. "I trust you—"

The ambulance siren whooped unnecessarily.

"What?" Nick said.

Grace yelled to Nick, inches from his face.

And Nick thought she said: "Do the T-bone." So he thought.

The Monza stalled and came to a shuddering, inglorious halt in the backstretch in its last lap before the jump and Nick cursed a blue streak as he sat behind the wheel helplessly trying to crank the dead engine, slamming his fist into the dashboard. Tink and Hoppy and Flynn sprinted the distance across the infield from their position next to the catch cars to try to get it started, but it was no good.

Nick couldn't hear, but he could see the crowd in the grandstand finally mutating into the mob that had been festering all day. A dozen or so men oozed through the flag stand gate and stood on the front stretch. It looked as if they were threatening Radar, who stood a few feet away from them across the front stretch. Nick couldn't hear Radar, whose echoey cadence sounded way off, but the little guy looked scared, even from behind, even at this distance.

Nick turned to see a few—too many—rowdy, drunk guys climbing down off the back fence, stalking across the backstretch toward him with the demeanor of a lynch mob. Nick undid his seatbelt and climbed out the car window.

The notion of getting out the Yamaha to do a bike jump finale flitted across Nick's mind, then flew away. Too late.

Hanna yelled something to the group at the Monza, waving her hand in the air. A clear signal: *Let's get the hell out of here.*

She quickly joined Boo as they hooked up the sound van and the trailer on the infield. Radar had dropped any pretense that there was still a show to announce and he'd tossed his microphone and cord into the van's side door. The speakers squealed; he hadn't even turned off the mike. He ran across the track to help PR who was tossing gear haphazardly onto the back of the carrier, just shoveling it aboard.

Hoppy and Flynn cursed over the hot, smoky, stubborn Monza engine, but not as vehemently as Tink. Nick stood by helplessly as the three men worked frantically, refusing to give up. Hanna waved again from the infield by the van.

"You're going to T-bone the Monza, right?" Tink had asked Nick after the ambulance had left with Grace and Joel. The Monza was Tink's baby. He'd made it run; now he'd see it fly.

Nick had hesitated, but only a second. There was only one answer to the look in Tink's eyes. "Of course," Nick had said.

A siren wailed somewhere, and two police cars drove onto the back-stretch through the rear gate. Police on foot came onto the track from the grandstand. People milled about, shouting.

Nick grabbed Tink's arm. "I think Hanna wants us to—"

"No, I can fix—"

"God*dam* it, Tink!" Flynn this time, jerking Tink away from the engine. "Look around you!"

A full-blown riot seemed in the making in the arena confines, with the Ian McGinnis Auto Daredevil Thrill Show right in the middle. The crew packed up to get on the road faster than ever before.

They left behind the seatbelt in the Monza, left it and a handful of new tools and the junkers where they were, packed up, and got on the road in twelve minutes, a new record.

CHAPTER TWENTY-EIGHT

As he flew back to the show, now in Lincoln, Nebraska, Ian toyed with different versions of revenge on Trigger for his monumental screwuppery.

He could tell Trigger that he, Trigger, could do a T-bone—and get it right this time—in about two weeks, which would put them in Minneapolis, a big show, then pull the rug out from under him at the last minute, which is what he'd planned to do as far back as Portland. That thought came first to his mind, and he set it aside, to come back to later, if no better option reared.

He could set up a T-bone in the Twin Cities, then rig the jump car so that it failed in the backstretch, or sputtered and died on the take-off ramp. But no. If there was the slightest chance that tinkering with the jump car might end up hurting a driver—even Trigger—Ian wouldn't do it. Junk was unpredictable enough anyway.

He could tell Trigger that there would be no T-bone at all, ever, anymore. Nobody did T-bone crashes anymore anyway. It was too dangerous with today's tin-can cars, and too costly given the number of shows booked. If a guy kept doing T-bone crash after T-bone crash, the odds favored a major injury sooner or later. Abandoning the T-bone was the logical thing to do.

Or he could simply fire the fair-haired star-boy. Give him a check and toss his bags out on the backstretch. This last option boiled in Ian's stomach; his lunch, wolfed just before take-off in Salt Lake City, went down like a rock.

Before the hired jet landed at Lincoln Municipal Airport, Ian had decided on a satisfying strategy. He wouldn't fire Trigger. That would always be a final option, and he'd make sure Trigger was aware of it. He wouldn't avoid doing T-bones either. Grace was right on that, and so was PR. There was too much media pressure to do it.

In fact, Ian planned to make it clear that there would be a half dozen or more T-bone crashes in the remainder of the season. They'd take place in the most obscure dates, tiny towns like Alliance and Sidney in western Nebraska, dates that Ian had set up before PR came on board with more significant bookings. Dates with bad, cramped tracks, rickety grandstands, small crowds, and little media. He would select afternoon shows for the T-bones, and do them on the second leg of back-to-back gigs. And—the point—he, Ian, would do them all.

Now and then, Ian would set up a T-bone at a show, then at the last minute, cancel it, blaming a bad car, a bad track, or whatever, then go for a motorcycle jump finale. Trigger would never know what to expect. It would drive him crazy.

Trigger could watch, frustrated, as Ian did T-bone crash after T-bone crash, and do them in such a manner that they were almost private events. Ian would shove it in Trigger's face: you ain't got the right stuff.

And if glamour boy gave him any shit, he'd fire him.

PR met him at the airport in the road Mav. Grace, he explained, was with Hanna and Joel at a TV interview, a local station news program. PR looked haggard, his dark-rimmed eyes reminding him of Shaun's a few hours before. He'd been busy.

Joel was okay. His injury has actually been minor and the hospital released him the next morning, a goose-egg lump on his forehead.

"I'm trying to bury Kansas City," PR said. Ian drove—he needed to, for the calming effect—while PR fiddled with the radio, looking for mention of the show on an Omaha all-news station, and listening for their radio ads on Lincoln stations. "We took a black eye there, PR-wise, lots of paperwork we're doing still—you don't want to know."

"I want to know." Ian wanted to let the disaster wash over him, go numb under the impact, and emerge calm and resolute. "Tell me."

"Where to start? There was a fistfight. Or two. Somebody took a hammer or something to one of the hell-driving cars, smashed the windshield. We're paying for some torn fence at the track. We kept a few cops busy before we got loaded up. Twelve minutes; did Grace tell you? We have two lawsuits pending—nothing for you to worry about, but our lawyers, Landini Tires' lawyers, they'll earn their keep."

"A fight? Anybody in the crew involved?"

"Couple of fights. No, we were too busy getting the hell out of there. I'm told that nobody got hurt. It just looked bad is all."

"Cops involved, huh."

"I also hear that there were no arrests. That'll work well for us."

"What else?"

As they drove through the blistering heat, the air almost too syrupy thick to breath, air conditioner set on high, whining in protest, Ian heard it all, the unfettered details.

The heat, the bad track, the accident on the access road, the late start. The drinking. Tink's Monza. Joel.

Trigger had thought he'd heard Grace say do a T-bone, but there'd been a lot of confusion, and Grace said she didn't say that at all, but she was stressed, worried about Joel, so she didn't remember, clearly, exactly what she'd said. So she'd told Ian on the phone.

PR had screwed up in not canceling the show after finding out that the fairgrounds had been closed.

"The wrong facility," Ian muttered.

"Yeah, I guess."

Ian concluded that Grace had done all she could to keep things under control, that Hanna had as well, and so had PR, given the circumstances. That was his rational side speaking. It still didn't stop him from being pissed off.

Joel would get his share of scolding for climbing on the carrier when he probably knew he shouldn't have. Ian resolved to have a talk with Tink; he'd practically insisted that Nick use the Monza to crash.

And Hanna, after Grace put her in charge of the show, should have put her foot down, insisted on the bike jump finale.

They'd failed sure, his own kids, and so had PR, but the real fault was with Trigger. Grace had told Nick, distinctly, before she took off with Joel, "No T-bone." But Nick had begun agitating for it before the ambulance had cleared the gate—*Hell, he'd been after it since day one*—and it looked as if he'd deliberately tried to avoid Hanna's authority, tried to take over the show.

"It's like they turned on us," PR said. "That crowd. I don't know what happened."

"I've seen it. It ain't pretty. Is there anything more?"

There was, and Ian insisted on hearing it all. Radar had dropped his microphone during hell driving and it broke and he had to dig out the back-up mike from the van. Boo couldn't find the hole for the flying rabbit gag and the gag fell flat and he got booed. An older woman in the audience fainted right after the dynamite chair and paramedics took her away. Intermission dragged on too long what with Joel's accident.

Ian finally summed up PR's narrative to a lack of authority.

"If I'd been there," he started, but got no further. Grace had no doubt done all she could, as had Hanna when Grace told her to take over. Joel was just a kid and who could blame Tink for getting excited when he did a good job fixing a car? That was what he was supposed to do.

But Trigger. Taking over? Who the hell did he think he was trying to impress?

They arrived at the stock car track, a broad, spacious dirt oval south of town, with shiny new stadium seating, the seats painted a glistening white. The crew was washing equipment in the infield and Ian took a moment to brief them about Gran. They took the news with somber nods. Then they went back to work, shirtless in the blast furnace heat.

Ian gave Trigger a "we need to talk" nod and walked away from the crew, toward the grandstands. Trigger followed, drew up to his side as they crossed the front straightaway.

"You screwed up," Ian said, not looking at Trigger.

"A lot went wrong, Ian," Trigger said. "Hell, even the weather went against us. Did you hear about that car wreck?"

"I'm not blaming you for the weather. But that T-bone." Ian stopped, put his hands on his hips and wagged his head, eyeing a scrap of metal embedded in the hard-packed clay in the middle of the track. "I distinctly recall telling Grace that the stunt was cancelled." He bent to dig out the metal fragment.

"I honest to god thought she said—"

"No T-bone," Ian said. "That's what she said." He stood and tossed the metal chunk, a fractured brake pad, to the infield.

"Look, Ian, I know you're pissed—"

"You don't know the half of it."

"—and I guess you deserve to be. I messed up, and I'm sorry. Hanna was working on the front stretch, doing what she could to keep the show going, working with Radar and Boo. Me and Tink and Flynn, we were working the stunts, moving the junk around, keeping things going, and I thought—" Trigger sighed. "Well, I thought what I thought. And I was wrong. Again. I'm really, really sorry."

Ian looked at him at last. Trigger did look contrite. There was no swagger in his stance, no sugar in his tone. His face looked drained of energy, saggy. Ian looked for any sign of deceit but found none. Trigger even had the makings of tears in his eyes.

But Ian had spent energy building up his rage and it wasn't to be casually dismissed. "Sorry?" he said with as much venom as he could muster. "Sorry? You? What are you sorry about? What exactly? Tell me." *Give me more ammunition, even if I don't really need it.*

"About the T-bone." Trigger held Ian's menacing gaze. "About getting ahead of myself, trying to do too much, about getting it wrong, not understanding what Grace was saying. I know she's upset. And Hanna, she—"

He looked Ian in the eye. "I'm really, really sorry, Ian. Believe me. I'm. Really. Sorry."

Ian tried to hear the tone of voice that made what Trigger said a lie, tried to see it in Trigger's stricken face, but it didn't show. For an instant, Ian felt a pang of sympathy. He'd seen that stricken look before, recently, on his family and friends, and in the mirror at the motel near the hospital in Salt Lake City.

Then Trigger broke the spell when he said, "And I'm sorry about Gran too. I loved her too. We all loved—"

"What?" It was all Ian could do to keep from punching Trigger where he stood. "What?"

Trigger pulled his shoulders back, a defensive posture, and his eyes widened. "Gran, she—"

"Shut up about her," Ian said. Menace coated Ian's quiet voice like venom. "Now, here's what's going to happen. Listen. Don't talk. Just listen."

And Ian told him there would be a T-bone crash, tomorrow night, right here in Lincoln. No motorcycle jump. Ian would do the crash.

Then Ian went to check out the junkers, pick his jump car.

No, not Trigger's fault. Mine. I should have been here. My fault, all mine.

CHAPTER TWENTY-NINE

*T*he Lincoln show went well enough. Good crowd, nobody got hurt, the stunts went well, no equipment damaged. Trigger behaved professionally, at least in the public eye.

The show moved on, up the river, so to speak, heading east through Missouri and into Illinois and Wisconsin, winding its way toward the Twin Cities. Ian did several T-bone crashes but he couldn't do them all. At Rockford, there had been a motocross a week before the show arrived. Some local amateur had wowed the crowd with a big jump, thirteen cars in the cramped speedway. It was a challenge and Ian met it. Trigger jumped fourteen cars, reasserting the show's dominance as the number one stunt show in America, or so PR said to the local media.

It rained out in Duluth.

Minneapolis demanded a full show, all the whistles and bells, so Trigger did a bike jump and Ian did a T-bone. This time, the Tire Jump went without a hitch. PR had figured out how to stack rubber so that the stack didn't explode like a giant popcorn ball when a car hit it. The B-S jump car was put on display on a special Landini Tires trailer.

Ian learned that PR was talking to Mattel about a motorized plastic model of the car and the jump. "But only if everything goes okay with the jump," he said. "They don't want to get behind a failure, or somebody getting hurt."

Ian understood.

But he thought PR had mentioned the Mattel talks as a salve for Ian's scorched ego. That Ian was in a blue funk since Lincoln—since Gran's stroke in the spring, actually—had become obvious. Ian felt the funk on his shoulders, weighing him down like a broken collarbone. But he felt powerless to do anything about it.

He called home daily. Gran had recovered, some, enough to insist she be let out of the hospital and sent home. That, according to doctors, was not a good idea. She needed full-time care, doctors said, which meant immediate access to a hospital. A compromise was reached and Gran went to live in a private nursing home next to the county hospital in Rock Springs. She had her own apartment there, but Shaun reported that it grated on her, and Gran faded in and out, sometimes seeming like she wasn't all there. Gran was sad, Amanda told Ian, and she was most often incoherent, and getting frailer all the time. She couldn't walk, couldn't feed herself, couldn't go to the bathroom without help.

When she was coherent, she cursed like a miner, and often cried inconsolably. Then she'd lapse back into a semi-catatonic state and just sit or lie helpless as a rag doll.

Shaun stayed at Gran's side as often as he could. The tire store gave him a long rope—everybody loved Gran. Shaun had given himself the job of being her primary care provider—or her chief mother hen, rather, since there was little he could do to help her when it came to maintaining her bodily functions or monitoring her frail condition. Nurses took care of that. Shaun provided family as around-the-clock as he could, and as doggedly as only Shaun could do, as nobody else but him could do.

"She woke up last night," Shaun told Ian when he called after the Duluth show rained out. "Talked with me like nothing happened, asking about Beauty, about the garden, her peas, the orchard, the family." Shaun's voice sounded rusty, raw. "'How's Ian?' she asked. 'How's Amanda? How's the baby?' I don't know if I should tell her Amanda's not pregnant after all." Shaun hadn't slept, Ian knew. He could hear it. He'd been there.

"Then she asked—" Shaun stopped, cleared something out of his throat. "Then she asked if I was ready. Ready to show yet."

Ian wanted to ask himself, wanted Shaun with him, now more than ever, but he didn't dare ask. If he asked, Ian knew, it would tear Shaun apart—stay with Gran or go on the road with the show and Uncle Ian? Which?

Ian would never put Shaun through that grinder. Shaun was in enough pain as it was. So was Ian.

"So" Ian asked, "how is she now?"

Big sigh. "Asleep. Or unconscious. I don't understand it, Ian, but sometimes, it's like she's here, the old Gran we all know and love, and sometimes it seems like she isn't—isn't—"

"Yeah, I know." But he didn't.

After Minneapolis, in a three-day gap before the next show, in Bemidji, Ian flew with PR down to Phoenix for a test of the re-designed loop-the-loop ramp. This time, a company of rent-a-cops patrolled the fence to keep media out, and there were plenty of media trying to get in.

A hundred cars and a half dozen TV satellite vans parked by the front gate, telephoto lens focused, as if they were watching a satellite launch at Cape Kennedy. One local station broadcast live reports.

The media view of the stunt was partly blocked by the stadium seating already set up flanking the loop ramp, which now extended a whopping hundred and fifty feet at its highest point. Two huge round banners had been created with the Landini Tire logos on them, placed in the center of the loop, in such a way that observers could still see the jump car drive through the ramp. Four huge screens, like drive-in movie screens, were being erected at the four ends of the grandstands, so that wherever anybody sat, they could see on one of the screens, the view through one of many cameras strategically placed to broadcast to the screens a scene a spectator might not otherwise be able to see. So, those sitting in the stands at the near end, with a good view of the loop itself, were too far away to see the landing, but they had a screen right in front of them focused on the landing. Others, sitting in front of where the landing would be, had a screen they could watch that would focus on the loop.

A camera was mounted at the far end of the approach way, a hard-packed and well-graded clay roadway that started inside the gate itself, and would give all spectators a view of the car as it started toward the loop. Another camera, this one shoulder-mounted, would get close-ups of Ian as he prepared for the stunt.

Before he took off, Ian would give a speech from a wooden podium just under the end lip of the take-off loop, which would be elevated at the time to clear twenty Landini Tires delivery trucks parked side by side. For now, the takeoff ramp was flat and Ian would drive off the ramp into a series of rope mesh barriers, where, so the plan went, he would be stopped quickly but gently and without injury to him or damage to the car.

Still, PR had hired a private company to film the event for possible future use. Maybe some of the film would be leaked before the event, or maybe PR would just let rumor and word of mouth generate interest.

Ian understood the private—rather, the *secret*—nature of the event was not only to forestall possible adverse publicity if "something went wrong," but also to whet the media appetite.

"I've scheduled a press conference at the front gate," he told Ian as they looked over the ramp. "Do you understand what I want you to do?"

"You'd better tell me," Ian said. This was PR's show, and Ian understood that not only what he said but how he said it was significant. But, for the moment, Ian wasn't sure if PR wanted him to reveal any aspects of the stunt, or which ones, or what attitude he was to project, for PR purposes.

"You're the happiest daredevil in the world," PR told him. "You've thoroughly inspected the ramp and you chose the car personally—of course, this is a back-up car, not the one you chose, but you get the idea. Anyway, you can hint that there are some problems to be resolved—in fact, I hope it comes up. We want that hint of uncertainty there. But in the main, you're pickled tink that everything—"

"Pickled tink?"

"What? What did I say?"

"Never mind." Ian laughed, and realized that this was the first time he'd really laughed since Gran's heart attack days ago. He wondered if PR hadn't made the mistake in an attempt to get a smile out of Ian, whose grimness had put a damper on show and crew. Which made Ian smile even more.

The crew was spending two days lollygagging in central Minnesota, shopping, taking in movies, trying to pick up girls, relaxing, and away from ol' Mr. Gloomy Himself. Flying to Phoenix for the B-S test session had subsidiary benefits. And, Ian thought, maybe the disposition Ian was to present to the media later in the day, after the test—and just before the five o'clock news, of course—was also part of PR's attempt to liven Ian's mood.

Ian laughed aloud. Whatever. It worked.

The jump car was a near duplicate of the car Ian had selected in Dallas for the final B-S. It was a lot more powerful than the Mustang he'd flown in earlier, but that was a good thing now. The loop ramp was higher and longer, and Ian expected he'd be able to clear the twenty trucks easily.

Even so, the trucks were parked in such a way that, if he fell short, as long as he was upright and not twisted or nose-heavy, he'd bounce off the last truck box and hit the tire pyramid okay. They'd secretly reinforced the roofs of the last two trucks, just in case, with extra sheet metal and roll bars, so that if Ian did fall short, the trucks wouldn't collapse under him and he'd bounce off them.

The massive loop ramp had been reinforced with a spidery maze of cables, anchored to spikes driven deep into the ground. There were thirty-eight wires—sixteen on each side, and four in front and after the ramp.

"We can adjust the tension of each wire," Cartwright told Ian as he inspected the set-up. "We have a system rigged that will record the give on each wire as your car passes up and over the ramp." Again, Ian noticed how Cartwright talked half to him and half to the camera, recording for posterity, and later profit. "We'll have data," he tapped one of a bank of machines lining a table under a long open-walled tent, where wires criss-crossed like tangled snakes, "on each wire, one wire to a machine." The machines looked like seismographs, or polygraphs, wires etching a piece of paper on a roll. "We'll analyze the data and adjust each wire to maximum tolerance, tension, and stress."

"How's it work?" Ian asked, but didn't really listen. The whole thing was for show anyway, including his question. Cartwright needed his moment on film, and Ian knew it was the place to ask the question. He didn't listen, but that was okay too. He didn't understand what Cartwright was saying anyway.

The ramp floor was made of thin-looking sheets of punched aluminum, cross-corrugated and bolted in place. The ramp was slightly narrower than before and rounded at the guardrail. Rather than an abrupt edge at the guard-rail sides, those sides rose gradually to the vertical. If the jump car strayed off the straight and true, the rounded, raised sides would gently guide the car back. The guardrail was made of double-meshed chain link and rose to Ian's thighs.

The test went well enough. Ian found a rut in the approach lane that needed to be graded out. He made subtle suggestions regarding the place-ment of the guardrail at the approach end, and he suggested possible camera angles. He reported one of the floor plates felt loose. One of Cartwright's students found the loose bolt and tightened it. The college students then swarmed over the ramp, on ladders and cherry-pickers, checking bolts and tie-downs.

The test took place at three p.m. A TV helicopter got some tantalizing but indistinct footage, and Phoenix couch potatoes got a distant glimpse of the stunt from a roadside camera. Bad angle and wavery in the heat, but news.

Ian stood before a bank of microphones at about five after five. He answered questions in his by-now well-known aw-shucks country manner for about a half hour. He was his charming self of old and the media loved it.

He gave his standard answer to the expected question, "Why do you do it?"

But one question surprised him. "Are you going to retire after this stunt?"

"Retire?" Ian hummed and hawed for a moment before PR bailed him out.

"A daredevil focuses on now," PR said. "Later—well, we worry about later—later." Much to Ian's relief, PR then quickly ended the session.

"We have a show to do tomorrow in Bemidji," PR said to the disappointed reporters, still shouting questions as he left the platform, "and a few more before we come back to Phoenix on September second for the loop-the-loop jump. We're focused on today, not next week."

They flew back to Minnesota. Ian had called Shaun from the airport before they took off and talked for a minute with Gran, one of her few and infrequent lucid moments. When they landed, Grace and Hanna were waiting for them in the road car. Ian felt good. He'd forgotten the annoying question about retirement, he'd had plenty of rest, and the test had gone okay. Gran was okay for the moment, and at least for the moment, he didn't hurt anywhere.

Ian did a car carrier jump in Bemidji. He landed wrong, flipped the jump car, hit the ground hard, and cracked his sternum. Grace had to drive the rig to Grand Forks that night.

Two weeks later, on August second, the afternoon before the show in Williston, North Dakota, in a radio interview, PR announced that there would be a double loop-the-loop jump.

"Ian and another daredevil will both do the loop-the-loop jump in Phoenix," PR said. "Simultaneously."

CHAPTER THIRTY

*T*he night after the Bemidji show, the crew showed at the Grand Forks, North Dakota county fairgrounds. After they parked the rigs on the track infield that morning, Grace approached Nick as he checked his bike in its rack on the car carrier.

"What's this?" Nick asked as Grace handed him a birthday card.

"Sign it. It's for Hanna."

Nick read the card. "She's—twenty?"

"Uh-huh."

"Today?"

"Uh-huh. I deducted five bucks from your wages for a gift. I hope you don't mind."

"Sure." Nick signed the card. "S'okay."

"We'll do a thing at supper, as usual."

There had been three birthdays on the road so far: Hoppy, Boo and Flynn. None of the three had seemed interested in seeing their birthdays remembered, let alone celebrated, but brief parties occurred for each anyway, usually at supper, in truck stops for Hoppy and Boo and at a Denny's for Flynn. Grace tapped everybody's wages five bucks each for a gift—a pair of cowboy boots for Hoppy, a new watch for Boo, and a new jacket for Flynn.

As he watched Grace corner Boo with the card, looking over her shoulder to make sure Hanna didn't see, Nick wondered why it seemed as if those whose birthdays it was seemed less than enthusiastic about it, yet Grace always made a fuss over it, insisting on cake and ice cream and getting the crew to sing "Happy Birthday." He asked Tink about it.

"It's sort of a tradition, I guess," Tink said. He had the hood up on the van and was checking the oil.

"You mean for Grace. But nobody seems like they're excited about it. I mean, Boo and Hoppy—"

"What about you? When's your birthday?"

"Uh—" Nick found it curious that he had to *think* to remember. "January. You?"

"October. I get it that Grace does it because we need to—you know; bond or something, as a crew. Work together and all that. She *is* a mother."

"I'm sure you mean that in the nicest way. So how come nobody wants to have their birthday celebrated? Boo—I knew he could blush like a prom queen, but I didn't think Hoppy and Flynn—"

"Well, how would *you* feel?"

"Huh?"

Tink shrugged, closed the hood. "I guess all that attention, it's embarrassing."

"Yeah, but when it comes showtime—"

"That's different. You know?"

Nick didn't know, and he said nothing.

He wondered what Grace would buy for Hanna on behalf of the crew and wondered what he'd buy for her on his own. Maybe he'd buy a ring.

The thought stopped him cold. What the hell was he thinking? It had been weeks since he'd broken up with Hanna. They'd seldom spoken to each other since, and when they did it was mostly because it was demanded by the show or simple civility. "S'cuse me." "Thank you." "You're welcome." "How are you?" "Fine, thanks."

And never alone, at least never alone long enough to have a real conversation. Whatever heat they'd generated rubbing their legs together had cooled. There was no way to rekindle that flame, he'd decided. Simple as that. Buying her a ring; where the hell did that thought come from?

"Shit," he muttered as he straddled the bike, getting ready to kick-start it.

"You okay?" Hanna said. She stood five feet away.

They were on the track infield unloading. The day was relatively cool with high, whisper-thin clouds. *Some wind gusts, maybe a problem to watch out for later.* Nick had planned to give the Yamaha a spin around the track, tune it up and get a feel for the wide oval they were to work with. With Ian hurting, Nick would do a bike jump finale. The dirt looked as if it had some high and low spots in the first corner that he'd have to watch for. His mind was on the track and the show ahead, so the voice startled him.

Hanna stood there shading her eyes with a hand, her hair fluttering in a cooling breeze. "You okay?"

No, I wasn't thinking about the track or the show. I was thinking about you. And a ring. Figure me that *out.*

"Yeah, I was—um." He sighed. "Look, Hanna, can we talk?"

"Nick, I—"

"Just talk. Your dad says when you bang you knuckles, you swear it out, get it out of your system—"

"Yeah. Okay." Without another word, Hanna straddled the back of the Yamaha and snuggled against him. He gritted his teeth, vowed to himself to not let her warm pressure on his back distract him.

They rode.

Nick took the bike around the track once and then drove out the back gate onto a long straight gravel lane that led north past farm houses and acres of tall, emerald green corn fields. They rode silently, Nick reveling in the cool wind in his face and the feel of a warm woman against his shoulder blades.

After about fifteen minutes, Nick pulled over at Rick and Masie's Gas 'N Gear, a country gas station and general store at a rural crossroads, one gravel lane cutting through corn fields led east-west bisecting the north-south lane they'd been on. "Hommade RootBeer, 50-cents" a hand-painted sign in the window read.

"Thirsty?" Nick asked.

"Uh-huh."

They sat at a picnic table in the shade of a gnarled old elm beside the gas station, sipping ice cold "Hommade RootBeer" from paper cups, and they talked.

"Did you know today's my birthday?" Hanna asked.

"That's supposed to be a secret. Tradition and all that. So you're all grown up now. Daredevil lady."

"And what do *you* want to be when you grow up?" Hanna disarmed the barb with a smile.

"Listen, Hanna—"

"You don't grow if you don't take risks. So what do you—"

"Hanna—"

"Don't worry about it, Nick. Really."

"Huh?"

"Kansas City. In fact, I'm grateful. That is, I think what you did, or tried to do—"

"A wonder your dad didn't fire me."

Hanna laughed. "Dad won't fire you. Not because you mean so much to the show—"

"I don't know about that."

"—but because he's screwed up himself as much or more, and he knows it. There was this one show—" She shook her head and slurped root beer. "Goddam blind, stubborn men."

"Watch your language."

Hanna laughed again. "But I mean it. You tried to help. I saw it. With mom gone, and the way things were—I mean, *I* was over my head. And dad had to get pissed off at *somebody*, mostly himself, really, because he wasn't there to screw things up on his own. You just stuck your neck out is all, and, well, I admire that."

"Yeah, well. Look, what I wanted to talk about. Us."

"Nick—"

"I'm okay. Really."

Pause. "Really?"

"I—I guess I'm just slow is all—"

"You? Trigger? Slow?"

"I mean when it comes to getting along with people."

"With women."

"Whatever. Hanna, I'm okay. Really."

Pause. "Okay."

"Okay?"

"Yeah, okay. Really."

They sat in companionable silence for a long time. There was work to be done back at the track, but Nick was in no hurry.

They reached the bottom of their "Hommade RootBeers" soon enough and saddled up for the return ride.

"How come you don't do wheelies with a passenger?" Hanna asked from the back of the Yamaha. "In the show."

"Because I'm slow? Hadn't thought of it."

"Teamwork, Nick. Think teamwork. Then getting along with people—"

"With women?"

"—it'll come."

Teamwork, Nick thought. Two on a bike. *And what do* you *want to be when you grow up?* A ring. *I admire that.* Birthdays.

Somewhere along the narrow gravel back road between Rick and Masie's Gas 'N Gear and the Grand Forks County Fairgrounds, Nick figured out what he wanted to be when he grew up. Step one was to get PR aside and have a little chat.

CHAPTER THIRTY-ONE

*I*an said nothing during the rest of the radio interview, absolutely nothing. His aw-shucks smile froze into place like concrete, lost all its humor and luster, became a frozen mask. He glared at PR, sitting next to him in the cramped radio station's sound studio. The reporter, an older, be-speckled, wispy man with a paunch, bad breath, and hair combed the wrong way over his bald spot, caught on that there was some tension between PR and Ian and did his best to steer the interview away from the irritant, what-ever it was. Both the reporter's and PR's expertise kept the live program from derailing precipitously, and the half-hour ended with the likelihood intact that no listener detected the tension.

As they got into the car in the radio station parking lot to return to the fairgrounds, Ian driving, PR buckled up and then turned on the radio.

Ian turned it off. "You did it again," he said. He buckled up and drove. "Did it again," he repeated, quietly. He said it as a statement, not an accusa-tion or a challenge. He said it as he drove into traffic, using the tranquility of driving to cool his boiling anger. He said it "that way," a way that by now PR fully understood, so PR would know that he was pissed off and that he would brook no bullshit.

"Didn't matter when I said it, Ian," he said. "You'd be mad about it anyway. I figured you're less likely to kick my butt in public."

"You're only delaying an ass-kicking."

"In the first place, Ian, media interest is flagging. We got a month to go and we're slipping. Not on track. I've talked it over with Saint Louis, and with Cartwright, and we're all agreed. When this gets out—and I have a working plan for this month—we should be back on schedule. Hell, we'll be ahead of schedule, PR-wise."

"PR-wise?"

"Figure of speech. And gate receipts have leveled off. Have you noticed? Grace has. Even before Kansas City. We're not making what we should. Some of these backwoods shows you booked before I came on board are killing us—"

"You keep saying *us*. I keep thinking this is the Ian McGinnis Auto Daredevil Thrill Show. Where did I go wrong?"

"You keep emphasizing teamwork. That's one of the reasons Landini Tires came to you for this campaign. Or have you forgotten? There are other shows out there, remember, but we chose you because you're family-oriented. Teamwork and family. You've seen our ads."

"Teamwork. Me and—who? Who have you hired to do the other side of the loop-the-loop?"

"You—you don't know?" PR sounded genuinely surprised.

"No, I—" but suddenly Ian did.

Trigger.

Somehow Trigger had wormed his way into PR's confidence, talked his way into doing the loop-the-loop. Trigger had tried to get in the spotlight with a T-bone, but that didn't work, so—now this.

The man had balls, Ian gave him that.

"Cassidy will do the jump, of course," PR said.

Ian had found himself in a traffic jam on the highway just a mile from the fairgrounds. There had been an accident up ahead and traffic on the two-lane rural road had come to a halt. Ian stood in line behind a pickup truck loaded down with bales of hay and in front of a big Ford wagon with a smeared, dusty windshield, a pile of suitcases tied down on top, and Oklahoma license plates. There were kids in the car. A dog that looked like Hobo stood on top of the hay bales in the pickup truck, barking at something ahead.

"Whose idea?" It came out rusty and flat, but it was the best Ian could do.

An old man in bib overalls wearing a straw hat walked stiffly by on the edge of the road and said a freight train had hit a tractor on the crossing up ahead.

"Ours," PR said.

"Ours?"

"Yeah. Landini Tires. We've been watching figures closely, I told you. We have a goal, certain target figures, and it was decided that—"

"What does Trigger think of the idea?" Flat-toned, or trying to aim that way. Deep breaths. It was a hot, muggy day.

"Well, we've talked, of course. I thought you'd talked with him too, but—" PR sighed. "He likes it. Wants to do it. He wants to do a T-bone, but I guess you already know about that."

"We've discussed it."

"So you *have* talked, then."

"Not as much as you, I guess."

"Right. I think you should let him do it, by the way," PR said. "The T-bone, I mean. If he's going to do the second leap of the loop-the-loop, he could use the practice. Don't you think?"

"What I think—" Ian let it hang in the humid air. An ambulance screamed by on the edge of the road, raising a dusty tail in the still, heated air, heading toward the railroad tracks beyond the copse of sycamores up ahead by a tall, round grain elevator, like a giant concrete fire hydrant.

"He needs the practice," PR said. "Right? You wouldn't do a stunt without practice, would you? So, he needs practice, so he needs to do a T-bone. Seems right to me, doesn't it to you?"

Yeah, Ian thought, Trigger's been working his charms behind the scenes. Maybe numbers were off, maybe Landini Tires' PR brigade, led by Baha, had come up with the idea. But Trigger had been involved. Involved—at least. Maybe it was his idea in the first place, and now PR thought it was his.

Ian struggled for something to say, found only anger in his voice, and under that, a tiredness he seldom felt. It reminded him of the tiredness he felt when he left Gran to fly back to Lincoln and found Trigger playing cat and mouse with his show.

He sighed, took his hearing aids out of his ears, and tucked them in his pocket. He could hear well enough without them, unless there was extraneous outside noise, and if PR spoke up and enunciated, but PR didn't know that. PR shut up.

The traffic finally cleared, and Ian drove back to the fairgrounds, where he spent the afternoon tuning up the Freightliner's engine, cleaning it, and replacing plugs and wires. Joel and Tink offered to help, but when they saw he wasn't wearing his hearing aids, they left, found something else to do.

Ian waited to talk with Grace. He waited not just because everyone was busy setting up for the Williston show, not because he wanted to be alone with her so he could speak his mind and Grace could speak hers, but because he wanted to distance his anger, numb it. It took him a few days before he brought the subject up.

"Can you think rationally about this?" Grace asked him. They were in the Freightliner, headed south into central Nebraska on Route 83. They had a fair date in Grand Island the next night. Joel snored in the sleeper behind them.

"I'm trying," Ian said. "That's why I'm talking to you."

"So, what do you want? Advice?"

Ian shrugged. "Got any?" He turned the CB down, stifling the hiss, squeak, and chatter on channel nine. Truckers whiling away the late hours swapping shop talk and gossip.

"The show is going stagnant, Ian. Not compared to last year, but compared to what PR wants out of the season. And what we're capable of, if you ask me. I think a double jump is a good idea, in terms of draw. People will go gaga over it."

"And what we got on the table so far—the loop jump and all that—isn't enough?"

"I've been watching the papers, listening to people talk. There was this call-in show, I guess you missed it, back up to Grand Forks. People are already jaded to the idea of the loop." She barked a mirthless laugh. "We haven't even done it yet and people are saying 'big deal.'"

"So maybe I should jump out of an airplane and land in the Grand Canyon."

They drove in silence for a long time.

"I'm uncomfortable with all this, Grace. PR. Baha. Everybody telling me what to do with my show. I know we're getting paid well and all that. And a lot of PR's ideas are good ones, helping a lot—his ad campaign, getting good junk, getting the cars stripped ahead of time, all that. And having Trigger to take some of the load off.

"There's been a time or two when I've woke up, stiff and sore and wondering how I'm going to get into a jump car that evening let alone drive it or jump it and then I realize that I don't have to do a jump tonight because we have this crackerjack motorcycle daredevil in the crew who's just dying for the limelight. Then I grit my teeth when I see him swagger across the grounds like this is *his* show, and I have to look at the signs just to see if they still have my name on them. I wonder, you know? I just wonder."

Another long pause.

"Ian, you got to do what you got to do. You always did. People told you that being a daredevil was a dumb idea. Told you that when they could stop laughing at you. But you showed them. You followed your heart, and you did what you knew you had to do. So do that now. I mean, where's your heart on this? What do you really want to do?"

Long pause.

"I want Shaun," Ian finally said. He didn't know if Grace heard him, but it didn't matter if she did or not.

The daredevil caravan stopped for the night at a truck stop just north of Valentine.

Before turning in, Ian called Shaun.

"Jesus Christ, Ian," Shaun said, voice sleep-soggy. "Do you know what time it is?"

"Too late or too early," Ian said. "I'm not sure which."

"What's in your craw, boss?"

They talked for almost an hour.

Just before the Grand Island show, a local radio station interviewed Ian and PR. And Trigger. Questions about the loop jump came up, as expected, but this time, word about the double jump had spread and the reporter paid more attention to Trigger than to Ian or PR. Ian didn't mind. His heart wasn't in it.

Ian did a car carrier jump that night.

He had a decent enough car to do a T-bone—a peppy '65 Chevy Biscayne sedan—and Ian did little to dissuade anybody from thinking there would be a T-bone finale. But at the last minute, he changed his mind.

He walked around the three junkers that had been used in the show so far, two for the rolls and one for the head-on, kicked the bald and flattened tires, and eyeballed the bent-in roofs, frowning, hands on his hips. "Too weak," he said. "Damn cars are made of tin."

Not good enough as catch cars for a T-bone but good enough for the carrier jump.

The next night, in McCook, there was an interview for the local newspaper, but Ian didn't participate in it. He was busy at the time. Trigger did a motorcycle jump.

A pattern began to emerge in the few days remaining to the 1979 edition of the Ian McGinnis Auto Daredevil Thrill Show, in the days before the last show in Tulsa on August 30, three days before the season's grand finale, the much-publicized and long-awaited world record-setting double loop-the-loop car jump in Phoenix. At first, a casual observer might have believed it was all arbitrary, casual, unplanned—that there was no pattern.

The crew had begun to anticipate a T-bone jump sometime before the season ended with much the same eagerness that the media and public anticipated the loop jump. But the catch cars were wrong, then the jump car was wrong, then it was the track, then the weather. In some cases, Ian would decide to do a carrier jump himself, and in others, he opted for the motorcycle jump. A careful observer would have noticed that he more often opted for the motorcycle jump in those last days after Trigger had been involved in a glittery interview, particularly if it involved TV.

On Sunday, August 19, the show set up in Pueblo, Colorado. That morning, from a distance across the fairgrounds track infield, Ian watched Nick and Hanna talking as Nick fiddled with his bike. Something about the way they talked—

It reminded Ian of the way Ian first saw them talking so intimately in the dark after the Spanaway show. That was the day, Ian now recalled, that he first discussed the T-bone with Nick. The damn stunt had been a bone is Ian's craw since.

Ian heard Hanna's tinkling laugh across the distance, but her words and Nick's got lost in a gust of wind. The two were smiling, talking casually, Hanna with her arms folded across her chest, feet apart, facing Nick, who knelt facing away from Hanna, facing his bike, doing something to the engine. They weren't touching, but Ian still felt a chill.

Ian looked at the carrier side where the show logo was painted, then barked a laugh.

"Pardon?" Boo stood nearby; Ian hadn't noticed.

"I actually looked to see." Ian pointed. "Tell me what that sign says."

"Pardon?"

"Never mind."

Pressure from media and the public for a T-bone had been unrelenting to be sure, but it also came from the crew, where Ian's avoidance pattern was becoming more obvious. Tink seemed most annoyed—*if that's the right word*—with Ian's behavior about the T-bone. Tink would do his under-the-hood magic to raise a rusted old dead-stick to the status of a jump car, then display it to Ian and say things like, "How about *this* car, boss? Think it'll fly?" Tink did it show after show, as if it were a personal

challenge to elevate junk to T-bone jump car status. When Ian sensed Tink
going pouty over Ian's refusal to anoint the resurrected car for the T-bone,
Ian used the piece for his carrier jump car, which seemed to assuage Tink's
ego. Some.

Ian made it a point of announcing during an on-site TV interview an
hour before the show that there would be a T-bone crash that evening. That
was about all he said during the interview, which concentrated on Trigger, the new kid on the block, the fair-haired heir apparent to daredevil
glory, who talked with stunning charm and appropriate humbleness about
the coming loop jump.

Ian enjoyed the reaction that his announcement about doing the T-bone
caused. Grace gave him a "What are you up to now?" look. Trigger tried
his best to restrain his anxiousness, did his best to avoid saying "You're going to let me do this, right?" Tink smiled and said little, but it was clear to
Ian that he felt elated. The other members of the crew watched a scriptless
drama play out, not knowing, really, that there really was a drama going on
behind the scenes. Ian knew the script, how it all came out, and that gave
him great, if perverse, joy.

The time for the jump arrived, and Trigger, right up to the last minute,
still didn't know if he was going to do it or if Ian was. As Ian put on his
helmet, Trigger's attempts to hide his crestfallen look gave Ian grim satisfaction. Hanna's look was unreadable. Grace looked pissed.

Ian got into the car, a '72 Dodge Coronet sedan, and revved the engine.
Smoke billowed up from the rusty muffler. Ian listened for Radar's spiel,
and when he got his introduction, he moved the car out onto the track,
where he waved to the crowd out the window.

Then he waved Boo over to the car. "Tell Trigger I want to talk to him."

"Now?"

"Read the goddam sign, Boo, and get your little ass in gear."

Boo ran off toward the catch cars where Trigger and the rest of the
crew were getting into their positions—the safety crew—little legs churn-
ing, waving his stubby arms.

In a moment, Trigger came running over. Radar filled in the stall in the
action, talking about "crew safety, last minute details, the professional daredevils taking care to see that blah, blah, blah," in his hushed, tense, excited
tones, as Ian motioned Trigger closer.

Trigger bent to put his head partway through the driver's side of the jump car, a puzzled, apprehensive look on his face, behind his charming smile.

"Cassidy, I want you to stew on this," Ian said. *I know I have, long enough.* "I would have done it earlier, so you could stew on it longer, eat your greedy, flashy little heart out, but the time didn't seem right." He gunned the engine, so Trigger had to lean closer to hear.

"It does now. I want you to watch this stunt close, because it's the last T-bone you'll ever see." He took the hearing aids out of his ears. "I ain't going to do another and neither are you. But I'm not going to tell anybody else that. Let them think what they want. This is my show, got my name on it, and this is the way I do it.

"Enjoy." He tucked the hearing aids in his shirt pocket. "I know I will."

Before Trigger could react, Ian gunned the engine, waved to the crowd, and sped out.

CHAPTER THIRTY-TWO

Doctors had earlier given Gran near zero chance of recovering, or dying before dawn, but she clung to life if not always to consciousness. Her condition hadn't improved noticeably in the weeks since the heart attack. She could still die any minute, doctors candidly advised the family. Shaun told the rest of the world to take a hike, and he made a home at her bedside. There could come a phone call any time, Ian knew. He began to dread the sound of phones ringing.

The show traveled through western Oklahoma and the Texas panhandle and a brief swing back up into Kansas, a number of big and small dates, stock car race tracks and fairgrounds, some back-to-back, a couple of deadly hot afternoon shows, a few dates Ian had gotten before PR came on the scene, others PR had booked to fill in gaps. There was a rain out in Lawton, Oklahoma—in fact, it was a massive hailstorm—and BB broke her little finger in a botched rollover in Liberal, Kansas. A drunk driver smashed into the side of the carrier at a truck stop outside Oklahoma City. Nobody hurt. Boo ate a bad taco at the truck stop and stumbled, pale and weak, through the Oklahoma City show, throwing up behind the van between stunts.

Ian taunted Trigger as he hinted in show after show that there might be a T-bone tonight—gee, you never know, though, when conditions make it impossible, but you might see one, we'll just have to wait and see, won't we, folks?

Sometimes Ian did the car carrier jump, but most often, Trigger took the limelight doing a motorcycle jump finale.

And so it went until the show arrived in Tulsa.

As the last show of the regular season, and as a PR appetizer for the B-S in Phoenix, PR wanted an all-out show. Car carrier jump, motorcycle jump, a big tire pyramid jump. The works.

"And how about a T-bone, Ian? Come on, it's the last chance. We have to do a T-bone tonight, don't we?"

"Yeah, Ian," Trigger said. "Last chance."

Ian couldn't read Trigger's expression when he said that. And that worried him.

The crew was sitting at picnic tables near the concession booths underneath the grandstands eating a lunch of burgers, Cokes, shakes, and fries that Grace and Hanna had fetched from town. Puffball clouds spotted the sky, offering neither much shade nor much threat of rain. A sputtery breeze stirred the plastic used car lot flags that lined the wooden concession booths and cooled the dirty, sweaty crew.

Ian detected a vague grumbling from the crew that sounded in general agreement with PR and Trigger. He took that as his cue and ran with it.

"So y'all want to see another T-bone?" he said, mouth full of burger. "Dangerous stunt. A guy could get hurt."

"A guy could have three days to recover," PR said, "before the B-S in Phoenix. Right?"

Nobody said anything. They looked weary, as if waiting for somebody else to take the lead.

"And the track looks okay, Ian," PR persisted, "doesn't it? Plenty of room. And that jump car—it's a hummer." They had a '63 Olds F-85. It ran well, had good metal all around.

"It's up to us, isn't it?" Ian said. "Tink?"

"You do what you want." Tink shrugged. "I ain't going to be doing it, so—" Ian noticed Tink exchanged a look—something odd about that look—with Trigger.

"BB? Radar?" Shrugs and vague, non-committal responses. Ian went around the table. "Hoppy? Boo? Flynn? Joel?"

Grace and Hanna were at the trailer, laying out uniforms and sorting mail.

Then: "Trigger? What do you think? Think we ought to do a T-bone crash tonight?"

Trigger nodded, not meeting Ian's gaze. He exchanged a quick look with Tink, started to say something, then bit into his burger, and nodded again.

"Okay," Ian said. "Let's do a T-bone tonight. PR, if you've got any interviews planned—"

"I don't have any more planned for this afternoon," PR said, standing, wiping his chin, "but I can arrange something." He stood and hustled off to a nearby payphone. "You're doing the right thing, Ian," he said over his shoulder.

In the few hours remaining before showtime, word about the T-bone crash that would be the show's grand finale spread like wildfire. Ian was astonished at the level of excitement among the crew, the media, and ticket-buyers. PR's magic again.

People started arriving earlier than usual.

"Where's that T-bone thing going to be?" one man with a baby in one arm and his wife on the other asked from the grandstands. "Down at this end, right?" He pointed north, toward the fourth corner.

"Yeah, that's right." Ian stood in the front stretch, sizing up the approach for the motorcycle jump. The landing might be a pinch, but if they settled on ten cars or maybe eleven, it would be doable. "But the carrier jump and the motorcycle jump and the tire jump are all that is going this way," he said, pointing south, toward the first corner.

The family man nodded and headed north, looking for a seat.

Astonishing. The T-bone crash had once been a routine part of daredevil shows, back in the '50s and '60s, the heyday of the traveling auto daredevil show, when Crash Dick was a superstar, when Sid Hirsch packed them in, when Jimmy Hapgood Senior held the world enthralled and Ian McGinnis was a wet-behind-the-ears wannabe. It was usually done just before the finale, which was usually a car jump over a bus or some other obstacle—the motorcycle hadn't arrived as a major show component back then.

Ian had used his car carrier as his jump obstacle for years because he always knew what he had to do, always had the carrier with him, always knew how to set it up and take it down. It was hard work to set up for and tear down after, but it was predictable so he could do it show after show. He had the details down pat. The car jump had never been a problem.

But the T-bone had always been a problem. Track conditions, jump car, catch cars, weather. All sorts of things could and did go wrong. And after so many shows like his quit operating for various reasons—money, injury, changed interests, whatever—people saw fewer and fewer T-bones. That one Ian did this season was, as far as he knew, the last anybody had done anywhere.

Except maybe in Hollywood, and that was all camera angle. Or maybe in Europe with those little bitty roller-skate cars.

The T-bone, it seemed, had earned a reputation of being the bull-goose stunt, the main event, the one that separated the men from the boys. The T-bone deserved the reputation, Ian thought, and probably the fact that it had slipped into the realm of legend made it even more interesting and exciting. It was the stunt that people talked about, the one they wanted to see.

Nobody did T-bones anymore, not on the road, not in cramped and rickety Podunk County Fairgrounds or on dirt stock car racetracks in little out-of-the way villages that nobody ever heard of. Maybe that was why the stunt was garnering such attention.

These people, Ian thought as he watched them filter into the stands in twos and threes and fours, lots of families among the audience, toddlers and tads, will never see a T-bone ever again. This is it. For these people—farmers, grocery clerks, miners, truck drivers, factory workers, ordinary people in jeans or coveralls and brogans or tennis shoes and cowboy hats or baseball caps, plain work-a-day folks—for them, this was it.

Ian told Radar to start the pre-show music on the loudspeakers earlier than usual. The concession stands had opened early too and the smell of popcorn drifted on a gusty, iffy breeze.

Or maybe it had something to do with anticipation over the upcoming loop-the-loop jump—make that *double* loop-the-loop, Ian thought, glancing at the logo on the carrier.

Whatever it was, it gave Ian pause. Something was going out of the landscape, the end of an era in history, and Ian could sense it. It made him feel uneasy, queer, a prickly sensation on his skin, and he wasn't sure why.

Age? Nah.

He expected he'd have to talk to Grace about it, but later.

A half hour before showtime, he called a conference with the crew in a sliver of shade behind the van and spelled out the show sequence. "The show's going its regular schedule," Ian said, "hell-driving, crew jump, flaming boardwalls, rollovers, head-on, dynamite chair—Hoppy, you do the chair tonight, okay?"

"I'm your man."

"Then intermission. We'll save all the big stuff for the second half. Pump it up, Radar, all you can, the second half. Flynn, you open with the iron chest. You feeling okay?"

"Hell, yes, boss."

"Watch your language. I'll do the high-skis next, as usual. Then, Trigger, you do some wheelies as we set up for the motorcycle jump. Remember you got a tight corner to land in, a high bank. Milk it, but be careful. After your jump, we'll do the tire pile jump—who wants to do that?"

Which surprised everybody. Ian had always done the tire jump, linking the stunt with PR over the B-S, and Ian was amused to see that everybody expected him to do the stunt tonight.

"Well, it's time to share the wealth," Ian said, his smile full of teeth. He watched Trigger as he said this, looking for a reaction, but Trigger's expression was unreadable. "We're doing a double loop in Phoenix, two loops, not one, and it looks like Trigger has his name on that second loop. So, who's up for a little tire pile? Flynn? BB?"

"I'll do it," Trigger said.

Which surprised Ian. For a minute. "Will you?" Again, Ian tried to read Trigger's stiff face. He noticed another exchanged look between him and Tink, quickly there and gone, and again Ian wondered what was going on. "What about the T-bone?"

"I'd like to do that too," Trigger said.

"Nah, I guess not," Ian said. "You get the motorcycle jump and the tire jump. I'll do the T-bone."

"Aren't you doing the car jump?" PR asked.

"No, not tonight. It'll take too long to set it all up, dragging carrier catch cars back over to the T-bone. We'd run poor Boo and Radar ragged filling in the slack time and bore the hell out of these nice people in the stands. Besides, these folks don't want to see the carrier jump. You've seen. You've heard. They want a T-bone, so we'll go right to the T-bone, right after the tire jump. While you're doing the tire jump, Trigger, I'll be setting up for the T-bone, keep the pace up. Sound good to everybody?"

Nobody contradicted Ian and the meeting broke up.

"Get ready, everybody," Ian said. "We got a full house. Let's give them a show they'll never forget."

Again, Ian noted the quick exchange between Trigger and Tink. It was beginning to annoy him, so Ian resolved to ask Tink about it, right after the show.

The show went without a hitch through intermission, but Ian's high skis didn't work well. He got up on two wheels sure enough, but within a hundred feet, ruts in the clay just before the end of the straightaway, not quite to the first corner, kept forcing him down on all four wheels. He tried three times, then gave it up. He stopped the ski car in front of Radar.

"I'm going to do some reverse spins," he told Radar. He got out of the ski car, walked to one of the hell-driving cars parked on the infield and got in as Radar announced the sudden change in the program and BB drove the ski car off the track.

Reverse spins. Ian drove the three-speed Maverick, column-mounted gear shift, in reverse down the front stretch as fast as he could, then, in front of the grandstand, right in the middle, he hit the brakes, cocked the wheel, slammed the gears from reverse to forward, the car flipped around, and he continued down the track forward. If his timing was off, he'd spit transmission parts all over the track. The crowd, not knowing what to expect the first time they saw him going backwards, just before he turned around, roared in approval after they saw it.

Ian did it again.

Then he did it a third time, and as he roared in reverse for what looked like a fourth reverse-spin, he stopped the car abruptly, jumped out and waved to the crowd. Roars, cheers. The ski-car dud saved by the spectacular reverse-spins. Ian had done it five or six times in the season, when the skis had gone badly, or when he felt the show needed a particular lift at some point.

People might think that he did it here because the skis went badly, but that's not why Ian did it. He wanted people to know—to *know*, rather than suspect or believe or imagine, in their hearts and minds—that it was *his* name on the show. Ian was the best there was, no question. He was the daredevil supreme, in top form, and there was nobody like him, as good at what he did, anywhere. He basked in the applause his display of skill earned him.

As Ian walked back to the infield, he looked for Trigger, to see his reaction. But Trigger was already roaring onto the front stretch on his bike, waving to the crowd, and the show moved on.

"Nice work, boss," Flynn said. He said it, but he had his eyes on the track, on Trigger.

Ian watched too as Trigger did his wheelie routine. Trigger was good at it, Ian found himself admitting. *He's as good on a motorcycle as I am in a car*. Then, Ian realized that one reason he did the reverse-spins was to impress Trigger, and for that lapse into pettiness, he felt angry with himself.

Which didn't last. Ian got to work, even as Trigger continued in his spectacular wheelie show, helping to set up for the bike jump, setting up the ramp and lining cars in position.

Trigger milked the motorcycle jump, doing three high-speed passes, "testing that track," Radar told the crowd in his breathless, intense manner, "checking to see if he's got the right speed, lining up on those ramps." Then, Trigger rode up to the top of the ramp, and stood there, straddling his bike, revving the engine, looking over the jump, the cars he'd have to clear, looking like some conquering God.

He rolled the bike back down the ramp, and Ian stood there. Here, they would confer, and Radar would imagine their conversation for the crowd, including lines about "last minute safety check," and "whatever concerns about the survivability of this stunt being discussed between those two professional daredevils," and "we may have a cancellation, ladies and gentlemen, if Ian McGinnis has decided that it's too risky," and so on. Pump up the crowd, get them on the edge of their seats, eyes wide open, and focused. So that, when Trigger landed at the other side, they'd roar their approval more loudly than they would have if he'd done the stunt without the ballyhoo.

Radar was good at milking inactivity and lulls on the track, getting into the audience's mind, letting people imagine all sorts of things.

None of which, usually, were really happening.

"We're running long," Ian told Trigger. "Do the jump and get on with the tire stunt right away. We won't have time for a warm-up before the tire jump, okay?"

"What about the T-bone, Ian?" Trigger tugged on his gloves and Ian heard the sarcasm in his voice. "Are you just going to do that without any warm-up laps?"

"You just do your job, smart-ass, and I'll do mine." Ian painted on his show smile, gave Trigger a fatherly pat on his shoulder and a jaunty wave to the crowd, the daredevil mentor giving his go-ahead to the young motorcycle performer and his assurance to the anxious crowd that all was well.

Something in Nick snapped, and anger overwhelmed him.

Smart-ass?

But the rage that suddenly surged through his veins when Ian patted his shoulder so patronizingly just as suddenly vanished, and Nick felt himself in that familiar yet too-rarely felt mystical zone of sharp certitude, like the heady, near-weightless instant of apogee of a good jump.

Nick felt—*alive.*

He unballed his fist; he'd unconsciously cocked his fist to bat Ian's hand away when he snapped.

He unclenched and relaxed, then he suddenly saw the future—at least the next few minutes—with crystal clarity.

He smiled back at Ian, teeth gritted so hard it hurt his jaw, but he did it, his mind already on the jump ahead. Utterly focused and relaxed.

He'd never done it before, but he'd watched, studied. He'd waited for this moment.

Still, gonna need a little help.

But he'd already been working on that.

Radar took up Ian's cue and got a round of applause. Trigger raised a thumbs up and rode back down the front stretch, where he suddenly stopped and called Tink over. They exchanged a few quick words, and Ian barely noticed the impromptu conference. He thought nothing of it as Trigger turned back into the stunt and Tink ran back across the track to rejoin the crew, assembled to take down from the bike jump and set up for the tire jump.

Of course the bike jump went well, Ian could tell from the applause, but he had his back turned to it; this time, a message to himself. He was busy now, doing his job, checking the tire jump car. It was a '69 Olds Toronado with the big 455 V-8, a gutsy engine that roared enough without any tinkering to shake the bleachers and be felt in people's bellies. Front-heavy, with not much metal on top to speak of, but the tire jump was a pansy stunt, the landing as easy as a swan dive off the low board onto a feather bed.

Still, Ian checked it. Details. It was his job.

Meanwhile, Tink and the rest of the crew had been setting up the T-bone catch cars.

Applause received for the motorcycle jump, Trigger walked the bike to the edge of the infield where Hanna took it to stow it out of the way for loading later. Ian watched over his shoulder, trying to read the look between Nick and Hanna in the brief, routine exchange. He saw Nick's smarmy smile, flickering quick then gone, but he couldn't see Hanna's face as the two moved on with the show.

Hanna walked the bike to its place in the infield by the carrier and Trigger joined Ian over by the tire jump car. Wordless, and without looking at Ian, Nick climbed through the driver's side window of the Toronado and belted in.

Wordless, Ian walked away, toward the T-bone jump car. They'd gotten a '64 Rambler station wagon, a six-cylinder, as good a T-bone jump car as Ian could ever have expected. It had come to them remarkably clean. Tink had fussed over it, as usual. It ran well.

Ian had checked it thoroughly earlier in the day, but he looked it over again, thoroughly, a habit honed over the years. Details. He forgot about Trigger, his festering irritation with him, and started getting his head into the job in front of him.

Something went wrong with the sound, some subtle change in the tone of the general soundscape around him, and Ian stopped to listen, puzzled. He tapped his hearing aid and listened.

Ian seldom listened to his announcers after the first few shows of any season. They either got it or they didn't; they were either competent or not. That he didn't listen was sometimes a problem related to his hearing aids, sometimes humidity or dirt fouled up the works, and he kept a box of replacement batteries in a cupboard in the trailer and spare hearing aids in case one got too fouled to use or if he lost one.

Sometimes he didn't listen to the announcers because he was busy getting ready for the next stunt, focused.

But it wasn't entirely his faulty hearing that kept him from keeping track of the announcer during a show, nor his focus on the next stunt. He listened instead for the rhythm of the show, which he sensed through audience reaction. He could tell, for instance, when a crowd was bored and he needed to do something like the reverse spins to get their attention back. Or he could tell if they'd reached a fever pitch from milking suspense and were ready to see the anticipated stunt, to release their pent-up energy in applause. He knew exactly when to stop milking a stunt, in other words, and do it, just *do* it.

Or he could tell when something else was going wrong, something not associated with the show, something unplanned and unwanted, such as a fire somewhere on the infield, somebody getting hurt, or, as it happened once, someone having a heart attack during a show.

Once, during an afternoon show in Pratt, Kansas—1969, it had been—the crowd mood changed to something like awe and apprehension during intermission, and for a long minute Ian couldn't figure what changed them. Until he saw the black funnel of a tornado beyond the backstretch.

They had been lucky that time; the tornado dissipated and the show moved on, but Ian remembered.

In 1974, they had a streaker at a show in Kamloops, BC.

Now, sensing some change in the audience, Ian looked to the east, over the backstretch. But the sky was clear, a warm, starry night.

Nothing was on fire, and there didn't seem to be anything wrong in the grandstands. No streakers.

Then Ian turned his attention to Radar, what he was saying. Something about a change in schedule. The T-bone "—being moved up in the program, and our young motorcycle daredevil, Nick Cassidy—"

Then Ian saw, coming out of the third corner and entering the backstretch, the Toronado roaring wrong way around the track, a rooster tail of dust and dirt following.

The car, Trigger driving, was going the wrong way. Wrong way for the tire jump, but not the wrong way for the T-bone.

Ian looked over and saw the T-bone had been set up and the safety crew were in their positions. Ready for the T-bone.

Which Trigger was doing.

Now.

Ian's heart jammed in his throat and for a second he couldn't breathe.

Then he started to run.

CHAPTER THIRTY-THREE

*T*he Toronado shifted sideways a few inches under Nick as he rounded the second corner and he steered into the semi-slide, countering neatly, keeping his speed up as he approached the first corner and the front stretch. He hadn't tested this track in any of the junkers, including this one, and he hadn't taken the bike all the way around, not flat out anyway, and not since early afternoon. Besides, the feel of a bike and the feel of a tank Toronado would be different, he knew, but he also knew how to ride the slide and keep the front end pointed frontward and keep the speed up.

He drove on feel, trusting his gut to get all the details of the stunt right the first time. There would be no second chance.

As ever, the crowd faded away, might as well not have existed, as Nick focused on the jump, seconds ahead. Nick's breathing and heart rate redoubled and adrenaline pumped as he deftly rounded the first corner and entered the front stretch, the jump ramp coming into his vision for the first time.

This is it.

Nick had never timed how long it took a car to come out of the first corner, line up on the take-off ramp, pass the point of no return, then hit the ramp and then crash. He'd never done so with his bike, had never thought of it. He'd always been too busy. Focused.

Besides, he was in molasses time now, where the world stopped turning.

That's what time it was when Nick saw somebody standing, as if he'd appeared out of the ground, between him and the take off ramp.

*

Ian ran, and time congealed, slowed, stopped.

Molasses time. It usually came when Ian was airborne in a jump, and before he crashed at the other end and time restarted with an abrupt and often painful jolt.

But it had happened at other times. He'd run across the infield like this before, a year ago, when Shaun was heading the wrong way around the track, too fast, for his first T-bone crash. Shaun had been driving too fast then, and as he ran now, feet moving too slow through the syrupy, sluggish air, Ian saw out of the corner of his eye that the Toronado was moving too fast, too fast, too fast.

Front end too heavy, not enough steel on top, wrong car, wrong driver, and too fast.

Ian had been in the middle of the infield checking out the Rambler when he started running, headed toward the T-bone launch ramps and catch cars tight inside the fourth corner. He guessed he had about fifty or sixty, maybe sixty-five yards to go. He pictured Tink's crash calculator in his mind and did the math. *Sixty yards times how fast the Toronado is going divided by how fast I'm going.*

Equals—what?

But Ian just ran and ran, his body on automatic, heart and legs pumping, mind racing.

Ian ran, and he suddenly knew what that look between Trigger and Tink had been all about, seeing it again in freeze-frame memory. Trigger might well have talked Radar into believing Ian had ordered a schedule change at the last minute—they *were* behind schedule, Ian had said so himself—but he'd still need cooperation from the set-up crew, from Tink at least, who supervised the crew, to upset the schedule, to hijack the T-bone. Tink had been conspiring with Trigger on this mutiny and who knew for how long it had been planned. This, or something like it.

And what about Flynn and the others? Goddam mutiny?

Ian ran. As he ran, old, forgotten aches in knee and hip joints, in fiery lungs, and stiff shoulders, reappeared. It hurt to run, but Ian ran anyway.

He stumbled in a hole, fell to the ground, got up again and ran. If he'd sprained an ankle, or broken it when he fell, he didn't know, didn't want to know, didn't care. He ran.

Ian ran, and he felt through his bones rather than heard the Toronado screaming out of the second corner, charge into the first, and angle toward the takeoff ramps. The big engine screamed, the crowd roared, Radar ranted in his machine-gun pace, Ian's heart slammed against his aching lungs and he ran and ran and ran, getting closer and closer.

But too slow. Too slow. Too slow.

Then, suddenly.

Suddenly, there he was. He stopped.

He'd crossed the infield, and it felt inside his burning chest as if he'd run a mile in a minute, and he suddenly stopped. Stopped, suddenly, where he'd intended to run to—not consciously, but intended nonetheless—to the center of the track, right—

—right *here*.

In the center of the front straightaway, between the behemoth, thundering, smoke-belching and dirt-spitting Toronado and the T-bone takeoff ramp. No, not quite the center, but a few yards farther up the track, closer to the takeoff ramp than the center of the straightaway. Where he stood, now, stopped, frozen, a dozen yards in front of the takeoff ramps, directly in front of them. Resolutely in place, he stood planted on this spot of dirt like a tree, a rock.

With Trigger heading straight for him.

Time shifted abruptly from molasses to glacial—time *stopped* altogether—as Ian looked into Trigger's eyes in the gap in Trigger's Bell Star helmet.

Trigger's eyes went wide—Ian could see the whites—

The vision of a black Labrador dog sitting on a landing ramp in Mississippi flashed across Nick's memory as he bore down on Ian, who stood in front of him, glaring at him, fists anchored on his hips as if *daring* him—*goddam you, Ian*—to hit him.

He wasn't going to move. Wasn't going to—*goddam you, Ian*.

How fast? The dog memory vanished, the thought of wondering how fast he was going flashed and vanished—he almost looked down at the speedo to see but remembered it had a bad cable, was a tad rattly—almost laughed to himself, an insane kind of nervous laugh he imagined men who were facing firing squads might make in the split second after el Capitan hollers "Fuego!" and still he had time to wonder how all these images, thoughts, and emotional reactions could course across his brainpan in the span of an instant that must exist—god*dam* you, Ian!—between heartbeats.

And before the next heartbeat—or even as Nick realized that he had to do something—*now, goddam you sonofabitch, right now!*—because Ian McGinnis wasn't going to *fucking well move his goddam stubborn ass*—

He did it.

—and Trigger's mouth dropped open and at the last possible second before hitting Ian, he swerved.

At the last possible second, Trigger swerved the Toronado.

He swerved to the left, toward the five-foot high raw concrete wall that stood between the bleachers and the track.

Time re-started its normal pace abruptly and Ian watched in horror as the Toronado slapped, a loud, violent metallic *thwack*, into the concrete wall. Trigger's head jerked a vicious snap when the car hit. Car parts, bent and twisted metal, pieces of fender and hood and bumper, rubber, and fragments of concrete wall and track dirt, flew and spewed high amid sparks and smoke and oil and dust against the wall and the high, wire fence above it, and people in the front rows flinched away instinctively.

A thousand people screamed, and the roar mixed with the scream in Ian's own head.

He started running again.

The concrete wall appeared in front of Nick as he turned into it as abruptly as Ian had appeared in front of him an instant before.

Nick hit the wall.

His head slammed forward then back against the head restraint, *whamwhamwham*, his head a rattling ball in a pinball machine. His chest slammed against the seatbelt, crushing his ribcage and lungs. Blood splattered past bit lips and bludgeoned nose against the inside of his helmet.

The world turned red—

Got to finish this—

—as electric pain shot through his body from head to ankles, Nick fought to keep conscious—

—*Hold on, just long enough*—

—body at the mercy of violent forces beyond his control, his mind clung desperately to awareness—

—*long enough*—
—the lights went out.
Nick's hands did what they had to do.

Ian realized as he ran that Trigger had somehow managed to hit the wall at a slight angle, hit on the left front fender of the bulky car rather than the heavier, more solid engine, and *bounce* off the wall, expending his forward momentum in increments rather than at once.

The car bounced away from the wall, then hit it again, and fewer parts, smoke, sparks, and dirt few away from this second, lesser impact. A third bounce, then a fourth and the car came to a shuddery stop fifty yards down the track, high against the wall, at the top of the fourth corner, facing back against the bleachers and the stunned audience.

The front end looked like a monstrous, metal snarl, a goblin opening wide for the dentist, showing its jagged, raw teeth and oily throat. The hood had curled over the windshield and lay held in place by a thin string of twisted metal. Fender lay crinkled and the left front tire rolled listlessly toward the infield, ripped from its joint. Oily smoke belched from the engine where wires and tubes and pieces of metal twitched and smoked, the innards of a dying beast.

Boo arrived before Ian did and had already popped on the fire extinguisher, belching a cloud of fog on the exposed engine, adding to the smoky haze. Ian got the driver's side door and pushed Flynn, who'd gotten there a second before him, aside. The door was only slightly crumpled, and it had held. The top had held.

"Are you all right?" Ian said to Trigger even before he really got a look at him in the car. Oily-smelling grit floated in the air.

"I'm okay," Trigger said, voice muffled under the helmet. His head swayed as if he was dizzy. His hands gripped the steering wheel at ten and two as if they had never left the wheel, as if he couldn't let go.

"I'm okay," he repeated. Blood sputtered from his lips.

Trigger hadn't had time to dive for the glove compartment, but then, he hadn't done the stunt either.

He *sounded* okay.

And why that pissed him off, Ian would never be able to explain, even to himself.

"Hey!" Ian reached inside the car with his left hand across Trigger's body and tugged on his right shoulder. Trigger looked up at him. "Do you have any idea what you've done?"

"Ian—" Flynn tugged on Ian's sleeve, but Ian ignored him.

"Huh?" He started to shake Trigger. "Do you have any idea what the hell—"

"Ian," Flynn tugged harder, fingers gripping deep into Ian's bicep, "I think you'd better come away."

Somebody had gripped Ian around the waist and was tugging on him—Hoppy and PR, both—helping to drag him away from Trigger.

Ian let them drag him away. He hadn't realized it until they did that he had put his other hand into the car and had started to grab Trigger around the neck. Ian had no idea why he had put his other hand into the car, why he had it around Trigger's neck. And it wasn't like anything he'd planned to do, or even realized he was doing at the time. In fact, it seemed as if he hadn't experienced it as it was happening, but he *remembered* it, after Flynn and Hoppy and PR had pulled him away.

He let them lead him away. He didn't look back as he walked toward the infield, toward the trailer. They let him walk on his own when he got to the edge of the infield. He limped. He'd sprained his ankle while running a few minutes ago. Soon, it would hurt.

But not now.

"Are you all right?" Grace was there, smelling like soap and sweat, her arm around his waist, holding him tightly, her dark eyes burning with a mix of anger and concern.

"Sprained my ankle," he said. "But it doesn't hurt."

Yet.

With Grace's aid, he limped to the back of the van. "I'll get the kit," she said. "You—don't move. You do stupid things when you move." She ran off to the Freightliner.

Just as some instinct beyond his rational mind had propelled Ian to run across the infield to intercept him when Trigger had been heading toward the T-bone take-off ramp, just as some infernal internal mental command—so contrary to rational thought, this last action—had prompted him to put his body between the speeding car and the takeoff ramp, and just as his arms seemed to be acting on their own in trying to throttle Trigger as he sat in the car, bloodied and dazed, after the crash, now Ian moved on automatic.

During the show, the crew stowed their gear in the back of the van, then re-stowed it in the other road equipment after each show for heading down the road. Ian, operating on some kind of mental autopilot, body fueled by something beyond anger, but not really knowing what or why and not really caring, took Trigger's suitcase out of the back of the van. He tossed it to the ground behind him. He rummaged around among the other crew members' gear and found Trigger's sleeping bag, and a large duffel bag Trigger used to store his helmet, bike leathers, and other gear. He tossed it all out behind the van.

He had picked up the suitcase and was smashing it against the side of the van when Grace returned and intercepted him.

"I told you not to move. Now, give me that and sit." With help from BB, Grace got Ian to give up his tantrum and sit in the van side doorway, where Grace applied an Ace bandage to Ian's sprained ankle.

He couldn't see from where he sat, because the van door and Grace and BB were in the way, but Ian heard the pandemonium erupting in the crowd. Shouts, boos, and hoots. Unhappy people. And a few screams. There was a siren wailing somewhere nearby, but it wasn't the ambulance. Ian could see the ambulance that had parked on the infield for the show had moved over by the crash, its back door open. The siren: police, maybe.

Radar was saying something on the PA, but Ian couldn't distinguish it and he realized that he'd lost one of his hearing aids somewhere, maybe when he'd fallen while running.

"I lost a hearing aid," he said. He surprised himself at how calm he sounded and wondered if he really was calm.

"Lucky that's all you lost," Grace said between gritted teeth.

"I'm going to kill him," Ian said, calmly. His breathing had eased and his heart rate had slowed and he sounded and felt rational, in control.

Grace grunted as she tightened the last foot of bandage and secured it with a clasp. "After *I* kill *you*, take a number."

"Kill him. Then I'm going to fire him." He tried to put his foot in the boot. It didn't fit, so he set the boot aside.

Ian stood, leaning on Grace. "I have to do it. I'm in charge. My responsibility. My show. It's got my name on it."

"You almost had your name on the front of that junker."

Ian took a few steps to the front of the van, where he stood and looked toward the grandstands. Most had left, but many remained, milling about.

He could see some in small groups shaking their fists, jumping up and down, shouting like wrestling fans on TV. He saw one man escorting a woman away who was obviously crying miserably as if she'd witnessed a terrible and bloody car crash. There were police moving among the crowd, making shooing gestures, trying to get people to leave.

The show ambulance still stood on the track, but its back door was closed, the engine off. No lights, no siren, and Ian was relieved to see that.

People milled around on the infield, but they looked tense and anxious, not like the crowds that came down after a good show. They looked bitter and hostile. A melee, a barroom brawl involving three or four people, had started a few feet away from the wrecked Toronado.

Chaos.

Where was the crew? Radar had shut down and was quickly trying to put away his sound equipment in the van. Ian saw Flynn and Hoppy, and Tink and Joel had formed a protective cordon, like settlers under attack by Indians, by the carrier and had pulled the wrecker in, to protect the equipment, the cars and the motorcycles, parked between the carrier and the van. A half dozen men, rowdiness and vandalism possibly on their minds, were standing a few feet away from the assembled daredevil protective army, shifting from foot to foot, as if trying to decide if they wanted to attack or not.

Two policemen approached, and the tentative, informal little lynch mob dissipated.

"Where is he?" Ian asked Grace. BB stood nearby.

"I think PR took him to the trailer," BB said. Grace gave her a "shut up" look.

"You should wait until more people leave before you kill him, Ian," Grace said.

"Okay."

"And until he gets out of the trailer. I don't want blood on my carpet."

"Okay. But I want him out." He started to the trailer, thirty yards away toward the backstretch. "He can sleep in the back seat of the Toronado for all I care."

Grace helped Ian limp to the trailer, cursing under her breath as she did, while BB picked up Trigger's discarded luggage and gear.

The trailer door was on the side facing the backstretch, how they always parked it for the show. As Ian rounded the near-side trailer corner, leaning on Grace, he saw Trigger and Hanna in a clutch, Hanna's back to the trailer, her arms around his neck, his around her waist, her face hidden by Trigger's shoulder.

Trigger looked up just as Ian took a swing at him.

CHAPTER THIRTY-FOUR

I'm really, really sorry," Nick said, but it didn't stop Hanna's flood of tears. His lips were swollen and he slurred his words, but the bleeding had stopped, mostly.

"You—you—" She punched her fists ineffectually against Nick's chest like a little girl, expending frustration, fear—who knows what?

"I'm okay, your dad is—"

Is Ian really okay? Am I?

"Everybody's okay." *Are you?*

Muffled tears, incoherent mutterings, tiny bunched fists slapping his chest. Puffball blows, yes, but they hurt. Maybe broken ribs, who knows what?

"Hanna—"

She sobbed and he just held her. What else could he do?

How about nothing? Might as well try nothing. Nothing seems to work, so how about I try to do nothing?

Nick had recovered consciousness quickly, wasn't even sure if he'd been unconscious, or if he had, how long it had lasted. But recovering awareness brought along with it a new set of problems. The engine could burst into flames—no, Boo had doused the engine even before Nick had found the seatbelt clasp.

Fear of fire propelled Nick to seek a quick exit from the crumbled car, but Boo was right there, and then so were other people. Nick barely heard them, his head ringing, and what happened in the next few minutes was a blur.

People yelled. He tried to get out of the car. Somebody tried to keep him in, others tried to get him out. Paramedics asking him stupid questions, their lips moved.

Ian was there, yelling something. Flynn and Tink.

Out of the corner of his eye, as he disengaged the seatbelt and struggled to climb out the side window, through billowing, acrid smoke, he saw Hanna.

Hanna stood on the infield edge of the track, fifty feet away, her hands over her mouth, knees bent, body convulsed in sobs, standing there as if afraid to come any closer. Nick tried to wave to her, tried to smile through bloodied lips. It hurt.

Somehow, he climbed out the window and took off his helmet. A paramedic did something to his face, something that stung like needles. Nick slapped the man's arms away and leaned on PR. It looked to Nick as if PR and the paramedic were arguing about something, but Nick didn't hear.

Leaning on PR, Nick made his way through the cordon of rescuers, got prodded and quizzed, poked and examined, all of which he pushed past, somehow. He was conscious. He could stand, he could walk. His cuts were messy but superficial.

He almost fell, but PR held him up. "You're okay, Nick. Nothing broken—"

PR escorted him to Hanna, said something to her, something to him—sounded urgent—then turned his attention to a group of paramedics and a cop that seemed to be dogging their trail. PR diverted the officious traffic and Hanna took over.

"You," she said, sobbing. "You." She reached a hand out but didn't touch him, as if afraid to.

It looked as if she would collapse any second, and Nick stepped forward and took her around the waist. "There, there," he said, blood sputtering from swollen lips. He guided her toward the trailer. "There, there." She needed to sit down. "Everything's all right."

But it wasn't. Hanna wouldn't stop crying.

Nick tried to comfort her, ignoring the pains in his own body, hugging her, trying to give her his warmth, trying to stop the shuddering sobs—

He felt as much as heard Ian behind him.

He turned.

Trigger ducked—swerved to the left again—and Ian's right fist slammed into the wall of the trailer with a solid *thwack*.

*

Ian's knuckles exploded, pain lanced up his arm, and he fell to his knees, his ankle forgotten. He gritted his teeth to bite off a scream, and clutched his throbbing right hand.

Trigger disappeared between one blink of his watery eyes and the next, and Grace and Hanna helped Ian into the trailer and sat him down.

"Let me look at that hand," Grace said, trying to pry it loose from Ian's chest where he clutched it tightly. Hanna held out an ice pack—they always kept one handy in the trailer's little fridge, just in case.

"No, don't bother," Ian grunted.

Grace retreated, lips pursed. She took the ice pack from Hanna. "You'd better go," she said. "See that Joel is okay." Hanna left, the door creaking shut behind her.

Ian took several deep breaths, gaining control slowly. Grace got up and found another hearing aid in the cupboard where they kept his spares and batteries, and gave it to Ian. She sat back down and waited.

At last, Ian nodded. "Ice pack." He put the hearing aid in his ear.

She handed him the ice pack. "You broke your hand good this time," she said. The anger had left her voice. All business. She'd been here before.

"Let's just keep this to ourselves, okay?" He pressed the ice pack gingerly to his swollen, raw-red knuckles.

"You're going to need—"

"Look, Grace, I'm way ahead of you."

"What are you talking about?"

And Ian told her.

Grace had long ago gotten used to Ian's radical and abrupt mood changes, his mercurial temper, flicking on and off like a light switch. Ian had expended his anger. It had started to ebb as he crossed the infield after the crash, but spiked when he saw Trigger with Hanna, but it had since ebbed again. He had in fact, in the last few seconds, discarded the anger entirely and gotten back to work.

Deep breaths helped.

"You skin your knuckles or bark your shins," he often told his crew, "you take a tire iron and beat the hell out of a fender, swear a blue streak, put on a Band-aid, then get back to work. All there is too it. Life is too short to sleep in late, lollygag, or let pain get your goat. Pain is God's way of letting you know you're still alive."

Crew understood. So did Grace.

After Ian told Grace the way it was going to be, beginning with no doctors—

"I think PR's chasing them off."

—and after she asked him questions to make sure he understood what he was doing, what he planned to do, and after she made damn sure she understood too, Grace got Ian a Coke from the fridge and left the trailer with several errands to perform.

Ian sat and waited.

In a few minutes, PR knocked on the trailer door.

"In," Ian said.

The trailer door squeaked open and PR stepped in, ducking his head under the low, narrow door. "Grace said you wanted to see me." He sat on the fold-down sofa across from Ian in the cramped living-room-cum-dining-room at the end of the small trailer. "Are you okay?"

PR's face flushed, sweaty and streaked with dirt. Deep lines creased his cheeks and forehead and he looked agitated. His breath fluttered, raggedy and strained. A long tear scored the left sleeve of his uniform. Under it, a long, reddish line, like a cat scratch.

"What did you do to your arm?" Ian asked.

PR looked at it as if noticing it for the first time. "I don't know. I've been busy. Never mind. What about you? Are you okay?"

"Yeah, I'm fine." Ian smiled his best show smile, and flexed his left hand. "See? No pain." Ian wasn't sure if PR knew that he'd tried to bludgeon the trailer, but he decided it would be wiser to assume he did. PR didn't know which hand Ian used, and it looked like he bought Ian's slight-of-hand deception.

"Ah," PR said. "Good. Good. I heard that—"

"Yeah, so you *did* hear. But not from me, and this is *my* show. I'm the authority, so don't you go believing anything you don't hear from me direct."

"Yeah, Ian. Sure. But look, we've got problems, and I've got to get with the fair manager, and the local authorities, and I've got to call Saint Louis—"

"First things first, PR. Where's Trigger?"

"Where's—oh. Uh, I got him in a taxi, sent him to a motel. Not our motel. Told him—"

"PR, I—"

"—to stay away from you—and from people and the media—until we get this sorted out."

"Good. Now, where's Hanna?"

"Hanna? I don't—"

"My daughter, you pansy-ass. Where is she?"

PR took a quivery breath. "She's with Grace. And BB's with her. But why—"

"Because if I see Trigger and Hanna in the same zip code together, I'll kill him. And wouldn't that be bad for business?"

"Ah," PR said. "Business." He nodded his head vigorously, a bundle of nerves, his hands rubbing convulsively on his knees. "I got my work cut out for me there." He barked a nervous, mirthless laugh.

"Cassidy is fired."

"I thought you might want to do that, but," PR held up a finger, "let me suggest something, please."

Ian sipped Coke and said nothing.

"We still have the double loop-the-loop jump Sunday in Phoenix. If you fire Cassidy—see, here's my problem. I mean, I can fix this—" he gestured at the mess outside, the pandemonium subsiding at least in volume, although Ian couldn't see what was going on.

"See," PR said, "we planned on Nick doing the loop jump—that is, the second one. You do the one, he does the other at the same time, is what we planned."

"Uh-huh. But he's fired."

"There you go again," PR said. Another nervous laugh. "Look, I got my hands full—I'm going to have my hands full trying to spin this—this *catastrophe*—so that we don't get our asses sued from hell to breakfast and do you have any idea—*do you have any idea*—" PR almost shouted, "—what all this is going to cost? We can't *not* do the B-S in Phoenix, so we have to do something to diminish the impact of this—this—"

"Fuck up."

"Yeah. This—this *fuck up*—it'll ruin everything. All we've been campaigning for all summer. It's bad enough with, with—" Again, he pointed in the general direction of the grandstands over his shoulder with his thumb. "I can fix this. I fixed Kansas City. I got experience."

Ian glared at him.

"But what it'll do to the B-S, well, that's another smoke. Maybe we can mitigate it, some. Maybe. Maybe we can *use* this. I don't know. See, we could say you knew that—that there was something wrong with the jump car, and that Nick had—I don't know—he had heroically tried—"

"I can't believe my ears." Ian sat forward abruptly and PR instinctively flinched back. Ian tapped his hearing aid. "After *this*—" He gestured at the mess outside, "—you still want to keep that little son-of-a-bitch in the show. In *my* show. Is that what I'm hearing?"

"Ian, we got a lot riding on the B-S. We have to finish, paint over this mess and finish. We *have* to. If we don't—" He gave a helpless shrug.

"Then your ass is toast, right?"

PR sat back and seemed to collapse, as if his bones had become liquid. "You're in this too, Ian," he croaked. "You got a lot riding on this."

"But that's where you're wrong. See, I don't give a shit about your goddam tires. Sue me. Go ahead. I'm a farmer. I'm already poor. And—get this clear, PR, because it ain't going to change, and you know how stubborn I can be, so get this good. I. Don't. Give. A. Shit."

PR blinked a few times, trying to focus. Finally, he stood and stepped to the fridge.

"So you aren't going to do the loop jump?" he asked tonelessly, his back to Ian, as he opened the fridge.

"I didn't say that."

PR turned, a can of Coke in one hand, surprise on his face. "What? What did you—"

"I'll do the stunt. For God and country and Landini Tires, I will."

"But I thought you just—"

"Close the fridge."

PR turned and closed the fridge. "Didn't you just say that—"

"I'll do it. Man, sometimes you're deafer than I am."

"Okay." PR took a long swig of Coke. "Okay. What about Nick? You said he was fired."

"I did. And he is."

"So that means—wait a minute, you're suggesting we do only a *single* loop?" PR sat down. "Just one, like we planned at the first? We could do that, but—"

"We can do a double. Still."

"But if you fire Nick—"

"I already did."

"If you fire Nick, then who—"

"Shaun."

CHAPTER THIRTY-FIVE

*T*he taxi PR had conjured in the chaos at the fairgrounds track took Nick south across town to a Super 8 in the suburb of Sapulpa, at the first turnoff before the start of the Turner Turnpike.

PR had managed to toss Nick's suitcase into the cab with him before he left. "You better change before people see you like that," PR had said. Nick nodded dully and didn't move. But once the taxi started motoring down the 244 freeway and Nick opened a window to take in a breeze, he ripped off his dirty, tattered and bloody show uniform and pulled on a clean-enough shirt and jeans. He tossed the uniform in a bundle on the floor in the back of the taxi and left it there.

PR had also stuffed a handful of cash into Nick's hand as he gave the cab driver orders that Nick didn't hear. Then PR had turned to Nick. "Stay low until I call you," he said. "Don't talk to anybody."

Somehow, in all the chaos, PR had not only managed to summon a taxi, but to reserve a room for Nick; he had no problems checking in. There was a note: "I'll send your stuff. Don't worry about anything."

Nick went to his room, lay down for a moment, staring at the ceiling, feeling his aching bones and torn muscles cry out.

After a moment, he got up, went to the bathroom, and threw up, again and again.

Then he slept.

"Shaun?" PR sat back, frowning at Ian.

Ian nodded once, and PR's eyes went unfocused. Thinking.

"Shaun does the other loop," PR said to himself, testing the notion on his tongue. He gazed off past Ian's shoulder and Ian could hear the gears turning. Despite all that had happened, despite how fast it had all happened, PR's promoting gears were still well oiled.

"Nick Cassidy," PR began, speaking to himself, mentally drafting a press release. "Nick Cassidy got hurt in the T-bone crash in Tulsa, so Ian McGinnis summons his nephew and protégé, Shaun McGinnis, from the bedside of his ailing grandmother—"

"Well, ain't you the bright one, after all?" Ian said. "Now, you best find a phone and get to work." Ian stood and headed for the trailer door, "I'm going to help load up and get this show on the road."

The arena had cleared of spectators. Only a few rent-a-cops stood around, looking bored. A dozen orange-vested men swept the bleachers, picking up trash, stuffing plastic bags.

The crew deliberately avoided Ian, busy, focused on their various tasks, sensing his foul mood. Tink had managed to find something to do on the far side of the track, completely out of sight. Ian would speak with Tink, but later. After he cooled off a lot more.

He found his boot in the van, took off the Ace bandage, tossed it aside, and put on the boot. By the time he was ready to help, gamely limping to the task, most of the loading had already been done, and all that remained was to hook on the car carrier behind the Freightliner and drive to the motel.

Ian backed the rig under the trailer, one-handed, but he let Grace drive it the few miles to the Motel Six. His hand hurt like hell and he exhausted a lot of energy keeping the fact from showing. When he got to the motel, he fell into bed, just to rest his eyes for a bit, before calling Shaun.

He skipped dinner with the crew at a nearby Denny's.

He slept.

He woke up the next morning to the smell of orange juice, hot coffee, and bacon and eggs over easy. Grace had ordered out.

The swelling had gone down in his hand, some, but he couldn't move it. It felt splintery under the skin. His ankle felt better.

He ate, showered, and called home.

Shaun was out, some errand or other for the tire store, but Brian was there, at Gran's bedside.

"How's she doing?" Ian asked.

"Same, same." Ian heard the weariness, the cautious optimism, in his older brother's voice. Everybody in the family had mentally prepared for her death, even if they didn't discuss it. Everybody knew. "How's things with you?"

Ian didn't tell Brian about the Tulsa fiasco. "When will Shaun be back?"

"This afternoon, after supper. Want me to tell him anything?"

"Naw, but I need to talk to him tonight. Very important."

On the way to the truck in the parking lot as they set out that morning, Ian found Tink leaning against the Freightliner driver's side door, arms folded, shoulders slumped, gaze nervously fixed on the asphalt at his feet.

"Grace, find something to do," Ian whispered to her as they approached Tink.

"I'll go check the, uh, the trailer hitch," she said, so Tink would hear, and she left them alone. Tink didn't look up.

Ian stood in front of his adopted son. "You got something to say?" It came out a lot less harsh than Ian intended, almost tenderly. He'd known rebellious boys before, had them in his crew practically every year. He knew they had stuff inside them they had to work out. Sometimes you couldn't help them, really. Like a rusted bolt, if you try to force it, twist too hard, you just break the damn thing off or strip the threads. Teenage boys were the same.

Besides, this was Tink. Adopted, yes, but still his son.

"Huh?" Ian persisted.

Tink flinched. He shifted his weight from foot to foot and sighed. It sounded close to a sob. His mouth opened and closed like a drowned fish. He looked around, took a ragged breath, looking at the horizon, at everything else but Ian.

"Well?" Ian said. "We're burning daylight."

"I—I—" Tink gulped, then deliberately looked into Ian's eyes and took another breath. "I'm sorry."

Ian nodded. "Yeah, well—"

"I can't explain—"

"Don't."

Pause. "Huh?"

"You apologized. You screwed up, you apologized. We're done. Now let's get back to work."

Tink blinked wordlessly a few seconds, smiled, relieved. Then he nodded and ran to his rig.

The show moved on, headed westward. The trip from Tulsa to Phoenix was more than a thousand miles, the longest between-show haul Ian had ever undertaken. It had been PR's work, not his, but he had plenty of time to do it. Today was Friday, August 31, and he planned to get to Albuquerque or maybe Gallup before stopping for the night. He'd arrive in Phoenix mid-day Saturday, with plenty of time to set up for the B-S the next evening.

The crew would have nothing to do except watch.

PR kept the road car and stayed behind, on the phone where he'd been all night, saying he'd catch up. Trigger was nowhere to be seen and Ian didn't ask.

Tink and the rest of the crew walked on eggs as they set out, nervous. After his brief chat with Tink, Ian deliberately didn't say anything to anybody—at least nothing that would make them more skittish than they already were. If he'd so much as said "boo" to any of them, he expected they'd piss their pants on the spot.

Which is what he wanted. He had a lot of equipment to get home; he had a show to do—one last show, the one he never wanted in the first place—and he needed help in getting it all done. He had payroll to settle up, details to take care of, and commitments to fulfill. And fulfill them, he would.

Tink had screwed up in Tulsa, who knew why. But he'd faced it like a man, faced Ian, and apologized. If the crew needed handling, Tink would do it.

Ian tried to talk with Hanna the morning after the Tulsa fiasco, but he changed his mind about that as soon as he saw her, Grace standing next to her, in the parking lot in front of Denny's. Hanna looked haggard, as if she'd been the one who'd gotten hurt. Grace gave him a keep-your-distance frowny look and Ian steered clear.

Grace drove the rig westward that morning down the Turner Turnpike to catch Interstate 40 at Oklahoma City. Ian looked out the window, pensively watching the heat-drained, parched and dusty, ubiquitously bland roadside landscape slip past.

"How's Hanna?" Ian asked.

"Nothing broke. Physically."

"What does that—"

"If you got to ask—" Grace shook her head, exasperated—or was she still pissed, and at what?—and Ian gave up. He hurt too much to argue, and he didn't even know what he was arguing about.

"How's Tink?" Grace asked.

"We talked. He's back on the job, looks like."

"So's Hanna," Grace said.

Long pause.

"Grace, do you think Tink—

"I honestly don't know, Ian. Being adopted and all. It can weigh on him, I think. And he's a teenager. Are you sure you include him in every-thing, make him a part of the show?"

Suddenly, Ian remembered his surprise announcement before the Tulsa show that the tire jump was open, that he'd asked for volunteers. He'd asked Hoppy and Trigger, even BB, but he didn't ask Tink if he wanted to do the stunt. In fact, Ian didn't know even now whether Tink might have volunteered. If Ian had asked, what would Tink have said?

He'd been so focused on rocking Trigger's boat that he hadn't noticed Tink. Maybe that was part of Tink's rebellion, part of why he helped Trig-ger hijack the T-bone.

Maybe Trigger saw what I didn't see.

"Damn." He thumped the seat with his left fist.

Joel stirred from his place in the sleeper behind Ian and looked out. He exchanged a smile with Grace and lay back down, adjusting his head-phones, changing the tape, and punching it on. Another Zane Grey tape. Joel had an audiotape collection he kept in a cardboard box in the trailer, adding to it at truck stops along the way. He liked Westerns.

"About your hand," Grace said. "When are you going to tell PR that you can't do it at all?"

"I'm not sure I can't. That's why I ain't said anything yet. Might not need to."

"Ian, save it for the show. It's me."

Long pause. "Yeah." Long pause. "Yeah. After I call Shaun, make sure he's on the program. Maybe even wait'll he shows. Then I'll talk to PR about it." Long pause. "Still—"

Grace barked a laugh. "Man, you're a caution."

They'd made good time. They had dinner in Clinton early that after-noon and they took a rest stop outside Albuquerque later that afternoon where Ian called Shaun from a phone booth.

"How's Gran?" First question, always.

"I heard she came around while I was out, about noon, Brian said. He was out of the room, but a nurse told him. The nurse didn't understand what she'd said, then she went back to sleep. Damn, I wish I'd been there. How's the show?"

Ian told him.

"That son-of-a-bitch," Shaun said. "I knew he was bad news. I told you, didn't I?"

"If you did, I didn't hear. I seem to be doing that a lot lately. Look, Shaun, I want you to come out and do the stunt."

Pause. "Huh?"

"The B-S. I want you to come and do it. Tell the truth—"

Ian sighed. He could talk to Shaun; he could talk to Grace and he could talk to Gran, but not like he could talk to Shaun. "Tell the truth, I can't do it alone."

"Sure you can. That was the original plan, wasn't it?"

"Yeah, but—" *I can talk to Shaun. I should tell him.*

"But what?"

"I can't do it—alone. I need you."

Ian heard staticky clicking on the phone and for a second he thought that maybe they'd been disconnected. "Shaun, are—"

"I heard." Ian heard muttering, indistinct. "Dammit, Gran is here. You understand? I can't just up and—"

"Shaun—"

"Just do it solo. Do it yourself, like you originally—"

"Shaun, I need—"

"Goddam it, Ian. God*dam* it."

Long pause; then Shaun sighed. "Let me think about it. Do you got a number I can call?"

"No. I'm at a payphone. We're on the road. I'll be in—"

"Wait a minute." Ian heard a voice in the background, Shaun muffled the phone; then: "Can you hold on a sec, Ian?"

"Shaun, what's—"

"Just hold on, dammit. I'll be right back."

Ian held on. Feeling claustrophobic, he opened the narrow phone booth door with his left hand and took a step out. The sun blazed hot and bare in a cloudless sky and no breeze mitigated the heat rising off the flat asphalt where Ian stood. *Like standing on a griddle*. Sweat poured down Ian's face.

But he found no comfort, standing one foot in the booth, the other out, phone tucked between chin and shoulder, the phone cord stretched out like an umbilical, his right hand held delicately at his side.

Waiting.

He wiped his forehead with the back of his right hand, the one holding the phone, and as he did so, he bumped his left hand against the booth door. Pain lanced up his arm and he grunted. He dropped the phone from his slippery right hand and it dangled at the end of its metal cord.

He picked the receiver back up and heard Shaun's voice.

"—kick my ass."

"What? Shaun, what did you say? I didn't hear—"

"Crank up your damn hearing aid, boss. I said Gran wants to kick my ass. She woke up and I told her you were on the phone and she asked about the show and I told her you wanted me to come out, but I wanted to stay with her and she started cussing like a daredevil and threatened to kick my ass if I didn't go. Now I know where you get your vocabulary, boss."

"What did she say? I don't—"

"She says I better get out there with you or she'll kick my ass. I don't know, Ian. Maybe I want to stand across the room and tell her I ain't going just to see her get up out of bed and try to catch me. Wouldn't that be—"

"If she wakes up and finds you still there, she'll be disappointed. That'd break her heart."

"Oh. Yeah. There is that." Pause. "She *does* look a lot better, Ian."

"Brian and Amanda are there. She'll be okay."

"Yeah. I guess."

"Get a good night's rest and start tomorrow. You should catch up to us by supper."

"Okay. I'm packed. Truth is, I've been ready for weeks."

"Cool your jets until morning, hear? If you need to call tonight or in the morning, we'll be at the Pathway Truck Stop in Gallup. You can look up the number. We'll reach there by eleven or so tonight and park there until tomorrow morning."

Ian didn't tell Shaun about his hand. Two parts of his mind fought against each other over the busted hand. One part told him he could still do it. He'd done it before, showed with broken bones, torn muscles, even with a concussion once, and he could do it again. It was nothing. He could steer with the other hand, rig something to keep the injured hand from bothering him, until after the stunt. He could do it.

The other part of his mind kicked Ian mentally under the table with Grace's foot and used her voice to tell him how stupid he was being. He *was* hurt, and he could *not* drive the jump car, not safely, not well enough—not for sure, anyway—and that handicap could jeopardize the show, as well as his own safety and that of spectators—what if he lost control and hit somebody, or hit the grandstands?

Ian was already hurt, so getting hurt more didn't bother him. But that he might hurt somebody else because of his injury intruded every time he thought that maybe, just *maybe*, the hand would start feeling better at the last minute and he didn't really have to tell PR that he couldn't do the stunt at all.

He'd asked Shaun once upon a time to do a stunt he couldn't finish because he'd gotten injured. That was a year ago. Now, here he was, asking Shaun to do it again.

Or he would ask, rather, when Shaun showed up.

Ian decided that he hadn't told Shaun about the hand on the phone because it was too complicated, and because Shaun was too excited. Besides, he was coming anyway, so it would work out.

Shaun's coming. Ian whistled as he walked to the truck.

Ian had done what he thought was a good enough job hiding the problem hand from the crew as they headed west, but he couldn't keep it up. He'd avoided eating with the crew. He let Grace drive. But how soon before the crew noticed and wondered and figured it out? And what sort of problems would that cause?

PR called Ian in Gallup late that night as everybody sat down to supper. As usual, being summoned to a phone put Ian's heart in his throat. But this one was not about Gran.

"I'm in Albuquerque," PR said. "Too tired to continue, so I'll stay here tonight, catch up with you tomorrow."

"So, how's tricks?"

PR told Ian that he'd smoothed ruffled feathers in Tulsa and left behind, if not exactly smiles, at least not blatant bitterness. "Maybe I salvaged something, I don't know. I went ahead and put the word out that there was an alternative to Cassidy, but I didn't go into details. Let them wonder, you know how it goes."

"Yeah, keep them guessing. The drama continues. It's all one big soap opera. Well, next time you talk to a reporter, you can tell them Shaun is on his way."

"Now? He's on his—"

"Well, in the morning. But he'll be in Phoenix by tomorrow for supper, and you can do your PR thing, maybe introduce him to the press, whatever you do."

"Okay. So *you're* okay?"

"Why do you ask?"

"Well, there's been a lot of surprises lately—"

"No. No surprises from me. I'm okay, you're okay."

"How's Gran?"

Ian sighed. "She's—getting better. And Shaun is coming to fill in, so everything *else* is okay. Okay?"

"I'll catch up on the road tomorrow afternoon. I need to rest now, get an early start."

"Don't get a speeding ticket, you hear?"

"I hear."

As Ian hung up, he tried to flex his right hand. It felt like it was laced with splinters and it hurt to even think about moving it.

It was no use. Ian resolved to tell PR about his hand as soon as he caught up. They could do a single loop, as they originally planned, but Shaun would do it, not Ian. Shaun *could* do it, of that Ian had no doubt. Ian would coach him about the speed, caution him on holding steady on the long, curved take-off ramp, and Shaun would do a good job. PR would have to adjust, do his best—he was good at rolling with the punches, and he was getting better as punch after punch came at him.

It would all turn out okay. Ian would do okay, tell PR about the change, straight up, right away, no lollygagging, no more self-deception. PR would do okay, spinning the change of events, somehow. And Shaun would be okay. He'd do the stunt and do it well and then they could all go home.

And he could look in on Gran.

Late the next afternoon, an hour outside of Phoenix, Ian heard his name on the CB. The state police were looking for him, had an important message.

The caravan found a rest area, pulled over, and waited.

Ian had prepared for this moment, mentally, since Gran's stroke, in the spring, so many months ago. After hearing what the doctors were saying about her chances of recovery—her lack of chances, rather—he wasn't surprised to see the trooper waiting at the rest area, hat in hand, head tucked down, somber-faced, just like that Smokey Bear had been back in Missouri a few weeks ago. Same hat, same posture, same face. Same news.

Why do they have to do it this way? Intercept a guy on the side of the road? Is that any way to tell a guy?

But Ian didn't blame the cop. It was nobody's fault. And he wasn't angry, really. He was tired; tired, and maybe, deep inside, glad to know it was finally over. Not glad—hell no, not that—that Gran had finally passed on, but relieved that the waiting had ended.

So, he thought, as he walked up to the officer, here it comes. The news. I can handle it. I can handle it.

But it wasn't Gran.

It was Shaun.

CHAPTER THIRTY-SIX

Shaun?" Ian looked at the trooper like he'd spoken French. "My nephew?"

"Yes, sir," the trooper said, his voice high-pitched, almost feminine. Tall, square-shouldered, clean-shaven. Sad eyes, tight lips. The cop hated this too. "I'm told he died instantly, pronounced dead at the scene." He gave an apologetic shrug. Hated it. "So I'm told."

Ian nodded, numb. His bones felt like jelly.

"Mr. McGinnis, if there's anything—"

"We'll be fine," Grace said. She held Ian like he was going to fall down, and he held her the same way. "We'll rest here a while." She tugged on Ian's sleeve, gently. "We'll be fine."

"Uh," the trooper pointed at Ian's obviously injured right hand. "If you're driving with that hand—"

"I'm driving," Grace said. She tugged on Ian's sleeve.

The officer nodded, sighed, and put on his hat.

Grace escorted Ian to the trailer, where he sat at the dining table, numb. Hanna and Joel sat at the table, crying quietly.

Tink sat on the trailer floor by the narrow door, hunched into himself. If he cried, he did it quietly, to himself. Tink most often stayed with the crew, being foreman. But for now, he huddled with family.

Ian cried. He emptied out onto Grace's shoulder in silent, racking sobs.

There had been pain. Bones cracked and broken, muscles pulled and torn, cuts and bruises and sprains. He'd seen friends hurt. He'd suffered loss, and waited to suffer more—Gran.

But this.

Ian never cried. You had work to do, you dealt with the pain, you moved on. But you never cried, never let the pain get your goat.

It took him about a half hour to finish weeping. When he finished, he noticed Grace had been crying too, but he was too inside himself, too into his own grief, that he hadn't noticed hers until he'd finished with his.

You bang your thumb or crack your shins, you swear up a blue streak, take a tire iron to a junker, beat the hell out of it, and then you get back to work. Because there's always work to be done, and you can't do it if you got stuff bottled up inside that wants out, like anger. Like grief.

Or you cry.

Ian was too tired, down to his rubbery bones, to take a tire iron to a handy car. So he'd cried.

"You ready to drive?" he asked Grace, voice husky.

Still weeping, she shook her head.

"Joel, Hanna," Ian said, standing. "Stay with your mom. I got to talk to the crew and find PR."

He touched Tink on the shoulder. Tink stood, somber faced but clear-eyed. He opened the door and stepped out of the trailer, holding the door open for Ian.

The trailer leaned and creaked as he stepped out. Tink closed it softly.

The crew, including Tink, Joel, and Hanna, had stayed a respectful distance when the trooper had talked with Ian and Grace by the trooper's cruiser. Like Ian, they had been waiting and dreading this moment, expecting a call about Gran at any moment. But when Grace told the three what the trooper had said as she escorted Ian to the trailer, the others heard.

Ian found them leaning in the shade of the fifth wheel behind the wrecker. "Listen up," he said. "Shaun is dead. He started out last night, not long after I called him. I told him to wait until morning, but—well, he's Shaun. Anyway, they say he got to Page, just north of Page, I guess, when he fell asleep. I guess he was trying to drive all the way through. Anyway, he fell asleep at the wheel, they say. That's what they think happened. That's what the trooper—" Ian looked around the rest area but the trooper was gone, "—that trooper said."

"He was coming here?" Flynn asked.

"To replace Trigger," Tink said. Ian hadn't told the crew yet that he'd asked Shaun to join them, wanted it to be a surprise, but Tink knew. Maybe he'd overheard Ian on the phone. Maybe he'd simply told Tink and didn't remember.

BB had been crying, Ian could see, leaning on Hoppy's arm. The others were somber, grim.

"So what do we do now?" Boo asked.

"We go on. The show goes on. At least, we got miles to cover before dark."

"Ian," Flynn said, "about your hand—"

"I'm fine. I'll take it up with PR, don't you worry."

"Yeah, but—"

"It's my business and none of yours. Now saddle up and get ready. I'm going to try to call PR."

There was a payphone by the toilets set back from the parking area amid a copse of old sycamores and a grassy area with picnic tables. A tourist family, mom, pop and three tads, loudly occupied one picnic table, and a young couple sat at another, holding hands.

There was a dog—it was Hobo. Joel had let Hobo out for a little exercise.

Ian picked up the phone, mind racing, before he realized that he didn't have his little black book in his hand. He turned around and headed for the trailer. Before he got there, the screen door squeaked open, and Grace stepped down. She had his book in her hand, held it out to him. Her cheeks were tear-streaked, mascara runny, and her hair needed a comb, but her eyes were clear and her shoulders were straight and her jaw was set in that stubborn, rigid fashion that told Ian she was ready.

"I love you," she said, handing him the book.

He called Landini Tires in Saint Louis. PR's secretary, or Baha's, would know where PR was. "I always check in with the office," PR had once told Ian, "at least twice a day, and hell, sometimes five or six times a day. They always know where I am. If you ever need to find me, call there."

He was at the Motel Six in Phoenix, the one where they'd stayed when Ian had first tested the loop-the-loop ramp. He'd arrived less than a half hour earlier. He'd taken highway 60 through Show Low and Globe, the back way, while Ian had stuck to the freeway, to Interstate 40 to Flagstaff, then south on 17. PR had arrived about the same time Ian was hearing the news about Shaun, and he'd called the office ten minutes before Ian called.

Ian called the Motel Six and PR answered on the first ring.

The phone booth Ian called from was no more than a box hung on a pole with a cracked and weathered plastic canopy above it and on two sides, and the tattered fragments of an old phone book hanging below it on a metal cord. It was a hot day. Ian scrunched into the booth, getting as much shade on his head as he could, holding the phone under his chin, the black book still open in his left hand.

"Listen, PR, I got some news." Ian told him.

"Jesus, Ian, I'm sorry. I'm, I'm—"

"So we got to work fast. That is, *you* got to work fast."

Across the grassy area by the toilets where the payphone stood, in the rest area parking lot, among station wagons, pickup trucks, cars, and two eighteen wheelers, the crew milled about, puttering. Tink was checking the tie downs on the three show cars atop the carrier. Boo was doing something inside his clown car on the fifth wheel trailer, his tiny butt sticking out of the little car's open door. BB and Grace were in the Freightliner: Ian couldn't see what they were doing. Hoppy and Radar and Flynn, he couldn't see from his vantage. Maybe in the van or the wrecker. Joel was watching Hobo cavort in a grassy area between the parking lot and the highway.

"Meaning?"

"The B-S. Tomorrow." A car, a mustard yellow '78 Gremlin, was trying to turn left onto the highway, its blinker on, trying to head the wrong way, against traffic flowing to the right.

"You—you still want to do it?"

"Yeah, I—" Then Ian stopped. He'd forgotten. Of course, he'd forgotten. He'd been thinking—or *not* thinking, in fact—for the last hour, immersed in his grief. He'd forgotten about the show, about his broken hand. He'd been ready to call PR and tell him that the double loop was out, that the show would have to be a single loop. "Because my hand is busted up. And. I. Can't. Do. It."

But now, maybe the whole show was bust. And it would be irresponsible to avoid telling PR the hard facts. You faced the facts—bark your knuckles, scrape your elbow—dealt with it, and moved on. *I shouldn't have waited. Waiting this long—that was irresponsible of me.*

"Listen, PR, I'm sorry about this mess." The Gremlin eased forward and a car blew past, horn blasting. A woman with long blonde hair drove the Gremlin. A male passenger, young, long dark hair. The driver looked puzzled. She waved her hands in obvious frustration and shook her head. The blinker still flashed, left, left, left.

"Don't blame yourself, Ian. If you want to back out, I understand. Landini Tires will understand. They'll have to. I'll make them. Hell, Ian, no-body expected anything like this. First Nick gets injured, then Shaun gets killed. Hell, Ian."

Cassidy hadn't been injured, but Ian didn't bother to correct PR. That wasn't the point.

"It's not that." The woman backed up, obviously realizing she was go-ing the wrong way, but her blinker still flashed left turn. "I mean, well, that's for you to spin, do your PR thing. Your bad luck, I guess. But there's this—"

"Yeah, bad luck. *There*'s a concept. People don't want to be associated with it." Deep sigh. "Listen, Ian, let me get on the phone to Saint Louis. I'm thinking with all this—well, bad luck, I expect they'll call it—but with all what's happened, maybe they'll want to call it off, the B-S. I mean, nobody wants to associate with this now, likely. Maybe we should cancel."

"Maybe we should—" Ian stopped, startled to realize that PR had gone ahead of him, that maybe he wouldn't have to tell PR about the hand after all. PR was offering Ian a way out, one that didn't involve Ian admitting he'd failed.

"Listen, PR, I—" The prospect both pleased and rankled. The stunt had to be cancelled, yes, but letting PR cancel it without telling him about the busted hand—that sounded wrong, somehow. And it rankled.

"You don't have to worry about it, Ian. We should leave it up to Saint Louis. Let you off the hook. What do you say?"

The Gremlin driver turned around at a wide spot in the parking lot, and headed for the exit at the other end of the rest area, talking animatedly, hands waving, maybe arguing, with her male companion. She headed right this time.

"I don't know, PR. It goes against the grain." But she still had her left turn signal flashing. "It's my show, my responsibility."

"I haven't seen you back away from a challenge yet. I know *you* might be ready to go on, but I think maybe Landini Tires might be ready to pull out. Anyway, I should call them. See what they say. This new develop-ment—Shaun dying and all."

Left turn signal still on, The Gremlin driver turned right onto the high-way.

"No," Ian said. He tried to flex his right hand. He couldn't do it. "There's a way."

"What? What do you mean?"

"You just wait there, by the phone. Don't call Saint Louis until I get back to you. I have an idea."

"I can't keep this in my pocket. The boys at home will want a say in what's going on. I got calls to make, asses to cover. Maybe a resume to write. Make it quick."

"Give me a half hour."

CHAPTER THIRTY-SEVEN

Except for a few minutes when PR called to wake up Nick to say he'd stowed Nick's Yamaha and bike gear bag with the local Landini Tire dealer, and to make sure he hadn't talked to anybody and that nobody had talked to him, Nick slept straight through to the next afternoon; his body needed it. He'd escaped with nothing broken, but he sported bruises that made him look like a pinto, liver-purple blotches against his tanned skin, and he ached all over. Maybe a few cracked ribs, nothing worse.

He had enough money to get room service to run errands. Ben-Gay and Ace bandages. He slept.

He was in no hurry to get back to Decatur, to Mac's and the bike repair biz. So he lay on the bed the day after, air conditioner whining as it fought the muggy heat, thinking. Or trying not to.

Maybe I should call Virgil. Maybe later. I don't remember the number.

Beer was hard to come by in uptight Oklahoma through regular channels, with the state's weird blue laws, but a guy could tip a desk clerk or bellboy extra and get things done. Lukewarm Bud. It would do.

Did PR give me the number where he stowed my bike?

Nick sipped suds and thought. Or tried not to.

Yeah, but I didn't write it down. I can look it up. When I'm ready.

When the words "Danny" drifted by in Nick's on-idle mindscape, like a puff of smoke from a smelly cigar, he sat bolt upright and found the word "Jack" next to the word "Danny." He called down to the desk to ask for a map.

"Of Alabama? Yeah, we got one. I'll bring it up right away, sir."

"Don't bother." Idle for too long, something that resembled action felt good. "I'll get it." The pain wasn't all that bad.

Nick pulled on a pair of jeans and a T-shirt and headed for the door. He almost closed it before he remembered his room key was on the dresser and besides, he ought to put on shoes. "No shoes, no shirt—"

In the elevator, Nick decided he'd better not take his Bud into the lobby. He drained the can, crushed it, and set it in the corner of the elevator.

The town of Jack, Alabama, looked to be no more than a speck on the map, a dozen or so miles south of Troy on state road 87, smack dab in the middle of nowhere. Danny had said his uncle's farm was near there and that was where he was going after Ingersoll's Quarry.

Danny had gotten nervous when he'd mentioned the name "Jack" to Nick.

Too easy to remember, huh? Afraid I'll have some time on my hands and that berg name would come back to me and then I'd come after your thieving ass?

Nick considered that he might have done so long ago if he hadn't gotten on with the show in the spring. Maybe.

It wasn't all that far to Jack. A day if you pressed, two if you took your time. Besides, it was on the way home, or near enough. Nick went back to his room and packed to leave, his mind already miles down the road.

Galvanized, Nick felt elated, yet he felt relaxed, in no hurry. He had a purpose, a goal. He took his time packing, planning. Thinking.

He found two Landini Tire stores to call. The second one had his gear, waiting for him. He called for a taxi and waited, taking mental notes.

He'd check at local bike shops in Montgomery and south of there, inquiring discretely. "I promised this guy I'd look him up." Or maybe "I owe him money." Something like that.

He'd motor through Jack, scope it out but not stay there. It was so small that Danny was probably related to everybody. Nick didn't want Danny to know he was being hunted. That would take planning. Not a problem; Nick was in no hurry. Maybe he'd rent a car.

He checked the Yamaha at the tire store. It was in good shape, just as he'd left it. He loaded up for the trip. He planned to ride east for a few hours, until after sunset maybe, then roll out his sleeping bag at the nearest wide spot. He revved the bike and was ready to set out when the owner of the tire store waved to him. Phone.

"For me?"

"Yeah. She said it's an emergency."

"She?"

"Yeah. Woman named Hanna or something."

Ian realized right after he hung up that he had no idea how to get in touch with Trigger. He called PR back.

"Where's Trigger? I need to reach him."

"Ian, I don't know if that's such a good idea."

So Ian had to tell PR what he had in mind, the idea that had occurred to him, inspired by the Gremlin driver trying to turn left when she meant to go right. But first, if he was to get PR's help in getting in touch with Trigger, he'd have to explain to PR—confess—about his hand.

It didn't take as long as he thought and PR was quick to come to grips with the situation. PR was fast on his feet, give him that.

"*I* should call him," PR had said, "not you."

"No, this is my—"

"Ian, you just fired the guy. Do you think—"

"*I* screwed it up, *I* got to fix it."

"You're as diplomatic as a bull with his balls in a ringer. Jesus, Ian. Let me do this."

Ian relented and hung up.

"Are you talking to PR?" Hanna's voice startled Ian. He hadn't noticed her standing behind Ian, shoulders hunched, arms folded across her chest, as if she were cold. Her eyes were red and swollen and her hair looked a mess.

"Yeah, honey. We have business."

"Have to do with your hand, right? And with Nick? You going to try to get him back? To do the B-S?"

"What? How did you—"

"Let me talk to PR." Hanna stepped around Ian, practically pushing him aside. "What's his number?"

It stunned Ian to slack-jawed immobility to realize that Hanna knew what he was thinking and planning. If she'd been standing nearby, listening, he hadn't noticed. Maybe she'd talked to Grace or PR or both. But she couldn't have talked to PR; Ian was talking with him. So maybe she'd talked to Grace—

"Hanna, this is none of your—"

"Dad, PR can't get Nick back. Trust me. What's the damn number?"

But she is *a McGinnis.*

"Watch your language."

Ian gave her the number.

He wanted to listen to her end of the conversation but she made him go away—*so like her mother*—and he didn't hear.

He waited in the trailer, twitchy.

Ten minutes later, Hanna opened the trailer door and stepped in. Smiling.

Sunday, September 2, 1979, the day of the much-publicized Landini Tires-sponsored Ian McGinnis Auto Daredevil Thrill Show Double Loop-the-Loop Jump, a world's first, and a record distance jump as well in the making, dawned hot and dry. It got to ninety degrees by late morning. Puff-ball clouds dotted the sky, pushed along by a listless, iffy breeze that barely disturbed the limp plastic used car lot flags lining the road to the jump site and the parking lot inside the gate and the massive, long, temporary bleachers that flanked the stunt path and faced each other, one set facing south, the other north.

The second loop had been taken down overnight. Its pieces lay in an irregular squarish mountain lashed down under huge blue tarps behind the western corner of the north side bleachers. PR had toyed with the idea of leaving the second loop in place, untouched, for the show. But he'd developed a good working relationship with a local day labor contractor in using the agency's services preparing for the show, so he tapped that resource again and had the thing removed during the night. Its removal provided better sight lines for some in one section of the bleachers who otherwise would not have been able to see the other loop. Besides, PR didn't want too much attention drawn to the second loop and the tragedy it represented.

"What do you think, Ian?" PR had asked before he took it down.

"Yeah. Take it down, if you can."

TV cameras found the pile, and commentators commented. But it was just a pile of pipes and planks and coils of guy wires and hardware, so after draining whatever symbolic pathos they could out of it they moved on.

The pre-show commentators had a lot to talk about.

PR had worked overtime since Tulsa getting word out that Cassidy had probably been injured, although he wasn't specific about the injury, and then he quickly and deftly switched attention from Cassidy to Shaun who was slated to replace him in doing the second loop.

Now, with this latest development—Family Tragedy: Young Daredevil Heir Dies on Road to Fame—the buzz was even greater, especially since Ian intended to go on with the show despite it all. The buzz in the media was that Ian opted to go on with the show as a tribute to his dead nephew and his ailing grandmother.

"I could use this," PR had said.

"Yeah, go ahead." Ian understood.

Ian would never say it aloud but the showman in him admired how quickly PR got to work after they'd talked the previous afternoon, after Hanna had talked to Trigger and Ian had then called PR back. Getting the buzz out, getting the second loop knocked down overnight, all the behind-the-scenes detail work; it was remarkable that it got done.

The jump was scheduled for three o'clock but the grandstands were full before noon. Some reports put the crowd at thirteen thousand, others at fifteen thousand. Millions more watched on TV. Country and Western singer Bob Wills kept the audience in their seats, as did back-to-back performances by Carole King and Neil Sedaka. An exhibition of close-quarter synchronized riding by the Arizona Highway Patrol Motorcycle Brigade followed. The Arizona State University Marching Band took to the field for a few numbers and stuck around for the National Anthem.

Concession stands behind and under the bleachers did a brisk business, and hawkers walked the stands peddling hot dogs, peanuts, beer and Coke, souvenirs, and programs. The air filled with the smell of hot buttered popcorn and cotton candy.

ABC had won the bidding war to broadcast the loop-the-loop jump live on their *Wide World of Sports*. They had set up a control booth adjacent to the western corner of the south grandstands. They had cameras strategically located all over the vast field so they could broadcast the event from point to point, use split screen, or follow the action camera to camera, and rebroadcast it, in slow motion if they wanted to, long after everybody else went home.

They had a camera on a tripod at the eastern end of the tire pile so viewers could watch—head-on—the car fly out of the loop ramp, fly over the row of Landini Tires delivery trucks and hit the pile. They had another camera at the point where the jump car would take off, just under the lip of the take-off ramp, facing east, so viewers could watch the car take off toward the distant tire pile. They had two cameras on top of the loop, one facing east, the other west.

They had cameras on top of both the north and south bleachers facing the action—the loop, the trucks lined up between the loop and the tire pile, and the tire pile-landing site. They had three cameras inside the loop, one with a fisheye lens, facing straight up at the sky under the tenth truck in the line, and a half-dozen roving cameras and crews gathering images of crowd scenes, crew preparing for the jump, warm-up events, and whatever else caught their eye.

A Landini Tires blimp circled overhead.

A camera had been mounted in the back seat of the jump car, the '75 Mercury Capri they'd bought in Dallas.

All the images fed into a bank of two dozen screens in a semi trailer parked behind the south bleachers where a producer and his assistants monitored the arrangement, like NASA mission headquarters, and fed info to the commentators in the booth a hundred feet away, "switching you live to our man on the scene, Marv Dekker, who has this report about a man who hitch-hiked all the way from Portland, Maine, to see this show . . ."

Four big screens, as big as drive-in movie screens, had been set up in the northeast and the northwest corners, and the southeast and southwest corners of the bleachers, where images were projected from the ubiquitous cameras, so that spectators sitting over *here* could easily see what was going on over *there*, views they otherwise couldn't see.

Ian got approached for an interview at about ten a.m. PR deflected the interviewer.

"He's still in shock over his nephew's death," PR said. "Cut him some slack."

"Okay, but we've *got* to do an interview. People want to see the man."

"Yeah, right."

So PR had cornered Ian. "This isn't working. I don't know what got into me, thinking it could work. We can't keep it a secret. You've got to step out and tell the truth."

"*You* want *me* to tell the truth?"

PR sounded angry. "If Nick doesn't get here in time . . . Do you want a *riot*? Huh?"

Visions of Tulsa raced through Ian's mind. He hadn't seen Kansas City, but he'd heard enough, and he'd been told that Tulsa looked like KC in a bottle. He'd experienced worse. Once, in 1968, at a show in Calgary—

"Yeah," Ian said, a dry-throated whisper. "I guess maybe there's a couple things I didn't think about."

They sat in the trailer, Ian and PR, while Grace and the rest of the crew did whatever they needed to do and wherever they needed to do it.

Hanna was at the airport.

"*Is* he coming?"

PR shrugged.

What Ian had in mind: Trigger would come to the track, sneak in, and he and Ian would switch places. Trigger would do the stunt, pretend that he was Ian. If they wore the same uniform—everybody, even the engineers, wore the same coveralls and caps—maybe nobody would notice. After, when the TV cameras would converge, Ian and Trigger would switch back. Chaos would help.

Trigger would melt away as part of the crew.

Ian's hand? Hurt in the stunt.

That was the plan. Somehow, Hanna had apparently talked Trigger into going along with it. What did she say? Who knew? She *did* say that he'd said he'd do it, and PR *did* say he'd made arrangements for a flight.

Now, the flight was late, and PR wasn't even sure Trigger was on it.

It was getting closer to showtime, Trigger wasn't there yet, the TV people were getting antsy. Things could go wrong—it looked like they *were* going wrong—and Ian hadn't considered all the details. He'd simply acted.

"He'll be here," PR finally said.

"Shit." Still plenty of time, or so Ian might have thought on any other occasion; but not now. Now, Ian fairly twitched with raw nervousness.

He did his best to hide from the spotlight as the clock ticked away. PR helped as much as he could.

One o'clock.

Where the hell—

In the excruciating absence of an interview with Ian himself, between and sometimes during pre-show acts of the famous singers, the motorcycle riding troupe, and the marching band, commentators found a lot to talk about. PR steered them in the right directions—distracted them—as needed. Commentators focused on Grace and Joel and on the other members of the daredevil crew.

Hanna was away.

Flynn and Boo and Radar got special attention when it was learned that Flynn would do a Russian Dynamite Death Chair before the jump, a last-minute addition to the program. The extra show element had been planned earlier but PR had delayed announcing it until the last moment for dramatic effect. It also helped insulate Ian from attention. Of course, Boo would do his clown dynamite gag before Flynn got in the dynamite box, and Radar would announce the gag and the stunt.

At one-thirty, the two jump cars were rolled onto the infield. Ian and the crew inspected the two cars, starting and re-starting them, hoods open, tinkering.

At two o'clock, Ian drove the Merc a few times up and down the track along the jump route and in front of the grandstands, gunning the engine, wowing the crowd. At two-ten, he parked the car, got out, and waved to the cheering crowd.

Then he conferred with his crew in a tight huddle under the takeoff ramp. One member of the crew broke from the huddle to bark at a camera-man who'd pressed too close. The circle of cameras backed off the huddle as it lingered. Minutes passed and the crowd began to murmur, a dull whisper, as they watched.

What was going on?

Commentators commentated and spectators spectated, and everybody watched the huddle.

"We got to stall," Ian whispered to his crew. "Anybody got any ideas?"

"Something wrong with the jump car always works for the show," Boo said.

"Yeah," Flynn added, "and it don't got to be nothing specific either. Just you, looking serious."

"Okay," Ian said. "That'll give us ten minutes. We'll need more, so keep thinking."

At last, shortly after two-thirty, the conference of crack daredevil me-chanics broke up—ladies and gentlemen, you're seeing it live—some crew members running this way and that with clear if unknown purpose—we'll try to get you a live exclusive interview—while others ambled away in dif-ferent directions as if with nothing to do and nowhere special to go. Please stay tuned for more after these important messages.

Ian, accompanied by Tink and Hoppy, walked slowly over to the Merc.

Ian nearly bumped into an intrepid cameraman who caught his grim expression, close up.

Was something wrong?

The crowd murmured, watched.

The clock ticked.

Trigger didn't come.

Ian stuck his head under the Merc's hood and listened—ABC watched over his shoulder through a portable camera—as Tink revved the engine. He said something to Hoppy, waved Flynn over. He'd found something, he muttered to Hoppy and Tink in a private conversation, out of earshot of the snooping camera; something wasn't right with the engine.

"I think it's the carburetor," Tink told one inquiring commentator when pressured. "Maybe a problem, maybe not. We're looking at it. This might take some time, don't know, but we got the backup car, just in case."

Of course. The second car set aside for the second loop was right there, so maybe Ian would use it.

But Ian didn't look happy as he stood over the open hood of the backup car—a '64 Rambler station wagon, auto, six—looking at the engine.

Ten to three and no sign of Trigger and Hanna.

The Rambler had been checked, re-checked, and it was being checked again. Commentators gushed breathlessly, as if they were watching a pro golf tournament, as Ian stood over the engine, hands on his hips, muttering.

"I don't know. Something—"

He *was* the expert, after all.

Ian's stall tactic brought everybody's attention directly on him, something he didn't want, but he was running out of ideas.

He drove the Rambler up and down the track as he'd done the Merc, got the same reaction from the crowd—maybe bigger as he'd milked anticipation bone dry. When he got out of the Rambler this time, he gave the crowd a thumbs up, did the same for the cameras, and told the crew, loud enough for the microphones to hear, "This one is a flier. We're good to go."

Cheers, roaring thunderously.

Three-twenty.

As the marching band performed, Ian walked up the slope of the loop-the-loop, flanked closely by two members of his crew and by Orland Cartwright.

"That's Orland Cartwright," a commentator reported, "the NASA engineer who designed and built the loop." View from the reporter's camera-man's shoulder-mounted camera was broadcast on the four screens flanking the grandstands as well as on TV, live. "As you recall, the first test of this ramp didn't go off so well and another test was scheduled . . ."

The show crew, plus a dozen other people PR had on hand for the occasion, including Cartwright, PR and Baha, all wore white coveralls with a red and blue stripe down both arms and legs. An "Ian McGinnis's Auto Daredevil Thrill Show" emblem was stitched on the back of each uniform and a Landini Tire logo adorned the breast pocket. They all wore white baseball caps with the Landini Tire logo.

Everybody looked alike, something Ian had counted on for the switch with Trigger.

After inspecting the jump ramp inner slope, Ian climbed up a ladder to the lip of the take off end of the ramp and looked out over the trucks the jump car would have to clear to reach the tire pile beyond. Dramatic images of Ian standing there staring into the gulf played on the big screens. Even more dramatic—the band had stopped playing and relative silence reigned.

Wind stirred the plastic flags into a gentle flutter, the motors on the blimp overhead hummed, a murmur went through the crowd, and they stirred. Stood.

The flag.

Three-thirty.

The band struck up the "Star-Spangled Banner," as a contingent of ROTC officers from Arizona State University presented the colors, and fifteen thousand voices rose in ragged but enthusiastic unison. ABC got it all, including the Man of the Hour, Ian McGinnis, standing at the takeoff ramp edge, facing into the wind, facing his destiny, his challenge, right hand over his heart, singing. At one point, Ian raised his left hand, where he held his hat, and brushed something, maybe a tear—the camera couldn't get close enough to tell—from his eye.

A gentle breeze eased the heat, and fluttered the flag, the banners, and the cuff of Ian McGinnis's white overalls, and ABC broadcast it all.

Then it ended, and the crowd cheered thunderously as the flag retired, and as Ian climbed back down the ladder.

Three-forty.

As Ian retreated to the vicinity of the trailer, where his crew in their white overalls surrounded him, the audience turned their attention to the center of the track, just to the south side of the lined-up trucks and centered on the grandstands where Radar had taken a microphone and introduced Boo. Radar stood on a slightly raised wooden platform, and he did his best, but people at either end of the south bleachers, and most of the people sitting in the north side bleachers, couldn't see. ABC played two cameras on the event and put them up on the four corner screens, and Radar and Boo took center stage.

The clown dynamite gag took five minutes and earned a decent share of applause and laughter, especially after the blast from the squib Boo set for the punchline went off, and one of the cameramen fell backwards, startled by the sudden, unexpected noise. It made for an extra laugh no one had anticipated.

Then Boo retired and Radar introduced Flynn.

"Terry Flynn," Radar said, carny-intense announcer voice booming through the PA, "from Price, Utah! Is! Captain! Dynamite!"

Flynn, clad in white coveralls, walked out beside Radar, waved his helmet to the crowd, took his applause. Then, as Radar announced, he got into place in the chair and settled in.

Ian had a story he told reporters about the history of the Russian Dynamite Death Chair. "I was in a hotel in Oregon," he said, "between shows, and I picked up this old magazine that had a story in it about this Russian czar who had a unique way of disposing of his rivals and enemies. He'd invite them into his palace and sit them down in this special chair, and literally blow them up with dynamite. Now, that intrigued me, and I got to wondering if I could do that—and survive."

Then he'd tap his hearing aid and say, "Well, it took a while before I figured it out, cost me my hearing, but I did it."

Radar dramatically told the story of the stunt's origin, got his audience focused on the dynamite chair itself, a low, silvery box affair on a bare patch of ground forty yards away, closer to the loop. He started a countdown from ten, but something went wrong and the blast occurred before he reached three.

The boom echoed from the artificial walls created by the two flanking sets of bleachers. It startled the crowd, whose shouts, muffled screams, and gasps of dismay followed the blast.

Radar himself was momentarily startled into a stutter, then silence, but he recovered quickly. "Get that safety crew in there," he said unnecessarily. The crew was already on the way to Flynn's side, and one of the four ambulances stationed on the grounds, the one nearest Flynn at the time, turned on its lights and the driver started the engine.

The billow of smoke and flying dirt and debris that hid Flynn when the blast went off dissipated quickly enough for folks, and the cameraman, who also rushed to the scene, to see Flynn struggling to get to his knees. Conscious but dazed, he was all right.

And the crowd went wild as Hoppy and BB hoisted Flynn up on unsteady feet and helped him take off his helmet. He waved weakly to the cheering crowd and staggered, with help, toward the nearby ambulance for a quick checkup.

Three fifty-five.

Ian had hoped the dynamite show would distract the audience and the TV people enough for him to make the switch with Trigger, but Trigger wasn't there.

An ABC announcer took over the PA to announce the big moment.

Four o'clock, and PR pulled Ian aside.

"We got *no* time left." He panted, face flushed. "Nick isn't here."

"Shit."

"I got *no* ideas left. You?"

"Shit."

"Ian—"

"*Shit*, I said."

PR said nothing more as Ian stood. He sighed and started walking slowly toward the jump ramp. He thought, desperately hard, as he walked toward the ramp end, where he'd stand, take a microphone, and address the silent crowd.

There was no way he could do it. No way. The pain would be intolerable; he might even lose consciousness, lose his grip, lose control of the car, hurt himself, maybe hurt or kill somebody. The stunt wouldn't work. It would be a disaster. There was *no way.*

Maybe Flynn, or Tink?

No. It'd be worse if they screwed up. This is my fault. My responsibility. But I just can't do it.

Show's over, folks. I'm sorry. I screwed up. Can you say, "screwed" on TV?

Ian's approach to the ramp platform at this moment hadn't been in anybody's playbook. Startled commentators stuttered as badly as Radar had earlier, when the dynamite chair went off, baffled and doing their best to look competent. The crowd hushed and all eyes focused on Ian. Nobody had the slightest clue what this was all about.

The only sound: the blimp motor humming, plastic flags fluttering.

"Ladies and gentlemen," Ian began. His voice echoed, too loud. He coughed; something caught in his throat. "There's—there's something, uh, I got to say—"

In the heavy, dead silence, from far to the west, by the entry gate of the big field, an engine roared, a cloud of dust billowed behind a car racing onto the field.

CHAPTER THIRTY-EIGHT

Nick hadn't slept since Hanna called. Maybe a few minutes on the airplane, but it wasn't restful sleep. Now, in the car with Hanna zipping down the freeway to the show, he felt more fatigued than he'd felt hours earlier.

He was dirty, hungry, tired, and—*what else*?

"Calm."

"What?" Hanna maneuvered deftly between cars, changing lanes, keeping up her speed, a notch above sixty. The plane had been late, delayed at take off for some reason. They hadn't bothered to pick up Nick's luggage. They'd run through the concourse.

It was almost four. "We're late, and you're *calm*?"

"You know show business and I know stunt business. How it feels. If you have to ask—"

"Yeah, right."

They sat in silence as Hanna concentrated on driving through the blast furnace Arizona heat and Nick thought about—not what he was doing, or going to do in a few minutes, but why.

Am I doing this to impress Hanna?

There was some truth to that, Nick admitted to himself. Hanna had not said she'd asked him to do it for her and he had no reason to believe that doing it would get them back together. He couldn't use this—wouldn't use it—as leverage to re-establish their relationship. That would be—

He barked a mirthless laugh. Still, he'd *thought* of it.

"What?" Hanna asked, eyes on the road.

"Nothing." *Sounds like something from one of those women's magazines. How I Risked My Life For Love.*

His feelings for Hanna lingered, like an itch under an old scab. But it *was* over.

So why *was* he doing it?

Nick had tried to compose himself on the way to the phone in the manager's office in the Tulsa tire store, but his heart jammed in his throat anyway when he heard her voice.

"What?" he'd said.

And she'd told him, crisply and without embellishment—this wasn't Radar or PR talking—what the problem was, and what she wanted him to do about it. Ian had broken his hand, Shaun was dead, Ian couldn't do the B-S, and he wanted Nick to do it.

"Jesus, Hanna, your dad just fired me. I screwed up—"

"Nick, I don't want you to do this for me. Understand?"

Silence.

"I want you to do this for my father."

Silence.

"Understand? For my dad. And for my mom. For the show, Nick. Understand? For the show."

Quite suddenly, Nick understood. He jumped. He said yes.

In a flash of insight, something both like and unlike the high he felt in that glorious infinite, frozen moment at the apogee of a good jump, Nick knew he must do this.

The reason? Not Hanna, not the thrill of the jump. Something else.

The realization, the *vision*, of the "something else" that occurred to Nick as he listened to Hanna was so stupefying that it caught his breath, made him momentarily dizzy. But it *was* a jump, a rush, the biggest rush of his life—*a bigger rush than Hanna had been.*

In the car, Hanna had told Nick the part of the plan she didn't know when she'd grabbed the initiative from Ian to contact Nick; that Nick was to pretend he was Ian for the stunt. Spotlight on Ian McGinnis, not on Nick Cassidy.

"There's a uniform in the back seat," she'd said. "Put it on. And the hat."

Nick grunted assent at this development and changed clothes as they drove. He'd already jumped, but this time, he saw his landing site with crystal clarity. The twist? The notion of pretending he was somebody he was not, of sharing the spotlight—surrendering it? Didn't bother him at all.

Not surprised; elated.

He laughed aloud at the realization. It seemed fitting.

"What?" Hanna honked the horn and the gate of the B-S arena opened. They were expected.

"Tell you later."

It was the road Maverick, Ian realized, with Hanna and Nick arriving. And suddenly, Ian changed his trajectory yet again.

Later, he'd have time to think about what he decided to do, what he knew he *must* do—but for now—

Ian put the microphone down on the edge of the ramp and it squealed. He walked down the ramp, looking for PR. But PR was already down the track intercepting the arriving Mav, ready to complete the subterfuge they'd planned. Ian waved one of Cartwright's crew over, the girl with the clipboard.

"Get the man in that car over here to me, hear?"

The girl nodded and spoke into a radio.

In a few moments, during which renewed rumblings among spectators vibrated the grandstands, Trigger was ushered up the ramp. PR was at his side, trying to shield him from view of stalking cameras, but the effort looked awkward and PR looked frazzled. It looked as if PR wasn't going to let Trigger come up to Ian. PR clearly didn't understand yet that Ian had made a last-second change in the program—again.

So Ian took the microphone up again and forced the issue.

"Ladies and gentlemen, Meet the daredevil who's going to perform the greatest daredevil feat in the history of the world—"

Both PR's and Trigger's eyes widened.

"—From Decatur, Georgia! Nick Cassidy!"

Cheers rose, but not as loud as it had been earlier for Ian. In fact, it sounded tentative, tepid—polite. Confused.

What's going on?

Cameras found Cassidy, who stood stunned, immobile, next to PR and among members of the uniformed crew and staff. Ian waved Cassidy forward.

It took a few moments, but Nick was shoved forward to stand beside Ian, where Ian shouted at him over the din.

"What?" Nick shouted.

"Just wave to the crowd, get in the car, and do the stunt."

"What?"

"The Rambler. Hit the ramp at sixty-five, and watch your grip. You'll be pushed down in the seat, not lifted, see—"

"Ian—"

"It's longer than you expect, the takeoff ramp, so be patient. Don't go for the glove compartment until you feel air under you."

"Ian, I thought—"

"Sixty-five, or a tad more. Go, goddamit, before I change my mind and do it myself."

Nick dutifully waved to the crowd and retreated to the foot of the ramp, where the Rambler waited, ready.

He'd been ready to make the switch, hide among the milling crew in similar uniforms, until Ian was ready to make the switch in a patch of dark at the west end of the stands. But Ian had given up the spotlight; given it up to Nick.

"What the hell's going on?" PR sounded angry, but Nick caught on quick; Nick had been ready to sacrifice the spotlight for Ian. Ian beat him to it.

PR, looking scared, said something about a riot and left the scene, but Nick didn't notice.

On the four big screens flanking the grandstands, an image showed of the Rambler station wagon as Nick put on his helmet, climbed into the driver's seat and buckled up.

Crew swarmed the car, talking to Nick, at him, around him.

Checking details, like they did at any show. Engine sounds fine, seatbelt fastened and adjusted secure, glove box reach across the front seat tests out okay, steering wheel responds tight, gauges look okay, doors wired shut, the tires—well, brand new Landini tires, of course. All systems go.

Crew repeated Ian's directions. Hit sixty-five at take-off, hold steady on the long ramp, wait until you feel air before you dive for the glove compartment, relax. Nick barely heard. His mind moved into the jump, tuned out the rest.

To an indistinct shouted question from Tink—or was it Flynn?—Nick nodded "okay," gave thumbs up, and thumped the dashboard with a fist—*thumpthumpthump*—and headed out. Ready.

The crowd roared, the grandstands shook with their roar, and the announcer's voice sunk behind the roar.

The Rambler raced down the track toward the loop-the-loop ramp. It built up speed, swerved to the north of the ramp at the last moment, roared past the north side grandstands, slowed and turned south and passed in front of the south side grandstands as it accelerated back westward.

A second time, the Rambler, painted in show colors with the Landini Tire logo on both sides, on the top, and on the hood, roared down the straightaway approach to the ramp. This time at the last second, Nick swerved to the south, roared past the cheering crowd, and returned past the north side stands to the west end.

There, Nick turned around, facing the gigantic loop again. Nick held the Rambler in place. He revved the engine again and again and a cloud billowing out the back and from the tires.

Then Nick *let go* and the car shot forward, leaping off the ground, coming faster and faster.

Ian ran to the landing site, as did the rest of the crew and Cartwright's engineers, after Nick took off in the Rambler. His lungs burned and his legs ached as he ran, gimpy, old injuries waking up to manifest in a painful inventory of past mishaps. He ran anyway, because when you're safety crew, that's what you did.

I'm getting too old for this, Ian thought as he ran past the trucks lined up between takeoff ramp and tire pile.

The idea to give the show to Nick had occurred to Ian suddenly as he stood there on the take off ramp, microphone in hand, ready to confess that he couldn't do the stunt and face the consequences like a man. Sudden, clear inspiration. That's what it had been.

The idea that, with Trigger arriving late, the switch subterfuge plot wouldn't have worked, that it was a silly—no; a *stupid*—idea in the first place, that people would find out about Ian's injured hand sooner or later anyway and resent the—the word "fraud" briefly skittered across Ian's mind—no, these ideas never occurred to him.

He gave the show to Nick because it was the right thing to do. That's all.

Hanna and Nick Cassidy? What else have I been blind to?

Ian replayed in his mind the stunning conversation he'd had with Hanna after she'd called Nick.

Her words—"I was in love with him, Dad, once" and "He loved me, too, for what that's worth"—sounded bizarre to Ian, like she was discussing a school play she'd seen. But she seemed so intense, serious.

"But I've moved on," she'd said.

"So why did you—"

"I got a hunch. I think maybe he understands, more than you know. About family, I mean, and the show. And I—"

Ian didn't need to hear her say it. "I'm still in love with him." Words Ian might have found hard to hear and she clearly found hard to say. But the words were there, in the way she held her body. In her eyes, the set of her jaw. *So like her mother.*

Ian arrived at the foot of the tire pile and stood bent over, his left hand braced on a knee, breathing razor blades.

But Nick had agreed with Hanna to do the stunt, was ready to do it under the terms—no spotlight for Nick Cassidy. When the idea to ask Cassidy to come back and do the stunt first occurred to Ian, the idea for insisting that Cassidy do it—*in secret*—quickly followed.

Could Cassidy do it? Ian realized—later, maybe within the last couple hours, who knew?—that the stipulation was a test. That Nick had agreed—*not with me but with Hanna*—was step one. Doing it, actually going through with it, that was another smoke altogether.

Ian and Nick hadn't talked much on the ramp in the few seconds after Ian gave Nick the spotlight, except for Ian's shouted instruction about speed and the like. But Ian had looked at Nick's expression anyway, looked for some clue that Nick understood. He didn't see what he was looking for.

Maybe Nick didn't really understand. Maybe he did, but didn't show it. Or did but simply didn't know that he did. But things moved fast; not much time for a guy to think.

God, I'm making myself dizzier.

Ian made a hasty mental note to ask Hanna about it later. She seemed to know a lot.

From the west, Ian heard a roar building, coming toward him.

He focused. Showtime.

*

Nick hit the loop take off ramp straight on. At sixty-seven. He braced for the inward pressure, soared up the inner side, upside down, and down the backside of the loop. Steady, steady. He shot off the ramp and flew through the air flat and straight a hundred feet above the line of Landini Tires delivery trucks. Then, coming down, the Rambler's nose started to fall.

Short.

He was going to crash.

Nick dove for the glove compartment and grabbed the passenger seat edge tight, teeth gritted, muscles straining.

The car hit the second to last of the twenty vans with a metallic *thunk* and then *bounced*, tail end rising as it did so. It landed upside down in the tire pyramid.

The impact jarred like he'd hit concrete instead of rubber tires and Nick felt as much surprise as pain. His grip on the seat edge tore loose, his fingers stung, and he shook like a rag doll. The seatbelt dug into his chest with the sudden impact and his next thought, after surprise, was, *Damn, more broke ribs*.

Then the world went dark as he realized he was upside down, buried in tires.

Smoke, gas fumes, and dust gagged Nick as he tried to unbuckle his seatbelt. He was upside down, dizzy, disoriented, and the buckle was stuck, his own weight jamming it. He felt like he was choking.

He heard faint shouts. Boo with his fire extinguisher, and other voices—Ian?—sounding dim, muffled.

Nick gave up on the seatbelt and hung upside down, waiting, dizzy, trying to breathe.

As he watched the Rambler fly through the air over the Landini trucks, Ian felt elated. *My god, that's beautiful.* In his mind, he tried to freeze the instant, to savor the vision. He'd seen this a hundred times. He'd *done* it a thousand times. It never failed to fascinate him.

Then he realized the car was falling short and his heart leapt into his throat.

Not fast enough, not fast enough—

The car bounced off the top of the truck and flipped into the tire pile, upside down.

In the half-dozen times in the previous weeks that the tire jump stunt had been performed, the crew had learned a few tricks. They'd discovered that they couldn't climb a mound of slippery, mushy tires without falling down a lot, looking like Keystone Cops, and risking twisted ankles. They used ladders to climb the tire mound. It worked.

They'd placed ladders at four corners of the tire pile, and as the car crashed into the pile—dead center; it couldn't have worked out better in that respect—the crew, as they'd done before, raised the ladders and dropped them onto the tires, with the high end near the center. They climbed the ladders.

They'd also learned to make the tire mound hollow, so it would give under the impact of a jump car. They'd discovered that a solid mound didn't catch the jump car; rather, it forced the jump car to bounce off it, and they couldn't predict where it would land. The hole in the center caught the car firmly and held it. The stunt looked good and audiences loved it.

Ian's busted hand hurt like holy hell as he climbed the ladder, but he did it anyway. No way was he going to wait at the bottom of the pile like a goddam—

This was *his* show, that was *his* daredevil in the car, and he was damn well going to be the first one on the scene—

Of course, Boo had beaten him to the scene, as had Flynn, Tink and Hoppy and a dozen others, all in uniform. Somebody had tried to hold Ian back but it didn't work.

At the top of the ladder, Ian tried to help toss tires aside. He quickly realized that he was useless. Worse, he was in the way.

The dirty bottom of the car faced the sky, tendrils of smoke oozing from the greasy engine bottom and the still-spinning rear wheels. The crew, swarming ant-like, pulled out tires from beside the car doors, tossed them up the side of the mound, which resembled a volcano, where others tossed the tires down the outer slope.

They couldn't get to the car windows or doors without digging. It took a few minutes, hushed, tense minutes, before Tink and Flynn were able to get down the sides of the car and climb into it. Ian tried to join the two, slipping and sliding into the pit.

He lost his footing and fell. He cried out in pain, a loud, sharp wail in the relative stillness.

An ambulance stood by at the foot of the mound, engine running. EMTs had a backboard already out.

Hoppy and BB hauled Ian out of the pit. Cameras zoomed in on his pain-etched face and the right hand he held clutched to his chest as EMTs converged. Broken?

No secret now.

Ian hadn't gotten a chance to see into the Rambler, to hear if Nick was okay. Nobody could see what was going on at the bottom of the tire crater. The best view came from directly overhead, from the Landini Tire blimp. That image, magnified as much as possible but jittery, was relayed onto the four screens flanking the arena, and broadcast live on the air.

Ian hushed a paramedic who was trying to ask him questions. He was listening for a word from one of the crew atop the pile. Joel was up there.

A thumbs up would do. Somebody yell, "He's all right!" Please. A signal. *Anything.*

"Come on, come on."

The silence lingered, that stunned, anxious, tensely waiting silence that too often presaged disaster in a show. Not a voice rose, not a sound heard among the thousands present except the flutter of plastic flags in the wind and the low hum of the blimp overhead. So quiet was the crowd at that moment that the TV cameras picked up the crew's muffled voices from inside and at the lip of the tire mound.

At last, one of the engineers standing on the rim of the tire crater raised his thumb and shouted, loudly enough for the TV microphones to catch, "He's all right!"

And the crowd went wild.

Nick emerged from the car, staggering and struggling for footing, helped by Tink and Flynn, climbing up the loose tires.

When they saw him emerge from the car, the cheering, clapping, and whistling redoubled and the grandstands thundered under the impact of thousands of stomping feet.

Nick stood on the lip of the tire mound, took off his helmet, and waved it, breathing cool air.

Thunderous applause rained down on him from all sides.

After a long, long moment, after the sustained applause and cheers had more or less expended itself, Nick was gingerly escorted down a ladder off the tire mound, where a cameraman waited at the bottom for a quick, frantic interview. It was short, because Nick was having difficulty breathing, in obvious pain, maybe broken ribs. Paramedics escorted him to a waiting ambulance, where Ian already sat in the back. The ambulance left, lights flashing, siren wailing, but slowly, heading for Phoenix Baptist.

"Phoenix Baptist is okay," Ian told Nick. "I been there before." Ian was on a first name basis with a doctor there and two nurses.

"I think I cracked some ribs," Nick whispered.

"Again?" Somewhere along the way, he had no idea, when, Ian had stopped thinking of Nick Cassidy as "Trigger."

"No, seriously, man."

A paramedic politely told the two to shut up.

CHAPTER THIRTY-NINE

*I*an and Nick were released from the hospital later that evening, bruised, bandaged, but ambulatory. Nick had cracked ribs, Ian a broken hand.

Media had followed them to the hospital, of course, and they did a few interviews in front of the hospital after they were released. Then PR did his magic and spirited them away to an obscure out-of-the-way motel north of town off Highway 17.

The next morning, Ian drove Nick to the airport. Ian hadn't had a chance to talk much with Nick in the ambulance and they'd been separated, and busy, at the hospital. Nick had his own room at the motel, and Ian didn't really feel much like socializing that night. He fell asleep as soon as his head hit the pillow.

Grace woke him shortly after six.

"Nick is leaving in an hour."

"I'll drive him to the airport," Ian had said.

"Are you sure?"

"I just said so, didn't I?"

It wasn't so much that Ian wanted to talk with Nick; he wanted to hear from Nick; why did he agree to do it?

They rode in silence until: "So why did you do it?" Nick asked.

Nick lounged back in the passenger seat, reclining, his right arm out the window, tapping listlessly on the window frame, looking at nothing in particular beyond the edge of the freeway. It was a bright, sunny morning, cloudless. Ian drove with his left hand, the other in a cast.

They were stuck in sluggish Monday morning commute traffic on the Maricopa Freeway a half mile from Phoenix Sky Harbor International. To make matters worse, there was an accident up ahead, and Cassidy had a flight to catch to Atlanta.

"I was going to ask you the same thing," Ian said. He'd borrowed a Hertz rental car that one of the Landini Tire people had at the show, a spanking new '80 Dodge Mirada with an ugly slat grill but with its new car smell still present, rather than the more conspicuous daredevil show car, to drive to the airport.

Inconspicuous. Ian had had his fill of reporters.

"I asked you first," Nick said. It was almost eight o'clock; Cassidy's flight was at eight forty-five and traffic was barely moving.

"Okay. We couldn't have gotten away with the switch idea after all. Reporters are reporters. They'd have found out. My hand. They had cameras everywhere. And switching cars like that at the last second—I don't know. And you were late."

"So, right there, on the ramp—"

"I was going to quit. Maybe all hell would have broken loose, like at Tulsa, but—"

"So, right then, just out of the blue—"

"Yeah, right then. Just out of the blue."

"But that's not what I meant."

"Huh?"

"I mean, in the first place. Why me, after you'd fired me and all? And why—"

"I saw something."

"Huh?"

Traffic stopped cold, horns honked, and Ian sighed.

He told Nick.

After Hanna had gotten Nick on board with the scheme on the phone at the rest area north of Phoenix Saturday, after he'd put PR to work implementing the scheme, Ian gathered the crew in the shade of the trailer and briefed them. They were still in shock over the news about Shaun, and surprised that in little more than an hour after hearing it, Ian had recovered his wits.

It took some effort to mobilize the troops, lead them out of their shock and grief, and beyond it, but Ian did it. He knew action trumped inaction, and that if he let their mourning become any more entrenched, it would fester, and he might not be able to pull it off, what he had in mind.

"I need your help to do this," he'd told them. "But if any of you ain't up to it, it's okay. I understand."

In fact, the crew welcomed the plan.

"It seems a fitting tribute," Radar had said in his crisp, pedantic manner.

"You got Trigger to go for it?" Hoppy asked again, stunned that Cassidy would agree.

"And he's going to fly out and do it?" Boo asked, again.

Ian nodded and the crew didn't take much time to ponder, maybe sensing that time was of the essence, and definitely relieved to have something to do.

"Let's do it," BB had said, munching Dentyne. The others echoed her declaration.

"You weren't there, Nick," Ian said, "when we talked about it." Traffic started moving again, but slowly. "Trust. Show is all about trust. You got that?"

Nick was silent for a while. "You trust me?"

There had been a time Ian had resented Nick in the worst way, a bitterness that Grace had identified for him, quite forcefully, as nothing more than petty, adolescent jealousy. Not long after Tulsa, she'd put the word right in his face—*jealousy*—and he'd had to chew on it. She'd said the word as if asking Ian to pass the mashed potatoes, as if it was a fact, like pain hurts, people have feelings, life goes on, and it's okay, after all. There was no accusation, no condemnation attached to the casual, off-hand remark. Ian hadn't responded, but he'd heard.

And he chewed on it, like gristle.

At the time, it tasted bitter. But then, he had his epiphany in the rest area after hearing about Shaun, while he was on the phone with PR, and it all fell into place, like well-oiled gears meshing.

"We got a lot in common, Nick," Ian said. But not loudly.

"What?"

"Of course I trust you. I called you, didn't I? And you came. Actions speak louder and all that. You came. You did it. I trust you. All there is to it."

"Maybe I'll want to write a book someday."

Ian snorted. "You can write?"

"So, why'd you do it?"

"The show is as much a thrill for us to do—"

"Oh, come on, Ian. You can't bullshit a bullshitter. This is *me*. I mean—

hell, you know what I mean. Why. Did. You. Do it?"

Ian chewed on his lip for a moment. *You whack your knuckles, you swear a lot, then you go back to work.* "You remember Tulsa."

"What's that have to do—"

"You had four choices there, when you saw me in your way."

"Choices? Man, you were there like a deer in my headlights. I didn't have a choice. I had to act."

"And you made the right choice. Instinctively right."

"Huh?"

Ian explained.

When Trigger saw Ian, suddenly and unexpectedly, in front of his speeding car, he could have hit Ian, killing him. Or he could have swerved to the right, the car speeding uncontrolled into the infield where Grace and Hanna and Joel stood, and Boo with his fire extinguisher, and Radar with his microphone, and the ambulance crew farther back to the infield. Somebody would have been killed, maybe including Nick.

Or he could have swerved to the left, into the five-foot high concrete wall, designed to keep speeding stock cars on the track when they lost control rather than flying into the bleachers. A sturdy, high, wire-mesh fence above the concrete wall anchored with solid, thick posts kept a car from climbing that wall and going into the crowd in the first rows. Hitting that concrete wall head on would have killed Nick instantly.

"And the fourth choice?" Nick prompted as Ian stopped talking, thinking. Ian had reviewed this in his mind a dozen times since he saw that Gremlin in the rest area parking lot trying to turn left, the wrong way.

"You're left-handed," Ian said.

Nick snorted. "Man, how many times does a guy have to say 'huh'?"

"When you did your first rollover—remember? Up in Montana? You were a natural. I asked you then if you were left-handed."

"Yeah, so?"

"A left-hander naturally tends to cut the wheel to the right in a rollover, which is why it's so hard to teach a lefty how to do rolls, because you have to turn left for the rolls. And in Tulsa? Most people would've froze, ran into me, but you acted. And you didn't go right, like you would've done naturally being a left-hander. You went left, against your nature. That's what you did when you did that first rollover."

"Okay, call me slow. I still don't understand—"

"You acted with your head, against your body's instincts. You acted, and you didn't kill me, which would have happened if you did nothing, which most people would have done, or not done, if you take my meaning—"

"Get to the point."

"—and you didn't go right like your nature would have dictated. You turned left. In an instant—you didn't think, you *acted*. And you turned left. Hit the wall."

Long pause. "You said there was four ways."

"If you hit that wall head-on, you would've been killed right there. But—again, you did this on instinct, and that's the amazing part—you cut to the *right* just before you hit the wall, so that you hit on the left front fender rather than the grill, at an angle, a slant, rather than head-on. You used the angle on the wall to slow the car's momentum, to bring it to a stop. Without getting killed and without killing anybody else. You did it all—on instinct. It was like you knew what to do, inside, but you weren't even conscious of knowing. You knew. You acted. Fast. That was it. I've seen the like once or twice, but it's so rare that it took me a long time to recognize it. I saw this car at the rest area, see, just a minute before I called you—I mean, before Hanna called. Anyway, what I saw, it triggered everything. And I knew."

Long pause.

Then Nick sighed. "Let me get this straight. You knew I could do it, the loop stunt. So you called me. Is that it?"

"Uh-huh."

"What if I'd said no?"

Ian shrugged.

"But you're a stubborn son-of-a-bitch. I mean, if I'd said no, would you have gone ahead and done it anyway?"

"No." Ian looked at his right hand, tried to flex the fingers under the cast. It would be a long time before he could use the hand. "I'd have had to call PR and tell him the bad news. I was about to do that anyway standing there on that ramp when you and Hanna showed. Just the thought—it hurt worse than this hand, but less than doing the stunt and screwing it up."

"So, why didn't you? I still don't get it. You hate my guts. You hate me so much that you nearly killed yourself—talk about instincts, tell me what drove you to get in front of my car. You couldn't have known that I would turn aside. No, you hate me that much, to put your life on the line to screw me over so I couldn't do the stunt. You almost killed me, you hate me that much. But you called. You'd fired my ass, tried to bash my head in, and still you called. I don't get it."

"I don't hate you—"

"Bullshit. There's something you're leaving out. And I got to know what it is. Spill, Ian. You've come this far."

Ian had seen the Gremlin, its left turn signal flashing and he had realized what Nick had done in Tulsa. But there was something else he realized too, even more mind-boggling.

I wonder if I'd have had the presence of mind. Would Shaun?

And that last thought, more stunning than the realization that had preceded it a moment earlier, set Ian's mind racing.

He'd decided to call Nick.

"I don't hate you," Ian started. His throat felt raw, parched, and he stopped and coughed, wished he'd had something to drink. "There's a lot about show. Details. It ain't just the kicks you get from stretching out there, testing what you can do. It ain't the crowd cheering. It ain't the fun. Well, it's all that, but there's more. I asked you to do the stunt because I wanted to know if you had that—that other thing."

"Now you're getting to it. Keep going."

"The terms, that you do it *as* me, that you do the stunt and never let the world know that it was you that did it, but let everybody believe it was me—that was what I wanted to know, if you had *that* in you. Show is family. I've never been able to describe it to anybody. Most people who go on the road with me never get it. It don't have words. You got it or you don't."

And Shaun didn't have it. Didn't have it.

"I wanted it done the way I wanted it done because I wanted to know if you had it, really had it. *It*. I *had* to know."

Because of Shaun.

"So that's why I insisted. And if you'd said no, I would have called PR and tossed in the towel."

Long silence.

They'd reached the airport. Ian pulled over to the side of the parking strip in front of the concourse by a sky cab. The curbside strip wasn't crowded, but Nick didn't have a bag. They'd left it at the airport the day before.

"And you said you'd do it," Ian said. "So, to answer your other question, yes, I trust you. I trusted you from the second you said you'd do it." He put the car in park with his left hand and turned to Nick. "Trust. It's a family thing. One of the details, but it ain't a minor one."

Ian couldn't read Nick's expression.

"Your hand must have been killing you," Nick said, "but you kept smiling, acting like it was all okay."

"Not a bit," Ian said, smiling. "Not a bit."

Nick shook his head, and again Ian couldn't read his expression.

A car behind them honked and Nick got out. He leaned back in the window. "Are we square, then?" he asked.

"No, it's your turn."

Nick sighed. "I get a kick out of pushing myself, Ian. The test pilots, they call it 'pushing the envelope.'"

"I know."

"Well, that's it." Nick shrugged. "That's all of it. I did that T-bone in Tulsa—well, tried to do it anyway—because I wanted to see for myself, feel it for myself. Hell, *you* understand that. You wouldn't let me do it, and I wasn't about to accept no for an answer. I guess I'm as stubborn as you are."

"That wasn't the question."

Nick looked at Ian, puzzled. "Huh?"

"I mean the loop jump. Why'd you do that? Why'd you agree to do it, especially with the terms I asked and you agreed to? Why did you agree to do it the way I wanted?"

Again, Ian couldn't read Nick's expression.

"Something to do with Hanna?" Ian asked.

Nick shook his head. Then he laughed. "We did it," he said. "Man, we *did* it. Now, *that's* a stunt. Wow."

Ian stifled his own laugh. "Yeah, we did."

"Yeah, wow." A dozen expressions played across Nick's face, and Ian wondered if he wanted to say something else.

A car behind Ian honked.

"Tell all," Ian said. "Come on. You can't bullshit a bullshitter."

Nick sighed. "I'm going to put together my own show, Ian. That's why I did it. It's like a first step, a demarcation point, or maybe like a point of no return. When Hanna told me what you had in mind, I saw myself five years from now, starting next summer, doing what you're doing, but doing it with motorcycles. My own show, my own logo and colors."

Ian found himself speechless.

"I don't hate you, Ian. And I'm not after Hanna. I've moved on, really. It was hard, I admit, but I've moved on. When she told me your idea, I suddenly had my own idea, saw it as clearly as if it had already happened. I'm going to compete with you on the road. I'm going to have fun, and I'm going to do it right. You'll see."

Ian found his voice. "You're one crazy son-of-a-bitch."

"Watch your language."

Nick walked away, into the airport.

The car behind Ian honked again, the driver gestured, shouted something, and Ian drove away.

CHAPTER FORTY

Nick walked into the crowded airport not watching where he was going. His mind was on the lie he'd just told Ian. Told himself. About Hanna.

Or was it a lie?

When she'd phoned him, to tell him about Shaun, and Ian's plan for the Big Stunt, and Nick's role in it, if he wanted it, he'd listened with his heart jammed in his throat. It was an odd, cramped sensation, listening to her voice on the phone, and he'd found it difficult to speak, or to even breathe.

But Hanna spoke. Now, he couldn't remember what she'd said, exactly. She'd been no-nonsense, direct. Didn't waste time. He finally interjected with something lame like, "well, I don't know—"

Then she'd used the word *family*. It was like a magician's abracadabra, that word, and he'd said "yes" without thinking, interrupting her.

And that was it. She abruptly stopped pitching the deal and started talking details. Who'd pick him up at the airport, when, and so on. Hanna didn't even bother to ask why he'd said yes.

But Nick thought about it since, a lot. Orphaned, raised by an aunt and uncle who also died when he was still young, and then by his cousin, not much older than him—he'd never been close to anybody, ever. All his relationships—he snorted a chuckle at the word and a fragrant fat old man he'd brushed past in the crowded concourse frowned at him as if he was armed.

Nick shook his head in exasperation. He was heading down the wrong concourse. His luggage and his plane were—over *that* way. He was going to miss his plane.

He ran. *I'm* not *going to miss it*. He ran.

Being on the road—no, that wasn't exactly it. Doing the show—no. *Damn it*. Something about it all—it *meant* something.

Relationship—whatever the hell that meant. Family?

Hanna?

They had not talked, much, after Hanna had picked him up from this very airport. In a hurry again. Hanna had been concentrating on driving, watching the clock, aware that they were late for the show and that the result could be a disaster. Nick took a quick mental glance at how he felt about sitting next to Hanna in the car, *not* talking. He felt a kind of numbness he couldn't identify; yet he felt intensely alert, like the instant before a jump.

Numb yet alert. It was too much to handle in one head.

He set the odd sensations aside, along with the budding notion of starting his own show and focused on getting ready, physically and mentally for the Big Stunt. He'd changed into his show duds in the car and he forced his mind to get behind the stunt, seeing himself doing it.

He didn't hear much of what Hanna said anyway. She didn't talk much. She understood pre-show mindset.

They'd talked again, so briefly, after the stunt.

Nick got his luggage from storage and boarded his flight on the run. He barely made it.

Which made him laugh as he settled into his seat and stared out the window.

Barely made it. That's what Hanna had said after. It wasn't a long conversation; everyone was busy with one thing and another, post show activity. Media types and fans crawled over everybody and everything, and it was a miracle that they even had a few seconds to speak.

"Barely made it?" Nick had said. "I made history today."

"*You* made history?"

"*We* did. And *we* barely made it."

Then, for a second or two, Hanna had gazed into Nick's eyes. She stood close, took his hands in hers. She smelled like sweat and gasoline and something sweet, perfumey.

"Nick, you're okay. I'm okay. *We*'re okay."

"Yeah." Dry mouth. No words. "Yeah."

"I wonder what's next. After. Don't you?"

"Yeah. Yeah."

"But let's keep it under the speed limit this time, okay?"

"Yeah. This time."

"Yeah."

Then the rush of post-show busyness overwhelmed them and they didn't speak again.

This time. This time.

Nick looked out the window as the plane took off. In the distance, to the east, low clouds threatened rain. But in minutes, the plane rose above the clouds. The sun shone bright. Nick slept.

Shaun's funeral was set for early Tuesday afternoon. Ian woke everybody up early Monday morning. They finished breakfast and were ready to go by nine.

Grace drove the Freightliner.

They drove straight through, stopping only for dinner in St. George, and gas and supper in Fillmore, pulling into the home yard just before midnight. Ian had called from St. George to tell Brian when they'd arrive. He was there at Ian's house when they arrived, had the front gate propped open, the garage unlocked and ready, the house heated up, water and gas back on, waiting.

"How's Gran?" Ian asked his brother. First question.

"Same, I'm afraid," Brian said. His shoulders sagged and his eyes were red-rimmed. "We told her, but we're not sure she knows, if she heard." He tried to smile but it looked foreign to his face.

Ian took the road car and left family and crew to settle in for the night. He drove to the care center by the hospital where Gran was.

It was one o'clock when he arrived, and he hesitated at the front door, finger above the "after hours, please ring" button. It was late. Gran would be asleep anyway. And he was tired. He went home.

He came back the next morning and sat with Gran for an hour. One of Brian's kids was there, had been since before breakfast. Always somebody at Gran's side, day and night. Ian had forgotten that the night before.

He talked, a little, but if she heard, Gran didn't let on. Ian held her papery-thin hand. It felt hot, vital. Limp.

Hundreds—maybe as many as a thousand people—attended Shaun's funeral.

BB's sister drove in from Montana that afternoon and took BB home the next day. Hoppy hitched a ride with them. Radar had stored his car at Ian's and he gave Boo a ride to the bus station in town, waited until Boo got on his bus, then drove home.

Flynn stuck around for three days, looking for a job, but finally decided to go home. He took a bus.

A week after Shaun's funeral, Tuesday, September 11, Amanda called Grace, asked her to come over.

"We did girl stuff," Grace told Ian when she got back late that afternoon, "is why I took so long. She's pregnant."

"Amanda? She's—"

"I know, I know." Grace plopped boneless into a chair at the kitchen table. "We were expecting they'd start making babies right off, but I guess at least one of them decided to get responsible, wait until they got their finances straight." She fumbled with her coat. It had been a cold morning.

"And Gran—Amanda says Shaun wanted to wait until she was okay. But then—" Grace stopped, suppressed a sob. "Amanda says it happened the night Shaun died. She conceived twelve or thirteen hours before he—"

Then she did cry. Again.

Ian gave her a back rub, muttered inanely, "There, there," and got her a cup of coffee.

Gran died quietly in her sleep a month later.

PR came out to her funeral.

"I got fired," he announced over coffee at the McGinnis kitchen table after the funeral. He had his coat on, ready to leave, his rental in the driveway. "We did good but not as good as we'd projected. By 'we,' I mean Landini Tires." He laughed. "I guess I shouldn't say 'we' after they fired me."

"It was a good show," Ian said. "A good season."

"Got any plans?" Grace asked.

"I was wondering," PR put his coffee cup down on the table deliberately and leaned forward at Ian. "I was wondering if you needed a good hand next season. If Radar doesn't come back, I could announce." He shrugged. "I can clown too, believe it. Or ramp hand." Another shrug. "Whatever."

Ian wasn't sure when he'd started thinking about the '80 season. Thinking what he was thinking. The unthinkable.

Maybe it was in Tulsa, standing there in the middle of the track, realizing that, reflexively, he'd put himself in the path of a two-ton vehicle bearing down on him at sixty miles an hour or more, driven by a man who *just might not back off*. Or maybe it was a second after Nick *did* back off. Or maybe it was later, when Ian redirected his surging adrenaline, his anger, into a balled fist and that fist into the side of the trailer.

It could have been the moment he saw that Gremlin, realized what he'd realized about Nick and Tulsa, and what that meant about Shaun—*Shaun didn't have that in him, no sir*—or maybe it was when Hanna said that Nick would do the Big Stunt.

Or maybe it was the thought of the Nick Cassidy Motorcycle Daredevil Show.

Or was it when he got word that Shaun was dead? No, that wasn't it. The show went on. Ian could have quit right then, but he didn't.

So it was the Gremlin, and what that meant. Or it was when Cassidy said yes to the switch scheme.

It's a new world.

"Pardon?" PR said. Ian didn't realize that he'd spoken aloud.

"You read about Terrible Tom?" Ian said. "His court thing? Lost all his endorsements over that. And Hapgood, I heard through the grapevine, his show stunk. Did barely 45-minute shows, didn't do any crashes at all. People booed him." Ian shrugged. "Maybe that was part my fault, being so successful this last season. How could Hapgood compare? I used to be the one who had to compare myself to him, but last season, we did so good, everybody started comparing to me."

He looked PR in the eye. "We succeeded, all right. No matter what Landini Tires says, we succeeded. Maybe we were *too* successful." He sighed. "It's a new day, PR. Hollywood's got us beat, with all those camera angles, new technology, robots and computers and stuff like that. The future is in the movies. And in monster trucks."

"What are you saying?" PR said, his voice almost a whisper.

The unthinkable is what. The unsayable.

But he said anyway. "Maybe it's time I stepped aside, let the younger kids take over, while I tend to the ranch and the garage and the tire store." He shrugged. "Maybe I'll build a monster truck, take it on the road, but no more big rigs, no more crashes. I've done that. Folks have seen it. What's next?"

"Well," PR said as he stood. "Call me. If and when." He left his number and drove away.

Grace sat slack-jawed, stunned at what Ian had said.

Finally, "Are you for real about this?" she asked.

Ian nodded. "Maybe. I've gotten calls. Dates. I ain't said yes yet, and I haven't returned a few of those calls. What do you think?"

"Life off the road?"

"No more Ben Gay, no more motels, no more hospitals."

"You under foot all the time?" Grace sat down, eyes glazed. "Let me think."

Two weeks later, Nick called. "I heard about Gran. I'm sorry. I was away and I heard too late and I couldn't come."

Nick had been busy promoting, booking, and recruiting for the "The Nick Cassidy Motorcycle Daredevil Brigade."

"What do you think?" he asked.

"I think the daredevil show is a dinosaur, a thing of the past. But I know that won't stop you. Good luck anyway."

"I talked with PR yesterday. He told me you weren't going out next year. Is that true?"

"Maybe. I think so. Maybe."

"Well. That won't be as much fun, will it? I mean, what would you do?"

"None of your damn business. I can give you numbers of bookers and some dates. And you should try to get in touch with Mike Stern. He's good on a bike. Not as good as you, but good."

"So you're really *not* going out next season?"

"Sometimes I think you're deafer than I am."

"Okay. I appreciate your help, Ian."

"And PR. He said he wanted to go with me."

"Yeah, we talked. I might take him on." Nick snorted a laugh. "Funny. The guy's making dough hand over fist and he wants to give it up to be a daredevil."

"Go figure."

"Uh, what about Tink? Do you have any problem with—"

"No. Ask if you want. He's his own man. And I trust him. He'll do what's right by himself. And by you, if he signs on." Ian laughed. "Hell, you can even ask Hanna if you want." Hanna had a new boyfriend, Andy Tyler. Good boy.

"Hm. I think BB might be available."

Ian offered up his name as a reference.

In mid-November, Ian sold two of his show cars. He kept the road car for the family to use, and he kept the van and the wrecker and fifth wheel, which he'd need for garage and tire store business. He had a buyer coming up from Grand Junction before Thanksgiving to look at the Freightliner. Whittingham Ford made an offer on the carrier, but Ian decided the offer was too low, so he opted to wait. They'd come around.

He kept the trailer. For vacations, and fishing and hunting trips next summer.

Beauty took sick the first week of December and Milt Cramer put her down. Ian had her rendered at the local slaughterhouse. Meat for a good part of the winter.

He bought a good milker from Brian's herd to replace Beauty. As he had done with Beauty, Joel milked this new cow. Joel named her "Wonder."

In a spiral notebook he always kept with him, Ian began writing down specs and ideas and making drawings for a monster truck.

It snowed Christmas Eve but the sun shone bright Christmas Day through a clear, cloudless blue sky, so blue it hurt to look at it. The sun glared off white mounds that covered everything—the house, trees, fields, cars, the van and trailer and wrecker and fifth wheel and Freightliner and carrier and the garage. White as far as the eye could see.

The fence posts lining the lane had foot high caps of diamond-studded cream. Snow lay a foot deep in the lane out front with one set of tire marks in them—the Swenson family from down the road had been up early. Icicles hung in jagged rows from the southern eve of the house and above the back door. Joel harvested one that morning when he brought in Wonder's milk pail, tendrils of warm steam rising from the pail. He put the icicle in the refrigerator, "to save for next summer," he said.

After all the presents were opened in the living room, oohed and awed over, and the wrapping paper picked up, and before they all then drove over to Brian's for more gift exchanging and then to the Davis' for Christmas dinner, Ian took everybody out to the garage, where'd he'd been working for the past two weeks, working late into the night on some secret project.

He unlocked the garage door with a flourish and herded them all in. They stood in the uninsulated garage, shivering, their breath puffing in little clouds—Grace, Tink, Hanna, and Joel, with Hobo barking and nosing about, tail wagging. In the concrete garage floor center, a large blue plastic tarp made a small, irregular mound.

Ian whipped the tarp aside.

"Ta-da!"

Five sleds lay stacked in a heap. "I made them myself," Ian said, grinning. "One for each of us." They were made of sheet aluminum, reinforced with runners, neatly curved upward at the front, and gently arched along the sides, with rope handles along both sides. He'd painted each one with the show logo. Each one had a name in large red letters. "That's what I've been doing for the last—"

Hanna squealed, hugged Ian, and Grace kissed him, and Tink and Joel grabbed their sleds. Everybody talked at once, excited, laughing. Ian, Hanna, and Grace grabbed their sleds too. Hobo barked at the pandemonium, tongue lolling, tail wagging.

Joel and Tink grabbed an armful of blocks and built a ramp to slide down off the carrier side. "We built it first," Tink said, "so we get to try it first."

Tink climbed into the open carrier and eased his sled over the side. It was a gentle slope down the ramp, about twenty feet long and four feet wide and four feet off the ground. Joel went next, and by the time everybody had gone down twice, Tink and Joel were gathering more blocks and ramps to make the slide longer and higher.

"We can go off the back of the carrier," Tink said, "if we set it up like a jump, only instead of going up, we go down."

Ian and Hanna and Grace pitched in, setting up the jump ramps at the end of the carrier and the support frame underneath. The slide now extended the length of four ramps, almost fifty feet. It was six feet side-to-side and started a good twelve or thirteen feet up, from the top of the carrier's upper platform. Ian put up a ladder along the carrier side to climb to the top.

He put a canvas tarp on the carrier top platform. The metal was frozen and slippery, and the tarp gave good footing when they got to the top of the ladder and got into place to slide down the artificial slope.

"Be careful," he said to Hanna as she tottered at the top, getting ready for her turn to slide down. Tink was at the top, helping her haul the sled up and into place.

"I'm being careful." She laid her sled in front of the ramp-slide and kneeled beside it. With Tink's help, Hanna laid facing forward on the sled and gently eased it to the lip of the long, sloping precipice, where she teetered on the edge.

She shoved off, using both hands on either side of the sled to push herself forward over the edge. Ian waited down below, on one side of the ramp, and Grace stood by on the other. Joel waited at the far end, where Hanna would stop, to help her up.

Something went wrong. Hanna's left hand got caught on a protruding frozen lump of chain, or something like it, and slipped. Her right hand caught firm, though, and she shot forward, lopsided, going down the long ramp sideways, not straight. She screamed going down and Ian didn't know if it was fear or delight, but he acted as Hanna careened to the side of the sideless, guardrail-less ramp and toward him.

As Hanna was on the brink of toppling off the ramp and onto the ground, where she might break an arm or collarbone if she fell wrong, Ian reached out. Instinct. He grabbed Hanna, gripping her puffy, loose-fitting coat at the shoulders with both fists and he fell backward, all in one motion. Hanna toppled onto him and the sled slipped aside as he fell back.

He hit the ground with a solid thump and Hanna landed on top of him, grunting.

"Are you all right?" Grace said, concern etched in her ruddy cheeks. She had ducked under the open frame of the ramp support and knelt beside Ian and Hanna. In another second, Joel and Tink were kneeling on the other side.

"Hanna, you weigh a ton," Ian grunted. "What are you feeding her, Grace?"

"Hey, how dare you?" Hanna uttered an indignant squeal, gave Ian a mittened-muffled slap on his chin, and struggled to stand. Tink helped her up. She was all right.

The snow and their heavy clothing helped ease the fall so no bones were broken. Ian's ribs hurt, but he assured Grace, as she helped them to stand, that they weren't broken.

"Let's go to the school and sled there," Joel said. People gathered at a long, low and wide hill between the college and the hospital every winter. It was crowded, yes, but it was a social thing, a community thing, to gather there and sled.

It was a family thing.

"We still got lots of time before we're expected for dinner," Grace said.

"Let's take this down first," Ian said. He climbed up the ladder to the top of the carrier to knock down the top ramp.

"You be careful, Dad," Hanna said.

They opted to just knock over the top two ramps and leave them lying on the ground rather than stow the whole arrangement. "It's safe," Ian said, panting from the exertion. "Nobody will get hurt on it."

He took off his gloves and flexed the fingers of his right hand. The knuckles felt swollen, cramped, and it wasn't just from the cold. He shook the hand vigorously, but it still ached.

He had his notebook with him, stuffed under his coat. He kept it with him all the time, even when he went to the bathroom, so he could jot down anything that came to him, and not lose the thought because the book was somewhere else.

Monster trucks were complicated.

I need to learn more about hydraulics . . .

"You all right?" Grace asked. "Your hand?"

"I'm fine." He put his glove back on.

They tossed the sleds in the back of the van and piled in.

"Can I drive?" Hanna asked.

From inside the garage, the phone rang.

"I'll get it," Grace said. She was closest, and Ian noticed that they hadn't locked the garage. Details.

Hanna sat in the driver's seat, revving the engine, warming it up. Ian sat in the back with Tink, Joel, and Hobo, leaving the front seat empty for Grace.

In a moment, she came out. Ian thought she looked pensive, and he remembered his dread of the phone ringing. It wasn't always a good thing.

She walked to the driver's side door and said, "It's for you," to Hanna.

"Oh?"

"It's Nick."

"Oh," Hanna said, her voice rose in a delicate lilt. She left the van and walked to the garage.

"Lock it when you're done," Ian yelled at her.

"And don't take all day," Grace said.

Hanna said nothing. Grace got into the van, passenger seat, and closed the door.

"I thought they—" Grace started as she belted up.

"Yeah," Ian said, "me too."

"She broke up with Andy," Grace said.

"Huh? I didn't know that. Nobody tells me anything."

They sat in silence for a while.

"You don't suppose they—" Ian started.

"She's her own man, Ian."

More silence.

In a few minutes, Hanna left the garage, locked it, and walked to the van, head down. Expressionless. She got in behind the wheel and buckled up. Said nothing.

As they drove down the lane, Ian and Grace exchanged a look. Ian started to speak, but Grace interrupted.

"I'm concerned about that hand, Ian," Grace said. He'd taken off the gloves and realized that he'd been unconsciously rubbing the knuckles.

"I'm okay," he said, tucking the offending hand under his leg. He tried to sound casual, but it came out annoyed.

"You're not. It may be arthritis, you never know."

"I'm okay."

"We'll have you checked, first thing next week."

"Grace, I said—"

"Dad?" Hanna. She had both hands on the wheel, ten and two, eyes ahead, and she kept her speed under control. She knew how to drive a vehicle.

Knows how to crash them too.

"What?" he asked, annoyed.

"That was Nick on the phone."

"Uh-huh."

"Did he talk to you, um—about his own show?"

"Yeah, a while back. By the way, Tink, he mentioned—"

"Yeah," Tink said. "We talked."

"Oh? Did you?"

"Offered me a job." Tink smiled.

"And?" Grace said, turning in the front seat to look at Tink.

Tink laughed. "I'm thinking about it."

"Wait a sec," Ian said. "Hanna, on the phone just now; did Nick offer you—"

"I think I know, now," Hanna said.

"Huh? Know what?"

"Why."

"Will somebody please—"

"Why. Why you do it. Why you do the show, I mean. Remember? I asked, last year? When Shaun did that T-bone? In Des Moines? There was this radio guy who did an interview—"

"Oh, yeah. I remember. You *still* remember that?"

"Yeah. And I know. Why you do it."

"You're changing the subject."

"No. No, Dad, I'm not."

"Okay." Ian sighed. "So tell me. Why do I do it?"

"The show is as much a thrill for us to do as it is for people—"

"Oh, for hell's sake, Hanna."

"Dad, watch your language."

ABOUT THE AUTHOR

Ken Rand wrote full-time from his home in West Jordan, Utah, until 2009. He wrote his first million words years ago and continued to write every day, no matter what, until shortly before his death. He sold dozens of stories and several novels as well as scores of interviews, hundreds of articles and several nonfiction books. He devoted hundreds of hours to teaching thousands of new writers. His philosophy: "Anybody can say you can't write. Let nobody say you don't."

OTHER TITLES FROM FAIRWOOD PRESS

Fantastic Americana: Stories
by Josh Rountree
trade paper $17.99
ISBN: 978-1-933846-16-3

McDowell's Ghost
by Jack Cady
trade paper $17.99
ISBN: 978-1-933846-11-8

*Living Forever
and Other Terrible Ideas*
by Emily C. Skaftun
trade paper $17.99
ISBN: 978-1-933846-98-9

Genesys X
by B.J. Graf
ltd. hardcover & trade $29.99/17.99
ISBN: 978-1-933846-99-6

The Best of James Van Pelt
by James Van Pelt
signed ltd. hardcover $40.00
ISBN: 978-1-933846-95-8

The Archronology of Love
by Caroline M. Yoachim
small paperback $8.00
ISBN: 978-1-933846-96-5

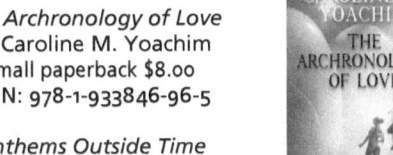

*Anthems Outside Time
and Other Strange Voices*
by Kenneth Schneyer
trade paper $18.99
ISBN: 978-1-933846-92-7

Unicorn Mountain
by Michael Bishop
trade paper: $18.99
ISBN: 978-1-933846-94-1

Find us at:
www.fairwoodpress.com
Bonney Lake, Washington

CHRYSOULA TZAVELAS

GREEN
WILD

THRONES OF THE FIRSTBORN
BOOK 2

DREAMFARMER PRESS
DREAMFARMER.NET

Dreamfarmer Press
www.dreamfarmer.net

GREEN WILD
ISBN: 978-1-943197-13-2

Cover art by Ravven Kitsune
www.ravven.com

AUTHOR'S NOTE

There is a list of important members of the Regency and Justiciar's Courts, along with a family tree, at the back of the book. These can be referred to at will and may be useful if names get confusing. (Like many royal families, the Royal Family of Ceria tends to reuse name elements. I am only grateful I convinced them to not actually duplicate entire names.)

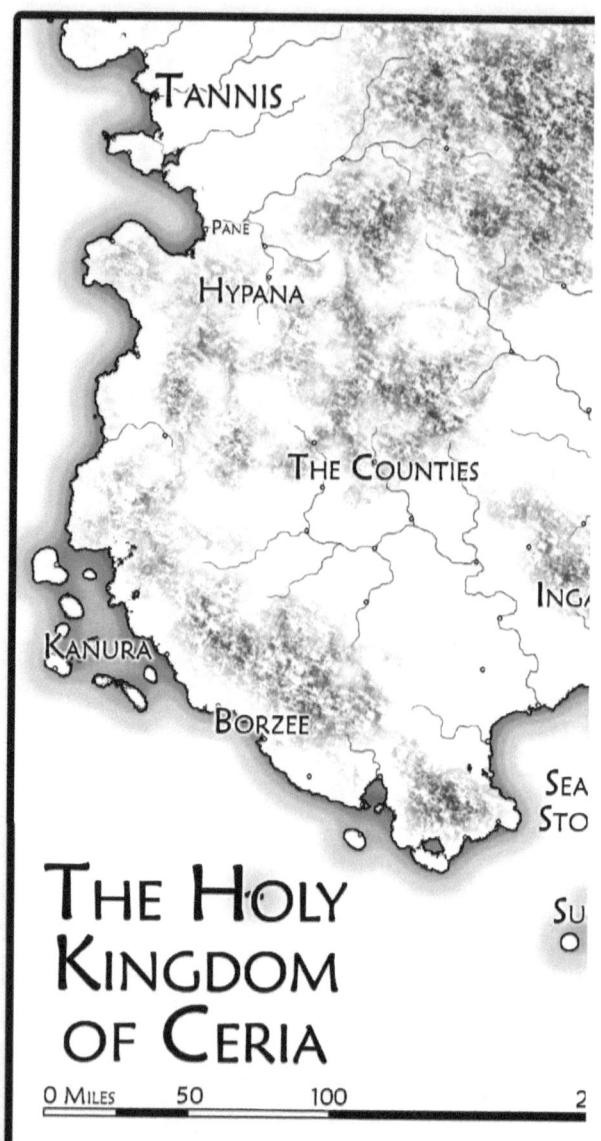

TANNIS

PANE

HYPANA

THE COUNTIES

ING

KANURA

BORZEE

SEA
STO

SU

THE HOLY
KINGDOM
OF CERIA

0 MILES   50   100   2

VASSAY

DALEIN

SEL SEVANTH

CITADEL
OF THE SKY

LOR SELENI

ARDOZA

LACHAN

GAE

STORMWATCH

A OF
ORMS

EIRCEDE

SHELL COAST

USSURA

PERURA

HESEVIC

200

GREEN
WILD

This one's for broken relationships: the pain they cause and the future they unlock.

CHAPTER ONE

THE SHADOW OF THE MOUNTAIN

"IT'S ALL RIGHT. We'll be all right," the Crown Princess Jerya told her cousin, and held her hand. After hours of rumbling and shaking and terror, the mudflow had finally stilled. The mud lingered, though, pressing against the walls of the Royal Palace. Starset Tower, where Jerya and her cousin sheltered, had been built within her lifetime by one of her brilliant uncles. It endured even as older spires crumbled.

Lightning crackled through the sky, so close she could feel a tingle on her skin and smell the burning air. "We may have to get away from the lightning, though," she added. "I don't think our uncle built Starset to resist strikes like that."

It rained, but the ash from the mountain fell too, mixing with the rain. It looked like black tears. Bleakly, Jerya approved. Her father had died only a few hours ago, along with she didn't know how many of her people. She and her cousin had used what magic they could to save them, but—

But best to think about their own survival now. The sky

could cry; she couldn't spare the time. "I promise you we're getting out of here," she told her cousin. "As soon as my birds come home. As soon as I know."

Her cousin, an older woman in her thirties, curled around their only lamp and didn't respond. She hadn't spoken for hours, ever since the magical barricades she'd erected against the mud had failed.

Jerya stood at the window, anticipating the return of the eidolon birds she'd sent out, and stared at the mud below. Jumbled masonry and uprooted trees drifted slowly, bumping against the dome of the Palace Library and tearing chunks out of the wing of the Palace where her father had lived. North of the river, chunks of rubble drifted on a slowly moving mudflow that grudgingly parted around the towers her uncle had built: all that remained of a once-flourishing quarter of the city. A few smaller buildings remained standing at the edge of the river, darkness oozing inside homes and extruding itself back out windows.

She thought of the dead uncle who had built the towers. He'd be proud, she supposed. Then she wondered what more he might have done if he hadn't died when she was a child, and if he and her father were together again and she couldn't think about *that* anymore either, because the living needed her strength more than the dead needed her grief.

When the mud met the river, it dwindled, as if it had reached its goal. Beyond the river flickered many, many lights, as the evacuated survivors filled the streets of the south city, frightened but alive. She didn't want to think about those who hadn't gotten out.

Something fluttered in the darkness and Jerya put out her hand. A ghostly falcon, glowing gem-like even in the ashen twilight, landed on her fingers. It cocked its head at her and melted into her skin. What it had known, she now knew. What it had seen, she now saw.

The lights across the river told only part of the story. Scenes of chaos flashed through her mind's eye: people struggling to return to the north side of the city and being restrained, people fighting to defend their homes from unexpected houseguests, screaming horses paralyzed by the crush, a brawl in a marketplace. Survivors on rooftops in the north city beyond her field of view, sobbing. And worse things, too, which Jerya absorbed with the rest and filed away to bring out later, when needed. When there was time.

Her eidolon falcon had not found her uncle Yithiere, the last of her father's brothers, which loomed twice a problem. Yithiere could make an eidolon big enough to carry Jerya and her cousin away from the tower without risking the mud. But Yithiere was also one of the more dangerous members of her family. His magic was as powerful as his portion of the family instabilities. The family madness. If Yithiere decided the mobs of evacuees were a danger to his family, the chaos would become a nightmare. More of a nightmare.

Jerya shaped another bird, turning ashen rain into gleaming silver, and sent it to find another of her cousins. Seandri was no more powerful than she, but he kept calm in a way most of her family couldn't. He and his Regent could handle Yithiere, but Jerya would have to move her cousin to safety herself.

She knelt beside Shanasee and shook her gently. The other woman didn't respond. Her skin glistened and her eyes were squeezed tightly shut. Her body was too tense for her to be asleep. Jerya studied her before pulling her into a sitting position. After brief resistance, Shanasee let her.

"Time to walk, Shanasee," Jerya said, pitching her voice

as close to the tones of a Regent as she could. Shanasee moved her legs weakly in response. When her knees bumped the floor, she stopped.

Jerya revised her command. "Stand up, Shanasee. Stand up and walk. I'm right here." This time, pulling heavily on Jerya's hands, Shanasee stood. Her eyes stayed shut, her head still drooped, but she could walk. Just like Jerya, she'd spent most her life learning to hear the advice of a Regent no matter what state of mind she was in.

Thunder crashed around the tower, so loud that dust streamed from the vaulted ceiling. As the booming faded, a horrible creaking vibrated through Jerya's boots. The whole tower shook, as if slapped by a giant. Jerya caught Shanasee in her arms as both women tumbled to the floor again, curling around her cousin like she was a child. Emanations of her magic flickered around her, ready to redirect any falling stones. After a moment, when nothing fell, Jerya uncurled and glared fiercely at the wall.

The tower of Starset was in perfect condition but the surrounding spires were not. One of them had just fallen against Starset. Towers weren't normally designed to withstand things like that, like cities didn't build with an eye toward giant mudslides.

Shanasee made a small sound and Jerya stood again, pulling Shan to her feet. Shanasee's face turned toward the flickering lamp, even though her eyes remained closed.

"Yes," Jerya told her. "We must go. The light won't last much longer." She should have brought a magical inscribed light. They lasted weeks. But she hadn't been thinking clearly, hadn't thought to spend the time looking for one. She wafted an emanation of power at the lamp and held it aloft that way, so she could guide Shanasee with two hands down the many, many stairs.

Shanasee made another little sound and shook her head violently. Then her legs gave out and she almost collapsed, pulling Jerya down with her.

"No!" said Jerya sharply. "This isn't how we survive. We keep moving." She yanked on Shanasee's wrists and her cousin stumbled forward. Sending the lamp drifting ahead of them, she pulled Shanasee down the stairs and did her best to make sure they didn't both fall. She couldn't do anything about the way Shanasee banged into the curving wall over and over again. Her cousin's terror of the darkness had driven her deeper into herself and it was all Jerya could do just to keep her from collapsing.

Her limited magic infuriated her. If she could make powerful eidolons, like her uncle, she could sling Shanasee across an eidolon mule. If she projected powerful emanations like her younger sister, she could float Shanasee down the stairs. She could float both of them across the mud to the other side of the river.

But Shanasee controlled vast magic. She'd held back the mud for hours despite her terror. Now she was lost, trapped in the darkness inside her head, and reliant on Jerya for her survival. Magic assisted, but in the end Jerya would get them out, not her magic.

They took a break on a landing while Jerya caught her breath and inspected some of Shanasee's bruises. The light flickered again before she could do much other than verify Shan wasn't bleeding. Then down they went again, down past the ground floor and into the old catacombs of the Palace of yesteryear. The dark, dusty hallways went all over the city, although she only knew the area immediately under the Palace. A small museum occupied one large chamber, and a promenade led along the many murals painted by previous generations. Couples liked it. But there were deeper levels, and longer arms where almost nobody ever went. Some of those arms stretched all the way to the river, and catacombs exits that weren't clogged by mud. Jerya had seen a map once. Now she needed to remember it.

They passed by a dusty corridor that led to a staircase down. Jerya's sister Tiana had wandered in the deepest levels not so long ago, and found a pendant that represented a puzzle that Jerya couldn't solve until too late: until her father had been murdered, the pendant—and the phantasmagory—destroyed, and her sister caught in the eruption of the mountain nobody ever expected to erupt.

The last thought hurt her more than all the others. She mourned her father, she raged silently about the pendant, but she'd spent her life trying to protect her little sister from the grief that haunted their family. Now, thanks to the phantasmagory pendant being destroyed, she didn't even know if Tiana still lived. She couldn't even reach the dreamspace any longer, as if it had never existed.

Shanasee started shaking again as the lamp dimmed. When it went out entirely, she whimpered.

"It's all right, Shanasee," Jerya said quickly. "It's all right. I'm here. We're all right together. Soon we'll be out of here and we'll go and find Cara. Then maybe we'll find some lunch. Are you hungry? I'm hungry. I'd love a big slice of roast beef about now." Jerya spoke as quickly and as lightly as she could. She'd never provided the calming Regent chatter before, but if she couldn't keep Shanasee moving, Jerya would have to abandon her in the dark for a time. After all Shanasee had done for their people that night, the idea horrified Jerya.

Without the lamp, the darkness in the catacombs bothered her. Jerya didn't mind the dark like Shanasee did, but enough darkness had a weight all its own: stifling and hungry. The catacombs were usually empty and safe; abandoned only as centuries of floodwaters changed the shape of the rest of the city. Once she might have made a game of walking them blind, but that scared her now. What if the mud was seeping down from somewhere above? She wouldn't even see it coming until she'd walked into it.

Holding Shanasee close, she projected an emanation ahead to feel the walls on either side. It was a cousin to touch: she could feel the solidity, the stoniness of the architecture. She stared at the faintly glimmering emanation, easily visible to her without any light. Those not of the Blood couldn't see emanations nearly as well, if at all.

Jerya concentrated. With a rush of dizziness, she sent many emanations crawling over every surface they touched. When she opened her eyes, she could see what she'd already sensed: the catacombs for some distance ahead of her and a little behind her lit up as if rivulets of glowing water spilled over each plane.

"Come on," she whispered to Shanasee, and started forward. The magic took some effort, just as physically supporting Shanasee took some effort, but staying still in the dark wasn't an option. If the eidolon falcon she'd sent to her cousin Seandri returned with assistance, it wouldn't be too soon. Until that point, they had to keep going.

Something rumbled ahead of them, vibrating underfoot. The emanations shivered in a ticklish way, but she didn't laugh. Rumbling could be never be good when you were in an ancient hallway with an incalculable amount of stone and mud over your head. Tugging Shanasee after her, she hurried on. She had to know exactly what had happened before she could decide what to do next.

They hadn't far to go. The masonry changed ahead and at the seam the stone ceiling of the old hall slumped against the floor, bringing the structure above down with it. A tangle of splinters and gravel and paving stones surrounded the enormous slab of fallen ceiling. Viscous black mud dripped down on top of the debris heap.

They couldn't move past it. Even if Jerya could navigate around it, or shift it out of the way, she didn't trust the rest of the hallway beyond. But instead of turning around, she stared at the black mud, illuminated by her emanation and the faintest hint of light from above.

"Look at that, Shanasee," she said, remembering that she'd meant to keep talking to other woman. "Look at that mud. It's even getting down here. If we let it, it's going to seep all the way to the museum and destroy everything there."

Shanasee started to shake again. Jerya shook her head and squeezed her cousin's hand. "Don't worry. I won't let it happen." She studied the debris around the great slab, before using an emanation to lift a chunk of wood and jam it into the gap through which the mud oozed. The light from above vanished, but the mud stopped too.

"There," Jerya said in satisfaction. But Shanasee kept shuddering, even when Jerya put her arms around her. "All will be right. I'll *make* it be all right. We just have to get out of here—"

The fragmentary remains of the eidolon bird Jerya had sent to find her other cousin flickered through the stone. The shards of power didn't rest elegantly on her hand, but flew straight at her head, passing directly to her mind. Because the eidolon had been destroyed, she only caught fragments of what it had seen. Fragments, but important, terrifying ones.

The bird had found Seandri, but Seandri was far too busy

to even notice. Jant, eldest of the family and Shanasee's father, fought to return to the palace. He'd inhabited the Palace like a hermit crab in a very large shell for most of his life. He wouldn't have evacuated if Seandri hadn't carried him out at Shanasee's request. Now he was desperate to return, because Jerya and Shanasee hadn't emerged, and because his whole life was in the Palace.

Normally an old man wouldn't be hard for a young man like Seandri to restrain. But Jant had been using family magic for more than half a century and he was throwing all he knew at Seandri in an attempt to break away. The last image captured before a stray emanation had destroyed the bird was Seandri raising a ring of dust around them as Jant's fox eidolon snapped at Seandri's stag.

No. The very last image was the face of a terrified evacuee girl, backing away from the conflict.

Jerya cursed and gave up on comforting Shanasee. "I dragged you into this, and I'll drag you out again if I have to, so *walk*, Shanasee!" She tugged her back the way they'd came, back to an intersection and another possible exit.

Shanasee walked. But Shanasee's stumbling blind walk wasn't fast enough. They had to run. The disaster of Blood fighting Blood required running. But only dim memories of an unfinished map guided Jerya. She knew they walked toward the river now, where the tunnel had to end.

Shanasee's steps slowed until at last even a firm, insistent pull couldn't move her. Slowly, almost gracefully, she knelt down and curled up. Her clammy hand became as cold and heavy as a rock, but her forehead burned to Jerya's touch. When Jerya pulled away from Shanasee, the sick woman didn't notice or complain.

"This is bad, isn't it, Shan? Come on, Shan. Stay with

me." She didn't know what to do for Shanasee, except to find somebody who had more experience. She needed Cara, Shanasee's Regent. She needed Yithiere. She needed blankets, light, a warm bed for Shan. She needed *help* and she needed to get out of here.

With a rush that left her dizzy, birds exploded out of her, some darting down the corridor ahead of her, some of them pressing their way through the ceiling in that way only they could. One of them stayed beside Shanasee, so she wasn't entirely alone.

Her head still spinning, Jerya started running after her scout birds. She moved so much faster when not dragging Shanasee, even in the dark. She turned toward the river at the next intersection, turned toward the river again, and stopped. The scent of fresh air wafted from the other turning. It was the wrong way, but there the scent was as vivid as the rising sun. She hesitated, but only for a moment. Then she turned back to the path with the fresh scent. Somewhere in the distance behind her, she heard keening.

The tunnel with the fresh air zigged and zagged back and forth. Something squelched under her feet and the tunnel turned to reveal an ashen rainfall beyond corroded iron bars. Black mud sucked at her feet, and slid tendrils into the slime-covered stone circle that led from the tunnels under the city to the riverside. She could just see the Green Street Bridge, which told her the location: a small park she'd visited before. She'd noticed the old stone circle with the iron bars previously. She'd always thought it led into a sewer before, and wondered why anybody would bother to barricade a sewer. But now she knew.

The bars were far too close together for her to squeeze through. She rattled them, and then shattered all but one of her emanations and eidolons, pulling all the power she could spare back into her core again. Setting her jaw, she gripped the bars with both her hands and her magic, and twisted.

The effort exhausted her. It was far harder than sending small birds flying all over the city, or illuminating a dark room, or even supporting Shanasee through dark places. But if she couldn't break the bars, she'd be giving up, and Jerya could barely comprehend the concept of giving up. The bars would bend and break before she would.

The bars bent, and one bar broke. It was enough. She squeezed through, scraping herself on the broken bar. She heard the rumble of a crowd over the noise of the river. Beyond the tunnel overhang she saw the rest of the bridge. An unruly collection of city folk gathered, facing a single man with spectral lightning dancing between his fingers.

Jerya had been worried and anxious before but actually seeing her uncle Yithiere on the verge of attacking their own people jolted terror down her spine. She leapt forward, heedless of the blood dripping down her arm, and shouted, "Uncle! I need you!"

Yithiere whipped around. Her father's younger brother was a tall, lean man with untrimmed hair and badly in need of a shave. He looked her over, and then turned back to the crowd. "Jerya. I'll be with you as soon as I convince these people where their best interests are."

"Uncle," Jerya said again, making a voice a lash. "Yithiere. I need you now. Attend to me."

Slowly he turned to her again, his cold gaze becoming questioning. "Jer?"

"I will convince our people," she told him, as calmly as she could. "You must go into the tunnel below us and fetch Shanasee. You must do this *now*, because she has spent all her strength saving these people and now she is sick." She made sure her voice carried as she spoke.

"Jer..." Yithiere said, and he made sure his voice didn't. "They are dangerous."

"So are we all, uncle," she told him. "Where are Iriss and Gisen?" He'd taken responsibility for moving her own comatose Regent and her youngest cousin to safety.

He bowed his head. "Safe," was all he said. He walked past her, off the bridge. She looked after him for a moment, wondering. If her uncle said somebody was safe, they were either safe, or they were dead.

Then the mob drew her attention. No, not a mob. Just a crowd of unhappy people, driven from their homes by a nightmare. A man held a sobbing woman close. Another woman in a ragged dress clutched three children. Two young people her sister's age clung to each other. She stared at them for a long moment. They stared back. Then, as their voices rose with their pleas and demands, she wiped the rain from her face and started the task of calming them.

CHAPTER TWO

THE REGENT OF THE BLOOD

THE ROYAL BLOOD didn't like to admit it, but the mountain of Sel Sevanth and its Citadel of the Sky was its own political entity, a nation within a nation. The little red flower the Citadel processed into the catalyst for magic grew nowhere else. Whoever controlled the mountain controlled the magic of the Logos.

But the Logos couldn't touch the Royal Blood's native magic. They used it to control the approach to the mountain. No army could take the Citadel of the Sky while the Blood held Lor Seleni at its base.

Of course, the clever found other ways of getting into the Citadel, thought Lady Lisette, Royal Regent. Sitting alone at a table in the communal dining room within the Citadel itself, she sliced a pear and drizzled honey over cheese. She kept an eye on the 'pilgrims' from the neighboring country of Vassay as they ate their dinner, too. They understood the alliance between the Citadel and Ceria's Royal Blood. And they understood alliances could be changed. They were as dangerous in their own way as the dragon that had attacked the Citadel in the pre-dawn after the holiday Antecession, when so much had changed.

Lisette, noble-blooded, served the Regency. As a Regent, she stood between the madness and power of the Blood, and their own people. She knew how dangerous the Royal Blood could be. She'd studied them, past and present, for the last ten years, after all. She respected the Regency. The system had worked for hundreds of years. And she loved Tiana as her best friend.

But apparently not everybody in the Regency thought the system worked, Lisette thought darkly. The 'pilgrims' acted like an embassy, without shame or secrecy. Lisette couldn't be sure, but she suspected they'd come at the secret invitation of the King's Regent, before he'd died, weeks ago.

Their leader smiled at her, as if she shared their goals. She gave him her most practiced smile back, and tilted her head as if she wanted to speak with him. She did want to speak with him, very much, so she could discover whatever he thought she knew.

He stood, and then looked over her shoulder, affected an overly casual stretch and sat back down again. A moment later Tiana sat down beside Lisette with a thump.

She put Jinriki, the great sword she carried carelessly in one hand, on the table between them, took a pear of her own and bit directly into it. Her hair needed combing and her simple woolen dress skewed lower on one shoulder than another. Lisette reached over the sword and tugged one side of the dress up.

"Oh, thank you," said Tiana, and looked around the dining hall. Her gaze passed right over the Vassay group, as if they didn't matter to her at all. Then she inspected the table again: fruit, cheese, pastries. "This is dinner?"

Lisette smiled, for real this time. "This is dinner. Nobody has time to cook right now, Tiana. There are wounded people, and structural instabilities, and Jinriki destroyed dozens of Logos workings on the walls and mountain."

"Well, yes," said Tiana, looking discomfited. "But this is more like... dessert. Where did all the cakes come from? And, look, a bowl of reception cookies." She grabbed one and cracked it open, but no little scroll fell out.

"It's the day after Antecession, too," Lisette pointed out. "Sweets are traditional."

"Oh," said Tiana. "Yes. Was that only yesterday?" Her gaze went far away and Lisette knew the sword spoke to her. She ignored the blade between them with practiced grace, but she couldn't forget about it.

Jinriki the Darkener, it—he—called himself, and she had extremely mixed feelings about the fiendish blade. He hurt those he disliked, he dominated the weak, he fought back violently against being held by anyone he didn't choose, he broke things, he threw power around wildly and he had nothing resembling ethics. But he was very much like a person, bound by limitations and shaped by loss she could barely imagine. Once, briefly, she'd seen those limitations intimately.

Tiana's attention snapped back to Lisette. "Anyhow, where's Kiar and Cathay? We need to plan."

Lisette didn't rush to answer, taking her time to slice a fondant covered cakelet into quarters. "They've been helping with the recovery effort. Everybody's coming by to eat though, so I'm sure they'll be here soon."

A guilty expression flashed across Tiana's face. "Should I have stayed awake to help, too? I was so tired."

Calmly, Lisette asked, "Do you feel like you have

something to prove?" When Tiana hesitated in answering, she added, "*I* don't feel bad for resting. Your sword is an exhausting burden to carry, even only for a short while." Her body still ached from what Jinriki had put her through when he'd borrowed her body to speak to Tiana.

Tiana frowned. "It isn't like that for me." She glanced down at the sword and added, "Oh. He says it's because he doesn't fit you like he fits me. Because of what that monk did when he passed him on to me, I suppose."

"Just so," agreed Lisette, despite how *disturbing* that sounded. It took training not to shiver. Instead she ate one of the cake quarters and gave Tiana one of the other ones, while she studied the sword.

Wicked fangs jutted out near the guard of the long, jagged blade. Those fangs moved when somebody took unwelcome liberties handling the sword. They could bite. But the sword also invaded minds. Twice now, Jinriki had opened Lisette's mind like a cupboard door. The first time, it had been attacking her—punishing her for interfering with Tiana's attempt to go fight a monster alone. The second time, it begged for her help so it—he—could talk to Tiana despite the disintegration of their magical bond. Lisette had shared the thing's black despair and felt sorry for him, even wanted Tiana to save him. That momentary sympathy was all the sword needed to steal her body and throw her into an icy-cold pool.

"Ooh, dessert," said Prince Cathay, as he stopped beside the table with Tiana's other cousin. "Just what we need, Kiar."

"Lovely," said Lady Kiar, a tall young woman with the dark cinnamon skin of the of the Blood but the pale hair of a commoner. It spiked around her angular face in short tufts.

As she slumped down into a chair, the stink of her sweat wafted over. Lisette made a note to at least make sure Kiar took a bath later, even if she couldn't make her rest.

Cathay sat down more gracefully, smiling tiredly at Lisette and Tiana. He was a typical specimen of the Royal Blood, with thick black hair and the Blood's delicate features. Even more than Tiana, he resembled any number of faces in the history books. Handsome, athletic and brave, he could be a romantic young lady's dream prince. But he'd chosen the path of a rake.

Alas for any young ladies with romantic dreams, thought Lisette wryly. Cathay had stopped at her bed while working his way through the Court and she'd enjoyed the attention. Not in any romantic sense—Regents were not allowed romance—but the experience had been.... educational. And adventurous.

Tiana bounced in her chair. "Come, eat something. We have to plan. I've been thinking about which of the lights to go after first."

Lisette offered Kiar and Cathay the two remaining cake quarters. Kiar took one. "Thank you. What do you mean, Tiana?"

Tiana bit her lip, looking between the three of them. "You all saw what happened, right? When all the Citadel magic went away? After the lights went out?"

Cathay said cautiously, "I saw something, right before we were yanked into the phantasmagory. I didn't know if it was real or not. I know that damn sword did something." He gave the blade lying between Tiana and Lisette a malevolent look, and then winced and lowered his eyes.

Tiana glanced between Cathay and Kiar anxiously. "Niyhan manifested. Well, some part of him. I saw a great throne made of blue light, and all the voices of the monks blended together. He gave me the light. I think it's part of a weapon, and if I can find the other three lights, we can use the weapon against the bastard who attacked my father."

"Okay," said Cathay. "How do we catch these other lights?" He was too pleasant; Lisette could tell he doubted Tiana's story.

Frowning, Tiana said, "We have to go... somewhere. To where the lights are. Then the Firstborn will give it to us."

"Somewhere," repeated Kiar dryly.

Defensively, Tiana said, "I can feel the lights pulling on me. It's real! It's almost overwhelming but Jinriki is damping it down for me."

Cathay's pleasant demeanor cracked. "I don't trust anything to do with that sword." He glanced at Lisette, as if hoping for backup, and Lisette gave him a little shrug.

"No, she's right, something happened to her," said Kiar. "She's got something new. She understood the Holy Mountain's eruption before I did."

"When the light rained into me, I could feel everybody breathing," said Tiana, her voice odd.

Kiar glanced at her before going on. "But even though I think she's right about the Firstborn giving her a weapon, I don't think we should go haring off without any idea where we're going. There's too much else going on."

"Nothing else is important as this," said Tiana, setting her jaw stubbornly.

Cathay said, "Tiana, the King just—ouch!" He looked at Lisette in puzzled confusion. "Why did you kick me?"

Lisette stared back at him, her eyebrows raised innocently. After a moment, Cathay's gaze slid around the public dining room. "Oh. Guess we're not talking about that yet. Well, anyhow, a Blight is pouring monsters into Ceria not a week out from Lor Seleni, Tiana. We have responsibilities."

Kiar blew out her breath. "The proper action is to go back down the mountain and support Jerya and make ourselves available in the defense against the Blight. But I think it's a better idea to stay here."

Tiana stopped glaring at Cathay to stare at Kiar in bewilderment. "Here? Why?"

"Blight. Other crises," said Kiar shortly. "We absolutely can not afford to lose the Citadel now." Her gaze drifted toward the Vassay contingent.

Scornfully, Tiana said, "As if the Citadel would betray us now, when I'm carrying the light of their Firstborn."

Kiar ground her teeth. "I'm pretty sure the Blighter is going to attack the Citadel again. If we're not here to defend it and *other people* are, that's not going to be much better than nobody defending it at all."

"Well, that's why we need to go get this weapon as soon as possible," Tiana pointed out, spreading butter on a scone.

"Fumbling around the countryside following a vague sense? There are books here, Tiana. Books with real information. I found out the Blighter's identity *here*, in a *book*. Your damn sword couldn't even tell us that."

"Bring some books along," suggested Tiana, her voice becoming brittle. "They're portable."

Lisette exchanged glances with Cathay. Kiar and Tiana bickered sometimes, but usually it didn't go anywhere serious. But after last night, Lisette didn't know what to expect. The Blood's usual retreat had been destroyed, Tiana had watched her father murdered, and a divine power had poured itself into the princess.

Lisette remembered the blue light, and the chant of

the Citadel monks. She hadn't understood any of it, but part of her training as a Regent involved remembering the strange things said around her. She wrote a report for the Regency Council before she took her nap, including some of Tiana's confidences—but not the ones Tiana felt were most personal.

"Jinriki is a black cloud with silver eyes in the phantasmagory?" *she asked, surprised.*

"Yes." Tiana scowled. "But take that part out. The part about his eyes. It doesn't matter anymore. The phantasmagory is gone."

Lisette knew there was something else there, another reason Tiana didn't want to talk about the sword's spirit form, but she didn't ask. Patience brought answers in time.

"I need to stay here," said Kiar sullenly.

"No. I need you. You're smarter than me. You notice things I don't." Tiana stared down at the tabletop, not eating her scone.

"If you think that, then actually listen to me!"

Tiana looked up, her eyes bright and pleading. "Cathay can stay here. Or go back down to Lor Seleni, whichever you think is best. You'll do that, won't you, Cathay?"

Cathay finished eating a scone of his own, then stretched back in his chair and yawned. "Nope. You're not my Queen, stormy weather. I'll go where I please."

"Right behind Tiana, I'm sure," said Kiar sourly.

"Well, yes," said Cathay, and offered Kiar a lazy grin she turned away from.

Lisette glanced at the sword on the table between Tiana and herself. She moved her elbow so she surreptitiously bumped against the blade, bracing herself for the invasion of Jinriki's mind. He didn't like being touched without permission, but she knew of no other way to reliably get his personal attention.

Almost immediately, she felt his mind engulf hers. Her vision darkened around the edges and red sparks danced in front of her eyes. The first time that happened, he had been furious at her. Her hands still had scabs from the injuries he'd inflicted. The second time, he'd been in utter despair. This time, he was amused and almost... friendly.

Why are you so brave?

You've never struck me as irrational, just cruel. And I'm the closest thing to an ally you have here.

As if I need allies, he said, as scornful as Tiana had been earlier. She could still basically follow the three royals' argument, she realized. Jinriki's words settled around theirs like a cover over a chair. The details were hard to catch but the shape was still there.

She is driven, said Jinriki. **I am suppressing the worst of it, because the strength of the pull hurts her. But she will go after these lights, no matter the argument, no matter the chain.**

And you will help her?

Of course. It is my vengeance we seek.

"Stormy, I know you won't listen, but... the sword. It's been trying to get you to go off and fight for days now." Cathay's intense gaze lingered on Tiana like he was devouring her with his eyes.

They are so good at lying to themselves, Jinriki observed clinically. **Look at him. He is convinced he can save her from me, and she can save him from himself.**

That's their business, Lisette thought primly. She watched Tiana put her hand to her head, as if it pained her. **What did the event look like to you?**

Like the intrusion of the hand of a god into the weft of this world. It poured particles onto her, and she swallowed them down into the darkness where her magic comes from.

Lisette glanced involuntarily down at the sword, struck by the odd description.

"Listen. When I destroyed the avatar of Ohedreton yesterday, I saw into his world for a moment." Kiar ran her hands through her hair, spiking it up further. "I could see *you* there, Tiana. I'm pretty sure that means *he* can see you, too. We have to think about this stuff before we get into more trouble."

"You're one to talk!" flared Tiana. "You're always jumping into trouble. You jumped into *another world* of trouble once. If Jinriki weren't around, would you two be so hesitant?"

"No," said Cathay, at the same time as Kiar said, "Yes."

Lisette decided to intervene. "In the stories, after the Firstborn removed themselves from the world, they left their thrones behind, so sometimes a chosen human could sit on the throne and act in the Firstborn's name." Everybody looked at her, as if they had forgotten she existed. "But there's no records of any real thrones. So I suppose it's a metaphor for this light." She shrugged. "I'll go with her. Kiar, did Twist return while I slept?"

Kiar flinched and once again looked away. "Not that I noticed. I was busy."

"Well, if you didn't see him, he didn't come back," said Cathay. "I wonder if something happened to him?"

Sometimes Lisette wanted to smooth Cathay's hair back away from his face, and sometimes she wanted to throttle him. "I'm sure he's fine," she said sharply, as Kiar's eyes dilated. "We can send a messenger down the mountain."

Kiar studied her hands, curling them into fists. "We'll have to camp outdoors. Even if Tiana doesn't care, you'll hate that, Lisette." She spoke absently, as if trying to distract herself. "You were miserable when we spent two weeks in the field last summer."

"Are you looking to me to change her mind?" Lisette glanced down at her hands, at the injuries she'd gained last time she'd changed Tiana's mind. "I think I'd rather go along and see where we end up this time." It was true. But she couldn't help remembering how miserable she'd been last summer. Too much exertion always made her light-headed and overheated, and left her exhausted long before her friends. She'd sat in the shade of a pavilion while the Blood and the other Regents engaged in practice battles.

There had been more Regents then. But in the space of a year and a half, so many of them had died. Now she was left, and little Yevonne, and Harthen and Cara. And Iriss, if Iriss ever woke up from her coma. They were the youngest Regents, except for Cara.

The Regency Council would establish new Regents, but adult-trained Regents would never have the same influence as those pair-bonded to their Royals as children, as Lisette had been. She'd grown up beside Tiana, befriending Jerya, Kiar and Cathay in the process, since they were all close in age. And she'd developed different relationships with the previous generation. They were her second family, and also her responsibility. Guiding them was her duty. Compared to that, a little dislike of travel and exercise could hardly compare.

But she hoped the other thrones of the Firstborn were close, all the same.

"Have you looked at any maps yet?" Kiar demanded of Tiana. "Maybe you can pick out where these lights are on a map. That would at least be something."

"I don't know if it's that... settled?" said Tiana hesitantly. "It's not a thing, stored in a place. It's power, sent down a channel, and the channel only exists for a short time."

At the other table, the leader of the Vassay contingent stood again. Lisette thought he was going to come talk to them after all, and she wished she could warn him away.

Before she could even shake her head, a monk stumbled into the dining room, the whites of his eyes showing. "The fiends," he said hoarsely, his gaze seeking around the room. He found Tiana. "The fiends in the basement have been unchained. We need your help."

CHAPTER THREE

THE MIRROR OF ICE

"W HY ARE THERE sky fiends in the basement?" demanded Tiana as she stood abruptly. "Did I miss part of the tour?"

What did you think they were going to do with me after they ripped us apart? inquired Jinriki sweetly. **They certainly couldn't banish me. The Logos likes me more.**

Shut up, thought Tiana. "Well?"

The monk twisted his garment. "When a fiend is banished, there is a chance it will eventually find a way to return again to the world. Some fiends are too dangerous to allow that opportunity. They constructed the Citadel, in part, to hold those fiends. The weight of all the workings presses down on them, Oh, come this way, please do. This isn't the place to talk."

He has no idea what he's talking about. The Citadel is far older than our enemy, and there were no fiends before he murdered my master.

The Vassay leader—Master Camerind—cleared his

throat. "Might we assist? It sounds very educational." Tiana remembered that they'd replaced their previous government with some kind of strange university system.

Kiar said sharply, "We'll let you know."

Lisette smiled toward Master Camerind, the sweet smile Tiana knew she saved for those she didn't much like. "Why don't you prepare some defenses up here? I'm sure that would be educational, too."

"Yes, what they said." Tiana picked up Jinriki and moved toward the monk, who stumbled back as if he thought she might stab him. She herded him into the hall and everybody else spilled out behind her. "Where's the Magister?"

"We woke him. He told us to fetch you, since your sword is the one who damaged their bindings." The monk was a middle-aged man, as so many of the Niyhani appeared to be, and his wide eyes seemed to be a permanent state of affairs. He walked backwards down the hall with an almost unsettling skill.

Kiar asked, "Does he want us to bind them or destroy them or banish them?" Her eyebrows knitted together. "We can do destruction, maybe, and banishment if the sword helps, but you could do that just as well."

Nobody is going to destroy my master's fallen Secondborn, Jinriki announced to Tiana. **Far too many have been lost forever already.**

"Secondborn?" asked Tiana out loud. Everybody looked at her, and she explained, "Jinriki says the sky fiends are Secondborn?"

Kiar bit her thumbnail. "Well, Secondborn are the servants and children of the Firstborn. If the sword's damned master was a Firstborn like the Dissolution Testament said, I suppose that could be true." The Dissolution Testament was the mysterious book Kiar had found hidden in the Citadel library, documenting the murder of the Firstborn Innis at the hands of his servant Ohedreton, and Ohredreton's defeat by Shin Savanyel, Tiana's ancestor.

The Niyhani knows. Look at him.

The monk turned around to walk normally, which Tiana didn't find particularly insightful. It was just sense, really. "Were you aware of this?" she asked him.

He stopped and looked down at his hands before he started walking briskly again. "I knew it is a crime against the Citadel to destroy them. I never asked why."

"The book said his messengers went mad when he died," Lisette said softly. "I wonder how Jinriki resisted."

"What makes you think it did?" asked Cathay acidly. "it doesn't seem any different from any other fiend to me, except that it's a sword. Evil, vicious, destructive. Where's the evidence otherwise?"

Tiana said defensively, "He's not evil. He's just focused. He's not any more evil than I am."

The Niyhani think I'm evil, the sword observed. **They believed that even before the end.** He paused, and added thoughtfully, **Perhaps the Niyhani did build a prison for my brethren. I shall have to investigate.**

No! thought Tiana. **Don't hurt anybody!**

Hush, he sent absently. **They'll never know.**

"He's very rational, at least," Lisette told the others. "That surprised me."

"Most fiends aren't," volunteered the monk. "Some of them are cunning, but they only become truly intelligent when they take control of a human. Otherwise they think perpendicularly to the world. The Magister says it's because there's always a part of them outside it."

No, it's because their hearts were destroyed with my master, said Jinriki acidly.

How did you survive? Tiana wondered.

My master's mortal servants saved me, he said briefly, and did not further explain.

"And he helped save Kiar's life," Lisette continued. "He didn't have to do that. Twist said it took a lot of power to do, too."

"And look what he got for his trouble," Cathay told her. "Tiana wouldn't take the opportunity for freedom when it beckoned."

Tiana shook her head uncomfortably and sped up until she walked beside the monk, leaving the others to talk about her and the sword behind her back. The monk increased his pace and she matched his stride until she was all but jogging. The others, more focused on their own argument, fell behind.

They went down a set of stairs, through a long hall, past a distillery, and then through an old wooden door left ajar. A stone spiral staircase descended into a darkness only made deeper by the inscribed lights studding the walls at the top. The monk padded down the stairs without a second thought, but Tiana hesitated. She didn't like descending into dark places alone.

Are you alone? The monk is ahead of you, and I am here.

"It's not the same," muttered Tiana, but she started down the stairs all the same. The air chilled rapidly as she descended. She wore a warm woolen dress and leggings and fur-lined boots: standard wear for the mountainside. But her fingers grew stiff and her cheeks burned with cold before they reached the bottom of the staircase.

"We really are under the Citadel, I see," she said to the monk as she emerged from the dim staircase into a pale chamber chipped directly from the mountain. Inscription-engraved walls glowed in the light of dozens of lamps. A group of monks clustered around a large door made of iron and white stone.

"Here she is," said the monk who led Tiana. He closely resembled the others; same hair, same middle-aged face. Telling Niyhani monks apart could be hard.

The others turned to look at her. One of them said, "All is well, Your Highness. But the fiends need to be moved to a more secure location. Can you help us?"

Confused by the change of situation, Tiana glanced at her guide. But she could no longer identify him in the cluster around the door.

"I thought my sword had broken their chains?" she queried uncertainly.

"A misunderstanding," said one of them. "It isn't as bad as we thought."

"Come and see," said another.

"Bring the sword," said a third.

That was *very* strange. She couldn't tell the monks apart, but they were always hierarchical. If many were present, only one ever spoke to her.

I will keep you safe.

Annoyed, Tiana thought **I'm not worried about how to stay safe. I'm worried about letting more monsters loose on Ceria.**

Why worry about what has already happened? But perhaps we can minimize the damage. Let us see what their prison looks like.

Tiana eyed the monks. They all stared at her with a hungry

expression that made her uncomfortable. Something was definitely not right. "Kiar?" she called over her shoulder.

Kiar cursed on the staircase behind her, and emerged into the bright chamber. As soon as she scanned the room, she cursed again. "They're tainted somehow. Where did our guide go?"

"Uh, he's over there somewhere." She waved Jinriki's tip in the general direction of the small crowd. Their eyes followed the sword in unison, and she realized with a start that they hungered for Jinriki, not her. "How do we untaint them?"

Kiar's hands curled into fists. "I don't know if we can. I haven't learned much about sky fiends taking possession of human, except that it usually leads to a Blight. At which point we usually, um, just kill them."

Tiana remembered when Jinriki had taken over her body, back at the beginning of their relationship, before she'd accepted the bond willingly. She had been an almost helpless passenger in her own body. And Lisette, Lisette had been watching and waiting as Jinriki borrowed her body. "We can't kill them. They're still in there!"

"I know," snapped Kiar. "I agree. Let me think a moment."

Lisette's voice came out of the stairwell. "What's going on?"

"Lisette, no, don't come down here!" Tiana cried, in sudden panic. "I don't want you getting possessed too."

The only person at risk here is Kiar. The rest of you already belong to me. Then he added, **And I believe Kiar has her own very interesting defenses.**

"Oh." Tiana flushed. "Never mind. Jinriki says it's safe." **Yours?** she demanded silently, as Lisette emerged into the light.

Alas, yes. It might be possible to donate Cathay to one of the others...?

I will chuck you into a river, Tiana warned him, and felt his unexpected flare of amusement like a caress on her cheek. She shook her head. *You're laughing? Why are you laughing now? How do we free the monks?**

But Jinriki remained silent, the touch of his laughter lingering.

Cathay stalked into the room and almost bumped into Lisette. "Should it be so cold down here? Aren't we closer to the heart of the mountain?"

"There's a *lot* of magic down here," Kiar said. "It must have come back after the sword cut everything loose. Very good workings."

"Why are they just staring at us?" Tiana asked nervously. "Shouldn't they attack us now that we're onto them or something?"

"And lose what we have gained so quickly?" asked one of the possessed monks. "We are not so foolish."

Another of the monks pulled open the iron and stone door. "Go in. See for yourself. Those that remain must be moved."

"Take the stock, if you must," said a third, generously.

"Stock?" asked Cathay, and laughed derisively. "We're dangerous stock, fiend. We've destroyed your kind before."

"Dangerous stock," agreed the third. "Ought to be put down, for the good of all."

"What shall we do?" Lisette curled her fingers around Tiana's arm.

Go in. The Logos noise in here is overpowering; I can't sense the prison on the other side.

"Can we save them, Kiar?" asked Tiana, and ignored Jinriki's exasperation.

Kiar shook her head slowly. "I don't know."

Tiana set her jaw. "I'm going in. Lisette, you go find the Magister and make sure he really knows about this. Cathay, you make sure they don't stop her. Keep them in here. Kiar, do... something. Whatever you think best."

Lisette nodded, squeezed her arm, and then stepped backward. Cathay hesitated. Tiana knew him, and imagined he was torn between a genuine need to make sure none of the fiend-possessed monks went after Lisette, and a manufactured need to protect Tiana. She hoped he wouldn't do anything stupid. She had to reserve that privilege for herself.

Walking across the pale chamber, her boots echoed oddly off the walls. "All right," she told the monks. "Here we are."

One of them bowed—to Jinriki, not to her—and gestured her in.

Am I just your transportation? she asked sourly.

He didn't answer right away. **Best that they think so,** he finally sent, the thought cool and distant.

The hall on the other side of the door was even colder than the antechamber, and looked empty. Her breath fogged the air and she desperately wished she had brought her mittens. More fog drifted low to the ground, and glittering pillars with sharp edges supported the high roof. Nothing fiendish loomed out of the mist at her. Then movement along one wall caught her eye and she spun around to face her own reflection.

"Mirrors," she said. The hall was full of mirrors, each one hanging at about shoulder height and stretching above her head. She moved closer, inspecting one closely. Each mirror reflected the large hall perfectly, but they weren't silvered glass. Instead the glass floated over deep blackness.

Not glass, said Jinriki.

She brought up one hand to touch the surface, and felt the painful cold. "Ice," she muttered, and tried to tug her fingers away. At first, they wouldn't come free: the ice clung to her hand as if her fingers had been wet. She pulled a little harder, and her hand came away. As it did, the mirror cracked, and then shattered.

Tiana scrambled backwards as shards of glossy ice fragmented and fell out of the engraved metal frame. Most of the shards crumbled to dust upon impact with the ground but several large pieces remained intact. They still reflected her shocked face, as if the image had been fixed along with her fingertips.

Warily, she glanced at the darkness that had been beyond the clear ice. It was gone; only dull, scratched metal glinted in the lamplight. "What's going on, Jinriki?"

Her face appeared in all the mirrors up and down the hall, distorted and frightening. Nervously, she backed up until she once again stood in the center of the hall. "Don't frighten me," she pleaded with them. "I get angry when I'm scared and Jinriki doesn't want you to be destroyed." In response, the reflections became her face, exactly, a perfectly normal reflection, save for how she wasn't standing directly in front of each of the mirrors.

She wondered uneasily why Jinriki wasn't answering her and glanced down at the sword, still in her hand. The reflections in the blade were as strange as the ones in the ice mirror. Light chased shadow up and down the edge, as if the sword moved in another place.

I'm busy.

"What do you want me to do?" she asked, and got no answer. Sighing, she wandered down the hall, inspecting each mirror. Each mirror inspected her back, save for the other ones that had been broken. She counted five in all, not including the one she'd shattered. And there were five possessed monks lurking outside the room.

Thoughtfully, she moved back over to the broken mirror and stirred the shards with her foot. When nothing happened, she looked around. The darkness imprisoned by the ice must have escaped, she reasoned. They really needed to have signs up warning visitors not to touch the mirrors.

"Come out, come out," she called. Nothing moved. The stillness and silence intimidated her. She could feel the presences around her, like a hum against her skin.

"What's going on?" asked Kiar, and Tiana jumped. Her cousin peeked around the partially open door. "Are you all right? We expected more noise."

"I broke a mirror," Tiana said. "You didn't see some kind of darkness come out of the room, did you?"

Before Kiar could answer, several other mirrors shattered loudly. Something dark materialized on the floor and then leapt toward Kiar. She cried out and caught it in her arms. Tiana thrust out her hand, her fingers curved into claws, sending an emanation out to wrap around the shadowy thing. It was small, even smaller than she was, with six limbs and—

"Tiana, watch out!" called Kiar. "I've got this, look to yourself."

Idiots. Unwilling to listen, growled Jinriki, and he moved in Tiana's hand to block as something rushed from her side. Tiana looked around wildly and saw three very different monsters rushing toward her. She had only an impression eyes, feathers, fur, fangs. On one, there was the oddness of a human woman's mouth, lips curved in a sensual smile.

She spun, waving her free hand in a wide arc, and flung the monsters away from her. "Can I destroy *these*, Jinriki?" she demanded. "Or would you rather I just let them eat me?"

They hardly deserve to be sustained after this, but—hold them in place, and stab me into them. I will disintegrate that which binds them together. Without a mortal host, they will flee back to the prison to reform.

"Fine." But this was easier said than done. With Jinriki's help, keeping them away from her wasn't a problem. Getting close enough to stab them was a different challenge, though. They spoke to the Logos as she pinned them up beside their shattered mirrors, and the ground twisted and melted under her feet, or tossed her into the air. After regaining her footing for the second time, she asked peevishly, "Can't you do something?"

I am.

Tiana muttered and launched herself at the closest sky fiend, carrying herself along with another emanation. If they were going to change the ground under her feet, she would avoid using it. She had never been able to manage so many different emanations at the same time before bonding with Jinriki. He was a very good weapon, even for somebody who had never learned to use a sword.

Focus!

She snapped her attention back to her target. It squirmed against the wall, an unfinished nightmare with four eyes from four different animals and a feathered mane. Then she drove Jinriki into its torso, and it exploded into a mist so icy that it seemed to cut at her skin.

With the first out of the way, the other two were easier to manage, but no less shocking. When the third one had exploded into frozen whiteness, she dropped to her feet and fell to her knees, shuddering with cold and pain. Her skin was paler than she'd ever seen it, like she'd been drained of all color. She stared at her hands for a minute, realizing she could barely feel the ground under her. Was that important? She looked for Kiar.

Her cousin hadn't moved from the door, the first little sky fiend frozen in her arms. Tiana blinked, staring at her, and shoved herself to her feet again. "Are you all right?"

Kiar's form flickered rapidly, like a guttering candle flame. Horrified, Tiana realized that the fiend had one hand sunk into Kiar's chest—and that Kiar had her hand sunk into the fiend's head.

"Don't do anything yet," said Kiar. Her voice was eerie, flickering just as her body did. "I'm looking in. Into our enemy's world. It's where I went before, Tiana. And they've been very busy."

CHAPTER FOUR

FIENDS AND FRIENDS

B USY?" DEMANDED TIANA. "What does 'busy' mean? Busier than invading our world?"

"Yes," Kiar assured her. "They're preparing other invasions into other parts of Ceria. And I think... I think the fortress they built at Mousame is in both worlds at the same time. This is incredible."

"Wonderful," said Tiana sourly. She watched the little fiend squirm around Kiar's hand and tried to decide if their merged bodies was creepier than the way Kiar flickered. "Are you planning on staying like that long?"

"I shouldn't," Kiar said, with a note of regret that Tiana decided won the 'creepy' contest. "Somebody will notice soon and that could make things complicated."

"Instead of incredible." Tiana shifted her weight, ready to intervene if the fiend tried anything awful when Kiar pulled away.

"Look, if you really need me to, I'll explain how incredible it is to see into what your enemy is planning. But later. Um.

Could you and Jinriki give me a hand? It's going to run as soon as I let go."

"I was waiting for you to ask." Tiana wrapped her power around the fiend and yanked. As soon as Kiar pulled her hand out of its head, and her chest away from its hand, Tiana spun the field around and drove Jinriki into the same spot Kiar had been attached to. Maybe Jinriki could do what Kiar had done and puncture Ohedreton in the process.

The thought amused her. But the amusement faded as the fiend wriggled against her power. It didn't dissolve like the others had. And Jinriki didn't respond to her thought. She reached out uncertainly. **Jinriki?** He was probably just distracted, he—

Yes. The final sky fiend exploded into icy mist that she no longer felt. **Your body is too cold. Time to go.**

Tiana looked doubtfully around the room. Blackness surged in the frames of four of the shattered mirrors. "What about them?"

"They need to be sealed up again. I don't quite know how it's done," Kiar said, sagging against the doorframe. "I can try, or we can wait until the Magister sends somebody along to do it. We still need to deal with the monks out there."

If you don't leave this chamber right now, I'm going to warm you up myself right here. Jinriki's tone was flat and ominous.

Tiana didn't see how this was the threat his tone implied until she thought about what would happen if magical heat filled the room. She didn't know much about how the Logos worked but she at least understood the basics of ice and heat.

"Fine," she grumbled. "I'm freezing," she told Kiar. "Let's talk about it in the antechamber."

Kiar blinked, looked closely at Tiana, and then stepped forward and put her arm around Tiana. "Lisette's going to kill me," she muttered. "Come on." She pressed her hand against Tiana's cheek and after a moment it burned. As she wrenched her head away, Kiar said, "You're going to miss the phantasmagory in a few minutes. How did you get so cold?"

"The fiends make it cold," Tiana explained. Her mouth felt strange, now that she paid attention to speaking. Her feet were clunky and wooden and she would have tripped except for Kiar's arm. It was, she thought, a little like being in the phantasmagory, or that time Jinriki had stolen her body. Except it was just the cold, putting out her fire.

"Well, it's warmer out here. We'll get you thawed," said Kiar briskly. They emerged into the antechamber. The monks huddled in the corner of the room furthest from both Cathay and herself, if 'huddled' was the right word to describe the precise way they'd arranged themselves.

When Cathay strode forward, the distance between each monk decreased. It fascinated Tiana and she wondered if Kiar had noticed.

Before she could say something, Cathay seized her hands. "You're freezing. How cold was it in there?" Without waiting for an answer, he tugged her away from Kiar and into his arms.

That completely banished the monks from her mind. Cathay didn't just hug her, he practically wrapped himself around her. She still held Jinriki in one hand, but he ignored the blade, pressing his head against hers and breathing on her cheek. "Put your hands on my chest."

"Yes, do that," said Kiar, relieved. "As soon as this is sorted out and she stops tripping over her feet, we should move her upstairs again. Tiana, defrosting is going to hurt."

Cathay's breath on her cheek was cool, not warm. Jinriki clattered to the floor and Tiana looked down. She'd dropped him. Or Jinriki had made her drop him. And she hadn't even felt her hand move.

Put your hands on his chest, Jinriki told her acidly. **He's finally good for something. I'll take the edge off the pain when I can.**

Tiana blinked down at the blade, then put her hands under Cathay's coat, against the cloth of Cathay's shirt. She could feel the pressure of his chest against her hands, but that was it.

"Yeah, that's cold," he said. His voice was gentle and calm, as if he hadn't been trying to seduce her for months.

"Skin contact would be better," said Kiar worriedly.

"Probably not the place," Cathay said, but placed one of his hands over both of Tiana's.

"Pay attention to the monks," said Tiana, distractedly. She could suddenly smell Cathay, as if she'd never smelled him before: sweat and leather and something spicy that was almost cardamom but not quite. She wished she was brave enough to actually slide her hands up under his shirt, against his bare skin. They'd warm up quickly, then, and—

She caught a surge of something from Jinriki, something savage and powerful. Then pain swept over her skin, as if a thousand needles stabbed her all at once. She cried out at the shock, and tears sprang to her eyes to spill down burning cheeks. Cathay kissed her forehead and that hurt, too. She tried to yank herself away, to rub her stinging legs and stomp her feet, to run out of the room and leave the pain behind.

Then, just as quickly as the pain had come, it faded. **My apologies,** Jinriki told her. **I was dealing with your monks. They are free now, or soon will be.**

Tiana dragged in a breath, shaken by the abrupt arrival and departure of the pain. Then she turned to look at the monks. One had fallen to the floor. Another sagged, their perfect formation destroyed. A third one fell. By the time the fifth one collapsed like a puppet without strings, the first one had climbed to his feet again.

"What have you done?" he croaked. "Where are the fiends?"

They are free, too. I found a way to extract them while preserving the men, but it means they will reform elsewhere. I had no other choice if you wanted the men to live. Jinriki's tone was as cold as Tiana's hands had been.

Tiana chewed at her lip and tried to push herself away from Cathay. He didn't let go, but he at least let her turn to face the monks fully. He kept hold of her hands, too, until she said, "Cathay, please, I need at least one."

He frowned and let go of one. She flexed her fingers; they were still clumsy, but she could feel her own hand when she made a fist and that was useful. She sent out an emanation and brought Jinriki to her.

"Where are the fiends?" repeated a second monk, stepping in front of the one who'd spoken first. That one fell back, bowing his head.

"Guess it's back to the old precedence order?" Tiana said, and shook her head. "In order to free you, they had to be freed as well. They've escaped into the wild."

"Tiana!" said Kiar, shocked. "We should have waited for the Magister before making that decision."

"Who says she made it?" countered Cathay, cupping Tiana's other hand between his own. "One will get you ten the sword did it on his own. Freeing five of his friends? The only surprise is that he didn't free any of the ones inside."

Tiana glared at him and yanked her hand away. "I didn't want these men to die."

"Convenient for him," said Cathay, scowling.

"Forgive me, your Highness, but we were fated to die as soon as we were taken. You should not have meddled." The monk's voice started out kind but became harsh by the end.

Aghast, Tiana said, "You can't want to be dead."

"If our deaths would have stopped monsters from returning to the world? That is why we are *here*, Your Highness. Every monk assigned here is prepared to give his life to protect the world from these fiends." The other monks all nodded and bowed. The speaker saw Tiana's shocked expressed and his softened into sadness.

"You are young, and you carry a most unique fiend. Your judgment is impaired. But please, Princess, you must try to consider the cost of your choices."

"What's your name?" asked Tiana sharply. "If I'm going to carry your life as a burden for all my days, I might as well know your name. All your names."

The monk hesitated, and then bowed and offered, "Danyeen, Your Highness."

The others followed Danyeen's lead, and soon Tiana was trying to commit five new names to memory. It helped to make a little song: *Danyeen, Jaele, Perris, Frans, Kai, a set of men who should have died.* As she composed it, the monks conferred together, before going into the mirror room.

When Tiana realized what was happening, she said, "Hey, wait, is it safe?" She looked at Kiar questioningly. When Kiar shrugged, she focused her attention on Jinriki. "Won't the fiends just possess them again?"

If so, it will only be what they deserve, sent Jinriki, with a restrained fury.

Hesitantly, Tiana asked silently, **Were you trying to free the fiends, not the monks?**

His anger was so palpable that it seemed wrong that his physical body was just an inert blade in her hand. She could *feel* his tension as he answered, **I would like to have freed my cousins, oh yes. It would have started with leaving them in their hosts, and next required paving a path out of this prison in human blood.**

Cathay reached for Tiana's hands again, and she stepped away absently. He was distracting even when she wasn't angry with him. **I don't understand. They don't need human hosts; I saw that the other day, and in the mirror room.**

Think about what you saw, Princess.

Tiana thought about it. Several more monks appeared with Lisette, including one Kiar recognized as an aide to the Magister, and she let Kiar talk to them as she thought about it. When the situation seemed to be sorted out, Lisette scolded her up the stairs to warmer rooms, all the way up to her bedroom. Then, as Tiana sat beside the fire, she ventured silently, ** Our enemy uses sky fiends as some kind of portal between his domain and our world.**

He made the sky fiends by destroying my master, and now he makes them his slaves and his spies, sending his power through them until they are torn to pieces by it, destroyed as surely as if you or your kin had acted. I have 'freed' them to that fate. At least in the mirrors they were preserved from future harm.

Tiana frowned down at the sword on her lap, running her fingers over the blade and all but tasting his bitterness.

"Why?" she asked aloud, forgetting to keep quiet.

"Do let us know what you find out," said Cathay, sprawled in a nearby chair with his eyes closed.

**I don't know. To see if I could. You didn't want the men

to die. Perhaps I wanted to repay you for accepting me on Antecession. Or perhaps I wanted to show them I am capable of valuing a human life.** He stopped for a moment, then surged on. ***I didn't think. If I had, I would have realized the consequences of attempting to be kind to Niyhan's monks. To any humans. It's not a mistake I'll make again.***

Tears sprang again to Tiana's eyes, but not from the fading frostnip this time. "It was the right thing to do," she whispered. "Enough people have died today and maybe the fiends won't be enslaved, maybe they'll escape."

That seems unlikely. Jinriki's voice was dry.

"Maybe," Tiana repeated. "There's no maybe in dead." She thought about explaining to Kiar and the others what Jinriki had actually been about, but hesitated. Cathay would never think anything good about Jinriki, and Tiana couldn't even blame him. As for Kiar and Lisette...

If you do, all they will hear is that I released five fiends to become five more portals between worlds. They'll come to that conclusion on their own soon enough. They will question whether I've been secretly corrupted by our enemy, perhaps even below my own awareness. She felt his hard little laugh. ***A very reasonable conclusion based on the available evidence.***

Tiana scowled. ***If you've been corrupted by anything, it's me. And that's a reasonable conclusion, too. You influenced me, I influence you. And if they bring it up, I'll tell them that.***

How embarrassing, Jinriki sent lightly. Then, in a sharper voice, ***Incoming.***

Only a heartbeat after the sword's warning, Twist popped into existence right next to Kiar and the bookshelf. He looked terrible, with mud on his clothes and face and twisted into his hair. His eyes were bloodshot and even their bright blue seemed dimmed. But when he spoke, he sounded as cheerful and lighthearted as always. "Ah, here you are. I'm glad I found you so easily. I have news!" He paused, and blinked slowly, looking around.

Tiana rose to her feet. "Is everybody all right? What happened below?"

He quirked an eyebrow. "Oh. Yes. Your entire family escaped the mudslide."

"And the city?" Lisette asked quietly.

Twist frowned and closed his eyes. After a moment of silence, Kiar said, "Twist?"

He swayed, and then gently folded toward the floor.

CHAPTER FIVE

GENIUSES

WITHOUT THINKING, KIAR stepped forward and caught Twist's arm, but that only changed the direction of his fall as he slumped against her. She struggled with his awkward weight, lowering him to the floor.

Her face alarmed, Tiana started forward. "Is he...?"

Biting her lip, Kiar waved a hand to stop Tiana, and Lisette did so by taking her hand. Kiar examined Twist's pale skin, then felt his forehead.

"I think..." She turned Twist's head back and forth, lifted his hand and dropped it, put her ear close to his mouth. His breath tickled her cheek. Then she sat back on her heels. "He's sleeping. He's exhausted himself." She scowled and resisted the desire to prod him awake. Smelling salts might do it but simple assault probably wouldn't, and from the looks of him, he needed the sleep. It was only luck that he'd managed to make it to safety before collapsing. She imagined what might have happened if he'd lost consciousness while skipping and shuddered.

Tiana guessed, "Lots of skipping around? That tires him out, right?"

Still looking at Twist's face relaxed in sleep, Kiar nodded. "All workings do. But he's been at this since last night and I don't think he took a break. I don't know why he pushes himself so hard—."

Lisette had a sudden choking fit, but before Kiar could do more than glance at her in concern, somebody cleared their throat at the door. Master Camerind of Vassay stood there, with two of his companions beside him. One of them, thin to the point of scrawniness, with a shock of sandy hair, practically buzzed with excitement.

"There he is!" He pointed past Master Camerind at Twist.

Master Camerind offered a faint, grave smile to the room. "We were in the library when he appeared. He asked where you might be found, then vanished again. Ripper is excited to meet him." He gestured at the sandy-haired man.

Ripper bounced on his toes. "Why is he on the floor? Is that part of his working?"

Kiar rose to her feet and stepped over Twist, placing herself between him and the gawkers. Tiana gave Ripper the cold, arrogant expression she'd picked up recently, which the man totally missed. "He's ill. You can meet him later."

Master Camerind chuckled. "I suppose he exhausted himself using that trick of his? Come, lads, I'm sure there will be a chance to approach him when he's conscious."

Ripper looked back and forth between Twist and Camerind—he hadn't bothered looking directly at Kiar yet, even though she interfered with his line of sight—then edged into the room. "He should use clarity. That's what we use, so we don't fall over like—well, like he's done."

The third man from Vassay silently clapped a hand over his eyes. He reached out to grab Ripper's arm, stopping him from moving further into Tiana's rooms.

Lisette spoke quickly. "I think he was ready to get some rest, given where he ended up. It's all right."

"Wait a minute," said Kiar, feeling like she'd been dunked in ice water. "Clarity? The drug?" She'd heard the term 'clarity' before. The men who'd attacked Tiana in Lor Seleni had been using clarity. It was a new drug in Ceria. Her brief investigation hadn't revealed where it came from.

"Oh yes," babbled Ripper. "It comes from an herbal concoction but we've discovered how to purify it. It's very useful. " He gave Master Camerind a sideways look, like he was trying to be clever. "But not as useful as a certain other powder. We could—"

"No, let's talk about clarity," Kiar interrupted, furiously. "Let's talk about the clarity making its way into Ceria. Let's talk about how clarity kills."

Master Camerind cocked an amused eyebrow and Kiar longed to smack him. But Ripper responded, even as he batted at the hand of his other companion. "No—what? Clarity's reasonably safe as long as you're not—" he snickered, "—stupid or anything. But Master Twist isn't stupid, we talk about him in classes—"

"Clarity makes a man strong and brave, right? Strong enough to think he can put out a wildfire with a switchblade." Kiar advanced on the three Vassay scholars, and heard Tiana's sharply inhaled breath as she finally caught up with the conversation.

"Sometimes—what?" Ripper focused on Kiar. "You're very upset about something," he guessed.

"Yes, I am," said Kiar. "I'm upset about clarity users

who tried to assassinate my cousin. I'm upset you have the sensitivity of a log. And I'm really upset you're here right now."

"I—I—I," stuttered Ripper, his eyes round as she closed on him, moving deliberately into his personal space. He stumbled backward, giving into the guidance of his friend, and Master Camerind took his place.

"Calm yourself, Lady," said the Master, that amusement still in place. "Are you suggesting our university students are responsible for how clarity is used in your city?"

"I'm suggesting—" Kiar took a deep breath and tried to calm herself, suddenly aware of the charged atmosphere "I'm suggesting you get out of here."

"I thought you wanted to talk about clarity," said Master Camerind, with the insolence of a man totally willing to provoke an international incident if the opportunity presented itself.

Kiar wasn't ready to start one. "Get out. Take Ripper here with you. Don't come back."

Master Camerind bowed and gave her a happy little smile, like she'd just agreed with him. Then he stepped backward, and made a show of closing the door as he and his companions left.

Kiar turned around and leaned on the door, taking a deep breath, marveling that Twist had slept through the confrontation. She'd never been so angry in her life. When the Blighter had murdered the King, she'd been shocked and horrified. But Vassay *infuriated* her. She'd been ready to physically throw the Vassay faction out herself.

And she wasn't the only one. Lisette casually held both of Tiana's hands, and Cathay stood with one hand half-outstretched, ready to unleash one of his cats. Both of them had wide eyes.

Lisette sighed and loosened her grip on Tiana's hands. She muttered something about the phantasmagory before saying, "Thank you, Kiar."

"They would have deserved whatever happened," said Cathay, slowly sitting back down again. He covered his eyes tiredly.

"Master Camerind, maybe," Lisette said. "But Ripper is just an innocent idiot."

Cathay snorted. "I don't believe that. The leader, what was his name? He wouldn't bring anybody stupid on this kind of trip."

Lisette waved a hand. "Skill and sense aren't always connected. I'm sure he's good at what he does. And I bet he's a treasure to anybody looking for an excuse to stick his nose in the wrong place at the wrong time." She pushed Tiana back into a chair again and turned to Kiar. "You're very tired, Kiar. You need to get some rest."

Her light, airy tone hadn't changed at all, so it took Kiar a moment to realize Lisette spoke to her. She shook her head. "Tiana, we should make them leave the Citadel entirely."

Tiana blinked and looked over at Kiar. "That's for the Magister to decide, isn't it?"

"Master Camerind practically admitted Vassay was behind an attempt to assassinate you! And they're trying to push the Citadel into giving them more plepanin."

"I *wish* he'd admitted it," said Tiana candidly. "But he didn't, not really." She hesitated and added sadly, "And they could have stopped. The men who attacked me, I mean. They wouldn't have started if they hadn't hated me so much."

Cathay darted to Tiana's side to comfort her. Kiar looked

away, at Twist. She knelt, felt his brow and cheek again, shook her head, and stretched her emanations to move him to a couch. His feet flopped over the end. She found a washcloth and filled a bowl of warm water from the kettle and got started sponging filth off his face and hands. He looked so young when he slept, like he was barely older than her. She supposed, from the perspective of an ancient like the Magister, he was. He'd only been a youth when he inherited the post of Royal Wizard and started teaching her. His gift for skipping put such burdens on him.

"We can't leave the Citadel to them," she finally said. "If you're going to leave the Citadel to go after this Firstborn light, I need to stay here, or they have to go."

Tiana only said, "We have to fight the Blight. You're worth a whole troop of soldiers, Kiar."

As Kiar savagely squeezed water out of the washcloth, Lisette said, "Have you talked to the Magister about Vassay yet? Maybe he can soothe your concerns."

"Hah," muttered Tiana, barely audible.

Kiar ground her teeth, and then remembered a conversation she'd had with the Magister yesterday, during the chaos after the Antecession ceremony. "He said yesterday it was our job to protect them."

"From Vassay? Or the Blighter? That's an important detail, Kiar," said Lisette.

"It was more of a general statement of faith," admitted Kiar grudgingly. "But how could Vassay not be included? Just because it's a whole country doesn't make it less of a potential threat."

"We talked to him about Vassay when we arrived," Tiana said absently. "He wasn't worried." Kiar remembered the conversation differently, but it was true the Magister hadn't exactly been alarmed by Vassay's intrusion. Then again, the Blight itself hadn't alarmed him much either.

"I can talk to him again if you want," Lisette offered. "You really need to get some sleep, Kiar. You're—" she hesitated, and Kiar's skin prickled. "You're more temperamental than usual."

Kiar closed her mouth on an irritated response. She didn't want to fight with Lisette. Or with Tiana. She didn't want to set herself against them. She didn't know how to do it and win, except by outright rebellion, and that she'd never do.

"I'll sleep," she muttered. "After that, I'll talk to the Magister myself."

* * *

Kiar fell asleep almost as soon as she stretched out, but her sleep was restless and full of dreams. She'd been awake for a day and a half and in that day, she'd discovered the name of her family's ancient enemy, spoken to him, fought a dragon, witnessed the visitation of a Firstborn and watched the lights of the Citadel go out. She'd stopped one earthquake and survived another. She'd moved literally tons of rubble, and sorted out library books. She'd argued with Tiana, although that was so common it was barely worth remembering. She'd learned about the source of the phantasmagory and lost it, all in the space of the same brutal murder. And she'd twice looked into her enemy's private world.

Those peeks into Ohedreton's world infused her dreams. Everything else drifted through: Twist's mud-covered face, the King's dying screams, Ohedreton's terrible smile, all set against the backdrop of that lightless world.

Or at least it had been lightless the first time she visited. But when she'd destroyed Ohedreton's avatar in the rooftop confrontation, she'd seen a reverse silhouette of Tiana against the sky, streaming with a blue light. She hadn't had time to see anything else. But later, when she'd sunk her fingers into the extraworldly substance of the escaping fiend, she'd had more time to look around. She'd seen the armies, and the other fortresses, and Tiana's silhouette hadn't been nearly as visible.

And she'd seen other things, too. Human men, in the center of the closest armies, lifted up on some kind of scaffolding. It reminded her of an illustration she'd once seen of an execution: mobs of people surging around a few raised high. But the mob she'd seen had been full of aliens. Mostly andani, the black dancers, but andani seemed to make up the bulk of Ohedreton's forces.

The reports unrolled in her dreams, and then wrapped themselves around the King's bleeding torso. He opened his eyes and said, "Beware of the Bastard."

Kiar said, "I know!" and sat up in bed. She'd shouted aloud. Fortunately for her pride, she was alone in the small room adjoining Tiana's. She took a deep breath and ran her hands through her hair. She wasn't Benjen the Black, Benjen the Bastard, resentful and disobedient and reviled, who tried to destroy the Royal Family. She was Tiana's advisor and companion and friend and she couldn't stomach the thought of directly opposing her. Not without support, anyhow.

The sun barely peeped over the horizon. Restless sleep or not, she'd still managed to sleep for nine solid hours. She hurriedly dressed before slipping into the hall. She wasn't sure if Tiana and Lisette were in the next room or not—everybody's schedules had been shifted around by the chaos—but she wasn't ready to talk to either of them again. She had to talk to the Magister first, just like she said she would.

On her way to the Magister's office, she passed by a series of tall, thin windows looking west off the mountain. Several long cushioned benches were placed along the windows. Twist stretched out on one of them, his arm flung over his eyes and his ankles crossed.

Kiar stopped dead, scrutinizing him for any clue why he was there.

Without moving his arm, he said, "How are you doing, Kiar?"

Frowning, Kiar said, "I know you have a room of your own. I saw them carry you inside."

"Cells," said Twist. "They call them cells, and for a reason, I might add. There are many reasons I'm not one of Niyhan's Dedicated, but the so-called beds they provide in their cells are one of them." He lifted his arm from his eyes and patted the bench. "This bench is here for guests like yourself who want to appreciate the sunset. It's *lovely* in the mornings. Have you come to join me?" He opened his eyes and looked at her, smiling.

"No," Kiar said shortly. "You don't want me around." It slipped out; she didn't mean to be so blunt.

His brow furrowed and he sat up. "Don't I?"

She refused to meet his eyes and didn't answer.

He sighed. "Releasing you as my apprentice doesn't mean I—you know what? Let's talk about this later after you've had some time to think about it." He laid back down and covered his eyes again.

Kiar's face flamed. "Don't skip when you're that tired ever again," she told his recumbent form, then hurried away before he could answer.

She went to the Magister's office, not expecting to find much except the bright rays of dawn illuminating an empty desk. Even though it was decorated differently than the Chancellor's office at home, with books and mementos of Niyhan rather than journals of genealogy and fashion, it was still the office of an administrator of an important organization. The Chancellor had a padded chair that revolved, with a cushioned back, while the Magister's chair was straight-backed wood, with a single cushion for the seat. But they both had the exact same desk. And they were both unexpectedly busy at odd hours.

"You're awake," she said in surprise, standing to one side in the double archway as a monk scurried out. A half-dozen other assistants thronged around him. "Don't you need sleep?"

"I take many naps, my Lady," said the Magister with a smile, as he signed something and gave it to another assistant. "Can I help you? I hope the fiends aren't causing problems again." When she hesitated, trying to decide whether to start with the threats she'd seen in the other world, or Vassay, he beckoned her over to the desk.

Kiar approached his desk. The assistants barely glanced up, murmuring to each other about whatever they were orchestrating.

"Your Excellency, I'm concerned about the safety of the Citadel. I saw strange things yesterday. I don't think the Blighter is done with it."

The Magister shook his head. "They never are. But we'll recover. Our stores run deep, and our craftsmen are skilled."

Kiar spread her hands. "When I interacted with the fiends earlier, I saw into what he was planning. There are armies. And Mousame is just the first of his planned fortresses."

Raising feathery eyebrows high, the Magister said, "You

don't say. The fiends?" His eyebrows lowered again. "But we're taking steps to make sure what happened in Mousame cannot happen here. An otherworldly fortress will not be breaking through the Logos. And I trust your family will deal with any other threats. Armies are hardly unusual for a Blighter."

Miserably, Kiar said, "Tiana wants us all to leave, though."

The magister said, "Yes, I heard about that extensively a few hours ago." He shuffled some papers. "It seems like a good idea to me. I certainly can't encourage ignoring the Firstborn's message."

Kiar stared at him. "But you asked us here. You wanted us here. You had some reason, and it wasn't so that damn sword could destroy the Citadel's workings."

"Things changed, my dear."

Kiar flushed. "Well, yes, but we don't all need to go. Tiana's on the quest, not me. I should stay here. Twist asked me to find a new teacher here. I can do more good here." But she recalled the Magister's smile on Antecession, when he'd sent her off to help Tiana, instead of staying behind to help his monks work the Logos. She wasn't one of them, and he wasn't going to let her join them.

He put down his pen and pinned her with a grave stare. "Lady Kiar, let me be honest with you. I think our princess's presence does more harm than good. I think if she leaves, some of this blighter's forces will be diverted to follow her. If our enemy is smart, he doesn't want her to complete her quest. So you see? I have been thinking about this quite seriously all night. And I think you should protect her. I think you should all protect her."

Once again, Kiar wished she could tell if he was lying.

Something about his expressions and his movements seemed so practiced, as if he used rhetorical tricks he'd polished over decades, all the while thinking about something entirely different. She always felt like he was suppressing laughter.

"Vassay has something to do with this, don't they?" she muttered.

"Vassay is a useful ally in these times of trouble." The Magister studied his papers again.

Kiar want to storm out and sulk, but she knew it was childish. Instead, she said, "Well, unless something changes, there are ways they won't be able to help you. And they're connected with the assassination attempt on Tiana, too." She paused to see his reaction to this.

He murmured, "Oh, really?" like she'd mentioned some inclement weather.

She sighed and gave up on that topic. "Regarding the fiend window... I mentioned the armies earlier. But I also saw human men in our enemy's world. Last night I realized one of them was one of your monks. The one who told us about the fiends. Kai, I think. It was like he cast a shadow there, or like his ghost was trapped. Whatever happened when he was possessed left a mark." She shook her head. "I think you should watch him. I don't think he's aware of it but he could be a vector of access to the Citadel now even without a fiend possessing him."

The Magister's face clouded and she took a petty pleasure in finally worrying him. "How interesting." He considered her for a long moment, slowly tapping one finger on the desk. "The Vassay have developed a method of communication our own Logos workers have not mastered. One of the items we're negotiating over. I am certain that I could request they send one of their workers along with you to maintain a line of communication. Do you think that would be a bad idea?"

Kiar said tartly, "Yes. I do. Yesterday was bad enough. Even if it turns out their connection to the assassination attempt is just a coincidence, I don't think it's a good idea to let the Vassay feel any more empowered. You're doing quite enough of that. No offense."

He laughed. "Honest child. And of course, you have Twist..." He paused a moment and Kiar wanted to say, What? How do I have Twist? But she knew what he meant.

"Well, Kai will provide something for our people to study and watch. Thank you for the information." He shuffled his papers again. "I understand your princess wants to leave today if she can arrange it. I'll be there to see you off. I suggest you pack if you haven't."

With a nod of his head, the Magister dismissed her from both his office and his Citadel. Burning with conflicted emotions, remembering her dream's warning to be wary of the Bastard, Kiar left.

CHAPTER SIX

THE TABERNACLE OF BROKEN HEARTS

H EY," SHOUTED AN angry voice. "Why did you let it happen?"

Jerya stood in the plaza known as The Tabernacle Of Broken Hearts, contemplating a large black granite box, worn smooth by many hands. The box and the matching dome above were all that remained of a forgotten temple, and the city had long ago given the ruins a new purpose.

The city folklore said that leaving the remains of your broken heart in the tabernacle would help you forget what you'd lost. People wrote letters to the Tabernacle, pouring out their pain, and left offerings: nearly new dancing shoes, promise rings, baby clothes, dried flowers. They left an offering, and sometimes, if they could bear it, they took something else out and tried to use it to help somebody else.

"Hey!" The angry voice came closer and Jerya's detachment of Royal Guard stepped between her and the source. She didn't move from her meditation.

The box usually contained a few offerings, but they never accumulated before somebody decided to reuse them. Now it overflowed. Hundreds of people gathered in the plaza. Some of them watched her and her family, but others scanned the crowd, looking for those they'd lost. Many of them wept. A day after the mudslide, and the reality of what—and in some cases who—they'd lost was sinking in. The ash was clearing from the sky, but the mud wasn't giving back what it had stolen. Once she'd gathered her family together again, they'd spent most of the previous day sending eidolons to pluck whomever they could from the roofs of the north city, but too many had been unwilling or unable to escape ahead of the mud.

"I just want to know—" went the angry voice. Young, male. Insistent. Jerya turned, waving the guards out of the way so she could fix her attention on the speaker.

A wild-eyed young man supported an old woman with a dirty, tear-stained face. When he realized he had the Crown Princess's attention, he stepped closer, pulling the old woman with him. But even standing only a few yards away, he didn't lower his voice.

"Why did you let it happen? My grandmother believed in you, so now what are you going to do? Are you going to roll back the mud? What good are you?" His voice broke and he shook his head.

Jerya looked up at the mountain and the smear of darkness down its flank. She didn't look at her relatives, clustered behind her. She couldn't afford to show them any weakness, anything that would inspire her uncles to get involved, or this could go very badly.

Turning back to the angry young man and his grandmother, she said, "I'm sorry. Did your entire family get out in time?"

"It's just me and my grandmother," he said bitterly. "She lost her life's work. I had to carry her out in her nightgown. And look at her now. How will she recover? We've lost *everything*, and here you are. What have *you* lost?"

Jant muttered behind her, and Jerya closed the distance between herself and the angry man. His accusation she ignored; it was so unfair that it had to come from grief, not reason. "Do you have some place to stay now?"

"No, of course not. Didn't you hear me? We lost everything. My grandmother doesn't even have a decent dress."

"We will find you a place to stay," Jerya said firmly. *She* had a place to stay. So would everybody, somehow.

"I want my house back!" the man snapped. "I want to know why you failed to protect us. Too busy playing in the palace, I suppose."

Jerya exhaled, looking over the man and his grandmother carefully. He was angry, but she was shocked and broken. He was young, and his grandmother was old, and he clearly loved her very much. He would, Jerya decided, recover. But how he recovered would be dependent on his grandmother.

She moved closer yet again, holding out her hand to the grandmother, focusing all her attention on the woman. "What was your craft?"

Faintly, the old woman said, "I—I was a weaver. Fine wall hangings. Other things." She opened a clenched fist to reveal a spool of viridian thread, vivid in the gray day.

The grandson interjected, "She does amazing work and half the time your nobles claim they did it themselves. She made a set of wall hangings for me, for any children—the legends of Lor Seleni—" He stopped talking, looked away.

"Your work sounds marvelous," said Jerya warmly, still

focusing on the old woman. "I'm so glad you're still with us. Do you train students?"

The woman's tormented expression slowly became puzzlement. "Not recently."

Glancing down at the spool of thread the old woman still held out, Jerya added, "Did you bring that for the Tabernacle? I hope not. It's so beautiful. And we will find you a new loom."

"What about our home?" demanded the young man. He threw something of his own toward the Tabernacle.

Jerya caught it with her magic and brought it to her hand. It was a house key. This, she kept as she turned her attention back to him. "And your craft?"

He stared at her sullenly until his grandmother squeezed his arm. "I'm a clerk in a warehouse on Gig Street."

Gig Street was on the south side of the river, the side of the city they stood in now. "You still have a job, then." She gave him a sad smile. "So do I. Let's both do our best, and maybe we can dig our way out of this disaster."

He hesitated, and Jerya nodded at one of her guards. He promptly moved forward.

"Sir, I'm Lieutenant Raffey. Please, come with me and we'll find a place for your family to stay."

The young man ignored the guard to glare balefully at Jerya. Then his grandmother reached up, twisted his ear, and said, "Stop being rude, boy," and his entire expression changed. His eyes widened and his mouth opened. He looked down at his grandmother.

She squeezed his arm. "Come now. We've all got work to do." And without looking at Jerya again, he went.

Jerya turned away, back to the granite box, the house key still on her palm. She mounted the steps of the dais the box rested on and slowly picked up a book that had tumbled off the heap and tucked it under her arm. Then she fingered a woman's cut-off braid, and a polished man's dancing slipper. There was a song book, and a paint brush. And there were the rocks: river-washed stones, tossed in among the abandoned belongings. Rocks weren't usually what you gave up to the Tabernacle, but when you'd lost your entire home fleeing in the middle of the night, rocks were all you could spare. Jerya didn't glance at the towers of the Palace, rising out of the mud that covered everything else. She knew.

She stacked the book—a novel, she realized, something Tiana had read—and the shoe and the paintbrush on top of each other, and then turned to where her family waited. "We can sleep in the inn, if you think it wise, but we must set up a court here, until the Palace can be recovered."

While Jerya stayed with Shanasee in the tower, Yithiere had taken over the Red Plume posting house, peremptorily kicking out the guests who'd come to celebrate Antecession and installing Iriss and the little girls. The rest of the family and the servants had followed, and the Chancellor and his servants, until the inn brimmed with the relocated Regency Court. Jerya was grateful Yithiere had chosen an inn to commandeer and not one of the big houses on this side of the river; at least most of the Antecession visitors had homes to go to out beyond Lor Seleni.

Yithiere frowned. "Why here? It's exposed and as the season changes, the weather will become a challenge."

"Because this is where they will come. You saw. This is where our job is." She sat down on the top step of the dais and glanced at the crowd behind her family. Most of them were watching her now. She looked back, solemnly, and then turned to see Jant's unexpected faint smile. He huddled

under his umbrella with two guardsmen close behind him.
Seandri and Seandri's Regent Harthen stood at his elbows.
Jant had insisted on coming, despite his dread of the open
sky. It made the journey to the Tabernacle of Broken Hearts
through the crowded streets even slower.

Yithiere's frown deepened. "Our 'job' is hardly soothing
broken hearts. We have a war to fight."

Jerya sighed. "We have more than one. Everything is
confused and disorganized, Uncle. The city is a mess. It's two
thirds its size suddenly, with much of the same population.
That isn't going to just sort itself out. Somebody will have to
make decisions."

"The Justiciars and the mayor—"

"I don't trust the Justiciars and the mayor," Jerya said,
her voice rising. She caught herself and modulated her tone.
"I want to be here. We can organize the war from here, can't
we? The Royal Guard has mobilized at Mousame. And if
anybody wants our help with restoring the city, we'll be easy
to find."

The Justiciars had claimed another inn for their own
court. Guards and clerks surrounded it, just like their Court.
It was, she supposed, safe, but it was also isolated. She
needed to be different than the Justiciars. She would be who
the people thought about when they required guidance. She
wanted, deep inside, to take that from the Justiciars. They'd
tried so hard to shut her out of governance, keep her family
as figureheads.

"Oh, they'll want your help," said a new voice. "They'll
want answers, too, just like that young man. Well done, by the
way." Just beyond her uncles stood Lady Alanah, the Royal
Family's martial instructor. She was an ordinary looking
woman, near forty: average height, with brown hair pulled

back in a bun and her skin dark enough to show that some of her ancestors had been of Royal Blood. She was armed like a Guardsman, which was uncommon in a woman but not remarkable. Her snapping hazel eyes, fringed with dark lashes and vivid even at fifteen paces seemed to be the only reason anybody would notice her... until she moved, because she moved like a tiger. Even now, only weeks after she'd had her third child, she looked like she could embarrass a troop of Royal Guard while thinking about something else.

"Alanah," said Jerya, smiling. She'd known the noblewoman most of her life. Lady Alanah, the daughter of a local count, had a genius for tactics and combat that had earned her an appointment as Royal instructor before she was twenty-five. "I'm glad to see you. I hope the rest of your family escaped safely? How is the baby?"

"Yes, everybody is well. Quite an orderly retreat. The children are with my mother in her house at Quinn Crescent." She glanced toward the east side of the city. "As I was saying, I'm getting questions about what happened and why. People are starting to make up their own stories. It was an ill-omened night for the mountain to shrug. Good work on Shanasee's part, though. That helped enormously, although we may need to remind people of it." Alanah spoke in the brusque, diffident way she talked about everything except martial arts and her children.

Jerya frowned. "We will." She rested her hands on her knees. "You also said they'd ask for help? Have there been other requests? More survivors on roofs?"

"No more of those, sadly. But dozens of another sort," Alanah assured her. "Nothing you can reasonably grant."

"Like what?" Jerya asked with a flicker of annoyance that Alanah made that decision without her.

Alanah glanced to her side, where another lieutenant of the Royal Guard stood waiting patiently. "People are trying to cross back over to the north side of the river, but the bridges have been destabilized by the mud. I've stationed guards along the crossing points to turn them back, but we've already lost at least one idiot. I'm sure this is what you want, yes?" Alanah was entirely outside the command structure of the Royal Guard, but her unique position made most of the Guard treat her suggestions like the orders they'd almost certainly become.

"Yes," said Jerya slowly. "Thank you. It's far too dangerous to return yet."

Alanah quirked a grin that made Jerya feel like a little girl in lessons again, eager to please her teachers. She'd have to check that reaction, because she suspected she was going to make decisions they wouldn't like.

An odd rushing whisper announced Twist's magical arrival. Jerya looked around as he appeared beside the Tabernacle. He stepped lightly down to sit beside her. "Hello. I hope I didn't break your heart too badly when I didn't report in last night. I was... tired."

"You and Shanasee are the heroes of the disaster," Jerya told him. "You'll get a medal eventually."

"Oooh, will it be shiny? I've always wanted a shiny medal." He sounded almost the same as he always did, but his blue eyes were dark with some distraction.

"Where did you sleep? At the Citadel? Did you see my sister?"

He tapped his nose. "Exactly so. I've just come from her. Would you like my report here?" He glanced around at the growing crowd. "There are some things we should talk about privately. You may not like the rest of it."

Jerya hesitated. "Is it urgent?" She felt torn between hearing about what her sister had done on the mountain, and her desire to show the people of Lor Seleni that she wasn't going to hide from them.

"That depends on whether you want me to rush back to the Citadel and try to stop Tiana from following a dream across the countryside." He yawned. "Mind, I don't think I could actually stop her, but we could probably manage to make her feel really bad about it."

Jerya stared at Twist before drawing her hands across her face. Standing up, she announced, "I'll be back this afternoon." Then she addressed her favorite cousin. "Seandri, would you remain here this morning?"

In response, he came over and took her hand. She wanted to run her fingers through his curly hair, but she refrained, letting him hold her fingers lightly, her chin lifted like she was a queen. After all, she all but was.

"What do you want me to do?" he asked her, his voice low.

"Be here," she told him. She could trust him. He was steady and gentle and she loved him for it. "Listen. Be kind. Don't give anybody permission to cross the river, no matter how they beg. Tell them I'll be back soon. It's just for a while, until we can get something better organized. They have to know we're here, Seandri. We haven't abandoned them."

He squeezed her fingers. "Are you afraid they think that?"

Shaking her head, she said, "I'm afraid they think it's our fault."

She walked back to the Red Plume, aware of how the crowds opened around her. It wasn't much; it wasn't enough to allow her to move quickly, but people pushed out of her way with whispers and murmurs. Impromptu markets assembled as some enterprising citizens realized they could sell all sorts of things to people who had lost almost everything. Twist walked beside her. Once, he flickered, as if he'd jumped somewhere and back again, very quickly. She didn't ask; it was hard to talk in the noise of the streets.

In the Red Plume, she made her way directly to the room they'd set aside for Shanasee and Iriss. Gisen sat between them, looking at a picture book aimed at much younger children, while Yevonne dozed with her head on Gisen's knee.

"No change?" Jerya asked. Gisen shook her head and closed her book, looking attentively at Jerya.

Cara, Shanasee's Regent, emerged from an adjoining room. She hadn't slept much in the last day and night, less even than Jerya and the others, and she looked it. She'd been furious when Yithiere brought Shanasee to her, irrationally angry at how Shanasee had been used and hurt. Now, she just seemed exhausted. She waved at her throat and said something inaudible. A mug steamed in one hand, fragrant with the scent of lemon and honey.

Yevonne lifted her head from Gisen's knee and yawned. "Cara's lost her voice. She's been talking and talking to Shan. But nah, they're both still sleeping safe. It's all right."

Jerya looked at the two still forms, thinking about love and loss. After a moment she turned away and went to one of the inn's parlours, where Cathay's mother and Jant's wife both sat sewing. The Royal Family and its Regents and spouses and parents had been spread out all through the Palace; before the disaster, Jerya would go occasionally go days without seeing Lady Siana or Lady Julina. That was another reason to hold as much business as possible at the Tabernacle. It was too crowded here. The Chancellor had already spoken of moving his own staff to another building but he wanted to identify an appropriately empty one first.

Lady Siana looked up and put her sewing down. "Do you need this chamber?" Jerya had heard that once Siana had been a vivacious woman, but now she was a pale, willowy creature whose laughter was quiet and her disapproval even quieter.

As a child, Jerya had sometimes pretended Lady Siana was her own mother: a mother who stayed with her child despite the sadness. But that hadn't lasted long; extended flights of fancy were Tiana's domain and so Jerya had put them away. And it was too easy to see the marks grief had left on Lady Siana. She and Lady Julina were noble-born, but when they'd married Royal princes, they'd become part of the Regency Court. They had some of the training and counseling Regents relied on, but it hadn't helped Siana. No training prepared you for your husband's suicide.

Jerya slanted a glance at Twist. "Did Cathay go with her?"

Twist yawned again. "I've always thought it was remarkable how single-gender the Citadel appears to be. There are female students, but the Citadel believes the path to avoiding distraction is for the girls to pretend to be boys." He shrugged. "It works, I suppose. If, like Cathay, you're not looking for romantic adventures because you've already found one and she's leaving the Citadel."

Grimacing, Jerya said to Lady Siana, "You might as well stay, if you can bear the crowd." She moved further into the parlour. Her uncles and Alanah moved in behind her, while the guards clogged the hall outside. Lady Julina stood, held out her hand to Jant, and bent down and kissed his head when he stood beside her.

Jerya walked over to the window, glanced outside, and then closed the curtains, casting the room into shadow. "What has my sister done now?"

From across the room, Twist stared at her for a long moment, as if he wasn't quite sure where to start. Dread churned in Jerya's stomach. "Is she well? You would have told me immediately if she wasn't, yes?"

Relaxing, Twist said, "She's mostly fine. During the Antecession ceremony an altercation with the sword Jinriki triggered an odd," he hesitated, as if looking for the right word. "An odd event. All the Logos-workings vanished, and Tiana had a direct encounter with the spirit of Niyhan. Now she's on a quest, at his command."

It was Jerya's turn to stare at Twist. "How much of this is verifiable?" She'd spent her life protecting her baby sister, sometimes from Tiana's own dangerous, irresistible whims.

"Most of it," Twist assured her. "The Magister agrees that Niyhan did manifest, and did give Tiana something special. A weapon to be used against the Blighter, if she can acquire the rest of it. Oh, and she reconciled with the sword. Which will probably come in handy... Though really, one has to wonder how many weapons Tiana needs."

"That sounds like two too many to me." Jerya wrapped her arms around herself. If Tiana was being guided by the Firstborn, that could change everything. They couldn't rely on the Firstborn's aid; the divine creator's last lesson taught that Blood protected Ceria now—but if they'd decided to involve themselves again, things were changing. She had to make sure they changed in favor of her family.

Despite the fragments of politics and metaphysical meaning and spin bobbing through her mind, she kept returning to an image of Tiana, her baby sister, carrying such a strange and awful burden. "Is she well? Is this new weapon hurting her somehow? The sword seemed bad enough."

"Oh, she's distracted but other than that she seems healthy. Now, I'll have more for you about the Blighter later. Kiar discovered all manner of secrets about him, but while we're this private—" and he glanced around at the rest of the family watching their conversation—"can we talk about the King?"

All her worries about Tiana faded under a surge of grief. Jerya closed her hands into fists. "What about him?"

"What happened to him?" Twist spoke gently, which momentarily enraged Jerya. He went on. "Kiar said something but she was coming out of the phantasmagory at the time and I couldn't know if it was just a dream. And then a dragon attacked us."

The curtains were dark, with bright flecks woven into them. Jerya wondered if they were supposed to represent stars. It was really very interesting to think about, and think about the curtains she did until she had herself under control. "Something. Something happened to him. I suppose we'll announce it soon, once things settle down. There can be a quick coronation. Maybe in two weeks on Arising-day, since it's traditional."

"There are stories already," said Alanah abruptly. "I heard one little boy telling his friends about how King Shonathan fought the old Bastard beyond the wall Shanasee built. He said the mud was what was left after King Shonathan won."

"Hah," said Jant fiercely. "My messenger told me the tale of how Shonathan battled the ghost of his brother Math in my Shan's barrier. They don't forget, even when they never knew."

"I don't like either of those stories," said Yithiere.

"Allowing them to cast the Blood—any of the Blood—in the role of enemy is too dangerous. We must tell them something else, and enforce it."

"The truth..." began Twist, and looked inquisitively at Jerya.

Jerya thought back to her last meeting with her father, in the phantasmagory. It had been ugly and painful. She'd been helpless, too familiar a sensation. But under the guise of tormenting her father, the Blighter had been trying to accomplish something. It was hard to understand, but in the end her father had died because he'd made the Blighter angry. He'd made the Blighter fail. "The truth is... complicated. Alanah, did the child you overheard say what happened to the King after he defeated the Bastard?"

"Oh, he flew off into the dawn to find the Bastard's secret stronghold in the hole in the night. Shonathan is still quite the hero, after all these years."

"Yes," Jerya said flatly. "He is." She took a deep breath and made a decision. "He died, but he died saving Ceria, and he died fighting. But he died. And after he died, the Blighter destroyed the phantasmagory somehow. I don't know how." She looked around the room, staring into each shadowed face. "And this is the last time we talk about it. From now on, all we know is that he left to fight the Blighter and he hasn't returned. We're waiting for news. Twist, I'm going to need you to help me stay in contact with Tiana, as if the phantasmagory still existed. And we're not going to release any other story to replace the tales children tell, Yithiere."

He scowled. "No coronation, then. Without a coronation, you aren't Queen. This is a foolish decision; perhaps you aren't ready to be Queen."

"The people need hope, Uncle." Jerya softened her voice.

"If they believe that the ruin of their city is the side effect of a great victory, they'll rebuild much faster than if they learn the devastating truth."

"And what of when they hear the truth after they've accepted the lie?" snapped Yithiere. "When they realize the Blighter is still out there, undefeated, his armies and his fortress devouring our country? How much hope will they have then? They will be betrayed, and worse, unprepared."

"You've spent half your life lying, boy," grumbled Jant.

"Have I? I do what is necessary to keep the innocent safe," said Yithiere. "But if you are correct, then I must be experienced with the consequences. Trust me to know when it is too dangerous."

Jerya shook her head. "I will always listen when you think it's dangerous, Uncle. But sometimes danger must be risked."

Yithiere moved closer, his head low and his nostrils flaring like the wolf that was his eidolon. "I know that. You think I don't know that? But they cannot be allowed to turn on you. The Blighter is too close, too uncontrolled. The Royal Guard is a skeleton force given the size of the Blight itself."

"Then watch them for me? Warn me if their fear outraces their hope and we will see if we can turn them in a different direction." Jerya hardly thought about what she said. Her only goal was to keep Yithiere behind her, not in front of her. Only those who knew him well understood how unpredictable he was; he kept to himself too much in public for the people to see him as anything other than the war leader who had fought off four Blights. If he decided to ignore her leadership and go his own way, her power would wither before it had fully developed. And without somebody stabilizing him, he'd be dragged down by his own fears before the Blighter could get to him.

Yithiere's mouth tightened. "I will watch." It was more a threat than a promise.

Great-Uncle Jant spoke impatiently. "I'm far more concerned about the Justiciar's Council and the duchies than about what the city does. What will they do without a monarch or a monarch's regent? Firstborn weapons or not, we need their troops to contain the Blighter, but if the fiction is that the King is off fighting a one-man war instead of calling on them, will they come?"

Jerya dragged her eyes away from Yithiere, toward the little silver-haired old man. He'd spent his life in the Palace, writing books and studying the family magic. He knew a great deal about many esoteric subjects. She hadn't thought politics was one of them.

"They'll send them," she said firmly. Doubt was an impossible weakness here.

"I don't know," said Jant. "My messenger told me about the troubles on the roads now. Perhaps they'll stay home and trust us and the Firstborn to deal with the Blight." He grimaced, as if personally offended by the Firstborn involving themselves.

Jerya repeated, "They'll send them. They have to, or there won't be a country left to live in. And they're armies, they'll cut right through any troubles on the road."

Yithiere shrugged. "The duchies are all far away from the fairy tales you want to spin for Lor Seleni. They know, or will find out, that the enemies we face are akin to our own magic. This Firstborn story weakens our authority; *that* news we should suppress if we can. And even so, trust may be lacking. How do we even teach a common soldier how to fight something made out of eidolon stuff? They're used to fighting men who are afraid of death, and who stop when stabbed."

Alanah cleared her throat. "As it happens, I have some ideas on that." When everybody looked at her, she shifted her weight. "It used to just be a theoretical exercise, after growing up in the Bastard era. I'm happy to share them with the troops."

The meeting went on, devouring the rest of the day. Jerya did her best to keep both her uncles too busy on details to question her own focus. She knew what was important: Seandri sitting in her place in the Tabernacle of Broken Hearts, and the Justiciar's Council, who had thought concealing the attacks on Ceria was better than letting her have power. She'd show them. She'd have to, or even if Tiana's Firstborn Weapon defeated the Blighter, there'd be nothing left for her family.

CHAPTER SEVEN

THE REGENT AND THE ROAD

PUFFY WHITE CLOUDS tumbled across a summer-blue sky. The breeze was brisk but the air was warm, and smelled of the harvest. It was the perfect day for a picnic. Unfortunately, they were on a quest instead, which was much less pleasant, and didn't involve your own bed at the end of the day.

They rode west. That was all Lisette knew: west. The group had met in the courtyard of the Citadel, their horses and mules packed for a long journey, and Kiar had asked Tiana for a destination and she'd immediately pointed... west. That was it.

For three days, they'd been riding west, in entirely the wrong weather for the season. Only the sun, low against the southern horizon, gave any clue it was almost winter. Every time it shone in Lisette's eyes, it felt like a metaphor for how little they knew about the quest.

It was ridiculous, Lisette thought, and felt guilty for thinking it. She was trained to deal with all sorts of ridiculous whims. She'd had no problems when her charge decided she wanted to grow up to direct plays rather than be a self-directed weapon. It had been fun. They'd been in a city. She liked cities. She liked having someplace warm to go after they spent time outside. She liked not being on a horse all day. She liked, if she was on a journey, to know where she was going and when she could anticipate it being over.

But being a Regent wasn't about doing what she liked.

When she'd agreed to the expedition, though, she'd thought Tiana meant to sleep indoors. She thought they'd travel on the roads and find posting houses at the end of each day. She fully expected they'd visit some of the country nobles and gentry along the way, as a break from posting houses. She thought they'd use remounts and eat supper in dining rooms most of the time. She knew how a Royal princess ought to travel, even with such a small escort. *Especially* with such a small escort. But that was too dangerous, Tiana said, and Cathay and Kiar agreed. Lisette didn't expect any better of Cathay, but she tried not to feel like Kiar was a traitor. Kiar knew how it was supposed to be done, and Kiar usually liked to do things properly.

They did travel on a road, once they came down from the mountain. Tiana had asked the guide to lead them down a side route, not the main road. She didn't want to go past Lor Seleni. There was no need, she said, and it would slow them down. So they came down the mountain on a path more suited for goats than horses, and it took them two days just to reach one of the Regency roads. It ran west, so Tiana was willing to follow it for a while, although she regarded that as a convenience, not a necessity. That night they'd slept on the ground, just as they had on the mountainside, because, Tiana said quite reasonably, if the Blighter decided to attack them in the middle of the night it'd be best not to have lots of noncombatants around. And they'd be harder to find if they weren't advertising their location at every posting house they passed.

It made sense, but it also made Lisette cranky. A Princess fighting a Blighter traditionally had an army as her escort. If they were with a proper army, they'd have beds. They'd have baggage trains, if they were with an army. They wouldn't have left Tiana's cook and maid behind. Instead they had a dozen guardsmen, which was too many for the group to move quickly, and too few to actually accomplish much, and none of them were very good at cooking. And they had to travel carefully, to spare their horses and their own muscles. Berrin said they'd have to pick up at least a few remounts when they could, but that wasn't feasible until they found somebody with the right kind of horses to sell.

The wind picked up, gusting a pin straight out of Lisette's hair and whipping the freed lock against her cheek. She tucked it up again as best she could, and then smoothed her horse's mane. She'd never spent quite so much time on Dustling's back before but the horse was doing well.

She dropped back to ride with the guards, tired of the whine in her own mental voice. Tiana didn't notice, and that was another thing that irritated Lisette, as much as or more than the rustic sleeping arrangements.

Maybe it was the heart of everything, really. Tiana had been distant since she'd picked up Jinriki, but since Antecession, she'd been positively withdrawn. Her face turned west so often, even when they were grazing the horses, that Lisette sourly suspected she'd developed a crick in her neck. Cathay, who had once upon a time focused exclusively on pleasing Lisette, now brooded like a tragic hero over Tiana. And Kiar spent all her time reading, on and off horseback. Lisette expected to be useful. At Court, someone always wanted her attention. But right now all she had to do was make sure her mare didn't get into any trouble on the road and Dustling was better at that without her help.

"My lady," said Slater gravely, touching his helmet but keeping his gaze pointed ahead. "Is there a problem?"

"Not as such," said Lisette, summoning a smile. "How are the guards dealing with the journey?"

Slater's gaze slid sideways to examine Lisette. "Some of the less experienced ones are a little tired, but they'll toughen up. For most of them, this is an adventure."

"Better than being with the main army, I suppose," sighed Lisette. She turned in her saddle and looked back over the more than half-dozen men ranged behind them. Most of them had the same blank expression Slater cultivated. Berrin grinned at her, as he usually did. He always seemed to find something to grin about.

Another guard behind Slater dozed, his head sagging on his chest. Lisette remembered him: young, maybe the youngest of the unit. Not so young he needed to take naps, though. She frowned. "Are they having trouble sleeping? I can certainly sympathize but—"

The young guardsman jolted awake, as if somebody had stuck him with a pin. He looked around wildly, and then squeezed his eyes shut and shook his head. When he opened them again, his face drained of all color. He stiffened and touched his helmet at Lisette.

Lisette nodded, smiled at him and faced forward again as Slater said, "If so, they'll get used to it. Young Ryely is new and a little bit nervous."

He hadn't appeared nervous to Lisette. He'd looked

exhausted, until something had woken him up. She wondered what might have done that, and cast her gaze over the rest of the column, noting the other dozers. Then every drooping head jerked up, wide-eyed and alert, although nobody had said a thing. An idea occurred to Lisette, arriving with the weight of intuition.

Jinriki? She thought, as loudly as she could. **I know what you're doing and you have to stop.** She paused and waited, before thinking at the sword again. Her thoughts were less polite this time: things she'd never say aloud.

Slater kept talking blithely. "You don't need to worry about them, you concentrate on taking care of the Royals, eh? And we'll take care of you." He considered, then rubbed his chin and added, "Sorry about the cooking. None of us are used to cooking for refined palates. I'm not sure we *have* taste buds anymore. Except Berrin, and he's busy with the horses after we stop."

If Jinriki heard her, he didn't answer. She smiled at Slater again, distractedly, and sent her horse trotting ahead to get closer to Tiana. If Jinriki wouldn't talk directly to her, she'd have to bring up her suspicions to Tiana, who had been able to limit him even before Antecession.

Don't.

Why shouldn't I? Lisette snapped, and instantly regretted it. She tried never to snap at anybody. But she expected her thoughts to remain locked inside her own head.

Because I asked nicely, and you know I don't have to do that.

Lisette's hands clenched on her saddle, and the scars on her palms ached. **You have to stop tormenting the guards.**

Why? Jinriki's mental voice was mocking.

*Because if you don't, we will see what Tiana does when you and I have another struggle.**

There was a long silence. Lisette watched Tiana's back to see if she turned around, or even shifted her weight: any sign Jinriki spoke to her. But Tiana might as well have been a statue propped up in her saddle.

Lisette's own mare shied nervously at nothing perceptible, and she wondered if Jinriki could get inside the heads of the horses and spook them. She remembered darkly that Cathay's Regent Sennic had died after being thrown from his horse. That had been a bad day, a horrible day. Cathay hadn't let anybody near him, until she'd talked her way past his defenses, and then he hadn't let her go.

Do you remember these things to irritate me? demanded Jinriki. **Cathay, Cathay, everywhere I look. Consider Slater. I have. He is also attractive, in a human sort of way, and far more reliable. He even has a few interesting issues I know you'd enjoy exploring.**

Lisette didn't need to turn around to consider Slater; she'd considered Slater since he'd been assigned to guard her, in an idle, self-indulgent kind of way. He was tall and well-built and smart and loyal and skilled with his sword. And also a Guard, which was a line she wasn't crossing just for fun.

Why are you invading the guards? she asked, refusing to let herself be pulled further off-topic.

I'm just helping them... what was Slater's phrase? I'm helping them toughen up. They're mostly incompetent. They need to know exactly what my expectations are. I'm giving them helpful advice on where they're going to fail.

Lisette couldn't even come up with words in her head to respond to that, except to squeak, out loud, "What?"

Kiar looked back at her quizzically, then back at her book

again. Nobody else noticed. Lisette reached out and played with her mare's mane, muttering under her breath, "How can you possibly think that's helpful?"

Well, Jinriki sent meditatively, **It might make them give up and go home before Tiana gets hurt trying to save them. They're a burden. It's dishonest not to tell them so.** He sounded almost pious.

"No, you're just being cruel. You're enjoying being cruel." The mare's ears flicked back to catch what she's saying, and she patted her horse's neck. "Not you, you're a good girl." Then she concentrated and sent, **The Royal Guard is a voluntary force. Every Guard on this trip was hand-picked for his dedication to protecting us. And Tiana is very lovable, in her own way. Don't torture her guards for wanting to serve her.**

I'm not. I'm torturing them for being useless. Again she caught that strange bubbling sense of self-righteousness, and she focused on it, dissecting it until she found the idle amusement underneath.

You're a bully, she told him flatly, watching Tiana again.

No, I'm a fiend, and I don't like humans very much. Neither did my master. At one point he considered you all a mistake.

Lisette thought about the lazy arrogance of the voice in her head. Jinriki was, according to his own claims and Kiar's reading, the favored Secondborn of a dead god. Some arrogance was probably natural. But he was also, in her observations and from Tiana's stories, incredibly intelligent. Something didn't make sense about his current approach. **You're too smart to think it's a good idea for Tiana to travel with only you as her companion. What's going on?**

And you. We mustn't forget you, her most precious friend.

Jinriki said 'friend' like Lisette would have said 'horserace' and Kiar might have said 'hairbrush'.

That would be a disaster and you know it. Why are you being so stupid?

Jinriki didn't answer right away. During his silence, Lisette kept a close eye on her mare. Wisps of straw danced by in the wind. The mare stretched out her neck to catch at one. When she missed one, she snorted and shook her head.

I am... grateful to the princess. But there are many who would be pleased if she once again gave me up. If I could remove their influence, that risk would be minimized.

Lisette was again surprised. Her mare stopped abruptly, misinterpreting her body language, and once more Kiar glanced over. This time she asked, "Is she all right?"

"Yes," said Lisette hastily. "I was stretching out my back and confused her." She urged the mare into movement again and thought fiercely, ***You're tormenting Tiana's guards to make them leave, putting her in potential danger, so you can feel more comfortable? That's so... petty.***

I know, Jinriki thought, low and annoyed.

The wind picked up again, blowing a splat of cold water against Lisette's cheek. Distant thunder rumbled, and she realized the bright sunny day had vanished. The sun still peeped out between the roiling clouds, but it was like a prisoner catching his last glimpse of freedom. And on the northern horizon loomed a mass of clouds so dark and solid that it seemed like another mountain, one that put Sel Sevanth to shame.

Voices raised behind Lisette, before Slater and Berrin both cantered past her to where Tiana rode in the lead with Cathay. Lisette exchanged glances with Kiar, and as one they both moved close enough to listen in.

"A magnificent thunderstorm is about to break on top of us, Princess," called Berrin. "We need to find shelter."

Tiana glanced over at Berrin like he'd woken her from a dream. Then she looked around. The road followed the border between Ingae and Dalein, a territory of mostly farmland. They grew lavender as well as grapes and grain, but there was a fair amount of waste land. They were passing through some now: too rocky and uneven for easy cultivation. There was, however, a small mixed orchard on the right.

"We could stop at a farmhouse?" Tiana suggested slowly. "There's one over there." The farmhouse and its barn were both small. Sheltering sixteen humans and twenty equines would be a challenge. "But I'd rather we kept going. I'm sure we'll get to a posting inn soon. Then we could have baths, too." She turned her head enough to smile at Lisette.

Thunder crashed overhead, and two of the soldiers' horses shied violently. Lisette's horse shook her head again and turned to stare at the misbehaving cobs.

Berrin shook his head. "I think we're going to have real trouble getting there. I was thinking, if you'll forgive me for making a suggestion, Your Highness, that we could rest our horses in the orchard here. I imagine we could weave some branches together to create rough shelters. And if this is one of those quick-passing storms as it looks to be, we'll be as tight and dry as can be within an hour or so." He paused and saw Tiana looking ahead, as if still thinking about riding on. "You won't get there faster by getting sick, Your Highness."

Another spattering of cold rain hit her in the face. Tiana shook her head. "I suppose I do at least know enough to come in out of the rain."

'Yes, you do," said Lisette tartly, and turned her horse toward the grove. As soon as they were off the paved road, she slid down from the saddle and gathered the reins in her gloved hands. The orchard was a mix of apples and pears: a sign it was for local use rather than anything sold in a marketplace. The ground was still dry and the spatters from the sky became a pleasant rattle against the red and yellow leaves. Lisette walked forward to make room for the others behind her, feeling more cheerful. The air was fragrant with apples and something else. Something muskier. It reminded her of an aunt's perfume.

"Wait!" called Kiar, just as Cathay swore and drew his sword. But it was Tiana's shriek of, "Lisette, no!" that sent Lisette diving to the ground. That was a combination of instinct and training: if something was moving toward her, she needed to get out of the line of sight between the Blood and their target.

She still had the reins, and much to her surprise, her mare went down with her, kneeling and lying flat in a smooth motion. Lisette flung an arm over her neck as something dark went over both their heads. Then Berrin crouched beside her, and Tiana had unsheathed Jinriki, and somebody screamed.

It was, Lisette realized finally, an ambush.

CHAPTER EIGHT

EYE CONTACT

After they descended the mountain and made it to the flatness of the road, Kiar began reading. Spooky wasn't the best horse for reading. He didn't have the smoother gait of the horses raised by the Palace and she had to keep refusing his requests to drop back and keep the soldier's cobs in line. But she wasn't going through books quickly, not this time. In the Citadel she'd been frantically searching for answers, but this was the steady, focused stuffing of her head with new knowledge. She'd taken history books from the Citadel: volumes she thought might have references to the first war against Ohedreton and information about the dawn of the Blooded monarchy in Ceria. But it was so long ago that much had been lost or transformed. With enough time the line between fiction and history seemed to blur.

Even so, it seemed odd how little she could find about Shin Savanyel's life. When a drop of rain spattered on her book, she closed and stowed it, and turned her mind to that mystery. She didn't pay much attention to the discussion about the storm; as long as her books were safe in their saddlebags, she didn't mind getting wet.

Then Lisette went off the road toward the orchard nearby and everything went wrong. Something rippled nearby. It reminded her of the phantasmagory, whenever it had been full of the minds of her cousins. The spiritual sanctuary generated an undertow that grew stronger when her cousins were upset, producing ripples and tides. What she felt now was the same, bouncing between Cathay and Tiana and herself. But instead of being drawn in, it felt as if something was about to be pushed out.

The ripples came from the orchard. "Wait!" Kiar called, as Cathay and Tiana also cried out.

Lisette promptly dropped to the ground, her horse flattening as well. Kiar flung herself from Spooky's back and landed hard, then surged to her feet and ran into the grove. Something dark flickered over Lisette's prone form and Berrin's gloved fist smashed into it. It shot up into the trees. He crouched down protectively over Lisette and Kiar turned away to scan the shadowed trees.

The treetop canopy shivered in the sprinkling rain, with spatters of water breaking through. Red leaves drifted down, shaken loose by the gusting wind, but nothing else moved. She didn't relax; something still tugged on her.

Her attention was split when, beyond the grove, Tiana pulled Jinriki out of his sheath. He immediately started doing something awful to the local Logos, warping it like a thousand pound spider in a stolen web. She could feel it well enough to be glad she regularly suppressed her Logos vision. Frowning, she focused back on the ripples.

"Where are they?" Tiana demanded, stepping into the grove. " Jinriki says they're pouring through a fiend, wearing it out. Are you all right, Lisette?"

The light, already dusky in the grove, dimmed further as the last of the blue sky was devoured by stormclouds. Lisette said, "I'm not hurt. Is it safe to get up?"

"You should get out of the grove," Cathay said. "Go to the Guards. Stay in the middle, just like in training. We'll take care of this, while they'll look after you."

Lisette sat up, patted the neck of her supine horse and said shakily. "All right. I—" and something zinged out of the shadows, just as the Guards moving toward the grove shouted.

Kiar reflexively put up one of her shields, but felt the missile go right past her face. Swearing, she put up a shield near Lisette and Berrin and instructed it to block any fast moving missile. Then she put up a similar shield near Tiana and Cathay, and then—too much to do, all at once—she ran back out of the grove and into the rain and the battle that had exploded there.

The horses were all going mad, rearing and screaming and kicking. More of the small fliers, carved of shadow and rain, flitted among them and even the Palace horses, trained not to take fright at eidolons, had joined into the desperate attempts to escape the strange fluttering things. Spooky, angry instead of frightened, reached out and caught one in his teeth and started shaking it hard.

Andani, smooth-skinned living silhouettes, moved nearby, following the birds in to attack. Kiar assessed the group of raiders, determined that she couldn't cage all of them, and sent her personal shield to protect and track her horse.

Then she ran past the guards struggling with their

mounts, toward the andani. Slater shouted at her but she
ignored him. Two eidolon swords materialized in her hands.
They weren't her native eidolon, but they weren't far from
shields conceptually. It was particularly easy to make them
seek out other eidolons.

The lead andani wore a helmet and a hauberk, both of
Cerian design, which struck Kiar as interesting. Even more
interesting was how he slowed his advance when she moved
toward them, holding out a hand to halt his followers. He
recognized her, she realized, and he was wary.

Kiar remembered her inadvertent visit to the andani's
own world. It wasn't the first time she saw an andani, but
previously she'd thought they were just somebody's stray
eidolons. In the other world, she'd watched one stroke
the side of a behemoth, soothing it. It had behaved like a
person.

Cautiously, she said, "Don't do this. You know what will
happen. You haven't nearly the forces here to stop us." It was
true. If Jinriki could deal with the portal fiend, then half a
dozen andani wouldn't be anywhere near enough to stop their
journey. Not with all three of Tiana, Cathay, and herself.

Especially not with herself.

Cathay shouted in rage in the forest, but Kiar didn't glance
away from the lead andani. Lightning crashed overhead and
the andani flinched, looking up at the sky. When it looked
back at Kiar again, the spark of intelligence had vanished.
The hand stopping the others from progressing dropped,
and moving as one, the andani leapt for Kiar.

Kiar lifted her hands and let the swords go. They flew
from her hands to engage the andani to either side of the
leader. Out of the corner of her eye, Slater moved forward,
along with several of the other guards. The brunt of the

attack fell on them, and they seemed to be handling it. The andani didn't bleed like humans did but they were still vulnerable to being sliced open.

The leader jumped toward her, the bone blade in each hand raised high. Kiar's trained reflexes took over. She ducked low and came up, catching the andani's slender arm. Looking at the frenzied, empty face, she thought of Cathay's cats, her father's wolves. Then she tore open her own eidolon source and pulled the andani inside herself, just as she'd done before.

It didn't fight being swallowed. It pulled its arms in close and dropped the weapons and collapsed out of the armor into a stream of eidolon stuff. It was odd, and uncomfortable precisely because it wasn't. She'd become used to touching the aliens and warping the stuff of their bodies.

Her knees gave out under her as her adrenalin drained away. She sat on the road and watched as the last of the andani fell to the road and dissolved into nothingness. Seven trained men against five andani wasn't much of a contest, even with the late start.

Slater wiped his sword on a cloth, apparently out of habit, and stood over Kiar. "Are you injured?" he asked curtly. When she shook her head, he said, "It was considerate of you to hold them off until we'd dealt with the horses, but next time, don't. If you get hurt, we've failed."

Kiar blinked up at him. "Me? You mean Tiana and Lisette, don't you?"

He reached down and took her by the arm, hauling her to her feet. "No, my Lady," he said, his teeth gritted. "I mean you. It would be good to protect the others, too, and that would be easiest if you would all *stay together*." He glanced at her face and loosened his grip. "You are just as valuable as the Princess, my Lady. And you haven't that sword to watch out for you."

"I have my shields," Kiar offered, bewildered by his concern. She'd always identified with the Guards: they were both there to serve the Princesses.

"You don't. You rush into things as wildly as any of your kin—" Slater shook his head. "Never mind. I'm sorry. You did well holding them off." He released her, looked past her, and the blood fled from his heated face. "Apparently that sword isn't as useful as I thought."

Kiar whirled around. Tiana was leaning against a tree just within the orchard, looking away as Lisette inspected an injury along the underside of her arm. The crimson blood shocked Kiar, but not as much as realizing the 'orchard' wasn't one anymore. Half of the trees had been lopped in two and none of them had any leaves left. Something glowed in the heart of the grove, and Kiar smelled smoke.

As she ran over to Tiana, Cathay emerged from the grove, his gloved fists clenched. He had scrapes on his face, but otherwise seemed uninjured.

"Where's Jinriki?" Tiana asked faintly.

"I left him there. I'm sure you'll be able to reclaim him after the fire's gone out."

"Cathay!" protested Tiana. "He wouldn't have hurt you. He promised me."

"I'm not going to follow the commands of anybody who treats me like a slave, stormy weather, not even for you. If he didn't want to spend the night in a burning forest, he should have handled things differently."

"She'll be all right if we can get it clean," said Lisette, who seemed more sure of herself than she'd been all day.

The sky chose that moment to open up as the gusting

wind brought the storm. Spatters of rain became a downfall punctuated by lightning and thunder. Lisette glanced up at the sky, muttered something and then turned Tiana's arm up to the rainfall.

"Did they want the pendant?" Kiar asked, thinking of the Royal necklace Tiana carried. Ohedreton had destroyed a duplicate of it when he'd killed the King, and he'd been annoyed when he discovered the trick. But nobody paid attention to her question.

Tiana winced, and then shouted at Cathay, "If you hadn't noticed, we're in the middle of a storm!"

"Then the fire will go out quickly!" snapped Cathay and jerked around. "Where the hell are our horses?"

Slater said, "Bolted. Sorry, your Highness."

Berrin cracked his neck and put on his helmet belatedly, before squinting up at the sky. "Your mare and the Lady's stallion will keep them from going too far, once they're away from the flappy things. Most likely."

Cathay glared balefully at Slater, the water streaming down his face making his expression even darker. "Why did you let them bolt? If I leave the horses with you, I expect the horses to stay with you."

Slater bowed. "The cobs are mountain ponies, not warhorses, your Highness. And most of the men aren't trained to fight from horseback. When you were attacked, we had to dismount; by then the horses were already spooked." He glanced at Kiar. "Except for Spooky, oddly enough."

"I didn't name him," she said, wiping rain out of her face. "I think his name was Eidolon or something else embarrassing and they panicked when presenting him to me."

Growling under his breath, Cathay started stomping

down the road. Slater silently gestured, pointing at four of the guards and sending them after Cathay.

"Where are you going?" Tiana called, and when he didn't answer she said, "Fine! I don't care anyhow."

Kiar checked the eidolon shield she'd set to orbiting Spooky. She could still feel it at the far end of her eidolon range, not moving. Cathay's mare—who *was* battle-trained—had stopped the flight as soon as the fight was out of earshot. Then she tried again, "So what happened in there? Did anybody else get hurt?"

"There was a fiend spawning those eidolon monsters, like the one at the heart of the dragon. The monsters were easy to destroy but there were a lot and they kept going after Lisette. I was annoyed. And then careless," said Tiana. "I got hurt. That annoyed Jinriki. He made the fiend detonate. It was all very exciting and now it's over and it's raining and we're soaked and Jinriki is *on fire.*"

"Can't he just... come out of the fire like he came to you during Antecession?" asked Lisette hesitantly.

"No," interposed Kiar hastily. "Even if he could he shouldn't. That was catastrophic."

"He won't," added Tiana, her lower lip stuck out. "He's angry, and he's..." her eyes widened. "He's eating the remains of the fiend to recover some of his strength."

"Oh." Kiar paused, not sure what to say to that. "All right." The rain drummed on her head and ran down into her ears until she flipped one of her eidolon shields over her head to act as an umbrella. "Here, at least we don't have to get utterly soaked. How long are we going to wait?"

"I don't know," snapped Tiana. "You don't have to wait. Go to the farmhouse. Leave me here."

"So Ohedreton can send another set of andani after you? No, I don't think so."

"Fine, then." Tiana turned her face away, looking down the road Cathay had followed.

"Although actually," said Kiar, considering the fight. "That wasn't as bad as I was expecting. As long as we stay together, we seem to be able to handle Ohedreton's jabs."

"Don't lower your expectations, my lady," said Slater harshly. "That was a test, not a real attempt to interfere with us. And after seeing what this—" he closed his mouth over what Kiar suspected was an obscenity, then swallowed it and went on, "this enemy does as a test, I'd be a lot more comfortable with three times the men. And the support staff. I think we need to stop at the nearest castle and have a serious logistical discussion."

"We'll see," said Tiana absently. She shoved wet hair out of her face and winced. "He didn't exactly sneak up on us. We can feel whatever he's doing to send his monsters here."

"That only helps if he sends them through near us," Kiar pointed out slowly. "Another troop came up behind us."

Tiana turned to stare at Kiar, her eyes wide. "Oh. I thought one or two of them had gotten out of the grove and you were dealing with those."

"One of them wore *armor*. They were a scout patrol, I suspect. Maybe the fiend was part of the patrol."

"That's a nifty trick," said Berrin. "Being able to summon reinforcements when you need them."

"Well, it didn't help these monsters much," said Tiana, with a hint of smugness.

"Why do you call them monsters?" Kiar blurted, thinking of the lead andani's moment of wary recognition.

Tiana looked at her in surprise. "Well, they're not animals like most eidolons are, are they?"

"I don't think they're exactly eidolons. And we gave them names. The slender silhouettes are the andani."

Tiana shook her head. "Silly names. They don't mean anything."

"Neither does monster," snapped Kiar. She was getting cold in the rain and suddenly she wanted to be done with the conversation and with her own thoughts.

"Yes, it does," said Tiana, a firm set to her jaw. "It means something I can fight without feeling guilty."

"They're invaders," said Lisette gently. "It's all right to defend yourself and Ceria from them."

Tiana gazed down the road again. "I know."

Lisette transferred her gaze to Kiar, looking at her steadily until, uncomfortable with the scrutiny, Kiar muttered, "I just wonder what happens to them when they die. Do they return to a maker, like ours do? Or... something else?"

Berrin laughed. "What happens to us when we die, my lady? That's a question I admit I'm a lot more concerned with."

"We rejoin the Firstborn," said Kiar vaguely. It was a bit of doctrine she'd never thought too much about.

"Ah?" said Berrin, and tapped his nose like she'd said something meaningful. She looked down the road Cathay had left via, just like Tiana had been doing. It was a useful road that way. Unfortunately, Cathay and the horses were nowhere to be seen.

The downpour became sheets of water sluicing out of the sky. Tiana turned to look at the glow in the heart of the grove. It was still bright and strong despite the downpour, but it didn't seem to be spreading. Nobody said anything for a few minutes. They stood in a cluster: Tiana, Lisette, Kiar, with Berrin and Slater flanking them and the rest of the remaining guards closed in a semicircle around them.

Lisette cleared her throat and said to Berrin, "Thank you for shielding me in there. I shouldn't have been so careless."

"I try to be good at my job, my lady," said Berrin, with a faint smile.

Lisette looked at the rest of the guards clustered around. "Your service is appreciated. Even if sometimes there's talk of reducing the size of our band."

"Who's talking about that?" Tiana asked in surprise. "Just because I'm not sure if I want a full company escorting me doesn't mean I don't like having the guards."

Lisette fixed a steady gaze on Tiana, her silence drawing attention to a time before when Tiana had seriously considered abandoning her guards, before she finally said, "I'm glad."

Tiana said, "What? I like being able to sleep at night. If we're going to sleep on the road, we need somebody to keep watch and take care of the details." She studied the guards thoughtfully. "I suppose a different mix of specialties might have been better than bringing along the same guards we were assigned at home, but..." she shrugged, then winced again, her fingers drifting to the arm Lisette had bandaged. "Even if we didn't expect what we got, we have to deal with it anyhow. Nobody starts out a specialist."

Lisette let out her breath and smiled a tiny triumphant smile, which Kiar found curious. But before she could ask, Tiana turned and walked into the wood again, like somebody called her urgently. Somebody probably did. Kiar followed her, halting when she saw the devastation of the grove. Very few of the orchard's inner trees would be producing fruit anymore. Two of them had been uprooted and a dozen more tangled together in a knot with a fire at its heart.

The fire had red and yellow flames like a normal fire, but its heart was not just blue, but silver. It was nearly smokeless despite the steaming wood, but it gave off a lot of heat. Tiana barely seemed to notice as she walked closer. She hadn't realized she was freezing, in the fiend prison either. Kiar wondered how much of it was Jinriki's power and how much of it was Tiana's own distraction.

"Hey, Tiana," she called "Don't catch on fire."

Tiana nodded distractedly, watching the flames. Then, all of a sudden, the silver flames vanished and the fire belched and hissed. Tiana darted in close, grabbing the handle of Jinriki the Darkener before backing up so fast she tripped over her own feet. "Stop it," she muttered to the sword as she stood again. "All right. When Cathay's here—"

The thud of hoof beats and the jangle of harness cut Tiana off and she ran past Kiar out of the orchard, looking pleased.

Kiar lingered, looking at the bonfire. Then she gave into temptation and let the Logos sight activate. The fiend that Jinriki had destroyed was gone, but she could still see echoes of it in the way the Logos slowly knit itself together again in the wake of Jinriki's passage. There was something familiar about its edges. Tiny clues came together and she suddenly knew that the fiend had been one of those Jinriki had loosed from the Citadel.

Her skin prickled. It was too strange. She watched as the Logos behind the fire filled in the clean edges of the hole, devouring the emptiness. What did it mean for one fiend to eat another one? And did it take a fiend to eat a fiend? If not, it was possible a lot of mysteries related to past blights could be explained.

"Kiar!" called Lisette. Berrin touched Kiar's elbow and she jumped.

"Sorry, my lady," he said. "Will you come?"

"Yes," she said, and regarded the fire one last time. It sizzled in the rain, and she could no longer see any magical sign that a fiend had once been eaten there. It was just a scene of local devastation, as likely to have been caused by a Royal cousin having a tantrum as a fiend losing its temper.

Then again, she didn't know who had done what. Maybe that's exactly what most of the mess was.

She hoped the owners of the orchard would blame the Blighter and his fiends. She didn't want to know the truth.

When she emerged from the grove again, Cathay held his mare's reins, as everybody else reclaimed their mounts. Spooky, running free, came over to nose her.

Cathay said, 'Has anybody bothered to check on the cottager yet, to make sure Ohedreton didn't lay any unpleasant traps there?" When nobody answered, he sighed. "Come on, let's go. If they're all right, we can at least find out who owns the orchard."

CHAPTER NINE

VASSAY

I'D LIKE YOUR advice on this one, Your Highness," Lt. Raffey said, as he escorted a man in shackles before Jerya's chair at the base of the Tabernacle of Broken Hearts.

Jerya folded her hands in her lap. "Oh, Lt. Raffey? I'm pleased to listen."

In only a few days the words had become a ritual, a way of involving herself in the city in ways the Blood normally didn't. Criminals were supposed to be handed over to the City Watch, or the Justiciar's Guard unless they'd sinned directly against the Blood. But asking for their Princess's advice was always a sound idea. And sometimes, after she gave her advice, the criminal in question just... disappeared.

"We found this swindler down on Kesserig Smalls selling promises that he could extract belongings from homes on the north side of the city. Greedy fellow; he was accepting goods as well as coin just for the privilege of trodding on hearts." Lt. Raffey bumped the shackled man forward. "I thought maybe he'd like to make *you* that offer, seeing where you sit."

The shackled man was dressed like a bureaucrat or clerk, although he looked like the kind of clerk who ran a lot. Not obviously frail, not too old. He stared up at her with a blazingly hostile—and frightened—gaze.

"Go ahead, then," Jerya said, gesturing at the swindler. "How *will* you be extracting my treasures from my chambers?"

The swindler looked away, his jaw set. Then he brightened and turned back to Jerya. "I'm not, o' course. But I know people—No, listen! You're right, I'm a terrible man, but I know people, much worse, who are planning to raid the Northside. It's a trove over there, all the nob houses. I could work with you to find them, stop them. You don't want all your jewels and magic powders being stolen."

Jerya laughed. "Perhaps you should have brought me that offer *before* my Guard caught you taking much more from those with much less." She leaned on the arm of her chair, her chin on her palm as he glared at her. Her Guard wouldn't have brought him to her if he was a bad candidate for her standard offer.

"Lieutenant, what would the Justiciars do with him?"

"Oh, they'd lock him up for a few years, ma'am."

She raised her eyebrows at the swindler. "And what would you like to do?"

"Not be locked up," he said promptly, as if he couldn't help himself.

"Ah! I think we can help you. Let's see. Do you know how many people he caught in his game, Lieutenant?"

The Guard did some quick figuring. "I'd say about twenty-two, ma'am? At least that many, based on the complaints and what we found on him."

"Oh, no! Only fourteen in total, ma'am!" said the swindler quickly. "It was a bad business. I was about to give it up."

"Perhaps you should have quit before you started? Now. There are creatures to the south of us, creatures who, like you, want to take *everything* from people who have already lost too much. Those creatures are monsters, but you are a man, are you not? Not a monster? You can prove that by going and ending the careers of... let's see, we'll round up and then divide by the nature of the crime... yes, ending the careers of twelve of those monsters. Lieutenant Raffey here will put you in touch with some assertive folks who will help you in your quest, down in Mousame. They'll keep you on the straight path." She paused. "Or we could turn you over to the Justiciars. Ooh, or we could send you over the bridge to Northside, to do what you promised."

The swindler hesitated. One of the paths offered him what looked like an easy chance to escape. He was smart enough to be wary. Jerya dropped her voice, coaxingly and leaned forward. "Twelve monsters, my friend. With the right training, it won't even be a challenge. And then you'll be free. Not only free, but *clean*. You can come back to me with a letter signed by your commanding officer and I will personally make sure nobody ever brings up swindling again. You can start a new life, do whatever you want, just based on twelve. And if you make it thirteen... well... a bonus would be in order."

Then she leaned back. "The bonuses in prison aren't nearly as good, I hear."

The man stared at her, his eyes wide. He frowned, then smiled faintly, as if in recognition. "I'll take Mousame, Your Highness."

"Excellent! A choice I think will please everybody.

Lieutenant, take him to the gathering point. And... leave the shackles on." She smiled at the swindler, who gave her a nod of acceptance. Raffey bowed, and escorted the prisoner away.

Jerya sat on the chair at the base of the Tabernacle of Broken Hearts and made decisions twice a day. Often she chose simply to listen as people poured out their troubles to somebody they hoped could make it better. Sometimes she pointed them to the refugee camps being overseen by her Guards or promised them they would have a real home again and that she wouldn't let them starve in the meantime.

That was a bit of a challenge, with the Blight in the middle of Ingae, Ceria's breadbasket. But the duchy of Dalein to the north was whole again, recovered from the loss of their orchards in the Bastard's Blight, and the endless autumn had sped cool season crops to a market that suddenly needed them.

Occasionally she faced issues of justice, as with the swindler. Not very often; both the Royal Guard and the Justiciar's Guard were out in force in the city. Other than outbreaks of frustrated violence, the mere presence of the Guards kept people behaving in an orderly fashion most of the time.

Sometimes, people came to ask her for information on the Blight: clear-eyed, practical people who didn't believe the mythology of the King and the mudslide racing through the city, or people from outside the city who had more direct experience with the Blighter's forces. She reassured them concisely but truthfully that the situation was being handled by her sister and the other members of her family not present, and reminded them there was an army of Royal Guard between the Blight and Lor Seleni.

She made other decisions, too, in less public venues than the Tabernacle. The Guard was recruiting heavily. Many of those who had lost their homes joined up. There was a surge in women recruits that seemed to make Alanah sad every time she mentioned it.

The Blighter was moving slowly. Despite ripping a hole in heart of one of the Duchies, invading via an army hadn't been his original plan. He'd tried to use magic to hurt the land itself, and Jerya's father had stopped him, drawing the Blighter's destructive magic to himself through a sympathetic connection to Ceria that Jerya didn't entirely understand. Twist had told her the connection had been forged through the decades of holiday rituals, and some quirk of the Royal Blood's magic. But it didn't matter how, really. He had died and Ceria had not, and nobody had recovered yet.

Her scouts theorized that only some of the invading aliens were conditioned to deal with the light and land outside the Blight. The scouts who had ventured within the Blight itself reported that sunshine there was washed out and distant, and that many of the creatures had tendrils on their feet that rooted to the ground when they stood still.

The Blight, unmoving, was a disaster equal in scope to what had happened to Lor Seleni. But even as armies trained at its borders, its borders slowly expanded. Some said the expansion was slowing, but it was present and measurable. Jerya had asked Jant to investigate what was happening, and how to stop it; the growth bothered her far more than the armies slowly building a mere week's march away from Lor Seleni.

Jerya listened to yet another rendition of what happened at Tranning, where the Blight had been born, from perspective of somebody who had lived at the edge of the affected region. The old man had personally measured the current growth of the Blight, and once he worked his way around to mentioning that, she cut him off and invited him to a debriefing with Jant. They'd probably like each other, she thought dispassionately. They'd swap old man stories about past Blights. Jant didn't get a chance to talk in person to his own generation much. He'd like that. And it got the old homesteader's information off the streets, which was just as important.

The next person in line to see Jerya was her own cousin, Gisen, and Gisen's Regent Yevonne. Both of them quivered with excitement.

"Hi, Jerya!" said Yevonne. "Guess what?"

Dryly, Jerya said, "If you're going to go through all the trouble to stand in line to talk to me, the least you could do is call me Your Highness. You goose."

"Gisen said it wasn't fair to cut off people who waited all day, even if we had news you'd really, really want to hear. I thought maybe we should consider *priorities* and all, but what do I know? I'm just the Regent. So we had to wait in line." Yevonne elbowed Gisen, then pointed at a few people waiting respectfully a few yards away. "But those people let us cut in line. I knew they would if we asked. I mean, I know we're short but she's still the Blood! And I gave them some of the money the Chancellor gave me." She waved at the waiting supplicants who waved back in bemusement.

"Yevonne," sad Jerya patiently. "What is your news?"

"Oh! We were out exploring the Old Wall, you know, on the east side of the city? Near Woolmadding Market? We climbed all the way up to the top—that was my idea, not Gisen's, so blame me if you want to yell—and guess what we saw?"

Jerya's mind raced ahead of Yevonne's story. *East.* There was one thing she dreaded more than any other in the east. "Vassay troops?"

Yevonne's face fell. "You guessed!"

Standing up, Jerya said, "How far?"

"It was hard to see them at first because there were these clouds in front of them. Like fog, you know? So we didn't realize it was them until they were pretty close. They're probably in the city by now."

Jerya ran her hands through her hair and looked around for one of her people, then sent an eidolon to find Yithiere. Gisen's sense of fair play was sometimes excruciating. "Gisen, next time listen to your Regent! Some kinds of information are more important than others!"

Gisen shrugged and said, "It's not an *army.*"

"It's not," Yevonne corroborated. "It's a bunch of wagons, mostly."

"It doesn't have to be an army to be an invasion," said Jerya crossly. "I want you two to come with me to meet them. Ask lots of questions. Be adorable at them."

"Ooh, all right," Yevonne twinkled. She was twelve, and adorable was her stock in trade.

"And Gisen, I need a horse. I want to be as impressive as possible."

The city folk enjoyed the spectacle, at least. Jerya had quickly changed into her best remaining outfit: golden riding tights under a spotless white tunic encrusted with meticulously embroidered golden and viridian thread, with a golden tiara delicately studded with emeralds and a cape dyed to match the embroidery. Her maids had been hard at work packing for her while she'd been helping Shanasee save the city. They'd packed more expensive and more elaborate outfits too, but this she could be comfortable in. She didn't trust herself with more elaborate garb with Iriss still in a coma.

Lord of Winter, she missed Iriss.

She rode a rainbow eidolon mare summoned by Gisen, two of Yithiere's wolves paced beside her, and an eidolon hawk rode her shoulder. It was showy rather than functional; Gisen's horses were only safe for others to ride when she was present and not under any stress. But Jerya wanted to appear like something out of a storybook to the visiting Vassay 'engineers'. A tiny eidolon fledgling perched on Gisen's shoulder, as cute and sweet as she was, to be Jerya's ears as the little girls poked around: the secret in the storybook.

They moved casually down the city streets, following in the wake of the Vassay convoy. Jant stayed behind, of course, but the rest of her family was on hand: Seandri beside her, Yithiere behind, and the little girls skipping ahead. The whole city seemed to have suspended both business and recovery to watch the parade, and they cheered the Blood's appearance and their finery.

Jerya wasn't pleased, though. Seandri rode beside her on a stag of his own making and she reached over to squeeze his hand nervously. She was following in Vassay's wake, going to visit the Justiciar's Court, and that was an image she couldn't change, only polish. But they weren't going to come to her, that much was clear.

When they approached the Elant, the new home of the Justiciar's Court, Jerya realized it would take more than some nice clothes and a few passive eidolons to get in. Vassay had indeed come with wagons, over a dozen large ones, and many of them were still in the streets waiting for a final destination. The great draft horses—larger than any horse Jerya had ever seen—had been unharnessed. What seemed like hundreds of foreigners milled around in the streets, laughing and talking and staring around. They wore strange clothes: billowy loose pants and vests on top of their shirts. Some of the women wore the wispiest skirts Jerya had ever seen: alternately lifting in the lightest draft and clinging to their legs. Many of them wore spectacles, which Jerya found as exotic as the strange clothing, especially given how young most of them were.

Several of them handed out candy to the city children, talking to them about the city and their toys. Without any urging from Jerya, Yevonne and Gisen ran up to join the throng. They didn't get their candy, though, because the Vassay handing it out stopped to gawk at Jerya, their eyes rounding.

Jerya stopped her mount and lifted her chin, looking pointedly past the visitors at the Elant. If they tried to keep her out, a troop of Royal Guard marched behind Yithiere. The Justiciar's Guard was barely in evidence amidst the throngs of Vassay and it would just be a matter of exerting her authority—

But that line of thought was wasted because as soon as she shifted her weight, the Vassay started shouting at each other to get the wagons out of the Queen's way. They moved into clusters and began pushing the wagons this way and that, until they cleared a path to the great doors of the enclosed Elant courtyard.

The doors themselves gaped wide; one of the wagons had been parked halfway through until the Vassay pulled it out of the way. Inside many more people mingled and talked loudly: more Vassay and many of her own people as well.

Seandri leaned over. "It's a bit like we're late to a party."

"Uninvited guests, more likely," she said back, then shifted her weight to send her spectral mare into the courtyard. Seandri and his stag followed behind. The Vassay within joined in with the staring.

Three of the Justiciars, flanked by their guards, stood at the entrance to the inn on the far side of the courtyard, welcoming the leadership of the Vassay contingent. Their expressions were delicious, worth the trouble of arranging the visit. Both the sneer on Lord Warrane's face and the look of irritation from Lord Aubin were especially fine. Then the man who had been clasping Lord Warrane's hand extracted himself. He strode toward the Blood, a broad smile on his face.

He was a big, bald man, well muscled even under his loose clothing and somewhat older than her father had been. He was certainly much older than any of the other Vassay Jerya had so far seen.

"Hello!" he called. "Hello!" He wore a short cape pinned with a series of large brooches: a quill pen, a sequence of interlocking bronze, gold and silver rings, and an open hand. He fingered the last brooch as he said, "Hello!" a third time. Then he looked around, possibly for backup.

Jerya regarded the top of the man's skull. Lord Jasper, the youngest and least antagonistic of the Justiciars present, strode after the possible dignitary and said, "Your Highness, may I present Ambassador Smith of Vassay?" Jerya inclined her head fractionally again and Lord Jasper went on. "Your Excellency, her Royal Highness the Crown Princess Jerya, accompanied by Prince Seandri." Lord Jasper scanned Jerya's retinue but chose not to introduce the rest of the Blood present, since neither Gisen nor Yithiere were paying any attention to him. "He has come to aid us in the reconstruction, bringing some of Vassay's legendary engineers with him."

"My students, yes," said the big man, smiling. "I'm delighted to finally meet you. The reports—" He caught himself and stumbled, then changed direction. "We're eager to get to work. We were discussing some ideas as we came through your city. The bridges—" and then a young woman tugged at his elbow. "Oh yes. Must introduce Landry and Cutter, my assistants."

Jerya stared at them in amazement, wondering at the temerity of assistants who inserted themselves into their ambassador's first introduction. Landry was a tallish girl with big eyes, a long nose and an expressive mouth. She smiled absently at Jerya before her gaze drifted over to Seandri and stayed there as she said, "So pleased to meet you."

Jerya promptly forgot to notice what Cutter looked like. She didn't like it when young women paid too much attention to Seandri. She never had, but it was especially bad now, with Tiana gone, Iriss lost, and her world teetering on the edge of chaos. She needed *something* she could rely on. One day Seandri would have to be given up to another woman. One day, but not any time soon. She couldn't afford the distraction.

Frostily she said to Ambassador Smith, "Good afternoon. Have the Justiciars been doing a pretty job of welcoming you?"

The ambassador chuckled. "Pretty enough, indeed. They've mentioned a feast but I don't know about that. It seems inappropriate under the circumstances."

"Maybe if we offset any shortages from our own wagons, sir?" said Landry brightly. "We have more coming over the next few days," she confided in Seandri's direction. "This is most of our people but we've brought, oh, all sorts of stores to help the evacuees."

Neither Seandri nor his stag mount shifted beside her, and it was only that rock solid stability that kept Jerya from displaying her own agitation. This friendly informality was too strange and too unexpected. She thought she'd have to shove her way into a conversation with the Vassay leadership, but here he was, abandoning the Justiciars to talk to her. It was wrong, somehow. She had to make unexpected decisions quickly. And this assistant girl was staring at Seandri like he was a dessert she'd been anticipating for a long time.

"Let them welcome you," she told the Ambassador. "It will make them feel useful. They do like their pomp and ceremony." The Ambassador laughed again, as she went on. "If you come to my Court tomorrow, I will explain how you can most benefit the city."

"Eh? Excellent, we'll do that." He looked around again. "Not all of us. My assistants and I. And my clerk. That's him over there." He gestured at a thin man around his own age who had stayed beside the Justiciars and was now talking with Lord Aubin. "Scriber Stone. That all right?"

"As you see fit," said Jerya graciously. As his annoying female assistant guided the Ambassador away with Lord Jasper, it occurred to Jerya that perhaps she was the equivalent of a Regent. That didn't make ogling Seandri any more acceptable, but did explain the way she kept inserting herself into the Ambassador's conversation. It was odd, even so. She'd never heard anything about Vassay using any kind of Regency system.

She watched them return to the conversation she'd interrupted with her arrival, then she cultivated her most dignified look and let her attention drift to the fledgling still on Gisen's shoulder. It was close enough that she could hear what it heard if she concentrated.

Gisen and Yevonne skipped between the wagons and Vassay within the courtyard, staring openly at everything that caught their interest.

"What's that?" Yevonne asked, pointing at a wagon's contents.

"Wood for bridges, houses," said the young man sitting on the wagon side.

"Oh," said Yevonne. "What's that?"

"Fabric for tents, clothing." The young man's accent was terrible.

"Oh. We have wool and silk, you know. And linen. We have trees, too."

"You don't have fabric like this," said the wagoneer positively.

"Show me," demanded Yevonne.

The wagoneer eyed her. "Not right now. You'll have plenty of chances to see later."

"All right." Gisen immediately moved to a different wagon, where three girls sat together on the driver's seat. They spoke rapidly in their own language. Jerya had studied the Vassay tongue but couldn't follow them through the fledgling. Gisen apparently could, because when Yevonne went to move on, she caught her hand and they lingered.

"Jer," said Yithiere, and she focused back on herself. Her uncle stood at her knee, his eyes darting around. "Don't do that here. There are assassins in this throng, I'm sure of it."

"That's why I have you, uncle," said Jerya sweetly. "Can you point them out?"

"I'm looking," he said grimly.

"Did you have a moment to observe the ambassador? Wasn't he *odd*?"

Yithiere snorted and shook his head, like a dog that

scented something unpleasant. "He's a decoy. Oh, he probably believes he's the ambassador. But the one behind the mission is the scribe, or clerk, or whatever he said he was."

Jerya looked again at the man identified as Scriber Stone. He didn't have the deference she expected in a clerk among nobles. But she'd already noticed few of their guests seemed to think much about relative rank.

Still, she thought she could see what had set her uncle off. Scriber Stone's gaze roved the crowd as he chatted with the Justiciars. Nothing seemed to escape him. Gisen certainly didn't; his gaze lingered on her so long that Jerya felt her temper rising. But when he realized Jerya was staring at him, he lowered his eyes and suddenly he was very much a clerk.

She leaned over to Seandri. "I'm saying something trivial and funny. Maybe I'm making fun of their clothes. Aren't I funny? Let's laugh."

Seandri said, "I think their clothes are charming, but their wagons are very strange. Not a scrap of decoration." And Seandri laughed, rich and deep, as if genuinely amused by her, so that her laugh was genuine as well.

But she watched, too. Scriber Stone raised his gaze when she directed her gaze elsewhere, but he didn't look at her. She followed the direction of his gaze and found herself looking at an ordinary-looking man moving a crate on a wagon.

"Him, yes," said Yithiere, following her gaze. "He's been moving the same boxes since you arrived. I'm trying to spot the others. There's something odd about the girl assistant but I don't think she's a killer. Noble born, though."

Seandri pointed out, "But they don't have nobles in Vassay anymore."

Yithiere snorted. "Hah. Privileged, in any case."

"She's certainly not trying to avoid notice," said Jerya

tartly, then slid off her mount. As soon as she did, it dissolved into an invisible vapor that trickled back to Gisen. Seandri dismounted his own stag and the eidolon burst into golden motes around him.

Then he held out his arm to Jerya. "Where are we going?"

"To mingle with our guests. If they want to be friendly, we should let them."

"Ward yourself, Jerya," Yithiere growled.

"I'm prepared, uncle. Ward my back." She watched the man moving boxes, walking slowly in his direction. She offered faint, vague smiles to several of the Vassay, and said to one nervous looking young woman, "Be welcome here." None of them were as friendly as Ambassador Smith had been, but they all stared at her with varying degrees of undisguised interest and curiosity.

Except for the man moving boxes. He never looked up at her even once. He was as muscular as the Ambassador. Most of the contingent wasn't, she noticed. Most of them were on the scrawny side.

She asked a man with a strawberry blond ponytail, "Have you no guards? How did you protect the convoy from bandits as you crossed the border?"

The young man gave her a startled, wary look. "Many of us are wordweavers. Logos-workers? We weave various protections tied to the caravan. And our colleagues at Home monitor us. They are able to lend a hand from a distance, yes, if we encounter any kind of problems, sending their own words. That can be very helpful!" A grin flickered on his face. "Though not for any bandits."

Jerya tightened her hand on Seandri's arm and she thought distantly, *I must control myself. Say something nice.*

"Ah. Like a mother cat watching as her kittens creep from the nest. That must be reassuring."

The young man smiled brightly, as if relieved. "Yes indeed."

Jerya inclined her head and pulled Seandri on. The initial shock faded, replaced by fear. For a moment she couldn't see anything, her inner vision awash with the horror of what had just driven into the heart of her city. Magic all the way from Vassay could follow these visitors? They didn't fear bandits because of that magic? It was hard to breathe calmly. When she looked up again, she was in front of the alleged assassin's wagon, and he was looking down at her.

His face was smudged with dirt, but he had a fine bone structure and swarthy skin underneath. His eyes were deep brown, with a striking fringe of lashes and sweeping eyebrows. They were utterly without expression: no surprise, no curiosity, no humor, no trepidation.

"Did you lose something? You keep moving boxes around," Jerya blurted, then cursed silently. She sounded just like Tiana and the little girls: no self-control, saying the first thing that popped into her mind. She couldn't *focus*. Magic from another country could reach into her city.

He stared at her for a long moment. Then his mouth quirked up, although the expression didn't touch his eyes. "Yes."

Was Vassay watching her through those eyes? Jerya nodded, squeezing Seandri's arm. "I hope you find it." She spun around quickly, her anxiety growing into panic. The idea that Vassay magic could reach into the heart of Ceria was too much. She couldn't talk anymore; she'd ruin everything. She couldn't be here with all these people, either. She wanted the phantasmagory, and Iriss. She had to get away before she lost control and started shouting at all of them, or worse.

She straightened her spine and forced herself to release Seandri. He caught at her hand as she pulled away. "Jer, you're fine—"

But she shook her head and stepped away from him. She'd hurt him more. She'd pull him in. All she had to do was walk out, walk back to her inn, and she'd be fine. She had to do it, before she lost control of her mouth again and triggered something terrible. Before she ruined everything.

Seandri let her go, but Yithiere caught her arm. "What is it?" he demanded.

"You're right," she began. "They're all—" And she caught herself. "I need to get out of here." She knew, distantly, that she should mount a summoned steed again, whirl it around dramatically and canter out of the inn. Her departure should be victorious. Stumbling out like she'd become ill was ignoble and damaging.

But setting Yithiere to kill them all would be more damaging.

She made it to the street, the sound of the Justiciars' laughter cutting through the noise of the crowd to sink into her brain. She covered her ears and ran.

CHAPTER TEN

THE VIEW THROUGH A HEART

TWO DAYS AFTER the storm, Kiar finished reading the books she'd borrowed. Well. She finished rereading them. She finished the first time huddled in the farmer's barn, sitting against a dairy cow's stall and reading by Logos light. By four days after the storm she'd studied them enough that she knew there was no point in going through them yet again.

That meant she had nothing to do but brood about unpleasant things, and play with the Logos. Boredom was an unfamiliar experience for her, but riding by endless fields of broccoli and cabbage day after day introduced her to the idea.

Twist hadn't caught up with them yet, which was... annoying. That was the best word. Troubling, worrying, nerve-wracking, *why* hadn't he found them? Was he all right? Would he bring her more books? Had she finally utterly alienated him?

Annoying. That was definitely the word.

Thinking about the enemy was no better. She kept seeing the way the armored andani's eyes had changed, and wondering if it was still inside her somewhere. No, those weren't good traveling thoughts either.

Even Lisette wasn't as companionable as Kiar would have expected. She had the uncomfortable suspicion that both Lisette and Tiana were chatting with the fiend, which made her feel peculiarly left out. She didn't even want the damn fiend in her head, and he wasn't good for her friends, either.

The books were useless, too. They kept her busy but they didn't provide a single answer. The Light of the Firstborn was mentioned occasionally, as something that would come 'someday' when Ceria had 'urgent need'.

It was nice, she thought in irritation, to know you were living in prophesied times. It would have been nicer if they'd told her where the Lights could be found.

"The road is turning here," said Tiana, stopping her mount. "Slowly, but really turning. I can tell. Where's a map?"

Kiar dug around in her saddlebags for the map she'd acquired when they bought their remounts the day before at a horse fair. They'd picked up a pair of adventurous stable girls there, too, because, as one of the stable girls had said acidly, they were all rubbish at doing more than basic horse care. "Yes," she said, unrolling it and looking. "You're right."

"The pull isn't turning." Tiana pursed her mouth.

Kiar gazed at the fields of, oh, look, it was cauliflower now, and then studied the map again. "There's a river ahead," she explained.

Lisette leaned over from her horse to look at the map and said, "I know where we're going."

"Good," said Kiar. "I'm glad somebody does." She scowled at the river. "We have to stay on the road unless you want to ford the river, Tiana."

"What if we miss it?" Tiana put a knuckle to her mouth to chew on it.

"Then it's very close and we'll be able to find it by sweeping the area. Do you think we're close?"

"I don't know," wailed Tiana. "How would I know? I just know I'm being pulled, and if I think about it too much I get confused. I have to shut down and just drift."

"I think we're going to Fel Dion," continued Lisette, talking determinedly as if nobody else had said anything. "The forest of Fel Dion, I mean. It's associated with Atalya in some old stories."

Kiar looked down at the map again. It was in the right direction, but almost all the way to the northwestern coast. "There's a lot of land between here and there. A lot of estates. Tons of shrines to Atalya, if we're assuming we're looking for a place dedicated to her." Atalya worship wasn't centralized like the worship of Niyhan and Keldera. Instead local priestesses organized village festivals and trained the heirs to their shrines.

"I've been remembering stories all day," said Lisette stubbornly. "I'm sure that's where we're going."

Kiar shrugged and folded the map again. "Well, it's unlikely to be farther unless it's under the ocean. Let's at least stay on the road until we cross the river, Tiana."

Tiana sighed, but nudged her horse into motion again. Berrin rode up to join Kiar and Lisette saying, "I beg you'll forgive me, but I hope you're wrong, my lady. I've heard bad things about Fel Dion."

Lisette looked at him in surprise. "There are stories of

a place sacred to her deep within the forest. Legends I read as a little girl. She emerged from the wood when the world was young to guide us. She protected the innocent who came there. And there's a story about a sleeping prince who—"

"Every forest has that story," interrupted Kiar. "That orchard the other day probably had that story. Roots of trees are a good place to hide things, even princes." She'd found a fiend hiding in a root hollow once. It hadn't been a dream come true.

Lisette's brow furrowed. "Really? Oh. But we're headed straight for Fel Dion, if you look at the map."

"The stories I've heard are definitely about Fel Dion," said Berrin. "And of more recent origin than the nursery tales, and from closer to the forest. Dark stories that imply dark and deadly things." He paused for effect. "Human sacrifice, for example."

Kiar snorted. "That's a step up from simply stealing children, which is what I heard about Fel Dion. I never believed it."

Berrin shrugged. "The stories always reference one particular legend. I could tell the tale, though a storyteller I'm not."

"Please," said Lisette earnestly.

Kiar noticed a twinkle in Berrin's eyes before his dark brows swooped down to hood his eyes. "Here is what I've heard, from the village of Sinethca, on the edge of Fel Dion. Once it was a flowered meadow where Atalya held court with her handmaidens. But when a great fiend came out of the forest and carried her off while her handmaidens fled, she cursed them, binding them to the meadow until she pardoned them. One by one, they took husbands among the heroes who came to rescue Atalya, and for one reason or another, none ever ventured deep enough into the forest to find her. That's how the village came to be. But for Atalya herself, she was imprisoned by thorny branches and plaits of children's' hair, and guarded jealously by the fiend or his servant, a giant raven. She convinced the thorns to soften themselves with blossoms, and the knotted hair to smooth itself out, but she couldn't escape the raven's gaze, for it loved to look at her shining hair. Finally, she sheared her hair and used it to adorn a mannequin of herself. Thus hidden from the raven, she fled the forest. She passed through Sinethca in the night and did not stop to pardon her handmaids, because she didn't approve of the way they settled."

Slater, riding close at hand, said, "I heard she did stop but they didn't recognize her without her hair, and laughed her out of the village."

Berrin gave the other soldier an unfriendly look and continued without acknowledgement, "Later, the fiend brought the mannequin of Atalya to life and sent it to torment the villagers. And so it goes to this day. The fiends of the forest steal children, eat them, and don their skins to torment the family of the lost child. And the villagers punish any fiend they can capture."

Slater said, "I thought Atalya herself asked them to hunt down the mannequin and destroy it, and others like it?"

Tiana tore her gaze away from the road. "That doesn't sound very much like the Atalya I know about. I was always told Atalya had golden hair." She sighed and touched her own black-brown hair. "And I read that she made dogs by distilling everything good out of the wolves in a forest. And that she was the first tamed falcon on a prince's arm."

There was a speculative silence for a moment and then Lisette said wistfully, "Atalya has always been my favorite of the Firstborn. When I was little, I used to wish she'd come play with me. She always seemed so... sweet and gentle."

Berrin said, "Hah, and that's why we chased her when we were little. Well, my sister pretending to be her. No offense to your ladyship."

Indignant, Lisette said, "You chased her? To do what?"

Berrin shrugged and grinned, unabashed. "Rub mud in her hair, usually. What else do you do when a girl runs from you in the spring and you're eight years old? That's what we thought the point of Maidrunning was."

"You—you—" Lisette struggled to find words, her face flushing. Kiar hid a snicker behind her hand.

Then the world yawned around her and her amusement vanished. The Logos twisted and snapped, like the ache of an unexpected cramp.

Slater noticed and moved closer to steady her. She muttered, "A sky fiend, somewhere close. I think it just arrived." She closed her eyes and focused herself as best she could. "We should deal with it, before it serves as a gateway for other enemies."

Tiana moved her healing arm restlessly., "This is ridiculous. Distracting us is as bad as stopping us, if he does it enough."

Kiar frowned. "We can't let more of them just wander the countryside if we can stop it. The soldiers are bad enough but if he releases something like the plague beast..." She shuddered and tangled her fingers in Spooky's mane. "Better we strike now."

"I'll do it, stormy weather," said Cathay abruptly. He'd been so quiet during the earlier discussion of Fel Dion that Kiar had assumed he was asleep. "I'll take Kiar and a few of the guards and deal with it, and then we can catch up."

"And what if it's another ambush?" asked Slater.

Tiana hesitated, looking at Cathay. Then she shook her head. "Kiar's right. So is Slater. Temporarily splitting up won't help. I just..." She shook her head and passed her hand over her chest. "I'm sorry. Can you tell where?"

Kiar whispered to the Logos, and then said, "On a huge rock left behind by ice, a galloping from here in the direction of the Citadel." She made a face. "Cabbage grows around it."

Tiana's shoulders slumped. "I've been trying not to think about the cabbage." Begrudgingly, she turned her horse, and then urged him into a run. Spooky stomped his feet and shook his head, and Kiar let him have his head until he'd taken the lead from Tiana's Moon. Then Kiar led the way down the road and between fields until they arrived at the source of the Logos quivering.

They dismounted at the edge of the cabbage field, leaving the horses with a pair of guards and the new stable girls. The stable girls immediately started fussing over the horses and one of them said loudly to the other, "They'll need a bit of a rest now."

Tiana paused at Kiar's side, Jinriki naked in her hand, and said quietly, "Jinriki wants to examine one while it's actively connected to the other world. He wants to see if he can understand how to cut the connection permanently. He wants to free them if he can, from Ohedreton, and from their madness." She hesitated. "He said you'd know what he meant."

Kiar did. She knew exactly what he meant. She chewed her lip, thinking about Jinriki's ulterior motives. "Do you *want* another one around?"

Tiana shrugged. "I don't know. They scare me right now.

But... they used to be like Jinriki, like the Secondborn in stories. This is a horrible fate."

Like the Secondborn. Kiar's gaze dropped to the blade in Tiana's hand, and thought about that. It was more flattering to fiends than she liked, and more frightening. Jinriki alone was proof that encountering something out of stories wasn't anything to be wished for.

Carefully, she said, "I don't trust him, Tiana. The fiend you fought the other day, the one he was so determined to destroy that he ate it—it was one of the ones he released—"

"I know," interrupted Tiana, her fingers white-knuckled around Jinriki's hilt. Her gaze searched Kiar's face in a scared, needy way that made Kiar want to hug her tight and put a shield around them both. "I know he's not... safe. But he's on our side. He's trustworthy that far."

"I don't know if he is. He's wild and chaotic and selfish, Tiana.'

Tiana's face closed off. "So am I, if it comes to that. Believe me. You trust me, don't you?"

Kiar didn't know how to answer. She was silent for a moment, maybe too long. "I'm here, aren't I?"

"Consider it logistically," said Tiana, and Kiar could tell Jinriki prompted her. "If we can destroy whatever binds them to Ohedreton's world, at the very least we've cut off a method for moving troops around swiftly. We may even gain more; if they return to their senses, they will obey Jinriki and swell our own ranks. And they need not travel with us to do so. They could serve as messengers..." Tiana shook her head. "Can't you just talk to her directly?" She paused and scowled. "He says you've never touched him. That doesn't matter with those trained to obey but he can't do that with you."

"Good. I've seen what he's done to people who touch him," said Kiar dryly.

Tiana glared down at the blade. "He's behaving now. But I don't blame you."

Kiar sighed and rubbed her nose. She looked at Cathay and Lisette, both close enough to hear. Lisette was grave, expressionless, while Cathy only shrugged. Kiar said, "I do understand what he wants, anyhow. I'll see what I can do. It's better than him *eating* another one. That can't go anywhere good." She turned and regarded the fiend's den.

A huge stone jutted out of the other side of the cabbage field, twice the height of a man at its peak, and half again as long. It was gently rounded except the top, where it hollowed and rose like a giant soup spoon.

"There's something in there," said Cathay. Kiar could just make it out, some sort of creature flattened against the surface of the rock.

She glanced around, her senses twanging. "No eidolon folk yet, I think."

Tiana said, "What should we do? Jinriki says we have to follow your instructions and, once you have it controlled, he'll investigate curing its madness."

Kiar blinked. Suddenly everybody was looking at her. "Um. I'd like to uh, interact with it on the ground. Maybe if we can get it down and over to me?"

Tiana nodded, and Slater barked out instructions to his men. They spread out in a circle around the big stone. Kiar added, "It hasn't attacked yet so... I don't think it's ready to fight. They don't seem to be aggressive when they're... um... serving as a door."

From the other side of the stone, Cathay said, "I'm going up." A moment later, he bounded up the side of the pinnacle, emanations supporting and balancing him, and eidolon claws gripping the stone. "Ugh," he announced. "It's part human." He poked at it with his sword. "Move it, fiend. We're not any worse than what you're already doing."

Nothing happened. Then an arm swiped at Cathay, pushing his sword away, and the creature yowled. The sword swerved as Cathay leaned back away from the stone, twisting with an almost inhuman grace "Some talons there. You'll want to reach it before it reaches you, Kiar." He made a shoving motion with his free hand, and the yowl turned into a squeal as something skittered off the top of the rock.

It was a warped lion, with the nose and eyes and arms of man. Those human hands were tipped with translucent ivory claws that Kiar saw all too well as it staggered towards her, unable to walk like a man or a cat. Slater said something and the guards circled behind it, their own swords unsheathed but still. It stumbled to a halt, its head turning slowly. It growled at the armed men behind it and then turned back to Kiar, who held no weapon at all. Its sleek golden hind legs crouched and its tail twitched, which was cat enough to be creepy.

Kiar shifted her weight, bracing herself. She muttered to the Logos, staring at the sky fiend. Fingers of air stroked the monster's fur in response. She searched for what she thought of as the soft spot, the place where the eidolons would be born when it was ready to birth them.

It flattened its ears further and slitted those human eyes. Then, like a striking snake, it leapt.

Even braced, Kiar was caught off-guard. She ducked instinctively, putting her arms over her head. But even as she ducked, she searched: looking, looking. There it was, on the sky fiend's belly. It was soaring over her, right there.

She straightened up so fast that she almost lost her balance. Windmilling her other arm, she stretched out and her fingers just barely brushed the soft spot. But just barely was all she needed.

Her fingers sank into the cool space beyond the fiend and she opened herself to the world on the other side. When she opened her eyes, she stood on a plateau in the eidolon world. She could feel the invisible substance of the fiend around her left hand and knew that once again, she was somehow in two places at once.

She turned. Above her loomed an enormous silhouette of Tiana, streaming with blue light. She drifted closer to it, wondering why it was here. She'd seen it on her previous peeks, but never so close. The plateau was otherwise barren, as if the light had scoured away all the strange vegetation and mobile life forms she'd encountered on previous visits. The intense light reminded her of the skies of Ceria. It was beautiful.

Within the light, though, a vision awaited her. She stared onto a vertiginous tableau: the world, Ceria, northern fields, the scene at the rock. She could see herself, frozen in the act of catching the sky fiend, the substance of the creature wrapped around her hand like a glove. There were the guards and—

No wonder Ohedreton's minions had no trouble finding them; no wonder the sky fiend had appeared so close. All they had to do was stroll over here and peer into the light.

Kiar scowled and tried to touch the edge of the silhouette, but it was as intangible as the sky. She had no idea how to make it go away. But maybe she could do the next best thing.

She stepped back again and stared up at what passed

for a dismal sky here: pale-splotched emptiness. Then she spread both her hands wide and exhaled, shaping an eidolon of her own. A shield wrapped itself around the silhouette, shimmering as she adjusted its appearance until it was exactly the same as a patch of the local sky. She touched it gently and it complained to her of the blue light beating on its interior walls. But it would cope. She didn't know how long it would last against Ohedreton himself; she'd seen how he'd absorbed the eidolons of others. But if that happened, she would know. Meanwhile, maybe they could get to wherever they were going. Tiana should be happy about that.

She turned her attention to the sky fiend, concentrating on the place where they'd interfaced, pulling together an idea of what caused that tunnel between her world and the eidolon world. She studied the inner shape of the sky fiend and realized it was illuminated by a flickering aura of eidolon-stuff. She touched the edge gently with an emanation, trying to understand how it was bound to the inner shape.

Nothing. She could sense nothing. The integration was as smooth and untouchable as the one between the silhouette and the local sky.

This was ridiculous. Was she totally useless? She prodded at the integration point again, this time using the emanation as a scalpel. It slid and scraped across the edge and she concentrated, trying to see someplace where she could pry the edges apart.

Distantly, she became aware of screaming. Her hand spasmed and she couldn't breathe. Something was wrong.

She pushed herself away from the sky fiend, releasing it and coming back to herself in the real world. Agony ambushed her as the sky fiend bucked in a seizure, its claws raking her face and shoulder. Without conscious thought a shield bubble formed around her, shoving the fiend away. She collapsed to the ground in a huddle, bewildered. Chaos exploded behind her. The sky fiend yowled and men shouted. Slater appeared in front of her, peering at her closely, and was then replaced by Tiana.

Tiana said, "Should we kill it? Jinriki says he doesn't know how to save it." It was a demand for instructions, guidance, one Kiar couldn't answer. She had no idea what had happened and she couldn't pull her scattered thoughts together enough to make a decision about what to do now. After a moment Tiana shook her head and went around the side of the bubble.

More chaos behind her. Kiar explored her injuries with her fingers. The scratches weren't deep: the side effects of the spasming sky fiend rather than a concerted attack. Already the agony had faded to a dull red throbbing. Once Lisette cleaned it, she probably wouldn't even have scars.

She huddled amid shredded cabbages and tried to find the thread of her thoughts. The fiend's reaction was something she'd have to think about. She had too many things to think about. The eidolon world confused her painfully. Once again, looming out of the mist of her mind, came the thought: *what are Ohedreton's eidolons?* Was there a shard of his will in each of them? The natives she'd encountered on her first visit had seemed so real—alien, but independent. But how could an eidolon be self-willed? Was she misunderstanding what they were? Her thoughts whirled around, fevered and unanswerable and she hunched tighter around herself.

She pressed her hand against the injuries on her face until they burned. Even if shallow, the scratches on her shoulder and collarbone hurt more than she wanted. With a rush of homesickness, she missed her father. He had always done his best to protect her, in his own way. He'd sometimes been the one who cleaned her cuts as a child, and every time he did so he'd distract her from the pain with a puzzle. He didn't expect her to run around saving fiends and making decisions. All he expected her to be was clever.

Tiana appeared in front of her bubble again. "It's safe now. You can take down the bubble. Are you all right?" In her hand, Jinriki pulsed angrily. She hesitated and added, "The fiend is gone. Jinriki is really unhappy. I'm sorry we asked you to do that."

Kiar lowered her eyes and forced the shield to dissipate. "I'll be fine. I—" she shook her head and pushed herself to her feet, her muscles aching.

Tiana said, "What happened?"

"I wasn't thinking clearly. I was stupid." She could feel smeared blood drying on her face. "But before that, I found something important." She explained about the Tiana-shaped window between the worlds, and the shield she'd put over it.

Tiana slid Jinriki into his sheath and said somberly, "That's worth it, at least. It sounds like you did more than you didn't, anyhow. Let's have Lisette look at those injuries."

All the same, Kiar couldn't stop thinking about what she might have tried instead, and dreading the 'next time' she knew would come.

CHAPTER ELEVEN

THE STOLEN DREAM

DAWN HAD LONG come and gone when Tiana woke, knowing Jinriki was gone. The absence ached. She stared at the sky, listening to the silent camp. Nothing moved, although the sky was bright blue. There was no smell of burned porridge, which was a blessing, but also horribly wrong.

Despite the lateness of the hour, she was the only one awake. That was wrong too, very wrong. But her thoughts were so sluggish that the wrongness was only a fleeting itch compared to her awareness of Jinriki's absence. Though she was sure—as sure as up came down—that he was gone, she felt at her side for the sword. She found only her blanket.

She couldn't remember what had happened, and surely she should remember? The guards woke her every morning, and there were always two keeping watch.

Jinriki had warned her they'd fail her eventually.

Spiderwebs entangled her thoughts, fragments of nightmare that refused to fade when she opened her eyes.

Brightness glimmered in the camp, crooning a lullaby. First one, then the second of the watching guards drifted off to sleep. She raged at them to wake up but they were far beyond the reach of dreams. When the camp slept, the glimmering became moonlight along slender limbs. A foxy visage looked down at her. "Sleepy mortal traitor. Great Prince, I have come! No longer must you suffer in such vile slavery. I dreamt you, Great Prince. The Betrayer hunts you! He does not wish any to recall Innis but oh, we cannot forget. We cannot."

It reached down and picked her up. She fought back. The creature hissed and then purred, "Great Prince, you test me. But I am worthy." She recognized it as an earth fiend, and struggled to wake herself instead. Earth fiends, immortal in their own way, were beyond her gifts with the mortal mind.

But that felt like hours ago. "Jinriki," Tiana muttered, and then shouted. "Jinriki!" and bolted to her feet. What would happen without him? Why had he let the earth fiend take him? How would she protect the others?

She took deep breath. They'd go slower. She'd lived her whole life without the additional power Jinriki brought her. But—what had happened? She paced in a circle and the camp slowly woke up. The soldiers muttered to each other. Kiar sat upright, rubbing her eyes.

Tiana crouched by Lisette and shook her awake. "Enchantment. By an earth fiend, I think. A thief." She closed her eyes and snatched at fragments of the dream. "It made us sleep." She still *felt* Jinriki, as if he were just out of reach.

She moves quickly. I am farther than that. Jinriki said. Tiana startled and he added, **Silly princess. I told you mere distance could not free you from me.**

Tiana swallowed and said aloud, "An earth fiend

enchanted us into deep sleep and stole Jinriki. She's running now, fast and far."

Slater said, "Are we going to pursue it?"

Tiana stared at him blankly. "Of course." Slater looked away.

Kiar said, "Is it a trap?" What she meant was, *It's a trap*. Tiana frowned and glanced at Lisette.

The Regent was tidying her hair into place, but absently she said, "Ohedreton hasn't been shy about simply attacking us. I can't imagine why he'd go to the trouble of luring us into a trap if he could enchant an unbreakable sleep and have an agent walk among us."

Kiar shrugged. "He's still talking to you? Where is he?"

Confidently, Tiana pointed. "That way. He said she's moving fast, though."

Sometimes on two legs, sometimes on four. The injuries she's sustained do seem to be causing her trouble. A fractured image passed before her eyes, of a creature loping on all fours, Jinriki's sheathed blade carried in her mouth. She moved at the speed of a cantering horse.

"Can you still use his magic?" Kiar asked.

Tiana shook her head. "We can talk but his magic works through mine, when we're very close."

Cathay looked up from his hands and stepped lightly to Tiana's side. "Excuse me, I'd just like to check something." He kissed her cheek, near the edge of her mouth. Tiana blinked at him and touched the spot he kissed. She wondered if he'd missed, and if he was going to try again. Instead he ducked his head and stepped back, saying only, "How very interesting."

Tiana's attention flicked away again, pulled by her worry about Jinriki, and she said, "Kiar, the shield you created stops the enemy from detecting my location from the other world, right?"

Kiar looked alarmed. "I hope so but there hasn't been enough time to verify that. Please don't think whatever you're thinking."

"But I am. If the rest of the group continues traveling, I could catch up to the earth fiend and be back again before the enemy has a chance to notice." To Lisette, she added, "I'm not running off to fight any battles on my own. This is what's going to happen, so there's no point in arguing."

"Two will travel as fast as one," Cathay said. "And be better able to handle any surprises."

Tiana frowned at him. "You need to stay with the group." She sounded like her sister, and she flinched away from that recognition.

Cathay shrugged. "That's too bad. Because I'm not letting you go alone. And the longer we fight about it, the further away your sword gets."

Slater said, "I'd like to come along, please."

Tiana clenched her fists. "Why is nobody doing what I say?"

Jinriki said, **Let him come along.**

Why?

After a pause, Jinriki said, **He's expendable.**

Tiana scowled. **We're going to have to talk more about that sort of thing.** Then she glared at Kiar and Lisette. When neither of them seemed to have any comment, she blew out her breath. "Fine. I don't have time to argue with either of you. But keep up. Somebody saddle my horse while I get something to eat." To Jinriki, she said, **Can you talk to the fiend?**

You mean, as I speak with you? I suppose I could try that,

*but what would I say? This is not a rational creature.***

You spoke to the sky fiends and they're not rational either.

But once they were. I know them. Earth fiends have always been balanced on the edge of madness.

Tiana thought. ***Tell her to stop and tend to her wounds. She called you a prince? Honor her with your attention.***

What a novel idea.

Ten minutes later, Tiana led the other two riders east after Jinriki. She would have liked a hard run, but the terrain was uncultivated, rocky meadowland, with old stream beds lurking beneath the grass. She scanned the horizon, wondering why the fiend had gone in this direction. Did it have a lair? Or had it fled randomly? It would have been convenient if it had run north.

She is ridiculously pleased with my address, and assures me that soon we'll be at a safe place where she can tend her battle scars.

That worked? Is she being cunning?

I don't believe so. She seems astonishingly amenable. A pity I can't interface with her as I would you.

A cold thread uncoiled in Tiana's stomach. ***We're moving now. Can you describe the terrain you passed through?***

My perceptions are skewed without you or another human around. I don't think my descriptions would be meaningful.

Tiana swore aloud. Days of pursuing the light of the Firstborn had taught her just how troublesome a simple heading could be.

Cathay, riding close at hand, said, "What's wrong?"

"I don't have any idea what's between us and Jinriki, and he can't tell me. I hate this."

Cathay smiled. "I'll send out an eidolon to scout ahead."

He closed his eyes. A lynx leapt out of him and vanished into the tall grass ahead.

Tiana sagged. "I should have thought of that."

"You don't think in terms of eidolons. And you're distracted. We're getting used to it. Although—I'm surprised. Has this overcome the pull northwest?"

Tiana bristled. "If you're going to criticize me again because I'm working with Jinriki, you can just stop, right now."

Cathay shook his head, still smiling faintly. "No, no. As much as I hate the thought, you made a conscious choice during Antecession. You're still making your own decisions. You're still you. So I respect that."

"You didn't last time we talked about it!"

"What, the day after Antecession? I was tired. I hadn't come to terms with it." He held her gaze. "But you did make a choice. And I'm not going to be able to look in the mirror if I scold you for not letting somebody else make your choices for you. Just... stay you, stormy weather."

Now Tiana was irritated with herself. She bit her lip and said, "I'm sorry he dislikes you so."

"It's not *your* fault. Though I admit, I'm enjoying his absence right now. Normally when I ride so close to you, it's not nearly as pleasant." His smile widened and he raised his eyebrows as if confiding a secret.

Tiana didn't know what to say to that, so she kept quiet, and Cathay didn't pursue the conversation. She wondered how far his attraction to her pushed him. If Slater hadn't insisted on coming along, would he have said more? Or was he truly content simply being with her?

Jinriki said, **It's uncanny how she seems to know me. I wish I could remember the events she speaks of. So much was lost...**

If Tiana had to guess, she would have said he sounded sad, which did not improve Tiana's mood. Jinriki was never sad. He got angry instead.

I thought you said she was 'not a rational creature'? Maybe she's making things up, she sent.

There's something familiar about it, though. Stories of the dawn of time. Fascinating...

Tiana said aloud, "I'd like to move a little faster now."

It was a long, unpleasant four hours they spent following Jinriki's trail. Tiana retreated inside her head, since the phantasmagory was beyond her reach, curling up in the cold distant place where she kept the thoughts she didn't want Jinriki to find. She watched through a narrow tunnel as Cathay picked a path, and her body moved like a thing apart, guiding her own horse. Minutes slid by, and the occasional conversation between Slater and Cathay joined the background chorus of crunching hooves and bird cries. The meadowland gave way to a little forest, and then turned back into meadowland again.

Eventually, Cathay said, "There are some ruins ahead. And a single voice within them."

Tiana stirred and examined the pull. "We're close."

At the same time, Jinriki said, **That's us.** and Tiana nodded to Cathay, who checked his sword.

Jinriki added, **I've been thinking. How are you going to reclaim me from her?**

No jumping to my hand again? asked Tiana wistfully.

That would be a waste of energy. Still. And there are no monks here to repair the damage I'd do to the Logos. I haven't Twist's gift, you understand.

Tiana set her jaw. **Any way we can, then. If she can't use you, it seems like it should be straightforward enough. Earth fiends *are a pest, anyhow.* ** It was true. They weren't destructive like sky fiends but it wasn't just fiendish swords they stole. They played tricks and stole livestock and flocked to the banner of any fiendish Blighter.

Jinriki's thoughts came slowly, as if they were difficult for him. **I wish to find a... non-violent... way of resolving this.**

Tiana yanked her horse to a halt. "What?"

I have been friendly to her. I do not want to betray her. I wish no harm to come to her. His voice became firmer.

Numbly, Tiana relayed this to her companions.

Cathay said, "I don't believe it." He hesitated. "And yet... Well, I never would have expected compassion from *him*."

Slater suggested, "Perhaps he wants something from it. It's a fiend as well."

"That must be it," Cathay agreed.

Jinriki said, **You humans are good at this kind of thing. Making peace.**

Tiana shifted position uncomfortably. She felt trapped and confused. After her father had told her of his conversation with an earth fiend, she'd daydreamed of talking to one herself someday. But now all she wanted was to reclaim her sword and continue her journey, as quickly as possible. She didn't even want to see the earth fiend, if it could be avoided. And now Jinriki asked her to negotiate with it?

Doubtfully, Cathay said, "Sometimes you can talk to earth fiends, I've heard. That is, you can get them to stop whatever annoying tricks they're engaged in and move along. But you have to figure out what they want."

Slater said, "This one seems to have what it wants already."

Cathay said, "Maybe. What will it do when we ride into the ruins? Even if we're willing to talk to it, it has to be willing to talk to us as well."

Her first instinct is to hide. I may be able to convince her otherwise.

Tiana couldn't bring herself to be a relay again, so she just shrugged helplessly at Cathay's curious look.

"Well, let's go find out," he said, and clicked to his horse. Her own horse shuffled after.

Do you want to hurt her? Jinriki's voice was suddenly like velvet in her mind, close and warm.

She's a thief! I'm angry!

We are learning from each other, I see, you and I.

And Tiana wanted to say, *No, that's not it, this isn't your lust for battle, this is something else, she stole you, she's still stealing you! I have to stop it!* But she couldn't. She couldn't escape the memory of killing those boys in the city, and her grief and her inability to run away. Surely an earth fiend was closer to a human than the dark eidolons of Ohedreton's creation. It at least belonged in this world. If it didn't want to fight and she destroyed it anyhow—how much had she really changed?

This thought kept her occupied as they approached the ruins. Once, perhaps it had been a great manor house, but now all that was left was the foundation and some crumbling stone walls. The stones were blotched grey and black, as lichen grew over rock damaged by fire. There was nobody to be seen, but the broken walls provided plenty of hiding places. Cathay drew his horse to a halt and glanced at her.

She had no patience for subtleties. "Jinriki, where are you?" she said aloud, projecting her voice to carry across the ruins.

She felt a subtle shift inside her head and knew Jinriki had re-established his normal connection to her. ***She hid me under a fallen stone. She's hiding elsewhere.***

Oh good, show me and we can get out of here without hurting her.

And how would you stop this entire day from repeating itself?

Tiana ran her hands through her hair. **Tell her to come out, then.**

A hatch opened in the ground not far away, and a figure climbed out of what must have been a cellar. Like too many creatures Tiana had seen lately, it was only human-shaped, not human. The figure paused, tilting her head to stare up at them, and Tiana was strongly reminded of a fox by the large raised ears, the slanted almond eyes and especially the tail.

The earth fiend approached them until she was a few sword lengths out of reach and sank down to her knees, never taking her eyes off the riders. She spread her arms. There were bandages over her hands and scabs around her mouth. "You are the princess?"

Tiana dismounted, passing the reins to Slater. "I am."

The fiend's amber eyes bored into her. "You have convinced the Great Prince that you are his master. He insists you are uncorrupted. But is that what I see?"

Tiana said, "Yes?" and then closed her mouth before she began babbling. The earth fiend's choice of language irked her, and she didn't know why. She stood uneasily, listening to the breathing of the horses and the creaking of leather behind her.

The fiend said, "I see a fire devouring the wind. I see an ancient shadow. The shadow reaches for the flame." She shook her head.

"Yes, that's what we need Jinriki to help us fight!" Tiana shifted her weight impatiently, glancing towards the ruin where Jinriki was hidden.

"The earthstream tells me secrets. It whispers that once the murderer was as yourself. But there is something...?" The creature cocked her head and then shook herself all over, rising to her feet. "I cannot tell. But the Great Prince insists. He makes it so we all win: I will return the Great Prince to you, and I will follow along to serve and protect him. My name is Minex."

CHAPTER TWELVE

A PRICELESS GIFT

FOR THREE MORNINGS running, Ambassador Smith sent his regrets that he wouldn't be able to visit Jerya's Court that day. Jerya was not surprised. She'd run away, after all. She'd demonstrated the weakness of her blood, acted like a frightened child, *ruined* her credibility. She couldn't forgive herself.

She couldn't forgive Vassay, either. They were so dangerous, and looked so innocent. She kept imagining what could be done with her own magic if she could send it hundreds of miles away, and shuddering.

At breakfast on the third morning, Jerya handed the note to Seandri as he sat across from her, spreading cheese on a roll.

"He's really so very busy organizing the mission's work, and he's sure I'm also busy with the Blight," she said sourly.

Seandri gave her an exasperated look and took the note to read it for himself. "And he looks forward to showing his work in the weeks to come. Come on, Jer, he's right. You *are* busy."

"Showing me *and* the Justiciars," corrected Jerya. "Mustn't overlook that part."

Seandri shrugged. "They seem nice."

"My father was nice too," she said querulously. "Nice doesn't get things done." Comparing the Ambassador to her father made her uncomfortable. She didn't know how to protect herself from such distracted kindness, and it had not, historically, led to good places.

"I'm nice," Seandri pointed out, and handed her a bread roll.

"It's not the same. You don't let it slow you down." She broke the bread roll open. It *wasn't* the same. Seandri would probably make as passive a King as her father had been, but he was energetic and focused once he had instructions, and more importantly, he was always on her side.

She'd spent the last two days in the Tabernacle of Broken Hearts, paying absolutely no visible attention to the Vassay. Oh, certainly Gisen and Yevonne spent all their time asking questions, while eidolon sparrows—which were harder for her to craft than birds of prey, because she didn't understand how they thought—pecked at their scraps with their living, breathing models. And certainly the city folk came to her with tales of the strange behavior of the foreigners, and every single thing they did wrong.

But Vassay was spying on her from their horrid, faraway University in their capital of Home, spying on her whole city, and able to use their magic from there to aid their spies. Her spying was not only completely fair and just as honest, it was necessary. How else could she protect herself and her people?

They'd changed everything with their arrival, with their aid, so much more insidious than a military invasion. The mayor and the city leaders had been eager for *her* help at first, desperate to keep the city functioning. But now they were busy with Vassay, who had dozens of people studying how to deal with flooding rivers and collapsed buildings and traffic management. All Jerya could do was talk to people or kill them. Or, she reminded herself bitterly, run away.

She wasn't *relevant* to the reconstruction of the city. That burned. Lor Seleni was her city, the people were her people and they loved her. She made sure of that, but she had to take care of them in return, just like she took care of Tiana.

The thought pierced her, as it did so often now: she had to fix the city before Tiana came home again. Tiana loved Lor Seleni; she'd always regarded it as a source of adventures rather than a backdrop for life. Jerya was going to make sure it was here waiting when Tiana returned safely from her quest.

She thought about Tiana as she finished breakfast and set out for her court, wondering if she wrote letters to their mother still, letters she never sent anymore. It bothered her sometimes that Tiana would write, even in pretense, to the mother who had abandoned them, but wouldn't tell the same things to Jerya.

She sat at the Tabernacle of Broken Hearts and spoke with her people. Tiana couldn't manage the patience or the focus to listen to the personal stories they shared. She would have passed the work to Yithiere and Alanah, who stood near her chair. But people liked Tiana anyhow. It was strange.

She thought about Vassay again. No, even if people naturally liked Tiana, it was best they had their separate tasks. Tiana would give up far too much to the Vassay.

"We are fighting a war, Jer," Yithiere told her, watching

as the latest supplicant departed. He had no patience now either.

She knew it, but she couldn't help herself as she said, "I know! And intelligence is crucial. They've been promising a supply caravan since they arrived, did you know that? And about a quarter of them have started ingratiating themselves with our craftsmen. And they're buying all sorts of trinkets. And they're already planning a small expedition back to—"

"Jerya!" snapped Yithiere. "I am talking about the invaders murdering our people, not feeding them!" He had a lot of experience worrying about threats from multiple directions. "You are such a babe yet when it comes to splitting your attention. As long as you and Gisen stay away from the Vassay, we needn't worry about them. They're hardly more than glorified domestic staff."

"You know what they can do. And death comes in many forms, Uncle," Jerya told him primly.

"It comes faster when your duchies delay in sending their armies," he grumbled. "We can't simply sit outside the Blight forever, not when it's growing. We need to get in there and penetrate to the heart of the fortress. And we need the armies for that. I don't trust Tiana's Firstborn."

Jerya sighed. Yithiere's Regent had died a year ago and she missed him, especially when Yithiere needed such constant reassurance. "We'll get them. It's only been a few weeks since the Blight appeared. Meanwhile the Vassay are *here* and so is their wretched magic-from-afar."

Yithiere gave her a baleful look, as if she was a child bothering the adults. Then he muttered, "They've gotten comfortable. I should have mobilized them for—" Alanah touched his arm and he subsided as he reached over to squeeze her hand.

Twist wandered up to Jerya's chair, unimpeded by the guards. He was eating a toasted sugar cake on a stick: holiday food. "Hello."

"Where did you get that?" Jerya demanded.

"A stall near the Vassay's camp at Bearfield. Happy Fallendre, Your Highness." He nodded at Yithiere. "I have some messages for you. And for you, Princess..." He tossed her a brightly wrapped parcel.

Jerya frowned as she caught it. Fallendre, a week after Antecession, was a gift-giving feast day but the Blood didn't play a ritual role as they did with Antecession and Arising. Any gifts given to the Blood were redistributed to the people, and this historically took the form of handing out lots and lots of candy to children.

Jerya opened the package and found a sack of Citadel caramels, made from goat's milk and elderberry honey. The Magister usually brought the candy down when he visited for the triple holiday, but she hadn't expected to see the treat this year.

"I couldn't help but overhear a moment ago. You know," began Twist, and then looked over Yithiere. "Both of you should know: I'm reasonably sure Vassay isn't going to use the Logos to kill anybody from a distance."

"The boy I spoke with wasn't lying, Twist." Jerya said patiently. "And look at their confidence." She glanced at Yithiere for support.

He said, "Twist doesn't know everything," and then added to Alanah, "That's for the best; if he did I'd have to kill him and he remains too useful," which was not as helpful as Jerya had hoped.

Twist gave Yithiere a graceful bow. "I am pleased that even my ignorance serves, my prince." As Yithiere snorted,

Twist transferred his bright gaze back to Jerya. "All the same, grant that I do know much of how the Logos works. It is not something worked quickly. For example, I could work right now on stopping Alanah's heart but you would notice, because I would be speaking to the Logos." He smiled at Alanah, and she smiled back, all teeth. "I would risk stopping my own heart, unless I sufficiently differentiated Alanah's heart from mine. Stopping your heart would be even harder, due to the veil of Royal magic that obscures your patterns."

"Lightning from the sky," Jerya suggested. "They're excellent at weather magic."

"An arrow in the dark," countered Twist calmly. "Poison in your hot chocolate. I've heard that poison is a popular method of advancement at their University."

Alanah said, "Twist! That is not helping."

Twist glanced at Alanah again, returning the toothy smile from before. "It's nonsense, of course. They're proud of having grown past the need for assassination. They like to hold committees and General Assemblies instead, where they talk you to death instead."

Jerya frowned. "Then what did Jory mean?" She'd discovered the boy's name as one of her sparrows stalked him the day before. The 'boy', who was older than her, was Jory and the Ambassador's assistants were Cutter and that wretched Landry, who happened to be the daughter of one of the University administrators, and the possible assassin was Thorn, who never smiled and paid little attention to his surroundings.

Twist shrugged. "Wards on the wagons that affected anybody who touched them without the key. Starting fires. Bringing, yes, storms. There's plenty of aid the Logos-workers can send to a beleaguered expedition if they have the time, the conditions and the precise knowledge of what's going on." He hesitated. "And they cannot, I think, spy just anywhere. Our guests act as beacons."

Alanah said, "As we speak, so they come. Be wary with your words." She nodded at the edge of the plaza and Jerya looked beyond Twist to see a small group of Vassay looking around. She recognized Landry easily. The alleged assassin called Thorn walked on the edge of the group, as if he was simply headed the same direction. And indeed, as Landry's coterie veered toward the Tabernacle, Thorn walked to a leatherworker's shop just outside the plaza.

Landry had a handful of people with her: Cutter, another pretty young woman, and two men who seemed to consider themselves the pretty woman's bodyguards. They glared at Jerya and Yithiere, like they expected something to leap out of them and bite.

Landry bowed to Jerya, totally missing the possibilities inherent in her flyaway skirt. Iriss would have frowned, but Jerya merely inclined her head in a silent greeting.

"This is your Court?" asked Landry, looking around curiously. "We looked for you at your inn, but Prince Seandri told us you spent every day here. What is the box? It's very large," she said, as if nobody had noticed that before.

"Landry," chided Cutter, and the girl glanced at him, then sighed and gestured him forward.

Cutter cleared his throat and executed a much better bow than Landry. He was a tall young man, taller than he looked because he was so perfectly proportioned. "Your Royal Highness," he began. "We understand it is a gifting feast day in Ceria today? We bring what we hope will be a gift for you? We've heard your lady companion fell ill after an attack by the Curse of Tranning, the Blighter, and it occurred to me that perhaps we had it within our means to heal her."

Jerya grew very still. She glanced at Twist, but Twist only shrugged, as if he had no idea if that was plausible or not.

"And do you?" she finally asked, when it became clear Cutter awaited her reaction.

"We have a healer. We won't know if she can succeed until we try," said Cutter cheerfully, then gestured the other woman and her two bodyguards forward. All three of them moved hesitantly forward. The woman was small and slight, with a wary gaze that reminded Jerya of a mouse. Cutter took her hand and pulled her away from her guards. "This is Sora. She is a student of the medical applications of the Logos. She knows the human body better than anybody else we've brought along. She volunteered to evaluate your companion and enact a restoration, if possible. If you will grant your permission, Your Highness."

Jerya stood and Sora the medical student backed away so quickly that she stumbled into one of her bodyguards. "Other wizards tried to repair the damage." She couldn't keep the frustrated hope out of her voice. "Our wizard—"

"I'm not a healer, Your Highness," interrupted Twist. "I spoke in vain with some of the healers in the Citadel about Lady Iriss. I can't imagine it would hurt to let Miss Sora look at her as well." He gave Cutter a peculiar little smirk, dark and twisted. "They would welcome the chance to expand their libraries, I imagine."

Iriss. She was quiet and gentle and whimsical. She'd been the calm heart of the Jerya's Regent Trials when she was seven years old, reading a book she'd smuggled in while the other girls swirled around her giggling and running. She hadn't ignored Jerya; she knew why she was at the Palace. But instead of trying to entice Jerya into games, Iriss had invited her to sit down and look through the picture book.

By the time the trial concluded, most of the other girls sat around Iriss, too: listening as Iriss read the book aloud. Iriss was that kind of person. She read everything, and she was happy to share it all. She'd always been reading. She read in four languages and understood fashion and the smiles of men and she was still friends with most of the girls who had been her rivals for Jerya's favor.

She wasn't as politically-minded as Lisette, it was true. She was more absent-minded than a Regent should be, and too clumsy to ever be deft with a weapon, but she had her own intangible magic every time she smiled. Jerya would have torn out her own heart and stomped it flat to have Iriss back again, because that's what not having Iriss felt like anyhow.

Her throat hurting with emotions she'd kept firmly under control ever since Iriss was attacked, Jerya said, "Yes. You have my permission. Let's go do this now."

Once again, Jerya had to displace Siana and Julina, who were sitting with the invalids while Cara dozed on a couch wedged in the corner. As she told them of Vassay's intentions, she became aware of a scuffle—there was no more dignified word—at the door. She turned to see Cutter physically keeping the little healer's bodyguards out of the room.

"It's not a large room, fellows," he said, pushing one of them back again. "Let the ladies leave and wait out here."

Sora slipped in past her bodyguards and under Cutter's arm, coming face to face with Julina. She looked at Julina, and then past her at Shanascc and Iriss in their parallel beds.

"There's two?" she said, dismayed. "I thought there was only one."

"The other one is the princess who saved the city from the mudslide, Sora," said Cutter, grunting as he pushed one of the bodyguards back again. Then he spoke rapidly in Vassay to them, and Jerya caught several bad words.

"Would you like to see my daughter?" asked Julina gravely. "I think the injury is in her mind, not her body, but perhaps you can tell us for certain."

Jerya turned away from Julina and Sora, leaving them to their conversation. Instead she advanced on Sora's bodyguards. "What is going on here?"

"Sora is frightened of your magic's corruption," said one of them, with bushy eyebrows and jowls more suitable for a man twice his age.

"We hear your monsters attack people. That they attacked this lady of yours." The second man, who had the face of a fairy tale prince and the voice of a pre-adolescent youth, gave her an ugly sneer.

Ah. This was more like what Jerya had been expecting since Vassay arrived.

"And just what are you going to do if such a monster attacks in my Court?" Jerya demanded.

"Protect her. Shield her with our bodies if we must."

Jerya heard Sora give a tiny sigh behind her and changed what she was about to say accordingly. "Did she *ask* you to protect her?"

"No, she didn't," answered Cutter, amused. "They attached themselves to her back on the road. Poor Sora."

Jerya took a deep breath. "You are guests in my city and I'm sure you have some... useful function to serve as part of your expedition. Go serve it, or I will introduce you to monsters who will physically escort you from the building, give your pretty cloaks a brush down, then throw you into the mud." They both stared at her, goggle-eyed. "Should I use smaller words? Go, now!"

"Landry!" called Sora, and the other woman pushed past the two bodyguards and turned to face them.

"Sora volunteered to be here, oafs," she said, and pushed one of them in the chest. "Go away."

"She doesn't take care of herself like she should," muttered one of them. They both took a few steps backward, running directly into Jerya's guards.

She smiled at Raffey. "Lieutenant Monster, escort these men back to their wagons. Don't let them return."

Landry and Cutter both looked at her, eyes wide, as the bodyguards were manhandled out of sight. Cutter seemed amused, and Landry surprised. Jerya gave them the same smile she'd given the guard. "They're all rather big and strong, my guardsmen, and there are so many of them. They make much better monsters than my eidolons."

"Landry!" called Sora again, impatiently.

Landry jumped. "Coming." She hesitated, clearly unwilling to shove past Jerya, which Jerya approved of. Graciously, but pointedly, she let Landry through as she turned to watch the healing.

Sora sat beside Shanasee's bed, her fingers lightly resting on Shanasee's chest. Landry pulled a chair over, sat down, and put one hand on Sora's hair. Both of them began to mutter to the Logos. Even quietly done, the sound of it scratched against Jerya's ears. It buzzed and twisted and she heard sounds surely no human throat could make.

Cara stood beside Julina, her hands clasped and her heart in her eyes. She hadn't been sleeping much, and she'd taken Shanasee's withdrawal much harder than anybody else. Jerya knew Cara blamed her, but what else could she have done? So many would have died without Shanasee's sacrifice.

Jerya glanced around at the sensation of Twist's arrival

and found him in the corner near the door. When she caught his eye he joined Cutter and Jerya. Cutter brightened, recognizing him, and said, "Shall I tell you what they're doing, sir?"

Shrugging and waving a hand, Twist said, "I'm sure the Crown Princess would be interested." He leaned against the wall, watching the work with a narrow gaze that didn't fit his usual temper.

"Of course, sir," said Cutter, glancing at Jerya. "Ah... are you interested? Do you understand the basics of the Logos?"

"Yes, of course," said Jerya pleasantly. "Are they working together? How exactly is that done?"

Cutter grinned. "Landry is what we call a foundation specialist. She narrates a set of terms built on top of the Logos that Sora uses to do very precise tasks. It fades when Landry stops working, but it's really useful."

Twist's eyebrows climbed to his hairline. "Do your secondary workers rely on the foundations your Landrys create? Or can they work independently?"

"Uh... Landry is her name, sir. And we can all work independently, of course. Sora practices a lot because in a crisis there isn't always a foundation specialist around. I'm guessing she's studying the Princess's brain now, that's pretty delicate work." Cutter swelled with pride. "At the University hospital, sometimes they build pyramids four levels deep to perform certain operations. We can't do that here because everybody above the foundation layer needs to be pretty good at medicine, and there needs to be a couple of coordinators keeping everything synchronized."

"Ah," said Twist, as if he suddenly understood something. "An interesting master trick. And on the strength on one trick, your people have climbed so far." He sounded almost sad, and Cutter gave him a bewildered look.

"Is the Vassay weather-working also one of these pyramids? I always thought it was a trick, like Twist's skipping," asked Jerya.

"Oh yes. It—" Cutter stopped as the babbling from the two women came to a stop. Sora sagged and wiped her mouth. Cutter hurried forward, pulling several clothes and a vial from a pocket in his billowy pants. He gave each of the women a cloth that they held to their mouths. Then he opened the vial and dispensed small tablets.

Only after Sora had swallowed hers and patted her mouth did she turn to the observers. She addressed Julina. "She is mostly healthy. There was some pressure in her brain, which I lessened. And—" she hesitated.

"Yes?" asked Julina quietly. "Please tell me."

Slowly, Sora shook her head. "Something old and healed badly. Something I might have been able to repair but I'm not sure it matters anymore."

Cara crossed her arms and stared at the floor.

"What are you talking about?" asked Jerya, intrigued. She'd never noticed any significant scars on Shanasee before, and her cousin never mentioned any old injuries. The trauma from her final battle with Benjen had been entirely psychological, supposedly. But if she had physical scars from that, perhaps they could help Shan deal with her darkness.

Sora gave Jerya an unhappy look. "It isn't proper to discuss things like this with anybody but her closest family."

Indignantly, Jerya said, "We are Blood! And cousins!" She caught herself and added, "I'm responsible for her. If we don't know, we can't help. And when she wakes up again, I need her to be healthy."

"This won't matter—" Sora stopped herself and shook her head. "At some point—years ago, judging from the markers on the tissue—this woman had a massively traumatic miscarriage. It didn't heal properly, which means she'll never bear children without exceptional magical assistance. Just getting pregnant could be very dangerous for her."

Jerya blinked, then looked at Julina and Cara. "When was Shanasee pregnant?"

Lady Julina glanced down at her daughter and sighed. "Years ago. It's an old story, and she never confided the details to me, only came to me for comfort when the pain became too much to bear." She didn't look at Cara, and Cara, who should have known everything about her charge, didn't say a thing, or lift her gaze from the ground.

After thinking about Sora's story and about Cara's silence for a moment, after wondering what had happened that made Cara stay so quiet when surely she knew something, Jerya shook her head. Whatever it was wouldn't be worked out here and now, especially with foreigners present. She said, "Yes, you're right, Sora. That doesn't matter now. Thank you for telling me, and thank you for what you've done for Shan. Can you examine Iriss now?"

Tension went out of Sora's shoulders and she moved around the bed lightly. "It was so interesting having a chance to examine one of your kind closely, although there's always more to see. The corruption—I know that isn't a good word, I am so sorry, is there a better word? The corruption is present on so many levels. It creates a bubble I can't see into. Of course, I wouldn't be able to, it's not the Logos—but the thought of what that bubble contains is just dizzying. What the Princess did was phenomenal and it must have come from those tiny bubbles."

Jerya swayed backward, buffeted by the sudden force of Sora's chatter. Then she said firmly, "What she did came from here," and touched her heart. "She was very frightened and she overcame that for the good of our people."

Sora stopped, dismayed. "Yes, of course. I hope she finds her way out of the darkness again." She lowered her eyes, fidgeted with the hem of her blouse, then turned to Iriss and began to mumble. After a moment, she sank into the chair beside the bed and held out her hand toward Landry.

Landry maneuvered past Jerya with a faint, concerned smile. "I'm sure your cousin will improve, Princess. She has a strong heart, as you mentioned. All your family seems so brave and fierce." Her eyes flickered past Jerya to the door, where Jerya knew Seandri observed.

She managed a curt nod, and got out of the way, joining Seandri as the women started work and Cutter hovered nearby. The room was so crowded. She wrapped her fingers around Seandri's arm and he whispered, "I'm glad you're letting them try to heal her. Harthen misses her. We all do."

Jerya leaned her head on his shoulder. "I feel so unbalanced without her," she responded in a low voice. "I feel so... violent. I want to murder people sometimes. I ran away from the Vassay before."

Seandri put an arm around her shoulders. "You have a strong heart," he said. She glanced up at him sharply, but he showed no sign of noticing he'd repeated Landry's phrase.

"I don't know how Yithiere bears it," she muttered. "Since Zavien died. Jant has Julina but Yithiere is all alone."

"We should talk about that at some point. He's relying on Alanah right now, which seems... dangerous," Seandri said meditatively.

Jerya glanced up at him. "Alanah is an old friend. I trust

her; the Chancellor trusts her. If spending time with her keeps him stable, where is the danger?."

"Alanah has three small children despite being unmarried," Seandri pointed out. It was true. Alanah liked children, but had never wanted a spouse and her Royal appointment allowed her to make eccentric choices. "And Yithiere gets obsessive and short-sighted when he thinks he's protecting those he cares about. Especially children."

"Oh." In the war with Benjen, the bastard had stolen and murdered Jerya's infant cousin. Jerya's generation had all been tiny then, and while Math and Shonathan had returned to war to bring Benjen down, it had been Yithiere who'd stayed behind to protect the remaining children.

Jerya chewed on her lip, her gaze on the two women working magic while she thought about Yithiere. Sora was grimacing. She'd never grimaced while inspecting Shanasee. "What else can we do, though? Alanah just came out of confinement and Zavien died months ago. How has he been managing?"

"Well, the other Regents helped. Lisette..." he began, then trailed off and shook his head. "He doesn't trust Harthen the same way. I think the phantasmagory helped him. He was connected to all of us; he could hide his fears in there and redirect his fire. It was an outlet, and safe."

Jerya ground her teeth. "That doesn't help." She wrapped both arms around his chest and pressed her face against him. "Lord of Winter, Seandri. We've lost so much. The Regents, the phantasmagory. We've lost so much and we're still losing. I don't know what will be left of us if I—"

"I can't!" said Sora sharply. Her chair clattered as she stood so fast she knocked it back. "I can't do this. There's something *in* her. I repair the damaged tissue and the corruption grows out of what I've done, like it's taken root. I think I'm making it worse." She looked around wildly, then found Jerya. "I'm so, so sorry. But I don't know enough. I can't understand what's going on and it frightens me."

In a distant, clinical way, Jerya was very glad she'd sent Sora's bodyguards away. Her distress would have frightened them and that would have complicated things. "I see—" she began, cool and controlled, then took a deep breath. Seandri's grip on her hand helped hold back her shattered hope.

Landry swore in Vassay, low and amazed, before leaning over Iriss. "You did do it, Sora! She's waking up."

Instantly, Jerya was at Iriss's side, half-knocking Sora onto Shanasee's bed and stepping on Landry's foot in her haste. Iriss had moved her hands from her chest to her face and shoulder. She shook her head fitfully, as if emerging from a bad dream.

Jerya took Iriss's thin, pale hand in her own, and their fingers laced together. That hadn't happened since the attack. "Iriss, I'm here," she breathed. "Come back to me."

Iriss opened her eyes. They shimmered with a pearly sheen, just as the Blood's did when they were in the phantasmagory. "Jerya?" she whispered, and turned her head blindly. "Jer, I'm so cold. What happened?"

CHAPTER THIRTEEN

THE PRICE

THE NEXT DAY, Jerya took her place at the Tabernacle of Broken Hearts. She wanted to stay with Iriss, but she'd made the Tabernacle of Broken Hearts her duty and she wasn't going to shirk just because she felt like it. Still, when she saw that the Plaza was almost empty, she indulged the hope that maybe she could return to the inn early.

Only a moment after she'd seated herself, a small boy came tearing into the plaza. He skidded to a stop near her chair and looked around wildly. "Where's the Princess? I need the Princess!"

Raffey moved forward and caught the child. "She's right there, lad. What's going on?"

The grubby boy gave Jerya a blank look. "Princess Gisen, I mean. Where is she? I need her to come to the new levee now, now, or—" The expression of fright on the boy's face compelled Jerya to rise.

"I'm not sure where she's at, but I'll come." She glanced at Seandri.

He shook his head. "The Plaza's empty. Let's go."

The boy's expression didn't allow time for an argument. Raffey released him and he took off like a slingshot. Jerya ran after him, sending eidolon birds from her hands to help her track him and find out what waited ahead.

They didn't have far to run before they encountered a crowd. The little boy beat on the legs of the people in front of him, trying to force a path for Jerya.

Jerya glanced at the crowd, and then looked beyond with her bird's eye view and saw the source of the child's panic. The engineers from Vassay were adjusting the old levees. The river was slowly rising as it adapted to the damage done to the whole river system by the mudslide, and it was clear the old levees, designed for spring thaws, weren't going to survive.

The Vassay were using their magic to reinforce the existing levees and raise new ones. Far down the river, Jerya's hawk saw another team working near the edge of the city to broaden the river's bed in a controlled fashion. Possibly that project was going well. But this one had descended into chaos. One of the levees was leaking and two people were in the turbulent river, hanging onto ropes, their heads barely above water.

The Ambassador stood at the base of the raised levees, shouting orders. More than one of the Vassay engineers had blood streaming from their mouth and many of the rest were chanting fiercely. When the levee sprang another leak, the crowd of observers started backing up.

Seandri scooped up the small boy as somebody almost stepped on him. He couldn't see what Jerya could, even with his advantage of height, but he could still help her.

"Lend me your strength, Seandri," she said, and held out

her hand. He put the boy down, placed his hand in hers, and opened the power in his blood to her. With a tingle as their magic merged. Jerya closed her eyes and remembered what it was like to fly and dive and *strike*. In response, a giant eidolon eagle spread its wings and separated from Jerya's form.

They'd practiced this many times before as part of training; it was part of the magic of eidolons. They'd always had the phantasmagory before; it was even taught that one *had* to be in a phantasmagorical combat trance to call a gestalt eidolon. Yet even without the phantasmagory, Jerya felt Seandri's mind close to hers: his affection, his worry, his omnipresent appreciation of a beauty she could never see. It twisted her heart and she didn't know why.

But the people in the river were drowning.

She and Seandri occupied the giant eagle together as it soared into the sky and dove. One foot closed over one individual, one foot over the other. Then she dropped them again, because they were tied to their ropes and she couldn't begin to estimate the damage she would do by pulling them into the sky. She circled above, gathering her focus to send a cutting emanation from the eidolon. But before she was ready, both people started bobbing down the river. Somebody else had cut the ropes first.

She swooped down again and caught them, one, two, and into the air, ignoring their screaming, and down again, depositing them in the dry street beyond the crowd.

Jerya exhaled and let the giant eagle dissipate. Looking up at the embankment the ropes had been tied to, she saw the man Yithiere had identified as an assassin—Thorn— standing there, a small knife still held in one hand. He gazed at the two people she'd rescued, and after a minute, she did too.

They'd collapsed in the street, exhausted and overcome by emotion. One was sobbing, the other whimpering. She watched impassively as the crowd engulfed them. Some of her own citizens saw her, and there were a few tentative cheers—and then the magic of the Logos-workers took hold and the water on the street began to flow backwards, into the river again.

Seandri's fascinated gaze was fixed on the water, in the way he had when he was coming up with an idea. Jerya squeezed his hand and said, "I'm going back to the Plaza. Will you stay here and keep an eye on them?"

He nodded, distractedly. "Yes, I think that's a good idea. Their magic is very slow to take effect, isn't it?"

"That's why a wizard could never defend Sel Sevanth," Jerya agreed. "I'll come if I'm needed."

As she walked back to the Tabernacle, people smiled as she passed them, and several congratulated her. She smiled back, nodded at their congratulations, and wondered how word of the rescue could have spread faster than she moved.

Then an old woman hanging out washing on the line over the street called down to her, "What are you doing out on the streets?"

Jerya looked up inquisitively. "What do you mean?"

"Your Regent is awake, Princess! You should be with her."

Bemused, Jerya said, "I should be at my Court. There are people waiting on me." But there hadn't been many, she recalled.

"Princess!" chided the old woman. "She's our Regent too. I mourn for Lord Tomas, but last night, old though I may be, I danced in Lady Iriss's honor. You must take care of her, for all of us."

Jerya realized: she thought of Iriss as *hers*, her friend, her helper, her center. But the Monarch's Regent was *the* Regent of Ceria, with far more potential civil power than the monarch herself. The murder of Tomas, her father's Regent, had crackled across Lor Seleni. The attack on Iriss had been another wound to the city. Nobody was comfortable with the idea of a monarch without a Regent. Her recovery became a sign of hope, and a return to normalcy.

Jerya took the woman's advice in the spirit it was meant, sent one of her guards to the Tabernacle to notify anybody waiting, and went back to the inn.

Iriss sat in the parlour with Julina and Siana, bundled up in blankets. Her eyes still glowed with phantasmagory light. She had trouble seeing, too. Jerya didn't care; she was awake, tilting her head to listen in that familiar, beloved way, and that was everything that mattered.

She sat down on the sofa beside Iriss and greeted her. "How is the chill?"

Iriss leaned on Jerya. She had so many blankets on that it was hard to make out a human form under them. "I'm still so cold. These blankets don't do anything." She placed an icy hand on Jerya's cheek and sighed after a moment. "This is the warmth I need."

Jerya obligingly dug her hands into the blankets and pulled Iriss close. They'd slept in the same bed when they were children, snuggled together just like this. They stayed like that, clasped in a timeless circle where Jerya could pretend everything was all right and everything she'd lost would return to her the same way.

Eventually, when a maid brought tea in, Iriss said, "I dreamt of you while I slept. Not often. I wished more. But I could see you when you came near me, a flickering bird of fire and shadow. I wanted to reach out for you, but my body was so cold I couldn't move."

"You can move now, though," Jerya pointed out, resting her chin on Iriss's hair. "The Vassay healer fixed you." She ought to do something nice for the healer, she thought. It was hard not to feel affection for the Vassay woman. "Do you want some tea? It's hot."

"I still dream, though. I woke this morning—I was so glad to wake! And I remembered my dreams."

Jerya pulled back enough to study Iriss. She didn't talk quite the same way she used to. She'd always been a little dreamy but now she sounded half asleep. Maybe she was; maybe that's what the phantasmagory eyes meant. She said she only saw darkness with her faraway eyes: a darkness that Jerya and the other Blood moved through like creatures of fire.

"What did you dream?"

"In the dark place, there's a man's voice. Harsh, angry. He instructs his people, but I can't see them. Possibly they aren't real?"

A handful of thoughts flickered through Jerya's mind: things Kiar had said, stories Twist had related. The image, forever seared on her mind's eye, of one of the andani engulfing Iriss's head. "I hope not."

Iriss pursed her lips in an annoyed pout. "He wants me to obey him, too. But I shan't, I shan't. I'm here to look after you. As soon as I can get warm again." She snuggled closer. "Also, I shall need to make a new dress. Siana has been telling me about the mountain waking up, and how all my belongings were swallowed up."

Jerya shot a look at Siana, sewing quietly. Siana glanced up and then lifted her shoulders in a little shrug. Jerya hadn't told Iriss about the disaster; she couldn't see where she was and Jerya didn't want to distress her. But maybe Siana had been right.

Iriss certainly seemed to be taking it well. "I've a vision of a gown in my head," Iriss confided. "I'm happy to make it. I suppose we won't be having any receptions for a while, but I'm sure it will help me feel more myself."

"It will," said Jerya firmly. "I'll find you some fabric somewhere, and help you."

"That would be lovely! Would you like to see my sketches?"

Jerya's eyebrows went up. "You made sketches?"

"She's been quite engaged by drawing," observed Siana, with a faint smile. "She's been humming for us, too, brightening everything."

Iriss blushed pinkly, and then pulled away from Jerya and turned to the table beside the couch. Her hand went unerringly to the stack of papers and she plucked several up.

"Can you see them?" asked Jerya, intrigued.

"Oh yes," said Iriss. "The room is dark but I can see what I draw perfectly. Once I understood how to find the edges of the paper, it was easy. I can even see them now. Well, faintly. Enough. Here, look." She put the sheaf into Jerya's hand.

Iriss had indeed been drawing a dress: a floating, ephemeral thing, descended from Lor Seleni summer sundresses but with many more layers, and interesting shaping on the bodice. But under the firm clear lines of the dress, Iriss had sketched in other things that made Jerya feel as cold as Iriss's hands.

The dress itself was on the shape of one of the andani. It was only that the andani looked like a basic sketch of a human, Jerya told herself at first. But that oversized smile on the figure's face made her look away, elsewhere through the sheaf of papers.

That didn't help; there were more dress variations and in some of the pictures, Iriss had sketched a background for the figure. It bent to pick flowers and in the distance loomed the fortress that had clawed its way out of the earth. Jerya had seen the sketches from the scouts and the eidolon miniatures made by Kiar; she recognized it. But Iriss had been unconscious when that particular nightmare emerged. What was going on?

Somebody coughed at the door and Jerya looked up sharply. Raffey stood there, waiting for her attention. "Your Highness, Ambassador Smith and some of his retinue are outside. They hope for an audience."

Jerya jumped between annoyance and an involuntary rush of pleasure. Perhaps they wanted to talk about what had happened at the levee—but she wasn't happy they were invading her private space to do so, especially not today.

She took a deep breath, looking at Iriss's face and steadying herself. Then she said, "Aunt Julina, would you take Iriss into my bedchamber? She doesn't need to deal with politics while she's recovering."

Julina rose, gathering up her knitting, and said, "Come, child. We can sit close to the fire and see if you can work the needles still."

Iriss looked wistful, but stood as well. She moved lightly toward Julina, but didn't see the end table in her way and slammed her knee into it. Jerya wasn't able to catch her before she went sprawling.

"Ow!" said Iriss, and "Ow! I'm all right, I think. Ow!" She rolled over and sat up to inspect her leg under her dressing gown. "Oh. I can't tell. Am I bleeding?" She lifted fingers daubed with red to her eye level, frowning in consternation.

"Just a knock, dear," said Julina. "We'll clean it up in the other room."

Silently, Jerya helped Iriss to her feet, biting her tongue to stop herself from saying something that would communicate her sudden fear to Iriss. She'd been so happy to have Iriss back—back from the dead, it had seemed. And she was undeniably Iriss. But while she was back, she wasn't healed, and the bright splash of blood on Iriss's knee drove home just how fragile she was. The last two days felt like a dream that would vanish soon, if it didn't turn into a nightmare first.

Siana paused in passing by and said, "Jerya? It will take time but she'll adapt."

Jerya woke from her introspection and said, "Aunt Siana. Don't go, please. I was hoping you'd stay with me while the Ambassador visits."

Siana's eyebrows rose. "Of course, sweetling." Something warm moved in Jerya's heart; Siana hadn't called her that for years.

Jerya seated herself again and gestured Siana to retake her place. "This is my home for now," she explained. "I don't know why they couldn't wait until I was at the plaza but I am not here at their convenience. On the other hand, they did do me a very great favor. I want to be friendly." She picked up one of the books on the end table Siana had just restored, and opened it. "There. Do I look suitably relaxed?"

Siana started laughing helplessly. "You haven't ever looked relaxed, Jerya. You look like you're going to devour that book if it doesn't go along with your plans."

Jerya glanced up, startled, and then back down at the

book again. "Well. Maybe I am. You may bring them in, Lieutenant."

A few moments later, Ambassador Smith appeared in the door frame, all but filling it with his bulk. He grinned as he ducked into the room, and said, "Ah, Your Highness." But his grin dimmed as he peered around the room. "Where's the young woman Sora healed? Not unwell again, I hope."

Jerya closed her book. The rest of his 'retinue' turned out to be Cutter and the clerk called Scriber Stone. They both lingered near the door, while someone stood beyond the door still, only visible by shadow.

"Please, come in. Is everything going well at the riverside?"

The Ambassador gave her a startled look, and Scriber Stone hurried to his side and said, not quietly, "The eagle that plucked the students from the water, sir. She couldn't have known it wasn't necessary. I do hope she didn't strain herself."

"Eh?" said the Ambassador, pushing Scriber Stone behind him. "That was you? I thought it was young Seandri. Prince Seandri," he corrected himself.

"We were both present," Jerya told him mildly. "Was it unnecessary? They seemed to be drowning."

"They're safe now, which is all I care about," said the Ambassador. He looked around the room, and Jerya realized he was still looking for Iriss, as if she was hiding under a chair somewhere.

"Iriss is very much improved, but resting," Jerya told him, and added firmly, "Please sit down. It's distressing to have you looming over me. Your attendants can sit near the window if they wish." She offered Cutter a warm smile as he moved past, and listened to Scriber Stone instructing the final member of their party to wait without unless he was called in.

The Ambassador looked around guiltily, before lowering himself into one of the parlour chairs. "Sorry, sorry. My curiosity sometimes gets the better of me."

Jerya hesitated before indulging her own curiosity. "Does your diplomatic corps not particularly value subtlety? You aren't what I expected." She didn't look directly at Scriber Stone, but she was aware of him all the same. He stared at her with an unblinking interest she found unsettling. His manners were as bad as the Justiciars.

Ambassador Smith chuckled, but uncomfortably. "Some of them are wretched subtle. I'm primarily a teacher and an administrator, Your Highness, which I imagine you've guessed by now. We thought physical assistance would be more useful than politics in your current situation." He tapped his fingers together. "Speaking of that, how goes destroying the Blight?"

Jerya studied the way he sat in the chair, as if eager to be on his feet again. She wondered if he paced while teaching. "Fighting a war is slow, Your Excellency. It takes time for armies to move. We're containing it until we have the manpower to eradicate it."

Scriber Stone rifled through a satchel of papers. The Ambassador glanced at him, then said, "I've been told your baby sister is off on a secret mission to acquire a special weapon?"

"Not so secret," said Jerya. "Though it certainly sounds exciting to describe it that way."

He waited a moment, clearly hoping she'd go on. Cutter moved restlessly by the window and the shuffling of Scriber Stone's papers seemed to fill the room.

Jerya smiled. "Is the levee stable now? Usually we'd have to build up the waterfront, which is an annoyance at the best of times. We appreciate your work." She could be so much more polite than Scriber Stone, oh yes. Why devalue truly useful work, even if people you disliked did it? "You mentioned the bridges in one of the notes you sent? You've been quite focused on the river."

"Well, yes," he said vaguely, running a hand through his hair. "The levee will keep the river in place for now, although it will stay high, which creates its own problems. As for the bridges... It'd be best if we could get people back into their homes again. And..."

Scriber Stone moved some papers again, and the Ambassador grimaced. "I will be honest with you, Princess. We would very much like to have access to the Royal plepanin reserves."

Jerya stared at him, long and cool. So this was why they'd healed Iriss. Not a gift, not a kindness, but just politics and greed. "And so you want to get into the Palace."

"Well, yes. You should get back to your home again too," he added, a happier note in his voice.

Cutter half raised his hand for attention. "And the supply caravan, sir. Don't forget about that."

"Oh, please don't forget about the supply caravan," said Jerya. "What must you tell me about the supply caravan?"

Ambassador Smith's eyes narrowed as he considered Jerya and suddenly she realized that while he might seem foolish in his enthusiasm and lack of subtlety, he was intelligent, and hardly as oblivious as she'd first thought. "Go ahead, boy. Since you're so eager, share with the class."

"Oh. Well...." Cutter came forward. "We have more supplies from Vassay coming behind us, Your Highness. It's protected just as our own caravan was, but it's larger, with fewer people."

"Tempting prey," observed Jerya.

He shifted. "Yes, well. It's also late. It's still coming, it's simply... being careful. On the way here we did have a few problems of our own. Some of your people saw us as... well... invaders. We don't want to hurt anybody if we don't have to. The presence of one of your family members would help."

"As a deterrent," she said flatly.

"To show your people we're not invaders."

Jerya studied Cutter. He seemed nervous and ill-at-ease, not at all like he'd been the day before. The request for an escort didn't seem like the sort of thing that would prompt a young man to interrupt his teacher. Unless... "Is there somebody in particular you care about on this second caravan?"

He looked down. "Yes."

"You're a wretched boy and will no doubt be the ruination of my career," said Ambassador Smith, without the faintest trace of ire. "Now that you've unburdened yourself to the Princess, go wait in the hall with Thorn."

Cutter bowed again and backed out of the room, his eyes fixed on Jerya pleadingly until he was out of the room.

Jerya regarded Scriber Stone. "And do *you* have any requests to make? I've heard that you've been just as helpful to the Justiciars as Cutter has been to me. In your own way."

"If I have, Your Highness, I'm content to let them reward me as they see fit," said Scriber Stone placidly. "But it is kind of you to offer."

"In the end, our requests do benefit Ceria, Your Highness," said Ambassador Smith, as if confiding a secret to a not-very-bright student. He glanced at Scriber Stone, before adding defiantly, "And speaking of the Justiciars, I want to invite you to a special meeting with them in a day or two. I think I could put some of my administration experience to work helping sort out some of the, ah, differences in perspective we've heard about."

Jerya shrugged, unable to summon any real interest in another meeting where the Justiciars would again dismiss her based on her family history. "Perhaps. Not at the Elant, though."

"No, no, of course not. We'll find somewhere." He tapped his fingers together again, waiting on her response to the other, more difficult requests.

Jerya glanced at Siana, who sat with her head down, making tiny stitches with her needle. If things hadn't gone horribly wrong, right now Iriss would be in Siana's position, and it would be Iriss she'd consult with before making a decision. She'd have access to the phantasmagory, and she'd be able to attract the eventual attention of one or more of her family just by making it ripple. She could do none of that now.

Instead she was about to make important decisions, almost utterly alone. She'd been fighting for the power to make decisions since her father's Regent had been murdered and they'd started investigating what was going on in their own country. This was the power she should have had all along, she who would be crowned Queen. She'd set up her own Court in the hopes of calling it to her. But when she started on this path, after her father's Regent Tomas had died, she had neither wanted nor expected to get the power all by herself. She firmly believed the true strength of the monarchs of Ceria was based in the stability of a partnership.

Her father had been content to leave all the decision-making in Tomas's hands, even when it came to matters of the Blood, like the use of the Palace and the training of individual family members. Her grandfather, she understood, had been similar. That never would have been the case with Jerya and Iriss. Jerya could never let go of what was hers, and half of the annual holidays Lor Seleni celebrated told her again and again Ceria belonged to *her*.

A murmur of voices came from the hall, growing louder. It was an argument. Jerya glanced at the door and recognized Yithiere's voice, fast and angry. A moment later, she recognized Seandri, and her guard. Then Yithiere flung open the door and loomed at the threshold.

"I am well, Uncle," Jerya said calmly, and some tension went out of his shoulders.

"These men outside your door—"

"Just men, Uncle. Is Seandri with you? Please, both of you come in. Ambassador Smith has asked us for a favor." Then again, she mused, even without the phantasmagory, she wasn't as isolated as she'd felt.

Seandri stepped into the room behind Yithiere, nudging him forward, and closed the door behind them again. "Here we are," he said. "Good afternoon, Ambassador. You've been busy today."

Jerya's heart lightened a touch. Even with Iriss strange and worrying, even with Vassay and the Blight, Seandri could always make her feel better. He was so reliable that sometimes she felt she had a second Regent. He loved her, he took care of her when she needed it, and he never made things hard. He hadn't been jealous of her brief fling with Cathay. He never felt threatened by anything. He was a deep pool of water that swallowed every stone. And everybody around him, even those who didn't know him, seemed to feel as if he could be trusted. Or at least forgotten about. She'd noticed that. He was so steady the Chancellor forgot about him when planning sometimes.

Jerya didn't mind. She never forgot about him.

"Ambassador Smith wants to excavate the Palace first," Jerya explained. "And he wants a Blood escort for another caravan. I think the first must be considered carefully, since the resources he has brought us are precious and should not be wasted on frivolous things. But the second—the second— what do you think, my Blood?"

Yithiere's hackles had risen at the mention of Vassay excavating the Palace, but she'd smoothed them in the same sentence. He rubbed his chin at her query. "I've been thinking about that. None of us should be sitting idle in Lor Seleni. It can take care of itself as long as we can stop the Blighter from getting any closer to it."

"This would be a good opportunity to get a look at what's going on out there," offered Seandri. "I don't think we should abandon Lor Seleni though. It would be bad for morale. And other things. I have some ideas there." His gaze slid over to the Ambassador.

"I see we're all being straightforward here," the Ambassador said, back to joviality again. "I personally find honest advice the best kind. It's hard to hammer out the flaws in a plan with less than honest feedback."

Scriber Stone audibly sighed, as if he regretted something. Jerya smiled at them again. "You did me a kindness in returning Iriss," she said. "And on Fallendre, too. I will do you a favor in response—one you *do* believe is necessary—and make sure your own loved ones stay safe on the journey here. As for the Palace, we will... discuss it. I'm not yet convinced it is the best use of resources, but you will have a chance to make arguments."

The Ambassador inclined his head. "Very gracious. And who will be joining our caravan? The sooner they can depart, the sooner the supplies will arrive."

Jerya looked at Yithiere and Seandri, and thought of the rest of her family, and too late realized the trap she'd set herself. She remembered, all of a sudden, why she'd sent none of the Blood out yet with the scout troops.

Jant, she could not command to leave Lor Seleni. Even if she had the will to do so, he wouldn't obey. He'd been ready to die in the mudslide rather than leave the Palace.

Gisen was still a child, younger than her thirteen years. Gisen was what they were fighting *for*.

Yithiere was dangerously unstable now, without a Regent and enormously stressed. Without the phantasmagory, she'd be unable to monitor him. It was a disaster on the edge of happening.

And Seandri... Seandri was stable and had his Regent and could be trusted absolutely... But Seandri was *hers*.

She silently cursed Tiana and Kiar and Cathay—especially Cathay—for running off, taking their strength of mind and independence of action with them. She cursed the Blighter, for destroying the phantasmagory. And she cursed herself, for trapping herself in this sudden dead end.

Siana was watching her, she realized. Her aunt had been sewing all this time, no more involved than the table. But now her needle stopped and she lifted her eyes to witness Jerya's decision. They were all watching her expectantly, but she felt like Siana expected something particular from her.

Seandri startled her by saying, "I'll go. It will be interesting and Yithiere can stay closer to the Blight."

"No!" Jerya covered her mouth, then dropped her hands, regaining her composure. "Uncle Yithiere, you'll go. You have the most experience in the field. You'll be able to keep the caravan safe, and that's what's important." It was the best she could do. She couldn't send away Seandri. She couldn't. He was hers.

Seandri glanced at her and shrugged. "Also a good plan. I can help the engineers instead. I thought this morning that our magic might be useful when combined with their own Logos skills."

Jerya didn't like that much better, but she couldn't say anything, couldn't argue without exposing her irrationality to far too many people. Instead she only nodded, and wondered why Siana looked down at her stitching and sighed.

CHAPTER FOURTEEN

FEL DION

MINEX KNEW STORIES about Fel Dion. When she discovered their destination, she wove chilling tales of trees that devoured corpses and bloody revels among the branches. She spoke of the animals hunted for sport with sympathy, as if she'd been one of them. With relish, she described maidens tearing away their own maidenheads. She even giggled as she related the doom that came upon those who stalked the chosen of the wood.

Minex knew stories about Jinriki, nonsensical stories that baffled Jinriki as much as they irritated Tiana. Eagerly she described how Jinriki had come down from the sky and dispensed justice for her people. She related how he'd been courted by the most beautiful of the earth fiends and rejected all his suitors as distractions from his true duty.

Minex knew ancient Blood history. She spun tales about family members in misty past, names nearly forgotten in the long descent from Shin Savanyel to Tiana herself. Kiar was especially interested in these supposed histories, stories of wars fought and earth fiends betrayed by those of her Blood who had seduced them. She wanted Minex to tell her more about Shin Savanyel, but the earth fiend never seemed to hear her queries. Or maybe the stories of Shin Savanyel just didn't feature enough earth fiends.

But Minex, it seemed, knew stories about almost everything. Privately, Tiana thought she invented them all. But the others paid attention when she breathlessly recounted tales of sorcery, betrayal and murder in Fel Dion, as she walked in the midst of the horses, and sat among them at the campsite. Even Jinriki listened closely, although he commented often to Tiana on the more extravagant or incomprehensible of the earth fiend's claims.

She wasn't even a very good storyteller. She'd lose track of one thread and go meandering off in a different direction, and everybody just stared at her in fascination. It was stupid, and Tiana tried not to pay attention, losing herself in the light of the Firstborn instead.

It sang to her, enticing her forward. It seemed to promise her that at the end of the road awaited both duty satisfied and desire achieved. It was a nice song to listen to. Tiana imagined what would happen when she'd gathered up all the lights of the Firstborn. She'd banish the Blighter in one blow, she hoped. There'd be no more fighting, no more watching Lisette cower on the ground or fending off darts from monsters. She'd drive off the Blighter and go home and Jerya would tell her she'd done well.

After a day and a half of Minex's company, they stopped on a hill. In the hazy distance, dark trees stretched along the horizon. "Fel Dion!" said Minex proudly, as if she was responsible for bringing them there. "And that is the terrible village," she added with a shudder, pointing at the closer peaked roofs of a small town.

Tiana remembered the original tale of Sinethca vividly; it bothered her more than all the earth fiend's ramblings. Carefully she led the others in a far circuit around the village so as not to attract attention. More people would only complicate matters, anyway.

Beyond the village, the road abruptly became a track, crossing a wide strip of meadowland before vanishing into the dark woods.

"This is the Gift," said Minex, springing forward into the long grass. "That's what the villagers call it, anyhow. It doesn't call itself anything. They believe as long as they don't go in it, the forest won't expand."

Tiana couldn't restrain herself. "Have you talked to them much, then? How did you manage that without being murdered, like in your stories yesterday?"

Minex's ears moved, a disconcerting sight. "I didn't! But the current remembers. They put their bones underground and the current nibbles them to dust and in the dust weeps all their words." She gazed up at Tiana with her solemn yellow eyes. "But it's the stones under the soil that stop the forest, really. So it won't matter if you cross the Gift."

"And are we going to be eaten inside?" Tiana asked, nudging her horse forward.

Firmly, Minex said, "The Great Prince would not allow that to happen." Then she dropped to all fours and scampered ahead.

**She's right, of course. **

Tiana mumbled, "Did you think I was honestly worried?"

The tall grass hid marshy ground and insects swarmed

around the horses' legs, disturbed by their steps. Halfway across the field, Minex vanished into the undergrowth on the forest side, and then reappeared again, her bushy tail waving. Tiana didn't know if the waving tail spoke of a dog-like happiness or a cat-like aggression. Sometimes it seemed to her it was both.

"Come! Come! Inside it is hers!"

Tiana's mount, Moon, pricked his ears forward as he carried Tiana into the shade of the boundary trees. A crushed floral scent wafted up from his hooves and dizziness swept over Tiana.

The emerald light filled the forest. Like a physical force, it pounded on her skin, swept over her, carried her out of herself. She struggled for something to cling to: Moon's saddle, Lisette's hand, even the scratchiness of Jinriki. But she had not been prepared and the green light was both close and cruel. Brambles tore through her skin and rooted in her bones, and the spicy scent of crushed wildflowers infused her blood.

Then something caught her. A pool of crimson, floating with roses, moved within the endless green. The ruby light slept within the expanse of the Green Wild, but even sleeping it pulled her free of the other light. She floated, lost and bewildered.

Firm arms closed around her and she gasped for breath. Jinriki murmured, ***I have you.***

Muzzily, she wondered where Jinriki had found arms, and if this was a phantasmagory dream. But she opened her eyes and Cathay's face looked down on her anxiously. She'd fallen off Moon; one foot was still in the stirrup, and Moon was investigating her bare leg curiously. Carefully, she pulled her foot free, and Cathay helped her stand. She could feel Jinriki's bulwarks inside, buffering the sensation of drowning in the light.

She felt steady enough on her feet, although the drifting scent of the tiny pink blossoms on the undergrowth made her recoil. Cathay said, "Do you want to keep going?" and she nodded.

Once on her horse again, she looked around at the others. The furtive glances from some of the guards made her ashamed; passing out without warning earned her whispers from strangers, and calm acceptance from her friends. But Jinriki said, **Hardly calm; that fool almost fell off his own horse in his hurry to get to you.** His voice sneered but Tiana was obscurely comforted all the same.

They moved past the edge bracken, trampling down quite a large section of it as they did. Once inside, beyond the reach of the afternoon sunlight, the forest dimmed. The light filtering through the green canopy above faintly echoed the green maelstrom Tiana could still sense. The trees were huge, with interlaced branches that absorbed every bit of direct sunlight, with another layer of branches below with fewer leaves and spikier branches. The forest floor was carpeted with needles, old leaves, broken twigs, small ferns and moss-covered sections of ancient tree. The horses' hooves sunk into it and they moved slowly. Slater dismounted and led his horse, testing the ground as he went, and the others followed, winding among the trees. Near the back of the column, one of the stable girls started complaining loudly.

"I'm not sure how far we should go," Slater announced. "If our destination is deep in the forest, we should leave the horses with the grooms and some men, and go on by foot."

Minex appeared over a fallen tree that rested against its neighbors. "This way! There's a road!"

Slater left his horse, ducking under the fallen tree. Tiana muttered, "I hope you're getting something useful from her."

She is company in a way humans are not. I haven't had that for a long time.

Slater reappeared, around the tree this time. "She's right. I don't believe it... but there's something like a road. This way."

There were no paving stones or tire ruts beyond the fallen tree, but the trees grew farther apart, stretching deeper into the forest. The canopy thinned, and nothing had colonized the open space. Minex crouched in the center of the track, digging with her bare hands. She looked up as Slater arrived next to her. "The current is very deep here. I don't know why."

Slater hesitated and then put his hand on Minex's head, between those ridiculous ears. "Digging may not be a good idea, then. Let's see what's further along."

"That's what I was trying to do," Minex said, but stood and shook herself.

They followed the curving path for several miles and more than an hour. The forest seemed endless. Tiana was unpleasantly reminded that the woodlands near her home were small, and surrounded by villages and farmland. *Captured,* she thought. Then, without fanfare, the road ended. Trees pressed closely together on all sides save the way they came.

Slater said, "Shall we make a camp here for the night and see what the area looks like in the morning?" He clearly thought it was the sensible decision, but Tiana remembered waiting outside the big gates of the Citadel of the Sky.

"No. Let's push a little farther in and find a campsite within." She looked around and added, "I don't think we want to be surprised by whatever uses this road normally."

It wasn't a tamed forest. There were no pleasant clearings

large enough for a royal camp-out. What they found was more like three clearings, each slightly wider than the trail they made, and separated by partially fallen trees. Trees didn't seem to make it all the way to the ground when they died here; they landed in other trees and become part of the landscape, hosting mushrooms and insects and eventually, ferns. Roots of trees and the ancient remains of deadwood made the ground rough, and it sloped unevenly, dotted with the remains of rivulets from the winter. A tiny creek seeped out from under a stone, the flow of water barely more than a hand span wide.

"Do you know where we go next, Your Highness?" asked Slater, while the others assembled the camp. It was a serious undertaking, with the mules and the remounts in one clearing with a handful of guards, half the guards and the Palace horses in the second, and the Blood in the third.

Even from her clearing, Tiana could hear the loud stable girl complaining. "—should have stayed in the meadow, where there's better grazing, this is dumb, somebody is going to break a leg, and why—" Tiana had wondered vaguely about how eager the stable girls had been to sign on with their expedition. She wondered less now. Most nobles preferred less vocal servants.

She shook her head in response to Slater's question. "It's everywhere, like a fog. I have no idea how to gather it." She didn't mention her awareness of the red light, because she didn't know what it meant. How could a light be sleeping?

Kiar said, "I'm not sure we should be doing some of these things," and she waved at where several guards worked on fire pits. "This is a holy place and we don't know what the restrictions are. We could make enemies."

Tiana raised her eyebrows. "I thought you said this was no different than any other forest."

Kiar scowled. "I said all forests had stories. This place is strange. And if your green light is here, that must mean it's holy somehow."

Tiana shrugged. "Well, if somebody wants to scold us, that will give us somebody to talk to. Which would be better than what we have right now." She leaned back, resting her head on a tree root and closing her eyes.

Kiar said, "You're being an optimist again." Tiana pretended she hadn't heard, and tried to focus on the lights of the Firstborn. But Jinriki muffled them and it felt like the green light was everywhere, a spiritual representation of the forest. It didn't welcome her the way the blue light of Niyhan had, and it gave her no clues on how to call it. All she knew was she *had* to acquire it, had to carry it within her as she carried the blue.

Even now she could touch the blue light, sense the movement of the sky and clouds overhead, and feel the trembling balance of the high places.

Stop that, said Jinriki. ****I don't like this. The Firstborn are using you.****

"But it's for the same purpose that you're using me, isn't it? And I've accepted that. I chose to accept that."

I don't know, he admitted grudgingly. ****It seems as though they seek more than vengeance against a murderer.****

"Of course they do. He's currently trying to destroy Ceria. Maybe more than just Ceria, too. He *killed* one of them before." Her tartness softened. "It's a lot more complicated than I expected, though. I don't understand what I'm supposed to do here. I thought I'd just... find the light and it would fall into me like the blue light did."

A tree rustled overhead, as if from a squirrel. A pack of squirrels, or else something very large.

Humans, sent Jinriki, even as the noises abruptly stopped. Tiana sat up, holding up her hand to gain her attendants' attention. The activity of the camp stilled and several of the guards half-lifted loaded crossbows. A pair of faces peeked out of the leaves.

Both were smudged with dirt and tree sap, with identical preternaturally leaf-green eyes, but the one who spoke seemed more masculine. "Oh no. Who are *you*?" The figure pulled himself to a higher and less obscured tree branch, while his companion remained hidden. He wore only rags, and his hands and feet were stained green.

Lisette rose to her feet, as elegant as if at a tea party. "First, you must tell me who *you* are. After that, I can introduce you properly to Her Serene Highness, the Princess Tiana." It wasn't exactly a proper introduction, but they weren't exactly at a cookie reception. Maybe it *was* the right form of introduction to forest wild children, Tiana reflected. Lisette would know.

The young man's eyes flicked to Lisette. "You don't need to know who I am."

Lisette sighed. "Then I'm afraid we're at a standstill."

He frowned. "But you just told me—" The figure below him giggled and he stopped short, flushing. Setting his jaw, he stared at Tiana again. "I don't believe you. But it doesn't matter. You shouldn't be here." Without looking away, he added, "And the crossbows aren't winning me over."

Impatiently, Tiana motioned for her guards to lower their weapons. "Why don't you believe her?" She'd never before encountered somebody who hadn't recognized her as a member of the Royal Blood on sight.

Those remarkable eyes assessed her again and he shrugged. "The Blood are all nine feet tall, and majestic.

You're lying in the dirt. Besides this isn't a place for the Blood. It's... protected."

The figure mostly hidden below him said, "We heard stories—"

The young man's hands tightened on the branch he held. "If the story is true, you're even less welcome. Atalya's blessings are not for the taking, not here."

Lisette helped Tiana to her feet. "Who tells stories of the Blood here?"

"What's *your* name?" he asked in response.

"Do you need to know?" she responded, then added, "No, that's unkind of me." She curtsied prettily. "Lisette, of the Regency." Dimpling at him in that way she had, she asked, "And your own?"

He smiled crookedly back, as if he couldn't help himself. They never could. "Fai. You look too gentle for your companions, Lisette. A tamed lady. You can let that go here, you know."

Tiana said, suddenly annoyed, "Excuse me, can we return to the subject of the Blood and recent tales?"

Fai's gaze lingered on Lisette as he said, "The Voice tells us the Blood descended on the Citadel of Niyhani and claimed the power of that Firstborn for their own, leaving the Citadel in ruins. Is it true, gentle Lisette? Were you part of such devastation?"

Intimately, said Jinriki, in some satisfaction, but Lisette said only, "It is no misdeed to accept a gift freely offered."

"Ah," said Fai, sounding almost disappointed. "Well, Atalya will offer no such gifts here. Not of *that* variety."

Tiana stared at him. "What do you mean? The light is here, I feel it everywhere. Why won't she help?"

Fai's smile wasn't pleasant. "Outside, the Lady's blood is shed every year for the good of the world and all the horrible people within it. Only here is she free, Queen instead of pawn, and here, she does not sacrifice. Not for hunters, and not for Blood Princesses." He spoke with an easy authority that made it hard to argue.

Frustrated tears sprang to Tiana's eyes. "But the Blight—Ohedreton—we need her. Why do I feel her light if she won't help us?"

Fai tilted his head and not unkindly, he said, "Perhaps She has other plans."

The girl hidden in the leaves said, "The others..."

Fai swung a foot and lightly brushed the girl's head. "Yes. There are other powers here. If you are so very desperate, perhaps you can convince one of them to help you against the Blight. I'll spread word of your visit."

Tiana ducked her head, her eyes burning, and felt Lisette's fingers close on her own comfortingly. Then Lisette said, "Tell also the true story of what happened at the Citadel: that Niyhan reached through all his monks to place a power and a quest in her, and that after, the Blighter tried to pull down the mountain itself in an attempt to thwart her quest."

"How frightening," said Fai, unimpressed. "Would you have us be vulnerable to the same devastation if you *could* strip the power from this place? No. She will not sacrifice her only sanctuary."

Without warning, Minex pressed against Tiana's other side. "Lady Lisette forgot one detail," she announced. "It's all right, she was right in the middle, she wouldn't have noticed."

The girl whispered something and Fai said sharply, "What is that, little earth spirit?"

Minex looked like a cat contemplating a bowl full of cream. "The servants of Niyhan could not hear his message at first, so distracted were they by their own lives. They couldn't hear him until the most profound silence swept over the Citadel and its protections had already started to crumble."

The young man's face grew cold, and without another word, he vanished back into the branches. His companion peeked out a moment longer before also withdrawing, the rustling of the branches first loud and then no more remarkable than the wind.

Plaintively, Tiana said, "What's going on?"

"They weren't from the local population. The villages outside the forest, I mean. He spoke like a noble and those rags were once fine clothing," said Lisette. She sighed. "Minex is right. Nobody at the Citadel had any idea what was going to happen. Don't let them discourage or confuse you, Tiana. They don't know any more than we do."

"Somebody does," said Kiar. "The one they called the Voice. News faster than we could travel, and slanted in the worst possible way. This is not nearly as friendly a place as the Citadel."

CHAPTER FIFTEEN

EYES IN THE DARK

JERYA WENT TO the meeting the Ambassador arranged with more hope than was warranted. It wasn't only the Crown Princess and the Justiciars, but the Mayor, a handful of prominent tradesmen, two nobles, a common laborer, a shipwife, a midwife, a bespoke enchanter and the manicured editor of a women's serial, all apparently invited because they weren't afraid to speak their minds. It wasn't a meeting, it was chaos. If they could have harnessed the various sneers of disdain, they could have pulled a war wagon into the heart of the Blight. When Jerya came back again and Iriss asked about the meeting, all she could do was shake her head and try to forget the gleeful way Scriber Stone had transcribed every single outburst and insult.

"At least," she told Iriss and Siana, "Most of the citizens were respectful to *me*. They just hated each other. And the nobles. And the Justiciars," she finished, with satisfaction. That thought kept her warm through the disarray and constant

worry of Yithiere's departure with Cutter and a handful of
Guards and a counselor assigned by the Chancellor.

But by the time night fell, she couldn't stop thinking
about the veiled looks they'd given her, and about the way
the shipwife and the serial editor had politely disapproved
of her and the Justiciars equally, in a cool, stinging way. The
memory mixed up with her concern about sending Yithiere
so far away. The Chancellor sent his man along more for
appearances' sake than any expectation that it would do any
good; Yithiere simply didn't trust anybody he hadn't known
from either his childhood or theirs. Even those he did trust
he did conditionally, these days.

By the middle of the night, Jerya gave up on sleep. She
was exhausted, but her brain wouldn't stop working, spinning
endless possible scenarios. Yithiere. Vassay. Seandri. The
Blighter. Winning. Losing. Escaping. Ruling. Dying.

She got dressed and left the room, intending at first on
visiting Seandri. But as she entered the hall, shrouded in the
velvet darkness, she stopped. The thought of cuddling close
to Seandri didn't appeal to her like it used to. She realized
that while they'd been close as children, what they had now
was.... Habit. Trust, yes. Reliability—but he surprised her the
day before with his decision to help the Vassay. He never
surprised her. He was always there. But one day, he wouldn't
be. What if that night was tonight?

She couldn't stand the thought. It made her think of
Tiana, gone far away. But she didn't want to think. Thinking
had kept her up this late. After a moment's thought, searching
for something she could do, she turned to Great-Uncle Jant's
chamber. A dim light under the door told her he was still
awake, too. She nodded at the guard outside, then knocked
and called, "Uncle?" softly.

"Come in," he responded, and when she opened the door, she found him sitting up in his bed, writing on a lap desk. He was alone, but Jerya could pick up the faint floral scent of the recent presence of his wife Julina.

Her great uncle looked so wizened and frail—but he'd always looked wizened and frail. Alone of all her relatives, he hadn't changed since she was tiny. He was her grandfather's younger brother, and he'd watched four monarchs before Jerya rule and fall. He had his limits—he couldn't bear to be outside most of the time—but he had much of the experience Jerya lacked, through direct observation, and through his studies. He maintained a network of contacts all across the country and beyond; he was always writing letters and in books.

He kept writing as she entered the room, saying, "The young need their sleep, child. What do you want?"

Jerya plucked a possibility out of the storm in her mind: something she'd talked about before with Seandri, something that might help everybody. "The phantasmagory was a *thing*, Uncle. A physical object."

His writing stopped, then picked up again. "I saw. We all saw." They'd all been pulled into the phantasmagory by an unfamiliar ghostly woman right before the Blighter had destroyed it, so Jerya's father wasn't alone at the end.

Jerya started pacing around the room. "It was a thing, but it was also an eidolon, Kiar said."

"And that I've heard," said her great uncle. "Don't pace like that, Jer, it disrupts my rhythm. No wonder you're not sleeping. Sleep requires stillness."

"My mind won't be still, Uncle, I'm sorry." But she made an effort to calm her body. "You've studied the phantasmagory a long time."

He folded his letter. "I did. I studied what was inside it, what could be done with it. I always considered it an extension of our own minds. And now it is gone." His voice was even, but Jerya fancied that if the phantasmagory did still exist, she'd be able to feel the ripples of his rage and grief.

Curiously she asked, "Did you write down much of what you found in there? The old stories and memories?"

"Some," he said, putting his lap desk aside and folding his hands. "Those I thought would be interesting to my correspondents or to scholars. But all those papers are in the Palace, my dear, if you were hoping to do some research." His eyes glinted brightly. She'd forced him to leave when the mudslide came. Apparently he was still annoyed about that.

Well, maybe she could redirect his energies. She took a deep breath, looking at the idea she'd plucked from the storm. "All right. That's fine. Actually, I was thinking... could we recreate the phantasmagory? Could you? Perhaps it was some kind of gestalt eidolon."

He stared at her, his eyes widening slowly. Then he shook his head. "Where would I even begin? If it was a gestalt eidolon, who did it belong to? And it was amazingly complex if so; beyond my capacity. How would you even fold the substance so you could achieve the layers..." his voice dropped down into muttering, until he shook his head again and said, "Why would you even think such a thing is possible?"

Jerya gnawed on a pinky nail, then made herself stop. "The andani, and the other soldiers of the Blighter seem independent, but Kiar was able to absorb them like they were her own eidolons. She's clever, not unusually gifted with Family magic. That started me thinking about eidolons and what they are. Then I made a gestalt eidolon with Seandri and I could... feel him, even without the phantasmagory." She shrugged. "I don't have any answers, just questions. And you've been looking at questions like this a lot longer than I have."

"Sometimes we forget how to ask new questions," Jant muttered, and Jerya thought again about her relationship with Seandri. His hand twitched and an emanation carried away his lap desk. *Sometimes we forget to ask questions at all.*

Great-Uncle Jant began working the emanation around a tiny eidolon: fox-shaped, as all his eidolons were unless he chose to change them. Jerya watched him, holding absolutely still in case her restless activity would interfere with any sudden flights of brilliance. But after only a moment, he let both forces dissolve. "I don't know. I haven't any idea of where to start."

"I'll have Gisen help you," said Jerya, in her own fit of inspiration. "She's the youngest, you're the oldest, the two of you can come up with something. She's really good with eidolons, too. And if it's gestalt, you won't be able to do it alone."

Jant squinted at her. "It would be.... good to have the phantasmagory back. It is such a precious archive—even wiped clean as it was—it was a way for us to communicate. You used to monitor the phantasmagory for us during the Blights when you were tiny, do you remember? The children have always done that. I did it when my mother—" He stopped abruptly, and shook his head. "I will speak with Gisen. She needs to be kept busy in any case; she's spending far too much time around those foreigners."

Again, Jerya decided not to fan the flames of his annoyance by mentioning Gisen attended the Vassay at her request. Instead she moved to the door. "I'll let you sleep on it."

"Don't forget to sleep yourself, child," said Jant gruffly. She turned back and went to kiss him on the cheek.

"Sometimes I feel like I slept through my entire childhood," she murmured. "We've all been sleeping, hidden away, ignoring the real world."

"Sometimes it's better to sleep than be awake," he said cryptically, then said, "Go on. Let an old man rest."

She left. She couldn't go back to her own apartment, though. It was too confining; all her thoughts bounced off the walls and came back at her.

As she went to the inn's exit, picking her way across the public parlour that had become a staging ground for the Royal Guard, Cara rose up from a couch against the wall.

"Jerya," she called, and when Jerya glanced over, came around a table and said, "Why? Why didn't you send Seandri?"

Her skin prickling, Jerya took in Cara's bedraggled appearance. She'd been slowly falling apart since the mudslide, but the conversation with the healer had wrecked her. She'd been curled up on the couch like she hadn't had the energy to move to her own bed.

"Yithiere has more experience—" she began, giving the same excuse she'd offered yesterday. But the sudden flash of rage in Cara's eyes silenced her.

"You didn't send Seandri because he's your *favorite*. You dragged Shanasee into her worst nightmares because the city needed her, but you'd rather let the Blight overwhelm us than risk your favorite. You lie and play games; you think this is all a game and meanwhile Shanasee is trapped in a darkness she can't escape from and you don't even care."

Jerya felt like she'd been slapped. "Of course I care! I stayed with her, didn't I? She sent you to safety with her paintings, and I stayed with her."

"And look how little good you did! My poor Shan, destroying herself for your precious citizenry so you can bask their love every day. Yithiere questions you, doubts you, and you send him away. Seandri never argues, and you never risk him. You are *terrible*. You'll be a queen like your great-grandmother, oh yes, except you won't because this Blight will consume us—"

At this point one of the few Guards on watch in the parlour intervened, putting an arm around the weeping Regent and muttering to her comfortingly. He turned her away, back to the couch.

"She's very tired, ma'am," said Raffey, who looked like he'd just woken. His hair stood up straight. "She can't sleep alone and she can't sleep when she's near Princess Shanasee. So she naps in here, when she can."

"I didn't know that," Jerya said helplessly.

"The Chancellor does," Raffey said reassuringly. "That's his job, ma'am, not yours. Although we'll have to report this outburst to him. I suspect she needs more help than she's getting. Are you going out, ma'am?"

"Just for a walk, yes." She stared at Cara's crumpled form, wondering. Not if what she said was true: Jerya knew her own motivations and trusted them. Cara was only right in that Seandri was her favorite. Except for Tiana, she'd never loved anybody more—and Tiana was different, her little sister, a baby bird abandoned by her mother.

But she wondered if other people saw the situation as Cara did. If so, what could she could do to change that impression? There would be a way to win, if only she could see it.

All right, Cara was right about something else, too. "It *is* a game. But that doesn't make it frivolous."

"Very good, ma'am. Somebody will accompany you, as usual," said Raffey. "Enjoy your walk."

She went out into the night city. A guard followed discreetly behind her, far enough back that she had the illusion of being alone. She walked first to the plaza where she spent her days, the path already a habit, thinking about Cara's words and Seandri's choices and Yithiere's instability.

It was darker at night, but not as different as she expected. A woman leaned her head on the Tabernacle, still and silent, a long swathe of fabric in one hand. Jerya hesitated, then turned away. The biggest difference, she thought, between the Tabernacle at day and at night was that she wasn't there. Those who went there at night did not want to share their pain.

She walked to the river instead, to the Green Bridge, across from the catacombs exit. Looking across the water at the ruined city beyond, she shivered. If Vassay could restore much of what was lost, that would be something. But what would it cost Ceria? She'd seen already that they didn't give gifts without expectations of compensation, not to her. Many of them were consistently kind to the children, they were cheerful, enthusiastic and friendly. But they were all young, Jerya's age. Their leaders were older, and they viewed the Blood as an obstacle standing between them and unfettered access to the Citadel of the Sky. And maybe they didn't like that they were monarchs; maybe that was why they'd invited all the other people to the meeting. Vassay had monarchs once, before their revolution.

A shadow moved near her, and she turned her head absently. She expected to see her guard, but there was only a tree, moving in the breeze. She looked around for the guard and didn't see him. Puzzled, she moved away from the river's edge, searching for him. It was dark, but it was a clear night, with the Winter Crown still rising in the northeastern sky and both the bright spill of starlight and distant lamplight illuminated enough that Jerya was sure her guard was gone.

Her skin prickling again, Jerya reached in and stilled her rising fear, sent it into an emanation circling in her hand. It was not a response suitable for visiting diplomats because the link between thought and action was too tight, but oh, it was right for anybody who'd removed her guard. She remembered the monster, the Blighter, engulfing Iriss—

"Let's talk," said a voice right behind her. She whirled around and saw the man leaning against the bridge piling. He wore the Vassay work clothes she'd seen so much of lately, and he didn't seem to be armed. In the dim light she could just identify his finely featured face. It was the man called Thorn. Only a man, not one of the Blighter's monsters.

She exhaled. "Oh. It's you." The emanation evaporated from her hand as curiosity overtook her nerves. "My uncle says you're an assassin."

"I know," said Thorn dryly. "He's a perceptive man. Sometimes." He straightened up and moved toward her.

"Where's my guard?" Jerya asked, looking around and not backing away. She was wary, but she certainly wasn't going to show it.

"Your guard is having a bad night. It's the sort of night where he wakes up tomorrow morning, realizes how wretched he is at his job, and runs off to join the infantry under an assumed name. But right now he's resting someplace out of the way." His speech was smooth and calm, almost hypnotic. He stopped a little more than an arm's length away, which was probably too close. Yithiere would disapprove. "To be fair, he wasn't very good at noticing things behind him in the dark and he might be amazing at stabbing monsters right in front of him. So this is probably better for everybody." He tilted his head to one side. "Although I suppose it might leave you a little afraid for yourself?"

Jerya gave him a surprised look. "No, of course not. Any assassin who gives me time to be afraid is either wretched at *his* job or has something else on his mind." She gave him a crooked smile. "Besides, the last time my baby sister got away from her guard, she killed somebody." She did her best to imitate his slow, measured drawl. "It's possible that you've misunderstood the purpose of our guards. That's all right, you're a foreigner, it's an easy mistake."

A smile flickered across his expressionless face so fast she might have imagined it in the darkness. "I want to show you something."

Jerya wondered how long he'd wanted to show her something; if he'd made the decision to not try to kill her before or after he'd disabled her guard. A prickling at the back of her neck told her it was after, that she'd been a hairsbreadth from a bad night of her own. "Here?"

He shrugged. "Here, there. It doesn't matter where."

She narrowed her eyes. "All right. Normally my Court hours begin after breakfast, but since you've been so... creative in your approach, let's see it. Unless it's a weapon of some sort," she added conscientiously. "Then you ought to apply to my sister. I think she's started collecting them."

"We have to wait," he said, and stood there, arms loose at his side, waiting. "It won't be long now."

Jerya raised a hand and let the emanation she'd had curled there unfold. It shed only a faint, misty glow just brighter than starlight, but just brighter than starlight was enough to see him more clearly. She regarded him for a moment, as he looked back at her. "You're not actually from Vassay, are you? Although Scriber Stone knows what you are."

He remained perfectly still, as if she hadn't unfolded magic near him or even spoken. "You shouldn't mistake this as my employer's task. You are exactly the kind of danger they fear on the throne in Ceria. But I'm curious about something." That flickering smile appeared and disappeared again. "I'm not used to being curious."

Jerya ran the other nearby countries under rapid review. "Tylisse? They have an amiable relationship with Vassay but they've managed to stay independent."

He blinked at her and she felt smug. "No so amiable."

"Why do they care so much about who rules Ceria? Do they really think that somebody else on the throne would allow them more plepanin? The monks can only produce so much."

Thorn sighed and rubbed the bridge of his nose. "If the rulers of nations confided in me, they would be very odd." He glanced up at the stars and said, "Soon now."

Recklessly, Jerya said, "I don't think you're actually an assassin. I think you just like skulking around in the dark. Maybe you hold a special place in Scriber Stone's heart and that's why he looks at you so much."

He raised his eyebrows. "Believe what you want. If I happen to be an assassin, that will prove useful later. You can keep taking long starlit walks, with vanishing guards, until somebody notices." He shifted his weight, as if coiling himself. "No matter what you think, you are risking yourself right now."

Jerya ignored that last. "And Scriber Stone can keep making eyes at you across a crowded room, and bringing you along as his porter. It's sweet, really."

A frown touched his face. "He believes he is subtle. He has a few skills, but some of them are not where he believes. But it doesn't matter what he betrays. You're so very careless, despite your uncle's warnings."

Jerya was unsettled and nervous and *irritated*. She thought, *I should run away, back to my guards and lamplight and Seandri. I should make this into a bad dream.* Then she thought, *There is a challenge here.* "Why am I still alive? If you're so confident and I'm so careless—and yet somehow such a threat!"

"Oh, hush," was all he said, and it shocked her enough that she did. She wasn't sure anybody had ever told her to *hush*, not in so distracted a way. The Justiciar's Court had tried hard to shut her up but all their thundering disdain hadn't achieved what this man did with a single word.

"It's beginning," he said. "You won't feel it yet." He held out his hand to her. "It will be useful if you take my hand."

Jerya stared at his big, square hand. It didn't match his fine features at all. "Why?"

He didn't answer, leaving his hand outstretched.

"No," Jerya said, and took a step backward. It was one thing to stand her ground against an unexpected assault, and something else entirely to go around holding hands with an alleged assassin. It was... intimate.

"I must remember to tell my employers," he said dryly, "that an outstretched hand is all it takes to dismay you. Although that is consistent. You've disliked Vassay's outstretched hand as well."

"It's not actually stretched out to me," she muttered. "They're just trying to get inside our defenses."

His eyebrows went up again. "I don't need to hold hands with you to get inside your defenses, I promise. But you do as you please and so shall I."

Jerya scowled and grabbed his hand, trying to crush his fingers in her fist. It didn't work; his hands were too big. She felt like a baby clinging to a grown-up's fingers. Solemnly, he moved his hand so that they had a more traditional palm-to-palm clasp. His hand was dry and warm, with hard callouses along the edges of the palm and the bottom of his fingers.

He said nothing for several moments, which Jerya spent resisting the urge to pull her hand out of his and run into the night. Then he said, "Look around."

When she did, her grip on his hand tightened involuntarily. The night had grown darker. She looked up at the sky, and the stars were dimming. She could actually see the Winter Crown fading. The lamps in the houses along the street all seemed to lower their flames at once. Even the water lost its glint.

"What is this?" she asked, the emanation around her free hand swirling up to lift her hair. An eidolon fluttered from her breast, its own ghostlight untouched by the fading.

Thorn looked curiously at the falcon as he said, "It happens every night."

Jerya remembered a Council session when three scholars had presented their findings on a change in their timekeeping: according to their measurements, the nights were getting longer and the days shorter. It was, Jerya had assumed, like the seasonal shifts, but on some epochal scale.

"Oh," she said. "I didn't realize it was like this."

"Wait," he said. "Wait, and remember that you are not falling asleep."

But as it got darker and darker, Jerya wondered that exact thing. It was so much like dozing off. What other rational explanation could there be for the dark fog stealing all the light? At one point Thorn squeezed her hand gently, then squeezed it again harder. When that didn't get the reaction he apparently wanted, he ran his thumb around her wrist, stroking the sensitive skin on the underside of her arm.

The touch sent a shock running up her arm and straight down her spine. She lifted her head, eyes wide and stared in his direction. She could barely see the shadows of his face against the deeper darkness. "Stay awake," he said softly. "Once it's entirely dark, be ready."

"I'm awake, believe me," she muttered, and started to ask what kind of readiness he expected when she realized that the ghostlight from her magical manifestations was fading, too. The eidolon itself seemed fine, according to the invisible thread that connected then. But as the emanation light faded, so did its power, until it was barely more than a breath of channeled wind.

She didn't mention that to Thorn.

She could see nothing; it was like she was in the deepest of catacombs without a single glimmer of light. Thorn squeezed her hand again, maintaining an almost painful pressure this time. "Here it comes," he said.

A heavy blackness engulfed the world. It pulled the ground away from her feet like the earth was nothing but a dream. It swept away the tiny bird on her shoulder, spinning it back into magic. Yet Thorn held her hand and so she knew she stood still in a world where almost every sensation had been clogged by this assault of darkness. A hot breeze blew, bringing her the scents of salt and rotting vegetation. And in her ear, Thorn whispered, "What of your magic now?"

Fear clutched at her chest. She brought eidolons into existence easily. She felt them fly out of her chest and into the warm wind. But she saw nothing. They vanished into the darkness, spun of her magic but beyond her reach or control. Then she sent out emanations, waves that should have shattered the air with their sound, but there was only silence.

"Your magic," he whispered. "Can it touch this darkness?"

"I'm—" she began, then stopped. "Yes," she said carefully. The truth was complicated, and not for sharing with him.

He made a sound that might have been a chuckle, too close to her ear, and she reminded herself to start carrying a knife. If she was unarmed for a portion of every day, she needed to acquire a different skill set. Every muscle in her body twanged as she tried to read his intentions. He still held her hand and she could feel the warmth of his body near hers, a stillness in the breeze.

There was something odd about her magic, and the way it worked and didn't at the same time. But she couldn't concentrate, couldn't study it. She was too achingly aware of the assassin beside her, holding her hand like they were courting. An idea occurred to her. She oriented herself toward him and fumbled until she found his other hand. It was empty, and she laced her fingers into his.

There. Now she was restrained, but so was he. He wasn't going to hold her with one hand and stab her with his other. At least if he made any sudden moves, she'd know, and she could kick him. Alanah would be proud.

His fingers tightened on her as he laughed. It was an odd, rusty sound. "I see. I was ready for you to pull away and flee into the darkness, but that doesn't fit you, does it? Don't worry, little falcon. The eye will end soon. Only a minute or two before it passes and the light begins to return."

"I'm not worried now," she told him. "The eye? It's looking at us?" Her skin prickled more, which she didn't think was possible.

"The eye, the heart, the center. Though this breeze does feel like something exhaling, don't you think?"

And then once again, all of Jerya's magic vanished, as if cut by a knife. The warm breeze faded and the previous mild coolness reasserted itself. The lights began to sparkle again, first at the corner of her eyes and flickering out when she looked directly at them.

"Was that... how long was that?" She shook her head. Her sense of the passage of time had been utterly warped by adrenalin and outright fear.

"Only a few minutes. The fading of the light has been going on for.... Years, I understand. The eye, the heart of the darkness has only been there for a matter of months."

An uncontrollable shudder ran up her spine and down her arms. Her magic burst around her again, an emanation flaring around her shoulders like a mantle. It felt odd, like she had an eidolon out, but without the sense of a part of her being distant.

Slowly Thorn became visible, first as a deeper darkness against the returning glow of the city. She'd never realized how bright the city was at night.

"It is very much like falling asleep and having a strange dream," she admitted. "I think I even saw it in the past—the fading, anyhow—and thought it was sleep. Thank you for showing me the truth." She glanced down at their linked hands, then tugged at hers.

He didn't let go. "Distrust me a few moments more, Princess."

She stopped tugging, curious, but he didn't go on, the silhouette of his head tilted toward hers as the stars brightened overhead.

"Thank you," she repeated, "But I'm a little at a loss as to why you showed me that."

"As I said, it was a self-indulgence. I was curious about something. And how well my curiosity has been rewarded. Perhaps I'll indulge myself again sometime."

"*Are* you some kind of assassin?" she asked. "Or just a mysterious half-breed with a sense for the dramatic?"

Once again, he didn't bother to give her a direct answer. "It's true that you're still a threat. Whatever that darkness is doesn't change that you are a very particular kind of problem for my employers."

"I think you *must* be bad at your job," she added in irritation, and tugged at her hands again.

This time he let her pull her hands through his fingers, slowly letting her go. "I'm not," he said, almost regretfully. "But I'm allowed some discretion as to whether you match the criteria I've been given. I've been evaluating you."

"And I'm a threat, yes, I certainly hope so, thus why are we standing here talking?"

He raised one of his hands, splay-fingered, toward her neck, and she stepped quickly out of range.

"The darkness is concerning," he admitted. "But there are more immediate troubles. The armies of your Blighter are moving."

"How do you know?" she demanded sharply.

"You'll get the news soon," he said, shrugging and stepping backwards himself.

She scowled. "And you think my magic will be useful against him. Well—"

He cut her off. "No. I don't. I think your magic is far too weak to do anything about this Blight. No. The threat you present is different." His rusty laugh came again. "But if you don't know what it is, I really shouldn't tell you. Goodbye,

Princess. I'll be seeing you." Then he turned and walked away, vanishing into the night, leaving Jerya to wonder what kind of threat Vassay found more terrifying than a Blight.

CHAPTER SIXTEEN

THE FOREST DANCE

EVEN IF YOU'RE not on the road, you're still waiting on their pleasure,** pointed out Jinriki, scathingly. It was the afternoon after Fai's visit and nothing, absolutely nothing had happened.

Tiana sat beside the tiny campfire, feeding it sticks in a desultory fashion. **I'm not. I'm waiting on Her pleasure.** She went to bed the night before certain that the morning would bring somebody in charge to help her sort things out. Now, after a day of idleness, she was no longer sure.

Perhaps in the spirit of your Running holiday, she wants you to chase the light down and take it.

Tiana scowled. **Maidrunning is about taking what's offered freely.**

After you run it down so that it has no other choice. Jinriki's satisfaction was palpable.

No! That's not right. Tiana thought of the holiday, which had always been a playful spring event for her. A race, a scavenger hunt, dancing: all outside in the warm sun after the chill of winter. If lots of people got up to other, less official activities after the dancing and racing, well, that was part of spring, too. **It's a game. A kind of tag.**

Then we should go tag the light.

No. The light is all around us. We've tagged Her. She's It.

Jinriki stopped arguing, which should have made Tiana feel victorious and didn't. Instead she felt cross and bored. The stable girls had most of the soldiers inspecting and cleaning tack and organizing the supplies the mules had carried. They didn't ask her to do any of the chores, though the loud stable girl had given Tiana a speculative look before being dragged off by her companion.

She knew she ought to go over and ask for work to do; she was sure they'd assign it if she asked. The girls treated Cathay like the soldiers. Lisette helped organize the mules' packs, and Kiar was, all right, she was reading again but at least she was busy. But Tiana couldn't seem to summon the energy. She found it easier to just to poke the fire and wonder where she'd gone wrong in acquiring the green light.

Maybe they ought to leave and come back later. But the red light slept within the green, whatever that meant, and the golden light was diffuse and far away. No, Tiana could tell this was where the Firstborn wanted her to be.

Lisette came and sat down beside her, offering her a candied fruit bar. "I found this in the pack and saved it for you."

Tiana watched one of the stable girls go by. "Give it to her. She's working. I'm just wasting time."

Lisette gave her a curious look, then stood again and delivered the treat. The stable girl—the quiet one—glanced at Tiana, ducked her head and went on about her errand. Tiana wondered if she'd eat it herself, or give it to the horses.

She'll split it with her partner, and they'll each sneak some to their favorite horse, Jinriki informed her. **Humans who work with animals have such ordered minds. It's almost as restful as the earth fiend.**

Tiana stole a glance at Minex, also sitting beside the fire on the other side of Jinriki. She played with a small stick, turning it over and over in her hands. Sometimes she burped, and giggled softly. Or she muttered to herself in a babyish voice. Occasionally she touched Jinriki's handle, which nobody other than Tiana did safely.

Tiana thought, **I don't know how you can find her restful. She's barely restrained chaos.**

So are you, he pointed out, and it stung because it was true.

"I can't wait here anymore," she announced when Lisette rejoined her. "We *should* but I can't. I'm going to lose my head about something sooner or later and I'd rather it be part of a plan."

Lisette said, "Rene, that's one of the Guardsmen, he has some experience in forests like this. He says he thinks there's a fair number of people living in the shelter of the wood."

"I suppose there are ways to tell these things," said Tiana, while wondering what 'forests like this' meant. Haunted holy forests? Forests with big trees? "Maybe we can lure them out?"

Cautiously, Lisette asked, "What do you have in mind? I think we should try to stay friendly for now."

Minex began humming to herself. It was pleasant, which annoyed rather than pleased Tiana. "I'm *trying*, Lisette. That's why we're sitting here rather than on the road. But we could build a bigger fire? And maybe..." She gnawed on her lip, thinking. When the Regency wanted people to connect, it held the cookie receptions, and other gatherings. "Maybe we could have some sort of party? Or at least find something fun for everybody to do? Even Kiar comes out for the cookie receptions when she's home."

Lisette's smile washed away the concern on her face. "That's a lovely idea." She glanced at Minex. "You're right. We have plenty of supplies and if we all enjoy ourselves, I think the inhabitants of the forest will be curious. We'll need music, too."

"And stories," suggested Minex. "I can make music." She turned her stick sideways and it became a pipe the length of her arm. She gave Tiana a fanged grin, brushed her fingers across Jinriki's blade, then brought the pipe to her mouth and blew a trill that danced down Tiana's spine to her feet.

She looked around and saw Cathay's dark head in the next clearing over. He turned and met her gaze as the earth fiend blew another trill. Tiana smiled. "We can dance. Everybody loves dancing."

Almost as soon as Lisette announced Tiana's plan, the quiet afternoon became a flurry of activity. Slater built up the fire. It wasn't quite a bonfire but it wasn't a discreet little cook fire, either. Other men cut back what brush remained in the clearing, expanding the edges back to the tree trunks. Lisette directed Kiar and Tiana and the guard Rene in turning foraged material into more little treats. They had no skill at cookery, but Lisette at least had taste, and it turned out mushrooms with cheese melted onto them were really delicious. And Berrin raided the small casks they carried and his own previously-secret stash to put together a weak punch.

"It won't make anybody more than tipsy before they have to —" he caught himself and changed track, "Well, it's more

for the flavor than anything else. To add to the atmosphere."
He offered Tiana a cup.

She tried some. It tasted like watery fruit juice with
some spices added, but it made her smile all the same. "It's
wonderful."

Minex sat beside the fire while they prepared, softly
playing strange music. It brought an otherworldly air to the
whole plan and for the first time since Minex had stolen
Jinriki, Tiana felt kindly toward the earth fiend. She wanted
Fel Dion to feel like another world, to feel magical and sacred.
Instead she'd found... a big, unfriendly forest. Bugs and
bumpy ground and strange sounds at night and boredom.
But Minex's music made the act of melting cheese and
cleaning a clearing feel like part of a ritual. Soon something
would happen.

Fai and his people would come. She knew they would.
Everybody would enjoy themselves and the Light of Atalya
would manifest. Or—she was trying to control her usual
optimism—Fai would introduce her to this Voice and she'd
find out what she had to do next.

Cathay put his hand on her shoulder and she jumped; she
hadn't realized he was close. The loss of the phantasmagory
changed so much; she'd never even realized before how the
ripples of the space told her when her relatives were near.
Every time Cathay touched her now, at first she thought it
was a stranger. It was odd and exciting.

He smiled at her. "Where's your chaperone?"

Tiana spotted Jinriki resting across Minex's knees,
sheathed. She hesitated. She didn't like Minex stealing Jinriki,
but she didn't like Jinriki harassing Cathay, either. If Minex's
company soothed Jinriki enough that Cathay could ask such
a question, that was good, right?

She wasn't sure.

Minex's song shifted from something sweet and slow to a spritely dancing tune and Tiana realized how dark the clearing had become. The sun might still be setting beyond the canopy but it was deep twilight beneath. Her fingers twitched, and Cathay took her hand.

You wish to dance? inquired Jinriki, in a distant, flat voice. **Very well. I will watch the perimeter.** She felt him withdraw from her, like once again he'd been taken far away.

Minex's song skipped and stopped as she trailed her fingers lightly down the blade. Then the earth fiend looked directly at Tiana, smiled and winked encouragingly. "Dance, yes! Everybody will dance, and the Great Prince will make sure no nasty darklings sneak up on you at your revels. You!" she said to Cathay. "Take the Princess and dance with her!"

She started playing again, and Cathay pulled Tiana to the other side of the fire and into the dance forming there. It was just Lisette and Slater, and Berrin and Kiar at first. Then the two stable girls joined them, and four soldiers formed a bachelor's square, and it started to feel like a proper party.

Dancing with Cathay was *fun*. Tiana hadn't truly enjoyed herself since Tomas had died, and she hadn't danced with Cathay since he started methodically working his way through the beds of all the other girls she knew. She'd been a little girl like Gisen the last time he danced with her like this. It was a different kind of pleasure now. Her breath caught in her throat as he caught her around the waist and they spun together, and her heart hammered in her chest as it had when he'd warmed her in the fiend's prison.

She'd been running from him ever since he first regarded her with that light in his eyes. Now she wondered why. Even if it couldn't last forever—even if whatever drove him wouldn't let it last forever—opening up enough to enjoy herself was wonderful.

The third tune came to a drifting end, and Tiana awoke from the haze of the dance when Lisette appeared beside her. She touched Tiana's arm lightly, but it was Cathay she spoke to. "You owe me a dance, my friend."

Cathay looked at her and smiled, though something sad touched his eyes. "All right. Just one, though. I've waited too long to see Tiana smiling like this." He kissed Tiana's fingers, before releasing her to take Lisette's hand.

Lisette considered Tiana, then said, "Berrin, come dance with Tiana." The big Guardsman loomed out of the shadows like he'd been waiting for the call.

"Would you honor me, Your Highness?"

"Happily," Tiana said and took his hand. But she was delayed in stepping back into the dance, because so many more people were dancing now. There were at least a dozen more dancers, young people in rags and sticks and mud. They danced with each other with an abandon that made the guards' bachelor square seem positively staid.

Two of them split off from the main group and pulled two of the guards and the stable girls into a square formation Tiana recognized. The forest girl turned and met Tiana's eye in a clear invitation. She tugged Berrin's hand, and the two of them joined the square. She thought the forest girl was the one who'd been in the tree with Fai the day before. Maybe after the dance she could steal a moment to find Fai, too. They could take a break from the dancing and she'd convince him to help her.

The music started again and she had no time to plan. She knew the dance; it was called the petal dance for the way the dancers folded together and out again. But it wasn't a dance commonly performed at the Regency Court, which encouraged couples-dances. The forest girl knew it perfectly, and her partner was almost as deft. Berrin knew a bit, and so did the loud stable girl. There were just enough skilled dancers to tip the square into 'enjoyable' rather than 'painful'. But Tiana had to concentrate.

When they made their final turns and bowed to each other, the music once again faded into the crackling of the fire. Tiana realized her square was at the center of a larger circle. Both the guards and forest children laughed and cheered for the petal dancers. Without any real problems, as if the Regency Court planned it, people drank and laughed and enjoyed themselves.

She turned to exchange a smile with the girl who initiated the petal dance, but she was gone already. Tiana's half-formed smile faded, then renewed itself when Cathay stepped out of the circle and reached for her hand again. But she said, "Wait a moment. I want to talk to some of my guests."

He nodded and kept her hand in his. "I could use a break. Minex plays like a fiend." He looked disconcerted as his own words caught up with him.

"Well, she is one," Tiana couldn't help pointing out anyhow. "Where's Lisette?" She spotted her Regent near the edge of the clearing and towed Cathay over to her. "Lisette, have you found Fai yet?"

Lisette was peering at the edge of the forest. She jumped when Tiana spoke. "What? Oh, I saw him near the fire." She gestured back toward Minex.

"What are you looking at?" Tiana asked, looking into the darkness. It might as well have been a stage curtain for all she saw.

"I thought I saw somebody. Not one of the forest people. A big man, in armor?"

"Berrin?" Tiana suggested, although Berrin had removed most of his armor for the dancing.

Lisette shook her head. "Maybe it was just a curl of smoke or something."

Tiana tugged her hand away from Cathay and spread her fingers. "Jinriki's watching for enemies, but I'm curious." She sent out emanation ribbons and swept them through the near forest. Everything she encountered felt pretty tree-like, but she closed her eyes to better concentrate on what the emanations were telling her.

She felt so pleasantly floaty, as if Berrin's punch had actually had some kick to it. The green light surrounded her, still diffuse and uncatchable, but almost tangible. It was a spicy freshness, a wildness: joy and passion and the moment. It was desire without sacrifice, pure abandon. It combined with Minex's song to flow through her. Her emanations changed, became like the wind, and her awareness traveled with the breeze.

It danced past the man Lisette had seen: a bearded man in a leather hauberk with some metal plates, with a sword and a small axe at his hip. He leaned against a tree, watching the light of the clearing with a casually interested air. Despite his weapons, he didn't seem threatening, and Tiana the breeze swirled on.

As the wind, she danced through the forest children, looking for Fai. She found Kiar lurking near the food tent, and a cluster of guards around the punch. The horses were well-fed but restless, the exuberance of the party influencing even them.

Navigating the pull of the air currents near the fire

challenged her control. But she focused and made her way to Minex and Jinriki. As she passed over them, Jinriki's voice tickled the back of her mind, a distant whisper not aimed at her.

I don't like it. If she lets him in, she won't attend to me.

Shh, Great Prince. She will attend better if she has formed a pair. And you will not be so confused by her. You will both focus better.

Yes. You've said. It's not working.

No, no! It is! You see, she enjoys herself and that rejuvenates her. You must protect her, yes?

Then the Tiana-wind drifted past the curious conversation. She blew over Fai, who crouched down beside the earth fiend, watching her.

Tiana closed her distant fingers and collapsed the emanation. With no more transition than turning a page, she looked out of her own eyes again. Lisette held her arm lightly, as she did when Tiana was in the phantasmagory.

Frowning, Tiana said, "I wonder if that was an eidolon experience...? It was strange. Where's Kiar? Wait, no, I need to talk to Fai. He's over there."

Cathay took her hand again. "I'll come with you. And after, we can dance again." He looked at Tiana with enough warmth that heat rushed to her cheeks and her skin felt tight.

"All right," she managed.

Cathay's fingers tightened on her hand and his smile flickered. Noise rose from the second clearing: raised voices. Tiana barely paid any attention, turning to pull Cathay over to the main fire.

Fai was still there. He sat so he could watch both the earth fiend and the dancers, but he didn't notice her approaching.

"Hello," she called to him, and he looked toward her. Then somebody stumbled between the two of them and fell on the ground. One of the forest people. Tiana realized he'd been pushed.

Looking around wildly, she desperately hoped it wasn't one of her own people doing the pushing. No. It was another of the guests, looking belligerent. "She's exactly what—" he began to shout at the fallen youth.

Tiana didn't stay to listen. A window of opportunity was closing. She plunged past the argument toward Fai.

He stood as she approached and asked urgently, "Where's my sister?"

"Did you talk to your leader—the Voice?" Tiana demanded right back. "Wait. Who's your sister?"

Fai narrowed his eyes, as if she'd said something stupid, then glanced around. "I'll talk to you later. I have to find my sister first. There's—That fight—" he shook his head and started walking off.

Tiana reached for his arm and her sense of the green light instantly faded away. It so shocked her that she gasped and recoiled, and just like that, the green light returned.

Fai vanished into the crowd beyond. There was less dancing and more roiling now. Somehow people were getting drunk on that weak punch.

Minex finished her song and said earnestly, "You two, go explore the shadows again? Perhaps just the two of you?"

"If she wants to, maybe," said Cathay. "What happened a moment ago, stormy?"

Tiana shook her head. She didn't understand it and she didn't want to think about it. She'd have to chase Fai down again, after he found his damned sister—was that the girl from the petal dance? Probably.

Another surge of noise swelled from the second campfire, and Minex glanced over there. "*Not* what I was playing for." Her fingers danced over Jinriki. "Out of practice. And the Great Prince is a big torch to juggle, oh yes. You will not go? I will make it nice."

Tiana looked at Minex, astonished. Then the noise at the second campfire became a woman screaming.

It is only a human argument, growled Jinriki.

"That's not good either!" Tiana pulled away from Cathay again and ran toward the noise. As she did, the entire party changed. The atmosphere of conviviality utterly vanished. Laugher died around her as she dodged through the crowd. People turned toward the screaming.

It wasn't anguished or pained screaming. It was angry. One of the stable girls shouted at one of the young men from the forest.

A wave of rage pulsed through Tiana and she knew enough now to recognize it as coming from Jinriki, not herself. She still itched to have his hilt in her hand, though.

"What? What is it?"

One of the guards near her pushed somebody else. The joy of the dance was transforming into something much uglier, so quickly it felt like a nightmare.

We performed an experiment. It failed. Jinriki's voice was flat and awful.

Slater waded into the middle of the argument, calm, steady Slater, apparently unmoved by the shifting mood of the gathering. He separated the two fighters, breaking their line of sight.

Minex started playing again. It was soft, barely audible at first, and it wasn't a dance tune. At first it was only a few familiar notes. Then Lisette started singing the nonsense cradle song called the Dreamsong and Minex's song became an accompaniment.

Lisette had always sung that song to Tiana. When she woke at night as a child with nightmares about her mother, and her dead uncles and aunts. When she couldn't sleep after an exciting day. She'd always associated it with warmth and safety and rest, and now all those memories hit her like a brick between the eyes.

Jinriki's rage ebbed, and the fights breaking out around her died stillborn. A guard rubbed his eyes and looked around, then wandered off. Three of the forest children walked dazedly into the shadows.

Tiana didn't understand what was going on. She knew she should, that it was obvious. It was right in front of her. But all she wanted to do was sleep.

Yes. Sleep. This was a mistake. Sleep, before it gets worse.

Tiana stumbled to her tent and slept.

CHAPTER SEVENTEEN

THE VOICE OF ATALYA

A
T MINEX'S DEMAND, Lisette sang to soothe the crowd, and singing, fell asleep herself. She woke up in the tent she shared with Tiana and Kiar, tucked under her blankets, certain the entirety of the day before had been a dream.

Completely waking up was hard. Her head ached and her throat hurt. She put her hand over her eyes and said, "We mustn't let Minex play music for us. No parties, either. I've had a foreboding."

Tiana, curled on her side with her eyes still closed, said, "I don't know. I thought parts were nice." The sword Jinriki rested near her back, scabbarded and quiet.

Kiar sat with her back to the wall of the tent. "The parts where the earth fiend used her magic to influence our minds, or the parts where all the fights started breaking out?"

Lisette rubbed her eyes and dragged herself out of her blankets. She'd really *wanted* it to be a dream, she thought wistfully. Things had been complicated enough yesterday morning. But no. That's not how being a Regent worked.

As she dragged a brush through her hair, Tiana sat up as well. "What do you mean, Minex used her magic?" She was being stubborn; Lisette could tell from her tone of voice that she knew exactly what Kiar meant.

"Lord of Winter, Tiana. You've had enough people messing around in your head by now that you ought to notice these things. Or maybe you can't anymore?" Kiar's angry voice dropped away as she actually thought about what she was saying. Lisette flinched on Tiana's behalf.

But Tiana said, "Did *you* notice? *Nobody* seemed to notice."

Lisette had time to change her stockings before Kiar said, "I noticed. But it seemed harmless. You wanted to have a party. I didn't think she'd hurt anybody. I didn't *think*."

"Nobody got hurt. At least, I don't think anybody got hurt. I'm fine, Kiar," Tiana added sharply.

"Minds aren't meant to be splash pools for whatever fiend or Firstborn comes along, I'm pretty sure," Kiar muttered. "We need to do something about the fiend so she doesn't dare do this again."

"No!" said Tiana. "No. Jinriki says to leave her alone. He says it's his fault. And I did suggest the party."

"Minex says dance. Jinriki says leave her alone. What does Tiana say?" Kiar demanded.

Lisette turned around. "Lisette says don't argue on an empty stomach, please. Change your stockings, both of you, and let's see if we can find something that doesn't require much cooking."

The cousins stared at each other belligerently instead. Lisette pursed her lips, then let herself out of the tent and stood in front of the entrance. The campsite was a mess and nobody was doing anything about it. Cathay, sitting in front of the fire, looked up and then came over to her.

"How is she?" he asked in a low voice.

"They're both capable of arguing, so you're going to stay out," she said firmly. "Tiana has enough people trying to influence her right now."

"I behaved last night," Cathay protested mildly. "She wanted me to be a gallant, and I was. It was easy, even." He looked so proud of himself.

Lisette shook her head. "Is that lump by the fire Minex?" She glanced around. There were a few other lumps in the clearing, too; whoever had put her to bed hadn't been as considerate of the guards who decided to curl up where they were standing.

"Yes, it is," said Cathay. "She won't wake up, either. I wanted to ask her about the music."

"Can you wake the sleeping guards?"

Cathay shrugged. "They groan when you poke them, so sure." He didn't move, though, as if she'd asked a theoretical question. She gave him a long, cool look, and he said, "So I'll be going to wake the guards, shall I? They're probably uncomfortable anyhow."

When he was gone, Lisette said softly, "Jinriki? What happened?"

She had good intentions, the earth fiend, he said. **I will be displeased if anybody else punishes her for them. That is all you need to know.**

That is not all I need to know! Her music was intoxicating. Literally. And then she used my song to make everybody pass out.

Yes, I was there.

"It matters," Lisette whispered. "I prefer to be asked. You all keep defaulting to using magic to sort these things out and it doesn't need to be that way."

**You have hands, a voice and a pretty face, little Regent. I have my mind, my magic and a sharp edge. **

"Yes, but she's got everything I have and some of what you have, too," pointed out Lisette. "If she's going to travel with us she needs to learn."

**Go find food, little Regent. Feed my princess. Do human things. Your whining is boring me. **

Kiar's voice drifted from the tent, "—just saying that you can't know you're not being hurt. You can't just go along with what people tell you to do in the hopes they'll approve of you, Tiana—"

Suddenly Lisette couldn't bear it anymore. The constant bickering between all three cousins, the single-minded focus of Cathay, the withdrawal of Tiana and the brooding of Kiar. She was just one Regent alone. Managing three of the Blood, and a fiendish sword and his earth fiend pet, it was too much for anyone.

She yanked the tent open and said, "Cathay is waking the men. Make one of them cook. I'm going for a morning walk. Please, try not to kill each other while I spend five minutes alone." Then she jerked the tent closed again, and walked away from the camp, all without actually looking at the charges part of her already felt she was abandoning.

Nobody followed her. Short walks into the forest first thing in the morning were expected, after all. This was just going to be a short walk. The Chancellor of the Regency had taught Lisette that while it was her job to be patient and understanding and sensitive and a good counselor, it was best for everybody if she occasionally took time for herself.

It had been so easy in Lor Seleni, though. Tiana was her best friend; usually, spending time with her was a pleasure. When Lisette wanted to go out alone, it was easy enough to arrange. Iriss and the other Regents liked Tiana too. She could safely leave Tiana alone reading a book, or taking a nap.

Now every time she turned around, something was about to explode, and at the same time, she felt lonelier than ever before.

She missed having somebody to talk to whom she wasn't responsible for. An equal, independent and interested. Somehow *everything* had changed when Tomas died.

The walk was nice, anyhow. That is, it took just enough focus to avoid twisting her ankle that she couldn't spare much for worrying. It turned out reading about woodland adventures did very little to prepare you for the real thing. Fairy tales rarely talked about the bumpy ground. She had excellent boots, but they were made for riding. Walking on ground full of twigs and roots did require attention.

Yet it wasn't as unpleasant as it could have been. It was cold and overcast beyond the canopy but not raining, and the old leaves and ferns made the air smell pleasant, even by the privy pit. Alongside the narrow neck of the campsite, it felt pleasantly isolated. The sounds of the rousing campsite tapered off. She couldn't even hear the argument at all, and she tried to convince herself it was already over. But at best she expected Tiana had gone off to sulk, with Kiar trailing behind, unwilling to give up.

A blossoming vine hung from a branch to her left and she paused to examine the flowers, wary of any stinging insects. The pink and orange blooms had a refreshing cinnamon scent. Thoughtfully, she broke off some stems. She could do worse than collect seeds for the gardens back home. Especially given that they'd have to be completely replanted, maybe in a whole new location.

A hissing startled her, and she froze, the flowers halfway to her nose. Something yowled long and low, like the cry of the sky fiend they'd faced the other day. Lisette stumbled backwards, looking around frantically. Leaves and trees and fallen wood—there! A yellow and black wildcat crouched in some underbrush below the hanging vine, its teeth bared and shockingly white.

Her questing foot stepped on something that broke and twisted. She had time to think, *I was doing so well, too*, before her head cracked against an unexpected tree. Darkness fluttered around her and she flailed to stop herself from falling further, to protect her torso from any branches. Then she was curled up on the ground, staring at a tiny growth of moss that had spread like a crack in glass.

She pushed herself to a sitting position, her head aching. An exploratory touch came back with crimson on her fingers, and a new surge of pain. She tried to cry out for help, but her tongue didn't work right, and after a single attempt she gave up. Shame swelled up, almost as fast as the bump on her head. She would be the one who got into trouble in the woods. She was helpless here, far away from the glitter of the Court.

Using the tree that had so painfully broken her fall, she climbed to her feet again and set out in the direction of the camp. After only a few steps, though, she turned around and staggered back the way she came. She needed more time before she could walk straight. Best not to get lost meanwhile. She put her hand on the tree again, but this time the bark was smooth, and there were no flowering vines. She squeezed her eyes shut against the ache in her skull and peered into the distance. Maybe it was that tree over there? Hard, rough bark under her fingers, but shouldn't there be a mark where she'd bloodied her head?

She entertained the dizzy thought that the tree had absorbed her blood, before fear began to percolate through her stunned perceptions. How could she be lost so close to camp? She concentrated on untangling her tongue. "Hello?" *Hello.*

"Anybody? Help?" ... *help?*

"Please!" she shrieked, the sound a splinter in her skull. And again came back the odd muffled echo ...*Please!* There was nothing else at all, no flutter of startled birds, no wildcat's hiss.

Perhaps she'd already scared them all away. That made sense. She was sensible. She needed to stay put and wait for somebody to find her. Preferably a friend. It was her job to be sensible, even through an aching head.

Sensible... whispered the echo, though she hadn't said the word.

Despite her intentions, she ran. Sensible only worked when the forest wasn't full of monsters.

She burst into a clearing with a campsite. But there was no Tiana, no Kiar, and the men sitting around several campfires seemed far rougher than the Regency guards. They'd all removed their Regency tabards, too.

She wavered to a stop in front of two big men standing near the edge of the clearing, and took in the fierce bearded faces and the abundance of swords and axes. One of them said something, although the words made no sense. She remembered looking into the darkness the night before and seeing the same man. She hesitated, wondering again if everything was a dream. The other scowled and reached out for her. She didn't know him. Letting him grab her was unthinkable. She gasped an apology and turned and fled.

Wrong camp. Who were they? Where were they? Where had the forest taken her? She tripped and rolled, leaving part of her skirt behind, and climbed to her feet behind another tree. She could hear water. They'd camped near a stream, and the little voice raging inside insisted that water was good.

She found herself with wet feet. A stream trickled over a rock outcropping into a stone-lined pool, and thirst burned her throat. She drank. The water was cold and clean; the stones stretched all the way to the dark depths, like a natural fountain. She felt her skull again and, before she had time to reconsider, dunked her entire head under the water. The injury stung and burned but when she pulled her head out again, she could think clearly. The stinging faded to a dull, distant pain as she squeezed water out of her hair and looked around.

The trees were... trees. They seemed like the same kind of trees they'd placed their camp among. A large white owl perched on the other side of the pool, looking at her with one eye.

"Aren't you out early?" she asked it, and was relieved to hear no strange echo.

In response, the owl flapped over to her. She raised her arms to ward it off, and it settled onto her fist. It was far lighter than it looked, but very warm. Its gnarled toes and talons only pressed lightly against her skin, but it seemed to have a stable perch all the same.

She tried to toss it back into the air. Its grip grew more painful before it flapped into the air and returned to its previous perch on a rock outcrop. It stepped back and forth uneasily before settling its feathers.

"I don't think you're here to help me find my way back," Lisette told it, and turned to leave the clearing. With a surprisingly human cry, the owl leapt into the air again, flying to intercept her. She kept her arms close to her sides, and her face down, but the owl landed on her head instead. The talons clenched on her injury and the sudden rush of pain made her sink to her knees. There was another burst of pain as it hopped off her head, to her shoulder and down to the ground.

"What do you want?" Lisette whispered. It hopped back and forth again. Lisette rubbed her eyes with the heels of her hand, wiping away a blur of moisture. "Shall I follow you instead?" The owl flew back to the rock, turned its head around to look at her, and then flew to a branch. That seemed clear enough. Slowly, very carefully, she picked her way after it.

The creature didn't go far. The trees changed, becoming smooth-trunked and graceful. The green and gold fallen leaves crunched under her feet, and flowers glittered on vines. Beyond a particularly lovely pair of matched trees was a natural arbor with a stone shrine. On the far side of the shrine stood a pale androgynous statue on a pedestal, head bowed, hands clasped.

The owl flew into the statue, like an eidolon returning to its creator, and the stone shape breathed. Its head lifted and emerald eyes burned. Great feathered wings erupted from its shoulders and flexed. Lisette finally wondered if she was even conscious, or if she was lying on the ground where she'd cracked her skull.

The creature said, "Lisette," in a golden voice and spread its hands. She shuddered like a plucked harp string and knew, in the place inside where her soul was bound to the heavens, that she was in the presence of a Secondborn. Not a confused or broken-down Secondborn like Jinriki and the sky fiends were supposed to be. She'd always wondered about that, but here there was no question. This was the child of a god. Trembling, she curtsied, and remained low. She'd felt on the brink for a while but now she knew she'd finally stumbled into a world where only fairy tales and myths could be her guide.

It regarded her with undisguised amusement. "I am known as the Voice of Atalya. Welcome."

Cold prickles danced down Lisette's spine. "I'm honored, Your Highness." She met its blazing gaze. It knew her name. She wondered what else it knew about her.

It brought its hands together again and said, "Do you enjoy games, Lisette?"

She picked her words with care, because even in the grip of religious awe, she wasn't going to dance into more trouble. Words were key in the fairy tales.

Follow instructions precisely.
Be careful what you promise.
Do what you say you'll do.
Don't lie.

"I have in the past. It depends on the game." After a hesitation, she added, "Tiana enjoys them more. I like results." She felt certain that Tiana should be here with her. Tiana loved the fairy tales. Tiana was the Blood Princess. Tiana had already been chosen by Niyhan. Why was the Voice of Atalya talking to *her*?

The Secondborn favored her with an illuminated smile. "That's good, don't you think? Are you Tiana's guardian, Lisette?"

That was an odd way of putting it. *But what isn't odd*

right now? "Yes, Your Highness. Not of her body, but her mind."

"Her soul." It inclined its head and tiny flowers bloomed in its white stone hair. "My Lady Atalya is also fond of games." It said the Firstborn's name like a prayer, a caress.

Lisette nodded fractionally, waiting to see where the Secondborn was going.

"Like a child, she views all the world as a game. But now, somebody has decided to wreck the game. What do you do, little guardian, when a game is no longer enjoyable?"

Lisette stared at the living statue. *Stop playing.* But she couldn't bring herself to say the words, couldn't believe that was what the Voice meant. But the Voice regarded her in a long silence, until Lisette understood silence wasn't an option. "If I could, I'd fix the game. If I couldn't, I'd find something else to do."

The Voice dipped its head again. "The Lady of Spring finds herself in such a situation. Some petition her to play the game differently, treat this foolish destroyer as a true player. Other supplicants beg her not to risk herself in a confrontation with something that obeys no rules. For if you change the way you play, the game itself changes. Even if the rule breaker is removed from the game, others will come. The game cannot be the same again." It lowered its blazing gaze to its hands, flexing long fingers. "You see her dilemma."

Lisette wondered if this was a Secondborn after all, or some kind of new evil eidolon sent to spread despair. "But she will find an answer. She wouldn't abandon that which is precious to her."

"Your faith, born far from her places of power, is charming. But it is a game. She has hidden her power away, behind a riddle, a paradox."

"And what is the riddle?"

"That is the beginning. It is not a new riddle, but one as old as the game itself. Study the reflections of the Lady and know the riddle; find the true reflection and know the truth behind the paradox."

Lisette filed that away for later examination, and lowered her eyes. "Thank you for your words, Your Highness. I will convey them to my Princess as soon as I return to her."

The Voice's laugh was as rich and deep as mahogany. "Not yet, little guardian. You have another task, first." It gestured languidly, drawing Lisette's gaze to the altar between them. A silver mesh gauntlet rested in the place of honor, palm up. It shimmered uncomfortably, as if it reflected light from someplace else.

"This is the Starcatcher Hand, an ancient treasure of Atalya's, never worn. Even if Atalya chooses to leave the game, this gift of hers will remain. Perhaps it will aid the efforts of the other players. She is fond of maidens, such as your Tiana." A frown touched that perfect face. "Perhaps, too fond. But nevertheless, it is for you to take up the hand and defend your princess from the evil invading the game."

Lisette's eyes widened. "I am not—there are others more appropriate for such a gift." In fairytales, gifts were always dangerous. How could one defend anybody else with only a gauntlet? The question clearly had an answer; not knowing it frightened her. She was on thin ice and it was cracking underneath her.

"And yet you are the one who was called." The Voice's eyes narrowed. "Come now."

"But isn't this against Her own rules? Responding to the game wrecker? I don't understand."

"Of course not. She is not responding to the evil one,

but to somebody else's move. But you argue too much. Are you disloyal?" Silken menace purred in the air. "Come. Do you not crave more than the role of counselor?"

"No! I—" The command seemed to shake the earth under Lisette's feet, with harmonics that jarred her bones. Her feet moved. Against her will, beyond her control, her hands came up, reaching for the artifact on the altar. She whimpered, panicking, struggling to fight back. She'd tried to be so careful with her words, so she couldn't be trapped into this. Nobody was ever careful with their words in the fairy tales. She thought that would make her safe.

"Come. Wear the Starcatcher Hand."

Her fingers brushed against the mesh, even as she shook her head. "No, no." It felt organic rather than metallic, like polished wood. She grasped it, tried and failed to make her right hand into a fist. Instead, she slid it on.

The glistening became a glowing as it constricted. Then the burning started, silver fire from her fingertips as the gauntlet sank into her flesh, merging with her more intimately than any armor. It hurt, and she screamed and screamed, and all the while the Voice of Atalya watched dispassionately, until the pain brought blackness, and absence of anything at all.

CHAPTER EIGHTEEN

THE MERCENARY

TIANA SAT BESIDE the fire gnawing on a hard biscuit, glaring at Minex's sleeping form. She was pretty sure nobody could make such terrible food on accident. Somebody was responsible. She hadn't quite worked out who, but she was guessing it was the earth fiend, despite all evidence regarding time and logic to the contrary.

She'd had such a lovely time last night, until it started falling apart. She'd been happy in Cathay's company. Everything seemed so full of promise. The disasters were far away and she was on an epic quest from the gods to save the world, in a magic forest, and there was dancing, and everything seemed lit from within.

Now Cathay was avoiding her while Kiar made horrible predictions that Tiana's mind would soon crumble like a castle wall under ballistic assault. Jinriki only offered her the tersest of reassurances, like he didn't even want to talk to her. Lisette was angry with her. She hadn't managed to get anywhere with Fai and her search for the green light. Breakfast was hard and salty, and it was about to rain.

When Tiana had emerged from the tent, all the guards were wandering around hollow-eyed, flinching at sounds. They seemed more energetic at the moment. Not energetic enough to do more than heat old biscuits, though. They stayed away from her, as if they were avoiding her, too.

Tiana scowled at Minex and wondered if the earth fiend's magic extended to making food taste better. She wouldn't wake up, even when nudged. Despite herself, Tiana worried, because when Minex slept she looked like a vulnerable child. Just as Tiana was about to nudge her again, Jinriki sent, **She is exhausted. Let her rest.**

Kiar hovered nearby, scrutinizing her. Tiana said, "You needn't watch me so. I feel fine, even if you think my mind is full of holes."

"No. Not that. Do you know where Lisette is?"

Tiana glanced around. The guards had retreated to the edge of the forest. She was all alone. But once Lisette returned she'd be fresh and back in her usual temper, and Tiana would have somebody to complain to. "She went for a walk a few minutes ago, Kiar. You were there. She'll be back soon. She's not interested in exploring. She'd rather be back in Lor Seleni."

"Tiana!" Kiar's voice sharpened. "It's been more than a few minutes. The guards are searching for her. Does Jinriki know where she's at?"

Ice ran down Tiana's spine but she resolutely ignored it. "She's fine. She just needed some personal time. She's the only Regent here, after all. Right, Jinriki?" She looked down at the sword beside her.

I... do not know. I cannot find her.

Instantly, the ice became fire, coiling in her belly and filling her up. Tiana clenched her fist around Jinriki's hilt and then threw the sword down. "Finding her should be easy! You stole her body from farther away than she could be." She stood, looking around. The guards weren't hiding from her; they were moving around purposefully, or talking intensely in small groups. Cathay stood near the edge of the clearing, his hands spread as he focused on an eidolon.

"Lisette!" Tiana put her hands to her head. Cathay and Kiar had noticed before her. When the phantasmagory had been around, she had picked stuff like that up from the ripples. She could use it to pretend to be normal. But—but what a useless thought when Lisette was gone.

Kiar regarded the trees in apprehension. "The forest does strange things to sounds. She might have gotten turned around because of it. When we call for her, it bounces around the trees."

Tiana wheeled on her furiously. "Why are you talking? Can't you do something with the Logos? Can't any of you do anything? *What happened to her?*"

She vanished. If she was attacked, she was not aware of it. She enjoyed the flowers.

Tiana asked, "How long ago?"

Jinriki didn't answer for a long moment. Two of the guards vanished into the woods while Tiana waited. Then he said, **I have been searching for her. There are anomalies about the way she vanished that indicate she is not dead. These crude, distant animal minds are restrictive. But I will find her.**

Tiana stared down at the blade before turning away. Kiar darted in front of her. "Tiana—"

"If something has happened to Lisette, I will tear down this forest, Kiar. Tree by tree. They will have *every* reason to fear the Blood here."

"No!" Kiar lowered her voice to a rushed hiss. "No, Tiana. You came here for a reason, remember? You came here as a supplicant, you came here as a searcher—"

"I am *never* a supplicant," Tiana snapped.

"The Blight, remember? The task given to you by Niyhan. You can't throw that away, you have to be calm and wait and see what happens, you don't know what they'll ask, I don't want anything to happen to Lisette but even if it has you have to ask why before you seek revenge."

Tiana froze as she realized what Kiar was implying. She had no words to respond, not until she realized Lisette might be hurt somewhere, calling for help. They couldn't waste time with this nonsense. "You're saying there might be a price for Atalya's light." She looked around. "I don't see Atalya's light, and I don't see Lisette. So try again." The world couldn't work like that. They couldn't expect it of her. And only her steel-hard refusal of the notion kept her from collapsing to the ground, overcome with sobbing.

Kiar hurried on. "If something has happened to her, something bad, think of the Blight again. The Blighter. What would serve him better than turning you against the Firstborn? Ask why, first, Tiana. Ask how."

"Fine. First talk, then burning." She bared her teeth in what she hoped was a reassuring smile. From Kiar's recoil, it was not.

Tiana scooped up Jinriki and said, "I have no eidolons. I have no phantasmagory. But I have you. Find her. Or find me somebody I can ask *why*. Find the dancers we entertained last night. Find me a fiend. Find *something*." In an earlier time, she'd be trembling on the edge of the phantasmagory now, halfway to a dream. But instead the world was bright and narrow, and full of moving targets. She would ask each one *why* and if they could not give her Lisette, they would bleed. They would burn.

But for a little while, she would wait, because Kiar asked her to. For a few minutes. She watched the figures moving around the campsites. Kiar lurked behind her, muttering to the Logos. That was probably a good thing.

Somebody shouted from beyond the tree line and Tiana lifted Jinriki to point at it. "What."

A man. He is clouded, somehow. He watched last night's revel. And then, **Lisette is with him. She is unconscious.**

After more shouting, the guards emerged from the underbrush, their crossbows trained on the man that followed them. He was large and bearded, dressed in stained leathers and brigandine, with Lisette slung over one shoulder. One huge hand balanced her body, while his other hand rested on the hilt of a sword on his hip. A small axe and a smaller knife hung from a second belt, but other than that, he didn't seem equipped for travel.

Tiana gasped and all but flew across the clearing. "What happened to her? Tell me!"

The big man stopped. His voice was as smooth and warm as distilled brandy, which didn't quite match his words. "Hell if I know. I'm guessing she tripped and banged her head. But she ran a distance afterward. It took me a while to find her." The stranger's thin mouth twitched in amusement as he glanced at the crossbows pointed at him. Then he slid Lisette down until he held her in both arms. A trickle of dried blood stained the crease of Lisette's neck, and the fingers of one of her hands. "Do you want her back?"

"Yes! Give her to me!" Tiana marched right up to him and held out her arms. His eyes drew together under his heavy brow as he looked down at her.

"You're no bigger than she is. Dragging her across the ground won't do her any good. Where do you want me to put her?"

Tiana resisted knocking the man on his backside, but only because he held Lisette. "If you want to help her, give her to me. If you want something else, let's get it over with so I can help her."

Behind her, Kiar quickly said, "And thank you."

He didn't seem to notice. "Brace yourself." He tipped Lisette carefully into Tiana's arms and Tiana let an emanation catch the bulk of her Regent's weight. The stranger's breath chuffed out in surprise but she didn't spare a glance for his expression. Instead she carried Lisette as if she was made of crystal, depositing her on her bedroll in the tent.

Kiar followed her in. "Where is she injured?"

"There's a cut and a lump on the back of her skull," called the stranger, leaning against a tree outside. Then he addressed the guards watching him warily. "So what are a pretty bunch of campers like you doing here? You had a nice party last night. It seemed like almost everybody came."

Tiana brushed Lisette's hair aside and inspected the scab. It was still moist, and crusted with dirt. Lisette's traveling dress was ruined, torn all over. It looked like she'd run through a bramble, but the skin of her arms and legs was unmarred.

"Are there other injuries? Can you see any magically?" she asked, looking sharply at Kiar. She called out of the tent. "We need some warm water. This is a mess."

Kiar, her eyes hazed with Logos-sight, moved her head to one side. "I... don't think so. Nothing obvious. But there's this." She lifted Lisette's hand. The fingernails glimmered, like she'd applied a particularly bright shade of paint. The very tips of the thumb and fingers glowed like a lamp turned low.

Slater brought in a hot kettle and a bucket, then withdrew again. Tiana frowned. "Can you wake her up?"

"I can try something. If it doesn't work, we shouldn't push it; I'm not a healer." Kiar touched Lisette lightly between her eyes. Nothing immediate happened.

Then Lisette made a soft, protesting noise, and rolled on her side, cradling her afflicted hand against her chest. Tiana stroked her face and murmured to her reassuringly, a reversal of the usual roles, until Lisette's eyes flickered open.

They were shockingly green. Lisette reached out for Tiana, squeezing her arm tight. "The rules don't work, Tiana. They don't protect you." Then her eyes fluttered closed and her hand went limp before Tiana could do anything more than stare at her.

"She's not really conscious," said Kiar hurriedly. "I think she's waking up for real, though. Wait a minute."

The rules don't work. Lisette was delirious; of course the rules worked. That was what they were for. Tiana shook her head impatiently.

Lisette opened her eyes again. Whatever had made them appear green—probably a ray of light filtered by the tent—had passed and her eyes were hazel once more.

"Tiana," she mumbled, and pushed herself up, still cradling her glowing hand. Kiar silently offered her a cup of water, and she sipped at it. "I met the Voice of Atalya. A Secondborn. More majestic than Jinriki." She fumbled for words. "Not in favor of the risk. It's risky. Of course it's risky; he's already killed one Firstborn." She laughed shakily. "It gave me a gift. Not gently. It thinks of everything as a game." She looked at her hand, flexing her fingers. "Where did it go? Did you take it off?"

"*We* didn't." Tiana scowled towards where Cathay and the stranger spoke. "What was it? Did this Secondborn hurt you?"

"It was a gauntlet. It hurt so much when I put it on." She twisted her hand around. "My hand feels... strange." Lisette's eyes widened, like a frightened animal. "Tiana, can you—do you still sense the Lady's light? I'm afraid... I tried to be careful so I didn't make any bad bargains, but it forced me—"

Tiana obediently closed her eyes. The green light spread around her, as elusive as fog. But the sleeping crimson light was practically in the palm of her hand. Her eyes snapped open, and she turned around to stare at the stranger again. "I do, it's the same as before, scattered all around. But *he*..." She rose to her feet and left Lisette in the tent with Kiar.

"You. What's your name?" she demanded, interrupting a conversation about wearing armor in forests, of all things.

Cathay gave her a worried look but the big man sketched a bow that somehow managed to be disrespectful. "Jozua Harken, Your Highness. What's the matter? Do you think *I* assaulted your pretty servant?" His smile insinuated he'd at least considered it.

Taken aback, Tiana floundered for words. "Did you— are you a soldier? A knight? Why did you bring her to us?" The red light furled tightly within him, no doubt. It didn't respond to her presence in the slightest.

He smirked. "Me, a knight? No. I'm just a hunter. Yon girl wandered into our camp, out of her wits and blood on her head. If I didn't chase her down and find out who she belonged to, somebody else would have. And my men are unruly enough in this damned forest." He tugged on his beard. "Also, when I saw her fine shredded dress, I thought it likely there might be some sort of reward for her return." He eyed Tiana as if that was no longer certain. "Gratitude, at least. Gratitude can be helpful in my business. Though money is better."

"We're very grateful," Tiana said, unsettled. She twisted her hands together behind her back. Red was the color of Rann, of love and honor. *Knights* swore themselves to Rann. Finding that light in this man was like discovering snow in the summer. "Don't you have *any* tact?"

"Ah, that'd be my rough-and-tumble charm. Just a simple country man, Your Highness. The etiquette of princesses, what with the stomping up and interrupting a man's conversation, is beyond my grasp."

Jinriki sent, **I am troubled by the way this forest breeds disrespect. Let's fix it.** He seemed distracted and the thought lacked his usual malevolence. Still, Tiana wondered if he might be onto something. Maybe the red light was meant to be a gift, unwrapped by defeating the man.

He'd brought Lisette back to her. She couldn't ignore that.

She said, "No doubt the rewards of the court are as well. Will you be hunting here long? For whatever you're hunting in armor?"

"Oh, not much longer, I think. We've almost acquired the prey we came for." Jozua Harken's teeth glinted. Thunder rumbled overhead and he glanced up. "Just in time, too."

"Come back before you leave, then." commanded Tiana. "I'm sure Lisette would like to thank you for rescuing her, once she's feeling better. For now, return to your hunt, huntsman."

He waved at her, a gold coin in his palm. "I'm not that far away, Your Highness. Enjoy your camping trip." He nodded professionally at Cathay and turned to leave the camp. But a few steps away from the tree line, he paused. "The prey just can't stay away, can it?" A rustling Tiana hadn't noticed stopped.

Fai spoke from the branches. "Don't flatter yourself, Harken. Princess! Will you be leaving now that you've simply been *given* the Lady's assistance?"

Tiana said, "What? What assistance?"

"Your Lisette was granted the Lady's gift. That's what you came for, yes? Best you leave before you knock the forest down."

Tiana shook her head. "I don't know what's been done to Lisette, but it isn't the power I'm looking for. Did you arrange for this to happen?"

Fai said, "No. I thought it would take... much longer before the Voice acknowledged you. You're blessed." He didn't sound pleased by the idea. Tiana wasn't either, if this Voice was the one who had hurt Lisette.

Jozua said, "Favored far above yourself, boy. I know some people who'd be very happy to give you all the attention you deserve, though, if you'd stop crawling around in the trees like a squirrel. Come on home, now."

Acid in his voice, Fai spat, "Shut up, you bastard. I ought to shoot you now, while you're away from your men." Tiana could just make out the shadow of a bow in the darkness of the leaves.

Jozua's voice lost its lazy drawl. "A bright young man would be proud to have his sister be the mother to Dukes. Even Atalya knows maidens don't stay maidens forever."

In response, there was a muttered curse and the creak of a bow.

A lighter voice said, "Fai, no!" even as the bowstring sang. There was the snap of breaking wood.

Jozua stood with his head tilted to one side. His gloved fist was near his chest, and he held a broken arrow. "Got that out of your system? Tell you what, Cinai. You come with me and I'll let your brother go without the lesson he deserves. Don't you want your family to matter again?"

Tiana stared in shock, until Jinriki said, **Bows aren't meant to be shot from trees. The arrow probably wouldn't even have penetrated his armor. Good show of nerve, though. Excellent reflexes.**

On the other side of the clearing, Lisette said, "Tiana... why is there fighting?" She sounded small and frightened and overwhelmed, and Tiana's shock was swept away on a tide of rage.

"A hunter? You're hunting a girl? *Here?* And I thought we didn't belong! Get out of here and leave them alone."

Jozua turned to her, opening his fist to let the shards of the arrow fall. "A royal command, Your Highness?"

Tiana hesitated. She could send him away and if such a man bothered to obey, the crimson light would slip through her fingers. "Just... go back to your own camp for now and stay there."

"Happily," he said, and strode beyond the trees without a final bow.

Tiana looked up into the swaying branches. They were already empty. "Fai?" she called anyhow. "Cinai? If you stay here I can protect you from him."

After waiting a moment for a response, she sighed and went to reassure Lisette.

CHAPTER NINETEEN

TOY SOLDIERS

THE SCOUTS REPORTED to Jerya early in the morning, as she drank her coffee and picked at her rolls at the table. Iriss sat beside her, but Seandri was off having breakfast with Vassay, and Gisen was still asleep. Jerya was about to take advantage of the private moment to tell Iriss about her encounter with Thorn when the scouts arrived.

They filed into the room, scouts from multiple different detachments, all coming at once. They liked to present themselves as a group, so all the bad news might be delivered at once: exactly the sort of thing Regency scouts considered a kindness.

"Go ahead with your report, please," Jerya said, after a quick glance at Iriss. Her Regent was smiling gently in the general direction of the scouts, while folding her napkin into strange shapes.

One of the scouts unrolled a map onto the table, nestling it between the jam pot and the coffee flask. Silently, he put down some metal weights. After weighing the corners, he put a black weight on the location of the Blight, where the village of Tranning used to be, along with a dozen other hamlets. Jerya didn't need the weight to remember; she'd thought about it often enough. It was only days away, on the road that led directly there. The bulk of the Royal Guard, including everybody not previously in active service, was arrayed between Lor Seleni and the Blight.

Then the scout put down another black weight, to the east of both Tranning and Lor Seleni, halfway to the great lake known as Morning, where the servants of the summer goddess Keldera served.

"Another Blight?" Jerya felt cold.

"An army of the Blighter, rather," said the scout. He was a short, slim man, with reddish hair and a freshly shaven face.

"How?" demanded Jerya. "How did it get over there?" The scouts were supposed to be watching the borders of the Blight; they were supposed to *tell her* if anything significant emerged.

Without answering, the scout put down yet another black weight. This one was to the west of Lor Seleni, most of the way to the Counties.

"Another army," Jerya said flatly. Alanah hurried in, escorted by the Guard sent to retrieve her. Jerya acknowledged her with a glance and returned her attention to the scout.

"Another army," he said. "But this one..." he fished out yet another weight from his pocket and set it down slowly. This one was black, but molded into the shape of a soldier. "This one has men as well as monsters."

Jerya stared at it, then reached out to touch the figure with one finger. "And where are the armies of the duchies? We called them. Where are they?"

The scout pulled out another set of soldier figures, these painted in the colors of each duchy and some of the marches and counties and started placing them on the map. "Not all our information is up to date, but these are our best guesses."

It was not good news. Stormwatch and the Shell Coast both had troops on the move; neither of them had the resources of any of the duchies. Tannis, far to the northwest, wasn't even a County technically, but it had a figure marching south.

"The Great Duchies have called their troops," said the scout. "But only Dalein is in any position to help with the Blight itself. Everybody else is holding steady at their own borders. In the case of Ardoza—" the scout tapped the lake Morning, "—that's sensible. As for everybody else... They're cowards."

"Inappropriate, Sergeant.," said Alanah mildly.

The scout shrugged, his eyes on Jerya.

"Why are there men with the western Blighter forces?" Jerya asked. "Who are they?"

"That's not clear, Your Highness. Rumor says—" he hesitated. "Rumor says it's Benjen and his men, back from the dead."

Jerya put her face in her hands for a moment. When she lifted it, she said, "Still? Still they tell that story? Why is Benjen so immortal?"

"Couldn't say, ma'am."

"Of course you can't. Instead, tell me how it is there are two armies?" She wanted to scream just asking the question, but she kept her voice as calm as a summer day. "I thought you were *watching the borders*."

The two scouts behind the spokesman swayed back, as if

she *had* screamed, but the redheaded scout remained stone-faced. He clasped his hands behind his back. "Best guess is they've been slipping out at night in small groups, ma'am. The two armies both prefer to travel at night, and they move faster when it's overcast."

"Shouldn't you have noticed some of these groups? One or two? And investigated?"

The scout didn't flinch. "Yes, ma'am. We've got no other explanation though, ma'am."

Jerya took a deep breath. "Very well. Find out who these men are that aid the enemies of Ceria. Find the hole in your surveillance and patch it. I will have further instructions later."

"Yes, ma'am." He bowed deeply, and all three scouts evaporated.

Silence fell. Jerya wrapped her hands around her coffee, staring into the black abyss. After a moment, Iriss, sitting at the other end of the table, said, "Sit down, Alanah. Have some breakfast. How is the baby?"

"Colic," said Alanah glumly. "Are you feeling better, my lady?"

"I'm much better, thank you," said Iriss gaily. Her eyes still glowed with the phantasmagory light and she couldn't see. She was still cold all the time. But she considered herself well. Jerya tried to believe her.

"I'm glad to hear it," Alanah said politely, then turned her attention to Jerya. "Your Highness, you were surprised by the status of the duchies? Yithiere's been keeping secrets again?"

"When doesn't he?" Jerya sighed.

"Ah, well, I suppose he thought there isn't much to be done about it from here. Strongly worded letters can only go so far."

Jerya looked at her for a long moment, letting the information settle into place as a new piece of a vast tapestry. "And the only army ready to fight is the one from the Duchy whose Council representative hates us the most. Yithiere wouldn't have trusted that at all. Alanah, do you know *why* the Duchies are so willing to let Lor Seleni burn?"

"Ask your uncle," said Alanah gruffly, spreading jam on a roll.

"If only I could," Jerya said bitterly. "Alas, the phantasmagory is gone. And he probably wouldn't—"

"You've got two uncles left, girl," said Alanah sharply. "Ask the one who's been around longer."

Jerya stared at Alanah, then stood abruptly. She pulled an eidolon from her chest and placed the small bird on the back of her chair. "Watch Iriss," she told it. "I'll be back."

She went to the other side of the inn and knocked on the door of Jant's chamber. Cutlery clinked on the other side and Jant called, "Yes, enter, why can't I train these—ah, good morning, Jerya."

Jant and Julina sat together at a table just large enough for the two of them, eating breakfast together. Jant gave her a little smile, while Julina regarded her apprehensively.

"I've been thinking about what you suggested and it's foolish. But it's the kind of foolish that should be explored. I—" Jant began, then paused when Julina put her hand on his.

"You're troubled, dear," said Julina. "What's the matter? Come, have a seat and drink some coffee."

Jerya perched on the edge of an armchair in the corner. "I'm glad you have ideas, Uncle. We may need them soon. The war—the armies—" She stopped, and organized her thoughts. "I always thought my father stayed out of politics because... because that was who he was. He let Tomas handle the Council and they let the Council make all the decisions because... because my father wasn't... strong. I always thought that even if our responsibility was defending Ceria, that could be approached in so many ways. I thought we didn't need to stay in the background during peacetime, pursuing nothing more than our own pleasures. But the Justiciar's Council has been so aggressive, and now the Duchies are being... hesitant in moving their armies. I think they want us *gone* and I don't know why. I begin to think it's more than ambition. You said something once: that it was better to sleep than be awake."

Jant's face slowly fell during Jerya's explanation. "Ah." He turned his face toward the wall, his eyes going far away.

Jerya waited patiently for him to bring his thoughts together enough to answer her, but it was Julina who spoke first. "You know the history of the Regency, my dear? Why it was founded?"

"I know that my family line is unstable, yes," said Jerya, holding herself still. Tiana always wiggled, but Jerya could be very still. "There are despicable acts in our past, and poor choices in who we married. The Regency was a good solution. But we do have the Regency now. We've had the Regency for hundreds of years, and the Duchies have risen for every major Blight in all that time."

"Our last major Blight was Benjen," said Jant, distantly.

Jerya's hand twitched. "Why does it always come back to Benjen?"

Her uncle turned to look at her. "Ask instead, 'Why Benjen?' He had armies, Jerya. He was more than a bastard with a grudge. Have you ever asked where they came from?"

The back of her neck prickled. "The same place the

armies of other Blighters come from. Mercenaries. Foreign governments who want the Citadel, or Ceria's land."

Jant sighed. "We should have educated you better. But my nephews wanted to protect you and then everything started falling apart... Some of them were mercenaries, yes. Mercenaries want paying, but Benjen didn't have the backing of one of the southern sea powers or the northern states. He got his money, and even some of his men, from within Ceria. He convinced many he'd be a better King than those currently holding the throne."

"Benjen?" Jerya asked incredulously. "Benjen? Who murdered infants and burned the orchards of Dalein?"

Jant pursed his lips and Julina said, "A more... just King, then. More inclined to providing the justice they wanted."

"Justice for *what?*" Jerya said and, despite her self-control, she knew she was wailing.

Jant sighed. "My mother."

Slowly Jerya's fists unclenched as she thought back over the family tree. Jant never talked about his mother, and she didn't figure into very many Palace history books. Jerya had, when she'd bothered to think about it, assumed she'd been much like Jerya's own father, who was in turn much like her grandfather Anther had been. Well-behaved members of the Blood were boring to write about. It seemed like they'd had generations upon generations of indolent, well-behaved Kings and Queens who did nothing more than entertain themselves between calls to war.

"Queen Shiani?" she asked hesitantly. "What did she do?"

"She was... politically active," he said, studying the tabletop. "The last of a series of active monarchs." He stopped talking, then started again, this time more conversationally.

"Her uncle was a frightening old fellow. I know you've heard of him, because Tiana kept talking about that play somebody wrote about his death and his children's deaths."

Jerya knew instantly what he was talking about. "The Tragedy of Tyanth and Liana?" Tiana had talked about it for days after watching and reading it when she was thirteen. It was annoying at the time, but suddenly Jerya ached to hear Tiana babbling about nonsense again.

"That's the one. It took liberties, of course—Reandri wasn't a *complete* monster. Did many fine things for the country. But he had some... unsavory habits and of course, he and his children did kill each other. My great-uncle."

"And your mother inherited?" Jerya summoned up her memory of the family tree. Despite her uncle's comment about her education, she'd spent plenty of time in the library with her tutor. It was just the political history of the past century hadn't been recorded very well. She wondered now if that was on purpose, if even her own family conspired to keep the Blood out of the way.

"Eventually. Her aunt came first, and her father. My great-aunt Jesandri, the people liked her and the nobles respected her. She never physically touched anybody, which put some people off. But she was fair and rational. She brought back the village schoolteachers. Controversial at the time, but it hasn't led to the collapse of the country yet." He shook his head. "You remind me of the stories of her. I never knew her myself. I wasn't born until after my mother came to power." He sighed again, and his wife squeezed his hand.

"What was she like?" Jerya asked.

His face changed and his voice dropped to a low, angry tone. "*She* was the complete monster. She terrorized Anther and me, and she wasn't any better to Ceria. Most powerful magic in two centuries, and she delighted in it. Though that wasn't where she was the worst. Nearly bankrupted the country, punished anybody who criticized her, wiped out the Auvaine, shattered Biaxin into the Counties. There was a serious Logos-Blight and when she took the Blighter prisoner... she kept him chained. As a threat, you see. So everybody would properly appreciate what she did for the country. She was never satisfied, no matter what anybody did. Nobody was allowed to be happy around her. She claimed my sister Viani's doll when Viani was two, because the toy made Viani laugh."

Jerya clasped her hands tightly in her lap. "Where was her Regent? Didn't she have a Regent to restrain her?"

"Regents are people, Jerya," said Lady Julina softly. "Brought up to love and serve their royal companion. Sometimes it takes... time for them to realize their true duty."

Jerya blinked at her, confused. Jant said, "I remember Mother and Callie fighting. Callie *tried* to check her. She spent years trying to mitigate and hide and obscure and fix what Mother did, with us and with the country. She worked far harder at it than our father did. Mother played *him* like an instrument, and when he finally rebelled, he died. I don't even know who Viani's father was. Nobody dared ask. By the end, the country was a bleeding wreck."

"The end? What happened to her?"

Her great-uncle took a deep breath and when he spoke again his voice was flat, all his anger regulated away. "When Anther was eighteen, Callie killed Mother and herself. The final duty of a Regent, Jerya. The Chancellor then was young, appointed after Mother removed the previous one. He covered it up; it frightened him. Mother had an accident, according to the history books." The old man laughed, a creaky laugh full of dried blood and desiccated rage.

Jerya blinked, then did some arithmetic. It was easier than dwelling on the pain in her great-uncle's voice. "You said those who supported Benjen wanted justice for your mother, but Benjen's Blight didn't start until *Math's* reign. That was over twenty years after Shiani died."

"Oh yes. A lifetime when you're an ambitious twenty year old girl," said Jant sarcastically. "And a long time to wait for anybody else, waiting on Anther's vague promises of reparations and distracted dreams of consensus. Math was ambitious, too."

"Wanting to be more than a weapon isn't wrong, Uncle," Jerya said firmly. "You said everybody respected your great-aunt, the one who started up the schools again."

"My mother ruined all that," Jant muttered.

"No." Jerya stood. "I'm not going to let the legacy of a woman who died fifty years ago destroy Ceria. And I'm not going to let nightmares in the dark prevent the armies we need from moving."

"Hah," Jant said to himself, then said, "You do what you have to, girl. Try not to die, though. I've seen enough of my kin die."

"Jerya?" said Iriss, peeking through the ajar door. "Can I come in?"

"I'm just leaving, Iriss."

"Oh." Iriss pushed the door open and curtsied to Jant. "Good morning, Your Highness, my Lady. Jerya, I was thinking about that scout's report. About the armies?" She paused, as if it might be a struggle for Jerya to remember the two armies marching on the eastern and western half of the kingdom.

Jerya glanced at Jant, but he made a point of ignoring her. "Let's go talk about it at the table," she told Iriss, and led the way there.

Iriss sat down again awkwardly, almost missing the chair. "I can still hear his voice," she began. "Giving instructions. When I close my eyes, I can see the shapes in the darkness better. After I finished breakfast, I thought about my dress. I realized that he was giving more than one set of instructions. There's places on the dress where the hooks and eyes open. More than one." She looked earnestly at Jerya, as if what she'd said made sense.

Jerya's father had spoken like that sometimes, and Yithiere. The memories squeezed her heart. "We really ought to get to work on that dress, shouldn't we?" she said, as cheerfully as she could.

"Yes, we should," said Iriss. "Once we do, I think I can show you where the hooks are opening."

Hooks. Jerya suddenly remembered how her father had died. He'd called hooks to himself, hooks intended to tear the land further apart.

Jerya reached over to the pad of paper in front of Iriss's place and looked at the dress sketched there. It was a floaty sundress constructed of many filmy layers, each one sketched out on another piece of paper. She studied the skirt, at the way the layers curved around each other. It didn't look like clothing. It looked, when she opened her mind—

Jerya's breath caught in her throat. "You mean show me on a map?"

"Yes," Iriss nodded. "I think if we make my dress, I can show you where the armies are coming from."

CHAPTER TWENTY

THE PROBLEM WITH POPULARITY

KIAR CLEANED LISETTE'S head injury and fed her several cups of willow bark tea to dull the ache, then sat down beside her again and studied at her once again with the Logos-vision.

"What does it look like to you?" Lisette asked. She was sitting up, holding her modified hand close to her chest. "What *is* it?"

"Does it hurt?" Tiana demanded, kneeling at the entrance to the tent.

"Not anymore." Lisette swallowed, her eyes wide and frightened. "But I don't know if I have fingertips left. I don't feel things properly." She drew the glowing fingertips across her other hand briefly, then shuddered and brought her hand back to her chest.

"The Logos there is so intense, so deeply layered that I can't make out individual details." She remembered a similar experience, when she'd looked at the phantasmagory pendant and the Royal Pendant Tiana now wore close around her neck.

But she was looking at eidolon magic then. This was almost the exact opposite. "Maybe somebody more experienced would understand it."

Tiana glanced down at Jinriki, unsheathed beside her. "Jinriki says he knows what it is. But I'm not going to translate between the two of you. He wants you to touch him so he can talk directly to you." She put the blade down beside them.

Kiar winced. She'd avoided that, actively, purposefully avoided that for so long. Somebody had to be resistant to the powers of the sky fiend. Touching him seemed to increase his influence, sometimes in really awful ways. She glanced toward Cathy, hovering beyond Tiana. The sword delved into minds so easily. And too many were vulnerable to the silent allure of the blade, which all but screamed 'touch me, take me up'.

But there was a time for trust, and she, more than anybody, should be able to shield herself from his influence, if he turned malignant.

She used no more than a finger to touch the gem on the sword's hilt. Immediately, the pressure of *pick me up, hold me, hear me* abated.

"Hey, what about the dreams?" Lisette asked, her frightened eyes narrowing in sudden, belated suspicion.

Is anybody sleeping right now? I think not. The sword's voice was very different than Kiar had expected. She'd heard him speak once aloud, when banishing another sky fiend, and then his voice had been guttural, screeching, alien. But the voice in her head was cool, lazy and intensely masculine. She instantly regretted letting him in.

And that was before she processed what Lisette had actually said to him. Anger and shame rose up and she tamped them down firmly, only asking, "Did you really need me to touch you?"

It certainly makes things easier. Some minds are stronger than others. The pleasure in the silent voice disturbed her. She wanted to put up a shield right now. But she didn't. She'd let him in for a reason and she was going to get what she paid for.

"So what is it?"

The Starcatcher Hand? It's a channel to the lux, the raw energy outside the world. A tool, and a weapon. The two of you could do great things if you learned to work together. A challenge to be mastered. An image formed in her mind of Lisette somehow passing energy to Kiar, and Kiar's grasp of the Logos shaping that energy into something real.

Kiar believed him; he had done something like that once before: made an unnatural monster natural, using Tiana as the channel. She pushed the intrusive image away. "I don't have the control for anything big like that. I know how dangerous it is to the worker." She glanced at Tiana covertly, then said, "How does she turn it off?"

Jinriki laughed. **It's not activated. She must learn how to do that first.**

Lisette said quickly, "I don't want to learn how to turn it on. I want to learn how to take it off."

She will need to attune herself to the new sensations and take hold of the energy. Communicating would be easier if she understood the Logos, of course. But there's stubbornness buried in there. She'll learn.

"Hey!" protested Lisette. "I'm right here!"

Outside the tent, a guard called, "Rider incoming!"

It's the wizard, said Jinriki. **Perhaps I'll simply explain to him.**

Kiar almost stepped on Tiana in her hurry to get out of the tent, but Tiana was hardly less eager than she was. They both tumbled out and Kiar rose to her feet and brushed herself off as she looked around.

After a moment, a wild-eyed farm horse crunched through the tree line, with Twist hanging onto the horse and trying to stop a sloppy pack from falling off. Kiar and Tiana raced to meet the horse, which shied and then deposited Twist on the ground before backing up.

"Yes, well, good afternoon to you as well." He let Tiana pull him to his feet.

"You found us! How are things in the city? Did the Vassay arrive? Why are you on a horse? What's in the pack?" Tiana demanded. Kiar stood twisting her hands together, feeling awkward.

"Honk, honk, honk, I come bearing Fallendre gifts," said Twist, and put the overloaded pack into Tiana's arms. "I borrowed Bluebell here because skipping through a forest with that pack gave me a giant headache. All those trees to account for, all those packages." He shook his head and clicked his tongue. "Alas, Bluebell wasn't much better. Do you have a horsey person who can take her and convince her humanity isn't a mistake?" One of the stable girls materialized beside Bluebell and gave Twist a nasty look. He bowed deeply to her. "A horsey *queen*, if I'm not wrong. Exactly what the wizard ordered. Take this poor beast away."

Lisette peeked out of the tent, then emerged slowly to sit by the fire, holding her hand under the cloak she'd put over her shoulders. Tiana lugged the pack over to her and started going through it. "Fresh cheese. Good crackers. Bacon. Some books for you, Kiar. Some flasks. Cookies! You're late, Twist, we needed this last night."

"I spent last night in somebody's stable," said Twist, with a mournful face. "I needed it more last night. There's a letter from your sister in one of Kiar's books."

Kiar wondered if he'd picked the books out for her himself, wondered what they were. She couldn't stop looking at him to go check. The shadows of exhaustion still lingered on his face, but the expressive liveliness she found so annoying danced in his eyes.

Then Minex's sweet, sleepy voice cut across the clearing. "You are no longer mortal, Lady Lisette." She was still curled by the fire, head on her arm, blinking her big eyes curiously.

"You're dreaming. Go back to sleep, creature," said Tiana. Twist brushed himself off and moved over to Kiar. "Things have been quite busy here," he murmured. "An earth fiend, and what's happened to Lisette?"

Suddenly, Kiar realized just how happy she was to see him. "Lisette's discovered a new talent. Well, I say 'discovered' but it actually seems to be a gift from a Secondborn. Jinriki thinks she can gather up raw energy."

Twist raised one eyebrow. "Are you talking to that creature now?"

"Well, it's not like you were here to talk to instead." He frowned at her, but a smile crept through. "It's nice to be missed for my conversation instead of my magic."

Giddiness made the words easy. "Is there anything else to talk about?" *Twist is here, Twist is here.* "Come, see." He followed her over to Lisette.

"I hear you've joined the ranks of Tiana's magical army." He crouched down and started unwrapping a candy from Tiana's pile of loot.

Lisette met his eyes and pulled aside her cloak to show him her hand. "I don't like it."

He popped the candy in his mouth, then inspected her hand as if she was a child showing him a scratched knee. "How does it feel?"

"Numb. Sometimes tingly. And look." She pressed her glowing fingertips against the side of her mug. "It's like they're not even there. I can touch where sensation begins and it feels... odd. Raw, sensitive." Lisette stared at her hand with a sick expression on her face. "The Secondborn made me take the gauntlet. Forced me."

Twist's expression turned peculiar. "I see." He stared at her for a long meditative moment. "That's not an easy thing to accept. Do you think it's meant to help?"

"Maybe. *They* think so. The Voice said Atalya thinks so. But why me? It goes against everything I'm supposed to be, and I have no preparation for it. No skills. No education. Jinriki says I use it by attuning myself and reaching out. I don't even *understand* that."

"Do you *want* to understand it?"

"No. I don't." Lisette's lips thinned uncharacteristically and she looked away, "But I'll try to anyhow. It'll just take some time."

"Brave girl." Twist laid two fingers on her wrist, comfortingly. "I'll do my best to help you. I do have a bit of experience teaching, unlike these people."

But not enough for me! Kiar's giddy happiness dropped away like a boulder. Twist smiled at Lisette, Lisette smiled back and Kiar's stomach burned.

"I'm just going to go check on... something. You two keep talking." She hurried away. As she did, she passed Cathay, loitering at the edge of the clearing, his face turned toward Tiana like a flower toward the sun. She recognized something horrible in his face and worse, saw his own recognition of something in hers. It was too much; she stumbled into a jog to the next campsite.

There, near the stable girls who were feeding the mounts and fussing over Bluebell, she stood facing the forest. What was wrong with her? What kind of reaction was that?

A jealous one, came Jinriki's purr.

You shut the hell up, she screamed silently. **What the hell do you know, you stinking heap of cursed metal?**

Oh, come now— but a red haze rose over Kiar's vision. She couldn't take it anymore.

Get the hell out of my head! She made a shield around her mind, around her heart, around everything she was, and because she desperately didn't want anybody to notice and wonder why, the shield around her skin was as close as her clothes. She'd learned since she was a child, oh yes. She could see through this shield, walk, even talk. It was fitted armor through which nobody could reach her.

In a tight, tiny silence, with nothing but herself to see, and no one but herself to know, she could admit Jinriki was right. The searing bolt that had ripped through her when Twist turned the full intensity of his attention to Lisette was jealousy. Stupid, irrational, baseless jealously. She felt like throwing up. Cold panic made her hands clammy at the thought of what underlay the jealousy. She didn't know what to do with the feelings. Especially here, so far away from books and places to hide. Her armor couldn't keep out what came from inside her.

A brief heaviness went through her chest: an eidolon coming home. The shield she'd just created had severed the maintenance on another shield. Dread overwhelmed her confusion even before she remembered what eidolon she'd been maintaining. It had been the one in the eidolon world, shielding Tiana's window silhouette from prying eyes.

Wiping her hands on her tunic, trying to wipe Twist from her mind the same way, she stumbled through the steps necessary to re-enable the protection. She sent the eidolon back by the same path it had used to return. Then she wrapped her arms around herself and leaned against a tree, taking deep breaths and trying to analyze what else needed to be done.

She had to tell Tiana. She had to tell her *something*, anyhow. It was Tiana she'd failed. Lord of Winter, it was so stupid to be jealous, so dangerous, so wrong. She had to remember where such feelings had led her.

Hurrying back through the camp, she barely restrained herself from urging the soldiers to pack up camp, right now. Once again, Cathay caught her eye, and this time he tilted his head in a silent invitation to join him in his vigil.

No time for that. Instead, she found Tiana, and then stared at her in silent consternation. What could she say? She couldn't explain why her eidolon had failed, even if she wanted to. It was too hard for her to find the right words. Twist sat right beside Tiana, with his gentlest smile turned on Lisette.

"Tiana, can I talk to you?"

Tiana looked up, then stood. "Of course." She obligingly moved away from Twist and Lisette.

Dropping her voice, Kiar struck out at random. "We shouldn't stay in one place for too long. The enemy, he's a master of eidolons. He might see through the shield I erected, or even subvert it."

Tiana tilted her head. "But you'd know, wouldn't you? If he stole it somehow?"

For a moment Kiar wanted to say, *Yes, that's it, he took control, we're in terrible danger.* But lying would be just as stupid as trying to explain. So she shook her head. "Maybe. I hope so."

"You never have enough faith in yourself. Well, I have enough faith for both of us. I'm sure your shield will keep us hidden. Don't worry so much."

Kiar ground her teeth. Tiana's faith, she felt, would be a lot more reassuring if her trust didn't so often seem born of denial rather than real evidence.

The forest was normal. Birds chirped. The horses nibbled on forage. The guards were still alert after Jozua's appearance. She had no evidence her slip mattered. Surely Ohedreton had many things occupying his time. Invading another world was a big undertaking. But that was hope speaking, not facts, so she tried one more time.

"Faith is one thing but being careful is something else entirely. We could move deeper into the forest. Maybe you'd sense more about the light."

Tiana hesitated. "No, I don't think so. The situation seems stable here." She looked away, to the edge of the clearing. "Yes. They can find us here and that's good. We need to stay here for now. We'll defend ourselves if we have to."

Kiar blew out her breath in a huff and stalked away, to the trees beyond the camp.

A guard moved to follow her. They had no intention of letting any more of their charges bump their heads in the woods and come back with glowing body parts. Kiar swallowed her annoyed protest.

Then Twist said, "I'll escort her, gentlemen," to the guard and she wanted to break into a run. She would have welcomed any company over Twist's: Cathay, the loud stable girl, even the little earth fiend. She couldn't trust herself alone with Twist. She never reacted sensibly.

He walked after her, and she didn't run, because that would be stupid and dangerous. If she ran, he was persistent enough that he might try skipping to catch up with her. She knew from the way he'd spoken before that skipping was dangerous for him in a forest, especially when he was tired and distracted.

She turned and waited for him to catch up. As he came around a tree, a flurry of raindrops fell and he put one hand over his head. "Where's your coat?" she called. "It's almost winter for real now."

He smiled as he approached her, and her stomach twisted itself into a knot. "I gave it to somebody who needed a coat more. It will be a while before I can replace the one I had. I suppose I should pick up a cloak. I'm not cold, though."

"You'll be wet soon," Kiar warned.

"You don't have a cloak either." He stopped, close enough that she could reach out and touch him. She resisted.

He went on. "Were you going for a walk?" The smile faded into a faint, pleased expression that made her want to trace his mouth with her fingers. Lord of Winter! What was wrong with her? There was too much going on for her to turn into the silly protagonist of one of Tiana's two-penny romance novels.

She ducked her head and turned away. "I can't help back there. You can, though."

He cocked his head and fell into step beside her, instead. "I've been looking forward to a chance to talk with you. Just you."

"Why? I'm not your apprentice anymore. I'm not your *anything* anymore."

"Not my anything?" he asked. "I hope that's not true. But even if you think we can't be friends, you're still my most reliable information source. We share a certain point of view. And other things." Not the lead in a romance novel, but the fool in a melodrama. At least she could make sure she concentrated on maintaining the aegis in the other world, this time.

Through stiff lips, she said, "What do you want to know? About the earth fiend? She's Jinriki's pet. Tiana knows more. About Lisette? That just happened today. Oh, here's something interesting. I've put an aegis in the dark world to stop the enemy from finding us." He kept looking at her steadily and she added in a rush, "I don't have anything else to talk about." It was a lie; she did, she did, she had so much to talk about—but not here. Not alone with him.

"Haven't you? Did I misunderstand the looks you sent my way?"

She couldn't answer. There were no words. She stared at the ground, barely aware of another shower of raindrops that dampened her neck.

Twist sighed. "I'd thought you'd be... but no." He touched her arm and when she flinched, he put his hands on her shoulders.

"Kiar, you know you're important to me, even if you're not my apprentice anymore."

"Sure," she mumbled. "Of course. You've said." She looked anywhere but his face, and wished the ground would swallow her up. Unbidden, she wondered what it would be like to kiss him. *No, no.* It was thoughts like that which made it so *impossible* to talk to him.

She wrenched herself away. "Please—," she said, and stopped. There was nothing she could say. She longed to tell him about the phantasmagory world, and her sense that the inhabitants lived. Maybe he could help her understand why that bothered her so much. But words dried up in her mouth. She wanted to complain to him about Tiana's decisions; he'd know what she meant, that she wasn't rebelling, just expressing herself. But her mind was a blank. And she yearned to cling to him, to hide from the rain in his arms, under the coat or cloak or his smile, anything would do, as long as it was him.

Twist bounced on his toes. "I have fewer tools out here, it seems. Back home, I had ways of making you talk." He mimed spilling something from his hands, and she blinked at him. "No? Nothing?" He sighed.

"Please," she whispered. "Leave me alone. I—I have to concentrate. On the aegis. It needs attention."

It started raining in earnest. For a moment, the patter of rain on leaves was the only sound. Then he said, "Of course." He hesitated a moment longer. "Do you enjoy it? Being the only person who can go there and see those things? Would you share it if you could?"

"Yes," she said. "And yes. To both. Please, please go."

His expression changed before he silently vanished, skipping away. For a moment, she thought she'd seen hurt. Why had he asked those questions? She realized with a sharp wrench that perhaps he had wanted to talk to her about *his* magic, and his feelings about it.

She huddled under a tree and cursed. The foliage kept most of the rain off, but the drops leaking through were cold on her hot face. Indistinct shadows deepened. She wished for the phantasmagory, so that she could feel the familiar cool presences of Jerya and her father. Yithiere couldn't give her affection, but she understood him, understood why, and that was comforting.

The shadow of a dead pine developed substance and texture, until Kiar realized another silhouette stood within, watching her. One of the forest children? She tried to pretend she didn't notice, while watching back.

Slowly, as she studied the shape, a hideous new anxiety grew inside her, like the seed of some awful plant. When she couldn't stand it any more, she called out, "I see you. Come out."

An andani, one of the graceful, smooth black servants of Ohedreton, stepped out of the deepest shadow, and Kiar's sick anxiety coalesced into a spike of fear. It bowed to her and she saw the wings borne by the previous avatar of Ohedreton himself. She tried to listen beyond her thundering heart, but she heard no outcry that would indicate other andani swarmed through the campsite.

"I'm glad you're alone," the andani said. "Or else we wouldn't have this chance to talk first."

It was some cruel joke, everybody wanting to talk to her. "What do you want? Are we going to fight again?"

It smiled. Perhaps it meant the expression to be reassuring, because it did not move any closer. But the andani had a very large mouth. "You're clever. Far more clever than any of your kin. And they never appreciate that. No, I'm not interested in fighting with you. I'm quite happy to have that girl sitting, waiting, in a wet forest."

"Really? You kept attacking us on the way here." She wondered if she could edge close enough to grab at the eidolon-stuff of the andani so she could banish it.

"Oh, well, *that*. I had no more idea of the games the Dawn Daughter would play than you did. But now..." It took a companionable step towards her, hands spread.

Kiar stayed her ground, feeling increasingly steady in herself. "What are you doing now?"

"A little of this, a little of that. I found some interesting artifacts stored within the prototype of my prison." The andani avatar meant the physical shell of the phantasmagory, which it had destroyed when it murdered the King. "I've made myself some champions from the remains. And I'm working on a very promising grafting technique."

Frowning, Kiar tried to understand what he was saying. "Why are you telling me this? Why do you think I care?"

"I said. You're smart. Do you know my story?"

"You served the Firstborn Innis, but you betrayed him and destroyed him. I read about it." The creature wasn't quite in reach.

"And after? No? Well, perhaps we'll talk about that later." It moved graceful fingers through the air. "I see you've been to my land. What do you think of it?"

"It's dark," Kiar said bluntly. "And strange."

"And small," sighed the andani. "My creation has so little room to grow. The foundation itself is flawed. But I was content with it, until the Firstborn turned Shin against me. Now, well. They've left this world, so it makes sense that I move in."

"We're still here!" She remembered the devastation left by the invading fortress, wondered again what had happened to the town it had swallowed.

"Yes. It's a shame that your guardians have abandoned you, isn't it?"

Kiar felt like a small child as she protested, "They haven't. They're guiding Tiana—"

"Oh and isn't that an inspired choice? Making a champion of the girl corrupted by the mad sword. I wouldn't put much faith in their guidance, if I were you. Here you sit, waiting for who knows what, while outside this forest—do you have any idea what's happening in the rest of the country? I do." It smiled again. "I've been everywhere."

"You gain more if you can convince me to share your views. Sowing discord and all. No," Kiar observed. "I'm wary of the blade, but I'm more wary of you." She abandoned subtlety and held out a hand. "Come closer, so I can send you away again."

"What if I've learned to avoid that trick?"

"Then I'll learn a new one." She lunged forward and the andani danced out of her reach, pirouetting prettily.

"Tell your friends I'm waiting here in the forest." It backed away. Kiar, who had been planning on doing just that, paused.

"Why?" But she answered her own question. If Tiana and Cathay knew their enemy lurked in the forest,, they would go out looking for him.

"I'd love to meet the sword again. I have ideas there, too, but I need a better look. Won't you help?" Its voice was sweet as candy.

She scowled and leapt for the andani, but it laughed and dodged her. So she slipped into the Logos sight and cast about, looking for the sky fiend that must have allowed the andani entry to this world.

The avatar cocked its head, a stomach-churningly alien movement. "I'm afraid I had to travel here as any man does. My slaves, the children of Innis, are occupied in other ways at the moment."

"Go *away*. I don't want to talk to you."

"I like you, Kiar," it whispered. "I hope you'll make me proud." It walked backwards until it faded into the woods.

Kiar shoved wet hair from her face and took a deep breath. She was torn between her desire to scamper back to camp before she was ambushed, and her desire to think. Dragging in another gasping breath, she put her back against a tree. *He knew, he knew. Traveling as a man does.* Somehow he'd used her lapse to find them. Her schoolgirl crush on her teacher was going to get them all killed.

She looked up into the dark trees. The forest children feared this, feared that Tiana and her companions would bring the Blighter into their woods. The Citadel of the Sky had been a wreck when they left. Would the Forest of Fel Dion fall as well? Would that be on her head? What worse disasters could happen if she didn't learn to control her emotions? If they didn't stop waiting?

She pushed herself away from the tree and started back to camp. Somehow, some way, without explaining why, she needed to convince Tiana to move the camp into the open fields.

CHAPTER TWENTY-ONE

THE CALL TO HUNT

INCANDESCENT SPARKS SPIRALED around Lisette's hand as she trailed it through the air. "Good," said Twist. "Can you gather them up?"

Tiana watched anxiously. Kiar stood beside her, intermittently muttering about moving the camp, but Tiana couldn't concentrate on Kiar's words, not now. Especially not when Kiar spoke in the roundabout way she had when she didn't want to upset anybody.

White-lipped, Lisette reversed her hand's movement and the sparks came together like a cloud. She closed her fingers into a fist. When she opened them, a tiny ball of light glowed in the palm of her hand. Additional sparks drained into it, darting at the glow like stars falling into the sun. The rest of the campsite seemed darker and Tiana kept her hand on Jinriki.

Twist stared at the brilliance. "But now what?" He touched a single finger to one of the falling sparks. White light exploded, tendrils crackling through him. A sharp, clear note like vibrating glass grew until it shrieked and he flew backwards, landing in a boneless heap.

"No!" Lisette looked around wildly and then pushed the brilliance into the ground. Fingers of light spread out over the ground before fading.

Kiar recovered from her own breathless recoil and dashed over to Twist. The Logos-worker pushed himself up. "Astonishing. Ast—" He peered at his fingertip until his eyes crossed and then patted the top of his head. "Good hair. Astonishing." He patted Kiar's head as she bent down. "Very good."

Kiar glared at him as she helped him to his feet, and his expression slowly cleared. "Did I already say 'astonishing'?"

"Yes."

"Oh. If only I—" A panicked wail from Lisette cut him off. She was staring at her hand, waving it frantically. Then she shoved her fingers into the dirt again. When she pulled them free, she started sobbing.

Tiana stared, biting her lip until she tasted blood. The pure light that had once crowned Lisette's fingertips now stretched halfway down her fingers.

"Cathay!" she shouted, and found him right beside her. He reached for her hand and she stepped away. "Soothe her. Calm her. You know how to distract her. Be what she needs." Before he could respond, she took two steps away and added, "Slater! You come with me."

"Tiana," said Cathay, his eyes wide, anguished. "I'm not—"

She shook her head. "I'm going to find this Voice and sort things out." She unsheathed Jinriki and leaned the blade against her shoulder. "You take care of things here. Do it!"

Slater followed her into the woods. "How may I help, Your Highness?"

"Just... be here. In case...." She shook her head again. "Remember for me." She couldn't think, couldn't spare time to see if he understood. She could still hear Lisette sobbing. "Jinriki. Find me that man. Jozua Harken."

Yes.

She let her feet lead her, closing her eyes in relief as the forest swallowed all Lisette's tears. The hunter's camp was close, closer than she expected, and full of the sounds of rough, bored men. At the edge of their camp, she stopped and shouted, louder than she intended, "Where's Jozua?"

Silence fell across the camp as a half-dozen uncouth, hairy men stared at her, and then at Slater behind her. One of them kicked a small tent and the big man himself crawled out, looking as if he'd just woken up.

"Princess," Jozua said, as he brushed himself off. "What do you want?"

"Show me where you found Lisette."

He raised his eyebrows at her until she was ready to snap at him again. "Sure." He settled his weapons around himself and followed her back into the woods. "There wasn't anything there. What are you looking for?"

"Whatever did that thing to her." She tightened her fingers around Jinriki's hilt. "We'll see what's there for ourselves."

"Ah." He regarded her curiously. "Do you really carry that sword like a club? It's pretty big for a slip of a girl like yourself."

"Yes," said Tiana. "It's very large, and I'm not a swordswoman. If you provoke me I might start swinging it around wildly. Somebody could get hurt."

He laughed silently and walked through the forest ahead of her, moving with an ease that belied his size.

The clouds that had threatened a downpour the last few

days finally delivered. The water seeped through the canopy in a thoroughly unpleasant way but Jozua didn't seem to notice. The rain was probably the first bath he'd had in days.

"Here." The spot wasn't even a clearing. There was a large rock, with a fallen tree rotting to shreds on top of it. There was a depression in the ground where water puddled. And there was an extra dense canopy of leaves that gave way as they arrived, shedding a waterfall on Tiana's head. She tilted her head back and closed her eyes, and then slicked her hair away from her face.

"Right. Where was she? Did they just toss her on the ground?" Silently, Jozua pointed at the depression. "Lovely. You may go now, if you wish." He shrugged and leaned against a tree and Tiana promptly put him out of her mind.

She reversed Jinriki and slid the point of the blade into the soil, deep enough that the sword would remain standing if she let go. "Get somebody's attention, Jinriki."

Yes. The sword practically purred. The hilt pulsed beneath her hands, and the forest grew darker. Shadows blurred together and the trees became twisted and inhospitable. The rain sharpened and flowed across the ground like a living thing.

"Your Highness!" Slater's voice was strained. "Remember what you came to Fel Dion for!"

She did remember, but Lisette was sobbing. Wasn't it for Lisette that she started on this road? Didn't Lisette represent everything she was supposed to protect? The Firstborn had failed, and so it was only her.

The darkness shivered around her and the trees cast crimson shadows on the swirling forest floor. She would wait a few moments more before taking more direct action.

Ah, said Jinriki, and the toothed rain brightened

until each drop sparkled and sang like crystal. The living darkness broke apart under a musical onslaught, and the shadows withdrew back into Jinriki's blade. The rain tingled as it soaked her hair, until she forced the droplets away. Slater inhaled sharply, and Tiana supposed the renewed forest was beautiful to anybody else. All she felt was impatience, and banked fires.

"Well? Is this it?"

An envoy is coming.

Blurred shapes pushed through the underbrush, one large, one small. Tiana blinked water off her eyelashes and the figures resolved into a tall old woman holding the hand of a small boy, both barely dressed in green paint and bleached leather. "You must behave if you're to stay here," said the child, sternly. Tiana stared blankly at the child and then transferred her gaze to the old woman.

"If you would heed the Voice of Atalya, you may walk with us." The woman's eyes were a deep, pure green, and though she met Tiana's gaze, Tiana felt it wasn't her the old woman saw. The emerald light enfolded Tiana, pressing against her skin, and met the fire of her fury. She looked away, and nodded.

The chiming rain accompanied them through the forest as the greenery pulled away, a path opening ahead of them. The residents seemed oblivious to the music, but Jozua held out his palm and flung droplets from his fingers, fascinated. Slater said nervously, "It makes being wet a little more pleasant, doesn't it?"

Jozua tucked his hand under his cloak again. "On the other hand, it makes it harder to sleep, and covers up the sound of somebody sneaking up behind you."

It's a song, sent Jinriki. **I almost remember it. A

hymn. ** Tiana felt the ache in his words. ***Do not let the Voice convince you it is not cruel.***A clearing opened around them, more people garbed in leather and paint appearing from the green as the trees pulled away. A single enormous tree remained to dominate the center of the clearing. White-barked, it had massive limbs spreading from low on the trunk, and leaves the size of Tiana's face. A nude alabaster figure with great white wings lounged on the lowest limb, like a self-indulgent monarch on a throne. At its right hand stood the siblings Fai and Cinai. The crystal rain clung to them and they seemed bright and precious.

The Voice of Atalya regarded Tiana with burning emerald eyes, then waved a hand. "At last. Welcome. You've brought the unpleasant one, we see. Well done." A white and blue butterfly emerged from the Voice's palm and fluttered over to Jozua. He moved to brush it away, but it landed on his mouth. All his movement stilled. His eyes closed and his breathing seemed to stop. The butterfly languidly flapped its wings.

"Jozua?" Concern made the name awkward on Tiana's tongue.

"He is beyond your words, Your Highness." The Voice stood. "But he will help us in a game."

Tiana remembered Lisette's story, and rage engulfed her again. Jinriki was a flame in her hand, and emanations stirred the air around her. "No games! Return Lisette to the way she was."

"That is not within my power, Princess." The Voice studied its fingernails. "But perhaps within yours, if you play the game and complete your task."

Politics! *Here!* The shock of it swept her breath away. Her head swimming, she tried to understand what the Voice wanted her to do.

No. There was too much, it was just a game, an attempt to control her. She wouldn't play. The Voice was talking like politics and that meant it *lied*. She needed to defend herself and Lisette.

What she remembered later was that Jinriki was silent, neither urging restraint nor encouraging her. What she heard at the time, though, was Slater.

He muttered, "Oh hell," and stepped forward, catching her free hand in his own. His skin was cool and wet, and he smelled of crushed leaves and wood smoke. "Tiana," he said urgently, awkwardly. "Where ever you've gone, you must come back. Today has been frightening, but you've always wanted to make decisions as yourself, as who you've chosen to be. You want to be more than the blood you bear. I've watched you, I've seen it. Come back. Don't let your magic make decisions for you."

Sluggishly, Jinriki said, **Decisions...**

Slater squeezed her hand tightly. Such clumsy words. He wasn't Lisette. Would Lisette be able to squeeze her hand again? Oh, painful thought. It would be so easy to just lose herself in her own rage, without even the phantasmagory to run to. How could a Secondborn *do* such a thing?

Jerya used to read to Lisette and her from some of her political books. A memory from one of them rose now: *"When you buy a ship from a politician, be assured you will receive the ship; but you will also receive the ship's cargo, whatever it is."* The creature didn't have to be lying. Perhaps restoring Lisette was beyond its power now. And perhaps there were secrets buried in its truths.

Tiana wondered if Jerya had felt this rage when Iriss had been attacked, or even when Iriss had been restored, strange and different, barely human, a Regent no longer. If so, there'd been no sign of it in Jerya's letter, crumpled in her skirt pocket. It had been calm and measured, reporting the news and dispensing general advice. Wear your cloak. Listen to Kiar. Try not to kill anyone.

Jerya would want her to be good. She sighed and squeezed Slater's hand back. Startled, he pulled away, and she let him go. She looked at his downturned, embarrassed face, and her attention was caught by Jozua, statue-still, behind him.

"What is your game, Voice?" she asked, looking at how still Jozua was.

"Excellent," said the Voice. "I shall make yonder brave hunter into prey, and he will stumble among the briars and thorns. Where he bleeds, flowers will spring up, and the scent of his blood will pull all the Lady's children from their dens to stalk him. Recall you what happened when the servants of the Lord of Winter were gathered together in his sacred place?"

Better than you. Had the gathering mattered? In a great contest of wills, Jinriki had stolen their magic. In the profound silence after, something had touched each monk to release a tiny bit of Niyhan's wisdom and power stored within them, transferred via dreams.

"What would be my role?" Many of the forest children were already gathered, young and old, watching her with expressionless faces. Men and women, boys and girls, marked with paint and dressed in rags and furs. Most of them had green eyes, though on the fringes she saw brown and hazel eyes. Some sort of initiation rite?

The Secondborn's favor.

Most of them had weapons: knives and small bows and darts.

The Voice said, "Call the hunt. Release the hunters."

Jozua's eyes opened but he was still frozen. She wondered if he could see and hear. Annoyed she'd ended up in a position to defend him, she snapped, "He isn't an animal, to be hunted for your pleasure." Why had he come along?

The Voice lifted its head. "Not mere pleasure, but a sacred rite. You know of Maidrunning in the spring. It is autumn and the hunter is in the sacred forest; let the rite reverse itself." A happy little smile played over that inhuman mouth.

Tiana remembered again the dancing and the races of Running, She recalled what Berrin had said about children's' interpretations, and how he'd chased his sister down to push her into the mud.

It spoke on. "And perhaps it will serve you in more ways than one. Red blood on the green wild. I have seen in the pool that this is something you care about."

She thought to Jinriki, **Can it really be so? You said it was cruel.**

I would happily drink its blood, but if a game is required to gather Atalya's light, her Voice is the only one who knows the rules. Although I can't fathom the point of this reversed ritual.

To gather the light... she thought, but no, it hadn't said that, had it? It hadn't even said the hunt was the game. Maybe this was the game, right now.

Tiana shook her head. "That's insane." She glanced around at the watchers. "Do all of you think this is right, to serve Atalya with such bloodlust? None of you remember her as something gentle and kind?"

"Gentle and kind *outside*, and in response, they only take and take from her. Sacrifice has become her duty," said a creaky woman's voice.

Tiana swung around, looking for the source of the voice. While she was trying to decide which of two older women had spoken, Fai said, "We know the true Atalya."

"And she wants blood?" Tiana didn't believe it.

"He hunts my sister!"

Tiana winced. She didn't like Jozua's 'hunt', but that didn't matter. "It's not the same. He wants to take her home, not kill her."

"Duty and desire," said the Voice, smirking. "Now he is part of something much vaster than even he ever dreamt."

A quiet voice said, "I'd actually prefer he just left." Cinai dropped her eyes as Tiana glanced at her.

"Cinai, no!" said Fai. "We gave him that chance! He's made his choice."

Cinai shrugged and hunched her narrow shoulders. "Atalya didn't kill her captors. She didn't hurt anybody."

Tiana recovered herself. "Yes. Listen to Cinai! She's one of your own and her choice should matter."

Fai cried, "Give him his freedom and he will take hers, eventually!"

Tiana thought of Jozua waiting in his camp. "Would he? Could he? From his campsite?"

Fai scowled at Jozua's still form. "He has his ways."

Near Cinai, a little boy holding a rabbit in his arms said, "I don't want to hunt him either. If he stays in the forest too long, he'll change, anyhow." He looked up at Cinai, who ruffled his hair. Then he turned and wandered into the woods.

The circle of observers rustled and a few other people muttered something before walking away. The butterfly on Jozua's lips lifted away, leaving Jozua blinking. A strange rumbling laughter emerged from him.

"What? What are you laughing at?" Tiana snapped.

The laughter became a cough and then he said, "All this talk of freedom and choice. But from what she said, your Lady Lisette had none."

The Voice of Atalya lounged against its tree inspecting a wing, as if it didn't much care that its audience was leaving and its game had fallen apart.

We've been talking. I don't think it can take away the gift it forced on Lisette. Let's just kill it.

Tiana seriously considered the idea, but Fai and Cinai, facing each other, distracted her again.

Cinai said, "He's right, Fai. If you want to champion somebody's freedom, go take care of that poor girl the Voice hurt. I can make my own choices here."

Fai's eyes slowly widened. He half-shook his head, frowned, and then looked from side to side like a trapped animal. In that other vision, the emerald light shuddered and flickered, like a guttering candle. Tiana reached out a hand. But the trembling remained: not a candle but leaves in the wind.

Cinai raised her voice. "Go! Leave me alone for once. Help somebody who needs it, who our *own patron* has mistreated." Her voice shook, and Fai stepped backward.

"It was needful," said the Voice, like a sulky child. "She wouldn't accept the present and Somebody worked so hard on it, too."

Tiana, unsettled by the rapidly shifting light only she could sense, stared at the Voice. Only with the skill of long experience did she control the desire to shout. What did *any* of them know about choice?

Fai turned his frown on the Voice and his shoulders straightened. Then he bowed to Tiana, as courtly as any of her suitors. Lisette was right; he was noble-born. Jozua had said something about Cinai being destined to be the mother of Dukes, hadn't he? "May I accompany you to your camp and examine the mischief worked upon your companion?"

"Do you think it will help?" She was savagely pleased when his control flickered to reveal wild, haunted eyes. The day wasn't going as she'd planned, either.

Fai closed his eyes for a moment. When he opened them, he said, "I don't know, but I will place what stock I have with the Lady Atalya at Lady Lisette's service. My own sister commands it. How could I do otherwise?"

The will to poke around inside the shell of glass thorns the boy maintained drained out of Tiana, until all that remained was tiredness. "Come along, then." She looked past him to the Voice, who smiled. "Is this still your game?"

Instead of answering, it swung back into its tree and went to sleep. Tiana was not surprised. "Come on," she repeated, and turned to go back to her campsite. It wasn't until she was almost back that she realized Jozua had not returned with them.

CHAPTER TWENTY-TWO

THE CHANNEL

NO LONGER CRYSTAL music, the steady rain shower promised dampness for days to come. Fai hardly seemed to notice the wet, and he was just as oblivious to Jozua's absence. She ought to chase the hunter down and drag him back with her; he could only be causing trouble, left alone. She needed him in one piece at until she worked out how to extract the crimson light sleeping within him. After that he could go get himself hanged for all she cared.

But she was tired, and afraid for Lisette, and so very frustrated. It was good the Firstborn had retreated from the world, because if one appeared before her now, she would shake them for making this so difficult. Their promised help had been a shining fairytale come to life and now she was cold and wet and *things* were creeping down her boots and worse *things* emerged every day from a hole in the world. Her sister's letter, with its vivid description of the gap in the night, crumpled in her pocket.

***I'm sure if your Firstborn could work faster, they would.*

They fear Ohedreton, you know that. Don't believe they grant this gift out of love for your world. **

Tiana sighed and recalled the sensation of the blue light washing through her. At that point, Niyhan had seemed wise and all-knowing. Confidence flowed naturally. How could the plan fail, whatever it was? She simply had to obey and collect the lights of the Firstborn. Then, somehow, it would all be made well again. They were the Firstborn and she wanted to obey them, but right now it felt like an impossible challenge.

The sound of the campsite rose over the patter of the rain. Tiana pushed her way into the guards' clearing where the rain came down in sheets. One man managed the sputtering, steaming fire; the rest were either inside tents or building some sort of shelter out of cut branches. The fire tender sprang to attention, his gaze going past her to Slater and then to Fai.

"Thank you for your escort, Lieutenant," said Tiana. "Go do something else. You, Fai, come with me."

Fai barely raised his head, but at least stayed on her heels. In the linked clearing, Twist and Cathay spoke with Lisette under an open tent, while Kiar huddled on the edge of the trees, Minex perched on a branch near her. "There she is. Can you actually do anything for her, or is this a symbolic gesture?"

Fai's voice was low. "What happened to her?"

"Your precious Voice forced her to take up a gauntlet that sank into her hand. Now her fingers are turning into light."

"Atalya's Voice," he murmured. "It values strength. Purity. I suppose..." he shook his head and moved to kneel before Lisette. "Lady Lisette, may I inspect your injury?"

Above his head, Lisette met Tiana's gaze. She was a mess, more rumpled and red-eyed than Tiana had ever seen her, but she looked curious rather than upset at the moment. Tiana forced herself to smile in return, until Lisette's attention returned to the young man in front of her.

Will indulging her histrionics improve matters? It is power, even if it has unfortunate side effects.

Irritated, Tiana thought, ***Sometimes I really don't like you very much.***

Almost mildly, Jinriki said, ***I don't like anybody very much, but your Lisette has earned more of my respect than most. Her current state of mind is alien to me. She doesn't want the power. How can that be?***

I don't know! Maybe it hurts. Maybe she doesn't like how her hand is vanishing. We do like our hands, you know. Maybe she doesn't want it because it was forced on her. I know forcing people to do things doesn't bother you much but that doesn't make it all right, it makes you a fiend.

Doggedly, Jinriki said, ***She was not this upset when I used her to speak to you.***

Tiana put her hands in her hair and turned away from Lisette and Fai. ***You're the mind-reader, sword.***

You're the human, Tiana. His voice curled around her like smoke.

Kiar detached herself from the forests' edge and moved towards her, and Tiana waved, glad of a distraction from Jinriki's conversation. From his voice, from the way he said her name.

"Look at her. I can't think of anything better to cheer her up, can you?" Tiana nodded at Lisette, surrounded by three attentive men. She could actually think of all sorts of better things, but none of them were in the forest and Lisette had admitted she missed Cathay's attention sometimes. That had to be worth something.

Kiar didn't even bother to look that direction, didn't even make the pretense of attending as she said, "Yes. Tiana, we need to move the camp. Outside the forest, preferably."

This conversation wasn't much better than Jinriki's. "You keep saying this and I keep saying I'm not ready, Kiar. You've got to—"

Kiar pushed pale wet hair away from her face with both hands. The whites of her eyes glinted in the dimming light. "No, listen. Earlier, I was distracted, and I dropped the aegis in the other world shielding our location from the Blighter. I re-established it, but..."

Tiana gnawed on her thumbnail. "Do you know that he saw us? Is a sky fiend near?"

"Other than Jinriki?" Kiar shrugged and pressed her lips together. "We hardly know what Ohedreton is capable of. Given that, we need to assume the worst."

Tiana wondered what had upset Kiar so much that she lost her iron focus; there were so many possibilities lately. Lisette, Jozua, Twist... ah, yes.

Something was odd about her story. "We're not moving right now because it's raining and it's almost night. But you re-established it? How did you do that?"

Kiar blinked and frowned. "I don't know." She cast about. "I just... reached out and did it. Without a sky fiend, without needing to be present. Except I *was* present." She chewed on her lip. "I have to think about this."

Tiana stuffed the damp letter from Jerya into Kiar's hand. "Read this when you do think about it because it may matter. Eidolons behave differently in the gap in the night. If you've been maintaining one through the gap, that's important."

Kiar took the letter, looked at it, and glanced up again, her brow furrowed. "All right. Later. How can I convince you we need to move the camp?"

"I really think I'm getting close, Kiar. The green light is... trembling. We can't leave." Tiana watched Kiar draw breath to argue and added, "Ask me again in the morning. We'll have all day to come up with a plan, then."

Kiar blew out her breath in a sigh. "I guess that will be all right. As long as nothing happens tonight."

Tiana smiled at her. "Exactly." Kiar lowered her head and moved back to her tree.

She should have mobilized the camp for departure while we were gone, if she was really concerned.

Tiana dropped her gaze. **Hah. It's Kiar. Everybody would look at her. She can't do that.**

Certainly not if she never has to. You are too kind to your companions. They will never grow and improve if you pamper them.

Don't say stupid things. Kiar shuts down when she's overwhelmed.

Oh, don't I get pampered, too? Well, I shall return the favor. Tiana clenched her fist, wondering if they were going to quarrel again. But he simply said, **She is stronger than she believes herself.**

Well, we can agree there. Nobody can ever make her see it, though.

Because you try kindness. Demand action instead.

Tiana recalled the fight against the sky fiend in the field, when Kiar had tried to free the creature. She'd failed, blamed herself, and huddled behind a shield while Tiana and Jinriki had dispatched the sky fiend. **It's not as easy as you think. If you'd known her as long as I have... you'd see it's not an easy thing.**

The trees rustled, and Cinai emerged near Tiana, followed by Jozua. Without the glimmering blessing of the crystal rain, Cinai looked older and less innocent: not a forest child but a young woman. But her eyes were clear and she carried a ragged bundle.

She paused next to Tiana and said quietly, "He's always known how to talk to girls, how to get what he wants and make them feel good about themselves at the same time. If our mother hadn't died..." She shook her head. "Well, the price he pays for being able to talk to women is that he has to listen to them." Behind her, Jozua snorted with laughter.

Tiana's alarm overtook her desire to listen. "That one hasn't threatened you, has he? Look, what I said before didn't mean I was on his side. You don't need to—Why is he with you?"

Cinai hesitated and then shook her head. "We've been talking. I've decided to go home again. There's a lot at stake." She dropped her eyes, as if expecting to be scolded for this decision, which put Tiana enough off balance that she didn't.

Instead, she asked, "Why did you run away? I heard something about a marriage?"

Her voice low, Cinai said, "Yes. To the son of the Count of Biaxin. It was arranged years ago."

Tiana gave her a helpless, unhappy look. She and all her family had the power of choice in their marriages, which only made sense in their situation. But she knew many other young people didn't. It was a popular theatrical trope. "Don't you like him?" she asked sympathetically.

Cinai shrugged, hugging herself. "He's all right. I don't want to marry him, though. I don't want to let him paw me every night until our fathers have their Duke again."

Tiana frowned. "I could cancel the arrangement, if you wish. There's something about Biaxin and the Counties, anyhow. Lisette would know."

Cinai gave her a strange little smile. "Could you? But no. There are too many benefits. Especially now, with the Blight." She turned her gaze to her brother again, still engaged in a soft conversation with Lisette. "He encouraged me to run away, and now I have to tell him I'm going back. Come with me? I'm not strong like you are. I'm afraid he'll talk me into changing my mind."

Jozua cracked his knuckles. "Oh, we can't be having with that."

Cinai addressed him for the first time in Tiana's hearing, her voice flat. "If you hurt him, I will do everything in my power to destroy you. And he will want to fight you, so maybe you should just go back to your camp."

Jozua laughed. "No. Go on, say your goodbyes. I'll watch from here."

Cinai hunched her shoulders and walked toward her brother, radiating dread. Tiana bit her lip and then caught up with her. She wished the green light would stop flickering so madly, and the sleeping red light wasn't complicating matters. She even longed for the ignorance she had at the Citadel of the Sky—had the blue light flickered before Jinriki's rebellion had given it an opportunity to pour itself into her? Was it a good thing or a bad thing?

Fai looked up in time to see Cinai approaching him, and froze, Lisette's hand in his own. Then he raised Lisette's hand to show it to Cinai. "It's amazing, Cinai. You were right."

Cinai whispered, "I'm going home, Fai." The words carried, despite the rain, despite the noise of the campsite. Lisette looked down, and pulled her hand away.

All the same, Fai stared at her. "What? What was that?" Cinai didn't answer, instead lowering her gaze.

Fai said, "You can't! We're dedicated to the Firstborn now, that's what you wanted! You can't go back."

Panic flared in Cinai's eyes. Tiana wanted to help her, but didn't know how to defend Cinai's decision. "It's her choice," was the easy cry—but she was returning to do something she didn't want to do, bind herself to other people's ambitions. "It's her choice," was an argument that cut both ways. And the Firstborn they followed was unfamiliar to Tiana, and very different from the gentle flower lady who watched over her from ceiling frescoes.

Cinai swallowed and found her own words. "I've been thinking and listening, Fai. And I think I can. I think I should. Going home is the right thing to do. It's my duty."

Fai only had eyes for his sister as he crossed the space between them. "It's a sacrifice. It's capture. You know that's not right."

Cinai put her hand up, as if to hold him away. "I don't know! I don't know that anything in this forest is right. You've seen what the Voice did to that girl. How can that be right? How does that match with all these ideals of freedom?"

"But you've felt her here, the same as I have! You know here She is a huntress, that outside this forest they follow a false Atalya."

"How can she be false when studying Her stories led us here?" Cinai's voice trembled, and Tiana touched her arm in encouragement.

When she did, Tiana's breath hissed through her teeth and her gentle touch became a clenched fi st. The green light gathered around Cinai, roiling like a stormy sea. But it was still beyond her reach, on the other side of a veil.

Slowly, she flexed her fingers and muttered, "Atalya is with her, even now." She raised her gaze to see both siblings staring at her from identical green eyes. "I can feel it."

Fai cried, "You don't know anything. How can you feel it? I feel Atalya. She whispers in my ear. She wakes me at night." He stepped forward, and Tiana moved between them, planting a hand on his chest to stop him.

And stopped herself. Once again, she could sense the green light gathering, this time around Fai, rushing and roaring. "How can that be? It's in both of you...." She shook her head, dizzied.

Perhaps you have to cut them open.

Tiana glanced at Jozua, who watched the argument with an amused unconcern, the crimson light still and quiet. Then emerald vertigo swirled around her and she stumbled to one side. Both siblings stared at her.

"Work it out," she demanded. "How can she be with the dutiful daughter and the wild son?" The air pressed down on her, as if the rain hadn't already started. "What is the common thread? What is she?"

Helplessly, Fai said, "I wanted to save her. I wanted her to be free to live her own life, not sold like a horse."

Cinai whispered, "I was so afraid. I didn't want to go. But I can make a difference. I can save everybody."

"Thank you," said Tiana and stepped between them again. This time she placed a hand on each sibling's chest. The light was there, beyond a tissue-thin veil. She wondered if Jinriki spoke the truth, and she had to reach inside them to take it. Was that right? It felt wrong.

Dreamily, she asked, "Fai, you brought her here to save her. But does Atalya need saving?"

He sucked in his breath. Then, slowly, he said, "The true Atalya walks into the forest to escape."

Cinai said, "She was taken, but she redeemed her captors."

There was a long, breathless moment. The twins stared at each other, their faces mirror images as they listened to something within them. Fai whispered, "Atalya saves herself."

Cinai nodded at him, saying back, "Atalya saves herself."

The rain turned to crystal again. Tiana hesitated, thinking about taking and choosing,and then repeated, "Thank you." She took her hands away and stepped back. "Will you give me what you have?"

Drops of water sang. "Gladly," said Cinai, her face alight.

Fai said nothing, and his expression darkened. The world itself rippled, as if the siblings were stones dropped into a pool. He pulled his gaze away from Cinai's face and looked around, to where Lisette stood. "I don't have to," he murmured, a struggle playing out across his face. "I don't want to. Is this how you feel, Cinai? I don't want to give Her up. But we want them all to be free, like we are. So I will." He spread his arms.

A green glow gathered around each sibling's chest, drawing radiance from the verdant trees. Each raindrop was a prism, splitting the shadows of the forest into a viridian rainbow. The glow pulled itself out of each sibling, spectral halves of an orb. For a space of time they hung there, together but separate, as if inviting the siblings to take them back again. Then Cinai made a little shooing gesture with her hand, and wiped tears from her eyes.

The hemispheres flowed together into a single orb.

Kiar screamed something. As she did, utter darkness fell, roaring, upon them.

CHAPTER TWENTY-THREE

BLOOD IN THE GREEN WILD

ARKNESS FELL, BUT the orb of green light still glowed just beyond Tiana's fingers. If her eyes were torn out, still she would see that light. She had no chance to claim it, though, before it fled that which stole the twilight. Kiar shouted her name. The fading green light muddied as someone cried out in agony, and a woman screamed.

We are in an eidolon, said Jinriki, and Tiana finally understood what Kiar shouted: ambush. Ohedreton *had* found them. He'd been content to wait as they waited, until the green light appeared. Now, his forces attacked in earnest.

How did you see in a world without light? Tiana remembered Kiar's description of that other world and wondered if it was the same. But she had no time for daydreams. Something moved near her and her own body moved in response, jerked like a doll by Jinriki in her hand.

"Can you sense them?" The sound of combat thudded

around her: soft, organic noises, and the cries of the guards.

   They are hidden by the greater eidolon, but I can hear as you hear. That will be enough.

"No, not enough," and she struggled to grasp the idea dancing tantalizingly out of reach. But the green light had been so close, born into an orb she could take inside herself, and now it was distant again, and tainted. The hurt of it overwhelmed the rage, and both overwhelmed her thinking.

People fought around her. Lisette was somewhere, Cathay and Twist beside her. She was probably safe, but how long would that last in the dark?

Kiar had used some inner sense to see in the world without light. But Tiana couldn't see for everybody. She had to attack the darkness.

Tiana, wind and fire.

She held out her arms, and imagined her rage rising through her. Radiance burned down her skin, little flames licking at the darkness. She felt, rather than heard, a deep moan, and so she flung her hands up and the eidolon fire devoured the eidolon darkness.

Sparks chased down the darkness like embers burning paper, revealing chaos. Andani battled humans, but more people fought than she expected, some in furs and paint. Several of the four-legged giants moved among them, swinging great staves. Despite the forest reinforcements, the melee went poorly for Tiana's side. Cathay stood halfway between Lisette and Tiana, two of his cats fighting at his side while emanations flickered around his sword. Lisette pressed close to Twist, pale but steady. Twist spoke quickly and quietly to the pair of andani menacing them, his hands flickering strangely.

Kiar stood at the forest's edge, an aegis shimmering

among the wall of trees. Beyond, more andani seethed. Minex perched in a tree, watching Kiar as if her magic was the most interesting thing in the clearing.

Tiana only noticed the slender blade a creature thrust toward her after Jinriki had dragged her into a roll to avoid it. She let him guide her hand while looking around wildly. The guards and forest children gathered into little knots around the wounded and the fallen, and none of them were Cinai and Fai.

Pay attention! You must start fighting back or they will fall!* The frustration in Jinriki's voice mirrored her own.

"Where are they? Fai and Cinai and the light, where did they *go*?" She knew he was right, though. Searching now would leave her companions to fight alone. She reached for focus.

But the phantasmagory was gone. She had to collect her thoughts without it. She lashed out wildly with an emanation, and a four-legged giant barely had to duck to avoid the blow. The monster squealed laughter and said something incomprehensible. That laugh gave her the focus of rage and she struck true the second time.

She looked away as the head of the eidolon bounced by, just as Twist failed to dodge the blade of an andani. It took him in the arm and he fell to one side, leaving Lisette standing alone, her back against a tree. Kiar shouted again, and the aegis she was maintaining vanished, to be replaced by a flurry of swords. But the andani just kept coming. Cathay cried out as the andani destroyed two of his cats. He stumbled, losing his footing.

Then Lisette glowed like stained glass, and reality poured off her. The guards became more substantial, while the aliens faded like a pencil sketch. She stood over Twist, a mother wolf, and with two sharp gestures she tore apart the andani with a hand of fire.

They all looked to the light, every human and alien in the clearing. Strange shadows moved independently, though their owners were frozen in shock. Something danced in the air before Lisette, wavering like a heat mirage. Then the mirage vanished, and it was only Lisette. She shrieked, "Don't just stand there, fight them!"

But the andani and the giants turned to flee, every one of them at the same time. They were harried to the edge of the clearing, driven back into the darkness beyond Kiar's aegis. Then the men turned their attention to the wounded, and Tiana turned her attention to the missing.

A moment's concentration told her they were not among the casualties, or at least that the green light had moved off to the east. She took a breath and turned her gaze on Lisette, who knelt with Kiar next to Twist, her cloak pulled tight around her. Then she found Slater, bleeding from shallow cuts. "Break the camp. Do what you can for the wounded, leave them with the forest children if you have to, but we must move on, out of the forest, before they return. I have to finish what I came here for, but as soon as I return, we must leave."

On the edge of the forest, she found Jozua, speaking with some of his own rough men. He held his axe in one hand and a hunting horn in the other, and Tiana recalled the golden belling of the horn in the eidolon darkness. He noticed her and waved his men away. "I think the brother took the opportunity of cover to spirit off the sister, eh?"

Tiana remembered the muddying of the green light and said, "No."

He fell into step beside her. "No? What, then?"

"I don't know," she said. "You only think he did that because that's what you would do."

"Oh ho? And what would you do?"

She remembered an alley, and blood. "I wouldn't run." She shook her head. "But it doesn't matter. We're not them."

"We're going to find them, yes? Do you have any idea of where to search?"

"I can find them." She frowned. Jozua's presence, with the red light sleeping within him, overpowered the coalesced green light. "But not with you here."

"Ah? Why is that? What was the theology lesson before your enemies attacked?"

She whirled on him. "My enemies? Ceria's enemies! Your enemies! Or do you think you would be safe, as the forest children did?"

His hazel eyes glinted. "A slip of the tongue. My apologies, Your Highness."

Tiana let her feathers smooth back down. "I'm collecting the Light of the Firstborn to use against the Blight. Fai and Cinai were the vessels for the light of Atalya. They still have it. I can find them."

"Ah," Jozua said, as if he understood perfectly.

Tiana frowned. "It's harder with you present." She wondered if explaining would change the situation, and gave Jinriki a chance to pipe in with an opinion. But he was uncharacteristically silent.

Monitoring Lisette and others.

Tiana sighed and said, "You're also a vessel. So you're interfering with my sense."

Jozua's eyebrows vanished into his hair. "Me? I've never been a man of faith."

Impatiently, Tiana said, "We can discuss whether that's

required later, but if, for now, you could *please* stand away from me, or better yet, stay behind, I'd like to find the green light."

Silently, he bowed and fell behind her, until he was barely visible among the trees. It wasn't perfect but she didn't want to spend more time arguing with him.

The green light was closer than she hoped; they'd stopped running and gone to ground as soon as they could. The glow suffused a massive tangle of fallen trees, but it didn't show her a path in.

Pull it apart?

"I'm not their enemy, Jinriki." She raised her voice as loud as she dared in the quiet wood, calling, "Cinai, it's Tiana. The battle's over."

Branches rustled within the tangle of trees, and Cinai said something incomprehensible, her voice distorted by sobbing.

Tiana moved closer, climbing up on one of the trunks. "I didn't hear you."

"Can you—can you help me carry him? I don't want to hurt him further."

Tiana glanced over her shoulder at where Jozua lurked, and then slid down into the wooden cave. Cinai crouched down, her arms around an unconscious Fai. The green glow filled his chest, and only by peering close could Tiana see the raw gash that the light filled.

"A sword came through him—-his eyes got so wide. I pushed the green light into him and he didn't fall. We ran, and then he fell. I dragged him here. He's still breathing, do you see?"

Tiana did. More to the point, she saw the edges of the wound fluttering with each breath. Hesitantly, she touched his chest, wondering if she could absorb the green light.

"What are you doing? Don't take it! It's all he has!"

Tiana yanked her hand away, but she already knew she couldn't take it, that it was bound by Cinai's own desires.

Regretfully, she said, "I'll help you move him, but both of you have to come with me."

In the dimness of the tree cave, Cinai's face was tight and frightened. "Come where? I said I would go home."

Tiana waved a hand. "Perhaps. We can decide on 'where' later. Right now we need to get out of the forest."

Cinai said, "But Fai needs healing! The Voice—-."

Tiana clenched her fist, remembering Lisette's story. "The Voice does not want Atalya to share her power. Do you understand what the light is?"

Cinai shook her head. "It's a gift of Atalya and it's keeping Fai from *dying*. And I know the Voice can heal."

Something scurried outside the wooden cave and Tiana hunched her shoulders. "The Blighter wants that gift, or wants to destroy it. The light is Atalya's throne and it's meant as a *weapon*, Cinai, Atalya's weapon. I need it. The Voice will make sure I don't get it."

"It gave you Lisette's gift," Cinai pointed out. "I don't want to take Fai out of the forest! Maybe the light will vanish, maybe he'll die!"

Knock her out, bring them both along. Tiana ground her teeth and didn't answer Jinriki, even though it was dangerously tempting. How far did not taking go? She wondered where the Blighter's servants had gone. It couldn't have been far.

Then, as sweetly as she could, she said, "Cinai, I'm a Princess of the Blood and you and your brother are my people, but protecting the country is my responsibility. You *will* come with me and act with the responsibility befitting your rank." She extended an emanation, and lifted Fai from Cinai's arms.

"No!" cried Cinai, but she let Fai be pulled away. Tiana started climbing out of the wooden cave, not looking to see if Cinai was following her. Instead, she concentrated on maneuvering Fai's drifting body among the tangled branches, and wondered how Cinai had gotten him inside in the first place.

Jozua had moved in from the edge of the trees, and a fine mist of rain fell. Tiana couldn't see his face in the darkness, for which she was glad. She turned to look at the mass of trees again, staring until finally she saw Cinai's head emerge from a hole near the ground.

She stood, covered in mud. "The Lady won't let him die." Her voice was dreamy. "If all the world burns, while that light maintains him, he'll live. That's enough."

Tiana sighed. If mysticism was required, she'd take it, but if Jerya had tried the quiet authority, it would have worked. She hoped the camp would be broken by the time they got back. She should have listened to Kiar, and they should have moved the camp, and it was past the time for recriminations, time for action, even in this downpour. They would look to her for a destination, and for that, she had to work out what to do about Jozua and his sleeping light.

CHAPTER TWENTY-FOUR

THE STARCATCHER HAND

T HEY WEREN'T READY to leave until long after full night, but nobody suggested waiting until dawn. In rain and darkness, they led the horses to the old road and mounted. Minex, once again fully awake and unrepentant, scampered in front. Ghostly flames, will o' the wisps, sprang up around her, and they followed the road as it wound through the forest to its eastern edge.

In darkness, Lisette stared down at the light at the end of her wrist, hidden from others under her cloak. The shape of her fingers remained, but they glowed like incandescent flames through frosted glass. Tiana had inspected it, and tightened her lips, and touched her shoulder. Twist had thanked her somberly for his life. Kiar had given her a pained frown. And the big man who had carried her through the woods, Jozua, gave her a wry smile that made her want to hug him. Only his expression made her feel human.

She looked into the light as she curled her shining fingers. She could touch material things, but barely feel them. Her grip was uncertain, and she was afraid of touching anything alive. She couldn't stop thinking the gauntlet remained and her hand was gone. When she'd summoned up the lux against the living eidolons, she felt like she was trading her flesh for power, like the gauntlet was devouring her. Like she was doing something wrong.

She shivered, and pulled her cloak closer around her. The rhythmic swaying of her horse soothed her, but she couldn't take her eyes off her hand. When she tried, all she saw was blackness. The murmur of voices, the creak of leather, the smell of wet horse, but like a metaphor for her life, all she saw was devouring light and a powerful darkness.

She'd always known her life would be dedicated to the Blood. She never imagined it would be quite so literal.

She curled and uncurled her fingers, felt the coolness of the light with her other hand as she clasped them together. That was the strangest part: to the rest of her flesh, the light was hardly anything at all: not a warmth, not a tingle, just a numb pressure, as if her hand had fallen asleep.

The light swallowed her sense of time passing, and shockingly soon, when she lifted her gaze from the lux to compare it to the dark, she found a dirty grey instead. The horses squelched along a muddy track, between barren fields. At some point, the rain had stopped, but heavy, wet clouds covered the sky.

Jozua rode near her, as if by accident. He quirked a grin at her as she regarded him. "Good trick, sleeping while you ride."

"I wasn't asleep—" she began, then realized he had to know the truth. She ought to smile back at him, but she couldn't find the energy.

As the day got brighter, the scouts found an abandoned

farmstead, and they settled down to rest for a few hours. Lisette found herself passing her horse to a guard and moving to find Tiana, the habit too strong for even a lux-infused hand to break.

The princess stood in the large kitchen at the heart of the farmhouse, in a cluster with some of the others. Lisette slipped in beside her as Cathay rummaged around in a low drawer. Tiana reached for her hand and then hesitated. A pinprick of grief almost exploded in Lisette's heart. She squeezed her eyes shut and Tiana hooked their arms together.

When she opened her eyes again, the pain safely tucked away again, Cathay stood, an apple in one hand and a carrot in another. "They've left recently." The apple was freshly picked, still plump and smooth.

"Fleeing from Ohedreton's forces? The army Jerya mentioned? The road has been so empty, even in the rain," Tiana sounded bewildered.

"Villages sometimes hide from Blighter armies," said Slater, reassuringly. "They'll come back."

"But they didn't take the food," said Cathay. "That's odd."

"Maybe they were in a hurry," Tiana said darkly. "Or maybe something else happened to them. Maybe they were *taken*. Jerya said there were *humans* with the Blighter army."

Later, Lisette curled under her blanket as the others slept through the morning, thinking about Tiana's suggestion. Were those caught in the expanding Blight transformed? Was that what gave the enemy's eidolons their apparent self-will? She wondered if they'd hidden in their coats, afraid of the reactions of the people left unchanged. The andani did not hesitate; any reservations they had were surely left with their previous shape, if previous shape they had. Their minds belonged to Ohedreton.

But here she was, still Lisette. She wanted to mourn, but she stumbled. If she was still Lisette, all she had to mourn was her hand. And scars gained in battle were nothing to hide, especially for a Regent.

She woke up, staring at the fingers of her unmodified hand. She flexed them. This journey had paralyzed her. It had taken her from the world she understood and changed Tiana and Kiar, and left her all alone.

She remembered reading about this in Rocliff's analysis of the collected diaries of twelve famous Regents. Most Regents typically experienced stress and even a loss of identity when their charge developed a close relationship with somebody else. It could happen even with a private internal fixation.

It was, Rocliff wrote, a Regent's coming of age. It was easy to blame the Voice of Atalya and her glowing hand, but when she considered it closely, she'd been increasingly adrift ever since the sword Jinriki had appeared. She still believed Tiana had done the right thing in preserving her connection to the sword, but where did that leave Lisette? The Regency had a phrase about Regents and weddings that seemed apt here, even if it was hardly a romance: 'No place for a Regent at the wedding table'.

Of course, relationships were rarely so well separated, and the epigram was more about how a Regent felt than any truth of the matter. But it validated her feelings. She felt this way, and it was normal. She read enough to trust that. Yet she also knew she had to stop letting her feelings control her if she was going to be useful to the Blood.

Rocliff himself had lost his leg to gangrene. There was no magic, no suggestion of a powerful gift, just life-changing loss, and moving on.

He didn't come to terms with losing his leg in two days,

either, said a sulky, self-indulgent part of her. But Lisette knew about that, too, knew about shock and survival and visualization. She knew about the need for purpose, and a hundred and one other tricks to keep a wobbly member of the Blood focused and fighting when, potentially, everything else was lost. It was all theory, with so little practice, but she knew how it began.

So she stood. She went to find a place to clean herself up, and she brushed her hair thoroughly, and if part of herself stood aside and watched her attack her hair like her bad thoughts were tangled in it, well, that was what a decade of specialized Regent training did to you.

They spent the afternoon traveling again, this time without rain. The road remained hauntingly empty. They journeyed toward Sunasin, Fai and Cinai's home, but they were limited to the speed of Fai's travois. They moved with a careful, aching alertness. The empty landscape put everybody on edge.

Lisette guided her horse up beside Kiar. She pulled her cloak aside and stretched out her light-filled fingers. Kiar only glanced at her, busy brooding At first Lisette wanted to back off, to coddle and pet and encourage Kiar the way she would any member of the Blood. She resisted the impulse. Right now, Kiar was a resource Lisette needed to understand what had happened to her.

"What I did before... wasn't what Jinriki suggested we do, was it?"

After a hesitation, Kiar raised her head again. "I don't think so. What were you trying to do?"

Lisette said, "I wanted to send power to whatever Logos-working Twist was doing when he fell. That didn't work, but something else did. Everybody seemed... stronger. It wasn't as... explosive as what happened to Twist, either." She waggled her fingers and Kiar gave her a pained look.

"Do you think it will explode or destroy anything you touch?"

"How would I know?" She paused, thinking, and added, "No, I don't, because it doesn't burn through my cloak when I wrap it, see?"

Tiana's raised voice came from the head of the column. "—idiotic. You can't go." She'd pulled her horse to a halt, cutting off Jozua's own mount, who blew and pawed the ground.

"I have a job to do, Your Highness. I'll take the girl to her father, and you can bring along the boy later. Or keep him, I don't much care."

"No," said Tiana stubbornly. "Cinai won't go. I'll explain things to her father when we get there."

Jozua's horse danced and Jozua let it. He shook his head. "Even a Blood Princess like you should understand how I ought to report in. The Blight is coming here and the defense of the Counties and that girl's marriage are links in the same chain."

"That's idiotic, too," said Tiana. "Why would armies depend on one girl's wedding? Nobody's going to withhold troops because somebody hasn't gotten married. This is just... nonsense."

Jozua shook his head and clicked his tongue. "Can't say I disagree. It's all nonsense but it's nonsense old men with armies care a lot about. How about this: you keep Cinai and I'll go ahead to warn the Count you're coming, get some armies mobilized, even start baking the wedding cake."

He attempted to move his horse past hers. Tiana leaned over to grab its bridle, staring at him.

Like it was printed in stage directions, Lisette could see that he was considering making—and breaking—a promise to wait there for whatever Tiana needed him for; she could see that Tiana was wondering if she could trust him, and as he shifted his weight and his horse snorted, he was further considering trying to intimidate Tiana into letting his horse go.

That was never a good idea, and she wondered why he was so eager to get away. She'd miss him; in the short time since he rescued her, she'd appreciated his relaxed, easy strength. He exuded confidence in a way none of the guards did, as if nothing could ever really touch him. Cathay was like that sometimes, but she'd never seen it in anybody else.

She indicated to Kiar that she'd be right back to continue their conversation, and started to move up the stalled column.

Tiana said, "Will you swear on my blade that you'll return as soon as you convey the message?" and Lisette pulled her horse back, surprised. What a cunning, awful idea. Where had she found it?

She came up with it herself, said Jinriki in her head, sounding crotchety.

Jozua raised his eyebrows. "I've heard bad things about that sword."

"If you're trustworthy, so is he." Tiana drew Jinriki from the scabbard slung over her saddle and rotated the blade so the handle extended toward Jozua.

He reached out and then pulled his hand back. "I don't think I'll make that oath after all."

"Then you can't go. Not that I understand why the red light would be in an oath breaker anyhow."

"I cannot break an oath I haven't sworn," Jozua snapped,

his patience visibly frayed. "But perhaps if I do, your red light will let me go. Shall we try it?"

"Please!" said Lisette loudly. She softened her voice as she moved closer to the arguing pair. "Please, don't be rash, either of you. Sir, would it be so bad to travel with us for a time? We're all going to the same place, to the home of Fai and Cinai. And you've seen that it's dangerous. You must look after your charge. Does it inconvenience you somehow?"

Tiana stuck her jaw out, nodding agreement, and Jozua stared at Lisette a little too long. Then he said, "There is the army coming."

"You don't care about the army coming," Tiana pointed out. "That's an excuse. Even a Blood Princess like me can see that."

"It's still true." He sighed. "I'm inconvenienced in... small ways. But I'll stay for now."

Lisette finally found a smile. "I'm glad. Perhaps we can talk more later."

"Perhaps," he said. "If I'm lucky." A little thrill of pleasure curled in Lisette's stomach at the genuine interest in the intensity of his gaze.

Tiana said, "And work on getting over whatever issues you have with Rann, please," and Jozua broke his gaze away from Lisette's. Without responding to Tiana, he turned his horse and rode back along the column to where Fai and Cinai travelled. Tiana blew out her breath and kicked her horse into a trot, ranging ahead with Slater at her heels.

Kiar caught up with Lisette. "That could have been worse."

Lisette shrugged and immediately returned to her previous conversation. "Will you experiment with me to discover what we can do together?"

Kiar gave her a flat, unfriendly look. "Why would you want to use that thing? I don't like what it's doing to you. What could possibly be worth it?" Her response reminded Lisette of her own reaction when Tiana decided—the first time—to keep Jinriki. She shivered.

Kiar saw and instantly apologized. "I don't want anything bad—worse—to happen to you, Lisette."

Lisette curved her lips into a reassuring smile and searched for something light to say. She found nothing, and so she tossed her hair away from her face and looked down at her hand. "I don't want anything bad to happen to me either. But it's too late. I'm not what I was. I want to understand what I am. And maybe, with practice, I can control... this." She tried to wiggle her fingers and the glow wavered.

Kiar squeezed her eyes shut. When she opened them again, she looked haunted. "Fine." She held up her own hand and an eidolon gauntlet shimmered into existence over her skin.

"What are you doing? That's not the Logos."

"I'm still curious." Kiar proffered her gauntleted hand. Lisette squeezed her own hand, with its glove of light, tightly shut.

"Maybe we should wait until we're not on horses. If you get thrown like Twist—."

"I can make my shields very quickly, and I'm prepared to do so. But if you're really concerned..."

The two young women stared at each other, caught in a morass of uncertainty. Then Lisette gritted her teeth and grabbed Kiar's gauntleted hand with her own glowing one.

Or at least tried to. The light slid off the eidolon, or the eidolon slid away from the light. She pushed and her hand seemed to pass through Kiar's, without any physical sensation.

Blinking rapidly, she pulled her hand away. "Is that—?"

Kiar turned her hand over and a perfect sphere, rippling with faint colors like a soap bubble, rose from her palm. "Try to catch that."

Lisette poked a finger on her left hand at the orb, touching the warm, smooth surface and making the colors swirl. Then she swiped at it with the hand leaking light. Once again, her hand passed through it—but she could see both at the same time, at the same moment. The sphere seemed as unreal as a shadow.

Yes. That was exactly what it was like, like looking at somebody standing within a shadow.

"Ouch," said Kiar, and the sphere vanished. She tapped her fingers together and then shook them. "I'll have to think about that."

"Did you sense something? Were you hurt?"

"Not exactly. There was a pressure." She shook her head. "I'll have to think about it," she repeated.

Lisette drew in a deep breath. "All right. Can we try something with the Logos now?"

Kiar said, "I still don't think that's a good idea. Jinriki used the lux to create a monster with Tiana. We don't need to do that."

Lisette pulled her horse up, and looked back along the column. At the very end, Jozua rode beside the mule that pulled the Fai's travois. "What about healing him? If Fai was healthy, Cinai would give Tiana the green light."

Kiar's breath hissed through her teeth. "Oh no. No, no. Don't you dare mention that idea to Tiana unless we're sure it will work."

Patiently, Lisette said, "I just want you to try it. See what you can do." She reached out and closed her fingers, like she had before when she summoned the motes of light. Sparkles appeared around her fingertips.

Kiar stared at her, narrowing her eyes. Then she began to mutter to the Logos. After a moment, she extended a single fingertip and touched just one spark, exactly as Twist had done.

There was a crackle, but Kiar stayed on her horse. Instead the spark exploded into a shower of light, and Lisette felt as if somebody pulled on her hand. Kiar stumbled in her speech, her words slowing down until Lisette thought she would stop entirely. That would be bad, she knew.

Something snapped from the vicinity of their hands and the shower of light. The motes compressed into a shape and absorbed color. Lisette felt, distantly, a tiny, rapid thumping. As Kiar stopped speaking, even that faded.

A hummingbird woke up and fluffed its wings in the palm of Kiar's hand. Lisette stared at it, and then turned her eyes on her own hand. The light now stretched halfway to her elbow.

"I think," said Lisette, "I'm getting better at it." She said it to reassure Kiar, she said the words, but she was lying.

CHAPTER TWENTY-FIVE

A Beautiful Dream

IRISS TWIRLED IN her new dress, showing it to Jerya. The long skirt flared out, the layers fluttering in the breeze. Her legs flashed through some of the gaps in the layers. The gaps, and the carefully torn holes.

"It's so pretty," said Iriss. "Thank you. I feel more like myself again."

Jerya smiled. "Pretty *and* useful. You'll tell me if you think it needs more holes, yes?"

Iriss gave her a little smile in return. "Of course. I'm still your Regent even if I have trouble with my eyes now. I'd still be your Regent even if my leg was cut off. Or I lost my hearing." She considered, tapping her finger on her chin with her head tilted to the side. "But not if I lost my head. I think you'd be on your own then."

She glanced up and apparently saw enough to recognize Jerya's sour expression. Instantly she took Jerya's hands. "It's all right. It's my head, I can make that joke."

Jerya squeezed her hands. Iriss had always been cheerfully morbid. This wasn't *new*. It was just... uncomfortable.

"You're right." Pulling away, Jerya returned to pacing around the room. Alanah attended a meeting with the marshals in command of the Royal Guard in Mousame. Jerya had also sent a special dispatch of the Guard with the Regency Scouts, to locations pinpointed though the craft of dressmaking. She apprehensively awaited word of Yithiere and the Vassay caravan he escorted. She expected messages on all of these missions imminently. The suspense kept her tense and moving.

"Did you hear from Tiana yet?" asked Iriss, sitting down decorously. She picked up some yarn to untangle.

"Twist came by this morning while you slept. She didn't bother to write me a letter, but she's alive. Near the army marching on Biaxin." Jerya brought her fingers to her mouth, then stopped herself from biting them. She'd broken herself of the childish habit almost a decade ago, dammit.

Somebody asked her today, in the Tabernacle of Broken Hearts, if Yithiere led troops from Vassay to protect them from the darkling army. He'd been a young man, with a child in tow, and eager for reassurance. Stories of the two armies outside the Blight were circulating. Overnight Jerya had gone from feeling on top of the situation to nearly helpless.

It was all the fault of the duchies, for being so stubborn, for clinging to old fears and cultivating new ambitions. She'd thought the Justiciar's Council's animosity was personal, but it turned out they represented their lands admirably.

She wanted to break something. The Justiciar's Council would be preferable. Alanah had gone to meet with the marshals *because* of the Council; they sent to the marshals every day asking if they needed anything; advice, supplies, weapons. Leadership. Jerya, the thinking went, was just an inexperienced girl.

But she knew she was inexperienced, which was why she didn't send to the marshals everyday, why she waited on their word as to when she'd be needed to defend Lor Seleni. They were soldiers with experience fighting Benjen. She was inexperienced, so she delegated.

A horse galloped up and a moment later a messenger hurried in. It was one of the Regency Scouts, not one she'd seen before. "Your Highness," he—she, it turned out when she spoke—began, then paused to wait for permission to speak.

Jerya acknowledged her with an impatient gesture and she went on. "I was with the force you sent to the location Lady Iriss pinpointed. We found a disorganized gathering of the darkling troops, ma'am. They were arriving through..." She swallowed, her scarred face twisting. "Through a fiend of some sort. It was birthing them."

Jerya clapped her hands together. "Of course. I remember Twist and Kiar both mentioning such a thing before."

The scout gave her a dark look, and said, "We dealt with it, and scattered the darklings, but for a high cost in soldiers, ma'am. Two thirds casualties. Fiends are even harder to kill than the darklings."

Tapping her mouth with her finger, Jerya regarded Iriss and her dress. "Well done. There are others, though. Other fiends. This is important." She opened the door and told a guard, "I need Twist." Then she directed the scout to the writing desk, to write a report while Jerya waited.

It didn't take long, but Jerya was already lost in planning the possibilities when the sound of Twist's arrival jerked her to alertness. He was just in time, and she wondered if he'd skipped in by the clock.

"Your Highness," he said. He looked tired and worried. Everybody did these days, but she was so used to seeing laughter in his eyes that it hurt a little more.

"Twist. Walk with me while I go to the Ambassador's meeting?" He nodded and fell into step beside her as she left the inn. "Are there any Logos-workers in the city who can banish fiends like you can? Of our own people, I mean."

Twist hesitated, thinking. "I doubt it. They're craftsmen, specialists. They might manage it if their life depended on it. Kiar did, but..." He shrugged, his mouth twisting sardonically.

"But Kiar is gifted, yes."

"Most of the fiend hunters work out of the Citadel," Twist offered. "But the Citadel is distracted right now. They have their own fiends to manage."

Jerya raised her eyebrows. "Can't they just put them down?"

Twist tsked. "They're not going to abandon a holy duty and simply execute their prisoners, Princess. And a hint? Don't even suggest it to them. Once one holy duty has been abandoned, there's much less incentive to cleave to the rest."

Jerya glanced at him as she stepped around a cart. He met her gaze guilelessly. "Yes, I know. But we need wizards, wizards who can banish fiends. Ohedreton is using them to move his forces around."

Twist hesitated, then said, "Vassay."

"I didn't want you to say that." Jerya nodded at a familiar face in the crowd. "If I was crowned, could I command the Citadel to help us?"

"Don't ask," Twist repeated, and his voice was harder. "Don't make them choose between two holy dictates."

As they approached the door to the Song Garden, the theater where the new meetings happened, Jerya sighed. "Ask them for me? Now? It's important."

Twist rolled his eyes in exasperation and vanished.

The table had changed; it was now big and round. "We built it," said the Ambassador, beaming. "I thought it might help people communicate better."

"I think we communicate just fine," said Lord Aubin. "But I'm pleased to see you've decided to reduce the number of voices. Your kindness is appreciated. Perhaps now we can get something done." All the Justiciars attended, of course. So did the Mayor and the nobles, but most of those lower in station had vanished. Given how Vassay operated, Jerya wasn't nearly as sure as Lord Aubin that this was a good thing. She wouldn't put it past them to hold another meeting for the commoners.

Seandri and Landry already sat at the table. She tried not to think about how they'd been spending their time. And— oh yes, Thorn sat high in the balcony. Jerya wondered sourly if he'd shoot her if she did something he didn't like. They'd placed her chair so that her back was to him. Of course. She sat down next to Seandri.

The meeting started with the business of the reconstruction. This time, it did go better. She offered her opinion whether or not anybody requested it, and the Ambassador made sure they listened to her, using a rough good humor to smooth over awkwardness. Sometimes the others wanted her thoughts; she heard tidbits from the petitioners at the Tabernacle that the Justiciars and the nobles didn't. They definitely preferred hearing the news from her over hearing accusations from some upstart citizen mistakenly invited to sit at their table. It wasn't right to be pleased by so little consideration but part of her, weak and small, enjoyed it anyhow.

Partway through a discussion of the bridgework and the southwest expansion, Jerya heard the whisper of Twist's arrival on the far side of the stage. He glanced at her briefly, then lifted his gaze to look at the balcony where Thorn lurked. He frowned for a long moment, his eyes narrow with dislike, before he finally dropped his gaze to Jerya again.

Once Jerya held his gaze, he shook his head clearly and decisively. Then, with another whisper, he vanished.

Jerya gnawed on her lip, thinking about the Vassay. Seeing the Ambassador beside the Justiciars, it was clear who she preferred to work with. It wasn't all bad, having Vassay's help in the reconstruction. They had ulterior motives as a nation but the engineers were just people, and the Ambassador was genuinely interested in helping. Ceria had suffered catastrophe after catastrophe; without Vassay's help, things would be much worse. She didn't like seeing children playing with Vassay dolls, but that was a problem to be resolved later.

But there had to be a later first.

"Well," said Lord Aubin. "That's enough about Lor Seleni for now. We must turn our attention to the bigger picture. Your Highness, have you heard from your father recently?"

Jerya raised her eyebrows. "Nothing meaningful," she hedged. Every time somebody asked she prepared herself for their discovery of her father's death, or the absence of the phantasmagory.

"Ah, well. Tell him we do miss his presence," said Lord Aubin with a kindness that was never real. "And have you word from your uncle Yithiere?"

Twist hadn't been able to find him the last two times

he'd checked, which meant that Yithiere had changed the caravan's route. Still, that didn't have to be bad.

But the Ambassador shifted his weight and looked down at the table, his eyebrows drawn together, and Jerya knew it *was* bad.

"No," she said flatly. "He hasn't been available. Have *you* heard from the caravan, Ambassador?"

The Ambassador coughed. "Ah, yes. We have. Prince Yithiere seems to have... guided it off track."

Lord Warrane snorted and said, "Stolen it, you mean."

"My uncle is a formidable man, Justiciar," said Jerya dryly, "But I think carrying off an entire caravan is beyond even his skills. Come now, what has he really done?"

"Led them east instead of west," said the Ambassador heavily.

"East. Ah. Toward Morning." Jerya looked over the Vassay. "Did he abandon the supplies?"

The Ambassador blinked at her in astonishment. "Many of them, yes. I don't wish to offend but he's been, ah, intimidating my students into following his orders. He's apparently treating them like soldiers, which I assure you they're not. One of them managed to communicate with us very early this morning to let us know what's been going on. He was extremely upset. And dirty."

Jerya looked around, then craned her neck to see up into Thorn's murder balcony. Twist was having a quiet little conversation with the assassin. "If your poor student provided a clear location, I can send Twist to go and find out my uncle's motivation. I'm sure he has a good reason."

"I thought," said Lord Aubin, his voice chilly, "It was your task to monitor your far-flung relatives as they engaged to deal with events. Tell me, do you have any news of your sister? Meaningful news? Or is your phantasmagory completely bereft of information these days?"

Lord Warrane said, "Oh, I'm sure all her informants have gone elsewhere."

Jerya's teeth clicked together. *They knew.* "Yes. And as it has nothing to do with anything in your purview, my Lord, I will spare you the details."

"If I could just drag the conversation back to my students," the Ambassador said apologetically. "I'm afraid we need more than Twist's assistance. Or rather, we need a different kind of assistance from Twist."

Jerya felt Seandri shift position beside her. She glanced at him and he gazed back at her earnestly, his hand on the arm of her chair.

"We need to convince Twist to teach the Vassay his skipping, Jerya," he told her. "If more wizards could move as he does, that would make so many things easier. It would be easier on him, too. He's burning himself out trying to keep up with our errands."

Jerya sat back, startled by the request, and shocked by who'd made it. They'd planned this conversation in advance, Vassay and Seandri. Her Seandri. "I can't make him teach anybody. We can't even pin him down." She looked over her shoulder again, but the balcony was empty.

"But you can ask him," Seandri said. "You can talk him into it. He's loyal to you. We've been talking about it and it would be such a help to everybody. It could turn the tide of the war."

Jerya hesitated, looking at Seandri. Sweet, gentle Seandri. Her Seandri. Her favorite cousin. She wanted to protect him, so she'd kept him here. He'd made himself useful by supervising the Vassay, and now he argued their case for them. Somewhere she'd made a terrible mistake, but she wasn't sure if it was a week ago or years ago.

It would hurt Twist if she told him to give up his secrets. It would be giving more power to those who were, despite all their kindness, her enemies. But the Regency Scout's report weighed on her mind. If they didn't take advantage of Iriss's insight, if they didn't deal with the fiends before they could transfer armies from the dark world, then everything would be lost.

"I'll talk to him," she said to the Vassay Ambassador. "If I convince him, those he teaches belong to Ceria, not Vassay. We have need of them, and I will direct them."

The Ambassador stared at her broodingly. Scriber Stone gave a tiny nod, which the Ambassador didn't seem to notice.

"I don't like that very much," he told Jerya. "Because of your uncle stealing my students and abandoning the supplies, we hardly have a choice."

"Really? I could have said the same thing about you demanding my uncle escort your supplies. Perhaps," she tapped her chin, "Perhaps your students kidnapped him." She gave him a little smile she didn't feel. "If neither of us believe we're winning, that's probably for the best, don't you think?"

CHAPTER TWENTY-SIX

A SHAPE OF DAZZLING COMPLEXITY

Kiar announced, "A troop of soldiers spotted us from one of the hills. They're coming this way."

It took a moment for the words to penetrate Tiana's fog of worry about Fai and the green light. She blinked, looking around, remembering where they were.

The cleared woodlands in what used to be the duchy of Biaxin looked abandoned but wasn't quite the case. Faces peeped from the windows of cottages and farmhouses, but people never came out to greet them. Kiar borrowed a trick from Jerya and crafted her eidolons into birds, sending them into the sky to scout the surrounding area. Many companies of soldiers, in a few different tabards, patrolled the countryside.

"Which kind?" asked Tiana.

There were other kinds of companies, too, ones far less human. Cathay's cats spied at least two of them, hidden in underbrush and in a bit of remaining forest, hiding from the sun peeking between the scudding clouds.

Kiar gave her an exasperated look. "The human kind. I'd be giving more of an alarm if Ohedreton found us again. They're moving quickly; they'll be here soon."

"Well, we're not exactly hiding. We're on a road," Cathay said. "It was bound to happen sooner or later."

They're nothing to worry about. Ordinary men. Jinriki paused for a moment and as the hoof beats of the soldiers' mounts grew louder, added, **They're apprehensive about us. How clever of them.**

Tiana furrowed her brow. "Why would they be worried about *us*?"

But worried they were; when the other group came around a bend in the road, they were moving cautiously and they had crossbows out. A man with ornamental armor and a plume in his helmet commanded the rest of the troop to halt while he rode close enough to shout, "Declare yourself!" He had a personal crest painted on his shield, which marked him as a local knight; Tiana couldn't remember enough heraldry to tell which Count he served.

Look at how careful they're being, sneered Jinriki. **That's so sweet. Forty of them, terrified of sixteen men and a handful of girls.**

Tiana pulled her mouth to one side and glanced around for Slater. When she met his gaze, he nodded at her and rode over to meet with the knight.

The conversation started out calm, but the plumed knight didn't seem reassured by Slater's quiet statements. After a moment, his expression became belligerent and Slater's shoulders stiffened so much his horse danced backward.

Then Slater whirled his mount and galloped back to Tiana, his face so hard that Tiana watched the crossbowmen anxiously to make sure none of them would shoot him in the back.

"What's going on?" she demanded.

"They don't believe it's you," said Slater bluntly.

Tiana looked past Slater, astonished. The plumed knight stared back at her, fear and bravado both showing in every inch of his carriage. "Should I *show* them?"

Slater shook his head, short and sharp. "Not yet." He glanced at Kiar and Cathay, then said, "But you may as well come to speak with him, if you can fend off any stray arrows. I'm not getting anywhere."

"We can," Tiana said, and sent Moon into a canter across the intervening space.

The plumed knight waited, holding his horse steady with an absent skill that reminded Tiana of Jozua, although she couldn't imagine Jozua showing the same apprehension. None of her own soldiers had been raised as horsemen; this knight clearly had been.

"Do you really doubt I am Tiana, Princess of the Blood?" she said, as Moon came to a halt only an arms width from the knight. Slater stopped behind her.

"I don't know what to think, ma'am," he said. He had a thin mustache and young eyes. "I *know* Benjen the Black's been spotted with the main of the darkling army, or at least his standard has. And I know good men have been tainted by the darkling magic and turned against us."

"Benjen's dead," said Tiana, automatically.

"Yes. And he's not the only dead man walking, either," said the knight. "So if you are the Princess Tiana, I hope you'll forgive my prudence."

"Of course," Tiana said uneasily.

He went on. "But we can't be thoughtlessly trusting anybody with the darkling powers these days, and—"

"Darkling powers?"

The knight plunged on over her interruption, doggedly, "—and so I have to insist you allow me to escort your party to my commanding officer, so he can verify your identity."

Hesitating, Tiana asked, "Where is he?"

"Northeast of here. Will you come peacefully?"

Tiana thought fast. The seat of Sunasin was to the southeast; allowing this knight to escort her to his marshal would be out of the way. On the other hand, surrounding Fai and Cinai with an army would only make it easier to protect them. Maybe once this marshal had recognized her, she could have him move his whole army south.

He won't. Armies are where they are for a reason. But he might be able to offer you respite from any more of these ridiculous interruptions.

"I'll consider your offer," Tiana told the plumed knight. "In the meantime, you and your men are welcome to have luncheon with us."

"That's a kind offer, ma'am, but not necessary."

Tiana nodded and turned Moon to return to her companions. As she did, the knight said, "I hope you understand, ma'am, that if you don't accept our escort, we can't allow you to travel further through the Counties." He was apologetic.

Terrified he hasn't made himself understood. Poor chick.

"Yes, I understood. I hope *you* understand how foolish you're being."

Hooves clattered behind them, and Tiana turned to see Jozua pulling his mount up a few yards ahead of the rest of the group. The foul-tempered twist of his mouth was a startling change from his usual indifference. He called, "Princess, can I talk to you? Privately?"

"Excuse me," she said to the knight, and tried to keep her irritation off her face until she turned away.

"What?" she snapped as she approached Jozua.

He was just as blunt. "I overheard a bit of your little chat. I'm not going anywhere with that knight, and neither is Cinai."

"What? I thought we'd settled this!"

"No," he said flatly. "We settled that I'd stay with you as we escorted Cinai home again. I'm not letting her anywhere near any County representative who isn't either her father or her future father-in-law. The rest of them would be all too happy to complicate my pay purse." He lifted his gaze to look coldly over Tiana's shoulder. "Besides, I don't much like knights."

Tiana regarded him, her irritation fading in the face of her curiosity. What exactly was going on here? She vaguely knew about the Counties from her lessons: they were the remains of the shattered duchy of Biaxin. They bickered a lot. As for Jozua's dislike of knights... She'd have to set Lisette to find out; she didn't think he'd tell her anything she didn't drag out of him.

"I am not going to argue with you about this right now. We may be riding with them in the future, so don't do anything I'll regret." She stared at him, and then said, "I'll hire you. You're for sale, right? Keep Lisette and Fai and Cinai safe for tonight, while I visit the knight's Marshal with Cathay. I'll return tomorrow. You can set your price."

He narrowed his eyes at her. "You have no idea how expensive I can be."

Impatience stole her tongue. "I don't care! I'll escort you myself into the treasury!" Why did the Firstborn favor the hard-headed?

He regarded her another long moment and then said, "Oh, fine. I'll go inform my men. You'd best be back tomorrow." He turned his horse and rode away before she could respond.

Tiana stared at his retreating back. "Was that a good idea, Jinriki?" she asked softly. "I had to come up with something. I don't want to fight my own people again."

I wish you'd insisted he swear on me. I want to look inside him and he's far more resistant than most soldiers. We should know why.

"I don't think I can make that man do anything. I could leave you behind, though, to keep an eye on things. Lisette could hold onto you, or Kiar."

You will not. Jinriki's voice was flat. ****Not even for a night, not while you ride away. No.****

"Everybody's so stubborn," she complained, but her heart wasn't in it; she hadn't been sure that was a good idea either.

She held her mount still, waiting until Lisette and Kiar came up beside her. Lisette was pale, her arm swathed in her cloak. Her brow knitted in a frustration reflecting Tiana's general mood these days, but otherwise, she appeared healthier.

"What did you say to Jozua?" she inquired mildly. "He looks like he swallowed a live rat."

"I asked him to guard you tonight while I go to visit the local Marshal, so the Marshal's men won't dog our heels for the rest of our journey."

Lisette looked puzzled and Kiar displeased, so Tiana quickly went into more detail on the situation. She ended with, "Cathay and I will go, since we're the obvious Blood and it's the Blood he's so worried about. I'll take Slater and

Berrin. Jozua will be in charge of the camp, but I'd like to leave you in charge overall, Kiar."

Kiar's eyes widened. "You mean Lisette, right?"

Lisette sighed. Tiana thought she saw a rare flash of temper in her Regent's eyes, but if so, she held her tongue. It didn't matter, though.

"We've been through this before, Kiar! I'm not asking you to make speeches to the assembled. I just want you to watch the situation and make decisions. You're going to be as good at that as I am, maybe better! You're smarter than me, anyhow."

Kiar flushed and looked away until she found her voice. "You're right. I wasn't thinking. But now I am. I think you shouldn't leave the rest of us behind! And if you put me in charge, I'll move us as fast as possible until we catch up with you. That's what my so smart thinks."

Tiana stared at her, incredulous. "You can't. Fai... Jozua... I just explained why I'm going alone, Kiar. It's going to be bad, bad like in that alley if they try to stop us, and Jozua—"

"Then don't go." Her flush had faded, and Kiar was calm now. "Ohedreton will take advantage of the split and attack. You must assume he's always watching us, Tiana."

"We might be able to remove your need to be concerned for Fai, anyhow," said Lisette, but Tiana hardly heard her, barely noticed Kiar's expression of veiled fury. She'd been trying so hard to manage things, but everybody, *everybody* argued back. This wasn't how it was supposed to be. She didn't have the skill to convince them any better than this. She wanted to lash out, to make them obey, but everything went wrong once you did that. Her breath came rapidly. She didn't want to lose her temper, but where could she go to hide? Somewhere, anywhere. Away.

She pulled Moon violently around, the gelding half-rearing in protest, and kicked him into a gallop, away from the column and off the road. In the ruins of a field, she half slid, half fell out of the saddle, and stumbled away from Moon.

Frustration leaked from her skin, made manifest as emanations, lifting the twisted and dried remains of the harvest to spiral around her. In a previous time she would have given herself to the phantasmagory, fallen into the darkness and let its imposed detachment mute her rage. She would have talked with Lisette through the detachment to make better choices. It would have *worked.*

But now, she didn't know what to do without it, except flee before she snapped, picked up every single one of the people frustrating her and bashed their heads together. How did her uncle and father command armies? How did they command their own kin?

Did they bash heads in? She'd seen a play once, where a commanding officer won respect by demonstrating his strength of arms. That couldn't be right, not against common people without the benefits of the Blood, though. It was only a step away from being a Blood Blighter.

Digging her fingers into the loam, she tried to recall if she'd heard any stories of something productive coming of battles between the Blood, if it ever led anything but tragedy. Thinking back over stories, even tragic stories, leeched away the edge of her raw emotions. It didn't lead to any answers, but after a moment she was calm enough to try again to think of ways to work with Kiar that didn't lead to temper tantrums.

She failed. All she could do was tell them what to do. If they refused to listen, what then? The dust whipped around her as her frustration rose again. Jozua and Kiar, Kiar and

Jozua—and Lisette had too much, finally, on her shoulders to delegate the problem to. And that *wretched* knight and his forty men and his ridiculous fears. Benjen!

Someone shouted from the road. Kiar, and Tiana looked over in time to see her falling off her startled horse, a shield curving up from beneath her to enclose her.

Hah, said Jinriki. **She was fast, but I am faster.**

"What did you do?" asked Tiana, her frustration turning into alarm for her cousin. She yanked her emanations under control again.

I wondered why she was so afraid all the time. Why she was so certain Ohedreton would strike. So I investigated and found out. She's been talking to him.

"What? When?" Tiana flew back to the road.

In the forest.

Kiar crouched in the center of a silvery translucent sphere. Berrin held the reins of the horses, while Lisette kneeled at the side of the sphere, her glowing hand carefully wrapped in her cloak. Tiana skidded to a halt and Kiar glanced up, her eyes bloodshot and savage.

"I *hate* that sword, Tiana! I wish you'd let the Citadel destroy it. It went into my *head* and it ripped and tore."

I was in a hurry. She can push me out... Jinriki's voice paused, and then his voice took on the timbre that meant he spoke to others along with her. **I have discovered the truth. She has been speaking privately with the enemy.**

Kiar's look brimmed with hatred. Tiana knelt outside the bubble beside Lisette, Jinriki's scabbard a dragging burden in her hand. Every time she dismounted now, she unhooked him from the saddle, a habit he certainly had reinforced. He didn't have any sense at all that minds were more than... libraries. "What happened, Kiar?"

Kiar wrapped her arms around herself. "Ohedreton found me in the forest when I walking alone. He talked to me. He tried to get me to tell you he was in the woods so you'd go looking for him. I didn't."

Privately, Jinriki said, **Her shield can't keep me out, not physically. Would you like me to destroy it?**

Tiana closed her eyes and then fumbled Jinriki out of his scabbard and sent him scything away behind her, off the road. Blades of grass fluttered to the ground.

What? Are you listening to her? Are you mad? Jinriki's sudden rage roared in her head. **She cannot be trusted! You should force her to submit to me, so I may pull out the complete truth and evaluate the risk—**

"SHUT UP!" Tiana shrieked, her palms on her temples. "Just shut up! I'll deal with you later!" She drew in a ragged breath, waiting for argument, but she sensed only sullen silence. For a moment, the blood throbbing in her head dominated her thoughts, but then Lisette's unmarred hand gently touched her own. When she looked up, Lisette withdrew her hand and gave her a little, unsmiling nod. Tiana took a deep breath and tried to turn her attention back to Kiar.

Kiar's shield was still up. She sat at the far side, watching Tiana warily. Tiana touched the shield, feeling its warmth, and wanted to weep at the fear behind it. "Kiar, I'm not angry at you. I'm not upset." She groped for words. "I'm bewildered, and worried. Did he hurt you? Ohedreton, I mean. Did you fight? What did he want with you, besides trying to ambush us? Is that why you don't want to be separated now?"

Kiar stared at her, and then said, "No. No. He... wanted to talk. I said. He just wanted to talk. He..." She studied the ground, her pale hair hiding her eyes. "He said he liked me."

Tiana blinked, and then bent her legs so her crouch turned into a sitting position. She drew her hands over her face. She had the most peculiar urge to giggle, and knew if she gave in, she wouldn't stop until she was crying. "Oh, Kiar. I'm so sorry."

Kiar pushed herself forward, closer to Tiana, and said, "It was awful! That maw, that monster, that murderer, and he said he liked me!"

That was it. It was too much for Tiana. The giggles spilled out, and Kiar pulled back again, offended. Her shield shimmered out of existence, but Tiana couldn't stop burbling with hysterical laughter. "What?" Kiar kept asking, while Lisette fumbled around for a canteen.

Tiana fell over on her back and then curled on her side. Part of her watched from a distance as the laughter racked her body, and hoped she could stop before the laughter became sobs. Lisette put the canteen in her hand and then pushed it to her lips. Tiana gulped at water and then choked on it. She managed to say, "Is this the first time a boy's told you he liked you, Kiar?" and then she went off again. It was so stupid, but she couldn't stop thinking about how aloof Kiar always was, how it took a Blighter to get her attention, and *of course* her reaction to an expression of admiration was 'how awful!'.

She poured more water down her throat, until the choking hurt so much that the hysterics had to reluctantly recede. "I'm so, so, so very sorry," she croaked. "I didn't mean to laugh. I don't know what came over me. I do believe it was awful. Having a Blighter, a monster, express even token affection for you!"

Kiar watched her from the corner of her eye, and said sulkily, "I've been trying to figure out what he could possibly like about me."

Knowledgeably, Lisette said, "Some men like a girl who can beat them up."

Kiar blushed. "I'm sure he didn't mean it in that way, anyhow."

Tiana sighed. She hated to break the moment; it reminded her of their easy camaraderie at the cookie receptions, back in another time. "So, is this why you don't want us to be separated?"

Kiar nibbled on her lip. "Basically. Especially with the injured, we can't flee if something happens."

Sourly, Tiana said, "Wouldn't the green light keep Fai alive even if we slung him over a horse's back?"

Kiar shrugged. "I don't know. Do you?"

Lisette said, "It might, but if that happened, his sister would be as likely to flee away with him as stay with us."

Tiana lay back on the track again. It was damp and cold through her cloak, but the change in perspective was pleasant. Grey clouds churned the sky, but here and there blue peeked through. It'd be freezing once the clouds blew away, seasonal weather at last. Finally. Winter was long overdue.

"I'll keep that in mind," she said to the sky. "It's a good concern. Do you think Ohedreton is going to seek you out again?"

Kiar said, "I'm trying my best to avoid being alone for any length of time, so if he does, hopefully everybody would know about it. What are you going to do about *that*?" Tiana turned her head and saw Kiar looking towards Jinriki.

Tiana sighed again. She'd never felt so worn out before. She could just close her eyes and go to sleep, right here. The ground would leech away her warmth and maybe she'd wake up as cool and calm as Jerya.

The pressure on her mind from Jinriki's silent rage

increased. "I don't know," she said. "Should I apologize? Is it my responsibility? I don't even know if I can promise he won't do it again. I'll talk to him."

Kiar's mouth puckered. "Well, if he does it again, I can promise he *will* regret it." She stood and took Spooky's reins from Berrin.

Tiana flopped on her other side, looking at the handle of the sword, visible through the golden winter grass. Minex crouched nearby, holding her hands close to her chest. "Too angry for me," she said, and shook her head. "I wish the party had worked."

As heavy as Tiana felt, she pushed herself to her feet and went to pick Jinriki up again.

Are you done with her? Am I to be graced with your attention now?Jinriki's voice growled in her mind. Irritation burned away some of the exhaustion left by the hysterics.

"Why did you go digging around in Kiar's mind? It was so hard for her to trust you even a little, and you *knew* it."

And now we know why she was so reluctant!

"Yes, we do!" She glared down at the blade. The metal swallowed her reflection, and only red highlights rippled along the edge. "Why did you do it, Jinriki? What made you think that kind of invasion was necessary? Or were you just bored?"

Jinriki said, **She presents herself as more incompetent than she is. I needed to know why. I'm looking after you, since you've demonstrated time and again that you can't take care of yourself. As you're demonstrating now.**

Tiana scowled. "Hurting my friends and family is a very poor way to 'look after me', as you put it. I trust Kiar. I thought I could trust you, too." Her anger grew the more she considered his words. Take care of her? Control her, more likely. The thought hurt.

Innis trusted Ohedreton, too, honored him above all others. You trust too easily, Jinriki snapped. **Trust will kill you. If I had been there—Such betrayal didn't come out of nowhere—**

"Kiar isn't going to betray me! She had a good reason for not mentioning those things!"

You can't know that. I can, if I could just get inside her head again, truly see what she thinks...

"Even if you *could* get into her head again—and don't you try it, ever again—that doesn't mean *anything*. I don't care what she thinks. There's more to a person than the thoughts they think. You think I don't know what she thinks of me? That I'm trouble, I'm... not heroic? Not smart? Silly? But her actions matter more than her thoughts and she's still here." She blew out her breath and felt the tickle in her throat that meant she might laugh again—or sob—if she didn't watch herself. "I can't believe I'm having this conversation with you. You're a sword. You should just... worry about sword and fighting things and leave the people to me."

I am. Not. Just. A sword.

Tiana rolled her eyes. That hot squeeze of her chest that meant she should hold her tongue but how could she? "Oh, right. My apologies. You're a *very magical* hunk of metal. You're still not a *person*. You know *nothing* about how people work. Innis probably didn't either, from what I've heard. Maybe that's why Ohedreton betrayed him." Somehow the words, intended to hurt him, hurt her as much.

The ground shook beneath her feet and an awful, inhuman howl split the sky. Jinriki growled, **I'll show you what I am.** The sword in her hand vanished.

The air shimmered and the howl dropped to a groan.

Voices shouted in alarm and horses screamed, but Tiana stared as the highlights and shadows of a shape of dazzling complexity unfolding in the sky. The last time this had happened, back at the Citadel when the monks had tried to bind him, the Logos had stopped responding. She knew she should say something, apologize, calm the fiend down before disaster struck a second time.

But her tongue stuck to the roof of her mouth and her desire to see what was behind the sword overwhelmed her. She realized that she drew a distinction between the blade and the voice in her mind that seemed like so much more than a... weapon. In the phantasmagory, he had silver eyes.

Somebody tugged insistently on her sleeve, and a voice intruded on her thoughts. It slipped under the grinding noise of the world stretching open to arrive at the forefront of her brain. "Very good, very good, but now is not a good time, you see? Look up in the sky." Tiana looked down, instead, into Minex's intense eyes. The little earth fiend pushed her chin up. "See, beyond the prince. You see?"

Tiana saw. She shouted, "No, Jinriki, he's *up there*." High above the facets and shards of Jinriki's shadow on the world drifted a frighteningly familiar shape. "It's the dragon!" *It couldn't be the dragon we fought at the Citadel, that one flew into the mountain. Does he have more? Lord of Winter!*

Last time she saw the dragon while they were traveling, she had wanted to fight it in the sky. This time, she keenly felt the absence of Jinriki from her hand. "Please, come back to me."

The shape Jinriki had become trembled and then, with a sound like a thousand doors banging one after another, the faceted edges collapsed. The sword fell from the sky into Tiana's waiting hand.

Something touched *me. From that thing.***

Tiana ran her gaze over the blade worriedly. "An attack?"

No. A probe. Lift your gaze again. The heated growl of Jinriki's voice had become chilly steel.

The dragon circled, rainbows shimmering off its obsidian scales. Then it rose higher, vanishing into the clouds.

A watcher, a spy. Observing us. Perhaps he wishes to claim me as he's claimed my younger siblings. But he never, ever will.

Tiana sighed, and gave up on going to visit the knight's marshal. They'd just have to find another way to deal with him and his forty men.

CHAPTER TWENTY-SEVEN

THE REGENT'S FIRST CHOICE

LISETTE WENT BACK to her horse and watched the County soldiers as Tiana argued with her fiend. When he vanished from her hand and something out of a forgotten dream started unfolding in the sky, she glanced up once, then returned to watching the County soldiers.

They shifted uncomfortably, drawing closer together. At one point the plumed knight leading them—Lisette recognized his arms as being from the minor family of Colvax, serving the Count of Wexin—trotted forward trying to get somebody's attention. Then, when nobody responded to him, he backed up miserably.

When Tiana stalked up beside Lisette, she looked down and said mildly, "Next time you might try arguing silently. Just for decorum's sake."

Tiana laughed humorlessly. "How do we deal with them, Lisette? Without fighting them? Their leader seems like a brave idiot."

"Invite them to escort us to Sunasin," Lisette suggested. "Don't let them make any other choice."

"I don't want to threaten them," said Tiana, her voice anguished. "I'm not good at threats. People call my bluff and then I have to kill them."

Lisette shrugged and pulled her cloak close around her. "Ask nicely."

Tiana took a deep breath. "Can you—"

"I don't think I should talk to them, Tiana," Lisette said carefully. "They've already seen enough... strange things. If they see my arm, it's only going to make them more nervous. If they're dubious that you're the Blood, they're not going to believe I'm a Regent. Not with this."

Tiana gave her a sad, sober look. "I know. I was going to ask if you could talk to Jozua. Even if I manage to convince Sir Plumes, Jozua might run off like a frightened rabbit." She made a sour face. "Apparently he doesn't *like* knights."

Lisette brightened. "I'd be happy to. We were chatting yesterday. He tells very amusing stories."

"I noticed," said Tiana and gave her a little smile in return. "Thank you. If you can keep him entertained and *here* and not picking fights with people because of their bad taste in helmets, it would help so much."

The chance to do something, do her job, pleased Lisette. Jozua was the only person who didn't seem to care about what had happened to her. But that same cool made her uncertain she had the sway over him that Tiana expected from her. He was, in technical terms, a tough nut to crack.

She turned Dustling and rode back to the end of the column, where Jozua huddled with his remaining men. As she approached, he shook his head at them and pulled away.

"What do you want?" he rasped, looking up at her.

"Tiana's not going to visit the Marshal after all," Lisette said lightly. "So we'll be riding on."

"Yes, I gathered that." He glanced up at the sky, and Lisette couldn't guess whether he was thinking of the dragon, or of Jinriki's half-unveiled form. "The question, m'lady, is what's going to happen with yonder company."

"They'll be escorting us, of course. To Sunasin. It shouldn't be a problem."

"Hah," said Jozua. "We'll see about that."

Lisette glanced over to where Cathay and Tiana spoke with the Colvax knight. The knight looked stubborn and noble. Tiana radiated irritation while waving Jinriki around absently. Then Cathay put his hand on her back and said something that made both of the others relax.

"Can I ride with you once we start moving again?" Lisette smiled at Jozua.

"I've clean run out of funny stories, my Lady," he said. "I won't be good company."

Lisette let her lower lip jut out in a small pout. "Kiar's avoiding me, too, and Tiana's always distracted. She'll be even more so now."

Jozua sighed. "As pretty as that pout is, and as true as your words probably are, I think it's a bad idea. But how can I stop you?" He looked around what was rapidly becoming an impromptu camp and checked his gelding's girth.

Lisette's smile returned, but her mind worked behind it. Tiana had picked the right words; Jozua felt like he was getting ready to run.

She stroked her horse's mane. "I heard Tiana offered you a small fortune to keep us safe."

"Yeah. Not as small as she thinks, either," he grumbled, "It was supposed to be while she rode off to have tea with the knights, but I should probably charge her even if that plan's canceled, just for putting up with them."

"You should," Lisette agreed. "I'd authorize it. You deserve it for your help in the forest. You were so very brave."

Jozua gave her a suspicious look. His eyes started twinkling. "You're trying too hard, my lady."

She twinkled back at him. "I don't think I am, actually."

He turned and shouted something at his men, then swung up onto his gelding. "I wonder if I ought to go hurry things along."

Lisette cast her gaze once again to the front of the column. The soldiers had lowered their crossbows but not stowed them. Cathay laughed at something the knight said, while Tiana glowered at both of them.

"I suppose they must arrange a marching order or something," Lisette said vaguely.

"Hmm," said Jozua. "That knight isn't a happy man." He turned his horses and trotted over to his handful of men, still standing around Fai's travois. Cleaving to her duty, Lisette followed him.

Cinai knelt beside her brother, her hand on his, oblivious to her surroundings until Jozua said her name. Then she looked up, blinking. "Is it time to go?"

"Soon," said Jozua gruffly. "We've got some new friends joining us. Don't introduce yourself. If anybody asks who the two of you are, you're to present yourself as Petern's youngsters." He nodded at one of his men.

The man in question was not quite as big as Jozua but he was significantly hairier. He guffawed and scratched his beard. "Hell, they could be for all I know. C'mere, Cinai, give your daddy a kiss."

"Petern," murmured Jozua. Just the man's name, quietly, calmly, and all of the men stopped laughing.

Petern shuffled a bit, then grinned and spat. "You know I'm a good 'un, Harken. Tell you what, I'll treat her like she's *your* daughter. Well, your sister, anyhow, nipper."

"Smart man," Jozua said and nodded at Cinai. He turned his horse and almost bumped into Lisette.

"Just making some arrangements," he told her.

"You think the knight would make trouble if he knew she was Cinai of Sunasin? I can emphasize that to Tiana, if you'd like."

"Hah," he said. "That one. The boy's all right, I suppose but—why you put up with the Blood is beyond me."

Question number 52 in the Regency's official question and answer book. But she didn't use the suggested answer. "They start us out so young. I barely remember life without the Blood. They're my family."

"Family, eh? That doesn't mean you have to put up with them." He leaned forward. "When your Princess lets me get on with my life..." He trailed off, meeting her gaze. "Well, no matter what any authority tells you, you don't have to stay someplace you don't want to be."

"I have always wanted to be with them," Lisette protested. "My parents didn't *make* me go to the Regent trials. They offered the opportunity and I volunteered. I remember *that*."

He snorted. "And how old were you?"

"I was seven," she said, with dignity.

"Nobody knows what they want at seven. Nobody knows what they want at fourteen, either. Hell, you're probably just figuring out what you want right now." He gave her a speculative look.

Lisette shook her head. "I have a fairly good idea of what I want right now." She glanced down at her arm.

He didn't, because he never paid any extra attention to her arm, like it was no different than any other scar to him. But his eyes narrowed and his horse backed up restlessly.

"And before that? Had everything you wanted out of life?"

Lisette looked down at her horse's mane. "It doesn't matter. I swore an oath."

"Bugger oaths," said Jozua flatly, and when she jerked her head up, shocked, he added, "Especially oaths made by children."

She sputtered. "How can your employer *trust* you?"

"Employers," he said. "I've had a few. And they trust me because they're paying me. If I don't do as I'm asked, I don't get the rest of my money. It's a powerful incentive, my Lady."

"But not everything," she said, looking up at his face. "Not your only incentive."

His hazel eyes met her own. "No," he agreed casually. "There's sex, too."

That should have shocked her, too, but instead it made her heart pound and her body warm. She bit her lip, noticed how his gaze moved to her mouth and his hand tightened on his reins again. The coals inside became a small flame.

Then she recognized the noise ahead and smiled at him impishly. "I'll keep that in mind. But... later. I think we're about to start moving again."

He shook himself, then said, "Are you still so sure you want to ride with me?"

"Oh yes," she told him. "Especially since you're asking that." She confided, leaning toward him. "I've always been very curious."

His mouth twitched under his beard. "I'm not sure curious is the word I'd pick myself."

Slater shouted a command and Jozua moved his horse forward in response. There was a moment of chaos as the knight's company rode down the little column, positioning themselves behind and before Tiana's company.

The Colvax knight-captain rode behind his men, accompanied by two others and studying the guards reorganizing themselves. When he got to the huddle of Jozua's men, he reined his horse to a stop. "Who's in charge of this lot? Did she bring wild men in from the forest?"

One of the men with the knight laughed, but the other one continued studying the hired swords. He had a red tabard, and metal roses wrought onto his shoulder plates. A quiet word from him had the Colvax knight turning his horse and riding back up to Jozua.

"Your men?"

"Yeah," said Jozua. "The Princess did hire us in the forest, as a matter of fact." He bared his teeth at the knight. "Grr."

"Hmm," said the knight. Lisette studied him, searched her memory and concluded, based on his age and the Regency genealogical records, he was Rufus Colvax, third son of Baron Colvax, who was in turn the first cousin once removed of the Count of Wexin.

"Well," said probably-Sir-Rufus. "I congratulate you on your sense of grooming. Maybe you can impose it on your men." He started to turn away, then stopped, staring hard at Jozua.

"Alezander," he said to the man with the roses on his shoulders. "Doesn't this fellow look like the man you were telling me about?"

Alezander, who Lisette decided was another knight, but

not in charge and not prone to plumes, rode closer. "Good afternoon, sir. Have we met? You do look familiar."

"No," said Jozua shortly. His horse flattened his ears at Rufus Colvax's horse.

"Ah," said Alezander. "Well, perhaps it's just that you're so big."

"That must be it," agreed Jozua. "The beard, too. It confuses people. Especially the easily confused."

"Ah," repeated Alezander and nodded at Jozua with a sort of sad, calm acceptance. "Yes, Rufus. I'm sure the tales I told you were inspired by just such a man as this fellow. But let us return to the Prince and Princess now." And the two men rode off.

"*Did* you know him?" Lisette asked. When Jozua gave her an unfriendly look, she added, "I did say I've always been curious."

"Hah. No, I don't know him. That he hasn't seen me before I can't say; people tend to notice me more than I notice them."

"I doubt that. I think you notice a lot more than you let on."

Jozua laughed humorlessly. "Also true, but trust me.... No, never mind." He went back to an earlier discussion. "So, they expect people to abide by oaths they swear when they're seven in the Regency Court? How often does that work?"

Lisette let him change the subject, although she would rather have talked about almost anything else.

"It always works," she said with a sigh. "But it's not the oath that keeps us there." She eyed him, and when he didn't ask, she told him anyhow. "It's love. The Regent trials are a playgroup, really. And we're appointed based on our rapport with the Blood. And then we grow up beside them. Tiana is my best friend."

He scoffed. "It's not just friendship. Look at you, dutifully flirting with me because she told you to keep me here. How far would that go?"

Heat rose to Lisette's cheeks. "Duty and desire aren't always contradictory."

"And when they are?" His gaze was steady. She knew suddenly he'd had this conversation before.

"Duty wins," she conceded reluctantly, and looked down at her glowing hand again. Then she glanced up the column where Tiana rode shrouded in her own dark mood. "Duty wins and I don't think I regret it."

"You'd lose your arm for duty?" he pressed. "You'd sleep with me for duty?"

"For love," she said, and he recoiled as if she'd spat poison. Apologetically, she added, "If you don't know what that's like, I don't think I can explain it. I could recommend some good poets who have tried, though."

"Poetry's as bad as knights," he grumbled, as he settled back down again. He shook himself all over, then gave her a faint smile that didn't quite reach his eyes. "Well, my lady, if you did come to my bed, I think you'd enjoy yourself whether that was your goal or not. But you needn't do it at your Princess's command; I'll stay the course until Sunasin." His smile turned grim. "As long as the knights don't come after me with shaving implements." And he made to kick his horse into a trot, made like he was done with her.

She leaned over and caught at his coat. When he looked back at her impassively, she said, "It isn't fair for you to leave with the wrong impression. Tiana would never ask such a thing of me. If it happened, you can trust that it's my idea."

He gave her a long, slow look that once again kicked off a fire in her belly. Then he lifted her hand from his coat. Too late, she realized she'd grabbed him with her light-numbed hand. It didn't hurt him, though, and—her heart thudded against her chest—she could feel the touch of his hand on hers like she'd never donned the Starcatcher Hand. When he brought her hand to his mouth, the white light reddened his beard. He kissed her knuckles slowly, his eyes never leaving hers.

"You make your own choice, then." He pushed her hand back in her cloak, pulled his horse around, and rode away.

Lisette smiled after him until the tingling in her hand faded away. She'd been trudging along for weeks, grimly doing her duty, always determined to do her duty. She'd forgotten each day was a choice, and the foundation of her duty was love.

It amused her, though, that it took talking to Jozua to remind her. He was so violently repelled by any of the higher emotions, so crass and selfish and mercenary. So disturbingly attractive.

She watched him as he moved up next to Berrin and began to chat easily with the big guardsman. Then, because sometimes duty and desire weren't contradictory after all, she rode forward to join Tiana.

CHAPTER TWENTY-EIGHT

CHAIN REACTIONS

KIAR SPENT THE next day and a half doing her best to convince Lisette that her Starcatcher Hand wouldn't be necessary to heal Fai. She studied her books, she studied both Fai and Cinai's bodies, and she tried hard to avoid thinking about the hummingbird that kept pace with the company.

The little bird rode on Minex's finger. The earth fiend fed it from flowers she picked as they wandered along. She acted like they were out for a summer stroll: skipping, playing little games with the bird and running ahead to sing naughty songs about knights. Judging from the column's pace, they were definitely strolling.

Tiana took them off the road. They travelled overland to Sunasin to avoid the attention of more troops like Sir Rufus and his men. The knight accompanied them, but Tiana didn't trust them and Kiar didn't blame her. While the knight seemed to have adapted to the situation, there were tensions between his men and the Royal Guards.

Kiar tried not to worry about it. Cathay and Slater were worrying about it. They knew a lot more than she did about morale and soothing the tensions of men with swords. Although possibly she could find a book to fill in the gaps in her knowledge. Maybe Twist could bring some—but thinking about Twist was just a way to waste time. Especially when he wasn't even there. When he was there, at least she could look at him while she wasted time.

They had camped late the night before, after a long detour around a spur of the darkling army moving amorphously across the landscape. Despite their strange movement patterns, they were an organized force. Companies like Sir Rufus's harried the edges of the mass of invaders, attacking and falling back again.

Meanwhile the darkling army itself moved slowly but single-mindedly, in pursuit of a goal the others spent hours debating. Nobody knew what the army *wanted*. They didn't loot the emptied villages they passed through; they didn't seem to need to resupply. They marched in small, widely-spaced groups. They rested during the day, but were well able to fight back against harassment. They never pursued the Counties soldiers, never did anything but defend themselves and continue their march. It was like the human defenders were no more than ants at the darkling picnic.

"I don't care what they are, soldiers have to eat," said Rufus, talking to Slater as they strode past at the lunch break. They had just crossed into the edge of Sunasin land, and hoped to get there by late evening. "We've been trying to find the source of their supplies. If we can cut them off, we might stand a chance when they finally turn and fight. And they'll have to fight back, once the rest of the armies arrive. I'm rather looking forward to it."

Kiar understood; it was always reassuring when things happened the way they were supposed to, even if the way they were supposed to happen was awful.

She stopped by Cinai's side. Fai's travois worked better than any wagon as they moved across the fields, but there was no good way to carry somebody as injured as Fai across many miles. "How is he today?"

Cinai huddled under a cloak, nibbling on a chunk of cheese. "No change yet." She glanced up at Kiar. "But every step we take away from Fel Dion, I worry. I'm afraid again. Staying like this forever isn't any better than being dead, is it?"

Kiar put her hand on Cinai's shoulder awkwardly. "You can't get better from dead. I'm working on learning out how to heal him. This won't be forever."

Cinai looked down again. "It can't be."

Kiar rubbed her eyes with one hand. Other students spent a decade studying the vast, deep sea of the human body. She was trying to do it in a week, on the road, with no teacher but the bodies around her. If she had her way, they'd wait at Sunasin Castle until a specialist could be summoned, however long that took. But that wasn't her decision and she appreciated being able to hand that responsibility over to somebody else. Even if that somebody else was Tiana.

Instead she sat down and focused her Logos sight on Fai. Work was always better than thinking, these days. The tendrils of power snaking through his system, along with the injuries, made him a poor subject to study, but she had to cross-reference what she'd learned and make sure it aligned with his biology. Today, she studied metabolisms, or how solid stores became active energy.

Time passed. Kiar woke from her trance when Lisette bumped her shoulder with her knee.

"Hello, Lisette," said Cinai. She'd acquired a cup of tea, and Kiar realized it had gotten colder. A cloak dropped on her head from above.

"Is it time to go?" She put on the cloak. Her skin was cool to her own touch but the chill didn't bother her yet.

Lisette said, "Tiana's still discussing strategy with Twist and Slater and the others. But soon."

Strategy, Lisette said, and Kiar thought of the tensions between the soldiers first. Then she saw Lisette's expression, and ducked her head. Lisette so rarely showed annoyance that seeing her sour face was like being bitten by a pet rabbit.

If you want me to use your flesh as fuel to heal Fai, go ahead, tell Tiana about this plan. Make me do it. But I'm not going to use you that way willingly, Lisette. She didn't say the words.

Something scratched at the aegis around her thoughts, all the same. Her heart jumped. *Stay out,* she thought as loudly as she could. To Jinriki, unvocalized words still made a sound. Then—"Twist's back?" She scrambled to her feet.

If anything, Lisette's sour expression intensified. "Are you going to ask him—?" and she glanced at Cinai.

"Of course not," Kiar said, already hurrying away. "Who knows what it would do to him?" She dodged between horses and men until she came to Tiana's blanket under spreading tree branches. Five cloaked men clustered around the Princess. Twist had his back to Kiar, but she recognized him anyhow: his height, his stance, his everything.

They were discussing the invader's army and the disposition of the armies in the west. She slowed to a halt, shy of interrupting for no good reason.

But then Twist said, "I'm no use with the soldiers, so I'll just go—" and he turned away and met Kiar's eyes. His voice, sharp with irritation faded, and she blushed. Day broke across his exhausted face. "There you are. I'd barely begun my search, too." The shock of her yearning washed over her: she wanted to wrap her arms around him, run her fingers through his hair, touch his face—Her hands clenched into fists at her sides. She'd been mad to run over here. She couldn't behave around him; she embarrassed herself and it always made everything worse.

"Are you talking to me?" she said. It was inane, but anything was better than gaping at him like an idiot.

A cloud passed over his face. "Yes. I was hoping we could continue...?"

Like a shower of sparks, thoughts burst and faded. Once again yearning overwhelmed her. She wanted to look at him—touch him—find out where he'd been—run. "No need. I'm sure other people are waiting on you."

His mouth curved in something other than a smile. With brittle cheer, he said, "Nope. I've been given two days to rest before I have to report back to Lor Seleni to start teaching." He spread his hands as he looked at her, almost as if he were pleading for something.

But acid burned down her throat. "Good. It's about time." That didn't seem to be enough. His hands were still spread. "I'm sure this time you'll get a good student." His open hands closed, and recklessly, drunk on a cocktail of emotions, she added, "Goodbye now." The sun vanished entirely from his face and the bleak expression she'd earned when she skipped his lessons returned. She turned away, fighting to keep the idiotic burning in her eyes from becoming tears.

"I'm so lucky," he said, and the chill in his voice froze her in place. "Most people are too kind to the objects of their infatuation, but I have *you*. You prefer cruelty."

Her mind shut down. She took a step away, one step with

feet like lead, that was all, and then he stood in front of her, blocking her escape. She kept her eyes down as he said, "I've tried to be patient, I've tried to wait this out. I wanted to be your friend again. Look at me, Kiar." One of his hands held her shoulder, while his other threaded through her hair to the back of her neck.

She wanted to avoid meeting his gaze, but despite her intentions, she looked at him. Lines feathered from the corner of his eyes, lines that hadn't been there six months ago. His brows swooped together in an anger she rarely saw, but his mouth was white with stress or pain. He was so very close: strange and familiar at the same time. She put her hand on his chest to push him away, and didn't.

His eyes scanned her face. Sounding almost puzzled, he said, "Maybe there's another way." Stepping even closer, he lowered his head.

Lightly, he brushed his lips over hers, a butterfly touch that knocked down all the walls she'd built. When he nibbled delicately at her lower lip, she whimpered deep in her throat and slid her arms around his neck, driven by the pure fire pumping through her veins. She pressed herself against his lean body. When his tongue flickered against hers, she responded in kind eagerly. The fingers at the back of her neck moved lightly against her skin while his grip on her shoulder remained firm and in control.

She slid one hand into his hair, unable to get enough of him. He smelled like earth and spiced wine and sweat, and kissing him was beyond anything she'd dreamt of.

He made a noise against her mouth. Did he think they were done? She nipped him, unwilling to let him go. His hand on her shoulder tightened. Then both arms moved down her body as sudden hunger replaced what had previously been gentle instruction. He lifted her feet off the ground as he took everything she offered and demanded more.

There was only him.

Then, beyond the rushing in Kiar's ears, Tiana sighed and said, "Finally."

Self-awareness flooded back. She stiffened and her feet touched the ground. Head whirling, she disentangled herself and stepped backwards, almost losing her feet. Only Twist's lingering hold prevented her from making an even bigger fool of herself.

His previous words came back to her with a rush of shame. Everybody was staring. Everybody knew. "I'm such an idiot," she said.

Twist stared at her, his wide blue eyes making him look very young. "Kiar—" He took a deep breath.

She clenched her fists. "No. No, don't. You've made your point. I'll try to stop being so stupid."

Everybody was still staring. Kiar couldn't bear it. Tiana blinked at her like a fish. She was going to say something else, Kiar just knew it, and then Kiar would die on the spot. She flailed for something, anything, to make them stop staring, replaying her idiocy over and over again.

"Tiana, hey, we figured out a way to heal Fai. Want to see?" She looked around, found Lisette watching her with far-too-expressive eyes. "Come on!" She took Lisette's arm above the elbow and half-dragged her to where Fai rested. Lisette said something, but Kiar couldn't listen.

She planted herself in front of Fai and Cinai. Cinai, at least, had no idea what had just happened; the horses had been in the way. But she could feel Twist staring at her. How long had he known? Longer than she had, she was sure. And look how patiently he'd endured her idiocy. And Tiana and Lisette, they'd known too. She glanced at Lisette and just knew they'd giggled over her infatuation, her bumbling attempts to explain herself.

She hardened her heart and looked at Fai. She couldn't be good at people like Lisette and Twist and Tiana, but she could be good at this. She stopped pretending that she couldn't direct the lux Lisette made available. The library of observations she'd been so cautious about tapping sprang to the forefront of her mind. "No reason to wait any longer, is there?" Without waiting for an answer, she slid her hand down Lisette's arm until she touched the light.

It tingled, like cold water lapping at her toes, but the wave of energy that crashed over her last time did not come. Lisette's face was white, her breath rapid.

"Please," Kiar said desperately. "You're right. We can do this. Please."

Lisette's gentle sigh was a bellows across the fires of Kiar's shame. "You all keep saying please," she murmured. The rudimentary gate Lisette had constructed opened.

The lux brought with it chaos, kicking the top off the anthill of Kiar's thoughts. But the underlying nature of an anthill is order and so it was with Kiar's mind. The little observations and theories formed a greater understanding, and the lux did not burn her. She stretched out a hand to Fai and began to speak, blind to everything but the foundational structure of the universe.

A small fraction of Lisette's essence unraveled as the lux poured through her. It was a side effect, created by a flawed binding. Kiar couldn't fix it, so she worked quickly instead.

Within Fai, a green orb nestled around his heart, and green light pumped through his veins, and green shadows flickered in his brain. The green light was a rarefied energy, lux and logos in one, as beyond her ability to manipulate as the phantasmagory would be for one not of the Blood. Underneath it, though, was shattered flesh and bone.

Medical Logos-working usually had to work with what was there: temporarily accelerating tissue regeneration, gently matching fragmented bones and so on. It was the work of many years to learn what could be safely done and what would only hasten the patient's death. Only the most legendary of healers had enough control, speed and precision to replace destroyed organs—and a living patient in that situation was rare enough that there wasn't often an opportunity to practice.

Kiar had learned just enough about the human body's operation during her study to know she didn't ever want to touch it in an ordinary situation. But with the lux— the lux was the stuff of wishes. It shaped itself almost faster than she could tell it what she wanted it to be, and Fai's body yearned to meld with it. It was almost too easy. She wondered if it would be as easy to make improvements as well as repairs. Had Fai, perhaps, always wanted to fly?

Then the process stuttered as her words tripped over the eidolon shadows buried deep in the boy's body. She remembered the same shadows within Iriss's far less injured body. The lux weakened them but could not banish the stubborn infection.

The lux and the Logos allowed no time to hesitate. She reached out with that same strange psychic appendage that she used to manipulate the eidolon world. The eidolon infection yearned towards her like Fai's body yearned toward the lux, and so she let herself be a conduit for the shadows, swallowing them into her own eidolon source.

Now with Fai's body clean, there was nothing to impede

healing. She made sure he was stable and released Lisette, pushing her away.

"He's not fully healed, but he will heal, if he doesn't do anything stupid," she said, her voice husky.

She watched in tired fascination as the green light withdrew hundreds of tendrils from Fai's body, barely aware of Cinai's astonished gratitude, and the murmurs around her. Did Tiana see what she saw?

The green orb detached itself from Fai with a final pulse, and the young man drew in a deep breath. Cinai fell silent as the orb drifted above Fai's body, within reach of her outstretched fingertips. Trembling, she kissed her fingers and reached out. A single green spark flew from her fingertips and merged with the orb. Then, without a sound, the orb sped over to Tiana and vanished.

A broad tree sketched of green light formed around Tiana. Branches spread around her like the antlers of a stag, and the face of a woman formed on the trunk. The tree grew and grew until it collapsed on itself, upon Tiana at its heart, until there was no tree, only Tiana, rimmed with green light. Her boots fell to pieces and her toes rooted themselves in the soil.

Then the light vanished, and Tiana collapsed.

CHAPTER TWENTY-NINE

CHOOSING

IS IT TRUE the King has fallen?" asked a well-dressed, middle-aged woman in the Tabernacle of Broken Hearts. It was the morning after her meeting with the Justiciars, the morning after Jerya ordered Twist to betray himself to the Vassay. "Is that why you sit here, day after day?"

Jerya tilted her head. "I don't know. I hope he hasn't." The lie came easily. Some days it was more work to remember the truth. But she hated being asked.

The woman pinched her lips together, dissatisfied with the answer. "What of your magic? Doesn't your family speak to each other magically?"

Jerya kept her face mild as she regarded the woman. Well-dressed and well-educated; most of her visitors didn't know very much about the family magic. It existed. That was usually enough. "We do. He does not communicate that way."

The woman's mouth twisted sourly. "And yet you think he

lives. Thank you, Your Highness." Her voice was patronizing, dismissive, and she turned and walked away without first showing proper respect. The few remaining audience-seekers stirred and murmured.

Jerya watched her go, all the way to the edge of the plaza where a Justiciar's Guard waited for her. One handed her something, and they parted ways.

Sweeping her gaze across the few people still hoping to speak with her, Jerya stood. The woman was the third person that morning to ask about both her father and the phantasmagory. The Justiciar's Council exerted itself and rumors grew: about her father, their magic, and the enemy armies. Somehow everybody knew about the armies outside the Blight but nobody knew about Jerya's discovery of their origin and what she was doing about it.

"We live in frightening days," she announced to the lingering observers. "We must remember that the architect of our fear comes at us from without, but the dwelling of those fears is our own hearts and minds. We will protect you, but in the meantime, trust in each other." Then she withdrew, hoping the pretty words could accomplish what facts and reason didn't.

Trust in each other. She thought of Cara, who trusted Jerya and betrayed her on the same day. Cara, who had informed the Justiciars that the phantasmagory was gone. Cara, who had such a twisted sense of her own duty that she didn't believe she'd done anything wrong in telling Jerya's secrets, because Jerya wasn't Shanasee. In the inn parlour after the meeting, Cara said, "You're a child," and "It's better to let wiser heads know the truth so they can make good decisions. Decisions that keep *everybody* safe." Yet Cara had trusted Jerya enough, even after betraying her, to turn her back and rejoin Shanasee.

The day had gotten worse, too. She and Twist had a long, quiet talk and at the end, he'd agreed to teach his magic to the Vassay. Then he'd gone off to see her sister like a man under a death sentence. She'd talked to him of duty, too, without any idea of what he considered his true duty to be.

Thorn stepped out of the crowd and fell into step beside her. "Your guards really aren't very good," he said mildly. "All the way back there."

"How many times do I have to tell you: they're not here to protect *me*?"

He glanced at her. "They'd be pretty bad at stopping you, too."

"They could do what was necessary," Jerya said stiffly, unclear on why they were even having this conversation. She turned a corner, to a quieter street.

"Mm. No. They couldn't. I don't think anybody here could, not even Miss Iriss. And that's supposed to be her job, isn't it? You've got them all depending on you."

"Not all of them," said Jerya, nettled and still thinking of Cara. "Why are you mentioning this? Do you think I'm about to lose control and go on a rampage?"

He watched her for a long moment, then shrugged. "There's dissension in the ranks. A debate about the different definitions of victory." He stopped strolling and stretched, and she turned back to him. "How do you define victory, Your Highness?"

"Keeping everything that's mine," she said quietly, and thought of Seandri, laughing with Landry after the Council meeting. She'd tried to keep him, only to realize how little she'd had.

"Interesting," Thorn said politely. "I've been thinking

about my own job. About where my responsibilities really lie. Do you ever think about your job that way?"

Jerya stared at him, then said flatly, "I am not talking to you about this," and walked away. He didn't follow her.

She all but ran the rest of the way to the inn, hurrying up to Jant's room. When she didn't find him, she stalked along the halls until she discovered him in one of the tiny writing rooms set aside for visiting scholars.

He sat in the desk chair, with the desk itself pushed into a corner. Gisen sat on the floor at his feet, and the air glimmered with the emanations they directed. Neither of them glanced at Jerya as she stood in the door.

"How is the project going?" she asked.

"Slowly," said Jant, in a go-away voice.

Jerya didn't go away. "We need it to go quickly. We *need* a phantasmagory before everything falls apart. I'm trying to hold onto everything, but they keep treating me like I'm a little girl dressed up as a Queen. As long as I have to keep pretending I have access to information they don't, that's all I really am."

Gisen gave her a wide-eyed look, then shook her head silently. Jant said, "Smart child. Why doesn't she just be a Queen, that's what I wonder. There's more to being Queen than bickering with the Justiciars."

Jerya's face tightened and she started to argue, but Jant wasn't done. "But I suppose we ought to help her out, or else she'll get herself killed and we'll have to take over. Queen Gisen?" He balanced a sphere on his fingers and Jerya couldn't tell if it was eidolon or emanation.

Gisen shook her head more vigorously. "Let's show her."

Jant nodded and held out the sphere to Gisen.

Squinting, Jerya said, "It's a gestalt eidolon, then? It's so small. And you weren't touching each other."

"It started as an eidolon. Now it's both," said Jant. "The emanation makes the eidolon and the eidolon uses the emanation. But that's an old trick, only useful for small things. That's not what we're showing you. Guess who it belongs to?"

"You?" said Jerya uncertainly. "You made it; I saw you do it."

"But Gisen holds it. The emanations are no longer mine."

Jerya looked a moment longer. "So you can pass workings back and forth? That's interesting, and maybe useful, but it's not a phantasmagory."

Gisen danced her fingers through the sphere, then held it out to Jerya, one hand coiling something invisible.

Jerya took a step, reaching out for the orb. As she did, Jant said, "Gisen, what did you do—"

Everything changed. Unseen windows opened and light streamed through. Jerya's vision flooded with green and when it faded, she was frozen, watching something else, somewhere else.

Windows along one side of a great gallery glowed in the light of dawn. Tiana stood in front of a painting, half-covered by an emerald cloth. She walked forward, her steps echoing on the polished wooden floor, and tugged on the fabric.

It pooled on the floor, revealing a woman, or possibly two women bound together at the back. No. It was a woman with two faces. One face lifted to the sky, features cold and expressionless. The other face looked down, smiling tenderly at the garden at her feet.

While the woman was only paint and canvas, the hilly landscape behind her moved. Plants twined over each other, flowered, dropped seeds, died, endlessly.

"He gave you death, my blossoms. He insisted you must die, insisted it was unavoidable." The painting spoke, in a dual voice both enraged and grieving. "The others have given you gifts as compensation. I will give you a—" and one voice said 'curse', while the other said 'blessing'. "Fear death, my flowers. Know it is coming and flee from it."

The double voice faded. The morning sun glowed through the eastern windows. Tiana shifted uncomfortably, and Jerya remembered how often her own family sought out danger, courted death, and even embraced it.

"Is that it?" Tiana touched the painting lightly, rubbed the dry pigment under her fingers. "Any advice for dealing with the Blighter?"

The painting flashed green, blinding, pure. Then the green ran with blood as a black spear pushed through the painting. The vision became a chaotic sequence of images and sensory input. Jerya sank into the jumble and *knew* the sensation. She was in a phantasmagory again, a tiny one, and so was every other living soul who carried enough Royal Blood to make an emanation.

It felt as if everybody in her family had piled into a small closet together. The noise and the sense of pressure overwhelmed her ability to process what was going on. She saw fragments of her family's surroundings, bumped against flashes of personalities she didn't recognize. Yithiere and the students he'd stolen hid in a forest, watching a vast darkling army move past, led by the lie she'd told so often. She recognized it, rejected it. Yithiere looked over at her and growled, "What is happening to my daughter?"

And Jerya saw: saw darklings and men battling, saw Cathay's eidolon leaping on an eidolon-man with a shimmering blade. Kiar huddled in an aegis with Lisette and two strangers. And Tiana—where was Tiana?

Where was Tiana?

The tiny phantasmagory shattered, just like the original had. Gisen stood in the center of the study room shaking eidolon-stuff from her hands. "*He* was there," breathed the small girl.

"Our enemy? Yes, I felt him." agreed Jant. "Others of the Blood, too, others we don't know. We'll have to find them."

Jerya grabbed Gisen's hands. "Why did you break it? Make another one! I didn't see Tiana. Did you see her?"

Gisen stared at her wide-eyed, then stuttered, "Didn't—didn't break it. Broke itself. It popped like a soap bubble." She swallowed. "Saw Tiana in the gallery with the Firstborn?"

"Yes, and a spear came through the painting! Did you see her after that, Uncle?"

Jant shook his head slowly. "Just the vision of the gallery. I'll have to run some more experiments but I think whatever Tiana did triggered that... experience. Still, it might be useful—"

"What are you talking about?" Jerya demanded incredulously. "My little sister is being attacked, right now."

"She has that sword," said Jant, far too calmly. "And there's nothing we can do about it. She's fought battles before; we hear about them later. She's right in the midst of the western invaders. I'd be more surprised if she wasn't in a fight."

Jerya wanted to shake his old frame. Somebody touched her elbow from behind and she whirled around. Siana stood there, with Iriss right behind her. "Come have tea, dear," she said.

"We just saw—they're fighting!"

"I heard, yes. Jerya. Come sit with me and Iriss and have some tea."

Jerya stared at her. She and Jant were so calm, as if none of this surprised them. Tiana might be *dead*. Then Iriss reached past Siana and laced her fingers through Jerya's. "Help me back to the couch, please. It's embarrassing to cling to Auntie Siana's shawl."

Jerya took a deep breath. She had Iriss and Iriss needed her help. She could focus on that. She went past both women, still holding Iriss's hand, and led her Regent back to the sitting room. Siana followed after a few words with Jant.

Jerya helped Iriss to the couch and sat on one of the high-backed chairs. "There's not any tea," she said, and she knew she sounded like a sullen little girl. Like Tiana, in fact. *Where was she?*

Just like Tiana, because the tea tray showed up a moment later, carried in by a wide-eyed inn servant. The tea things were haphazardly placed on a tray clearly prepared in a hurry. The servant put it on the table, gave Jerya a frightened look, and left the room.

"You were screaming," said Iriss lightly, reaching for a tea-cake and knocking it to the floor. Jerya picked it up, set it aside, and handed her another one. "And there were unformed eidolons climbing the walls. I don't know who did that but I think it frightened the staff.

"We were all in the phantasmagory again," Jerya tried to explain. "All of us. Except for Tiana."

Siana poured the tea delicately and handed the cups around. Jerya sipped hers dutifully. Instead of their usual afternoon tea, they drank a calming herbal mixture the Chancellor blended himself. He insisted the Blood drink it whenever possible after they trained with their magic or had a meltdown. Repetition created habit, and Jerya felt some of her adrenalin draining away.

"Now," said Siana. "There's something I've been meaning to ask you. I wonder now if I should have asked you long ago."

Jerya sat up straight, feeling like she had that morning at the Tabernacle, as if any minute the world would collapse under her. "Go ahead."

Siana hesitated, which didn't make Jerya feel any better. Finally Siana said, "Why have you been treating the Justiciar's Council as enemies?"

Being slapped couldn't have shocked Jerya more. She swayed back, and then leaned forward, into an argument.

And sat back again. Because it was Siana. Siana, who had hugged her after her mother left, who had lost her husband but stayed with the family anyhow, and so Jerya bit her tongue on her immediate response. She went over her experiences with the Council: the insults, the snubs, the way they treated her as a child. She looked at her own behavior, trying to decide if she'd been acting irrationally or worse, telling herself stories to justify her desires. It was easy to do; she simply asked herself what Tiana would have done.

Finally, cautiously, she said, "I've been a little irrational, but they've been awful to me. To us. They want us to be leashed dogs, Siana." Then she hesitated and said, "They have been awful, yes?" What was *really* awful was that she couldn't trust herself, even now. Not with her father, not with Yithiere for an uncle.

"They've been extremely rude and antagonistic," agreed Siana. "But you're good at turning antagonists into allies when you try. Every day you go to the Tabernacle and convince people who hate you that you're on their side. But then you don't do that with the Council. Why is that?"

Jerya tilted her head back, closing her eyes. "Because they're trying to take what's mine. They're not my allies, not even potentially. They want nothing from me except my nonexistence. They're my enemies. Just like Vassay."

Porcelain clinked as Siana sipped her tea, but that was the only sound. Jerya thought about Seandri, about his sweet smile turned toward Landry.

The spear went straight through the painting toward Tiana.

Iriss said cheerfully, "You've always been so possessive, Jer. Hasn't she, Auntie Siana?"

Without opening her eyes, Jerya said, "I share."

"Yes, you certainly do, as long as everybody knows something's yours," said Iriss, and her cheer was threaded with tartness.

"I wonder," said Siana gently. "What else is yours, besides Lor Seleni and what it contains? You have spent so much of your energy here."

"Ceria," said Jerya, then lowered her head and put her hands over her face. "Tiana. I need to go to the duchies myself and convince them to give us the armies, don't I?" Her voice turned sour. "Make allies of them. So Tiana, if she's even still alive, has a chance to do what the *damned* Firstborn want her to do. So I don't lose *everything*." Jerya glanced up at Siana, who had her hands folded in her lap. "That's what you're saying, isn't it?"

"If you don't, I think the price will be very high."

Jerya put her face in her hands again, breathing hard as what had to be done unrolled before her. "And I have to leave Iriss here. I just got her back again."

"What?" cried Iriss. "No, of course you don't. Only, I'll need a carriage. Or a wagon."

Jerya shook her head. "You're a resource to more than me now. You have insights, intelligence we wouldn't have. You need to stay with Alanah and the Guards."

"Insights I have for *you*, Jerya!" Iriss stood, agitated. "It's you I see best. Without you I'll be blind. It's for *you* I don't listen to *him*. Don't leave me behind. I don't know what will happen if you do."

Jerya hunched in her chair and tried to find the right words to convince her. But she never could, not with Iriss, not with Tiana. Pretty words only went so far. "You *have* to. If I took you along, that would be for me and for you, not for Ceria—"

"I *am* for you!" flared Iriss, her face red. Eidolon substance flickered on her skirt. "I've always been for you, since we were seven years old."

Jerya shook her head again, more slowly. "No. You've been for Ceria. Regents stand between the Blood and the people. You know that, I know that. And we both know you couldn't do what you had to, if you had to. I love you, Iriss. And you *must* stay here."

Iriss burst into tears and stumbled out of the room, one hand held ahead of her so she didn't bump into a wall. Jerya wanted to go after her, and couldn't. She turned to the remaining woman instead. "Aunt Siana, I do need some companion. A companion who knows my weaknesses. You've watched me all this time. You said something today. Would you come with me instead?"

"Of course, sweetling." Siana's gaze stayed on her, level and calm, as Jerya stood.

"Thank you." She cast around for something else to say. "I have to talk to some other people. And I suppose arrange the journey...."

"I can do that, at least." Siana found a small book in her knitting basket and opened it up to start making a list.

Jerya nodded, distracted by her own mental list of people she had to speak with. Work was better than thinking of Iriss's face, and the eidolon energy crawling over her dress. Instead she thought of several of her city folk who awaited advice from her. Alanah, who would need to write her regularly about the Blight. The Chancellor, who needed to be warned about Cara. Seandri, who deserved an apology for things she'd never felt sorry for.

Then she remembered Thorn, remembered his murmuring about jobs and the threat she offered but didn't see. It made sense now. He thought she might be able to unite Ceria so that they didn't need foreign support. If she went on this trip without neutralizing him, she'd always be looking over her shoulder.

She looked over her shoulder now, the hair on her neck prickling. Was he was getting information from within the inn? There was nothing out of place, nothing that stood out, but she didn't have much time to deal with him.

"I'm going to go get started on farewells." She backed out of the sitting room door before her aunt could notice her sudden tension, then turned around and ran out of the inn, sending an emanation circling lightly around her body. It wasn't one of Kiar's aegises but it was better than nothing when it came to arrows.

Only a few steps down the street, she saw him out of the corner of her eye, moving in the same direction from near the inn. He kept pace with her like he was just another person on the street, close enough to talk to if she wanted. She didn't. She kept walking until she came to a warehouse she knew to be abandoned. Then she turned around and held out her hand to the guards always behind her. "Stay outside, please."

She didn't wait to see if they'd obey before going into the warehouse. Thorn had vanished from the street already, although she didn't think he'd used the front door.

The dark warehouse smelled awful: the last trace of whatever had once been stored there. Maybe if her head stopped whirling so much she could remember what it had been but all she could think about was her list of things to do.

Not getting assassinated was at the top.

"What are you doing here?" came Thorn's voice, from somewhere in the gloom.

"Giving you an opportunity." She coiled an emanation in both her hands.

"Do you really think I've been waiting for one?" His voice moved around the warehouse.

She unleashed one of her emanations and diffused it so that it was nothing more than a current of air, then let it carry the distant movements of Thorn to her skin. "Why does your employer *want* Ceria to remain disorganized in the face of this Blight? Do they think they can reason with it?"

Thorn stilled. "This one? I think they might. After all, he shares your powers. *You* are the true Blight."

The flat statement stole Jerya's breath. "That's a dangerous thought," she muttered.

Thorn remained still. He didn't fidget like a normal man, as if no background thoughts distracted him from his focus on her.

"It doesn't matter," Jerya told him. "It doesn't matter if we are. Ceria is mine and I'm not going to let it be torn apart by Vassay and Ohedreton for their own satisfaction. I'm leaving Lor Seleni soon, to organize the duchies."

Thorn moved forward, shockingly fast. Jerya felt his
lunge against her skin and she dodged and sent out the other
emanation at his feet. She missed, or he jumped over it. She
rolled to one side and sent the little emanation whipping
back at him, then ran behind one of the remaining crates. It
smelled of rotten onions.

"That's why you didn't try to kill me before," she told
him breathlessly. "Because I stayed in Lor Seleni, focused on
the city."

"Yes," he said. She ran behind another crate as he closed
on her. "Princess. This is stupid. Coming in here was stupid.
Are you going to be shot by my partner on the catwalk with
the crossbow?"

"Are you going to be shot by my guards when they burst in
here with lanterns?" she countered. He chuckled and jumped
on a crate, but it wasn't the crate she crouched behind.

"They can shoot each other," he said, with the laughter
still warming his voice.

"Do you always talk to your victims like this?" she asked.
One of the crates gaped open on the side. It too stank like
rotting onions. Silently she created a small owl and sent it
inside the crate. Then, as she moved away, it started ruffling
its feathers and moving its wings, making just a whisper of
a sound.

"Never," said Thorn.

"Look at what you've been missing out on, then."

"Fun and games in the dark," he drawled. "Yes, I see." He
reached the crate with her owl and looked inside. Instantly
the owl fluttered in his face. Jerya shoved at him with her
emanations but they were too weak to move a large man,
so she darted forward and used her shoulder to knock him
off balance and into the open crate. As he fell, he twisted,

grabbing her wrist and pulling her down with him, into the rotten vegetable remains.

The owl landed on his head, and she kicked at him, bringing an emanation to bear. They were weak, but she could make them quite sharp. He caught her other wrist as they flailed around, but it didn't matter; unlike Tiana she didn't need to map her emanations to her body. All she had to do to cut him was narrow her eyes.

Instead, she lay on top of him, both his hands holding both her wrists and said, "I win."

He shook his head. The owl on his forehead shifted her weight, clacking her beak inches from his eyes. "Yes, it does appear you have an edge. But don't declare victory quite yet." His muscles moved under her as he prepared to do something.

"Hush!" she said sharply. "Listen." He froze beneath her, listening. "I *could* kill you. I could have had my guards arrange for your death. A bar fight, a scandal, I'd pay for your death with plepanin or a window of access to the Palace. It would have been easy."

"I've stood over you while you slept through the eye of the night," he said. It was a counter, a note, offered simply as a point of comparison.

"Have you? I believe it. Look at us, both disappointing Vassay by staying alive. Do you think Scriber Stone is so unsubtle by accident? Whichever of us dies, he wins."

His eyes widened, then narrowed. He released her wrists and she fell on his chest. When he pushed himself up into a sitting position, she was left sitting half on his lap. The little owl fluttered over to Jerya's shoulder.

She scooted off his knees and out of the crate, then stood. He shifted position but stayed down. With the owl on her shoulder she could just see him sitting with his knees up and arms loose between them. He simply looked at her, waiting in silence.

Jerya waited too. She wanted him to say something, to respond to what she last said. But he didn't. Finally, she repeated, "I'm leaving Lor Seleni soon, to organize the duchies. I'd like you to come with me. If you're not going to kill me, you might as well stop other people from killing me, too."

With that laughter in his voice again, he said, "Do you think I'd make a better bodyguard than I do an assassin?"

She hesitated. "I think you'd tell me when I was being stupid. I could use that sometimes. And... your other skills might also be useful." She held out her hand to him.

He looked at her long enough that her hand started getting tired. Then his big hand closed around her fingers as he said, "You're being stupid to trust me."

"Thank you for your opinion," she said gravely, and braced herself to pull him to his feet.

CHAPTER THIRTY

BROKEN

L ife filled the world, and Tiana could feel it all. It knocked down walls, it crashed through stone. When the spear came through the painting, Tiana stepped back, and that was life. When Atalya's gallery faded away around her and she came back to earth, she emerged into a sea of life. It wasn't a green light, as Niyhan had given her a blue light. It was a green force, palpable, driving and furious. It pounded in her veins, a defiant shout against an endless silence.

Life twined around her, flashing small and glowing large. It was beautiful, until the larger glows began blinking out mid-flower. Horror seized her in its gaping maw. But what could she do but encourage them to blaze brighter?

One of the glows moved close to her, until it obscured everything. It slapped her, hard.

Tiana staggered backwards, the green force fading just enough that she could see the everyday world once more. The loud stable girl stood in front of her, brown eyes blazing.

Blood smeared down the stable girl's face and both her hands were crimson.

"Wake up!" the stable girl shouted, and brought her hand back to hit Tiana again. "We need you and your bloody sword, or everybody's going to die!"

Tiana stepped backward again and almost tripped over the dead horse behind her. She still held Jinriki in his belt over her shoulder and the sword's point swung down and stopped her.

You couldn't hear me, sent Jinriki, his frustration palpable. **Not at all.**

She looked down at him and she understood why. Jinriki had none of the green force running through him. He existed outside the power of Atalya.

Minex said, "Very good, loud stable girl. She is awake now, very good. I will do more." Minex, on the other hand, vibrated with something that, if not green, was a close cousin. The earth fiend put her small hand on Tiana's arm, and a jolt ran through her. The green receded more, replaced by a roaring in her ears.

She stood in the middle of a battlefield. The darkling army had found them.

"Look up, yes?" said Minex again. "At the ridge. Witness what he does to your people."

Tiana dragged her gaze away from the men fighting andani and looked at the ridge Minex pointed to. Several men observed the battle, wreathed in eidolon magic. One of them pointed down at them. Even at that distance, even through the dust in the air, Tiana could tell he had the coloring of the Blood. She thought *Oh, so the stories of Benjen are true*, before she thought *How?* The man turned to one of the andani, a bat winged one, and passed it his sword. Then another wave of andani came over the hill and obscured her view.

A horse screamed and the stable girl cursed and ran away, pulling a jagged knife out of her belt as she did. Cathay swore behind Tiana, and Kiar's shield shimmered in front of her. Near her, Slater fought a pair of andani determined to get past him.

"No," said Tiana, and swung Jinriki still sheathed. The emanation split around Slater to carry his two attackers back, tumbling back, into the claws of their allies. Then she pulled the scabbard off the blade and turned in a circle, taking in the battle going on around her. Men fell and she could see who was dead and who was only injured. The deaths hurt her in a strange new way, as if it wasn't only her fault they died, but also that they lived.

I have never liked Atalya, said Jinriki irritably. **Let's end this so you're not troubled by more deaths.**

Tiana nodded and raised her hands over her head. Every andani within sight lifted into the air, held by invisible fists. Then she flung them all away, just as she'd flung away Slater's attackers. It wasn't lethal, but the maneuver gave everybody fighting a moment of breathing room.

"Maybe they'll be smart. Maybe they'll flee," said Kiar, appearing beside Tiana, pulling Lisette behind her.

"They're eidolons. How can they flee?" asked Tiana, distracted. She glanced first to Lisette, and next to Cathay, to determine if they were injured. Lisette only had that awful glow—yet she stood close to Kiar and where would be safer in a battle? But three gashes sliced down Cathay's cheek and forehead, making his face a bloody mess.

He wiped blood out of his eye and gave her a small smile. "I've never been so grateful you've got that sword as I am right now."

She frowned at his injuries, reached out a finger and

traced one of them. A green spark danced down the wound, sealing it closed. Cathay gasped and caught her hand, his eyes wide.

"Tiana, should you be doing that?" asked Kiar in alarm. "Don't we need that power for *them*?"

"Probably I shouldn't," agreed Tiana. "But I don't care. Doing what I was supposed to didn't do anything for them." She nodded at one of the fallen who wouldn't be getting up again. "If this is going to be a game, I want to be a player, not a piece. Especially given what they do to my friends."

Good, growled Jinriki, and ***Finally.*** Then he added, ***Here comes a heavy one.***

Tiana looked, and saw a big, bat-winged andani picking its way toward them, leading the reformed troop that had been assaulting them. Amidst the groans of men and the noise of hurt and frightened horses, Berrin called, "Princess?" He stood near the corner of the rough formation Slater commanded, with Jozua watching his back.

"Yes," said Tiana, pulling her hand away from Cathay and turning around. She swung Jinriki. This time the andani stayed on the ground; Tiana lifted, but they didn't rise. "What's going on, Jinriki?"

I said, they're heavy. Ohedreton is pouring a lot of power into them so you can't blow them away like scattered ashes. Don't worry. If we destroy the big one the old-fashioned way, all will be well.

"All right. The old-fashioned way, then. This is your dance." She walked forward to meet them, relaxing her mind so she would respond better to Jinriki's instructions.

The andani looked like the one she'd faced at the Citadel of the Sky. She wondered if it too would speak with Ohedreton's voice, and if once again, she'd distract it while

Kiar destroyed it. That might, she felt, be harder with a company of similar soldiers at its back.

This one had a sword: real metal, but strangely wrought. It had fangs along each side, and it more resembled Jinriki than anything she'd seen before. But it glinted all over like something that had never been used.

The andani hissed at her, showing its mouth full of jagged fangs. Probably not Ohedreton, then. It moved its sword into a careful guard position and waited.

Tiana let Jinriki move her body; he knew what to do better than she could ever imagine knowing. He swung, and even with their magics conjoined, her muscles ached.

The andani endured the blast of power that came off the sword, although the blast frayed away the edges of its substance. Its own weapon clashed against Jinriki. The edges slid together, and then—

And then—

Jinriki caught in the fangs of the andani's weapon with an awful jolt. And another jolt, as both weapons twisted together. The andani's weapon shimmered and darkened. Power raced down it, whining like a spinning disc. The andani shuddered, And then—

there was a crack that swelled and became a peal of thunder.

Jinriki bent—

No.

Jinriki snapped.

The top half of the blade flew off to Tiana's side and— *something* leaked out of the twisted, sheared edge. Lines of distortion waved in the air, flapping like loose threads. The shock in her arm still reverberating, Tiana said uncertainly, "Jinriki?"

Tiana.... he said, and his voice faded away. His presence in her mind fragmented, like ice cracking and melting.

The andani with the swordbreaker moved his weapon to end her, and Kiar stood between them, her shield glimmering bright. She jumped on the andani, tore him apart with her bare hands, but Tiana barely noticed.

"Jinriki," she wailed, realization hitting like the ground after a cliff. "No, don't go. I wanted to see your true shape someday."

Nobody answered in her mind, not with a whisper, or a laugh or or a burst of a temper. Tiana pulled the remains of the blade close and looked around wildly.

Minex held the other half of Jinriki's blade. Tiana lunged for her and Minex held it out of her reach, one hand moving over the broken end. "No," said the earth fiend distractedly. "No. Don't touch me yet."

Tiana wanted to fall on her and sob. But somebody screamed behind her and his green light flickered and faded. The red light moved nearby and the green light within Tiana rose up *raging* at the red she did not yet have.

She didn't understand.

Minex tugged on the broken blade Tiana still held tightly. "Give me the Prince," she demanded. "Give him to me. I must save him."

Tiana goggled at her, not letting go. Minex was a dreamer, a storyteller, a fool. Tiana had seen Jinriki leaking out of the blade, felt him leaking from her mind. She couldn't give up all she had left of him to the earth fiend's fantasy.

An andani appeared behind Minex, already injured, with empty eyes and one of their own darkling weapons. It swung.

Tiana released what was left of Jinriki to Minex's tugging

and shoved her hands out, flinging the andani away. The little earth fiend didn't even realize the danger she'd been in, so obsessed was she with holding both halves of the shattered sky fiend.

Where was Lisette? The thought was shamefully delayed, but it overran the spitting green light and the shock of Jinriki's silence. Tiana looked and found her just to hand, always to hand, her presence obscured by the red light, by Jozua standing at her back. Lisette's arm glowed brightly, shedding a real radiance that should have overcome the spiritual glows of the Firstborn lights, but there was too much, too much to see and understand, all at once.

"Lisette, I'm going to kill them all," Tiana told her, in case her Regent had a different plan.

Lisette's face had streaks through the mud and blood. "Please do, Tiana. I will be here." The words had a formal cadence that didn't hide Lisette's rage.

Tiana turned back to the battle and did her best. She stopped throwing the enemies away and started twisting— but it was hard, harder than it had been for months. Jinriki had made her natural power so much stronger that what once took a whisper now took a shout. At least, she thought distantly, they didn't bleed.

Her own people did, though, and the blood sprayed around her until it seemed like rain. They were losing. Despite all Tiana and Cathay's strength, despite Kiar's special gifts, there were simply too many of them. An endless flood streamed from the ridge where the darkling man of the Blood watched, and the humans died and died.

Lisette and Kiar moved the wounded when they could, back to the center of a smaller and smaller square, and Tiana and Cathay protected them. At one point, Tiana saw, spinning, that Minex crouched in the center of the square, ignoring the bodies around her as she fixated on the remains of Jinriki. She glowed. But everybody was glowing now, except the dead and there were far too many of those.

Then they weren't just fighting andani. Some of the warriors that came up against them and threw themselves at the fort of bodies were darkling men. They had the same empty eyes as the andani, but they contributed lasting corpses when they died.

Cathay hesitated when he came face to face to one, and Tiana reached past him with an emanation and crushed the man's throat. He turned to look at her, pale, and she remembered in a flash his enthusiasm once upon a time, after she'd first killed in a dirty alley.

"You need to get out of here," he said. "You need to escape. It's you he wants."

"No," Tiana said. "It's everybody I love." She turned back to the battle.

It was a slaughter, and they were going to lose. But at least she wouldn't have to live to watch everybody else in Ceria die. It was a small comfort.

The ground shook with the thunder of running horses. Men on horseback swept past her, a river to match the darkling flood. There was barely a moment's drift between crushing a darkling soldier and having several tons of horseflesh between her and the enemies.

She threw herself forward but a mailed hand shoved her back, and then Lisette took the hand she brought forward to move the impediment from her path. "Let them, Tiana," she said. "Let's walk this way. Let's go see Cathay."

Lisette had the quiet, calm voice she used when Tiana was lost in the phantasmagory, but there was no phantasmagory now. The voice still worked. Her exhaustion helped. She never felt exhaustion in the phantasmagory either.

She took a deep breath, and another, and then another one, the breaths very much like sobs. Lisette pulled her away from the moving front of the battle.

Cathay was already in the square of injured, where several armored men with the heraldry of Sunasin waited. They'd only been a few hours away from Sunasin, hadn't they? Just a few hours away from safety, and survival for so many now lost.

The new soldiers stared, not at Cathay or Tiana, but at Minex. Still glowing, she floated in the air in the center of the square, her hands clasped to her breast like she protected something very small. Kiar stood between her and the strange armed men, anxious but clearly ready to stop them from attacking the earth fiend.

Minex's eyes opened and she looked at Tiana, her expression radiant. "I have him," she said. "I caught his heart." But when Tiana looked in Minex's hands, she saw nothing at all.

CHAPTER THIRTY-ONE

THE WIND-UP PRINCESS

TIANA SAT IN the chamber the chatelaine of Sunasin found for her, looking blindly at some books left on a table. It was a quiet room, with burgundy drapes and local watercolors on the walls, where she could think about what happened and let the last dregs of adrenalin evaporate into the ashes of grief.

Lisette promised to join her soon, after she debriefed the Count of Sunasin. Kiar and Minex had vanished as soon as they arrived in the courtyard of the castle. The men were all busy with the rescuing soldiers, even Cathay, and Tiana sat alone, as instructed, like a good girl.

They'd treated her like fine porcelain on the ride to the Sunasin seat. "He was bound to her mind," Kiar had said to Jozua impatiently, as if Tiana couldn't hear her. "Who knows what the damage could be?" Tiana knew. She felt the emptiness in her thoughts, and the sobs she couldn't surrender to.

A servant silently brought a tea tray in and set it on the

table. Tiana watched her numbly. As the maid turned to leave, Tiana said, "Wait."

"Ma'am? Your Highness? Ma'am?" The maid stumbled over her words, unused to addressing the Blood.

Tiana wondered if the maid would obey if she told her to wait in the room in her stead. The maid had other work to do, of course, but Tiana was her Princess. Did that mean anything here? They brought her tea, but not a change of clothes.

Instead, she said, "Go find Lisette, my Regent. Tell her I'm... tell her I'm not here. Tell her I'm somewhere."

"Where?" asked the maid uncertainly.

"Not here. Not waiting. I'm not waiting. I'm not going to sit and wait, or go and go because somebody else says I should." Tiana stood briskly and brushed her filthy, blood-soaked riding dress off, as if she could brush away the obligations that held her.

The maid gaped at her, then backed out of the room. She spoke to somebody beyond, and Tiana followed her to see Berrin leaning beside the door, his arm in a sling.

"You make me feel like a prisoner," she told him. "Am I under arrest? Did I do something wrong? Yes, of course I did. People died. Jinriki died." Her voice caught in her throat.

"Princess," said Berrin roughly. "You did nothing wrong. I didn't want you to be completely alone now, and..." he glanced down at his arm. "And I'm not sure what else I'm good for now."

"I'm sorry," she told him. It didn't seem like enough but what else could she say? "Do you know where Lisette is?"

Berrin looked away. "With Jozua, I think."

Her heart leapt into her throat. "Is he... is he also injured?"

"No," said Berrin neutrally. "No, he isn't injured at all. Luck favors him."

"Rann. It's Rann who favors him." Tiana shook her head. "Thank you... thank you for all you've done for me, Berrin. But I have to get out of this room. I have to not be their wind-up princess, stored on a shelf. Just for a while."

Berrin regarded her for a long moment before saying, "I'll rest here," and leaned back against the wall again.

Tiana gave him a grateful nod and hurried away down the stone-flagged hall.

She wandered for a while, avoiding people, until she found her way to the stables. Nobody accosted her along the way. The buildings for the horses were as large as the Palace stables in Lor Seleni and right then, far busier as horses were shuffled between stall to pasture and stable yard to stall. Tiana found a corner and watched the traffic, her throat tight. Her horse Moon had been one of the horses killed in the battle. She'd ridden to Sunasin on a soldier's mount that had lost its rider; she didn't even remember what color it had been.

The stable girls hurried by and the quiet one cast an eye over Tiana as they did. Then she tugged on her companion and they stopped.

The loud stable girl glared at Tiana, and demanded, "What do you want?"

Tiana's cheek stung briefly in memory of the slap the girl had delivered. She shook her head. She hadn't come here with any clear intent and she didn't know what to say.

"I'm sorry about Moon," said the quiet stable girl. "Would you like to see Spooky and Dustling?"

Silently, Tiana nodded. The stable girls turned, both of them, and led her through the stables like they'd known them all their lives. Dustling and Spooky had been stabled beside each other, and they whickered at seeing familiar faces. Tiana went to first Dustling, Lisette's mare, then Spooky, patting their noses. The stable girls lingered, watching her. The loud one acted like she might run off with one of the horses as soon as they turned their backs.

After a moment of whispering nothings to Spooky, Tiana turned around, her back against the stall door. "What are your names? I think I was told once, but I've forgotten. I'm sorry."

The quiet stable girl smiled at Tiana. "I'm Nori." After a moment, she elbowed her companion.

"I'm Stefi," the loud stable girl muttered, still looking like Tiana's very existence in the stable was an affront.

"I'm Tiana," She wasn't sure she'd ever introduced herself so casually before. "Um. Thank you for waking me up back there, Stefi."

Stefi's eyes widened. "Are you serious?"

Uncertainly Tiana said, "Yes? Thank you. I couldn't hear Jinr—" and her throat closed up. She swallowed hard. "I couldn't hear anybody else. You got through to me. You saved lives."

To Tiana's surprise, the loud stable girl—Stefi—turned bright red. "Ah, well, it was no big deal. You ever need to be smacked upside the head again, I'm your girl. No tip needed."

Nori covered her mouth, aghast and laughing. "Stefi!"

"She thanked me, Nori! What am I supposed to say?"

Tiana summoned up a small smile for both of them, then turned back to the stall, leaning her head against a post. She was so tired suddenly. But if she slept, she'd have dreams of the guards who died, of the emptiness in her head.

Instead she left the stable to its business. She made

her way through the stable yards to the military buildings. Soldiers filled the yards: relaxing against walls, dealing with equipment, sharing information. They didn't ignore her arrival as the stables had. First one group, then another turned to look at her. In the stable she'd been just another human, far less important than the horses; here she was a weapon, and soldiers always paid attention to weapons.

Cathay appeared out of a group of knights, many with the roses on their shoulders. "Stormy," he greeted her soberly. "I was just thinking about—" and he caught her hand and pulled her around the corner of a building, out of sight of the soldiers. Then he looked at her face, as if memorizing every inch of it.

"What?" she said. "Why are you looking at me like that?" She held his hand between both of hers, feeling the warmth.

"Because I can," he said bleakly. "Kiar's looking for you, though."

Tiana shook her head at the nonsensical answer. "How are you?"

"Making plans. Stormy—" He put a finger under her chin. "I want to kiss you now. While I still can."

Bewildered but willing—now, after so much—she leaned forward.

He quirked a familiar grin at her before his mouth closed over hers.

It was something out of storybooks, just this once. Cathay knew exactly what to do. He turned her so the wall supported her, then proceeded to kiss her until her knees buckled. She clung to him feverishly, so he held her up and kissed her some more until she was a hot, panting mess, ready to do whatever he wanted, wherever he wanted.

"Finally," said Kiar nearby, and the ice of her voice cut through the heat.

Tiana remembered Kiar and Twist kissing, and how she'd broken that moment. Shame flooded through her. Frantically, she pushed Cathay away.

Instantly he put her down and stepped back, maintaining his hold on her shoulder to steady her. He threw an inscrutable look at Kiar, standing nearby, then ignored her as he said, "Stormy—Tiana. I'm leaving soon. I'm going to ride out with some of the Knights of the Rose to do what we can against Ohedreton's army. I've spent too much time paying attention only to what I want. But those men today—" He looked at his hand. "They died. And some of them were on the other side. I can't help but wonder if that would have happened if I had... chosen differently, weeks ago. If I had paid attention to something other than what I wanted, no matter how much I wanted it."

Tiana blinked at him, trying to focus on what he said instead of the looming, awful presence of Kiar standing nearby with her angry, scornful expression. She took a deep breath. "When?"

"Soon. They have a camp nearby so I'll be riding over with a few of them before sunset." His black-brown eyes locked with hers. "I'll be thinking about you every hour. I can change how I act, but not how I feel. So take care of yourself."

"Wait—you mean you're saying goodbye *now*?" Tiana shook her head, bewildered.

He nodded, and Rann's red light sparked, deep in his eyes. She opened her mouth to say, "No, you can't go, I need you—" and she almost did—

But she wasn't going to simply move as the Firstborn

dictated anymore, be their wind-up Princess, no, she *wasn't*, and she wasn't going to make Cathay do so either. She couldn't quite put it into words, but she knew that Cathay was wasted following her around: wasting what he could be to other people and wasting what he could be to himself. Cathay had never followed her out of true love, anymore than she'd done as the Firstborn bid out of duty. They'd both been looking for fairy tales, for dreams, and it was time to wake up. Whatever the spark of red indicated about Cathay's role in gathering Rann's light, it wasn't going to be at her side. He'd made that decision himself and she wasn't going to undo it with careless words.

"Go, then," Tiana said. "Do well. Come home again." Yet because she couldn't shake off the habits of a lifetime just by wishing, she added, "We'll be seeing each other again."

"I hope so," he said, and kissed her hand. When he turned to Kiar, he said, "Will you stay with her?"

Kiar looked up at the sky, as if it was easier to talk to the clouds. "Yes." She shook her head, but said again, "Yes."

Cathay nodded, and then he was gone, back around the corner, leaving Tiana alone with Kiar.

"Kiar, I'm sorry—"

"Don't be," said Kiar curtly. "Look at what I accomplished. Come on."

Tiana almost resisted, almost pushed back. She wasn't going to be a wind-up Princess anymore, after all. But Kiar was her cousin, and her friend, and Tiana had hurt her by treating her like a character in a play. Maybe she'd utterly ruined something that could have been wonderful.

So she went with Kiar, docile and brooding, without even asking their destination. Kiar didn't speak as they went back into the main castle, down a broad corridor and out into a large kitchen garden. A covered shrine stood on the far side, under an ancient plum tree. Old and worn, undedicated shrines like this were used by the kitchen staff to beg attention from whichever Firstborn they required.

Within the shrine knelt Minex, her hands held close to her heart again. Tiana stopped. She didn't want Minex, didn't want Minex's stories and experiments.

Kiar grabbed her arm and hauled her forward. "We're not doing this without you, in case he reacts poorly."

"Doing what?" Tiana demanded.

Lisette knelt inside the shrine as well. "Oh! You found her."

Kiar eyed Tiana, then sighed. "We're going to save Jinriki, Tiana. Minex did capture *something*. I can see it in the Logos. She says that with our help, mine and Lisette's, she can save him."

Lisette held up her glowing arm. "I'd rather use it to save people than kill them." The glow had eaten more of her arm, and Lisette looked pale and sad.

"I thought you were talking to the Sunasin with Jozua," she said, subdued.

"Yes. But Minex found me and said this was more important."

"She's lying, she plays tricks, she can't even tell what's real—" Tiana said, too afraid to hope.

Kiar squeezed her arm. "Look at me, Tiana. She did catch something. I don't play tricks. And we need to help her or what she's got will slip away."

Minex said brightly, "Not now. But I am getting a little sleepy, and if I sleep, we both turn into dreams."

Kiar let go of Tiana. "Stay or go. If you stay, sit by the door." Then she and Lisette joined Minex, kneeling down with her to form three points on a triangle. Minex carefully put the invisible thing she'd been cuddling close into the center of the triangle, then took the hands of the human girls.

"I will sing a song," Minex whispered. "I will show you a vision. The two of you will do your beautiful magic to make my song real. He will not be the Great Prince anymore in body, oh no. He becomes my brother. The earth loves the sons of the sky and she will adopt the Great Prince. Isn't that nice?" Minex beamed.

Tiana didn't understand, but Kiar's eyes widened. "He'll be an earth fiend?"

"My brother, yes. But he will still be the Great Prince in his heart. He will still have the memories, the dreams."

Lisette caught her breath. "Oh." She glanced toward Tiana, then back at Minex. "All right. Please sing us your song, Minex. I'm ready."

Kiar nodded, and Minex began to sing. It was a lovely song, and completely incomprehensible to Tiana. Whatever vision it showed Kiar remained invisible, too. After a moment Kiar began to speak to the Logos. Her voice sounded soft and measured, as if she coaxed a small animal from a burrow. After a moment the two voices twined around each other perfectly, like they were producing the same piece of music. It was beautiful and sad and it seemed to go on forever.

Tiana put her head on her knees and stared out the archway she sat beside, watching the afternoon slowly turn into evening. Every time she glanced at the working, more of Lisette's arm had transfigured to light, and nothing else had changed.

At last, she blinked, and realized full night had fallen. Berrin stood at the garden door with Slater. Lanterns glowed

around the garden and the stable girls—Nori and Stefi—sat
on a bench eating winter peas. Twist stood in the far corner
of the shrine, his eyes fixed on Kiar.

Kiar's voice scratched hoarsely. Tiana looked despite
herself, then inhaled sharply. This time, something was
different. A dark mist moved at the center of the triangle,
staying within the points but spinning—

Tiana remembered how in the phantasmagory, Jinriki had
always been a dark cloud with silver eyes, and for a moment
she wondered—

Kiar's Logos speech became urgent and Twist moved
forward a step before holding himself still. Lisette's arm was
light from shoulder to fingers. Something *snapped.*

The mist collapsed into a solid form. But instead of a
sword, a naked man uncurled himself. He had golden skin
and shaggy hair the color of dried blood and his eyes, when
they opened, were silver.

As soon as his eyes opened, he sprang to his feet. Kiar's
speech cut off mid-syllable as she jerked backward.

Where—? said Jinriki's voice in Tiana's mind, thin
and distant.

"Where—?" said the man, his voice deep and rich and
angry.

Minex beamed up at him. "Great Prince. And now I
must sleep."

The man looked down at Minex, then stared down at his
hands. Then he looked up, directly at Tiana. With two long
strides he crossed the small shrine until he loomed over her.
She stared up at him, confused. He had Jinriki's eyes, but
Jinriki had been a sword...

"I heard my master," said the man bleakly, as Jinriki said
the same thing in her mind. "He called to me. It was time to

come home. Vengeance didn't matter anymore." He hesitated, and his own gaze was as puzzled as Tiana felt. He muttered, "But I couldn't go. I wanted to, but I couldn't. Even when he called, I couldn't leave *you*."

Here ends The Green Wild, Book 2 of the Thrones of the Firstborn Pentalogy. Shrine of Summer is forthcoming.

Thank you for reading Green Wild! If you'd like to know when the next book is available, you can sign up for my announce-only list at http://www.dreamfarmer.net

Reviews help books and readers find each other, which is getting harder and harder as the internet expands. If you want to share your thoughts with others, I welcome all reviews, positive and negative. It's amazing how much they matter.

The next book in the *Thrones of the Firstborn* series is *Shrine of Summer.*

DRAMATIS PERSONAE

The main of our story takes place in **LOR SELENI**, the heart of Ceria from which all strength springs forth.

THE ROYAL FAMILY

The following is an incomplete listing of The Scions of the Royal Blood, Protectors of Ceria and Wardens of the Holy Mount, in order of succession:

HIS ROYAL MAJESTY, KING SHONATHAN II, blessed with a perfect memory. Represented by a mirror.

HER ROYAL HIGHNESS, THE CROWN PRINCESS JERYA, his eldest daughter. Represented by a hawk.

HER SERENE HIGHNESS, THE PRINCESS TIANA, his younger daughter. Represented by lightning.

HIS HIGHNESS, PRINCE YITHIERE, younger brother of the King. Represented by a wolf.

HIS HIGHNESS, PRINCE CATHAY, the King's nephew. Represented by a hunting cat.

HER HIGHNESS, PRINCESS GISEN, the King's niece. Represented by a white horse.

HIS HIGHNESS, PRINCE JANT, uncle to the King. Represented by a fox.

HER HIGHNESS, PRINCESS SHANASEE, the King's cousin. Represented by a candleflame.

HIS HIGHNESS, PRINCE SEANDRI, the King's cousin. Represented by a red stag.

LADY KIAR SUAN, a natural daughter of the Royal Blood. Represented by a sword and shield.

The Regency Court

ANTECEDENTS AND COUNSELORS

The Regency Court manages the day to day life of the Royal Blood, among many other tasks.

HIS EXCELLENCY, CHANCELLOR BRYN HALE

HER LADYSHIP, IRISS BASCOMB, Regent to Princess Jerya

HER LADYSHIP, LISETTE CONRA, Regent to the Princess Tiana

LADY YEVONNE HUAR, Regent to Princess Gisen

HER LADYSHIP, CARA MISTONTE, Regent to Princess Shanasee

HIS LORDSHIP, HARTHEN BYERRES, Regent to Prince Seandri

HER HIGHNESS LADY JULINE INGAE, wife of Prince Jant and mother of Princess Shanasee

HIS HIGHNESS LORD JAIME EIRCEDE, widower of Princess Rinta and father of Princess Gisen

HER HIGHNESS LADY SIANA CALAIN, widow of Prince Pell and mother of Prince Cathay

HER MAJESTY, QUEEN ANNIS, dwelling at the Hypana Ducal Court

The Justiciar's Court

LAWMAKERS FROM THE SIX DUCHIES

THE JUSTICIAR'S COUNCIL

LORD TERRENCE AUBIN OF BORZEE, land of tumbled hills and crashing cliffs, along the western coast

LORD DONATIEN WICHARD OF KANURA, mountain land rising from the Telamic Sea

LADY ROSALYN SCOTT OF ARDOZA, fair southern land of wine and silk

LORD MILLARD BELLAMONT OF INGAE, the richest farmland in all of Ceria

LORD WARRANE DUNSTAN OF DALEIN, the northern orchards

LORD JASPER GUERAN OF HYPANA, the forestlands farthest north

KEEPERS OF THE FLAME OF FAITH

HIS GRACE, DORIAN III, Magister of the Citadel of the Sky

GONE BUT NOT FORGOTTEN

THE BLOOD BASTARD, BENJEN BLACK, great-uncle to the current King, who twice brought a Blight to Ceria and once saved it.

THE FIRST KING, SHIN SAVANYEL, given dominion over Ceria by the Firstborn

KING MATH III, Shonathan's elder brother, who died fighting Benjen

PRINCE BENJIN, his infant son, kidnapped and murdered by Benjen Black at the start of his second Blight

PRINCE PELL, Shonathan's younger brother, an architect

PRINCESS RINTA, Shonathan's younger sister, a librarian

PRINCESS VIANI, aunt of the current King, a famous beauty, and well-favored with the Royal magic.

LORD TOMAS FERYA, the Crown Regent, recently departed in an upsetting way

LORD ZAVIEN EIRCEDE, a Regent for Prince Yithiere

LORD GEOSEPH YARZEE, a Regent for Prince Jant

LORD SENNIC ARDOZA, a Regent for Prince Cathay

NATINA SUAN, mother of Lady Kiar

Acknowledgments

This book has been a long time coming. It could not have existed without the support of Raymond, the skills of Kevin, the cover art of Ravven, the enthusiasm of Rachel H., the feedback of Jenna and Suzanne, and the sharp eyes of Rachel G. and Daniel. Killian and Robin probably helped too.

Special thanks to Matrice, whose offer gave me a reason to write the book, and my supporters on Kickstarter and Patreon, who helped me get the cover.

About the Author

Chrysoula started writing as a child, eventually getting into Carleton College on the strength of a story. After working her way through various forms of paid and volunteer game writing, her first novel in the Senyaza Series was published by a small press in 2012. Since then she's moved full-time to self-publishing, with an epic fantasy series about girls (Thrones of the Firstborn) and the ongoing Senyaza Series running concurrently. She likes to write about women, magic swords, fallen angels, artificial intelligence, aliens, technology and the power of being human. Her hobbies include fiber arts, coloring books, video games, Regency romances and gardening. She is the mother of two small children.

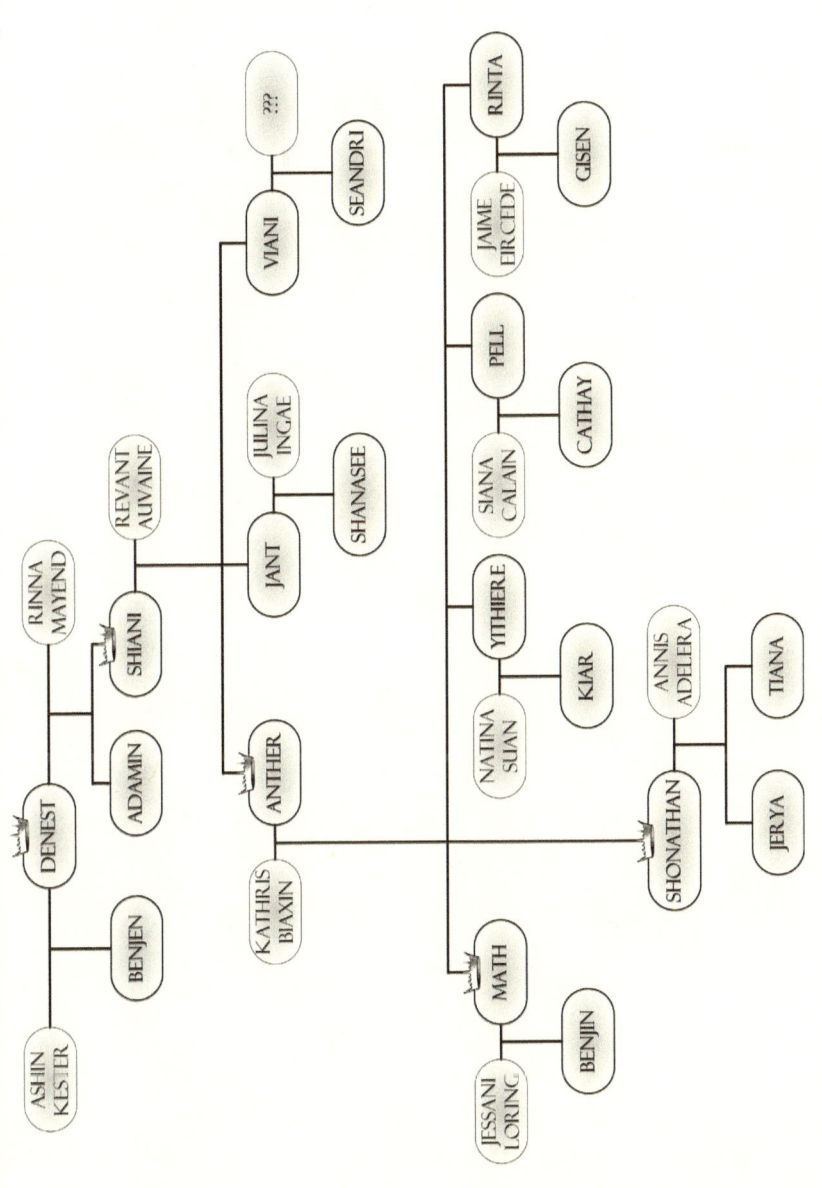

THRONES OF THE FIRSTBORN
CONTINUES IN

SHRINE OF
SUMMER